The Magic Mountain

[Complete & Annotated]

THOMAS MANN

ILLUSTRATED & PUBLISHED

BY

E-KİTAP PROJESİ & CHEAPEST BOOKS

www.cheapestboooks.com

www.facebook.com/EKitapProjesi

Copyright, 2020 by e-Kitap Projesi

Istanbul

ISBN: 978-625-7120-25-8

E-ISBN: 978-625-7120-15-9

© BOOK COVER: Die Gralsburg (*Oil on Cardboard, 1895*), Hans Thoma (German, 1839–1924)

About the Book & Author

Paul **Thomas Mann** (1875 – 1955) was a German novelist, short story writer, social critic, philanthropist, essayist, and the 1929 Nobel Prize in Literature laureate. His highly symbolic and ironic epic novels and novellas are noted for their insight into the psychology of the artist and the intellectual. His analysis and critique of the European and German soul used modernized versions of German and Biblical stories, as well as the ideas of Johann Wolfgang von Goethe, Friedrich Nietzsche and Arthur Schopenhauer.

Mann was a member of the Hanseatic Mann family and portrayed his family and class in his first novel, Buddenbrooks. His older brother was the radical writer Heinrich Mann and three of Mann's six children, Erika Mann, Klaus Mann and Golo Mann, also became significant German writers. When Adolf Hitler came to power in 1933, Mann fled to Switzerland. When World War II broke out in 1939, he moved to the United States, then returned to Switzerland in 1952. Mann is one of the best-known exponents of the so-called Exilliteratur, German literature written in exile by those who opposed the Hitler regime.

* * *

The Magic Mountain (*German: Der Zauberberg*) is a novel by Thomas Mann, first published in German in November 1924. It is widely considered to be one of the most influential works of twentieth-century German literature.

Mann started writing what was to become The Magic Mountain in 1912. It began as a much shorter narrative which revisited in a comic manner aspects of Death in Venice, a novella that he was preparing for publication. The newer work reflected his experiences and impressions during a period when his wife, who was suffering from a lung complaint, resided at Dr. Friedrich Jessen's Waldsanatorium in Davos, Switzerland for several months. In May and June 1912, Mann visited her and became acquainted with the team of doctors and patients in this cosmopolitan institution. According to Mann, in the afterword that was later included in the English translation of his novel, this stay inspired his opening chapter ("*Arrival*").

The outbreak of World War I interrupted his work on the book. The savage conflict and its aftermath led the author to undertake a major re-examination of European bourgeois society. He explored the sources of the destructiveness displayed by much of civilised humanity. He was also drawn to speculate about more general questions related to personal attitudes to life, health, illness, sexuality and mortality. Given this, Mann felt compelled to radically revise and expand the pre-war text before completing it in 1924. Der Zauberberg was eventually published in two volumes by S. Fischer Verlag in Berlin.

The narrative opens in the decade before World War I. It introduces the protagonist, Hans Castorp, the only child of a Hamburg merchant family. Following the early death of his parents, Castorp has been brought up by his grandfather and later, by a maternal uncle named James Tienappel. Castorp is in his early 20s, about to take up a shipbuilding career in Hamburg, his home town. Before beginning work, he undertakes a journey to visit his tubercular cousin, Joachim Ziemssen, who is seeking a cure in a sanatorium in Davos, high up in the Swiss Alps. In the opening chapter, Castorp leaves his familiar life and obligations, in what he later learns to call "the flatlands", to visit the rarefied mountain air and introspective small world of the sanatorium.

* * *

The Magic Mountain

Table of Contents

Foreword

*T*he story of Hans Castorp, which we would here set forth,

not on his own account, for in him the reader will make acquaintance with a simple--minded though pleasing young man, but for the sake of the story itself, which seems to us highly worth telling—though it must needs be borne in mind, in Hans Castorp's behalf, that it is his story, and not every story happens to everybody—this story, we say, belongs to the long ago; is already, so to speak, covered with historic mould, and unquestionably to be presented in the tense best suited to a narrative out of the depth or the past.

That should be no drawback to a story, but rather the reverse. Since histories must be in the past, then the more past the better, it would seem, for them in their character as histories, and for him, the teller of them, rounding wizard of times gone by. With this story, moreover, it stands as it does to--day with human beings, not least among them writers of tales: it is far older than its years; its age may not be measured by length of days, nor the weight of time on its head reckoned by the rising or setting of suns. In a word, the degree of its antiquity has noways to do with the passage of time—in which statement the author intentionally touches upon the strange and questionable double nature of that riddling element.

But we would not wilfully obscure a plain matter. The exaggerated pastness of our narrative is due to its taking place before the epoch when a certain crisis shattered its way through life and consciousness and left a deep chasm behind. It takes place—or, rather, deliberately to avoid the present tense, it took place, and had taken place—in the long ago, in the old days, the days of the world before the Great War, in the beginning of which so much began that has scarcely yet left off beginning. Yes, it took place before that; yet not so long before. Is not the pastness of the past the profounder, the completer, the more legendary, the more immediately before the present it falls? More than that, our story has, of its own nature, something of the legend about it now and again.

We shall tell it at length, thoroughly, in detail——for when did a narrative seem too long or too short by reason of the actual time or space it took up? We do not fear being called meticulous, inclining as we do to the view that only the exhaustive can be truly interesting.

Not all in a minute, then, will the narrator be finished with the story of our Hans. The seven days of a week will not suffice, no, nor seven months either. Best not too soon make too plain how much mortal time must pass over his head while he sits spun round in his spell. Heaven forbid it should be seven years!

And now we begin.

CHAPTER I

Arrival

*A*n unassuming young man was travelling, in

midsummer, from his native city of Hamburg to Davos--Platz in the Canton of the Grisons, on a three weeks' visit. From Hamburg to Davos is a long journey—-too long, indeed, for so brief a stay. It crosses all sorts of country; goes up hill and down dale, descends from the plateau of Southern Germany to the shore of Lake Constance, over its bounding waves and on across marshes once thought to be bottomless.

At this point the route, which has been so far over trunk--lines, gets cut up. There are stops and formalities. At Rorschach, in Swiss territory, you take train again, but only as far as Landquart, a small Alpine station, where you have to change. Here, after a long and windy wait in a spot devoid of charm, you mount a narrow--gauge train; and as the small but very powerful engine gets under way, there begins the thrilling part of the journey, a steep and steady climb that seems never to come to an end. For the station of Landquart lies at a relatively low altitude, but now the wild and rocky route pushes grimly onward into the Alps themselves.

Hans Castorp—-such was the young man's name—-sat alone in his little greyupholstered compartment, with his alligator--skin hand--bag, a present from his uncle and guardian, Consul Tienappel—-let us get the introductions over with at once—-his travelling--rug, and his winter overcoat swinging on its hook. The window was down, the afternoon grew cool, and he, a tender product of the sheltered life, had turned up the collar of his fashionably cut, silk--lined summer overcoat. Near him on the seat lay a paper--bound volume entitled *Ocean Steamships;* earlier in the journey he had studied it off and on, but now it lay neglected, and the breath of the panting engine, streaming in, defiled its cover with particles of soot.

Two days' travel separated the youth—-he was still too young to have thrust his roots down firmly into life—-from his own world, from all that he thought of as his own duties, interests, cares and prospects; far more than he had dreamed it would when he sat in the carriage on the way to the station. Space, rolling and revolving between him and his native heath, possessed and wielded the powers we generally ascribe to time. From hour to hour it worked changes in him, like to those wrought by time, yet in a way even more striking. Space, like time, engenders forgetfulness; but it does so by setting us bodily free from our surroundings and giving us back our primitive, unattached state. Yes, it can even, in the twinkling of an eye, make something like a vagabond of the pedant and Philistine. Time, we say, is Lethe; but change of air is a similar draught, and, if it works less thoroughly, does so more quickly.

Such was the experience of young Hans Castorp. He had not meant to take the journey seriously or commit himself deeply to it; but to get it over quickly, since it had to be made, to return as he had gone, and to take up his life at the point where, for the moment, he had had to lay it down. Only yesterday he had been encompassed in the wonted circle of his thoughts, and entirely taken up by two matters: the examination he had just passed, and his approaching entrance into the firm of Tunder and Wilms, shipbuilders, smelters, and machinists. With as much impatience as lay in his temperament to feel, he had discounted the next three weeks; but now it began to seem as though present circumstances required his entire attention, that it would not be at all the thing to take them too lightly.

This being carried upward into regions where he had never before drawn breath, and where he knew that unusual living conditions prevailed, such as could only be described as sparse or scanty—it began to work upon him, to fill him with a certain concern. Home and regular living lay not only far behind, they lay fathoms deep beneath him, and he continued to mount above them. Poised between them and the unknown, he asked himself how he was going to fare. Perhaps it had been ill--advised of him, born as he was a few feet above sea--level, to come immediately to these great heights, without stopping at least a day or so at some point in between. He wished he were at the end of his journey; for once there he could begin to live as he would anywhere else, and not be reminded by this continual climbing of the incongruous situation he found himself in. He looked out. The train wound in curves along the narrow pass; he could see the front carriages and the labouring engine vomiting great masses of brown, black, and greenish smoke that floated away. Water roared in the abysses on the right; on the left, among rocks, dark fir--trees aspired toward a stonegrey sky. The train passed through pitch--black tunnels, and when daylight came again it showed wide chasms, with villages nestled in their depths. Then the pass closed in again; they wound along narrow defiles, with traces of snow in chinks and crannies. There were halts at wretched little shanties of stations; also at more important ones, which the train left in the opposite direction, making one lose the points of the compass. A magnificent succession of vistas opened before the awed eye, of the solemn, phantasmagorical world of towering peaks, into which their route wove and wormed itself: vistas that appeared and disappeared with each new winding of the path. Hans Castorp reflected that they must have got above the zone of shade--trees, also probably of song--birds; whereupon he felt such a sense of the impoverishment of life as gave him a slight attack of giddiness and nausea and made him put his hand over his eyes for a few seconds. It passed. He perceived that they had stopped climbing. The top of the col was reached; the train rolled smoothly along the level valley floor.

It was about eight o'clock, and still daylight. A lake was visible in the distant landscape, its waters grey, its shores covered with black fir--forests that climbed the surrounding heights, thinned out, and gave place to bare, mist--wreathed rock. They stopped at a small station. Hans Castorp heard the name called out: it was "DavosDorf." Soon he would be at his journey's end. And suddenly, close to him, he heard a voice, the comfortable Hamburg voice of his cousin, Joachim Ziemssen, saying: "Hullo, there you are! Here's where you get out!" and peering through the window saw his cousin himself, standing below on the platform, in a brown ulster, bareheaded, and looking more robust than ever in his life before. He laughed and said again: "Come along out, it's all right!"

"But I'm not there yet!" said Hans Castorp, taken aback, and still seated.

"Oh, yes, you are. This is the village. It is nearer to the sanatorium from here. I have a carriage. Just give us your things."

And laughing, confused, in the excitement of arrival and meeting, Hans Castorp reached bag, overcoat, the roll with stick and umbrella, and finally *Ocean Steamships* out of the window. Then he ran down the narrow corridor and sprang out upon the platform to greet his cousin properly. The meeting took place without exuberance, as between people of traditional coolness and reserve. Strange to say, the cousins had always avoided calling each other by their first names, simply because they were afraid of showing too much feeling. And, as they could not well address each other by their last names, they confined themselves, by established custom, to the thou. A man in livery with a braided cap looked on while they shook hands, quickly, not without embarrassment, young Ziemssen in military position, heels together. Then he came forward to ask for Hans Castorp's luggage ticket; he was the concierge of the International Sanatorium Berghof, and would fetch the guest's large trunk from the other station while the gentlemen drove directly up to supper. This man limped noticeably; and so, curiously enough, the first thing Hans Castorp said to his cousin was: "Is that a war veteran? What makes him limp like that?"

"War veteran! No fear!" said Joachim, with some bitterness. "He's got it in his knee—-or, rather, he had it—-the knee--pan has been removed."

Hans Castorp bethought himself hastily.

"So that's it?" he said, and as he walked on turned his head and gave a quick glance back. "But you can't make me believe you've still got anything like that the matter with you! Why, you look as if you had just come from manœuvres!" And he looked sidelong at his cousin.

Joachim was taller and broader than he, a picture of youthful vigour, and made for a uniform. He was of the very dark type which his blond--peopled country not seldom produces, and his already nut--brown skin was tanned almost to bronze. With his large, black eyes and small, dark moustache over the full, well--shaped mouth, he would have been distinctly handsome if his ears had not stood out. Up to a certain period they had been his only trouble in life. Now, however, he had others.

Hans Castorp went on: "You're coming back down with me, aren't you? I see no reason why not."

"Back down with you?" asked his cousin, and turned his large eyes full upon him. They had always been gentle, but in these five months they had taken on a tired, almost sad expression. "When?"

"Why, in three weeks."

"Oh, yes, you are already on the way back home, in your thoughts," answered Joachim. "Wait a bit. You've only just come. Three weeks are nothing at all, to us up here—-they look like a lot of time to you, because you are only up here on a visit, and three weeks is all you have. Get acclimatized first—-it isn't so easy, you'll see. And the climate isn't the only queer thing about us. You're going to see some things you've never dreamed of—-just wait. About me—-it isn't such smooth sailing as you think, you with your 'going home in three weeks.' That's the class of ideas you have down below. Yes, I am brown, I know, but it is mostly snow--burning. It doesn't mean much, as Behrens always says; he told me at the last regular examination it would take another half year, pretty certainly."

"Half a year? Are you crazy?" shouted Hans Castorp. They had climbed into the yellow cabriolet that stood in the stone--paved square in front of the shed--like station, and as the pair of brown horses started up, he flounced indignantly on the hard cushions. "Half a year! You've been up here half a year already! Who's got so much time to spend——"

"Oh, time——!" said Joachim, and nodded repeatedly, straight in front of him, paying his cousin's honest indignation no heed. "They make pretty free with a human being's idea of time, up here. You wouldn't believe it. Three weeks are just like a day to them. You'll learn all about it," he said, and added: "One's ideas get changed."

Hans Castorp regarded him earnestly as they drove. "But seems to me you've made a splendid recovery," he said, shaking his head.

"You really think so, don't you?" answered Joachim; "I think I have too." He drew himself up straighter against the cushions, but immediately relaxed again. "Yes, I am better," he explained, "but I am not cured yet. In the left lobe, where there were rales, it only sounds harsh now, and that is not so bad; but lower down it is still *very* harsh, and there are rhonchi in the second intercostal space."

"How learned you've got," said Hans Castorp.

"Fine sort of learning! God knows I wish I'd had it sweated out of my system in the service," responded Joachim. "But I still have sputum," he said, with a shoulder--shrug that was somehow indifferent and vehement both at once, and became him but ill. He half pulled out and showed to his cousin something he carried in the side pocket of his overcoat, next to Hans Castorp. It was a flat, curving bottle of bluish glass, with a metal cap.

"Most of us up here carry it," he said, shoving it back. "It even has a nickname; they make quite a joke of it. You are looking at the landscape?"

Hans Castorp was. "Magnificent!" he said.

"Think so?" asked Joachim.

They had driven for a space straight up the axis of the valley, along an irregularly built street that followed the line of the railway; then, turning to the left, they crossed the narrow tracks and a watercourse, and now trotted up a high--road that mounted gently toward the wooded slopes. Before them rose a low, projecting, meadow--like plateau, on which, facing south--west, stood a long building, with a cupola and so many balconies that from a distance it looked porous, like a sponge. In this building lights were beginning to show. It was rapidly growing dusk. The faint rose--colour that had briefly enlivened the overcast heavens was faded now, and there reigned the colourless, soulless, melancholy transition--period that comes just before the onset of night. The populous valley, extended and rather winding, now began to show lights everywhere, not only in the middle, but here and there on the slopes at either hand, particularly on the projecting right side, upon which buildings mounted in terrace formation. Paths ran up the sloping meadows to the left and lost themselves in the vague blackness of the pine forest. Behind them, where the valley narrowed to its entrance, the more distant ranges showed a cold, slaty blue. A wind had sprung up, and made perceptible the chill of evening.

"No, to speak frankly, I don't find it so overpowering," said Hans Castorp. "Where are the glaciers, and the snow peaks, and the gigantic heights you hear about? These things aren't very high, it seems to me."

"Oh, yes, they are," answered Joachim. "You can see the tree line almost everywhere, it is very sharply defined; the fir--trees leave off, and after that there is absolutely nothing but bare rock. And up there to the right of the Schwarzhorn, that tooth--shaped peak, there is a glacier—-can't you see the blue? It is not very large, but it is a glacier right enough, the Skaletta. Piz Michel and Tinzenhorn, in the notch—-you can't see them from here—-have snow all the year round."

"Eternal snow," said Hans Castorp.

"Eternal snow, if you like. Yes, that's all very high. But we are frightfully high ourselves: sixteen hundred metres above sea--level. That's why the peaks don't seem any higher."

"Yes, what a climb that was! I was scared to death, I can tell you. Sixteen hundred metres—-that is over five thousand feet, as I reckon it. I've never been so high up in my life." And Hans Castorp took in a deep, experimental breath of the strange air. It was fresh, and that was all. It had no perfume, no content, no humidity; it breathed in easily, and held for him no associations.

"Wonderful air," he remarked, politely.

"Yes, the atmosphere is famous. But the place doesn't look its best to--night. Sometimes it makes a much better impression—-especially when there is snow. But you can get sick of looking at it. All of us up here are frightfully fed up, you can imagine," said Joachim, and twisted his mouth into an expression of disgust that was as unlike him as the shoulder--shrug. It looked irritable, disproportionate.

"You have such a queer way of talking," said Hans Castorp.

"Have I?" said Joachim, concerned, and turned to look at his cousin.

"Oh, no, of course I don't mean you really have—-I suppose it just seemed so to me for the moment," Hans Castorp hastened to assure him. It was the expression "all of us up here," which Joachim had used several times, that had somehow struck him as strange and given him an uneasy feeling.

"Our sanatorium is higher up than the village, as you see," went on Joachim. "Fifty metres higher. In the prospectus it says a hundred, but it is really only fifty. The highest of the sanatoriums is the Schatzalp—-you can't see it from here. They have to bring their bodies down on bob--sleds in the winter, because the roads are blocked."

"Their bodies? Oh, I see. Imagine!" said Hans Castorp. And suddenly he burst out laughing, a violent, irrepressible laugh, which shook him all over and distorted his face, that was stiff with the cold wind, until it almost hurt. "On bob--sleds! And you can tell it me just like that, in cold blood! You've certainly got pretty cynical in these five months."

"Not at all," answered Joachim, shrugging again. "Why not? It's all the same to them, isn't it? But maybe we do get cynical up here. Behrens is a cynic himself—-but he's a great old bird after all, an old corps--student. He is a brilliant operator, they say. You will like him. Krokowski is the assistant—-devilishly clever article. They mention his activities specially, in the prospectus. He psycho--analyses the patients."

"He what? Psycho--analyses—how disgusting!" cried Hans Castorp; and now his hilarity altogether got the better of him. He could not stop. The psycho--analysis had been the finishing touch. He laughed so hard that the tears ran down his cheeks; he put up his hands to his face and rocked with laughter. Joachim laughed just as heartily—it seemed to do him good; and thus, in great good spirits, the young people climbed out of the wagon, which had slowly mounted the steep, winding drive and deposited them before the portal of the International Sanatorium Berghof.

Number 34

On their right as they entered, between the main door and the inner one, was the porter's lodge. An official of the French type, in the grey livery of the man at the station, was sitting at the telephone, reading the newspaper. He came out and led them through the well--lighted halls, on the left of which lay the reception--rooms. Hans Castorp peered in as he passed, but they were empty. Where, then, were the guests, he asked, and his cousin answered: "In the rest--cure. I had leave to--night to go out and meet you. Otherwise I am always up in my balcony, after supper."

Hans Castorp came near bursting out again. "What! You lie out on your balcony at night, in the damp?" he asked, his voice shaking.

"Yes, that is the rule. From eight to ten. But come and see your room now, and get a wash."

They entered the lift—it was an electric one, worked by the Frenchman. As they went up, Hans Castorp wiped his eyes.

"I'm perfectly worn out with laughing," he said, and breathed through his mouth.

"You've told me such a lot of crazy stuff—that about the psycho--analysis was the last straw. I suppose I am a bit relaxed from the journey. And my feet are cold—-are yours? But my face burns so, it is really unpleasant. Do we eat now? I feel hungry. Is the food decent up here?"

They went noiselessly along the coco matting of the narrow corridor, which was lighted by electric lights in white glass shades set in the ceiling. The walls gleamed with hard white enamel paint. They had a glimpse of a nursing sister in a white cap, and eyeglasses on a cord that ran behind her ear. She had the look of a Protestant sister—-that is to say, one working without a real vocation and burdened with restlessness and ennui. As they went along the corridor, Hans Castorp saw, beside two of the white--enamelled, numbered doors, certain curious, swollen--looking, balloonshaped vessels with short necks. He did not think, at the moment, to ask what they were.

"Here you are," said Joachim. "I am next you on the right. The other side you have a Russian couple, rather loud and offensive, but it couldn't be helped. Well, how do you like it?"

There were two doors, an outer and an inner, with clothes--hooks in the space between. Joachim had turned on the ceiling light, and in its vibrating brilliance the room looked restful and cheery, with practical white furniture, white washable walls, clean linoleum, and white linen curtains gaily embroidered in modern taste. The door stood open; one saw the lights of the valley and heard distant dance--music. The good Joachim had put a vase of flowers on the chest of drawers—a few bluebells and some yarrow, which he had found himself among the second crop of grass on the slopes.

"Awfully decent of you," said Hans Castorp. "What a nice room! I can spend a couple of weeks here with pleasure."

"An American woman died here day before yesterday," said Joachim. "Behrens told me directly that she would be out before you came, and you might have the room. Her fiancé was with her, an English officer of marines, but he didn't behave very well. He kept coming out in the corridor to cry, just like a little boy. He rubbed cold cream on his cheeks, because he was close--shaven and the tears smarted. Night before last she had two first--class haemorrhages, and that was the finish. But she has been gone since yesterday morning, and after they took her away of course they fumigated the room thoroughly with formalin, which is the proper thing to use in such cases."

Hans Castorp took in this information with a sprightly, yet half--distraught air. He was standing with his sleeves pushed back before the roomy wash--hand--basin, the taps of which shone in the electric light, and gave hardly a glance at the white metal bed with its fresh coverlet.

"Fumigated it, eh? That's ripping," he said loquaciously and rather absurdly, as he washed and dried his hands. "Methyl aldehyde; yes, that's too much for the bacteria, no matter how strong they are. H_2CO. But it's a powerful stench. Of course, perfect sanitation is absolutely essential." He spoke with more of a Hamburg accent than his cousin, who had broken himself of it since his student days. Hans Castorp continued volubly. "But what I was about to say was, probably the officer of marines used a safety--razor; one makes oneself sore with those things easier than with a wellsharpened blade—at least, that is my experience, and I use them both by turns. Well, and salt water would naturally make a tender skin smart, so he got in the way, in the service, of rubbing in cold cream. I don't see anything strange about that ..." He rattled on: said that he had two hundred Maria Mancinis (his cigar) in his trunk, the customs officers had been very courteous; and gave his cousin greetings from various people at home. "Don't they heat the rooms here?" he broke off to inquire, and ran to put his hands on the radiator.

"No, they keep us pretty cool," answered Joachim. "The weather would have to be different from this before they put on the heat in August."

"August, August!" said Hans Castorp. "But I am cold, abominably cold; I mean in my body, for my face burns shockingly—just feel it!"

This demand was entirely foreign to the young man's nature—so much so that he himself was disagreeably impressed as he heard himself make it. Joachim did not take up the offer, but merely said: "That is the air—it doesn't mean anything; Behrens himself is purple in the face all day long. Some people never get used to it. Come along now, do, or we shan't get anything to eat."

Outside they saw the nursing sister again, peering short-sightedly and inquisitively after them. But in the first storey Hans Castorp suddenly stopped, rooted to the spot by a perfectly ghastly sound coming from a little distance off round a bend in the corridor. It was not a loud sound, but so distinctly horrible that Hans Castorp made a wry face and looked wide-eyed at his cousin. It was coughing, obviously, a man coughing; but coughing like to no other Hans Castorp had ever heard, and compared with which any other had been a magnificent and healthy manifestation of life: a coughing that had no conviction and gave no relief, that did not even come out in paroxysms, but was just a feeble, dreadful welling up of the juices of organic dissolution.

"Yes," said Joachim. "That's a bad case. An Austrian aristocrat, you know, very elegant. He's a born horseman—a gentleman rider. And now he's come to this. But he still gets about."

As they went, Hans Castorp discoursed earnestly upon the gentleman rider's cough.

"You must realize," he said, "that I've never heard anything like it before. It is entirely new to me, and naturally it makes a great impression. There are different kinds of cough, dry and loose, and people always say the loose one is better than the other, the barking kind. When I had croup, in my youth" (he actually said "in my youth"!), "I bayed like a wolf, and I can still remember how glad everybody was when it got looser. But a cough like this—I didn't know there was such a cough! It isn't a human cough at all. It isn't dry and yet isn't loose either—that is very far from being the right word for it. It is just as if one could look right into him when he coughs, and see what it looks like: all slime and mucous—"

"Oh," said Joachim, "I hear it every day, you don't need to describe it to me." But Hans Castorp could not get over the coughing he had heard. He kept repeating that he could see right into the gentleman rider's vitals; when they reached the restaurant his travel-weary eyes had an excited glitter.

In the Restaurant

It was charming in the restaurant, elegantly appointed and well lighted. The room lay to the right of the hall, opposite the salons, and was, Joachim explained, used chiefly by new arrivals, and by guests eating out of the usual meal hours or entertaining company. But it also served for birthday feasts, farewell parties, even to celebrate a favourable report after a general examination. There were lively times here in the restaurant on occasion, Joachim said, and champagne flowed freely. Now, no one was here but a solitary lady of some thirty years, reading a book and humming; she kept tapping the table-cloth lightly with the middle finger of her left hand. After the young people had taken their places, she changed hers, in order to sit with her back to them. Joachim explained in a low voice that she suffered from shyness as from a disease, and ate all her meals in the restaurant, with a book. It was said that she had entered her first tuberculosis sanatorium as a young girl, and had never lived in the world since.

"So compared with her, you are only a novice, with your five months; and still will be when you have a year on your back," said Hans Castorp to his cousin; whereat Joachim, with his newly acquired shoulder--shrug, took up the menu.

They had sat down at the raised table in the window, the pleasantest spot in the room, facing each other against the cream--coloured hangings, their faces lighted by the red--shaded table--lamp. Hans Castorp clasped his freshly washed hands and rubbed them together in agreeable anticipation——a habit of his when he sat down to table, perhaps because his ancestors had said grace before meat. They were served by a friendly maid in black frock and white apron. She had a pleasant, throaty voice, and her broad face was indisputably healthy--coloured. To his great amusement, Hans Castorp learned that the waitresses here were called "dining--room girls." They ordered a bottle of Gruaud Larose, and Hans Castorp sent it back to have it warmed. The food was excellent: asparagus soup, stuffed tomatoes, a roast with vegetables, an exceedingly well--prepared sweet, cheese, and fruit. Hans Castorp ate heartily, though his appetite did not turn out quite so stout as he had thought. But he always ate a good deal, out of pure self--respect, even when he was not hungry.

Joachim paid scant honour to the meal. He was tired of the cooking, he said; they all were, up here, and it was customary to grumble at the food. If one had to sit up here for ever and a day——! But, on the other hand, he partook of the wine with gusto, not to say abandon; and repeatedly, though with careful avoidance of emotional language, expressed his joy at having somebody here with whom one could have a little rational conversation.

"Yes, it's first--rate you've come," he said, and his gentle voice betrayed some feeling. "I must say it is really an event for me——it is certainly a change, anyhow, a break in the everlasting monotony."

"But time must go fast, living up here," was Hans Castorp's view.

"Fast and slow, as you take it," answered Joachim. "It doesn't do at all, I tell you. You can't call it time——and you can't call it living either!" he said with a shake of the head, and fell to his glass again.

Hans Castorp drank too, though his face was like fire. Yet he was still cold, and felt a curious restlessness in his limbs, at once pleasurable and troubling. His words fell over each other, he often misspoke and passed it over with a deprecating wave. Joachim too was in a lively humour, and their conversation continued in a still freer and more convivial vein after the humming, tapping lady had got up suddenly and left the room. They gesticulated with their forks as they ate, nodded, shrugged their shoulders, talked with their mouths full. Joachim wanted to hear about Hamburg, and brought the conversation round to the proposed regulation of the Elbe.

"Epoch--making," said Hans Castorp. "Epoch--making for the development of our shipping. Can't be over--estimated. We've budgeted fifty millions for immediate expenditure and you may be sure we know what we're about."

But notwithstanding all the importance he attached to the projected improvement, he jumped away from the theme and demanded that Joachim tell him more about life "up here" and about the guests—-which the latter straightway did, being only too pleased to be able to unbosom himself. He had to repeat the story of the corpses sent down by bob--sleigh, and vouch for its truth. Hans Castorp being taken by another fit of laughing, his cousin laughed too, with hearty enjoyment, and told other funny things to add fuel to their merriment. There was a lady sitting at his table, named Frau Stöhr, the wife of a Cannstadt musician; a rather serious case, she was, and the most ignorant creature he had ever seen. She said diseased for deceased, quite seriously, and she called Krokowski the Asst. And you had to take it all in without cracking a smile. She was a regular gossip—-most people were, up here—-and published it broadcast that another lady, a certain Frau Iltis, carried a "steriletto" on her person.

"That is exactly what she called it, isn't that priceless?" They lolled in their chairs, they flung themselves back and laughed so hard that they shook; and they began to hiccup at nearly the same time.

Now and then Joachim's face would cloud over and he would remember his lot.

"Yes, we sit here and laugh," he said, with a long face, his words interrupted by the heaving of his diaphragm, "we sit here and laugh, but there's no telling when I shall get away. When Behrens says half a year, you can make up your mind it will be more. It *is* hard, isn't it?—-you just tell me if you don't think it is pretty hard on me. I had already been accepted, I could have taken my exams next month. And now I have to drool about with a thermometer stuck in my mouth, and count the howlers of this ignorant Frau Stöhr, and watch the time slipping away. A year is so important at our age. Down below, one goes through so many changes, and makes so much progress, in a single year of life. And I have to stagnate up here—-yes, just stagnate like a filthy puddle; it isn't too crass a comparison."

Strange to say, Hans Castorp's only reply to all this was a query as to whether it was possible to get porter up here; when Joachim looked at him, in some astonishment, he perceived that his cousin was overcome with sleep, that in fact he was actually nodding.

"But you are going to sleep!" said Joachim. "Come along, it is time we both went to bed."

" 'You can't call it time,' " quoth Hans Castorp, thick--tongued. He went with his cousin, rather bent and stiff in the knees, like a man bowed to the earth with fatigue. However, in the dimly lighted corridor he pulled himself sharply together on hearing his cousin say: "There's Krokowski sitting there. I think I'll just have to present you, as briefly as possible."

Dr. Krokowski sat in the bright light at the fire--place of one of the reception--rooms, close to the folding doors. He was reading a paper, and got up as the young people approached.

Joachim, in military position, heels together, said: "Herr Doctor, may I present my cousin Castorp from Hamburg? He has just arrived."

Dr. Krokowski greeted the new inmate with a jovial and robust heartiness, as who should say that with him all formality was superfluous, and only jocund mutual confidence in place. He was about thirty--five years old, broad--shouldered and fleshy, much shorter than either of the youths before him, so that he had to tip back his head to look them in the face. He was unusually pale, of a translucent, yes, phosphorescent pallor, that was further accentuated by the dark ardour of his eyes, the blackness of his brows, and his rather long, full whisker, which ended in two points and already showed some white threads. He had on a black double--breasted, somewhat worn sack suit; black, open--worked sandal--like shoes over grey woollen socks, and a soft turndown collar, such as Hans Castorp had previously seen worn only by a photographer in Danzig, which did, in fact, lend a certain stamp of the studio to Dr. Krokowski's appearance. Smiling warmly and showing his yellow teeth in his beard, he shook the young man by the hand, and said in a baritone voice, with rather a foreign drawl: "Welcome to our midst, Herr Castorp! May you get quickly acclimatized and feel yourself at home among us! Do you come as a patient, may I ask?"

It was touching to see Hans Castorp labour to master his drowsiness and be polite. It annoyed him to be in such bad form, and with the self--consciousness of youth he read signs of indulgent amusement in the warmth of the Assistant's manner. He replied, mentioning his examinations and his three weeks' visit, and ended by saying he was, thank God, perfectly healthy.

"Really?" asked Krokowski, putting his head teasingly on one side. His smile grew broader. "Then you are a phenomenon worthy of study. I, for one, have never in my life come across a perfectly healthy human being. What were the examinations you have just passed, if I may ask?"

"I am an engineer, Herr Doctor," said Hans Castorp with modest dignity.

"Ah, an engineer!" Dr. Krokowski's smile retreated as it were, lost for the moment something of its genial warmth. "A splendid calling. And so you will not require any attention while you are here, either physical or psychical?"

"Oh, no, thank you ever so much," said Hans Castorp, and almost drew back a step as he spoke.

At that Dr. Krokowski's smile burst forth triumphant; he shook the young man's hand afresh and cried briskly: "Well, sleep well, Herr Castorp, and rejoice in the fullness of your perfect health; sleep well, and *auf Wiedersehen!*" With which he dismissed the cousins and returned to his paper.

The lift had stopped running, so they climbed the stairs; in silence, somewhat taken aback by the encounter with Dr. Krokowski. Joachim went with his cousin to number thirty--four, where the lame porter had already deposited the luggage of the new arrival. They talked for another quarter--hour while Hans Castorp unpacked his night and toilet things, smoking a large, mild cigarette the while. A cigar would have been too much for him this evening——a fact which impressed him as odd indeed.

"He looks quite a personality," he said, blowing out the smoke. "He is as pale as wax. But dear me, what hideous footgear he wears! Grey woollen socks, and then those sandals! Was he really offended at the end, do you think?"

"He is rather touchy," admitted Joachim. "You ought not to have refused the treatment so brusquely, at least not the psychical. He doesn't like to have people get out of it. He doesn't take much stock in me because I don't confide in him enough. But every now and then I tell him a dream I've had, so he can have something to analyse."

"Then I certainly did offend him," Hans Castorp said fretfully, for it annoyed him to give offence. His weariness rushed over him with renewed force at the thought.

"Good--night," he said; "I'm falling over."

"At eight o'clock I'll come fetch you to breakfast," Joachim said, and went. Hans Castorp made only a cursory toilet for the night. Hardly had he put out the bedside light when sleep overcame him; but he started up again, remembering that in that bed, the day before yesterday, someone had died. "That wasn't the first time either," he said to himself, as though the thought were reassuring. "It is a regular death--bed, a common death--bed." And he fell asleep.

No sooner had he gone off, however, than he began to dream, and dreamed almost without stopping until next morning. Principally he saw his cousin, Joachim Ziemssen, in a strange, dislocated attitude on a bob--sled, riding down a steep course. He had a phosphorescent pallor like Dr. Krokowski, and in front of him sat the gentleman rider and steered. The gentleman rider was indistinct, like someone one has heard cough, but never seen.

"It's all the same to us up here," remarked the dislocated Joachim; and then it was he and not the gentleman rider who was coughing in that horribly pulpy manner. Hans Castorp wept bitterly to hear, and then perceived that he must run to the chemist's to get some cold cream. But Frau Iltis, with a pointed snout, sat by the road--side with something in her hand, which must be her "steriletto," but was obviously nothing else than a safety--razor. This made Hans Castorp go from tears to laughing; and thus he was tossed back and forth among varying emotions, until the dawn came through his half--open balcony door and wakened him.

CHAPTER II

Of the Christening Basin, and of Grandfather in His Two--fold Guise

*H*ans Castorp retained only pale memories of his parental

home. His father and mother he had barely known; they had both dropped away in the brief period between his fifth and seventh birthdays; first the mother, quite suddenly, on the eve of a confinement, of an arterial obstruction following neuritis—-an embolus, Dr. Heidekind had called it—-which caused instantaneous cardiac arrest. She had just been laughing, sitting up in bed, and it looked as though she had fallen back with laughter, but really it was because she had died. The father, Hermann Castorp, could not grasp his loss. He had been deeply attached to his wife, and not being of the strongest himself, never quite recovered from her death. His spirit was troubled; he shrank within himself; his benumbed brain made him blunder in his business, so that the firm of Castorp and Son suffered sensible financial losses; and the next spring, while inspecting warehouses on the windy landing--stage, he got inflammation of the lungs. The fever was too much for his shaken heart, and in five days, notwithstanding all Dr. Heidekind's care, he died. Attended to his rest by a respectable concourse of citizens, he followed his wife to the Castorp family vault, a charming site in St. Katherine's churchyard, with a view of the Botanical Gardens.

His father the Senator survived him a short time; then he too passed away, likewise of inflammation of the lungs. His death agony was sore, for unlike his son, Hans Lorenz Castorp had been a man of tough constitution, and firmly rooted in life. Before his death, for the space of a year and a half, the grandfather harboured the orphaned

Hans Castorp in his home, a mansion standing in a narrow lot on the Esplanade, built in the early years of the last century, in the northern--classic style of architecture. It was painted a depressing weather--colour, and had pilasters on either side the entrance door, which was approached by a flight of five steps. Besides the parterre, which had windows going down to the floor and furnished with cast--iron grilles, there were two upper storeys.

In the parterre were chiefly reception--rooms, and a very light and cheerful diningroom, with walls decorated in stucco. Its three windows, draped with wine--coloured curtains, looked out on the back garden. In this room, daily, at four o'clock, for the space of eighteen months, grandfather and grandson dined together, served by old Fiete, who had ear--rings in his ears and silver buttons on his livery, also a batiste neckcloth like his master's, in which he buried his shaven chin just as Hans Lorenz Castorp did in his. Grandfather said thou to him and addressed him in dialect——not with any humorous intent, for he had no bent that way, but in all seriousness, and because it was his custom so to do in his dealings with the common people——the warehouse hands, postmen, coachmen, and servants. Hans Castorp liked to hear it, and very much he liked to hear Fiete reply, in dialect too, bending over as he served and speaking into his master's left ear, for the Senator could hear much better on that side. The old man would listen and nod and go on eating, sitting erect between the table and the high back of his mahogany chair, and scarcely at all bending over his plate. And his grandson, opposite, watched in silence, with deep, unconscious concentration, Grandfather's beautiful, thin, white old hands, with their pointed nails, and, on the right forefinger, the green seal ring with the crest; watched the small, deft, practised motions with which they arranged a mouthful of meat, vegetable, and potato on the end of his fork, and with a slight inclination of the head conveyed it to his mouth. Then he would look at his own hands, and their still clumsy movements, and see in them the hope foreshadowed of one day holding and using his knife and fork as Grandfather did.

Again, he would wonder whether he should ever bury his chin in such another neck--band as that which filled the wide space inside Grandfather's extraordinary collar, with its sharp points brushing the old man's cheeks. He doubted it. One would have to be as old as Grandfather for that; in these days, save for him and his old Fiete, nobody, far and wide, wore such collars and neckcloths. It was a pity; little Hans Castorp liked the way Grandfather's chin nestled in the high, snow--white band. Even after he was grown, he recalled it with pleasure; something in the depth of his being responded to it.

When they had done, they folded their table--napkins and put them in their silver rings—-a job at which Hans Castorp never acquitted himself very well, for they were the size of small tablecloths. Then the Senator got up from his chair, which Fiete drew away behind him, and went with shuffling steps into his "office" to get a cigar. Sometimes the grandson followed him in.

This office had come to exist because of a peculiarity in the arrangement of the lower floor—-namely, that the dining--room had been planned with three windows instead of two, and ran the whole width of the house; which left space for only two drawing--rooms, instead of the usual three, and gave to one of them, at right angles to the dining--room, with a single window on the street, a quite disproportionate depth. Of this room, therefore, some quarter of the length had been cut off, and turned into a cabinet. It was a strip of a room, with a skylight; twilighted, and not much furnished—-there was an *étagère*, on which stood the Senator's cigar case; a cardtable, the drawer of which held whist cards, counters, little marking--boards with tiny teeth that clapped open and shut, a slate and slate--pencil, paper cigar--holders, and other such attractions; and finally, in the corner, a rococo case in palisander--wood, with yellow silk stretched behind its glass doors.

"Grandpa," little Hans Castorp might say, standing on tiptoes to reach the old man's ear, "please show me the christening basin."

And the grandfather, who had already pulled back the skirts of his long cashmere frock--coat and taken the bunch of keys from his trouser pocket, forthwith opened the door of the glass case, whence floated odours odd and pleasant to the boy's sense. Inside were all manner of disused and fascinating objects: a pair of silver--branched candlesticks, a broken barometer in a wooden case with allegorical carving, an album of daguerreotypes, a cedar--wood case for liqueurs, a funny little Turk in flowing silk robes, under which was a hard body with a mechanism inside. Once, when you wound him up, he had been able to leap about all over the table, but he was long since out of repair. Then there was a quaint old model of a ship; and right at the bottom a rat--trap. But from one of the middle shelves Grandfather took a much--tarnished, round silver dish, with a tray likewise of silver, and showed them both to the boy, lifting them separately and turning them about in his hands as he told the story he had so often told before.

Plate and basin, one could see, and as the little one heard once again, had not originally belonged together; but, Grandfather said, they had been in use together for a round hundred years, or since the time when the basin was made. The latter was very beautiful, of simple and elegant form, in the severe taste of the early nineteenth century. It rested, plain and solid, on a round base, and had once been gilt within, but the gilding had faded with time to a yellow shimmer. Its single decoration was a chaste garland of roses and serrated leaves about the brim. As for the plate, its far greater antiquity could be read on the inside: the date 1650 was engraved there in ornamental figures, framed in curly engraved lines executed in the "modern manner" of the period, florid and capricious devices and arabesques that were something between star and flower. On the back, engraved in a variety of scripts, were the names of its successive owners, seven in number, each with the date when it had passed into his hands. The old man named each one to his grandson, pointing with beringed index finger. There was Hans Castorp's father's name, there was Grandfather's own, there was Great--grandfather's; then the "great" came doubled, tripled, quadrupled, from the old man's mouth, whilst the little lad listened, his head on one side, the eyes full of thought, yet fixed and dreamy too, the childish lips parted, half with awe, half sleepily. That great--great--great--great—-what a hollow sound it had, how it spoke of the falling away of time, yet how it seemed the expression of a piously cherished link between the present, his own life, and the depth of the past! All that, as his face showed, made a profound impression. As he listened to the great--great--great, he seemed to smell the cool, earthy air of the vault of St. Michael's or Saint Katherine's; the breath of regions where one went hat in hand, the head reverently bowed, walking weavingly on the tips of one's toes; seemed, too, to hear the remote and set--apart hush of those echoing places. Religious feeling mingled in his mind with thoughts of death and a sense of history, as he listened to the sombre syllable; he received therefrom an ineffable gratification—-indeed, it may have been for the sake of hearing the sound that he so often begged to see the christening basin.

Grandfather set the vessel back on the tray, and let the boy look into the smooth, faintly golden inside, which caught the light from the window in the ceiling.

"Yes," he said, "it will soon be eight years since we held you over it, and the water flowed into it from your baptism. Lassen, the sexton of St. Jacob's, poured it into our good Pastor Bugenhagen's hand, and it ran out over your little topknot and into the basin. We had warmed it, so it should not frighten you and make you cry, and you did not; you cried beforehand, though, so loud that Bugenhagen could hardly get on with the service, but you stopped when you felt the water—and that, let us hope, was out of respect for the Holy Sacrament. A few days from now it will be forty--four years since your blessed father was a baby at the baptismal font, and it was over his head the water flowed into the basin. That was here in this house, where he was born, in front of the middle dining--room window, and old Pastor Hezekiel was still alive. He was the man the French nearly shot when he was young, because he preached against their burning

and looting. He has been with God these many years. Then, five-
andseventy years ago, I was the youngster whose head they held
over this selfsame basin; that was in the diningroom too, and the
minister spoke the very words that were spoken when you and your
father were baptized, and the clear, warm water flowed over my head
precisely the same way—there wasn't much more hair than there is
now—and fell into this golden bowl just as it did over yours."

The little one looked up at Grandfather's narrow grey head,
bending over the basin as it had in the time he described. A familiar
feeling pervaded the child: a strange, dreamy, troubling sense: of
change in the midst of duration, of time as both flowing and
persisting, of recurrence in continuity—these were sensations he had
felt before on the like occasion, and both expected and longed for
again, whenever the heirloom was displayed.

As a young man he was aware that the image of his grandfather
was more deeply and clearly imprinted on his mind, with greater
significance, than those of his own parents. The fact might rest upon
sympathy and physical likeness, for the grandson resembled the
grandfather, in so far, that is, as a rosy youth with the down on his
chin might resemble a bleached, rheumatic septuagenarian, Yet it
probably spoke even more for that which was indeed the truth, that
the grandfather had been the real personality, the picturesque figure
of the family.

Long before Hans Lorenz Castorp's passing, his person and the
things for which he stood had ceased to be representative of his age.
He had been a typical Christian gentleman, of the Reformed faith, of
a strongly conservative cast of mind, as obstinately convinced of the
right of the aristocracy to govern as if he had been born in the
fourteenth century, when the labouring classes had begun to make
head against the stout resistance of the free patriciate and wrest from
it a place and voice in the councils of the ancient city. He had little
use for the new. His active years had fallen in a decade of rapid
growth and repeated upheavals, a decade of progress by forced
marches, which had made continual demands on the public capacity

for enterprise and self--sacrifice. Certainly he had no part or lot, old Castorp, in the brilliant triumph of the modern spirit that followed hard upon. It was not his fault; he had held far more with ancestral ways and old institutions than with ruinous schemes for widening the harbour, or godless and rubbishing plans for a great metropolis. He had put on the brakes; he had whittled things down wherever he could; and if matters had gone to his liking, the administration would have continued to wear the same old--fashioned, idyllic guise as, in his time, his own office did.

Such, in his lifetime and afterwards, was the figure the old man presented to the eye of his fellow burghers; and such, in essentials, was he also to the childish gaze of little Hans Castorp, who knew naught of affairs of state, and whose formless, uncritical judgments were rather the fruit of mere lively perceptions. Yet they persisted into later life, as the elements of a perfectly conscious memory--picture, which defied expression or analysis, but was none the less positive for all that. We repeat that natural sympathy was in play here too, the close family tie and essential intimacy which not infrequently leaps over an intervening generation.

Senator Castorp was tall and lean. The years had bent his back and neck, but he tried to counteract the curvature by pressure in another direction; drawing down his mouth with sedulous dignity, though the lips were shrunken against the bare gums, for he had lost all his teeth, and put in the false ones only to eat. It was this posture also which helped to steady an incipient shaking of the head, gave him his look of being sternly reined up, and caused him to support his chin on his neckcloth in the manner so congenial to little Hans Castorp's taste.

He loved his snuff--box—it was a longish, gold--inlaid tortoise--shell one—and on account of his snuff--taking, used a red pocket--handkerchief, the corner of which always hung out of the back pocket of his coat. If this foible added a quaint touch to his appearance, yet the effect was only of a slight negligence or licence due to age, which length of days either consciously and cheerfully permits itself, or else brings in its train without the victim's being aware. If weakness it were, it was the only one the sharp eye of the child ever noted in his grandfather's exterior. But the old man's everyday appearance was not his real and authentic one, either to the seven--year--old child, or to the memory of the grown man in after years. That was different, far finer and truer; it was Grandfather as he appeared in a life--size portrait which had once hung in the house of Hans Castorp's own parents, had moved over with him to the Esplanade on their death, and now hung above the great red satin sofa in the reception--room.

The painting showed Hans Lorenz Castorp in his official garb as Councillor: the sober, even godly, civilian habit of a bygone century, which a commonwealth both self--assertive and enterprising had brought with it down the years and retained in ceremonial use in order to make present the past and make past the present, to bear witness to the perpetual continuity of things, and the perfect soundness of its business signature. Senator Castorp stood at full length on a red--tiled floor, in a perspective of column and pointed arch. His chin was dropped, his mouth drawn down, his blue, musing eyes, with the tear ducts plain beneath them, directed toward the distant view. He wore the black coat, cut full like a robe, more than knee--length, with a wide trimming of fur all round the edge; the upper sleeves were wide and puffed and furtrimmed too, while from beneath them came the narrow under--sleeves of plain cloth, then lace cuffs, which covered the hands to the knuckles. The slender, elderly legs were cased in black silk stockings; the shoes had silver buckles. But about his neck was the broad, starched ruff, pressed down in front and swelling out on the sides, beneath which, for good measure, a fluted jabot came out over the waistcoat. Under his arm he held the old--fashioned, broad--brimmed hat that tapered to a point at the top.

It was a capital painting, by an artist of some note, in an old--masterish style that suited the subject and was reminiscent of much Spanish, Dutch, late Middle Ages work. Little Hans Castorp had often looked at it; not, of course, with any knowledge of art, but with a larger, even a fervid comprehension. Only once—-and then only for a moment—had he ever seen Grandfather as he was here represented, on the occasion of a procession to the *Rathaus*. But he could not help feeling that this presentment was the genuine, the authentic grandfather, and the everyday one merely subsidiary, not entirely conformable—a sort of interim grandfather, as it were. For it was clear that the deviations and idiosyncrasies presented by his everyday appearance were due to incomplete, perhaps even unsuccessful adaptation; they were the not quite eradicable vestiges of Grandfather's pure and genuine form. The choker collar and band, for instance, were old--fashioned; an adjective it would have been impossible to apply to that admirable article of apparel whose interim representative they were: namely, the ruff. The same was true of the outlandish top--hat Grandfather wore, with the bellshaped crown, to which the broad--brimmed felt in the painting corresponded, only with a higher degree of actuality; and of the voluminous frock--coat, whose archetype and original was for little Hans Castorp the lace--and fur--trimmed ceremonial garment.

Thus he was glad from his heart that it should be the authentic, the perfect grandfather who lay there resplendent on that day when he came to take last leave of him. It was in the room where so often they had sat facing each other at table; and now, in the centre, Hans Lorenz Castorp was lying in a silver--mounted coffin, upon a begarlanded bier. He had fought out the attack on his lungs, fought long and stoutly, despite his air of being at home in the life of the day only by dint of his powers of adaptability. One hardly knew whether he had won or lost in the struggle; but in any case there he lay, with a stern yet satisfied expression, on his bed of state. He had altered with the illness, his nose looked sharp and thin; the lower half of his body was hidden by a coverlet on which lay a palm branch; the head was lifted high by the silken pillow, so that his chin rested beautifully in the front swell of the ruff. Between the hands, half--shrouded in their lace cuffs, their visibly cold, dead fingers artfully arranged to simulate life, was stuck an ivory cross. He seemed to gaze, beneath drooping lids, steadfastly down upon it.

[39]

Hans Castorp had probably seen his grandfather several times at the beginning of this last illness, but not toward the end. They had spared him the sight of the struggle, the more easily that it had been mostly at night; he had only felt it through the surcharged atmosphere of the house, old Fiete's red eyes, the coming and going of the doctors. What he gathered as he stood now by the bier in the dining--room, was that Grandfather had finally and formally surmounted his interim aspect and assumed for all time his true and adequate shape. And that was a gratifying result, even though old Fiete continually wept and shook his head, even though Hans Castorp himself wept, as he had at sight of the mother he had abruptly been bereft of, and the father who, so little time after her, lay in his turn still and strange before the little boy's eyes. Thus for the third time in so short a space and in such young years did death play upon the spirit and senses——but chiefly on the senses——of the lad. The sight was no longer strange, it was already right familiar; and as on those earlier occasions, only in still greater degree, he bore himself in the presence of death with a responsible air, quite self--controlled, showing no nervous weakness, if some natural dejection. He was unaware of the practical result the loss would mean to his own life, or else with childlike indifference was instinctively confident that he would be taken care of somehow; thus, at the bier, he displayed both an uncomprehending coolness and a detached alertness of observation, to which were added, on this third occasion, a feeling and expression of connoisseurship. And something more, a peculiar, precocious variation: he seemed no longer to think of tears——either the frequent outburst of grief or the contagion from the grief of others——as a natural reaction. In three or four months after his father's passing he had forgotten about death; but now he remembered, and all the impressions of that time recurred, precise, immediate, and piercing in their transcendent strangeness.

Reduced to order and put into words, they would have been something like the following. In one aspect death was a holy, a pensive, a spiritual state, possessed of a certain mournful beauty. In another it was quite different. It was precisely the opposite, it was very physical, it was material, it could not possibly be called either holy, or pensive, or beautiful—not even mournful. The solemn, spiritual side expressed itself in the ceremonial lying--in state of the corpse, in the fan--leaved palm and the wealth of flowers, all which symbolized the peace of God and the heavenly kingdom, as did even more explicitly the ivory cross stuck between the dead fingers of what was once Grandfather, and the bust of Christ by Thorwaldsen at the head of the bier, with towering candelabra on either side. It was these last that gave a churchly air to the scene. All such arrangements had their more precise justification in the fact that Grandfather was now clothed forever in his true and proper guise. But over and above that *raison d'être* they had another, of a more profane kind, of which little Hans Castorp was distinctly aware, though without admitting it in so many words. One and all of them, but expressly the flowers, and of these more expressly the hosts of tuberoses, were there to palliate the other aspect of death, the side which was neither beautiful nor exactly sad, but somehow almost improper—its lowly, physical side—to slur it over and prevent one from being conscious of it.

It was this other aspect of death that made Grandfather himself look so strange; not like Grandfather at all, more like a life--size wax doll, which death had put in his place to be the centre of all this pious and reverent spectacle. He who lay there——or, more correctly, that which lay there——was not Grandfather himself, but a shell, made, as Hans Castorp was aware, not of wax, but of its own substance, and only of that. Therein, precisely, was the impropriety. It was scarcely sad at all——as things are not which have to do with the body and only with it. Little Hans Castorp regarded that substance, waxy yellow, and fine--grained like cheese, of which the life--size figure was made, the face and hands of what had been Grandfather. A fly had settled on the quiet brow, and began to move its proboscis up and down. Old Fiete shooed it cautiously away, taking care not to touch the forehead of the dead, putting on a seemly air of absent--mindedness——of obscurantism, as it were——as though he neither

might nor would take notice of what he was doing. This correctness of demeanour obviously had to do with the fact that Grandfather was now no longer anything but body. But the fly, after a circling flight, came to rest on Grandfather's fingers, close to the ivory cross. And Hans Castorp, watching, thought he detected, more plainly than ever before, a familiar, strange exhalation, faint, yet oddly clinging——he blushed to find that it made him think of a former schoolfellow, who was avoided by his classmates because he suffered from a certain unpleasant affection——for the drowning out of which the tuberoses were there, and which, with all their lovely luxuriance and the strong-
-ness of their scent, they yet failed to overpower.

He stood three times by his Grandfather's bier. Once alone with old Fiete; once with Great--uncle Tienappel, the wine merchant, and his two uncles, James and Peter; the third and last time when a group of harbour hands in their Sunday clothes came to take leave of the head of the house of Castorp and Son. Then came the funeral. The room was full of people, and Pastor Bugenhagen of St. Michael's, the same who had baptized little Hans, preached the sermon in a ruff. He was most friendly with the boy as they drove out together to the cemetery, in the first carriage behind the hearse. Thus did another epoch in the life of Hans Castorp come to an end, and again he moved to a new home and new surroundings, for the second time in his young life.

At Tienappels', and of Young Hans's Moral State

The change was no loss to him; for he entered the home of his appointed guardian, Consul Tienappel, where he wanted for nothing. Certainly this was true so far as his bodily needs were concerned, and not less in the sense of safe--guarding his interests——about which he was still too young to know anything at all. For Consul Tienappel, an uncle of Hans's deceased mother, was administrator of the Castorp estate; he put up the property for sale, took in hand the business of liquidating the firm of Castorp and Son, Importers and Exporters, and realized from the whole nearly four hundred thousand marks, the inheritance of young Hans. This sum Consul Tienappel invested in trust funds, and took unto himself two per cent of the interest every quarter, without impairment of his kinsmanly feeling.

The Tienappel house lay at the foot of a garden in Harvest-ehuderstrasse; the windows looked out on a plot of lawn in which not the tiniest weed was suffered to flourish, then upon public rose--borders, and then upon the river. The Consul went on foot every morning to his business in the Old Town—-although he possessed more than one fine equipage—-in order to get a little exercise, for he sometimes suffered from cerebral congestion. He returned in the same way at five in the afternoon, at which time the Tienappels dined, with due and fitting ceremony. He was a weighty man, whose suits were always of the best English cloths; his eyes were watery blue and prominent behind his gold--rimmed glasses, his nose was ruddy, and his square--cut beard was grey; he wore a flashing brilliant on the stubby little finger of his left hand. His wife was long since dead. He had two sons, Peter and James, of whom one was in the navy and seldom at home, the other occupied in the paternal wine trade, and destined heir to the business. The housekeeping, for many years, had been the care of an Altona goldsmith's daughter, named Schalleen, who wore starched white ruffles at her plump, round wrists. Hers it was to see to it that the table, morning and evening, was richly laden with cold meats, with crabs and salmon, eel and smoked breast of goose, with tomato ketchup for the roast beef. She kept a watchful eye on the hired waiters when Consul Tienappel gave a gentlemen's dinner; and she it was who, so far as in her lay, took the place of a mother to little Hans Castorp.

So he grew up; in wretched weather, in the teeth of wind and mist, grew up, so to say, in a yellow mackintosh, and, generally speaking, he throve. A little anæmic he had always been, so Dr. Heidekind said, and had him take a good glass of porter after third breakfast every day, when he came home from school. This, as everyone knows, is a hearty drink—-Dr. Heidekind considered it a blood-

-maker—-and certainly Hans Castorp found it most soothing to his spirits and encouraging to a propensity of his, which his Uncle Tienappel called "dozing": namely, sitting staring into space, with his jaw dropped and his thoughts fixed on just nothing at all. But on the whole he was sound and fit, an adequate tennis player and rower; though actually handling the oars was less to his taste than sitting of a summer evening on the terrace of the Uhlenhorst ferry--house, with a good drink before him and the sound of music in his ears, while he watched the lighted boats, and the swans mirrored in the bright water. Hear him talk, sedate and sensible, in a rather low, monotonous voice, just tinged with dialect; observe him in his blond correctness, with his well--shaped head, which had about it some stamp of the classic, and his self--possessed, indolent bearing, the fruit of innate, inherited, perfectly unconscious self--esteem—-you would swear that this young Castorp was a legitimate and genuine product of the soil in which he flourished, and strikingly at home in his environment. Nor would he, had he ever put such a question to himself, have been for a single second doubtful of the answer.

Yes, he was thoroughly in his element in the atmosphere of this great seaboard city: this reeking air, compact of good living and a retail trade that embraced the four corners of the earth. It had been the breath of his father's nostrils, and the son drew it in with profound acquiescence and a sense of well--being. The exhalations from water, coals, and tar, the sharp tang in the nostrils from heaped--up stacks of colonial produce; the huge steam--cranes at the dock--side, imitating the quiet, the intelligence, and the giant strength of elephants at work, as they hoisted tons of sacks, bales, chests, vats, and carboys out of the bowels of seagoing ships and conveyed them into waiting trains and scales; the business men, in yellow rubber coats like his own, streaming to the Bourse at midday, where, as he knew, there was oftentimes pretty sharp work, and a man might have to strengthen his credit at short notice by giving out invitations to a big dinner—-all this he felt, saw, heard, knew. Besides it all, there was the field in which later was to lie his own particular interest: the confusion of the yards, the mammoth bodies of great ships, Asiatic and African liners, lying in dry--dock, keel and propeller bare, supported by props as thick as tree--trunks, lying there in monstrous helplessness, swarmed over by troops of men like dwarfs, scouring, whitewashing, hammering; there were the roofed--over ways, wrapped in wreaths of smoke--like mist, holding the towering frames of rising ships, among which moved the engineers, blueprint and loading scale in hand, directing the work--people. All these were familiar sights to Hans Castorp from his youth upwards, awaking in him only the agreeable, homely sensations of "belonging," which were the prerogative of his years. Such sensations would reach their height when he sat of a Sunday forenoon with James Tienappel or his cousin Ziemssen—-Joachim Ziemssen—-in the pavilion at Alster, breakfasting on hot cuts and smoked meat, with a glass of old port; or when, having eaten, he would lean back in his chair and give himself up to his cigar. For therein especially was he true to type, that he liked good living, and notwithstanding his thinbloodedness and look of over--refinement clung to the grosser pleasures of life as a greedy suckling to its mother's breast.

Comfortably, not without dignity, he carried the weight of culture with which the governing upper class of the commercial city endowed its children. He was as clean as a well--cared--for baby, and dressed by the tailor in whom the young men of his social sphere felt most confidence. Schalleen took beautiful care of his small stock of carefully marked linen, which was bestowed in a dressing--chest on the English plan. When he studied away from home, he regularly sent back his laundry to be washed and mended, for it was a saying of his that outside Hamburg nobody in the kingdom knew how to iron. A rough spot on the cuff of his dainty coloured shirts filled him with acute discomfort. His hands, though not particularly aristocratic in shape, were well tended and fresh--skinned, and he wore a platinum chain ring as well as the seal ring inherited from Grandfather. His teeth were rather soft and defective and he had a number of gold fillings.

Standing and walking, he rather stuck out his abdomen, which hardly made an athletic impression; but his bearing at table was beyond cavil. Sitting very erect, he would turn the whole upper part of his body to speak to his neighbour (with selfpossession, of course, and a little *platt*) and he kept his elbows well in as he dismembered his piece of fowl, or deftly, with the appointed tool, drew the rosy flesh from a lobster's shell. His first requirement after a meal was the finger--bowl of perfumed water, his second the Russian cigarette---which paid no duty, as he had a convenient way of getting them smuggled in. After the cigarette the cigar; he favoured a Bremen brand called Maria Mancini, of which we shall hear more hereafter; the fragrant narcotic blended so soothingly with the coffee. Hans Castorp protected his supply of tobacco from the injurious effects of steam--heating by keeping it in the cellar, whither he would betake himself every morning to load his case with his stock for the day. It went against his grain to eat butter served in the piece instead of in little fluted balls.

It will be seen that we mean to say everything that may be said in Hans Castorp's favour, yet without fulsomeness, not making him out as better, or worse, than he was. He was neither genius nor dunderhead; and if, in our description of him, we have avoided the use of the word mediocre, it has been for reasons quite unconnected with his intelligence, hardly even with any bearing upon his whole simple personality, but rather out of regard for his lot in life, to which we incline to ascribe a certain importance above and beyond personal considerations. His head--piece sustained without undue strain the demands made upon it by the course at the Realgymnasium---strain, indeed, was something to which he was quite definitely disinclined, whatever the circumstances or the object of his effort; less out of fear of hurting himself than because he positively saw no reason, or, more precisely, saw no positive reason, for exertion. This then, perhaps, is why we may not call him mediocre: that, somehow or other, he was aware of the lack of such a reason. A man lives not only his personal life, as an individual, but also, consciously or unconsciously, the life of his epoch and his contemporaries. He may regard the general, impersonal foundations of his existence as definitely settled and taken for granted, and be as far from assuming a critical attitude toward them as our good Hans Castorp really was; yet it is quite conceivable that he may none the less be vaguely conscious of the deficiencies of his epoch and find them prejudicial to his own moral well--being. All sorts of personal aims, ends, hopes, prospects, hover before the eyes of the individual, and out of these he derives the impulse to ambition and achievement. Now, if the life about him, if his own time seem, however outwardly stimulating, to be at bottom empty of such food for his aspirations; if he privately recognize it to be hopeless, viewless, helpless, opposing only a hollow silence to all the questions man puts, consciously or unconsciously, yet somehow, puts, as to the final, absolute, and abstract meaning in all his efforts and activities; then, in such a case, a certain laming of the personality is bound to occur, the more inevitably the more upright the character in question; a sort of palsy, as it were, which may even extend from his spiritual and moral over into his physical and organic part. In an age that affords no satisfying answer to the eternal question of "Why?" "To what end?" a man who is capable of achievement over and above the average and expected modicum must be equipped either with a moral remoteness and single--mindedness which is rare indeed and of heroic mould, or else with an exceptionally robust vitality. Hans Castorp had neither the one nor the other of these; and thus he must be considered mediocre, though in an entirely honourable sense.

All this that we have said has reference to the inward state of the young man not only during his school years, but also in those that followed, after he had made choice of his civil profession. On his way through his forms at school, he had now and again to take one for the second time. But in the main his origin, his good breeding, and also a pretty if unimpassioned gift for mathematics got him forward; and when he received his one--year service certificate, he made up his mind to continue at school, principally, it must be said, because he thus prolonged a situation he was used to, in which no definite decisions had to be taken, and in which he had further time to think matters over and decide what he really wanted to do, which he was far from knowing after he had arrived at the top form. Even when it was finally decided——to say when Hans Castorp finally decided it would be saying too much——he had the feeling that it might quite as well have been decided some other way.

So much, however, was true, that he had always liked ships. As a small boy he had filled the pages of his note--books with drawings of fishing--barks, five--masters and vegetable--barges. When he was fifteen, he had had a front seat at the christening ceremony of the new double--screw steamer *Hansa*. He had watched her leave the ways at Blohm and Voss's, and afterwards made quite a happy water--colour of the graceful ship, done with a good deal of attention to detail, and a loving and not unskillful treatment of the glassy green, rolling waves. Consul Tienappel hung it in his private office, and somebody told him that it showed talent, that the artist might develop into a good marine painter——a remark which the Consul could safely repeat to his ward, for Hans Castorp only laughed good--humouredly, and not for a moment considered letting himself in for a career of being eccentric and not getting enough to eat.

"You haven't so much, you know," his Uncle Tienappel would say to him. "James and Peter will get most of what I have; that is to say, it stops in the business, and Peter will draw his interest. What belongs to you is well invested, and brings you in something safe. But it's no joke living on your interest to--day, unless one has at least five times what you have; and if you want to be somebody here in this town and live as you have been brought up to, you'll have to earn a good bit more to put with it, you mark my words, my son."

Hans Castorp marked them. He looked about for a profession suitable in his own eyes and those of his fellow citizens. And when he had once chosen——it came about at the instance of old Wilms, of the firm of Tunder and Wilms, who said to Consul Tienappel at the Saturday whist--table that young Castorp ought to study ship--building; it would be a good idea, he could come into his office and he would keep an eye on him——when he had once chosen, he thought very highly of his calling. It was, to be sure, confoundedly complicated and fatiguing, but all the same it was very first--rate, very solid, very important. And certainly, being peaceful in his tastes, he preferred it to that of his cousin Ziemssen, the son of his mother's half--sister, who was bent on being an officer. But Joachim Ziemssen was rather weak in the chest, and for that reason a calling which would keep him in the open, and in which there was no mental strain or fatigue to speak of, might be quite the right thing for him, Hans Castorp thought with easy condescension. He had the greatest respect for work——though personally he found that he tired easily.

And here we revert to our suggestion of a few pages back: the idea that an unfavourable influence exerted upon a man's personal life by the times in which he lives may even extend to his physical organism. Hans Castorp respected work——as how should he not have? It would have been unnatural. Work was for him, in the nature of things, the most estimable attribute of life; when you came down to it, there was nothing else that was estimable. It was the principle by which one stood or fell, the Absolute of the time; it was, so to speak, its own justification. His regard for it was thus religious in its character, and, so far as he knew, unquestioning. But it was another matter, whether he loved it; and that he could not do, however great his regard, the simple reason being that it did not agree with him. Exacting occupation dragged at his nerves, it wore him out; quite openly he confessed that he liked better to have his time free, not weighted with the leaden load of effort; lying spacious before him, not divided up by obstacles one had to grit one's teeth and conquer, one after the other. These conflicting sentiments on the subject of work had, strictly speaking, to be reconciled. Is it, perhaps, possible, if he had been able to believe in work as a positive value, a self--justifying principle, believe in it in the very depth of his soul, even without being himself conscious of doing so, that his body as well as his spirit——first the spirit and through it the body as well——would have been able to devote itself to his task with more of joy and constancy, would have been able to find peace therein? Here again is posed the question of Hans Castorp's mediocrity or more than mediocrity, to which we would give no hard and fast answer. For we do not set up as the young man's encomiast, and prefer to leave room for the other view: namely, that his work stood somewhat in the way of his unclouded enjoyment of his Maria Mancini.

To military service he was not inclined. His being revolted against it, and found ways of making difficulties. It may be, too, that Staff Medical Officer Dr. Eberding, who visited at Harvestehuderstrasse, heard from Consul Tienappel, in the course of conversation, that young Castorp was leaving home to begin his technical studies, and would find a call to the colours a very sensible interruption to his labours. Working slowly and deliberately——he kept up his soothing habit of porter breakfasts while he was away——he filled his brain with analytic and descriptive geometry, differential calculus, mechanics, projection, hydrostatic; reckoned full and empty displacement, stability, trim moment, and metacentre; and sometimes he got very sick of it. His technical drawings, the draughts and designs of frames, waterlines and longitudinal projections, were not quite so good as the picturesque representation of the *Hansa* on the high seas; but wherever it was in place to call in the sense perceptions to help out the intellectual, wherever he could wash in the shadows and lay on the cross--sections in the conventional colours, there Hans Castorp showed more dexterity than most.

When he came home for the holidays, very clean, very well dressed, with a little red--blond moustache that became his sleepy, young patrician face, obviously *en route* to a considerable position in life, people looked at him, the people who concerned themselves with the affairs of the community and made it their business to know all about family and social relations——and that, in a self--governing city--state, meant most of the population——they looked him well over, his fellow citizens, and asked themselves what public rôle young Castorp was destined to fill. He had traditions, his name was old and good, they would certainly have to reckon with him one day, as a political factor. Some day he would sit in the Assembly, or on the Board of Directors, he would help make the laws, he would occupy some honourable office and share the burdens of sovereignty. He would belong to the executive branch, perhaps, or the Finance or Building Commission. His voice would be listened to, his vote would count. It would be interesting to see what party he would choose. Appearances were deceiving, but he did not look as a man does whom the democrats can count on; and his likeness to his grandfather was unmistakable. Would he take after him, and be a drag, a conservative element? It was quite possible—-but so was the opposite. He was an engineer, studying ship--building; on the technical side, in touch with world commerce. He might turn out to be a radical, a reckless spender, a profane destroyer of old buildings and landscape beauties. He might be as unfettered as a Jew, as irreverent as an American; he might prefer a ruthless break with tradition to a considered development of natural resources; he might incline to plunge the state into foolhardy experimentation. All that was conceivable. Was it in his blood to feel that their Worships in the Senate, before whom the double sentry at the *Rathaus* presented arms, were likely to know best in all contingencies; or would he side with the opposition in the Assembly? In his blue eyes, under their reddish--brown brows, his fellow citizens read no answer to their curious questioning. And he probably knew none himself, Hans Castorp, this still unwritten page.

When he took the journey upon which we have encountered him, he was in his twenty--third year. He had spent four semesters at the Dantzig Polytechnic, four more at the technical schools of Braunschweig and Karlsruhe, and had just previously passed his first final, quite respectably, if without any fanfare of trumpets. And now he was preparing to enter the firm of Tunder and Wilms, as volunteer apprentice, in order to get his practical training in the ship--yards.

But at this point his life took the following turn. He had had to work hard and steadily for his examination, and came home looking rather paler than a man of his blond, rosy type should do. Dr. Heidekind scolded, and insisted on a change of air; a complete change, not a stay at Norderney or Wyk on Föhr—-that would not mend matters this time, he said; if they wanted his advice, it was that Hans Castorp should go for a few weeks to the high mountains before he took up his work in the yards. Consul Tienappel told his nephew and foster--son he approved of the plan, only that in that case they would part company for the summer, for wild horses couldn't drag him into the high mountains. They were not for him; he required a reasonable atmospheric pressure, else he might get an attack. Hans Castorp would be good enough to go by himself—-let him pay his cousin Ziemssen a visit.

It was an obvious suggestion. Joachim Ziemssen was ill—-not ill like Hans Castorp, but in all seriousness, critically. There had been a great scare, in fact. He had always been subject to feverish catarrh, and one day he actually spat blood; whereupon he had been rushed off to Davos, heels over head, to his great distress and affliction, for he had just then arrived within sight of the goal of all his hopes. Some semesters long, he had complied with the wish of his family and studied law; then, yielding to irresistible inward urging, he had changed over, presented himself as ensign and been accepted. And now, for the past five months, he had been stuck in the International Sanatorium Berghof (directing physician Hofrat Behrens) and was bored half sick, as he wrote home on postcards. If Hans Castorp wanted to do himself a good turn before he entered his post at Tunder and Wilms's, what more natural than that he should go up to Davos and keep his poor cousin company for a while—-it would be agreeable on both sides.

It was midsummer before he made up his mind to go. Already the last week in July. He left for a stay of three weeks.

CHAPTER III
Drawing the Veil

*H*e had been so utterly weary, he had feared to oversleep;

but he was on his legs rather earlier than usual, and had a superfluity
of leisure in which to perform the accustomed ritual of his morning
toilet, in which a rubber tub, a wooden bowl of green lavender soap,
and the accompanying little brush played the principal parts. He had
even time to do some unpacking and moving in. As he covered his
cheeks with scented lather and drew over them the blade of his silver-
-plated "safety," he recalled his confused dreams and shook his head
indulgently over so much nonsense, with the superior feeling a man
has when shaving himself in the clear light of reason. He did not feel
precisely rested, yet had a sense of morning freshness.

With powdered cheeks, in his Scotch--thread drawers and red
morocco slippers, he walked out on the balcony, drying his hands.
The balcony ran across the house and was divided into small separate
compartments by opaque glass partitions, which did not quite reach
to the balustrade. The morning was cool and cloudy. Trails of mist
lay motionless in front of the heights on one side and the other, while
great cloud--masses, grey and white, hung down over the distant
peaks. Patches and bands of blue showed here and there; now and
then a gleam of sunshine lighted up the village down in the valley, till
it glistened whitely against the dark fir--covered slopes. Somewhere
there was music, very likely in the same hotel where there had been a
concert the evening before. The subdued chords of a hymn floated
up; after a pause came a march. Hans Castorp loved music from his
heart; it worked upon him in much the same way as did his breakfast

[53]

porter, with deeply soothing, narcotic effect, tempting him to doze. He listened well pleased, his head on one side, his eyes a little bloodshot.

He could see below him the winding road up to the sanatorium, by which he had come the night before. Among the dewy grass of the sloping terrace short--stemmed, star--shaped gentians stood out. Part of the level ground had been enclosed for a garden, with flower--beds, gravel paths, and an artificial grotto under a stately silver fir. A hall, with reclining--chairs and a galvanized roof, opened towards the south; near it stood a flag--pole, painted reddish--brown, on which the flag fluttered open now and then on its cord. It was a fancy flag, green and white, with the caduceus, the emblem of healing, in the centre.

A woman was walking in the garden, an elderly lady, of melancholy, even tragic aspect. Dressed all in black, a black veil wound about her dishevelled grey--black hair, with wrinkled brow and coal--black eyes that had hanging pouches of skin beneath them, she moved with rapid, restless step along the garden paths, staring straight before her, her knees a little bent, her arms hanging stiffly down. The ageing face in its southern pallor, with the large, wried mouth drawn down on one side, reminded Hans Castorp of a portrait he had once seen of a famous tragic actress. And strange it was to see how the pale, black--clad woman unconsciously matched her long, woeful pace to the music of the march.

He looked down upon her with pensive sympathy; it seemed to him the sad apparition darkened the morning sunshine. But in the same instant he became aware of something else, something audible: certain noises penetrating to his hearing from the room on the left of his own, which was occupied, Joachim had said, by a Russian couple. Again he felt a discrepancy; these sounds no more suited the blithe freshness of the morning than had the sad sight in the garden below——rather they seemed to befoul the air, make it thick, sticky. Hans Castorp recalled having heard similar sounds the evening before, though his weariness had prevented him from heeding them:

a struggling, a panting and giggling, the offensive nature of which could not long remain hidden to the young man, try as he good--naturedly did to put a harmless construction on them. Perhaps something more or other than good nature was in play, something to which we give a variety of names, calling it now purity of soul, which sounds insipid; again by that grave, beautiful name of chastity; and yet again disparaging it as hypocrisy, as "hating to look facts in the face"; even ascribing it to an obscure sense of awe and piety——and, in truth, something of all these was in Hans Castorp's face and bearing as he listened. He seemed to be practising a seemly obscurantism; to be mentally drawing the veil over these sounds that he heard; to be telling himself that honour forbade his taking any cognizance of them, or even hearing them at all——it gave him an air of propriety which was not quite native, though he knew how to assume it on occasion.

With this mien, then, he drew back from the balcony into his room, in order not to listen further to proceedings which, for all the giggling that went with them, were plainly in dead earnest, even alarming. But from indoors the noise could be heard even more plainly. He seemed to hear a chase about the room; a chair fell over; someone was caught and seized; loud kissing ensued——and the music below had changed to a waltz, a popular air whose hackneyed, melodious phrases accompanied the invisible scene. Hans Castorp stood towel in hand and listened, against his better judgment. And he began to blush through the powder; for what he had all along seen coming was come, and the game had passed quite frankly over into the bestial. "Good Lord!" he thought. He turned away and made as much noise as possible while he concluded his toilet. "Well, at least they are married, as far as that goes," he said to himself. "But in broad daylight——it's a bit thick! And last night too, I'm sure. But of course they are ill, or at least one of them, or they wouldn't be here--that may be some excuse. The scandalous part of it is, the walls are so thin one can't help hearing everything. Simply intolerable. The place is shamefully jerry--built, of course. What if I should see them, or even be introduced? I simply couldn't endure it!" Here Hans Castorp remarked with surprise that the flush which had mounted in his freshly shaven cheek did not subside, nor its accompanying warmth: his face glowed with the same dry heat as on the evening before. He had got free of it in sleep, but the blush had made it set in again. He did not feel the friendlier for this discovery towards the wretched pair next door; in fact he stuck out his lips and muttered a derogatory word in their direction, as he tried to cool his hot face by bathing it in cold water—-and only made it glow the more. He felt put out; his voice vibrated with ill humour as he answered to his cousin's knock on the wall; and he appeared to Joachim on his entrance like anything but a man refreshed and invigorated by a good night's sleep.

Breakfast

"Morning," Joachim said. "Well, that was your first night up here. How did you find it?"

He was dressed for out--of--doors, in sports clothes and stout boots, and carried his ulster over his arm. The outline of the flat bottle could be seen on the side pocket. As yesterday, he wore no hat.

"Thanks," responded Hans Castorp, "it was well enough, I won't try to judge yet. I've had all sorts of mixed--up dreams, and this building seems to possess the disadvantage of being porous—-the sound goes straight through it. It's annoying.—-

Who is that dark woman down in the garden?"

Joachim knew at once whom he meant.

"Oh," he said, "that's Tous--les--deux. We all call her that up here, because it's the only thing she says. Mexican, you know; doesn't know a word of German and hardly any French, just a few scraps. She has been here for five weeks with her eldest son, a hopeless case, without much longer to go. He has it all over, tubercular through and through, you might say. Behrens says it is much like typhus, at the end—-horrible for all concerned. Well, two weeks ago the second son came up, to see his brother before the end—-handsome as a picture; both of them were that, with eyes like live coals—-they fluttered the dovecots, I can tell you. He had been coughing a bit down below, but otherwise quite lively. Well, he no sooner gets up here than he begins to run a temperature, high fever, you know, 103.1°. They put him to bed—-and if he gets up again, Behrens says, it will be more good luck than good management. But it was high time he came, in any case, Behrens says.—-Well, and since then the mother goes about—-whenever she is not sitting with them—-and if you speak to her, she just says: *'Tous les deux!'* She can't say any more, and for the moment there is no one up here who understands Spanish."

"So that's it," Hans Castorp said. "Will she say it to me, when I get to know her, do you think? That will be queer—-funny and weird at the same time, I mean." His eyes looked as they had yesterday, they felt hot and heavy, as if tired with weeping, and yet brilliant too, with the gleam that had been kindled in them yesterday at the sound of that strange, new cough on the part of the gentleman rider. He had the feeling that he had been out of touch with yesterday since waking, and had only now picked up the threads again where he laid them down. He told his cousin he was ready, sprinkling a few drops of lavender--water on his handkerchief as he spoke and dabbing his face with it, on the brow and under the eyes. "If you like, we can go to breakfast, *tous les deux*," he recklessly joked. Joachim looked with mildness at him, then smiled his enigmatic smile of mingled melancholy and mockery—-or so it seemed, for he did not express himself otherwise.

After looking to his supply of cigars Hans Castorp took coat and stick, also, rather defiantly, his hat—-he was far too sure of himself and his station in life to alter his ways and acquire new ones for a mere three weeks' visit—-and they went out and down the steps. In the corridor Joachim pointed to this and that door and gave the names of the occupants—-there were German names, but also all sorts of foreign ones—-with brief comments on them and the seriousness of their cases.

They met people already coming back from breakfast, and when Joachim said good--morning, Hans Castorp courteously lifted his hat. He was tense and nervous, as a young man is when about to present himself before strangers——when, that is, he is conscious that his eyes are heavy and his face red. The last, however, was only true in part, for he was rather pale than otherwise.

"Before I forget it," he said abruptly, "you may introduce me to the lady in the garden if you like, I mean if it happens that way, I have no objection. She would just say: *'Tous les deux'* to me, and I shouldn't mind it, being prepared, and knowing what it means——I should know how to look. But I don't wish to know the Russian pair, do you hear? I expressly don't wish it. They are a very ill--behaved lot. If I must live for three weeks next door to them, and nothing else could be arranged, at least I needn't know them. I am justified in that, and I simply and explicitly decline."

"Very good," Joachim said. "Did they disturb you? Yes, they are barbarians, more or less; uncivilized, I told you so before. He comes to the table in a leather jacket, very shabby, I always wonder Behrens doesn't make a row. And she isn't the cleanest in this world, with her feather hat. You may make yourself quite easy, they sit at the 'bad' Russian table, a long way off us——there is a 'good' Russian table, too, you see, where the nicer Russians sit——and there is not much chance of you coming into contact with them, even if you wanted to. It is not very easy to make acquaintance here, partly from the fact that there are so many foreigners. Personally, as long as I've been here, I know very few."

"Which of the two is ill?" Hans Castrop asked. "He or she?"

"The man I think. Yes, only the man," Joachim answered, absently. They passed among the hat--and coat--racks and entered the light, low--vaulted hall, where there was a buzzing of voices, a clattering of dishes, and a running to and fro of waitresses with steaming jugs.

There were seven tables, all but two of them standing lengthwise of the room. They were good--sized, seating each ten persons, though not all of them were at present full. A few steps diagonally into the room, and they stood at their places; Hans Castorp's was at the end of a table placed between the two crosswise ones. Erect behind his chair, he bowed stiffly but amiably to each table--mate in turn, as Joachim formally presented him; hardly seeing them, much less having their names penetrate his mind. He caught but a single name and person——Frau Stöhr, whom he perceived to have a red face and greasy ash--blond hair. Looking at her he could quite credit the malapropisms Joachim told of. Her face expressed nothing but ill--nature and ignorance. He sat down, observing as he did so that early breakfast was taken seriously up here.

There were pots of marmalade and honey, basins of rice and oatmeal porridge, dishes of cold meat and scrambled eggs; a plenitude of butter, a Gruyère cheese dropping moisture under a glass bell. A bowl of fresh and dried fruits stood in the centre of the table. A waitress in black and white asked Hans Castorp whether he would drink coffee, cocoa or tea. She was small as a child, with a long, oldish face——a dwarf, he realized with a start. He looked at his cousin, who only shrugged indifferently with brows and shoulders, as though to say: "Well, what of it?" So he adjusted himself as speedily as possible to the fact that he was being served by a dwarf, and put special consideration into his voice as he asked for tea. Then he began eating rice with cinnamon and sugar, his eyes roving over the table full of other inviting viands, and over the guests at the six remaining tables, Joachim's companions and fellow victims, who were all inwardly infected, and now sat there breakfasting. The hall was done in that modern style which knows how to give just the right touch of individuality to something in reality very simple. It was rather shallow in proportion to its length, and opened in great arched bays into a sort of lobby surrounding it, in which serving--tables were placed. The pillars were faced halfway up with wood finished to look like sandalwood, the upper part white--enamelled, like the ceiling and upper half of the walls. They were stenciled in gay--coloured bands of simple and lively designs which were repeated on the girders of the vaulted ceiling. The room was further enlivened by several electric chandeliers in bright brass, consisting of three rings placed horizontally one over the other and held together by delicate woven work, the lowest ring set with globes of milky glass like little moons. There were four glass doors, two on the opposite wall, opening on the verandah, a third at the bottom of the room on the left, leading into the front hall, and a fourth, by which Hans Castorp had entered through a vestibule, as Joachim had brought him down a different stair from the one they had used yesterday evening.

He had on his right a plain--looking woman in black, with a dull flush on her cheeks, the skin of which was downy--looking, as an older person's often is. She looked to him like a seamstress or home dressmaker, the idea being suggested by the fact that she took only coffee and buttered rolls for breakfast; since his childhood he had always somehow associated dressmakers with coffee and buttered rolls. On his left sat an English spinster, also well on in years, very ugly, with frozen, withered--looking fingers. She sat reading her home letters, which were written in round hand, and drinking tea the colour of blood. Next her was Joachim, and then Frau Stöhr, in a woollen blouse of Scotch plaid. She held her left hand doubled up in a fist near her cheek as she ate, and drew her upper lip back from her long, narrow, rodent--like teeth when she spoke, obviously trying to make an impression of culture and refinement. A young man with thin moustaches sat next beyond. His facial expression was of one with something bad--tasting in his mouth, and he ate without a word. He had come in after Hans Castorp was already seated, with his chin sunk on his breast; and sat down so, without even lifting his head in greeting, seeming by his bearing plumply to decline being made acquainted with the new guest. He was, perhaps, too ill to have thought of or care for appearances, or even to take any interest in his surroundings. Opposite him there had sat for a short time a very lean, light--blonde girl who emptied a bottle of yogurt on her plate, ladled it up with a spoon, and took herself off. The conversation at table was not lively. Joachim talked politely with Frau Stöhr, inquired after her condition and heard with proper solicitude that it was unsatisfactory. She complained of relaxation. "I feel so relaxed," she said with a drawl and an underbred, affected manner. And she had had 99.1° when she got up that morning—what was she likely to have by afternoon? The dressmaker confessed to the same temperature, but she on the contrary felt excited, tense, and restless, as though some important event were about to happen, which was certainly not the case; the excitation was purely physical, quite without emotional grounds. Hans Castorp thought to himself that she could not be a dressmaker after all; she spoke too correctly, even pedantically. He found her excitation, or rather the expression of it, somehow unsuitable, almost offensive, in so homely and insignificant a creature. He asked her and Frau Stöhr, one after the other, how long they had been up here, and found that one had five, the other seven months to her credit. Then he mustered his English to inquire of his neighbour on the right what sort of tea she was drinking (it was made of rose--hips) and if it tasted good, which she almost passionately affirmed; then he watched people coming and going in the room; the first breakfast, it appeared, was not regarded as a regular meal, in any strict sense.

He had been a little afraid of unpleasant impressions, but found himself agreeably disappointed. The room was lively, one had not the least feeling of being in a place of suffering. Tanned young people of both sexes came in humming, spoke to the waitresses, and fell to upon the viands with robust appetite. There were older people, married couples, a whole family with children, speaking Russian, and half--grown lads. The women wore chiefly close--fitting jackets of wool or silk—the so--called sweater—in white or colours, with turnover collars and side pockets; they would stand with hands thrust deep in these pockets, and talk—it looked very pretty. At some tables photographs were being handed about—amateur photography, no doubt—at another stamps were being exchanged. The talk was of the weather, of how one had slept, of what one had "measured in the mouth" on rising. Nearly everybody seemed in good spirits, probably on no other grounds than that they were in numerous company and had no immediate cares. Here and there, indeed, sat someone who rested his head on his hand and stared before him. They let him stare, and paid no heed.

Hans Castorp gave a sudden angry start. A door was slammed——it was the one on the left, leading into the hall, and someone had let it fall shut, or even banged it, a thing he detested; he had never been able to endure it. Whether from his upbringing, or out of a natural idiosyncrasy, he loathed the slamming of doors, and could have struck the guilty person. In this case, the door was filled in above with small glass panes, which augmented the shock with their ringing and rattling. "Oh, come," he thought angrily, "what kind of damned carelessness was that?" But at the same time the seamstress addressed him with a remark, and he had no time to see who the transgressor had been. Deep creases furrowed his blond brows, and his face was contorted as he turned to reply to his neighbour.

Joachim asked whether the doctors had come through. Yes, someone answered, they had been there once and left the room just as the cousins entered. Then it would be better not to wait, Joachim thought. An opportunity for introducing his cousin would surely come in the course of the day. But at the door they nearly ran into Hofrat Behrens, as he entered with hasty steps, followed by Dr. Krokowski.

"Hullo--ullo there! Take care, gentlemen! That might have been rough on all of our corns!" He spoke with a strong low--Saxon accent, broad and mouthingly. "Oh, so here you are," he addressed Hans Castorp, whom Joachim, heels together, presented.

"Well, glad to see you." He reached the young man a hand the size of a shovel. He was some three heads taller than Dr. Krokowski; a bony man, his hair already quite white; his neck stuck out, his large, goggling bloodshot blue eyes were swimming in tears; he had a snub nose, and a close--trimmed little moustache, which made a crooked line because his upper lip was drawn up on one side. What Joachim had said about his cheeks was fully borne out; they were really purple, and set off his head garishly against the white surgeon's coat he wore, a belted smock of more than kneelength, beneath which showed striped trousers and a pair of enormous feet in rather worn yellow laced boots. Dr. Krokowski too was in professional garb; but his smock was of some shiny black stuff and made like a shirt, with elastic bands at the wrists. It contrasted sharply with the pallor of his skin. His manner suggested that he was present solely in his capacity as assistant; he took no part in the greeting, but a certain expression at the corners of his mouth betrayed the fact that he felt the strain of his subordinate position.

"Cousins?" the Hofrat asked, motioning with his hand from one to the other of the two young men and looking at them with his bloodshot eyes. "Is he going to follow the drums like you?" he addressed Joachim, jerking his head at Hans Castorp. "God forbid, eh? I could tell as soon as I saw you"——he spoke now directly to the young man——"that you were a layman; there's something civilian and comfortable about you, not like our sabre--rattling corporal here! You'd be a better patient than he is, I'll wager. I can tell by looking at people, you know, whether they'll make good patients or not; it takes talent, everything takes talent——and this myrmidon here hasn't a spark. Maybe he shows up on the parade--ground, for aught I know; but he's no good a' being ill. Will you believe it, he's always wanting to clear out! Badgers me all the time, simply can't wait to get down there and be skinned alive. There's doggedness for you! Won't give us even a measly half--a--year! And yet it's quite pretty up here; I leave it to you if it isn't, Ziemssen, what? ... Well, your cousin will appreciate us, even if you don't. He'll get some fun out of it. There's no shortage in the lady market here, either; we have the most charming females. At least, some of them are very picturesque on the outside. But you ought to have better colour yourself, you know, if you want to please the sex. 'The golden tree of life is green,' as the poet says——but it's a poor colour for the complexion, all the same. Totally anæmic, of course," he broke off, and without more ado put up his index and middle fingers and drew down Hans Castorp's eyelid. "Precisely! Totally anæmic, as I was saying. You know it wasn't such a bad idea of yours to let your native Hamburg shift for itself awhile. Great institution, Hamburg——simply revels in humidity——sends us a tidy contingent every year. But if I may take the occasion to give you the benefit of my poor opinion—— *sine pecunia*, you understand, quite *sine pecunia*——I would suggest that you do just as your cousin does, while you are up here. You couldn't turn a better trick than to behave for the time as though you had a slight *tuberculosis pulmonum*, and put on a little flesh. It's curious about the metabolism of protein with us up here. Although the process of combustion is heightened, yet the body at the same time puts on flesh.——Well, Ziemssen, slept pretty well, what? ... Splendid! Then get on with the out--of--doors exercise——but not more than half an hour, you hear? And afterwards stick the quicksilver cigar in your face, eh? And be good and write it down, Ziemssen! That's a conscientious lad! Saturday I'll look at the curve. Your cousin better measure too. Measuring can't hurt anybody. Morning, gentlemen. Have a good time——morning—— morning——" Krokowski joined him as he sailed off down the hall, swinging his arms palms backward, directing to right and left the question about sleeping well, which was answered on all sides in the affirmative.

Banter. Viaticum. Interrupted Mirth

"Very nice man," Hans Castorp said, as after a friendly nod to the lame concierge, who was sorting letters in his lodge, they passed out into the open air. The main entrance was on the south--west side of the white building, the central portion of which was a storey higher than the wings, and crowned by a turret with a roof of slatecoloured tin. You did not issue from this side into the hedged--in garden, but were immediately in the open, in sight of the steep mountain meadows, dotted with single fir--trees of moderate size, and writhen, stunted pines. The way they took—-it was the only one they could take, outside the drive going down to the valley—-rose by a gentle ascent to the left, behind the sanatorium, past the kitchen and domestic offices, where huge dustbins stood at the area rails. Thence it led in the same direction for a goodish piece, then made a sharp bend to the right and mounted more rapidly along the thinly wooded slopes. It was a reddish path, firm and yet rather moist underfoot, with boulders here and there along the edge. The cousins were by no means alone upon it: guests who had finished breakfast not long after them followed hard upon their steps, and groups of others, already returning, approached with the stalking gait of people descending a steep incline.

"Very nice man," repeated Hans Castorp. "He has such a flow of words I enjoy listening to him. 'Quicksilver cigar' was capital, I got it at once.—-But I'll just light up a real one," he said, pausing, "I can't hold out any longer. I haven't had a proper smoke since yesterday after luncheon. Excuse me a minute." He opened his automobile- -leather case, with its silver monogram, and drew out a Maria Mancini, a beautiful specimen of the first layer, flattened on one side as he particularly liked it; he cut off the tip slantingly with a sharp little tool he wore on his watch--chain, then, striking a tiny flame with his pocket apparatus, puffed with concentration at the long, blunt- -ended cigar until it was alight. "There!" he said. "Now, as far as I'm concerned, we can get on with the exercise. You don't smoke—-out of sheer doggedness, of course."

"I never do smoke," answered Joachim; "why should I begin up here."

"I don't understand it," Hans Castorp said. "I never can understand how anybody can *not* smoke—-it deprives a man of the best part of life, so to speak—-or at least of a first--class pleasure. When I wake in the morning, I feel glad at the thought of being able to smoke all day, and when I eat, I look forward to smoking afterwards; I might almost say I only eat for the sake of being able to smoke—-though of course that is more or less of an exaggeration. But a day without tobacco would be flat, stale, and unprofitable, as far as I am concerned. If I had to say to myself to--morrow: 'No smoke to--day'—-I believe I shouldn't find the courage to get up—-on my honour, I'd stop in bed. But when a man has a good cigar in his mouth—-of course it mustn't have a side draught or not draw well, that is extremely irritating—-but with a good cigar in his mouth a man is perfectly safe, nothing can touch him—-literally. It's just like lying on the beach: when you lie on the beach, why, you lie on the beach, don't you?—-you don't require anything else, in the line of work or amusement either.—-People smoke all over the world, thank goodness; there is nowhere one could get to, so far as I know, where the habit hasn't penetrated. Even polar expeditions fit themselves out with supplies of tobacco to help them carry on. I've always felt a thrill of sympathy when I read that. You can be very miserable: I might be feeling perfectly wretched, for instance; but I could always stand it if I had my smoke."

"But after all," Joachim said, "it is rather flabby--minded of you to be so dependent on it. Behrens is right, you are certainly a civilian. He meant it for a sort of compliment, I dare say; but the truth is, you are a civilian—-incurable. But then, you are healthy, you can do what you like," he added, and his eyes took on their tired look.

"Yes, healthy except for the anaemia," said Hans Castorp. "That was certainly straight from the shoulder, his telling me I look green. But it is true—-I've noticed myself that I look green in comparison with the rest of you up here, though it never struck me down home. And it was nice of him to give me advice gratis like that—-'*sine pecunia*,' as he put it. I'll gladly undertake to do as he says, and live just as you do. After all, how else should I do while I'm up here? And it can't do me any harm; suppose I do put on a little flesh, then, in God's name—-though it sounds a bit disgusting, you will admit."

Joachim coughed slightly now and then as they walked, it seemed to strain him to go uphill. When he did so for the third time, he paused and stood still with a frown.

"Go on ahead," he said. Hans Castorp hastened to do so, without looking round. Then he slackened his pace, and finally almost stopped, as it seemed to him he must have got a good distance ahead of Joachim. But he did not look round.

A troop of guests of both sexes approached him. He had seen them coming along the level path half--way up the slope; now they were stalking downhill directly towards him; he heard their voices. They were six or seven persons of various ages: some in the bloom of youth, others rather older. He took a good look at them, from the side, as he walked with bent head, thinking about Joachim. They were tanned and bareheaded, the women in sweaters, the men mostly without overcoats or even walkingsticks, all of them like people who have just gone casually out for a turn in the open. Going downhill involves no sustained muscular effort, only an agreeable process of putting on the brakes in order not to finish by running and tripping head over heels; it is really nothing more than just letting yourself go; and thus the gait of these people had something loose--jointed and flighty about it, which communicated itself to the appearance of the whole group and made one almost wish to be of their lively party. They came close up to him, he saw their faces clearly. No, they were not all brown: two of the ladies were, on the contrary, distinctly pale; one of them thin as a lath, and ivory--white of complexion, the other shorter and plump, disfigured by freckles. They all looked at him, smiling rather boldly. A tall young girl in a green sweater, with untidy hair and foolish, half--open eyes, brushed past Hans Castorp, nearly touching him with her arm. And as she did so she whistled—-oh, impossible! Yes, she did though; not with her mouth, indeed, for she did not pucker the lips, but held them firmly closed. She whistled from somewhere inside, and looked at him with her silly, half--shut eyes—-it was an extraordinarily unpleasant whistle, harsh and penetrating, yet hollow--sounding; a long--drawn--out note, falling at the end, like the sound made by those rubber pigs one buys at fairs, that give out the air in a wailing key as they collapse. The sound issued, inexplicably, from her breast——and then, with her troop, she had passed on.

Hans Castorp stood and stared. In a moment he turned round, understanding at least so much, that the atrocious thing must have been a joke, a put--up job; for he saw over his shoulder that they were laughing as they went, that a stodgy, thick--lipped youth, whose coat was turned up in an unseemly way about him so that he could put both hands in his trouser pockets, turned his head and laughed quite openly. Joachim approached. He had greeted the group with his usual punctiliousness, almost pausing, and bowing with heels together; now he came mildly up to his cousin.

"Why are you making such a face?" he asked.

"She whistled," answered Hans Castorp. "She whistled out of her inside as she passed. Will you have the goodness to explain to me how?"

"Oh!" Joachim said, and laughed curtly. "Nonsense, she didn't do it with her inside. That was Hermine Kleefeld, she whistles with her pneumothorax."

"With her what?" Hans Castorp demanded. He felt wrought up, without knowing why. His voice was between laughter and tears as he added: "You can't expect me to understand your lingo."

"Oh, come along," Joachim said. "I can explain it to you as we go. You looked rooted to the spot! It's a surgical operation, they often perform it up here. Behrens is a regular dab at it. When one of the lungs is very much affected, you understand, and the other one fairly healthy, they make the bad one stop functioning for a while, to give it a rest. That is to say, they make an incision here, somewhere on the side, I don't know the precise place, but Behrens has it down fine. Then they fill you up with gas——nitrogen, you know——and that puts the cheesy part of the lung out of operation. The gas doesn't last long, of course; it has to be renewed every two weeks; they fill you up again, as it were. Now, if that keeps on a year or two, and all goes well, the lung gets healed. Not always, of course; it's a risky business. But they say they have had a good deal of success with it. Those people you saw just now all have it. That was Frau Iltis, with the freckles, and the thin, pale one was Fräulein Levi, that had to lie so long in bed, you know. They have formed a group, for of course a thing like the pneumothorax brings people together. They call themselves the Half--Lung Club; everybody knows them by that name. And Hermine Kleefeld is the pride of the club, because she can whistle with hers. It is a special gift, by no means everybody can do it. I can't tell you how it is done, and she herself can't exactly describe it. But when she has been walking rather fast, she can make it whistle, and of course she does it to frighten people, especially when they are new to the place. Also, I believe she uses up nitrogen when she does it, for she has to be refilled once a week."

Then it was that Hans Castorp laughed. His excitement, while Joachim was speaking, had fixed for its outlet upon laughter rather than tears; and he laughed as he walked, his hand over his eyes, his shoulders bent, shaken by a succession of subdued chuckles.

"Are they incorporated?" he asked as soon as he could speak. His voice sounded weak and tearful with suppressed laughter. "Have they any by--laws? Pity you aren't a member, you could get me in as a guest, as—-as associate half--lunger.—-You ought to ask Behrens to put you out of commission, then perhaps you could learn to whistle too; it must be something one could learn—-well, that's the funniest thing ever I heard in my life!" he finished, heaving a deep sigh. "I beg your pardon for speaking of it like this, but they seem very jolly over it themselves, your pneumatic friends. The way they were coming along—-and to think that was the Half--Lung Club. Tootle--ty--too, she went at me—-she must be out of her senses! It was utter cheek—-will you tell me why they behave so cheekily?"

Joachim sought for a reply. "Good Lord," he said, "they are so *free*—- I mean, they are so young, and time is nothing to them, and then they may die—-perhaps—-why should they make a long face? Sometimes I think being ill and dying aren't serious at all just a sort of loafing about and wasting time; life is only serious down below. You will get to understand that after a while, but not until you have spent some time up here."

"Surely, surely," Hans Castorp said. "I'm sure I shall. I already feel great interest in the life up here, and when one is interested, the understanding follows.——But what is the matter with me—it doesn't taste good," he said, and took his cigar out of his mouth to look at it. "I've been asking myself all this time what the matter was, and now I see it is Maria. She tastes like papier mâché, I do assure you——precisely as when one has a spoilt digestion. I can't understand it. I did eat more than usual for breakfast, but that cannot be the reason, for she usually tastes particularly good after a too hearty meal. Do you think it is because I had such a disturbed night? Perhaps that is how I got out of order. No, I really can't stick it," he said, after another attempt.

"Every pull is a disappointment, there is no sense in forcing it." And after a hesitating moment he tossed the cigar off down the slope, among the wet pine--boughs. "Do you know what I think it has to do with?" he asked. "I feel convinced it is connected with this damned heat I feel all the time in my face. I have suffered from it ever since I got up. I feel as though I were blushing the whole time, deuce take it! Did you have anything like that when you first came?"

"Yes," said Joachim. "I was rather queer at first. Don't think too much of it. I told you it isn't so easy to accustom oneself to the life up here. But you will get right again after a bit. Look, that bench is in a pretty place. Let's sit down awhile and then go home. I must take my cure."

The path had become level. It ran now in the direction of Davos--Platz, some third of the height, and kept a continuous view, between high, sparse, wind--blown pines, of the settlement below, gleaming whitely in the bright air. The bench on which they sat leaned against the steep wall of the mountain--side, and near them a spring in an open wooden trough ran gurgling and plashing to the valley.

Joachim was for instructing his cousin in the names of the mist--wreathed Alpine heights which seemed to enclose the valley on the south, pointing them out in turn with his alpenstock. But Hans Castorp gave the mountains only a fleeting glance. He sat bent over, tracing figures on the ground with the ferrule of his cityish silvermounted walking--stick. There were other things he wanted to know.

"What I meant to ask you," he began, "the case in my room had died just before I got here; have there been many deaths, since you came?"

"Several, certainly," answered Joachim. "But they are very discreetly managed, you understand; you hear nothing of them, or only by chance afterwards; everything is kept strictly private when there is a death, out of regard for the other patients, especially the ladies, who might easily get a shock. You don't notice it, even when somebody dies next door. The coffin is brought very early in the morning, while you are asleep, and the person in question is fetched away at a suitable time too——for instance, while we are eating."

"H'm," said Hans Castorp, and continued to draw. "I see. That sort of thing goes on behind the scenes, then."

"Yes——for the most part. But lately——let me see, wait a minute, it might be possibly eight weeks ago——"

"Then you can hardly say lately," Hans Castorp pounced on him crisply.

"What? Well, not lately, then, since you're so precise. I was just trying to reckon. Well, then, some time ago, it was, I got a glimpse behind the scenes——purely by chance——and I remember it as if it were yesterday. It was when they brought the Sacrament to little Hujus, Barbara Hujus——she was a Catholic——the Last Sacrament, you know, Extreme Unction. She was still about when I first came up here, and she could be wildly hilarious, regularly giggly, like a little kid. But after that it went pretty fast with her, she didn't get up any more—her room was three doors off mine—and then her parents arrived, and now the priest was coming to her. It was while everybody was at tea, not a soul in the passages. But I had gone to sleep in the afternoon rest and overslept myself, I hadn't heard the gong and was a quarter of an hour late. So that at the decisive moment I wasn't where all the others were, but behind the scenes, as you call it; as I go along the corridor, they come toward me, in their lace robes, with the cross in front, a gold cross with lanterns—it made me think of the *Schellenbaum* they march with, in front of the recruits."

"What sort of comparison is that?" Hans Castorp asked, severely.

"It looked like that to me—I couldn't help thinking of it. But listen. They came towards me, marching, quick step, three of them, so far as I remember: the man with the cross, the priest, with glasses on his nose, and a boy with a censer. The priest was holding the Sacrament to his breast, it was covered up, and he had his head bent on one side and looked very sanctified—it is their holy of holies, of course."

"Exactly," Hans Castorp said. "And just for that reason I wonder at your making the comparison you did."

"Yes, but wait a bit—if you had been there, you wouldn't have known what kind of face you would make remembering it afterwards. It was the sort of thing to give you bad dreams—"

"How?"

"Like this: I ask myself how I am supposed to behave, under the circumstances. I had no hat to take off—"

"There, you see, don't you?" Hans Castorp interrupted him again. "You see now, one ought to wear a hat. Naturally I've noticed that none of you do up here; but you should, so you can have something to take off when it is proper to do so. Well, but what then?"

"I stood against the wall," Joachim went on, "as respectfully as I could, and bent over a little when they were by me—it was just at little Hujus's door, number twentyeight. The priest seemed to be pleased that I saluted; he acknowledged very courteously and took off his cap. But at the same time they came to a stop, and the ministrant with the censer knocks, and lifts the latch, and makes way for his superior to enter. Just try to imagine my sensations, and how frightened I was! The minute the priest sets his foot over the threshold, there begins a hullabaloo from inside, a screaming such as you never heard the like of, three or four times running, and then a shriek——on and on without stopping, at the top of her lungs: Ah--h--h--h! So full of horror and rebellion, and anguish, and——well, perfectly indescribable. And in between came a gruesome sort of begging. Then it suddenly got all dulled and hollowsounding, as though it had sunk down into the earth, or were coming out of a cellar."

Hans Castorp had turned with violence to face his cousin. "Was that the Hujus?" he asked abruptly. "And how do you mean——out of a cellar?"

"She had crawled down under the covers," said Joachim. "Imagine how I felt! The priest stood on the threshold and spoke soothingly, I can see now just how he stuck his head out and drew it back again while he talked. The cross--bearer and the acolyte hesitated, and couldn't get in. I could see between them into the room. It was just like yours and mine, the bed on the side wall left of the door, and people were standing at the head, the relatives of course, the parents, talking soothingly at the bed, where you could see nothing but a formless mass that was begging and protesting horribly, and kicking about with its legs."

"You say she kicked?"

"With all her might. But it did her no good, she had to take the Sacrament. The priest went up to her, and the two others went inside the room, and the door closed. But first I saw little Hujus's head come up for a second, a shock of blond hair, and look at the priest with staring eyes, that were without any colour, and then with a wail go down under the sheet again."

"And you tell me all that now for the first time?" Hans Castorp said, after a pause.

"I can't understand how you came not to speak of it yesterday evening. But, good Lord, she must have had strength, to defend herself like that. That takes strength. They ought not to fetch the priest before one is quite weak."

"She was weak," responded Joachim.——"Oh, there's so much to tell, one doesn't have time to pick and choose. She was weak enough! It was only the fright gave her so much strength. She was in a fearful state when she saw she was going to die; and she was such a young girl, it was excusable, after all. But grown men behave like that too, sometimes, and it's deplorably feeble of them, of course. Behrens knows how to treat them, he takes just the right tone in such cases."

"What kind of tone?" Hans Castorp asked with drawn brows.

" 'Don't behave like that,' he tells them," Joachim answered. "At least, that is what he told somebody lately——we heard it from the Directress, who was present and helped to hold the man. He was one of those who make a regular scene at the end, and simply won't die. So Behrens brought him up with a round turn: 'Do me the favour not to behave like that,' he said to him; and the patient became quite calm and died as quietly as you please."

Hans Castorp slapped his thigh and threw himself back against the bench, looking up at the sky.

"I say, that's pretty steep," he cried. "Goes at him like that, and simply tells him not to behave that way! To a dying man! But after all, a dying man has something in a way——sacred about him. One can't just——perfectly coolly, like that——a dying man is sort of holy, I should think!"

"I don't deny it," said Joachim. "But when one behaves as feebly as that——"

"No," persisted Hans Castorp, with a violence out of proportion to the opposition he met, "I insist that a dying man is above any chap that is going about and laughing and earning his living and eating his three meals a day. It isn't good enough"—-his voice quavered—-"it isn't good enough, for one to calmly—-just calmly"—-his words trailed off in a fit of laughter that seized and overcame him, the laughter of yesterday, a profound, illimitable, body--shaking laughter, that shut up his eyes and made tears well from beneath their lids.

"Sh--h!" went Joachim, suddenly. "Keep quiet," he whispered, and nudged his uncontrollably hilarious cousin in the side. Hans Castorp looked up through tears. A stranger was approaching them from the left, a dark man of graceful carriage, with curling black moustaches, wearing light--coloured check trousers. He exchanged a good--morning with Joachim in accents agreeable and precise, and then remained standing before them in an easy posture, leaning on his cane, with his legs crossed.

Satana

His age would have been hard to say, probably between thirty and forty; for though he gave an impression of youthfulness, yet the hair on his temples was sprinkled with silver and gone quite thin on his head. Two bald bays ran along the narrow scanty parting, and added to the height of his forehead. His clothing, loose trousers in light yellowish checks, and too long, double--breasted pilot coat, with very wide lapels, made no slightest claim to elegance; and his stand--up collar, with rounding corners, was rough on the edges from frequent washing. His black cravat showed wear, and he wore no cuffs, as Hans Castorp saw at once from the lax way the sleeve hung round the wrist. But despite all that, he knew he had a gentleman before him: the stranger's easy, even charming pose and cultured expression left no doubt of that. Yet by this mingling of shabbiness and grace, by the black eyes and softly waving moustaches, Hans Castorp was irresistibly reminded of certain foreign musicians who used to come to Hamburg at Christmas to play in the streets before people's doors.

He could see them rolling up their velvet eyes and holding out their soft hats for the coins tossed from the windows. "A hand--organ man," he thought. Thus he was not surprised at the name he heard, as Joachim rose from the bench and in some embarrassment presented him: "My cousin Castorp, Herr Settembrini."

Hans Castorp had got up at the same time, the traces of his burst of hilarity still on his face. But the Italian courteously bade them both not to disturb themselves, and made them sit down again, while he maintained his easy pose before them. He smiled standing there and looking at the cousins, in particular at Hans Castorp; a smile that was a fine, almost mocking, deepening and crisping of one corner of the mouth, just at the point where the full moustache made its beautiful upward curve. It had upon the cousins a singular effect: it somehow constrained them to mental alertness and clarity; it sobered the reeling Hans Castorp in a twinkling, and made him ashamed.

Settembrini said: "You are in good spirits—-and with reason too, with excellent reason. What a splendid morning! A blue sky, a smiling sun—-"with an easy, adequate motion of the arm he raised a small, yellowish--skinned hand to the heavens, and sent a lively glance upward after it—-"one could almost forget where one is."

He spoke without accent, only the precise enunciation betrayed the foreigner. His lips seemed to take a certain pleasure in forming the words. It was most agreeable to hear him.

"You had a pleasant journey hither, I hope?" he turned to Hans Castorp. "And do you already know your fate—-I mean has the mournful ceremony of the first examination taken place?" Here, if he had really been expecting a reply he should have paused; he had put his question, and Hans Castorp prepared to answer. But he went on: "Did you get off easily? One might put"—-here he paused a second, and the crisping at the corner of his mouth grew crisper—-"more than one interpretation upon your laughter. How many months have our Minos and Rhadamanthus knocked you down for?" The slang phrase sounded droll on his lips. "Shall I guess? Six? Nine?

You know we are free with the time up here——-"

Hans Castorp laughed, astonished, at the same time racking his brains to remember who Minos and Rhadamanthus were. He answered: "Not at all——-no, really, you are under a misapprehension, Herr Septem——-"

"Settembrini," corrected the Italian, clearly and with emphasis, making as he spoke a mocking bow.

"Herr Settembrini——-I beg your pardon. No, you are mistaken. Really I am not ill. I have only come on a visit to my cousin Ziemssen for a few weeks, and shall take advantage of the opportunity to get a good rest——-"

"Zounds! You don't say? Then you are not one of us? You are well, you are but a guest here, like Odysseus in the kingdom of the shades? You are bold indeed, thus to descend into these depths peopled by the vacant and idle dead——-"

"Descend, Herr Settembrini? I protest. Here I have climbed up some five thousand feet to get here——-"

"That was only seeming. Upon my honour, it was an illusion," the Italian said, with a decisive--wave of the hand. "We are sunk enough here, aren't we, Lieutenant?" he said to Joachim, who, no little gratified at this method of address, thought to hide his satisfaction, and answered reflectively: "I suppose we do get rather one--sided. But we can pull ourselves together, afterwards, if we try."

"At least, *you* can, I'm sure——-you are an upright man," Settembrini said. "Yes, yes, yes," he said, repeating the word three times, with a sharp *s*, turning to Hans Castorp again as he spoke, and then, in the same measured way, clucking three times with his tongue against his palate. "I see, I see, I see," he said again, giving the *s* the same sharp sound as before. He looked the newcomer so steadfastly in the face that his eyes grew fixed in a stare; then, becoming lively again, he went on: "So you come up quite of your own free will to us sunken ones, and mean to bestow upon us the pleasure of your company for some little while? That is delightful. And what term had you thought of putting to your stay? I don't mean precisely. I am merely interested to know what the length of a man's sojourn would be when it is himself and not Rhadamanthus who prescribes the limit."

"Three weeks," Hans Castorp said, rather pridefully, as he saw himself the object of envy.

"*O dio!* Three weeks! Do you hear, Lieutenant? Does it not sound to you impertinent to hear a person say: 'I am stopping for three weeks and then I am going away again'? We up here are not acquainted with such a unit of time as the week—-if I may be permitted to instruct you, my dear sir. Our smallest unit is the month. We reckon in the grand style—-that is a privilege we shadows have. We possess other such; they are all of the same quality. May I ask what profession you practise down below? Or, more probably, for what profession are you preparing yourself? You see we set no bounds to our thirst for information—-curiosity is another of the prescriptive rights of shadows."

"Pray don't mention it," said Hans Castorp. And told him.

"A ship--builder! Magnificent!" cried Settembrini. "I assure you, I find that magnificent—-though my own talents lie in quite another direction."

"Herr Settembrini is a literary man," Joachim explained, rather self--consciously.

"He wrote the obituary notices of Carducci for the German papers—-Carducci, you know." He got more self--conscious still, for his cousin looked at him in amazement, as though to say: "Carducci? What do you know about him? Not any more than I do, I'll wager."

"Yes," the Italian said, nodding. "I had the honour of telling your countrymen the story of our great poet and freethinker, when his life had drawn to a close. I knew him, I can count myself among his pupils. I sat at his feet in Bologna. I may thank him for what culture I can call my own—-and for what joyousness of life as well. But we were speaking of you. A ship--builder! Do you know you have sensibly risen in my estimation? You represent now, in my eyes, the world of labour and practical genius."

"Herr Settembrini, I am only a student as yet, I am just beginning."

"Certainly. It is the beginning that is hard. But all work *is* hard, isn't it, that deserves the name?"

"That's true enough, God knows—-or the Devil does," Hans Castorp said, and the words came from his heart.

Settembrini's eyebrows went up.

"Oh," he said, "so you call on the Devil to witness that sentiment—-the Devil incarnate, Satan himself? Did you know that my great master wrote a hymn to him?"

"I beg your pardon," Hans Castorp said, "a hymn to the Devil?"

"The very Devil himself, and no other. It is sometimes sung, in my native land, on festal occasions. '*O salute, O Satana, O ribellione, O forza vindice della ragione! ...*'

It is a magnificent song. But it was hardly Carducci's Devil you had in mind when you spoke; for he is on the very best of terms with hard work; whereas yours, who is afraid of work and hates it like poison, is probably the same of whom we are told that we may not hold out even the little finger to him."

All this was making the very oddest impression on our good Hans Castorp. He knew no Italian, and the rest of it sounded no less uncomfortable, and reminded him of Sunday sermons, though delivered quite casually, in a light, even jesting tone. He looked at his cousin, who kept his eyes cast down; then he said: "You take my words far too literally, Herr Settembrini. When I spoke of the Devil, it was just a manner of speaking, I assure you."

"Somebody must have some *esprit*," Settembrini said, looking straight ahead, with a melancholy air. Then recovering himself, he skillfully got back to their former subject, and went on blithely: "At all events, I am probably right in concluding from your words that the calling you have embraced is as strenuous as it is honourable. As for myself, I am a humanist, a *homo humanus*. I have no mechanical ingenuity, however sincere my respect for it. But I can well understand that the theory of your craft requires a clear and keen mind, and its practice not less than the entire man. Am I right?"

"You certainly are, I can go all the way with you there," Hans Castorp answered. Unconsciously he made an effort to reply with eloquence. "The demands made to--day on a man in my profession are simply enormous. It is better not to have too clear an idea of their magnitude, it might take away one's courage: no, it's no joke. And if one isn't the strongest in the world——It is true that I am here only on a visit; but I am not very robust, and I cannot with truth assert that my work agrees with me so wonderfully well. It would be a great deal truer to say that it rather takes it out of me. I only feel really fit when I am doing nothing at all."

"As now, for example?"

"Now? Oh, now I am so new up here, I am still rather bewildered——-you can imagine."

"Ah——-bewildered."

"Yes, and I did not sleep so very well, and the early breakfast was really too solid.——-I am accustomed to a fair breakfast, but this was a little too rich for my blood, as the saying goes. In short, I feel a sense of oppression——-and for some reason or other, my cigar this morning hasn't the right taste, something that as good as never happens to me, or only when I am seriously upset——-and to--day it is like leather. I had to throw it away, there was no use forcing it. Are you a smoker, may I ask? No? Then you cannot imagine the annoyance and disappointment it is for anyone like me, who have smoked from my youth up, and taken such pleasure in it."

"I am without experience in the field," Settembrini answered, "but I find that my lack of it is in no poor company. So many fine, self--denying spirits have refrained. Carducci had no use for the practice. But you will find our Rhadamanthus a kindred spirit. He is a devotee of your vice."

"Vice, Herr Settembrini?"

"Why not? One must call things by their right names; life is enriched and ennobled thereby. I too have my vices."

"So Hofrat Behrens is a connoisseur? A charming man."

"You find him so? Then you have already made his acquaintance?"

"Yes, just now, as we came out. It was almost like a professional visit—-but gratis, you know—- *sine pecunia*. He saw at once that I am anæmic. He advised me to follow my cousin's regimen entirely: to lie out on the balcony a good deal—-he even said I should take my temperature."

"Did he indeed?" Settembrini cried out. "Capital!" He laughed and threw back his head. "How does it go, that opera of yours? 'A fowler bold in me you see, forever laughing merrily!' Ah, that is most amusing! And you will follow his advice? Of course, why shouldn't you? He's a devil of a fellow, our Rhadamanthus! 'Forever laughing'—-even if it *is* rather forced at times. He is inclined to melancholia, you know. His vice doesn't agree with him—-of course, else it would be no vice. Smoking gives him fits of depression; that is why our respected Frau Directress has taken charge of his supplies, and only deals him out daily rations. It even happens sometimes that he yields to the temptation to steal it, and then he gets an attack of melancholia. A troubled spirit, in short. Do you know your Directress already, too?

No? You have made a mistake. You must remedy it at the earliest opportunity. My dear sir, she comes of the noble race of von Mylendonk. And she is distinguished from the Medici Venus by the fact that where the goddess has a bosom, she has a cross."

"Ah, ha ha!—-capital!" Hans Castorp laughed.

"Her Christian name is Adriatica."

"Adriatica!" shouted Hans Castorp. "Priceless! Adriatica von Mylendonk! Isn't that splendid! Sounds as though she had been dead a very long time. It is positively mediaeval."

"My dear sir," Settembrini answered him, "there is a good deal up here that is positively mediaeval, as you express it. Personally, I am convinced that Rhadamanthus was actuated simply and solely by artistic feeling when he made this fossil head overseer of his Chamber of Horrors. You know he is an artist, by the bye. He paints in oils. Why not? There's no law against it—-anybody can paint that likes. Frau Adriatica tells all who will listen to her, not counting those who won't, that a Mylendonk was abbess of a cloister at Bonn on the Rhine, in the thirteenth century. It can't have been long after that she herself saw the light of day."

"Ha ha! Why, Herr Settembrini, I find you are a mocker!"

"A mocker? You mean I am malicious? Well, yes, perhaps I am a little," said Settembrini. "My great complaint is that it is my fate to spend my malice upon such insignificant objects. I hope, Engineer, you have nothing against malice? In my eyes, it is reason's keenest dart against the powers of darkness and ugliness. Malice, my dear sir, is the animating spirit of criticism; and criticism is the beginning of progress and enlightenment." And he began to talk about Petrarch, whom he called the father of the modern spirit.

"I think," Joachim said thoughtfully, "that we ought to be going to lie down."

The man of letters had been speaking to an accompaniment of graceful gestures, one of which he now rounded off in Joachim's direction and said: "Our lieutenant presses on to the service. Let us go together, our way is the same: the 'path on the right that shall lead to the halls of the mightiest Dis'—ah, Virgil, Virgil! He is unsurpassable. I am a believer in progress, certainly, gentlemen; but

Virgil—-he has a command of epithet no modern can approach." And on their homeward path he recited Latin verse with an Italian pronunciation; interrupting himself, however, as he saw coming towards them a young girl—-a girl of the village, as it seemed, and by no means remarkable for her looks—-whom he laid himself out to smile at and ogle most killingly: "O la, la, sweet, sweet, sweet!" he chirruped. "Pretty, pretty, pretty! 'Then come kiss me, sweet and twenty,' " he quoted as they passed, and kissed his hand at the poor girl's embarrassed back.

"What a windbag it is," Hans Castorp thought. He remained of that opinion still, after the Italian had recovered from his attack of gallantry and begun to scoff again. His animadversions were chiefly directed upon Herr Hofrat Behrens: he jeered at the size of his feet, and at the title he had received from a certain prince who suffered from tuberculosis of the brain. Of the scandalous courses of that royal personage the whole neighbourhood still talked; but Rhadamanthus had shut his eye—-both eyes, in fact—-and behaved every inch a Hofrat. Did the gentlemen know that he—-the Hofrat—-had invented the summer season? He it was, and no other. One must give the devil his due. There had been a time when only the faithfullest of the faithful had spent the summer in the high valley. Then our humourist, with his unerring eye, had perceived that this neglect was simply the result of unfortunate prejudice. He got up the idea that, so far at least as his own sanatorium was concerned, the summer cure was not only not less to be recommended than the winter one, it was, on the contrary, of great value, really quite indispensable. And he knew how to get this theory put about, to have it come to people's ears; he wrote articles on the subject and launched them in the press—-since when the summer season had been as flourishing as the winter one.

"Genius!" said Settembrini. "In--tu--ition!" He went on to criticize the proprietors of all the other sanatoria in the place, praising their acquisitive talents with mordant sarcasm. There was Professor Kafka. Every year, at the critical moment, when the snow began to melt, and several patients were asking leave to depart, he would suddenly find himself obliged to be away for a week, and promise to take up all requests on his return. Then he would stop away for six weeks, while the poor wretches waited for him, and while, incidentally, their bills continued to mount. Kafka was once sent for to go to Fiume for a consultation, but he would not go until he was guaranteed five thousand good Swiss francs; and thus two weeks were lost in *pourparlers*. Then he went; but the day after the arrival of the great man, the patient died. Dr. Salzmann asserted that Kafka did not keep his hypodermic syringes clean, and his patients got infected one from the other. He also said he wore rubber soles, that his dead might not hear him. On the other hand, Kafka told it about that Dr. Salzmann's patients were encouraged to drink so much of the fruit of the vine—-for the benefit of Dr. Salzmann's pocket--book—-that they died off like flies, not of phthisis but cirrhosis of the liver.

Thus he went on, Hans Castorp laughing with good--natured enjoyment at this glib and prolific stream of slander. It was, indeed, great fun to listen to, so eloquent was it, so precisely rendered, so free from every trace of dialect. The words came, round, clear--cut, and as though newly minted, from his mobile lips, he tasted his own wellturned, dexterous, biting phrases with obvious and contagious relish, and seemed to be far too clearheaded and self--possessed ever to mis--speak.

"You have such an amusing way of talking, Herr Settembrini," Hans Castorp said.

"So lively, so—-I don't quite know how to characterize it."

"Plastic?" responded the Italian, and fanned himself with his handkerchief, though it was far from warm. "That is probably the word you seek. You mean I have a plastic way of speaking. But look!" he cried, "what do my eyes behold? The judges of our infernal regions! What a sight!"

The walkers had already put behind them the turn in the path. Whether thanks to Settembrini's conversation, the fact that they were walking downhill, or merely that they were much nearer the sanatorium than Hans Castorp had thought——for a path is always longer the first time we traverse it——at all events, the return had been accomplished in a surprisingly short time. Settembrini was right, it was the two physicians who were walking along the free space at the back of the building; the Hofrat ahead, in his white smock, his neck stuck out and his hands moving like oars; on his heels the black--shirted Dr. Krokowski, who looked the more self--conscious that medical etiquette constrained him to walk behind his chief when they made their rounds together.

"Ah, Krokowski," Settembrini cried. "There he goes——he who knows all the secrets in the bosoms of our ladies——pray observe the delicate symbolism of his attire: he wears black to indicate that his proper field of study is the night. The man has but one idea in his head, and that a smutty one. How does it happen, Engineer, that we have not spoken of him until now? You have made his acquaintance?"

Hans Castorp answered in the affirmative.

"Well? I am beginning to suspect that you like him, too."

"I don't know, really, Herr Settembrini. I've seen him only casually. And I am not very quick in my judgments. I am inclined to look at people and say: 'So that's you, is it? Very good.' "

"That is apathetic of you. You should judge——to that end you have been given your eyes and your understanding. You felt that I spoke maliciously, just now. If I did, perhaps it was not without intent to teach. We humanists have all of us a pedagogic itch. Humanism and schoolmasters——there is a historical connexion between them, and it rests upon psychological fact: the office of schoolmaster should not——cannot——be taken from the humanist, for the tradition of the beauty and dignity of man rests in his hands. The priest, who in troubled and inhuman times arrogated to himself the office of guide to youth, has been dismissed; since when, my dear sirs, no special type of teacher has arisen. The humanistic grammar--school——you may call me reactionary, Engineer, but *in abstracto*, generally speaking, you understand, I remain an adherent——"

He continued in the lift to expatiate upon this theme, and left off only when the cousins got out as the second storey was reached. He himself went up to the third, where he had, Joachim said, a little back room.

"He hasn't much money, I suppose," Hans Castorp said, entering Joachim's room, which looked precisely like his own.

"No, I suppose not," Joachim answered, "or only so much as just makes his stay possible. His father was a literary man too, you know, and, I believe, his grandfather as well."

"Yes, of course," Hans Castorp said. "Is he seriously ill?"

"Not dangerously, so far as I know, but obstinate, keeps coming back. He has had it for years, and goes away in between, but soon has to return again."

"Poor chap! So frightfully keen on work as he seems to be! Enormously chatty, goes from one thing to another so easily. Rather objectionable, though, it seemed to me, with that girl. I was quite put off, for the moment. But when he talked about human dignity, afterwards, I thought it was great——sounded like an address. Do you see much of him?"

Mental Gymnastic

Joachim's reply came impeded and incoherent. He had taken a small thermometer from a red leather, velvet--lined case on his table, and put the mercury--filled end under his tongue on the left side, so that the glass instrument stuck slantingly upwards out of his mouth. Then he changed into indoor clothes, put on shoes and a braided jacket, took a printed form and pencil from his table, also a book, a Russian grammar——for he was studying Russian with the idea that it would be of advantage to him in the service——and, thus equipped, took his place in the reclining--chair on his balcony, throwing his camel's--hair rug lightly across his feet.

It was scarcely needed. During the last quarter--hour the layer of cloud had grown steadily thinner, and now the sun broke through in summerlike warmth, so dazzlingly that Joachim protected his head with a white linen shade which was fastened to the arm of his chair, and furnished with a device by means of which it could be adjusted to the position of the sun. Hans Castorp praised this contrivance. He wished to await the result of Joachim's measurement, and meanwhile looked about to see how everything was done: observed the fur--lined sleeping--sack that stood against the wall in a corner of the loggia, for Joachim to use on cold days; and gazed down into the garden, with his elbows on the balustrade. The general rest--hall was populated by reclining patients, reading, writing, or conversing. He could see only a part of the interior, some four or five chairs.

"How long does that go on?" he asked, turning round.

Joachim raised seven fingers.

"Seven minutes! But they must be up!"

Joachim shook his head. A little later he took the thermometer out of his mouth, looked at it, and said: "Yes, when you watch it, the time, it goes very slowly. I quite like the measuring, four times a day; for then you know what a minute—or seven of them actually amounts to, up here in this place, where the seven days of the week whisk by the way they do!"

"You say 'actually,' " Hans Castorp answered. He sat with one leg flung over the balustrade, and his eyes looked bloodshot. "But after all, time *isn't* 'actual.' When it seems long to you, then it *is* long; when it seems short, why, then it is short. But how long, or how short, it actually is, that nobody knows." He was unaccustomed to philosophize, yet somehow felt an impulse to do so.

Joachim gainsaid him. "How so?—-we do measure it. We have watches and calendars for the purpose; and when a month is *up*, why, then up it is, for you, and for me, and for all of us."

"Wait," said Hans Castorp. He held up his forefinger, close to his tired eyes. "A minute, then, is as long as it seems to you when you measure yourself?"

"A minute is as long—-it *lasts* as long—-as it takes the second hand of my watch to complete a circuit."

"But it takes such a varied length of time—-to our senses! And as a matter of fact—-I say taking it just as a matter of fact," he repeated, pressing his forefinger so hard against his nose that he bent the end of it quite round, "it is motion, isn't it, motion in space? Wait a minute! That means that we measure time by space. But that is no better than measuring space by time, a thing only very unscientific people do. From Hamburg to Davos is twenty hours—-that is, by train. But on foot how long is it? And in the mind, how long? Not a second!"

"I say," Joachim said, "what's the matter with you? Seems to me it goes to your head to be up here with us!"

"Keep quiet! I'm very clear--headed to--day. Well, then, what *is* time?" asked Hans Castorp, and bent the tip of his nose so far round that it became white and bloodless.

"Can you answer me that? Space we perceive with our organs, with our senses of sight and touch. Good. But which is our organ of time—-tell me that if you can. You see, that's where you stick. But how can we possibly measure anything about which we actually know nothing, not even a single one of its properties? We say of time that it passes. Very good, let it pass. But to be able to measure it—-wait a minute: to be susceptible of being measured, time must flow evenly, but who ever said it did that?

As far as our consciousness is concerned it doesn't, we only assume that it does, for the sake of convenience; and our units of measurement are purely arbitrary, sheer conventions—-"

"Good," Joachim said. "Then perhaps it is pure convention that I have five points too much here on my thermometer. But on account of those lines I have to drool about here instead of joining up, which is a disgusting fact."

"Have you 99.3°?"

"It's going down already," and Joachim made the entry on his chart. "Last night it was almost 100°——that was your arrival. A visit always makes it go up. But it is a good thing, notwithstanding."

"I'll go now," said Hans Castorp. "I've still a great many ideas in my head about the time——a whole complex, if I may say so. But I won't excite you with them now, you've too many degrees as it is. I'll keep them all and return to them later, perhaps after breakfast. You will call me when it is time, I suppose. I'll go now and lie down; it won't hurt me, thank goodness." With which he passed round the glass partition into his loggia, where stood his own reclining--chair and side--table. He fetched *Ocean Steamships* and his beautiful, soft, dark--red and green plaid from within the room, which had already been put into perfect order, and sat himself down.

Soon he too had to put up the little sunshade; the heat became unbearable as he lay. But he was uncommonly comfortable, he decided, with distinct satisfaction. He did not recall in all his experience so acceptable an easy--chair. The frame——a little oldfashioned, perhaps, a mere matter of taste, for the chair was obviously new——was of polished red--brown wood, and the mattress was covered in a soft cotton material; or rather, it was not a mattress, but three thick cushions, extending from the foot to the very top of the chair--back. There was a head--roll besides, neither too hard nor too yielding, with an embroidered linen cover, fastened on by a cord to the chair, and wondrously agreeable to the neck. Hans Castorp supported his elbow on the broad, smooth surface of the chair--arm, blinked, and reposed himself. The landscape, rather severe and sparse, though brightly sunny, looked like a framed painting as viewed through the arch of the loggia. Hans Castorp gazed thoughtfully at it. Suddenly he thought of something, and said aloud in the stillness: "That was a dwarf, wasn't it, that waited on us at breakfast?"

"Sh--h," went Joachim. "Don't speak loud. Yes, a dwarf. Why?"

"Nothing. We hadn't mentioned it."

He mused on. It had been ten o'clock when he lay down. An hour passed. It was an ordinary hour, not long, not short. At its close a bell sounded through the house and garden, first afar, then near, then from afar again.

"Breakfast," Joachim said and could be heard getting up.

Hans Castorp too finished with his cure for the time and went into his room to put himself to rights a little. The cousins met in the corridor and descended the stair. Hans Castorp said: "Well, the lying--down is great! What sort of chairs are they? If they are to be had here, I'll buy one and take it to Hamburg with me; they are heavenly to lie in. Or do you think Behrens had them made to his design?"

Joachim did not know. They entered the dining--room, where the meal was again in full swing.

At every place stood a large glass, probably a half litre of milk; the room shimmered white with it.

"No," Hans Castorp said, when he was once more in his seat between the seamstress and the Englishwoman, and had docilely unfolded his serviette, though still heavy with the earlier meal; "no, God help me, milk I never could abide, and least of all now! Is there perhaps some porter?" He applied himself to the dwarf and put his question with the gentlest courtesy, but alas, there was none. She promised to bring Kulmbacher beer, and did so. It was thick, dark, and foaming brownly; it made a capital substitute for the porter. Hans Castorp drank it thirstily from a half--litre glass, and ate some cold meat and toast. Again there was oatmeal porridge and much butter and fruit. He let his eyes dwell upon them, incapable of more. And he looked at the guests as well; the groups began to break up for him, and individuals to stand out. His own table was full, except the place at the top, which, he learned, was "the doctor's place." For the doctors, when their work allowed, ate at the common table, sitting at each of the seven in turn; at each one a place was kept free. But just now neither was present; they were operating, it was said. The young man with the moustaches came in again, sank his chin once for all on his breast, and sat down, with his self--absorbed, care--worn mien. The lean, light blonde was in her seat, and spooned up yogurt as though it formed her sole article of diet. Next her appeared a lively little old dame, who addressed the silent young man in Russian; he regarded her uneasily, and answered only by nodding his head, looking as though he had a bad taste in his mouth. Opposite him, on the other side of the elderly lady, there was another young girl—-pretty, with a blooming complexion and full bosom, chestnut hair that waved agreeably, round, brown, childlike eyes, and a little ruby on her lovely hand. She laughed often, and spoke Russian. Hans Castorp learned that her name was Marusja. He noticed further that when she laughed and talked, Joachim sat with eyes cast sternly down upon his plate.

Settembrini appeared through the side door, and, curling his moustaches, strode to his place at the end of the table diagonally in front of that where Hans Castorp sat. His table--mates burst out in peals of laughter as he sat down; he had probably said something cutting. Hans Castorp recognized the members of the Half--Lung Club. Hermine Kleefeld, heavy--eyed, slid into her place at the table in front of one of the verandah doors, speaking as she did so to the thick--lipped youth who had worn his coat in the unseemly fashion that had struck Hans Castorp. The ivory--coloured Levi and the fat, freckled Iltis sat side by side at a table at right angles to Hans Castorp—-he did not know any of their table--mates.

"There are your neighbours," Joachim said in a low voice to his cousin, bending forward as he spoke. The pair passed close beside Hans Castorp to the last table on the right, the "bad" Russian table, apparently, where there already sat a whole family, one of whom, a very ugly boy, was gobbling great quantities of porridge. The man was of slight proportions, with a grey, hollow--cheeked face. He wore a brown leather jacket; on his feet he had clumsy felt boots with buckled clasps. His wife, likewise small and slender, walked with tripping steps in her tiny, high--heeled Russia leather boots, the feathers swaying on her hat. Around her neck she wore a soiled feather boa. Hans Castorp looked at them with a ruthless stare, quite foreign to his usual manner——he himself was aware of its brutality, yet at the same time conscious of relishing that very quality. His eyes felt both staring and heavy. At that moment the glass door on the left slammed shut, with a rattle and ringing of glass; he did not start as he had on the first occasion, but only made a grimace of lazy disgust; when he wished to turn his head, he found the effort too much for him——it was really not worth while. And thus, for the second time, he was unable to fix upon the person who was guilty of behaving in that reckless way about a door.

The truth was that the breakfast beer, as a rule only mildly obfuscating to the young man's sense, had this time completely stupefied and befuddled him. He felt as though he had received a blow on the head. His eyelids were heavy as lead; his tongue would not shape his simple thoughts when out of politeness he tried to talk to the Englishwoman. Even to alter the direction of his gaze he was obliged to conquer a great disinclination; and, added to all this, the hateful burning in his face had reached the same height as yesterday, his cheeks felt puffy with heat, he breathed with difficulty; his heart pounded dully, like a hammer muffled in cloth. If all these sensations caused him no high degree of suffering, that was only because his head felt as though he had inhaled a few whiffs of chloroform. He saw as in a dream that Dr. Krokowski appeared at breakfast and took the place opposite to his; the doctor, however, repeatedly looked him sharply in the eye, while he conversed in Russian with the ladies on his right. The young girls——the blooming Marusja and the lean consumer of yogurt——cast down their eyes modestly as the doctor spoke. Hans Castorp did not, of course, bear himself otherwise than with dignity. In silence, since his tongue refused its office, but managing his knife and fork with particular propriety. When his cousin nodded to him and got up, he rose too, bowed blindly to the rest of the table, and with cautious steps followed Joachim out.

"When do we lie down again?" he asked, as they left the house. "It's the best thing up here, so far as I can see. I wish I were back again in my comfortable chair. Do we take a long walk?"

A Word Too Much

"No," answered Joachim. "I am not allowed to go far. At this period I always go down below, through the village as far as the Platz if I have time. There are shops and people, and one can buy what one needs. Don't worry, we rest for an hour again before dinner, and then after it until four o'clock."

They went down the drive in the sunshine, crossed the watercourse and the narrow track, having before their eyes the mountain heights of the western side of the valley: the Little Schiahorn, the Green Tower, and the Dorfberg—-Joachim mentioned their names. The little walled cemetery of Davos--Dorf lay up there, at some height; Joachim pointed it out with his stick. They reached the high road that led along the terraced slope a storey higher than the valley floor.

It was rather a misnomer to speak of the village, since scarcely anything but the word remained. The resort had swallowed it up, extending further and further toward the entrance of the valley, until that part of the settlement which was called the "Dorf" passed imperceptibly into the "Platz." Hotels and pensions, amply equipped with covered verandahs, balconies, and reclining--halls, lay on both sides of their way, also private houses with rooms to let. Here and there were new buildings, but also open spaces, which preserved a view toward the valley meadows.

Hans Castorp, craving his familiar and wonted indulgence, had once more lighted a cigar; and, thanks probably to the beer that had gone before, he succeeded now and then in getting a whiff of the longed--for aroma——to his inexpressible satisfaction. But only now and then, but only faintly; the anxious receptivity of his attitude was a strain on the nerves, and the hateful leathery taste distinctly prevailed. Unable to reconcile himself to his impotence, he struggled awhile to regain the enjoyment which either escaped him wholly, or else mocked him by its brief presence; finally, worn out and disgusted, he flung the cigar away. Despite his benumbed condition he felt it incumbent upon him to be polite, to make conversation, and to this end he sought to recall those brilliant ideas he had previously had, on the subject of time. Alas, they had fled, the whole "complex" of them, and left not a trace behind: on the subject of time not one single idea, however insignificant, found lodgment in his head. He began, therefore, to talk of ordinary matters, of the concerns of the body——what he said sounded odd enough in his mouth.

"When do you measure again?" he asked. "After eating? Yes, that's a good time. When the organism is in full activity, it must show itself. Behrens must have been joking when he told me to take my temperature——Settembrini laughed like anything at the idea; there's really no sense in it, I haven't even a thermometer."

"Well," Joachim said, "that is the least of your difficulties. You can get one anywhere——they sell them in almost every shop."

"Why should I? No, the lying--down is very much the thing. I'll gladly do it; but measuring would be rather too much for a guest; I'll leave that to the rest of you. If I only knew," Hans Castorp went on, and laid his hands like a lover on his heart, "if I only knew why I have palpitations the whole time——it is very disquieting; I keep thinking about it. For, you see, a person ordinarily has palpitation of the heart when he is frightened, or when he is looking forward to some great joy. But when the heart palpitates all by itself, without any reason, senselessly, of its own accord, so to speak, I feel that's uncanny, you understand, as if the body was going its own gait without any reference to the soul, like a dead body, only it is not really dead——there isn't any such thing, of course——but leading a very active existence all on its own account, growing hair and nails and doing a lively business in the physical and chemical line, so I've been told——-"

"What kind of talk is that?" Joachim said, with serious reproach. " 'Doing a lively business'!" And perhaps he recalled the reproaches he had called down on his own head earlier in the day.

"It's a fact——-it *is* very lively! Why do you object to that?" Hans Castorp asked. "But I only happened to mention it. I only meant to say that it is disturbing and unpleasant to have the body act as though it had no connexion with the soul, and put on such airs——-by which I mean these senseless palpitations. You keep trying to find an explanation for them, an emotion to account for them, a feeling of joy or pain, which would, so to speak, justify them. At least, it is that way with me——-but I can only speak for myself."

"Yes, yes," Joachim said, sighing. "It is the same thing, I suppose, as when you have fever——-there are pretty lively goings--on in the system then too, to talk the way you do; it may easily be that one involuntarily tries to find an emotion which would explain, or even half--way explain the goings--on. But we are talking such unpleasant stuff," he said, his voice trembling a little, and he broke off; whereupon Hans Castorp shrugged his shoulders——-with the very gesture, indeed, which had, the evening before, displeased him in his cousin.

They walked awhile in silence, until Joachim asked: "Well, how do you like the people up here? I mean the ones at our table."

Hans Castorp put on a judicial air. "Dear me," he said, "I don't find them so very interesting. Some of the people at the other tables look more so, but that may be only seeming. Frau Stöhr ought to have her hair shampooed, it is so greasy. And that Mazurka—or whatever her name is——-seemed rather silly to me. She keeps giggling and stuffing her handkerchief in her mouth."

Joachim laughed loudly at the twist his cousin had given the name.

" 'Mazurka' is capital," he said. "Her name is Marusja, with your kind permission—it is the same as Marie. Yes, she really is too undisciplined, and after all, she has every reason to be serious," he said, "for her case is by no means light."

"Who would have thought it?" said Hans Castorp. "She looks so very fit. Chest trouble is the last thing one would accuse her of." He tried to catch his cousin's eye, and saw that Joachim's sunburnt face had gone all spotted, as a tanned complexion will when the blood leaves it with suddenness; his mouth too was pitifully drawn, and wore an expression that sent an indefinable chill of fear over Hans Castorp and made him hasten to change the subject. He hurriedly inquired about others of their tablemates and tried to forget Marusja and the look on Joachim's face—-an effort in which he presently succeeded.

The Englishwoman with the rose tea was Miss Robinson. The seamstress was not a seamstress but a schoolmistress at a *lycée* in Königsberg—-which accounted for the precision of her speech. Her name was Fräulein Engelhart. As for the name of the lively little old lady, Joachim, as long as he had been up here, did not know it. All he knew was that she was great--aunt to the young lady who ate yogurt, and lived with her permanently in the sanatorium. The worst case at their table was Dr. Blumenkohl, Leo Blumenkohl, from Odessa, the young man with the moustaches and the absorbed and care--worn air. He had been here years.

They were now walking on the city pavement, the main street, obviously, of an international centre. They met the guests of the cure, strolling about, young people for the most part: gallants in "sporting," without their hats; white--skirted ladies, also hatless. One heard Russian and English. Shops with gay show--windows were on either side of the road, and Hans Castorp, his curiosity struggling with intense weariness, forced himself to look into them, and stood a long time before a shop that purveyed fashionable male wear, to decide whether its display was really up to the mark.

They reached a rotunda with covered galleries, where a band was giving a concert. This was the Kurhaus. Tennis was being played on several courts by long--legged, clean--shaven youths in accurately pressed flannels and rubber--soled shoes, their arms bared to the elbow, and sunburnt girls in white frocks, who ran and flung themselves high in the sunny air in their efforts to strike the white ball. The well--kept courts looked as though coated with flour. The cousins sat down on an empty bench to watch and criticize the game.

"You don't play here?" Hans Castorp asked.

"I am not allowed," Joachim answered. "We have to lie—-nothing but lie.

Settembrini says we live horizontally—-he calls us horizontallers; that's one of his rotten jokes. Those are healthy people, there—-or else they are breaking the rules. But they don't play very seriously anyhow—-it's more for the sake of the costume. As far as breaking the rules goes, there are more forbidden things besides tennis that get played here—-poker, and *petits--chevaux*, in this and that hotel. At our place there is a notice about it; it is supposed to be the most harmful thing one can do. Even so, there are people who slip out after the evening visit and come down here to gamble. That prince who gave Behrens his title always did it, they say."

Hans Castorp barely attended. His mouth was open, for he could not have breathed through his nose without sniffing; he felt with dull discomfort that his heart was hammering out of time with the music; and with this combined sense of discord and disorder he was about to doze off when Joachim suggested that they go home. They returned almost in silence. Hans Castorp stumbled once or twice on the level street and grinned ruefully as he shook his head. The lame man took them up in the lift to their own storey. They parted, with a brief "See you later" at the door of number thirty--four; Hans Castorp piloted himself through his room to the balcony, where he dropped just as he was upon his deck--chair and, without once shifting to a more comfortable posture, sank into a dull half--slumber, broken by the rapid beating of his unquiet heart.

Of Course, A Female!

How long it lasted he could not have told. When the moment arrived, the gong sounded. But it was not the gong for the meal, it was only the dressing--bell, as Hans Castorp knew, and so he still lay, until the metallic drone rose and died away a second time. When Joachim came to fetch him, Hans Castorp wanted to change, but this Joachim would not allow. He hated and despised unpunctuality. Would he be likely, he asked, to get on, and get strong enough for the service, if he was too feeble to observe the hours for meals? Wherein he was, of course, quite right, and Hans Castorp could only say that he was not ill at all, but only utterly and entirely sleepy. He confined himself to washing his hands; and then for the third time they went down together to the dining--hall.

The guests streamed in through both entrances, they even came through the open verandah door. Soon they all sat at their several tables as though they had never risen. Such at least was Hans Castorp's impression——a dreamy and irrational impression, of course, but one which his muddled brain could not for an instant get rid of, in which it even took a certain satisfaction, so that several times in the course of the meal he sought to call it up again and was always perfectly successful in reproducing the illusion. The gay old lady continued to talk in her semifluid tongue at the care--worn Dr. Blumenkohl, diagonally opposite; her lean niece actually at last ate something else than yogurt; namely, the thick cream of barley soup, which was handed round in soup--plates by the waitresses. Of this she took a few spoonfuls and left the rest. Pretty Marusja giggled, then stuffed her dainty handkerchief in her mouth——it gave out a scent of oranges. Miss Robinson read the same letters, in the same round script, which she had read at breakfast. Obviously she knew not a word of German, nor wished to do so. Joachim, *preux chevalier*, said something to her in English, which she answered in a monosyllable without ceasing to chew, and relapsed again into silence. Frau Stöhr, sitting there in her woollen blouse, gave the table to know she had been examined that forenoon; she went into particulars, affectedly drawing back her upper lip from the rodent--like teeth. There were rhonchi to be heard in the upper right side, and under the left shoulder--blade the breathing was still very limited; the "old man" said she would have to stop another five months. It sounded very common to hear her refer thus to Herr Hofrat Behrens. She displayed, moreover, a feeling of injury because the "old man" was not sitting at her table to--day, where he should by rights be sitting if he had taken them "*à la tournée*"—-by which she presumably meant in turn—-instead of going to the next table again. (There, in fact, he really was sitting, his great hands folded before his place.) But of course that was Frau Salomon's table, the fat Frau Salomon from Amsterdam, who came *décolletée* to table even on week--days, a sight which the "old man" liked to see, though for her part—-Frau Stöhr's—-she never could understand why, since he could see all he wanted of Frau Salomon at every examination. She related, in an excited whisper, that last night, in the general rest--hall up under the roof, somebody had put out the light, for purposes which she designated as "transparent." The "old man" had seen it, and stormed so you could hear it all over the place. He had not discovered the culprit, of course, but it didn't take a university education to guess that it was Captain Miklosich from Bucharest, for whom, when in the society of ladies, it could never be dark enough: a man without any and all refinement—-though he did wear a corset—-and, by nature, simply a beast of prey—-a perfect beast of prey, repeated Frau Stöhr, in a stifled whisper, beads of perspiration on her brow and upper lip. The relations between him and Frau ConsulGeneral Wurmbrandt from Vienna were known throughout Dorf and Platz—-it was idle any longer to speak of them as clandestine. Not merely did the captain go into the Frau Consul--General's bedroom while she was still in bed, and remain there throughout her toilet; last Thursday he had not *left* the Wurmbrandt's room until four in the morning; that they knew from the nurse who was taking care of young Franz in number nineteen—-his pneumothorax operation had gone wrong. She had, in her embarrassment, mistaken her own door, and burst suddenly into the room of Herr Paravant, a Dortmund lawyer. Lastly Frau Stöhr held forth for some time on the merits of a "cosmic" establishment down in the village, where she bought her mouthwash. Joachim gazed stonily downwards at his plate. The meal was as faultlessly prepared as it was abundant. Counting the hearty soup, it consisted of no less than six courses. After the fish followed an excellent meat dish, with garnishings, then a separate vegetable course, then roast fowl, a pudding, not inferior to yesterday evening's, and lastly cheese and fruit. Each dish was handed twice and not in vain. At all seven tables they filled their plates and ate: they ate like wolves; they displayed a voracity which would have been a pleasure to see, had there not been something else about it, an effect almost uncanny, not to say repulsive. It was not only the light--hearted who thus laced into the food—-those who chattered as they ate and threw pellets of bread at each other. No, the same appetite was evinced by the silent, gloomy ones as well, those who in the pauses between courses leaned their heads on their hands and stared before them. A half--grown youth at the next table on the left, by his years a schoolboy, with his wrists coming out of his jacket sleeves, and thick, round eye--glasses, cut all the heaped--up food on his plate into a sort of mash, then bent over and gulped it down; he reached with his serviette behind his glasses now and then and dried his eyes—-whether it was sweat or tears he dried one could not tell.

There were two incidents during the course of the meal of which Hans Castorp took note, so far as his condition permitted. One was the banging of the glass door, which occurred while they were having the fish course. Hans Castorp gave an exasperated shrug and angrily resolved that this time he really must find out who did it. He said this not only within himself, his lips formed the words. "I must find out," he whispered with exaggerated earnestness. Miss Robinson and the schoolmistress both looked at him in surprise. He turned the whole upper half of his body to the left and opened wide his bloodshot blue eyes.

It was a lady who was passing through the room; a woman, or rather girl, of middle height, in a white sweater and coloured skirt, her reddish--blond hair wound in braids about her head. Hans Castorp had only a glimpse of her profile. She moved, in singular contrast to the noise of her entrance, almost without sound, passing with a peculiarly gliding step, her head a little thrust forward, to her place at the furthest table on the left, at right angles to the verandah door: the "good" Russian table, in fact. As she walked, she held one hand deep in the pocket of her close--fitting jacket; the other she lifted to the back of her head and arranged the plaits of her hair. Hans Castorp looked at the hand. He was habitually observant and critical of this feature, and accustomed when he made a new acquaintance to direct his attention first upon it. It was not particularly ladylike, this hand that was putting the braids to rights; not so refined and well kept as the hands of ladies in Hans Castorp's own social sphere. Rather broad, with stumpy fingers, it had about it something primitive and childish, something indeed of the schoolgirl. The nails, it was plain, knew nothing of the manicurist's art; they were cut in rough--and--ready schoolgirl fashion, and the skin at the side looked almost as though someone were subject to the childish vice of finger biting. But Hans Castorp sensed rather than saw this, owing to the distance. The laggard greeted her table--mates with a nod, and took her place on the inner side of the table with her back to the room, next to Dr. Krokowski, who was sitting at the top. As she did so, she turned her head, with the hand still raised to it, toward the dining--room and surveyed the public; Hans Castorp had opportunity for the fleeting observation that her cheek--bones were broad and her eyes narrow.——A vague memory of something, of somebody, stirred him slightly and fleetingly as he looked.

"Of course, a female!" he thought, or rather he actually uttered, in a murmur, yet so that the schoolmistress, Fräulein Engelhart, understood. The poor old spinster smiled in sympathy.

[101]

"That is Madame Chauchat,'" she said. "She is so heedless. A charming creature."

And the downy flush on her cheek grew a shade darker—as it did whenever she spoke.

"A Frenchwoman?" Hans Castorp asked, with severity.

"No, she is a Russian," was the answer. "Her husband is very likely French or of French descent, I am not sure."

Hans Castorp asked, still irritated, if that was he—-pointing to a gentleman with drooping shoulders who sat at the "good" Russian table.

"Oh, no," the schoolmistress answered, "he isn't here; he has never been here, no one knows him."

"She ought to learn how to shut a door," Hans Castorp said. "She always lets it slam. It is a piece of ill breeding."

And on the schoolmistress's meekly accepting this reproof as though she herself had been the guilty party, there was no more talk of Madame Chauchat.

The second event was the temporary absence of Dr. Blumenkohl from the room—-nothing more. The mildly disgusted facial expression suddenly deepened, he looked with sadder fixity into space, then unobtrusively moved back his chair and went out. Whereupon Frau Stöhr's essential ill breeding showed itself in the clearest light; probably out of vulgar satisfaction in the fact that she was less ill than Dr. Blumenkohl. She accompanied his exit with comments half pitying, half contemptuous.

"Poor creature," she said. "He'll soon be at his last gasp. He had to go out for a talk with his 'Blue Peter.' "

Quite stolidly, without repulsion, she brought out the grotesque phrase—-Hans Castorp felt a mixture of repugnance and desire to laugh. Presently Dr. Blumenkohl came back in the same unobtrusive way, took his place, and went on eating. He too ate a great deal, twice of every dish, always in silence, with the same melancholy, preoccupied air.

Thus the midday meal came to an end. Thanks to the skilled service—-the dwarf at Hans Castorp's table was one of the quickest on her feet—-it had lasted only a round hour. Breathing heavily, and not quite sure how he got upstairs, Hans Castorp lay once more in his capital chair upon his loggia; after this meal there was rest--cure until tea--time—-the most important and rigidly adhered--to rest period of the day. Between the opaque glass walls that divided him on the one side from Joachim, on the other from the Russian couple, he lay and idly dreamed, his heart pounding, breathing through his mouth. On using his handkerchief he discovered it to be red with blood, but had not enough energy to think about the fact, though he was rather given to worrying over himself and by nature inclined to hypochondria. Once more he had lighted a Maria Mancini, and this time he smoked it to the end, no matter how it tasted. Giddy and oppressed, he considered as in a dream how very odd he had felt since he came up here. Two or three times his breast was shaken by inward laughter at the horrid expression which that ignorant creature, Frau Stöhr, had used.

Herr Albin

Below in the garden the fanciful banner with the caduceus lifted itself now and again in a breath of wind. The sky was once more evenly overcast. The sun was gone, the air had grown almost inhospitably cool. The general rest--hall seemed to be full; talking and laughter went on below.

"Herr Albin, I implore you, put away your knife; put it in your pocket, there will be an accident with it," a high, uncertain voice besought. Then: "Dear Herr Albin, for heaven's sake, spare our nerves, and take that murderous tool out of our sight," a second voice chimed in.

A blond young man, with a cigarette in his mouth, sitting in the outside easy--chair, responded pertly: "Couldn't think of it! I'm sure the ladies haven't the heart to prevent me from amusing myself a little! I bought that knife in Calcutta, of a blind wizard. He could swallow it, and then have his boy dig it up fifty paces from where he stood. Do look—-it is sharper than a razor. You only need to touch the blade; it goes into your flesh like cutting butter. Wait a minute, I'll show it you close by." And Herr Albin stood up. A shriek arose. "Or rather," said he, "I'll fetch my revolver; that will be more interesting. Piquant little tool—-useful too. Send a bullet through anything.—-

I'll go up and get it."

"No, no, don't, pray don't, Herr Albin!" in a loud outcry from many voices. But Herr Albin had already come out to go up to his room: very young and lanky, with a rosy, childish face, and little strips of side--whisker close to his ears.

"Herr Albin," cried a lady's voice from within, "do fetch your greatcoat instead, and put it on; do it just to please me! Six weeks long you have lain with inflammation of the lungs, and now you sit here without an overcoat, and don't even cover yourself, and smoke cigarettes! That is tempting Providence; on my word it is, Herr Albin!"

He only laughed scornfully as he went off, and in a few minutes returned with the revolver in his hand. The silly geese squawked worse than before, and some of them even made as if they would spring from their chairs, wrap their blankets round them, and flee.

"Look how little and shiny he is," said Herr Albin. "But when I press him here, then he bites." Another outcry. "Of course, he is loaded—-to the hilt," he continued. "In this disk here are the six cartridges. It turns one hole at each shot. But I don't keep him merely for a joke," he said noticing that the sensation was wearing off. He let the revolver slip into his breast pocket, sat down again, flung one leg over the other, and lighted a fresh cigarette. "Certainly not for a joke," he repeated, and compressed his lips.

[104]

"What for, then—-what for?" they asked, their voices trembling.

"Horrible!" came a sudden cry, and Herr Albin nodded.

"I see you begin to understand," he said. "In fact, you are right, that *is* what I keep it for," he went on airily, inhaling, despite the recent inflammation of the lungs, a mass of smoke and breathing it slowly out again. "I keep it in readiness for the day when I can't stand this farce any longer, and do myself the honour to bid you a respectful adieu. It is all very simple. I've given the matter some study, and I know precisely how to do it." Another screech at the word. "I eliminate the region of the heart, the aim is not very convenient there. I prefer to annihilate my consciousness at its very centre by introducing my charming little foreign body direct into this interesting organ."—Herr Albin indicated with his index finger a spot on his close--cropped blond pate. "You aim here"—-he drew the nickel--plated revolver out of his pocket once more and tapped with the barrel against his skull—"just here, above the artery; even without a mirror the thing is simple—-"

A chorus of imploring protest arose, mingled with heavy sobbing. "Herr Albin, Herr Albin, put it away, take it from your temple, it is dreadful to see you! Herr Albin, you are young, you will get well, you will return to the world, everybody will love you! But put on your coat and lie down, cover yourself, go on with your cure. Don't drive the bathing--master away next time he comes to rub you down with alcohol. And stop smoking cigarettes—-Herr Albin, we implore you, for the sake of your young, your precious life!"

But Herr Albin was inexorable. "No, no," he said "let me alone, I'm all right, thanks. I've never refused a lady anything yet; but you see it's no good trying to put a spoke in the wheel of fate. I am in my third year up here—-I'm sick of it, fed up, I can't play the game any more—-do you blame me for that? Incurable, ladies, as I sit here before you, an incurable case; the Hofrat himself is hardly at the pains any longer to pretend I am not. Grant me at least the freedom which is all I can get out of the situation. In school, when it was settled that someone was not to move up to the next form, he just stopped where he was; nobody asked him any more questions, he did not have to do any more work. It's like that with me; I am in that happy condition now. I need do nothing more, I don't count, I can laugh at the whole thing. Would you like some chocolate? Do take some—no, you won't be robbing me, I have heaps of it in my room, eight boxes, and five tablets of Gala--Peter and four pounds of Lindt. The ladies of the sanatorium gave it to me when I was ill with my inflammation of the lungs—"

From somewhere a bass voice was audible, commanding quiet. Herr Albin gave a short laugh, a ragged, wavering laugh; then stillness reigned in the rest--hall, a stillness as of a vanished dream, a disappearing wraith. Afterwards the voices rose again, sounding strange in the silence. Hans Castorp listened until they were quite hushed. He had an indistinct notion that Herr Albin was a puppy, yet could not resist a certain envy. In particular, the school--days comparison made an impression on him; he himself had stuck in the lower second and well remembered this situation, of course rather to be ashamed of and yet not without its funny side. In particular he recalled the agreeable sensation of being totally lost and abandoned, with which, in the fourth quarter, he gave up the running—he could have "laughed at the whole thing." His reflections were dim and confused, it would be difficult to define them; but in effect it seemed to him that, though honour might possess certain advantages, yet shame had others, and not inferior: advantages, even, that were well--nigh boundless in their scope. He tried to put himself in Herr Albin's place and see how it must feel to be finally relieved of the burden of a respectable life and made free of the infinite realms of shame; and the young man shuddered at the wild wave of sweetness which swept over him at the thought and drove on his labouring heart to an even quicker pace.

Satana Makes Proposals
That Touch Our Honour

After a while he lost consciousness. It was half past three by his watch when he was roused by voices behind the left--hand glass partition. Dr. Krokowski at this hour made the rounds alone, and he was talking in Russian with the unmannerly pair on the next balcony, asking the husband how he did, it seemed, and inspecting the fever chart. He did not, however, continue his route by the balconies, but skirted Hans Castorp's section, passing along the corridor and entering Joachim's room by the door. Hans Castorp felt rather hurt to have Krokowski circle round and leave him out—-even though a tête--à--tête with the gentleman was something he was far from hankering after. Of course he was healthy, he was not included with the other inmates; up here, he reflected, it was the sound and healthy person who did not count, who got no attention—-and this the young man found vastly annoying.

Dr. Krokowski stopped with Joachim two or three minutes; then he went on down the row of balconies, and Hans Castorp heard his cousin say that it was time to get up and make ready for tea.

"Good," he answered, and rose. But he was giddy from long lying, and the unrefreshing half--slumber had made his face burn anew; yet he felt chilly; perhaps he had not been well enough covered as he lay.

He washed his eyes and hands, brushed his hair, put his clothing to rights, and met Joachim outside in the corridor.

"Did you hear that Herr Albin?" he asked, as they went down the steps.

"I should say I did," his cousin answered. "The man ought to be disciplined—- disturbing the whole rest period with his gabble, and exciting the ladies so that it puts them back for weeks. A piece of gross insubordination. But who is there to denounce him? On the contrary, that sort of thing makes quite a welcome diversion."

"Do you think he would really do it——put a bullet into himself? It's a 'very simple matter,' to use his own words."

"Oh," answered Joachim, "it isn't so out of the question, more's the pity. Such things do happen up here. Two months before I came, a student who had been here a long time hanged himself down in the wood, after a general examination. It was a good deal talked about still, in the early days after I came."

Hans Castorp gaped excitedly. "Well," he declared, "I am certainly far from feeling fit up here. I couldn't say I did. I think it's quite possible I shan't be able to stop, that I'll have to leave——you wouldn't take it amiss, would you?"

"Leave? What is the matter with you?" cried Joachim. "Nonsense! You've just come. You can't judge from the first day!"

"Good Lord, is it still only the first day? It seems to me I've been up here a long time——ages."

"Don't begin to philosophize again about time," said Joachim, "You had me perfectly bewildered this morning."

"No, don't worry, I've forgotten all of it," answered Hans Castorp, "the whole 'complex.' I've lost all the clear--headedness I had——it's gone. Well, and so it's time for tea."

"Yes; and after that we walk as far as the bench again, like this morning."

"Just as you say. Only I hope we shan't meet Settembrini again. I'm not up to any more learned conversation. I can tell you that beforehand."

At tea all the various beverages were served which it is possible to serve at that meal. Miss Robinson drank again her brew made of rose--hips, the grand--niece spooned up her yogurt. There were milk, tea, coffee, chocolate, even *bouillon;* and on every hand the guests, newly arisen from some two hours' repose after their heavy luncheon, were busily spreading huge slices of raisin cake with butter.

Hans Castorp chose tea, and dipped *zwieback* in it; he also tasted some marmalade. The raisin cake he contemplated with an interested eye, but literally shuddered at the thought of eating any. Once more he sat here in his place, in this vaulted room with its gay yet simple decorations, its seven tables. It was the fourth time. Later, at seven o'clock, he sat there again, for the fifth time, and that was supper. In the brief and trifling interval the cousins had taken a turn as far as the bench on the mountain--side, beside the little watercourse. The path had been full of patients; Hans Castorp had often to lift his hat. Followed a last period of rest on the balcony, a fugitive and empty interlude of an hour and a half.

He dressed conscientiously for the evening meal, and, sitting in his place between Miss Robinson and the schoolmistress, he ate: julienne soup, baked and roast meats with suitable accompaniments, two pieces of a tart made of macaroons, butter--cream, chocolate, jam and marzipan, and lastly excellent cheese and pumpernickel. As before, he ordered a bottle of Kulmbacher. But, by the time he had half emptied his tall glass, he became clearly and unmistakably aware that bed was the best place for him. His head roared, his eyelids were like lead, his heart went like a set of kettledrums, and he began to torture himself with the suspicion that pretty Marusja, who was bending over her plate covering her face with the hand that wore the ruby ring, was laughing at *him*— though he had taken enormous pains not to give occasion for laughter. Out of the far distance he heard Frau Stöhr telling, or asserting, something which seemed to him such utter nonsense that he was conscious of a despairing doubt as to whether he had heard aright, or whether he had turned her words to nonsense in his addled brain. She was declaring that she knew how to make twenty--eight different sauces to serve with fish; she would stake her reputation on the fact, though her own husband had warned her not to talk about it: "Don't talk about it," he had told her; "nobody will believe it, or, if they do, they will simply laugh at you!" And yet she would say it, say once and for all, that it was twenty--eight fishsauces she could make. All of which, to our good Hans Castorp, seemed too mad for words; he clutched his brow with his hand, and in his amazement quite forgot that he had a bite of pumpernickel and Cheshire still to be chewed and swallowed. When he rose from table, he had it still in his mouth.

They went out through the left--hand glass door, that fatal door which always slammed, and which led directly to the front hall. Nearly all the guests went out the same way, it appeared that after dinner a certain amount of social intercourse took place in the hall and the adjoining salons. Most of the patients stood about in little groups chatting. Games were begun at two green extension--tables: at the one, dominoes; at the other, bridge, and here only the young folk played, among them Hermine Kleefeld and Herr Albin. In the first salon were some amusing optical diversions: the first a stereoscope, behind the lenses of which one inserted a photograph—-for instance, there was one of a Venetian gondolier—-and on looking through, you saw the figure standing out in the round, lifelike, though bloodless; another was a kaleidoscope—-you put your eye to the lens and slightly turned a wheel, when all sorts of gay--coloured stars and arabesques danced and juggled before it with the swift changefulness of magic. A third was a revolving drum, into which you inserted a strip of cinematographic film and then looked through the openings as it whirled, and saw a miller fighting with a chimney--sweep, a schoolmaster chastising a boy, a leaping rope--dancer and a peasant pair dancing a folk--dance. Hans Castorp, his cold hands on his knees, gazed a long time into each of these contrivances. He paused awhile by the card--table, where Herr Albin, the incurable, sat with the corners of his mouth drawn down, and handled the cards with a supercilious, man--of--the--worldly air. In a corner sat Dr. Krokowski, absorbed in a brisk and hearty conversation with a half--circle of ladies, among them Frau Stöhr, Frau Iltis, and Fräulein Levi. The occupants of the "good" Russian table had withdrawn into a neighbouring small salon, separated from the card--room by a portière, where they formed a small and separate coterie, consisting, in addition to Madame Chauchat, of a languid, blond--bearded youth with a hollow chest and prominent eyeballs; a young girl of pronounced brunette type, with a droll, original face, gold ear--rings, and wild woolly hair; besides these, Dr. Blumenkohl, who had joined their circle, and two other youths with drooping shoulders. Madame Chauchat wore a blue frock with a white lace collar. She sat, the centre of her group, on the sofa behind the round table, at the bottom of the small salon, her face turned toward the card--room. Hans Castorp, who could not look at the unmannerly creature without disapproval, said to himself: "She reminds me of something, but I cannot tell what."

A tall man of some thirty years, growing bald, played the wedding march from the *Midsummer Night's Dream* three times on end, on the little brown piano, and on being urged by some of the ladies, began the melodious piece for the fourth time, gazing deep and silently into their eyes, one after the other.

"May I be permitted to ask after the state of your health, Engineer?" inquired Settembrini, who had lounged up among the other guests, hands in pockets, and now presented himself before Hans Castorp. He still wore his pilot coat and check trousers. He smiled as he spoke, and Hans Castorp felt again the sobering effect of that fine and mocking curl of the lip beneath the waving black moustaches. He looked rather stupidly at the Italian, with lax mouth and red--veined eyes.

"Oh, it's you!" he said. "The gentleman we met this morning on our walk—at that bench up there—-near the—-yes, I knew you at once. Can you believe it," he went on, though conscious of saying something *gauche*, "can you believe it, I took you for an organ--grinder when I first saw you? Of course, that's all utter rot," he added, seeing a coolly inquiring expression on Settembrini's face. "Perfectly idiotic. I can't comprehend how in the world I——"

"Don't disturb yourself, it doesn't matter," responded Settembrini, after fixing the young man with a momentary intent regard. "Well, and how have you spent your day, the first of your sojourn in this gay resort?"

"Thanks very much—-quite according to the rules," answered Hans Castorp.

"Prevailingly 'horizontal,' as I hear you prefer to call it."

Settembrini smiled. "I may have taken occasion to express myself thus," he said.

"Well, and you found it amusing, this manner of existence?"

"Amusing or dull, whichever you like," responded Hans Castorp. "It isn't always so easy to decide which, you know. At all events, I haven't been bored; there are far too lively goings--on up here for that. So much that is new and unusual to hear and see—-and yet, in another way, it seems as though I had been here a long time, instead of just a single day—-as if I had got older and wiser since I came—-that is the way I feel."

"Wiser, too?" Settembrini asked, and raised his eyebrows. "Will you permit me to ask how old you are?"

And behold, Hans Castorp could not tell! At that moment he did not know how old he was, despite strenuous, even desperate efforts to bethink himself. In order to gain time he had the question repeated, and then answered: "I? How old I am? In my twenty--fourth year, of course. I'll soon be twenty--four. I beg your pardon, but I am very tired," he went on. "Tired isn't the word for it. Do you know how it is when you are dreaming, and know that you are dreaming, and try to awake and can't? That is precisely the way I feel. I certainly must have some fever; otherwise I simply cannot explain it. Imagine, my feet are cold all the way up to my knees. If one may put it that way, of course one's knees aren't one's feet—-do excuse me, I am all in a muddle, and no wonder, considering I was whistled at in the morning with the pn—-the pn—-eumothorax, and in the afternoon had to listen to this Herr Albin—-in the horizontal, on top of that! It seems to me I cannot any more trust my five senses, and that I must confess disturbs me more than my cold feet and the heat in my face. Tell me frankly: do you think it is possible Frau Stöhr knows how to make twenty--eight different kinds of fish--sauces? I don't mean if she actually can make them——that I should consider out of the question——I mean if she said at table just now she could, or if I only imagined she did——that is all I want to know."

Settembrini looked at him. He seemed not to have been listening. His eyes were set again, they had taken on a fixed stare, and he said: "Yes, yes, yes," and "I see, I see, I see," each three times, just as he had done in the morning, in a considering, deriding tone, and giving a sharp sound to the *s*'s.

"Twenty--four?" he asked after a while.

"No, twenty--eight," Hans Castorp said. "Twenty--eight fish--sauces. Not sauces in general, special sauces for fish——that is the monstrous part of it."

"Engineer," Settembrini said sharply, almost angrily, "pull yourself together and stop talking this demoralized rubbish. I know nothing about it, nor do I wish to. You are in your twenty--fourth year, you say? H'm. Permit me to put another question, or rather, with your kind permission, make a suggestion. As your stay up here with us does not appear to be conducive, as you don't feel comfortable, either physically or, unless I err, mentally, how would it be if you renounced the prospect of growing older on this spot——in short, what if you were to pack to--night, and be up and away with the first suitable train?"

"You mean I should go away?" Hans Castorp asked; "when I've hardly come? No, why should I try to judge from the first day?"

He happened, as he spoke, to direct his gaze into the next room, and saw Frau Chauchat's full face, with its narrow eyes and broad cheek--bones. "What is it, what or whom in all the world does she remind me of?" But his weary brain, despite the effort he made, refused an answer.

"Of course," he went on, "it is true it is not so easy for me to get acclimatized up here. But that was to be expected. I'd be ashamed to chuck it up and go away like that, just because I felt upset and feverish for a few days. I'd feel a perfect coward. It would be a senseless thing to do, you admit it yourself, don't you?"

He spoke with a sudden insistence, jerking his shoulders excitedly——he seemed to want to make the Italian withdraw his suggestion in form.

"I pay every homage to reason," Settembrini answered. "I pay homage to valour too. What you say sounds well; it would be hard to oppose anything convincing against it. I myself have seen some beautiful cases of acclimatization. There was Fräulein Kneifer, Ottilie Kneifer, last year. She came of a good family——the daughter of an important government official. She was here some year and a half and had grown to feel so much at home that when her health was quite restored——it does happen, up here; people do sometimes get well——she couldn't bear to leave. She implored the Hofrat to let her stop; she could not and would not go; this was her home, she was happy here. But the place was full, they wanted her room, and so all her prayers were in vain; they stood out for discharging her cured. Ottilie was taken with high fever, her curve went well up. But they found her out by exchanging her regular thermometer for a 'silent sister.' You aren't acquainted as yet with the term; it is a thermometer without figures, which the physician measures with a little rule, and plots the curve himself. Ottilie, my dear sir, had 98.4°; she was normal. Then she went bathing in the lake——it was the beginning of May; we were having frost at night; the water was not precisely ice--cold, say a few degrees above. She remained some time in the water, trying to contract some illness or other——alas, she was, and remained, quite sound. She departed in anguish and despair, deaf to all the consolations her parents could give. 'What shall I do down there?' she kept crying. 'This is my home!' I never heard what became of her.——But you are not listening, Engineer. Unless I am much mistaken, simply remaining on your legs costs you an effort.

Lieutenant!" he addressed himself to Joachim, who was just coming up. "Take your cousin and put him to bed. He unites the virtues of courage and moderation——but just now he is a little groggy."

"No, really, I understood everything you said," protested Hans Castorp. "The 'silent sister' is a mercury thermometer without figures——you see, I got it all."

But he went up in the lift with Joachim and several other patients as well, for the conviviality was over for the evening; the guests were separating to seek the halls and loggias for the evening cure. Hans Castorp went into his cousin's room. The corridor floor, with its strip of narrow coco matting, billowed beneath his feet, but this, apart from its singularity, was not unpleasant. He sat down in Joachim's great flowered arm--chair——there was one just like it in his own room——and lighted his Maria Mancini. It tasted like glue, like coal, like anything but what it should taste like. Still he smoked on, as he watched Joachim making ready for his cure, putting on his house jacket, then an old overcoat, then, armed with his night--lamp and Russian primer, going into the balcony. He turned on the light, lay down with his thermometer in his mouth, and began, with astonishing dexterity, to wrap himself in the two camel's--hair rugs that were spread out over his chair. Hans Castorp looked on with honest admiration for his skill. He flung the covers over him, one after the other: first from the left side, all their length up to his shoulders, then from the feet up, then from the right side, so that he formed, when finished, a neat compact parcel, out of which stuck only his head, shoulders, and arms.

"How well you do that!" Hans Castorp said.

"That's the practice I've had," Joachim answered, holding the thermometer between his teeth in order to speak. "You'll learn. To--morrow we must certainly get you a pair of rugs. You can use them afterwards at home, and up here they are indispensable, particularly as you have no sleeping--sack."

"I shan't lie out on the balcony at night," Hans Castorp declared. "I can tell you that at once. It would seem perfectly weird to me. Everything has its limits. I must draw the line somewhere, since I'm really only up here on a visit. I will sit here awhile and smoke my cigar in the regular way. It tastes vile, but I know it's good, and that will have to do me for to--day. It is close on nine—it isn't even quite nine yet, more's the pity—-but when it is half past, that is late enough for a man to go to bed at least halfway decently."

A shiver ran over him, then several, one after the other. Hans Castorp sprang up and ran to the thermometer on the wall, as if to catch it *in flagrante*. According to the mercury, there were fifty degrees of heat in the room. He clutched the radiator; it was cold and dead. He murmured something incoherent, to the effect that it was a scandal to have no heating, even if it was August. It wasn't a question of the name of the month, but of the temperature that obtained, which was such that actually he was as cold as a dog. Yet his face burned. He sat down, stood up again, and with a murmured request for permission fetched Joachim's coverlet and spread it out over himself as he sat in the chair. And thus he remained, hot and cold by turns, torturing himself with his nauseous cigar. He was overcome by a wave of wretchedness; it seemed to him he had never in his life before felt quite so miserable.

"I feel simply wretched," he muttered. And suddenly he was moved by an extraordinary and extravagant thrill of joy and suspense, of which he was so conscious that he sat motionless waiting for it to come again. It did not—-only the misery remained. He stood up at last, flung Joachim's coverlet on the bed, and got something out that sounded like a good--night: "Don't freeze to death; call me again in the morning," his lips hardly shaping the words; then he staggered along the corridor to his own room.

He sang to himself as he undressed—-certainly not from excess of spirits.

Mechanically, without the care which was their due, he went through all the motions that made up the ritual of his nightly toilet; poured the pink mouth--wash and discreetly gargled, washed his hands with his mild and excellent violet soap, and drew on his long batiste night--shirt, with *H.C.* embroidered on the breast pocket. Then he lay down and put out the light, letting his hot and troubled head fall upon the American woman's dying--pillow.

He had thought to fall asleep at once, but he was wrong. His eyelids, which he had scarcely been able to hold up, now declined to close; they twitched rebelliously open whenever he shut them. He told himself that it was not his regular bed--time; that during the day he had probably rested too much. Someone seemed to be beating a carpet out of doors—-which was not very probable, and proved not to be the case, for it was the beating of his own heart he heard, quite outside of himself and away in the night, exactly as though someone were beating a carpet with a wicker beater. It had not yet grown entirely dark in the room; the light from the little lamps in the loggias, Joachim's and the Russian pair's, fell through the open balcony door. As Hans Castorp lay there on his back blinking, he recalled an impression amongst the host received that day, an observation he had made, and then, with shrinking and delicacy, sought to forget. It was the look on Joachim's face when they spoke of Marusja and her physical characteristics—-an oddly pathetic facial distortion, and a spotted pallor on the sun--browned cheeks. Hans Castorp saw and understood what it meant, saw and understood in a manner so new, so sympathetic, so intimate, that the carpet--beater outside redoubled the swiftness and severity of its blows and almost drowned out the sound of the evening serenade down in the Platz—-for there was a concert again in the same hotel as before, and they were playing a symmetrically constructed, insipid melody that came up through the darkness. Hans Castorp whistled a bar of it in a whisper—-one *can* whistle in a whisper—-and beat time with his cold feet under the *plumeau.*

That was, of course, the right way not to go to sleep, and now he felt not the slightest inclination. Since he had understood in that new, penetrating sense why Joachim had changed colour, the whole world seemed altered to him, he felt pierced for the second time by that feeling of extravagant joy and suspense. And he waited for, expected something, without asking himself what. But when he heard his neighbours to right and left conclude their evening cure and re--enter their rooms to exchange the horizontal without for the horizontal within, he gave utterance to the conviction that at least this evening the barbaric pair would keep the peace.

"I can surely go to sleep without being disturbed; they will behave themselves," he said. But they did not, nor had Hans Castorp been sincere in his conviction that they would. For his part, to tell the truth, he would not have understood it if they had. Notwithstanding which, he indulged in soundless expressions of utter astonishment as he listened.

"Unheard of," he whispered. "It's incredible—-who would have believed it?" And between such exclamations joined again in the insipid music that swelled insistently up from the Platz.

Later he went to sleep. But with sleep returned the involved dreams, even more involved than those of the first night—-out of which he often started up in fright, or pursuing some confused fancy. He seemed to see Hofrat Behrens walking down the garden path, with bent knees and arms hanging stiffly in front of him, adapting his long and somehow solitary--looking stride to the time of distant march--music. As he paused before Hans Castorp, the latter saw that he was wearing a pair of glasses with thick, round lenses. He was uttering all sorts of nonsense. "A civilian, of course," he said, and without saying by your leave, drew down Hans Castorp's eyelid with the first and middle fingers of his huge hand. "Respectable civilian, as I saw at once. But not without talent, not at all without talent for a heightened degree of oxidization. Wouldn't grudge us a year, he wouldn't, just one little short year of service up here. Well, hullo--ullo! gentlemen, on with the exercise," he shouted, and putting his two enormous first fingers in his mouth, emitted a whistle of such peculiarly pleasing quality that from opposite directions Miss Robinson and the schoolmistress, much smaller than life--size, came flying through the air and perched themselves right and left on the Hofrat's shoulders, just as they sat right and left of Hans Castorp in the dining--room. And the Hofrat skipped away, wiping his eyes behind his glasses with a table--napkin——but whether it was tears or sweat he wiped could not be told.

Then it seemed to the dreamer that he was in the school courtyard, where for so many years through he had spent his recesses, and was in the act of borrowing a leadpencil from Madame Chauchat, who seemed to be there too. She gave him a halflength red pencil in a silver holder, and warned him in an agreeable, husky voice to be sure to return it to her after the hour. And as she looked at him——with her narrow, blue--grey eyes above the broad cheek--bones——he tore himself by violence away from his dream, for now he had it fast and meant to hold it, of what and whom she so vividly reminded him. Hastily he fixed this occurrence in his mind, to have it fast for the morrow. Then sleep and dream once more overpowered him, and he saw himself in the act of flight from Dr. Krokowski, who had lain in wait for him to undertake some psychoanalysis. He fled from the doctor, but his feet were leaden; past the glass partitions, along the balconies, into the garden; in his extremity he tried to climb the red--brown flagstaff——and woke perspiring at the moment when the pursuer seized him by his trouser--leg.

Hardly was he calm when slumber claimed him once more. The content of his dream entirely changed, and he stood trying to shoulder Settembrini away from the spot where they stood, the Italian smiling in his subtle, mocking way, under the full, upward--curving moustaches——and it was precisely this smile which Hans Castorp found so injurious.

"You are a nuisance," he distinctly heard himself say. "Get away, you are only a hand--organ man, and you are in the way here." But Settembrini would not let himself be budged; Hans Castorp was still standing considering what was to be done when he was unexpectedly vouchsafed a signal insight into the true nature of time; it proved to be nothing more or less than a "silent sister," a mercury column without degrees, to be used by those who wanted to cheat. He awoke with the thought in his mind that he must certainly tell Joachim of this discovery on the morrow.

In such adventures, among such discoveries, the night wore away. Hermine Kleefeld, as well as Herr Albin and Captain Miklosich, played fantastic rôles—-the last carried off Frau Stöhr in his fury, and was pierced through and through with a lance by Lawyer Paravant. One particular dream, however, Hans Castorp dreamed twice over during the night, both times in precisely the same form, the second time toward morning. He sat in the dining--hall with the seven tables when there came a great crashing of glass as the verandah door banged, and Madame Chauchat entered in a white sweater, one hand in her pocket, the other at the back of her head. But instead of going to the "good" Russian table, the unmannerly female glided noiselessly to Hans Castorp's side and without a word reached him her hand—-not the back, but the palm—-to kiss. Hans Castorp kissed that hand, which was not overly well kept, but rather broad, with stumpy fingers, the skin roughened next the nails. And at that there swept over him anew, from head to foot, the feeling of reckless sweetness he had felt for the first time when he tried to imagine himself free of the burden of a good name, and tasted the boundless joys of shame. This feeling he experienced anew in his dream, only a thousand--fold stronger than in his waking hour.

CHAPTER IV
Necessary Purchases

"*A*s your summer over now?" Hans Castorp ironically

asked his cousin, on the third day.

There had come a violent change of scene.

On the visitor's second full day up here, the most brilliant summer weather prevailed. Above the aspiring lance--shaped tips of the fir--trees the sky gleamed deepest blue, the village down in the valley glared white in the heat, and the air was filled with the sound, half gay, half pensive, of bells, from the cows that roamed the slopes, cropping the short, sun--warmed meadow grass. At early breakfast the ladies appeared in lingerie blouses, some with open--work sleeves, which did not become them all alike. In particular it did not suit Frau Stöhr, the skin of whose arms was too porous; such a fashion was distinctly not for her. The masculine population too had in various ways taken cognizance of the fine weather: they sported mohair coats and linen suits——Joachim Ziemssen had put on white flannel trousers with his blue coat, and thus arrayed looked more military than ever.

As for Settembrini, he had more than once announced his intention of changing.

"Heavens, how hot the sun is!" he said, as he and the cousins strolled down to the village after luncheon. "I see I shall have to put on thinner clothes." Yet after this explicit expression of his intentions, he continued to appear in his check trousers and pilot coat with the wide lapels. They were probably all his wardrobe could boast. But on the third day it seemed as though nature suffered a sudden reserve;

everything turned topsy--turvy. Hans Castorp could scarcely trust his eyes. It happened when they were lying in their balconies, some twenty minutes after the midday meal. Swiftly the sun hid its face, ugly turf--coloured clouds drew up over the south--western ridge, and a wind from a strange quarter, whose chill pierced to the marrow, as though it came out of some unknown icy region, swept suddenly through the valley; down went the thermometer—-a new order obtained.

"Snow," said Joachim's voice, behind the glass partition,

"What do you mean, snow?" Hans Castorp asked him. "You don't mean to say it is going to snow now?"

"Certainly," answered Joachim. "We know that wind. When it comes, it means sleighing."

"Rubbish!" Hans Castorp said. "If I remember rightly, it is the beginning of August."

But Joachim, versed in the signs of the region, knew whereof he spoke. For in a few minutes, accompanied by repeated claps of thunder, a furious snow--storm set in, so heavy that the landscape seemed wrapped in white smoke, and of village and valley scarcely anything could be seen.

It snowed away all the afternoon. The heat was turned on. Joachim availed himself of his fur sack, and was not deterred from the service of the cure; but Hans Castorp took refuge in his room, pushed up a chair to the hot pipes, and remained there, looking with frequent head--shakings at the enormity outside. By next morning the storm had ceased. The thermometer showed a few degrees above freezing, but the snow lay a foot deep, and a completely wintry landscape spread itself before Hans Castorp's astonished eyes. They had turned off the heat. The temperature of the room was 45°.

"Is your summer over now?" Hans Castorp asked his cousin, in bitter irony.

"You can't tell," answered the matter--of--fact Joachim. "We may have fine summer weather yet. Even in September it is very possible. The truth is, the seasons here are not so distinct from each other; they run in together, so to speak, and don't keep to the calendar. The sun in winter is often so strong that you take off your coat, and perspire as you walk. And in summer——well, you see for yourself! And then the snow, that puts out all one's calculations. It snows in January, but in May not much less, and, as you observe, it snows in August too. On the whole, one may say there is never a month without snow; you may take that for a rule. In short, there are winter days and summer days, spring and autumn days; but regular seasons we don't actually have up here."

"A fine mixed--up state of affairs," said Hans Castorp. In overcoat and galoshes he went with his cousin down to the village, to buy himself blankets for the out--of--doors cure, since it was plain his plaid would not suffice. For the moment he even weighed the thought of purchasing a fur sack as well, but gave it up, indeed, felt a certain revulsion from the idea.

"No, no," he said, "we'll stop at the covers. I'll have use for them down below, and everybody has covers; there's nothing strange or exciting about them. But a fur sack is altogether too special——if I buy one, it is as if I were going to settle down here, as if I belonged, understand what I mean? No, for the present we'll let it go at that; it would absolutely not be worth while to buy a sack for the few weeks I'm up here."

Joachim agreed, and they acquired two camel's--hair rugs like his own, in a fine and well--stocked shop in the English quarter. They were in natural colour, long, broad, and delightfully soft, and were to be sent at once to the International Sanatorium Berghof, Room 34: Hans Castorp looked forward to using them that very afternoon. This, of course, was after second breakfast, for otherwise the daily programme left no time sufficient to go down into the Platz. It was raining now, and the snow in the streets had turned to a slush that spattered as they walked. They overtook Settembrini on the road,

[123]

climbing up to the sanatorium under an umbrella, bare--headed. The Italian looked sallow; his mood was obviously elegiac. In well--chosen, clearly enunciated phrases he complained of the cold and damp from which he suffered so bitterly. If they would only heat the building! But the ruling powers, in their penuriousness, had the fire go out directly it stopped snowing—-an idiotic rule, an insult to human intelligence. Hans Castorp objected that presumably a moderate temperature was part of the regimen of the cure; it would certainly not do to coddle the patients. But Settembrini answered with embittered scorn. Oh, of course, the regimen of the cure! Those august and inviolate rules! Hans Castorp was right in referring to them, as he did, with bated breath. Yet it was rather striking (of course only in the pleasantest sense) that the rules most honoured in the observance were precisely those which chimed with the financial interest of the proprietors of the establishment; whereas, on the other hand, to those less favourable they were inclined to shut an eye. The cousins laughed, and Settembrini began to speak of his deceased father, who had been brought to his mind in connexion with the talk about heated rooms.

"My father," he said slowly, in tones replete with filial piety, "my father was a most delicately organized man, sensitive in body as in soul. How he did love his tiny, warm little study! In winter a temperature of twenty degrees Réaumur must always obtain there, by means of a small red--hot stove. When you entered it from the corridor on a day of cold and damp, or when the cutting tramontana blew, the warmth of it laid itself about you like a shawl, so that for very pleasure your eyes would fill with tears. The little room was stuffed with books and manuscripts, some of them of great value; he stood among them, at his narrow desk, in his blue flannel night--shirt, and devoted himself to the service of letters. He was small and delicately built, a good head shorter than I—imagine!—but with great tufts of grey hair on his temples, and a nose—-how long and pointed it was! And what a Romanist, my friends! One of the first of his time, with a rare mastery of our own tongue, and a Latin stylist such as no longer exists—-ah, a '*uomo letterato*' after Boccaccio's own heart! From far and wide scholars came to converse with him—-one from Haparanda, another from Cracow—- they came to our city of Padua, expressly to pay him homage, and he received them with dignified friendliness. He was a poet of distinction too, composing in his leisure tales in the most elegant Tuscan prose—-he was a master of the *idioma gentile*,"

Settembrini said, rolling his native syllables with the utmost relish on his tongue and turning his head from side to side. "He laid out his little garden after Virgil's own plan—-and all that he said was sane and beautiful. But warm, warm he must have it in his little room; otherwise he would tremble with cold, and he could weep with anger if they let him freeze. And now imagine, Engineer, and you, Lieutenant, what I, the son of my father, must suffer in this accursed and barbarous land, where even at summer's height the body shakes with cold, and the spirit is tortured and debased by the sights it sees.—-Oh, it is hard! What types about us! This frantic devil of a Hofrat,

Krokowski"—-Settembrini pretended to trip over the name—-"Krokowski, the fatherconfessor, who hates me because I've too much human dignity to lend myself to his papish practices.—-And at my table—-what sort of society is that in which I am forced to take my food? At my right sits a brewer from Halle—-Magnus by name—-with a moustache like a bundle of hay. 'Don't talk to me about literature,' says he. 'What has it to offer? Anything but beautiful characters? What have I to do with beautiful characters? I am a practical man, and in life I come into contact with precious few.' That is the idea he has of literature—-beautiful characters! Mother of God! His wife sits there opposite him, losing flesh all the time, and sinking further and further into idiocy. It is a filthy shame."

Hans Castorp and Joachim were in silent agreement about this talk of Settembrini's: they found it querulous and seditious in tone, if also highly entertaining and "plastic" in its verbal pungency and animus.

[125]

Hans Castorp laughed good--humouredly over the "bundle of hay," likewise over the "beautiful characters"—-or, rather, the drolly despairing way Settembrini spoke of them.

Then he said: "Good Lord, yes, the society is always mixed in a place like this, I suppose. One's not allowed to choose one's table--mates—-that would lead to goodness knows what! At our table there is a woman of the same sort, a Frau Stöhr—-I think you know her? Ghastly ignorant, I must say—-sometimes when she rattles on, one doesn't know where to look. But she complains a lot about her temperature, and how relaxed she feels, and I'm afraid she is by no means a light case. That seems so strange to me: diseased and stupid both—-I don't exactly know how to express it, but it gives me a most peculiar feeling, when somebody is so stupid, and then ill into the bargain. It must be the most melancholy thing in life. One doesn't know what to make of it; one wants to feel a proper respect for illness, of course—-after all there is a certain dignity about it, if you like. But when such asininity comes on top of it—- 'cosmic' for 'cosmetic,' and other howlers like that—-one doesn't know whether to laugh or to weep. It is a regular dilemma for the human feelings—-I find it more deplorable than I can say. What I mean is, it's not consistent, it doesn't hang together; I can't get used to the idea. One always has the idea of a stupid man as perfectly healthy and ordinary, and of illness as making one refined and clever and unusual. At least as a rule—-or I don't know, perhaps I am saying more than I could stand for," he finished. "It was only because we happened to speak of it"—-He stopped in confusion. Joachim too looked rather uncomfortable, and Settembrini lifted his eyebrows and said not a word, with an air of waiting politely for the end of his speech. He was, in fact, holding off until Hans Castorp should break down entirely before he answered. But now he said: "*Sapristi*, Engineer! You are displaying a most unexpected gift of philosophy! By your own theory, you must be yourself more ailing than you look, you are so obviously possessed of *esprit*. But, if you will permit me to say so, I can hardly subscribe to your deductions; I must deny them; my position is one of absolute dissent. I am, as you see, rather intolerant than otherwise in things of the intellect; I would rather be reproached as a pedant than suffer to pass unchallenged a point of view which seemed to me so untenable as this of yours."

"But, Herr Settembrini, I——"

"Permit me. I know what you would say: that the views you represent are not, of necessity, your own; that you have only chanced upon that one of all the possible ones there are, as it were, in the air, and you try it on, without personal responsibility. It befits your time of life, thus to avoid the settled convictions of the mature man, and to make experiments with a variety of points of view. *Placet experiri*," he quoted, giving the Italian pronunciation to the *c.* "That is a good saying. But what troubles me is that your experiment should lead you in just this direction. I doubt if it is a question of sheer chance. I fear the presence of a general tendency, which threatens to crystallize into a trait of character, unless one makes head against it. I feel it my duty, therefore, to correct you. You said that the sight of dullness and disease going hand in hand must be the most melancholy in life. I grant you, I grant you that. I too prefer an intelligent ailing person to a consumptive idiot. But I take issue where you regard the combination of disease with dullness as a sort of aesthetic inconsistency, an error in taste on the part of nature, a 'dilemma for the human feelings,' as you were pleased to express yourself. When you professed to regard disease as something so refined, so——what did you call it?——possessing a 'certain dignity'——that it doesn't 'go with' stupidity. That was the expression you used. Well, I say no! Disease has nothing refined about it, nothing dignified. Such a conception is in itself pathological, or at least tends in that direction. Perhaps I may best arouse your mistrust of it if I tell you how ancient and ugly this conception is. It comes down to us from a past seething with superstition, in which the idea of humanity had degenerated and deteriorated into sheer caricature; a past full of fears, in which well-being and harmony were regarded as suspect and emanating from the devil, whereas infirmity was equivalent to a free pass to heaven.

[127]

Reason and enlightenment have banished the darkest of these shadows that tenanted the soul of man——not entirely, for even yet the conflict is in progress. But this conflict, my dear sirs, means work, earthly labour, labour for the earth, for the honour and the interests of mankind; and by that conflict daily steeled anew, the powers of reason and enlightenment will in the end set humanity wholly free and lead it in the path of progress and civilization toward an even brighter, milder, and purer light."

"Lord bless us," thought Hans Castorp, in shamefaced consternation. "What a homily! How, I wonder, did I call all that down on my head? I must say, I find it rather prosy. And why does he talk so much about work all the time? It is his constant theme; not a very pertinent one up here, one would think." Aloud he said: "How beautifully you do talk, Herr Settembrini! What you say is very well worth hearing——and could not be more——more plastically expressed, I should think."

"Backsliding," continued Settembrini, as he lifted his umbrella away above the head of a passer--by, "spiritual backsliding in the direction of that dark and tortured age, that, believe me, Engineer, is disease——a disease already sufficiently studied, to which various names have been given: one from the terminology of aesthetics and psychology, another from the domain of politics——all of them academic terms which are not to the point, and which I will spare you. But as in the spiritual life everything is interrelated, one thing growing out of another, and since one may not reach out one's little finger to the Devil, lest he take the whole hand, and therewith the whole man; since, on the other side, a sound principle can produce only sound results, no matter which end one begins at——so disease, far from being something too refined, too worthy of reverence, to be associated with dullness, is, in itself, a degradation of mankind, a degradation painful and offensive to conceive. It may, in the individual case, be treated with consideration; but to pay it homage is——mark my words——an aberration, and the beginning of intellectual confusion. This woman you have mentioned to me——you will pardon me if I do not trouble to recall her name——ah, thank you, Frau Stöhr——it is not, it seems to me, the case of this ridiculous woman which places the human feelings in the dilemma to which you refer. She is ill, and she is limited; her case is hopeless, and the matter is simple. There is nothing left but to pity and shrug one's shoulders. The dilemma, my dear sir, the tragedy, begins where nature has been cruel enough to split the personality, to shatter its harmony by imprisoning a noble and ardent spirit within a body not fit for the stresses of life. Have you heard of Leopardi, Engineer, or you, Lieutenant? An unhappy poet of my own land, a crippled, ailing man, born with a great soul, which his sufferings were constantly humiliating and dragging down into the depths of irony——its lamentations rend the heart to hear."

And Settembrini began to recite in Italian, letting the beautiful syllables melt upon his tongue, as he closed his eyes and swayed his head from side to side, heedless that his hearers understood not a syllable. Obviously it was all done for the sake of impressing his companions with his memory and his pronunciation.

"But you don't understand; you hear the words, yet without grasping their tragic import. My dear sirs, can you comprehend what it means when I tell you that it was the love of woman which the crippled Leopardi was condemned to renounce; that this it principally was which rendered him incapable of avoiding the embitterment of his soul? Fame and virtue were shadows to him, nature an evil power——and so she is, stupid and evil both, I agree with him there——he even despaired, horrible to say, he even despaired of science and progress! Here, Engineer, is the true tragedy. Here you have your 'dilemma for the human feelings,' here, and not in the case of that wretched woman, with whose name I really cannot burden my memory. Do not, for heaven's sake, speak to me of the ennobling effects of physical suffering! A soul without a body is as inhuman and horrible as a body without a soul——though the latter is the rule and the former the exception. It is the body, as a rule, which flourishes exceedingly, which draws everything to itself, which usurps the predominant place and lives repulsively emancipated from the soul. A human being who is first of all an invalid is *all* body; therein lies his inhumanity and his debasement. In most cases he is little better than a carcass——"

"Funny," Joachim said, bending forward to look at his cousin, on Herr Settembrini's farther side. "You were saying something quite like that just lately."

"Was I?" said Hans Castorp. "Yes, it may be something of the kind went through my head."

Settembrini was silent a few paces. Then he said: "So much the better. So much the better if that is true. I am far from claiming to expound an original philosophy——such is not my office. If our engineer here has been making observations in harmony with my own, that only confirms my surmise that he is an intellectual amateur and up to the present, as is the wont of gifted youth, still experimenting with various points of view. The young man with parts is no unwritten page, he is rather one upon which all the writing has already been done, in sympathetic ink, the good and the bad together; it is the schoolmaster's task to bring out the good, to obliterate for ever the bad, by the methods of his profession.——You have been making purchases?" he asked, in a lighter tone.

"No," Hans Castorp said. "That is, nothing but——"

"We ordered a pair of blankets for my cousin," Joachim answered unconcernedly.

"For the afternoon cure——it's got so beastly cold; and I am supposed to do as the Romans do, up here," Hans Castorp said, laughing and looking at the ground.

"Ah ha! Blankets——the cure," Settembrini said. "Yes, yes. In fact: *placet experiri*," he repeated, with his Italian pronunciation, and took his leave, for their conversation had brought them to the door of the sanatorium, where they greeted the lame concierge in his lodge. Settembrini turned off into one of the sitting-rooms, to read the newspapers before luncheon. He evidently meant to cut the second rest period.

"Bless us and keep us!" Hans Castorp said to Joachim, as they stood in the lift.

"What a pedagogue it is! He said himself that he had the 'pedagogic itch.' One has to watch out with him, not to say more than one means, or he is down on you at once with all his doctrines. But after all, it is worth listening to, he talks so well; the words come jumping out of his mouth so round and appetizing—-when I listen to him, I keep seeing a picture of fresh hot rolls in my mind's eye."

Joachim laughed. "Better not tell him that. He'd be very put out I'm sure, to hear the sort of image his words call up in your mind."

"Think so? I'm not so sure. I get the impression that it is not simply and solely for the sake of edifying us that he talks; perhaps that's only a secondary motive. The important one, I feel sure, is the talk itself, the way he makes his words roll out, so resilient, just like a lot of rubber balls! He is very pleased when you notice the effect. I suppose Magnus, the brewer, was rather stupid, after all, with his 'beautiful characters'; but I do think Settembrini might have said what the point really is in literature. I did not like to ask, for fear of putting my foot in it; I am not just clear about it, and this is the first time I have ever known a literary man. But if it isn't the beautiful characters, then obviously it must be the beautiful words, and that is the impression I get from being in Settembrini's society. What a vocabulary! and he uses the word virtue just like that, without the slightest embarrassment. What do you make of that? I've never taken the word in my mouth as long as I've lived; in school, when the book said '*virtus*,' we always just said 'valour' or something like that. It certainly gave me a queer feeling in my inside, to hear him. And it makes me nervous to hear him scolding, about the cold, and Behrens, and Frau Magnus because she is losing weight, and about pretty well everything. He is a born objector, I saw that at once, down on the existing order; and that always gives me the impression that the person is spoilt——I can't help it."

"You say that," Joachim answered consideringly, "and yet he has a kind of pride about him that makes an altogether different impression: as of a man who has great respect for himself, or for humanity in general; and I like that about him; it has something good, in my eyes."

"You are right, there," Hans Castorp answered. "He's even austere; he makes one feel rather uncomfortable, as if you were——well, shall I say as if you were being taken to task? That's not such a bad way to describe it. Can you believe it, I had the feeling he was not at all pleased at my buying the blankets? He had something against it, and he kept dwelling on it."

"Oh, no," Joachim said after reflecting, in some surprise. "How could he have? I shouldn't think so." And then, thermometer in mouth, with sack and pack, he went to lie down, while Hans Castorp began at once to wash and change for dinner——which was rather less than an hour away.

Excursus on the Sense of Time

When they came upstairs after the meal, the parcel containing the blankets lay on a chair in Hans Castorp's room; and that afternoon he made use of them for the first time. The experienced Joachim instructed him in. the art of wrapping himself up, as practised in the sanatorium; they all did it, and each new--comer had to learn. First the covers were spread, one after the other, over the chair, so that a sizable piece hung down at the foot. Then you sat down and began to put the inner one about you: first lengthwise, on both sides, up to the shoulders, and then from the feet up, stooping over as you sat and grasping the folded--over end, first from one side and then from the other, taking care to fit it neatly into the length, in order to ensure the greatest possible smoothness and evenness. Then you did precisely the same thing with the outer blanket——it was somewhat more difficult to handle, and our neophyte groaned not a little as he stooped and stretched out his arms to practise the grips his cousin showed him. Only a few old hands, Joachim said, could wield both blankets at once, flinging them into position with three self-assured motions. This was a rare and enviable facility, to which belonged not only long years of practice, but a certain knack as well. Hans Castorp had to laugh at this, lying back in his chair with aching muscles; Joachim did not at once see anything funny in what he had said, and looked at him dubiously, but finally laughed too.

"There," he said, when Hans Castorp lay at last limbless and cylindrical in his chair, with the yielding roll at the back of his neck, quite worn out with all these gymnastic exercises; "there, nothing can touch you now, not even if we were to have ten below zero." He withdrew behind the partition, to do himself up in his turn.

That about the ten below zero Hans Castorp doubted; he was even now distinctly cold. He shivered repeatedly as he lay looking out through the wooden arch at the reeking, dripping damp outside, which seemed on the point of passing over into snow. It was strange that with all that humidity his cheeks still burned with a dry heat, as though he were sitting in an over-heated room. He felt absurdly tired from the practice of putting on his rugs; actually, as he held up *Ocean Steamships* to read it, the book shook in his hands. So very fit he certainly was not—-and totally anæmic, as Hofrat Behrens had said; this, no doubt, was why he was so susceptible to cold. But such unpleasing sensations were outweighed by the great comfort of his position, the unanalysable, the almost mysterious properties of his reclining-chair, which he had applauded even on his first experience of it, and which reasserted themselves in the happiest way whenever he resorted to it anew. Whether due to the character of the upholstering, the inclination of the chair-back, the exactly proper width and height of the arms, or only to the appropriate consistency of the neck roll, the result was that no more comfortable provision for relaxed limbs could be conceived than that purveyed by this excellent chair. The heart of Hans Castorp rejoiced in the blessed fact that two vacant and securely tranquil hours lay before him, dedicated by the rules of the house to the principal cure of the day; he felt it——though himself but a guest up here——to be a most suitable arrangement. For he was by nature and temperament passive, could sit without occupation hours on end, and loved, as we know, to see time spacious before him, and not to have the sense of its passing banished, wiped out or eaten up by prosaic activity. At four o'clock he partook of afternoon tea, with cake and jam. Followed a little movement in the open air, then rest again, then supper——which, like all the other meal--times, afforded a certain stimulus for eye and brain, and a certain sense of strain; after that a peep into one or other of the optical toys, the stereoscope, the kaleidoscope, the cinematograph. It might be still too much to say that Hans Castorp had grown used to the life up here; but at least he did have the daily routine at his fingers' ends.

There is, after all, something peculiar about the process of habituating oneself in a new place, the often laborious fitting in and getting used, which one undertakes for its own sake, and of set purpose to break it all off as soon as it is complete, or not long thereafter, and to return to one's former state. It is an interval, an interlude, inserted, with the object of recreation, into the tenor of life's main concerns; its purpose the relief of the organism, which is perpetually busy at its task of self--renewal, and which was in danger, almost in process, of being vitiated, slowed down, relaxed, by the bald, unjointed monotony of its daily course. But what then is the cause of this relaxation, this slowing--down that takes place when one does the same thing for too long at a time? It is not so much physical or mental fatigue or exhaustion, for if that were the case, then complete rest would be the best restorative. It is rather something psychical; it means that the perception of time tends, through periods of unbroken uniformity, to fall away; the perception of time, so closely bound up with the consciousness of life that the one may not be weakened without the other suffering a sensible impairment. Many false conceptions are held concerning the nature of tedium. In ought that the interestingness and novelty of the time-

-content are what "make the time pass"; that is to say, shorten it; whereas monotony and emptiness check and restrain its flow. This is only true with reservations. Vacuity, monotony, have, indeed, the property of lingering out the moment and the hour and of making them tiresome. But they are capable of contracting and dissipating the larger, the very large timeunits, to the point of reducing them to nothing at all. And conversely, a full and interesting content can put wings to the hour and the day; yet it will lend to the general passage of time a weightiness, a breadth and solidity which cause the eventful years to flow far more slowly than those poor, bare, empty ones over which the wind passes and they are gone. Thus what we call tedium is rather an abnormal shortening of the time consequent upon monotony. Great spaces of time passed in unbroken uniformity tend to shrink together in a way to make the heart stop beating for fear; when one day is like all the others, then they are all like one; complete uniformity would make the longest life seem short, and as though it had stolen away from us unawares. Habituation is a falling asleep or fatiguing of the sense of time; which explains why young years pass slowly, while later life flings itself faster and faster upon its course. We are aware that the intercalation of periods of change and novelty is the only means by which we can refresh our sense of time, strengthen, retard, and rejuvenate it, and therewith renew our perception of life itself. Such is the purpose of our changes of air and scene, of all our sojourns at cures and bathing resorts; it is the secret of the healing power of change and incident. Our first days in a new place, time has a youthful, that is to say, a broad and sweeping, flow, persisting for some six or eight days. Then, as one "gets used to the place," a gradual shrinkage makes itself felt. He who clings or, better expressed, wishes to cling to life, will shudder to see how the days grow light and lighter, how they scurry by like dead leaves, until the last week, of some four, perhaps, is uncannily fugitive and fleet. On the other hand, the quickening of the sense of time will flow out beyond the interval and reassert itself after the return to ordinary existence: the first days at home after the holiday will be lived with a broader flow, freshly and youthfully——but only the first few, for one adjusts oneself more quickly to the rule than to the exception; and if the sense of time be already weakened by age, or—-and this is a sign of low vitality—-it was never very well developed, one drowses quickly back into the old life, and after four--and--twenty hours it is as though one had never been away, and the journey had been but a watch in the night.

We have introduced these remarks here only because our young Hans Castorp had something like them in mind when, a few days later, he said to his cousin, and fixed him with his bloodshot eyes: "I shall never cease to find it strange that the time seems to go so slowly in a new place. I mean—-of course it isn't a question of my being bored; on the contrary, I might say that I am royally entertained. But when I look back—-in retrospect, that is, you understand—-it seems to me I've been up here goodness only knows how long; it seems an eternity back to the time when I arrived, and did not quite understand that I was there, and you said: 'Just get out here'—-don't you remember?—-That has nothing whatever to do with reason, or with the ordinary ways of measuring time; it is purely a matter of feeling. Certainly it would be nonsense for me to say: 'I feel I have been up here two months'—-it would be silly. All I can say is 'very long.' "

"Yes," Joachim answered, thermometer in mouth, "I profit by it too; while you are here, I can sort of hang on by you, as it were." Hans Castorp laughed, to hear his cousin speak thus, quite simply, without explanation.

He Practises His French

No, after all, he was by no means, even yet, adjusted to his surroundings. Neither in familiarity with the features peculiar to life as lived up here—-a familiarity impossible to achieve in so few days, which, as he was quite aware, and had even said to Joachim, he could hardly hope to acquire in the three weeks of his stay—-nor in the adaptation of his physical organism to the prevailing peculiar atmospheric conditions. For this adaptation was bitterly hard; so hard, indeed, that it looked as though it would never be a success.

The daily routine was clearly articulated, carefully organized; one fell quickly into step and, by yielding oneself to the general drift, was soon proficient. After that, indeed, within the weekly round, and also within other larger divisions of time, one discovered the existence of certain regular variations of the programme, which showed themselves, one at a time, a second one sometimes appearing only after the first had repeated itself. But even the phenomena of everyday life held much that Hans Castorp had still to learn: faces and facts already noted had to be conned, new ones to be absorbed with youth's receptivity.

Those great--bellied vessels, for example, with the short necks, which he had noticed the first evening standing in the corridors before certain doors. They contained oxygen; he had asked, and Joachim informed him. That was pure oxygen, six francs the container. The reviving gas was given the dying in a last effort to kindle or reinforce their strength. They drew it up through a tube. For behind those doors where such vessels were placed lay the dying—-the *"moribundi,"* as Herr Hofrat Behrens called them when Hans Castorp met him one day in the first storey. Purple of cheek, in his white smock--frock, he rowed along the corridor, and they went down the steps together.

"Well, and how are you, you disinterested spectator, you?" said Behrens. "Are we finding favour in your critical eye, what? Thanks so much. Yes, yes, our summer season, it's not too bad, there's something to be said for it. I've spent a little money myself to push it. But it's a pity you won't be here in the winter—-you're stopping only eight weeks, I hear? Ah, three? That's nothing but a week--end!—-won't pay you to take off your hat. Oh well, just as you think. Only it is a pity you won't be here for the winter; that's when the nobs come," he said comically, "the international nobs, down in the Platz; they don't come except in winter—-you ought to see them, if only for the sake of your education. Regular high--flyers. You ought to see the jumps they make with those skis of theirs. And then the ladies! O Lord, the ladies! Birds of paradise, I tell you, and regularly out for

[137]

adventure. Well, I must go in here, to my *moribundus*, number twenty--seven. Last stage, you know—off centre. Five dozen fiascos of oxygen he's had all together, yesterday and to--day, the soak! But he will be going to his own place by middle--day. Well, my dear Reuter," he was saying as he entered, "what do you say—shall we break the neck of another bottle?" The sound of his words died away as he closed the door. But Hans Castorp had had a moment's glimpse into the background of the room, where on the pillow lay the waxen profile of a young man with a little chin beard, who slowly rolled his great eyeballs toward the open door.

This was the first dying man Hans Castorp had ever seen; for his father and mother, and his grandfather too had died, so to speak, behind his back. How full of dignity the young man's head, with the little beard thrust upward, had lain upon his pillow! How speaking the glance those unnaturally great eyes had slowly turned upon the door!

Hans Castorp, still quite absorbed by that glimpse, instinctively tried to make his own eyes as large, as slowly gazing and meaningful as those of the dying man, walking on as he did so, toward the stairs, and encountering a lady who came out of a room behind him and overtook him at the landing. He did not at once realize that it was Madame Chauchat; she, on her side, smiled at the eyes he was making at her, put her hands to the braids at the back of her head, and passed before him down the stairs, soundless, supple, with her head somewhat thrust out.

Acquaintances he made scarcely any in these early days, nor for a long time afterwards. The daily routine was not favourable. Hans Castorp, too, was of a retiring disposition, felt himself very much the "disinterested spectator," as Hofrat Behrens had called him, and was in general content with the society and conversation of his cousin Joachim. The corridor nurse, indeed, continued to crane her neck after them, until Joachim, who had already favoured her with a little converse now and then, introduced his cousin. She wore the ribbon of her pince--nez tucked behind her ear, and spoke with excruciating affectation. On closer acquaintance, indeed, one got the impression that her reason had suffered on the rack of continual boredom. It was hard to get away from her, she showed such evident distress whenever the conversation gave signs of languishing; when the cousins seemed about to go on their way, she sought to hold them by a stream of words, by glances and despairing smiles, until, for very pity, they refrained. She spoke at random, of her papa, who was a jurist, and of her cousin, who was a physician—obviously with the idea of presenting herself in a good light and impressing them with her cultured origin. Her present charge, she said, was the son of a Coburg doll--manufacturer, named Rotbein; the disease had attacked young Fritz's intestinal tract. That was hard for all concerned; the gentlemen could understand how hard it was, for one who came from cultured surroundings and had the delicacy of feeling of the upper classes. And one couldn't turn one's back a minute. A little time ago she had just gone out a few minutes—to get some toothpowder, in fact; when she came back, there sat her patient in bed, with a glass of stout, a salame, a thick wedge of rye bread, and a pickle before him. All these clandestine dainties his family had sent to give him strength. The next day, of course, he was more dead than alive. He was himself hastening his own end. But that would be only a mercy for him, a blessed relief. For her, Sister Berta, however—whose real name was Alfreda Schildknecht—it would mean little or nothing; she would just go on to another case, in a more or less advanced stage, either here or elsewhere; such was the prospect that opened before her—and there was no other.

Yes, Hans Castorp said, her calling was a hard one, but satisfying, he should think. Of course, she answered, it was. Satisfying, but very hard.

Well, kind regards to the patient—and the cousins tried to take leave.

But she so hung upon them, with words and looks, that it was painful to see, putting forth all her powers to hold them only a little longer—-it would have been cruel not to have vouchsafed her another few minutes.

"He is asleep," she said. "He does not need me. I came out here for a second or so." She began complaining about Hofrat Behrens, whose manner with her was altogether too free, considering her origin. She much preferred Dr. Krokowski, she found him so full of soul. Then she returned to her papa and her cousin, her mental resources being exhausted. In vain she struggled to hold the young men, letting her voice rise until it was almost a shriek as she saw them moving. They escaped her finally and went; she kept on looking after them awhile, her body bent forward, her gaze so avid it seemed as though she would fairly suck them back with her eyes. Her breast was wrung with a sigh as she turned and went into her patient's room.

Hans Castorp made but one other acquaintance in these days: the pale, black--clad Mexican lady he had seen in the garden, whose nickname was Tous--les--deux. It came to pass that he heard from her own lips the tragic formula; and being forearmed, preserved a suitable demeanour and was satisfied with himself afterwards. The cousins met her before the front door, as they were setting forth on their prescribed walk after early breakfast. She was restlessly ranging there, with her pacing step, her legs bent at the knee--joints, wrapped in a black cashmere shawl, a black veil wound about her disordered silver hair and tied under her chin, her ageing face, with the large writhen mouth, gleaming dead--white against her mourning. Joachim, bare--headed as usual, greeted her with a bow, which she slowly acknowledged, the furrows deepening in her narrow forehead as she looked at him. Then, seeing a new face, she paused and waited, nodding gently as they came up to her; obviously she found it of importance to learn if the stranger was acquainted with her sad case, and to hear what he would say about it. Joachim presented his cousin. She drew her hand out of her shawl and gave it to him, a veined, emaciated, yellowish hand, with many rings, as she continued to gaze in his face.

Then it came: "*Tous les dé, monsieur,*" she said. "*Tous les dé, vous savez.*"

"*Je le sais, madame,*" Hans Castorp answered gently, "*et je le regrette beaucoup.*"

The lax pouches of skin under her jet--black eyes were larger and heavier than he had ever seen. She exhaled a faint odour as of fading flowers. A mild and pensive feeling stole about his heart.

"*Merci,*" she said, with a loose, clacking pronunciation, oddly consonant with her broken appearance. Her large mouth drooped tragically at one corner. She drew her hand back beneath her mantle, inclined her head, and turned away.

But Hans Castorp said as they walked on: "You see, I didn't mind it at all, I got on with her quite well; I always do with such people; I understand instinctively how to go at them—-don't you think so? I even think, on the whole, I get on better with sad people than with jolly ones—-goodness knows why. Perhaps it's because I'm an orphan, and lost my parents early; but when people are very serious, or down in the mouth, or somebody dies, it doesn't deject or embarrass me; I feel quite in my element, a good deal more so than when everything is going on greased wheels. I was thinking just lately that it is pretty flat of the women up here to take on as they do about death and things connected with death, so that they take such pains to shield them from contact with it, and bring the Eucharist at meal--times, and that. I call it very feeble of them. Don't you like the sight of a coffin? I really do. I find it a handsome piece of furniture, even empty; when someone is lying in it, then, in my eyes, it is positively sublime. Funerals have something very edifying; I always think one ought to go to a funeral instead of to church when one feels the need of being uplifted. People have on good black clothes, and they take off their hats and look at the coffin, and behave serious and reverent, and nobody dares to make a bad joke, the way they do in ordinary life. It's good for people to be serious, once in a way. I've sometimes asked myself if I ought not to have become a clergyman—-in a certain way it wouldn't have suited me so badly.——I hope I didn't make any mistake in my French?"

"No," Joachim answered, " *'Je le regrette beaucoup'* was perfectly right as far as it went."

Politically Suspect

Regular variations in the daily routine began to discover themselves. The first was Sunday, Sunday with a band on the terrace, which, it appeared, played there once a fortnight. Hans Castorp had arrived in the latter half of one of these periods. He had come on a Tuesday, and thus the Sunday was his fifth day up here——a day whose springlike character contrasted with the late extraordinary change and relapse into winter. It was mild and fresh, with pure white clouds in a pale blue sky, and gentle sunshine over vale and slopes, which displayed once more the green proper to the season, for the recent snow had been fated to speedy melting.

All hands, it was plain, took pains to observe Sunday and distinguish it from the rest of the week, management and guest seconding each other in their efforts to this end. At early breakfast there was seed--cake, and each guest had before his place a small glass with a few flowers, mountain pinks and even Alpine roses, which the gentlemen stuck in their buttonholes. Lawyer Paravant from Dortmund had put on a black frock--coat with a spotted waistcoat, and the ladies' toilets were suitably festal and diaphanous. Frau Chauchat appeared in a flowing lace matinée, with open sleeves. As she entered and the glass door crashed into its lock behind her, she paused a second facing the room and gracefully as it were presented herself before she glided to her table. The garment so became her that Hans Castorp's neighbour, the Danzig schoolmistress, was quite ravished. Even the barbaric pair at the "bad" Russian table had taken notice of the day: he by exchanging his leather jacket for a short coat, and the felt boots for leather shoes; she, though she still wore the soiled feather boa, by putting on a green silk blouse with a neck--ruche. Hans Castorp wrinkled his brows when he saw them, and coloured——he seemed, since he had been up here, to blush so easily.

Directly after second breakfast the concert began on the terrace; there were all kinds of horns and woodwind, and they played by turns sprightly and *sostenuto*, until nearly luncheon--time. The morning rest, during the concert, was not obligatory. A few guests did regale themselves with this feast for the ears, at the same time lying on their balconies; in the garden rest--hall a few chairs were occupied. But the majority sat at the small, white tables on the covered platform, while the more frivolous spirits, finding it too prim to sit upon chairs, encamped on the stone steps that led down into the garden, where they presently gave evidence of their high spirits. These were youthful patients of both sexes, most of whose names or faces Hans Castorp knew by now. There were Hermine Kleefeld, and Herr Albin——who carried about a great flowered box of chocolates, and offered them to all the guests, he himself eating none, but with a benevolent, paternal air smoking gold--tipped cigarettes; there were the thick--lipped youth who belonged to the Half--Lung Club, the thin and ivory--coloured Fräulein Levi, an ash--blond young man who answered to the name of Rasmussen and carried his hands breast--high, with the wrists relaxed, like a pair of flippers; Frau Salomon from Amsterdam, a woman of full bodily habit, in a red frock, who had attached herself to the group of young folk; the tall, thin--haired young man who could play out of the *Midsummer Night's Dream* sat on the step behind her, his arms about his bony knees, and gazed steadfastly down on the tanned back of her neck. There was a red--haired Greek girl, another of unknown origin with a face like a tapir's; the voracious lad with the thick eye--glasses, and another fifteen--or sixteen--year--old youth, with a monocle stuck in his eye, who carried his little finger, with its abnormally long nail shaped like a salt--spoon, to his mouth when he coughed, and was manifestly a first--class donkey——these, and numerous others.

The person with the finger--nail, Joachim related in a low voice, had been only a light case when he came. He had had no fever and had been sent up merely as a precautionary measure, by his father, who was a physician. The Hofrat had advised a stay of three months. The three months had passed, and now he had 100 to 100.5 degrees of fever and was seriously ill. But he lived so wide of all common sense that he needed his ears boxed.

The cousins sat at a table by themselves, rather apart from the others, for Hans Castorp was smoking with his dark beer, which he had brought out from breakfast. From time to time his cigar gave him a little pleasure. Rendered torpid, as often, by the beer and the music, he sat with his head on one side and his mouth slightly open, watching the gay, resortish scene, feeling, not as a disturbing influence, but rather as heightening the general singularity, and lending it one mental fillip the more, the fact that all these people were inwardly attacked by well--nigh resistless decay, and that most of them were feverish. They sat at the little tables drinking effervescent lemonade; the group on the steps were photographing each other. Postage stamps were exchanged. The red--haired Greek girl sketched Herr Rasmussen's portrait on a drawing--pad, but would not let him see it. She turned this way and that, laughing with wide--open mouth, showing her broad far--apart teeth——it was long before he could snatch it from her. Hermine Kleefeld perched on her step, eyes half open, beating time to the music with a rolled--up newspaper; she permitted Herr Albin to fasten a bunch of wild flowers on the front of her blouse. The youth with the voluptuous lips, sitting at Frau Salomon's feet, turned his head upwards to talk with her, while behind them the thin--haired pianist directed his unchanging gaze down the back of her neck. The physicians came and mingled with the guests of the cure, Hofrat Behrens in his white smock, Krokowski in his black. They passed along the row of tables, the Hofrat letting fall a pleasantry at nearly every one, till a wave of merriment followed in his wake; and so down the steps among the young folk, the female element of which straightway trooped up sidling and becking about Dr. Krokowski, while the Hofrat honoured the sabbath by performing a "stunt" with his bootlaces before the gentlemen's eyes. He rested one mighty foot upon a step, unfastened the laces, gripped them with practised technique in one hand, and without employing the other, hooked them up again crosswise, with such speed and agility that the beholders marvelled, and many of them tried to emulate him, but in vain.

Somewhat later Settembrini appeared on the terrace. He came out of the diningroom leaning on his cane, dressed as usual in his pilot coat and yellow check trousers, looked about him with his critical, alert, and elegant air, and approached the cousins' table. "Bravo!" he said, and asked permission to sit with them.

"Beer, tobacco, and music," he went on. "Behold the Fatherland! I rejoice to see you in your element, Engineer—-you have a feeling for national atmosphere, it seems. May I bask in the sunshine of your well--being?"

Hans Castorp looked lowering—-his features took on that expression directly he set eyes on the Italian. He said: "You are late for the concert, Herr Settembrini; it must be nearly over. You don't care for music?"

"Not to order," responded Settembrini. "Not by the calendar week. Not when it reeks of the prescription counter and is doled out to me by the authorities for the good of my health. I cling to my freedom—-or rather to such vestiges of freedom and personal dignity as remain to the likes of us. At these affairs I play the guest, as you do up here: I come for a quarter--hour and go away—-it gives me the illusion of independence. That it is more than an illusion I do not claim—-enough if it please me!

It is different with your cousin. For him it all belongs to the service—-that is the light, is it not, Lieutenant, in which you regard it? Ah, yes, I know, you have the trick of hugging your pride, even in a state of slavery. A puzzling trick; not everybody in Europe understands it. Music? You were asking if I profess to be an amateur of music? Well, when you say amateur" (Hans Castorp could not recall saying anything of the sort), "the word is perhaps not ill chosen; it has a slight suggestion of superficiality——yes, very well, I am an amateur of music——which is not to say that I set great store by it; not as I love and reverence the Word, the bearer of the spirit, the tool and gleaming ploughshare of progress.——Music? It is the half--articulate art, the dubious, the irresponsible, the insensible. Perhaps you will object that she can be clear when she likes. But so can nature, so can a brook——what good is that to us? That is not true clarity, it is a dreamy, inexpressive, irresponsible clarity, without consequences and therefore dangerous, because it betrays one into soft complacence.——Let music play her loftiest rôle, she will thereby but kindle the emotions, whereas what concerns us is to awaken the reason. Music is to all appearance movement itself——yet, for all that, I suspect her of quietism. Let me state my point by the method of exaggeration: my aversion from music rests on political grounds."

Hans Castorp could not refrain from slapping his knee as he exclaimed that never in all his life before had he heard the like.

"Pray do not, on that account, refuse to entertain it," Settembrini said with a smile.

"Music, as a final incitement to the spirit of men, is invaluable——as a force which draws onward and upward the spirit she finds prepared for her ministrations. But literature must precede her. By music alone the world would get no further forward. Alone, she is a danger. For you, personally, Engineer, she is beyond all doubt dangerous. I saw it in your face as I came up."

Hans Castorp laughed.

"Oh, you shouldn't look at my face, Herr Settembrini. You can't believe how the air up here sets me on fire. It is harder than I thought to get acclimatized."

"I fear you deceive yourself."

"How so? I know, at least, how deucedly hot and tired I am all the time."

"It seems to me we should be grateful to the management for the concert," Joachim said reflectively. "I wouldn't contradict you, Herr Settembrini, because you look at the question from a higher point of view, so to speak, as an author. But I find one ought to be grateful up here for a bit of music. I am far from being particularly musical, and then the pieces they play are not exactly elevating, neither classic nor modern, but just ordinary band--music. Still, it is a pleasant change. It takes up a couple of hours very decently; I mean it breaks them up and fills them in, so there is something to them, by comparison with the other days, hours, and weeks that whisk by like nothing at all. You see an unpretentious concert--number lasts perhaps seven minutes, and those seven minutes amount to something; they have a beginning and an end, they stand out, they don't so easily slip into the regular humdrum round and get lost. Besides they are again divided up by the figures of the piece that is being played, and these again into beats, so there is always something going on, and every moment has a certain meaning, something you can take hold of, whereas usually——I don't know whether I am making myself——"

"Bravo!" cried Settembrini. "Bravo, Lieutenant! You are describing very well indeed an aspect of music which has indubitably a moral value: namely, that her peculiarly life--enhancing method of measuring time imparts a spiritual awareness and value to its passage. Music quickens time, she quickens us to the finest enjoyment of time; she quickens——and in so far she has moral value. Art has moral value, in so far as it quickens. But what if it does the opposite? What if it dulls us, sends us to sleep, works against action and progress? Music can do that too; she is an old hand at using opiates. But the opiate, my dear sirs, is a gift of the Devil; it makes for lethargy, inertia, slavish inaction, stagnation. There is something suspicious about music, gentlemen. I insist that she is, by her nature, equivocal. I shall not be going too far in saying at once that she is politically suspect."

He went on in this vein, and Hans Castorp listened without precisely following; first on account of his fatigue, and second because his attention was distracted by the proceedings of the lightheaded young folk on the steps. Did his eyes deceive him, or was the tapir--faced girl really occupied in sewing on a button for the monocled youth---and, forsooth, on the knee--band of his knickerbockers? She breathed asthmatically as she sewed, and he coughed and carried his little finger, with the saltspoon--shaped nail, to his mouth. Of course they were ill---but, after all, these young folk up here did have peculiar social standards! The band played a polka.

Hippe

Thus Sunday passed. The afternoon was marked by drives undertaken by various groups; several times after tea a carriage and pair drove up the winding road and halted before the portal to receive its occupants---these being, for the most part, Russian ladies.

"Russians drive a great deal," Joachim said to Hans Castorp, as they stood before the entrance and amused themselves with watching the carriages move off. "They will be going to Clavadel, or into the valley of the Flüela, or as far as Klosters. Those are the usual objectives. We might have a drive too while you are up here, if you like. But for the present I think you have enough to do to get used to things, and don't require more diversion."

To which Hans Castorp agreed. He had a cigarette in his mouth, and his hands in his trouser pockets; and stood so to watch the lively little old Russian lady, as she, with her lean grand--niece and two other ladies, took their seats in a carriage. The ladies were Madame Chauchat and Marusja. Madame Chauchat had put on a thin dust--cloak belted in at the back, but wore no hat. She sat down beside the old dame in the body of the carriage, while the two girls took their places behind. All four were in lively vein and chattered without stopping in their soft, spineless tongue. They chattered about the top of the carriage, which was hard for them all to get underneath, about the Russian comfits the great--aunt had brought for them to munch, in a little wooden box lined with cotton--wool and lace paper, and was already handing round.---

Hans Castorp distinguished with interest Frau Chauchat's slightly husky voice. As always whenever he set eyes on that heedless creature, the likeness reasserted itself which had puzzled him for a while and then been revealed in a dream. But Marusja's laugh, the expression of her round, brown eyes, staring childlike above the tiny handkerchief she held over her mouth, the full bosom, which was yet so ailing within, reminded him of something else, something which gave him a sudden thrill and made him glance cautiously at his cousin without turning his head. No, thank goodness, Joachim had not gone mottled, like that other time; his lips were not so painfully compressed. But he was gazing at Marusja, and his bearing, the expression in his eyes, was anything but military. Indeed that absorbed and yearning look could only have been characterized as typically civilian. However, he pulled himself quickly together and stole a glance at Hans Castorp, which the latter had only just time to avoid, by turning his own eyes away and staring up into the sky. He felt his heart give a sudden beat—without rhyme or reason, of its own accord, as it had taken to doing up here.

The Sunday was not further remarkable, except perhaps for the meals, which, since they could not well be more abundant than they already were, displayed greater refinement in the menu. At luncheon there was a *chaud-froid* of chicken, garnished with crayfish and stoned cherries; with the ices came pastry served in baskets of spun sugar, and fresh pineapple besides. In the evening, after he had drunk his beer, Hans Castorp felt heavier in the limbs and more chilled and exhausted than on the day before; toward nine o'clock he bade his cousin good-night, drew his *plumeau* up to his chin, and slept like the dead.

But next day, the first Monday spent by the guest up here, there came another regularly recurring variation in the daily routine: the lectures, one of which Dr. Krokowski delivered every other Monday morning in the dining-room, before the entire adult population of the sanatorium, with exception of the "moribund" and those who could not understand the language. The course, Hans Castorp learned from his cousin, consisted of a series of popular--scientific lectures, under the general title: "Love as a force contributory to disease." These instructive entertainments took place after second breakfast; it was not permissible, Joachim reiterated, to absent oneself from them--or, at least, absence was frowned upon. It was thus very daring of Settembrini, who surely must have more command of the language than anyone else, not only never to appear, but to refer to the entertainment in most disparaging terms. For Hans Castorp's part, he straightway resolved to be present, in the first place out of courtesy, but also with unconcealed curiosity as to what he should hear. Before the appointed hour, however, he did something quite perverse and ill--judged, which proved worse for him than one could possibly have guessed: he went out for a long, solitary walk.

"Now listen to me," had been his first words, when Joachim entered his room that morning. "I can see that it can't go on with me like this. I've had enough of the horizontal for the present; one's very blood goes to sleep. Of course it is different with you; you are a patient, and I have no intention of tempting you. But I mean to take a proper walk after breakfast, if you don't mind, just walking at random for a couple of hours. I'll stick a little something in my pocket for second breakfast; then I shall be independent. We shall see if I am not quite a different chap when I come back."

Joachim warmly agreed, as he saw his cousin was in earnest in his desire and his project. "But don't overdo it," he said; "that's my advice. It's not the same thing up here as at home. And be sure to come back in time for the lecture."

In reality young Hans Castorp had more ground than the physical for his present resolve. His over--heated head, the prevailing bad taste in his mouth, the fitful throbbing of his heart, were, or so he felt, less evil accompaniments to the process of acclimatization than such things as the goings--on of the Russian pair next door, the table--talk of the stupid and afflicted Frau Stöhr, the gentleman rider's pulpy cough daily heard in the corridor, the utterances of Herr Albin, the impression he received of the manners and morals of the ailing young folk about him, the expression on Joachim's face when he looked at Marusja—-these and a hundred observations more made him feel it would be good to escape awhile from the Berghof circle, to breathe the air deep into his lungs, to get some proper exercise—-and then, when he felt tired at night, he would at least know why. He took leave of Joachim in a spirit of enterprise, when his cousin addressed himself, after breakfast, to the usual round as far as the bench by the watercourse; then, swinging his walking--stick, he took his own way down the road.

It was about nine o'clock of a cool morning, with a covered sky. According to programme, Hans Castorp drew in deep draughts of the pure morning air, the fresh, light atmosphere that breathed in so easily, that held no hint of damp, that was without associations, without content. He crossed the stream and the narrow--gauge road to the street, with its scattered buildings; but left this again soon to strike into a meadow path, which went only a short way on the level and then slanted steeply up to the right. The climbing rejoiced Hans Castorp's heart, his chest expanded, he pushed his hat back on his forehead with the crook of his stick; having gained some little height he looked back, and, seeing in the distance the mirror--like lake he had passed on his journey hither, he began to sing.

He sang what songs he had at his command, all kinds of sentimental folk--ditties, out of collections of national ballads and students' song--books; one of them, that went:

Let poets all of love and wine,

Yet oft of virtue sing the praises,

he sang at first softly, in a humming tone, then louder, finally at the top of his voice. His baritone lacked flexibility, yet to--day he found it good, and sang on with mounting enthusiasm. When he found he had pitched the beginning too high, he shifted into falsetto, and even that pleased him. When his memory left him in the lurch, he helped himself out by setting to the melody whatever words and syllables came to hand, heedless of the sense, giving them out like an operatic singer, with arching lips and strong palatal *r*. He even began to improvise both words and music, accompanying his performance with theatrical gesturings. It is a good deal of a strain to sing and climb at the same time, and Hans Castorp found his breath growing scant, and scanter. Yet for sheer pleasure in the idea, for the joy of singing, he forced his voice and sang on, with frequent gasps for breath, until he could no more, and sank, quite out of wind, half blind, with coloured sparks before his eyes and racing pulses, beneath a sturdy pine. His exaltation gave way on the sudden to a pervading gloom; he fell a prey to dejection bordering on despair.

When, his nerves being tolerably restored, he got to his feet again to continue his walk, he found his neck trembling; indeed his head shook in precisely the same way now, at his age, in which the head of old Hans Lorenz Castorp once had shaken. The phenomenon so freshly called up to him the memory of his dead grandfather that, far from finding it offensive, he took a certain pleasure in availing himself of that remembered and dignified method of supporting the chin, by means of which his grandfather had been wont to control the shaking of his head, and to which the boy had responded with such inward sympathy.

He mounted still higher on the zigzag path, drawn by the sound of cow--bells, and came at length upon the herd, grazing near a hut whose roof was weighted with stones. Two bearded men approached him, with axes on their shoulders. They parted, a little way off him, and "Thank ye kindly, and God be with ye," said the one to the other, in a deep guttural voice, shifted his axe to the other shoulder, and began breaking a path through crackling pine--boughs to the valley. The words sounded strange in this lonely spot: they came dreamlike to Hans Castorp's senses, strained and benumbed. He repeated them, softly, trying to reproduce the guttural, rustically formal syllables of the mountain tongue, as he climbed another stretch higher, above the hut. He had in mind to reach the height where the trees left off, but on glancing at his watch resisted.

He took the left--hand path in the direction of the village. It ran level for some way, then led downhill, among tall--trunked pines, where, as he went, he once more began to sing, tentatively, and despite the fact that he felt his knees to tremble more than they had during the ascent. On issuing from the wood he paused, struck by the charm of the small enclosed landscape before him, a scene composed of elements both peaceful and sublime.

A mountain stream came flowing in its shallow, stony bed down the right--hand slope, poured itself foaming over the terraced boulders lying in its path, then coursed more calmly toward the valley, crossed at this point by a picturesque railed wooden footbridge. The ground all about was blue with the bell--like blossoms of a profusely growing, bushy plant. Sombre fir--trees of even, mighty growth stood in the bed of the ravine and climbed its sides to the height. One of them, rooted in the steep bank at the side of the torrent, thrust itself aslant into the picture, with bizarre effect. The whole remote and lovely spot was wrapped in a sounding solitude by the noise of the rushing waters. Hans Castorp remarked a bench that stood on the farther bank of the stream. He crossed the foot--bridge and sat down to regale himself with the sight of the foaming, rushing waterfall and the idyllic sound of its monotonous yet modulated prattle. For Hans Castorp loved like music the sound of rushing water——perhaps he loved it even more. But hardly had he settled himself when he was overtaken by a bleeding at the nose, which came on so suddenly he had barely time to save his clothing from soilure. The bleeding was violent and persistent, taking to stanch it nearly half an hour of going to and fro between bench and brook, snuffing water up his nostrils, rinsing his handkerchief and lying flat on his back upon the wooden seat with the damp cloth on his nose. He lay there, after the blood at length was stanched, his knees elevated, hands folded behind his head, eyes closed, and ears full of the noise of water. He felt no

[153]

unpleasant sensation, the blood--letting had had a soothing effect, but he found himself in a state of extraordinarily reduced vitality, so that when he exhaled the air, he felt no need to draw it in again, and lay there moveless, for the space of several quiet heart--beats, before taking another slow and superficial breath. Quite suddenly he found himself in the far distant past, transported to a scene which had come back to him in a dream some nights before, summoned by certain impressions of the last few days. But so strongly, so resistlessly, to the annihilation of time and space, was he rapt back into the past, one might have said it was a lifeless body lying here on the bench by the waterside, while the actual Hans Castorp moved in that far--away time and place——in a situation which was for him, despite its childishness, vibrant with daring and adventure.

It happened when he was a lad of thirteen, in knee--breeches, in the lower third form at school. He stood in the school yard in talk with another boy of like years, from a higher form. The conversation had been begun, rather arbitrarily, by himself and, dealing as it did with a narrowly circumscribed subject of a practical nature, could in no case be prolonged; yet it gave him the greatest satisfaction. It took place in the break between the last two periods, a history and a drawing hour for Hans Castorp's form; the pupils were walking up and down, or standing about in groups, or lounging against the glazed abutments of the school--building wall. A murmur of voices filled the red--tiled court--yard, which was shut off from the street by a wall topped with shingles and provided with two entrance gates. Supervision was exercised by a master in a slouch hat, who munched a ham sandwich the while.

He with whom Hans Castorp spoke was called Hippe, Pribislav Hippe. A peculiarity of this given name was that you were to pronounce it as though it were spelled Pschibislav; and the singularity of the appellation suited the lad's appearance, which did indeed have something exotic about it. Hippe was the son of a scholar and history professor in the gymnasium. He was, by consequence, a notorious model pupil, and, though not much older than Hans Castorp, already a form higher up. He came from Mecklenburg and was in his person obviously the product of an ancient mixture of races, a grafting of Germanic stock with Slavic, or the reverse. True, his close--shorn round pate was blond; but the eyes were a grey--blue, or a blue--grey—an indefinite, ambiguous colour, like the hue of far--distant mountain ranges—-and of an odd, narrow shape; were even, to be precise, a little slanting, with strongly marked, prominent cheek--bones directly under them. It was a type of face which in this instance, far from seeming an abnormality, was distinctly pleasing, though odd enough to have won for him the nickname of "the Kirghiz" among his schoolmates. Hippe already wore long trousers, and a blue jacket belted in at the back and closed to the throat, the collar of which was usually whitened by a few scales of dandruff. Now, the thing was that Hans Castorp, for a long time, had had his eye upon this Pribislav; had chosen him out of the whole host, known and unknown, in the courtyard of the school, taken an interest in him, followed him with his eyes—-shall we say admired him?—-at all events observed him with peculiar sympathy. Even on the way to school he looked forward with pleasure to watching him among his fellows, seeing him speak and laugh, singling out his voice from the others by its pleasantly veiled, husky quality. Granted that there was no sufficient ground for his preference, unless one might refer it to Hippe's heathenish name, his character as model pupil—-this latter was, of course, out of the question—-or to the "Kirghiz" eyes, whose grey--blue glance could sometimes melt into a mystery of darkness when one caught it musing sidewise; whichever it might be, or none of these, Hans Castorp troubled not a whit to justify his feelings, or even to question by what name they might suitably be called. For, since he did not "know" Hippe, the relation could hardly be one of friendship. But in the first place there was not the faintest need of calling it anything; it could never be a subject of discussion; that would be out of place, and he had no desire for it; and, in the second, giving a thing a name implies, if not passing judgment on it, at least defining it; that is to say, classifying it among the familiar and habitual; whereas Hans Castorp was penetrated by the unconscious conviction that an inward good of this sort was above all to be guarded from definition and classification.

But whether well or ill founded, and however far from being the subject of conversation, or even from being touched on in Hans Castorp's own mind, these feelings of his flourished there in great strength, as they had done for almost a year now—-or a year as nearly as one could fix the time, for it was hard to be precise about their beginnings. For about a year, then, he had carried them about in secret, which spoke for the loyalty and constancy of his character, when one reflects what a great space of time a year is at that age. But alas, every characterization of this kind involves a moral judgment, whether favourable or unfavourable—-though, to be sure, each trait of character has its two sides. Thus Hans Castorp's "loyalty"—-upon which, be it said, he was not prone to plume himself—-consisted, baldly, in a certain temperamental heaviness, sluggishness, and quiescence, a fundamental tendency to feel respect for conditions of duration and stability; and the more respect, the longer they lasted. He inclined to believe in the permanence of the particular state or circumstances in which he for the moment found himself; prized it for that very quality, and was not bent on change. Thus he had grown used to his silent and remote relation to Pribislav Hippe, and considered it a regular feature of his life; loved the emotions it brought in its train, the suspense as to whether he was likely to meet him that day, whether Pribislav would pass close by him, even look at him; loved the subtle and wordless satisfaction imparted by his secret, loved even the disappointments inseparable from it—-the greatest of which was Pribislav's absence from school. When this happened, the school yard became a desert, the day lacked all charm, hope alone lingered.

The affair had lasted a year, up to that intrepid and culminating moment; after which, thanks to Hans Castorp's constancy of spirit, it lasted another. Then it was over. And it is a fact that he marked no more the loosening and dissolving of the bond which united him to Pribislav than he had previously marked its beginnings. Moreover, in consequence of his father's taking another position, Pribislav left the school and the city; but that was all one to Hans Castorp; he had already forgotten him before he went. One may put it that the figure of the "Kirghiz" had glided out of the mist into Hans Castorp's life, and slowly grown vivid and tangible there, up to that moment of the greatest nearness and corporeity, in the school court; had stood awhile thus in the foreground, then slowly receded, and, with no pain of parting, dissolved again into the mist.

But that moment, that bold, adventurous situation, into which Hans Castorp found himself transported after all these years, the conversation—-an actual conversation with Pribislav Hippe—-came about thus. The drawing--lesson was the next period, and Hans Castorp found himself without a pencil. His classmates needed their own, but he had among the other pupils this and that acquaintance, of whom he might have sought a loan. Yet he found it was Pribislav who after all stood nearest to him, with whom, in secret, he had had to do; and with a joyous impulse of his entire being he determined to seize the opportunity—-for so he called it—-and ask Pribislav for a pencil. It was rather an odd thing to do, since he did not, in reality, "know" Pribislav at all; but this aspect of the affair escaped him in his recklessness, or he chose to disregard it. So there he stood before Pribislav Hippe, among the bustling crowd that filled the tiled court--yard; and he said to him: "Excuse me, can you lend me a pencil?"

And Pribislav looked at him, with his "Kirghiz" eyes above the prominent cheekbones, and spoke, in his pleasantly husky voice, without any surprise, or, at least, without showing any.

"With pleasure," he said. "But you must be sure to give it me back, after the period." And drew his pencil out of his pocket, a silver pencil--holder with a ring in the end, which one screwed in order to make the red lead--pencil come out. He displayed the simple mechanism, their two heads bent over it together.

"Only be careful not to break it," he added.

What made him say that? As if Hans Castorp had been intending to handle it carelessly or keep it after the hour!

They looked at each other, and smiled; then, as there remained nothing more to say, they turned, first their shoulders and then their backs, and went.

That was all. But never in his life had Hans Castorp felt so supremely content as in this drawing hour, drawing with Pribislav Hippe's pencil, in the immediate prospect of giving it back into the owner's hand—-which followed as a matter of course out of what had gone before. He took the liberty of sharpening the pencil a little, and cherished three of the red shavings nearly a year, in an inner drawer of his desk—-no one seeing them there could have guessed what significance they possessed. The return of the pencil was of the simplest formality, quite after Hans Castorp's heart—indeed, he prided himself on it no little, in the vainglorious state his intimacy with Hippe produced.

"There," he said. "And thanks very much."

And Pribislav said nothing at all, only hastily tried the screw and stuck the pencil in his pocket.

Never again did they speak to each other; but this one time, thanks to the enterprise of Hans Castorp, they had spoken.

He wrenched his eyes open, amazed at the depths of the trance in which he had been sunk. "I've been dreaming," he thought. "Yes, that was Pribislav. It's a long time since I thought of him. I wonder what became of the shavings. My desk is in the attic at Uncle Tienappel's; they must be there yet, in the little inner back drawer. I never took them out, never thought enough about them to throw them away! That was certainly Pribislav, his very own self. I shouldn't have thought I could remember him so clearly. How remarkably like her he looked—-like this girl up here! Is that why I feel interested in her? Or was that why I felt so interested in him? What rubbish!

Anyhow, I must be stirring, and pretty fast, too." But he lay another moment, musing and recalling, before he got up. "Then thank ye kindly, and God be with ye," he said—-the tears came to his eyes as he smiled And with that he would have been off, but instead sat suddenly down again with his hat and stick in his hand, being forced to the realization that his knees would not support him. "Hullo," he thought, "this won't do. I am supposed to be back in the dining--room punctually at eleven, for the lecture. Taking walks up here is very beautiful—-but appears to have its difficult side. Well, well, I can't stop here. I must have got stiff from lying; I shall be better as I move about." He tried again to get on his legs and, by dint of great effort, succeeded. But the return home was lamentable indeed, after the high spirits of his setting forth. He had repeatedly to rest by the way, feeling the colour recede from his face, and cold sweat break out on his brow; the wild beating of his heart took away his breath. Thus painfully he fought his way down the winding path and reached the bottom in the neighbourhood of the Kurhaus. But here it became clear that his own powers would never take him over the stretch between him and the Berghof; and accordingly, as there was no tram and he saw no carriages for hire, he hailed a driver going toward the Dorf with a load of empty boxes and asked permission to climb into his wagon. Back to back with the man, his legs hanging down out of the end, swaying and nodding with fatigue and the jolting of the vehicle, regarded with surprise and sympathy by the passers--by, he got as far as the railway crossing, where he dismounted and paid for his ride, whether much money or little he did not heed, and hurried headlong up the drive.

"*Depêchez--vous, monsieur,*" said to him the French concierge. "*La conférence de M. Krokowski vient de commencer.*" Hans Castorp tossed hat and stick on the stand and squeezed himself with much precaution, tongue between his teeth, through the partly open glass door into the dining--room, where the society of the cure sat in rows on their chairs, and on the right--hand narrow side of the room, behind a covered table adorned with a water--bottle, Dr. Krokowski, in a frock--coat, stood and delivered his lecture.

Analysis

Luckily there was a vacant seat in the corner, near the door. He slipped into it and assumed an air of having been here from the beginning. The audience, hanging rapt on Dr. Krokowski's lips, paid him no heed——which was as well, for he looked rather ghastly. His face white as a sheet, his coat spotted with blood——he might have been a murderer stealing from his crime. The lady in front of him did, indeed, turn her head as he sat down, and measured him with narrow eyes. With a sense of exasperation he recognized Madame Chauchat. Deuce take it——was he never to have a moment's peace? He had thought that, having arrived at his goal, he could sit here quietly and rest a little; and now he had to have her under his nose. In other circumstances he might conceivably have found her nearness rather pleasant than otherwise. But now, worn out and harassed as he felt, what was it to him? It could only make new demands on his heart and keep him from drawing a long breath during the whole lecture. With Pribislav's very eyes she had looked at him, and at the spots of blood on his coat; her look had been rather bold and ruthless too, as a woman's would be who let doors bang behind her. How badly she held herself! Not like the ladies of Hans Castorp's social sphere, who sat erect at their tables, turned their heads towards their lords and masters, and spoke with mincing correctness. Frau Chauchat sat all relaxed, with drooping shoulders and round back; she even thrust her head forward until the vertebra at the base of the neck showed prominently above the rounded *décolletage* of her white blouse. Pribislav had held his head like that. But he had been a model pupil and full of honours (which was not the reason why Hans Castorp had borrowed his pencil), whereas it was abundantly clear that Frau Chauchat's bad carriage, her doorslamming, and the directness of her gaze all had to do with her physical condition; yes, were even expressive of that want of restraint in which young Herr Albin rejoiced, which was not honourable at all, yet possessed boundless advantages all its own.

Hans Castorp's thoughts, as he sat and looked at Frau Chauchat's flaccid back, began to blur; they ceased to be thoughts at all and began to be a reverie, into which Dr. Krokowski's drawling baritone, with the soft-sounding *r*, came as from afar. But the stillness of the room, the profound attention that rapt all the rest of the audience, had the effect of rousing him too. He looked about. Near him sat the thin-haired pianist, with bent head and folded arms, listening with his mouth open. Somewhat farther on was Fräulein Engelhart, avid-eyed, with a dull red spot on each cheek; Hans Castorp saw the same signal flame on the faces of other ladies——on Frau Salomon's, and Frau Magnus's, the same who was wife to the brewer and lost flesh persistently. Frau Stöhr sat somewhat farther back, an expression of ignorant credulity painted on her face, truly painful to behold; while the ivory-complexioned Levi, leaning back in her chair with half-closed eyes, her hands lying open in her lap, would have looked like a corpse had not her breast risen and fallen with such profound and rhythmical breaths as to remind Hans Castorp of a mechanical waxwork he had once seen. Many of the guests had their hands curved behind their ears; some even held the hand in the air half-way thither, as though arrested midway in the gesture by the strength of their concentration. Lawyer Paravant, a sunburnt man who looked to have had the strength of a bull, even flicked his ear with his forefinger to make it hear better, then turned it again to catch the words that flowed from Dr. Krokowski's lips.

And what was Dr. Krokowski saying? What was his line of thought? Hans Castorp summoned his wits to discover, not immediately succeeding, however, since he had not heard the beginning and lost still more while musing on Frau Chauchat's flabby back. It was about a power, the power which——in short, it was about the power of love. Yes, of course; the subject was already given out in the general title of the whole course, and, moreover, this was Dr. Krokowski's special field; of what else should he be talking? It was a bit odd, to be sure, listening to a lecture on such a theme, when previously Hans Castorp's courses had dealt only with such matters as geared transmission in shipbuilding. No, really, how did one go about to discuss a subject of this delicate and private nature, in broad daylight, before a mixed audience? Dr. Krokowski did it by adopting a mingled terminology, partly poetic and partly erudite; ruthlessly scientific, yet with a vibrating, singsong delivery, which impressed young Hans Castorp as being unsuitable, but may have been the reason why the ladies looked flushed and the gentlemen flicked their ears to make them hear better. In particular the speaker employed the word love in a somewhat ambiguous sense, so that you were never quite sure where you were with it, or whether he had reference to its sacred or its passionate and fleshly aspect——and this doubt gave one a slightly seasick feeling. Never in all his life had Hans Castorp heard the word uttered so many times on end as he was hearing it now. When he reflected, it seemed to him he had never taken it in his own mouth, nor ever heard it from a stranger's. That might not be the case, but whether it were or no, the word did not seem to him to repay such frequent repetition. The slippery monosyllable, with its lingual and labial, and the bleating vowel between——it came to sound positively offensive; it suggested watered milk, or anything else that was pale and insipid; the more so considering the meat for strong men Dr. Krokowski was in fact serving up. For it was plain that when one set about it like that, one could go pretty far without shocking anybody. He was not content to allude, with exquisite tact, to certain matters which are known to everybody, but which most people are content to pass over in silence. He demolished illusions, he was ruthlessly enlightened, he relentlessly destroyed all faith in the dignity of silver hairs and the innocence of the sucking babe. And he wore, with the frock--coat, his négligé collar, sandals, and grey woollen socks, and, thus attired, made an impression profoundly otherworldly, though at the same time not a little startling to young Hans Castorp. He supported his statements with a wealth of illustration and anecdote from the books and loose notes on the table before him; several times he even quoted poetry. And he discussed certain startling manifestations of the power of love, certain extraordinary, painful, uncanny variations, which the majestic phenomenon at times displayed. It was, he said, the most unstable, the most unreliable of man's instincts, the most prone of its very essence to error and fatal perversion. In the which there was nothing that should cause surprise. For this mighty force did not consist of a single impulse, it was of its nature complex; it was built up out of components which, however legitimate they might be in composition, were, taken each by itself, sheer perversity. But—-continued Dr. Krokowski—-since we refuse, and rightly, to deduce the perversity of the whole from the perversity of its parts, we are driven to claim, for the component perversities, some part at least, though perhaps not all, of the justification which attaches to their united product. We were driven by sheer force of logic to this conclusion; Dr. Krokowski implored his hearers, having arrived at it, to hold it fast. Now there were psychical correctives, forces working in the other direction, instincts tending to conformability and regularity—-he would almost have liked to characterize them as bourgeois; and these influences had the effect of merging the perverse components into a valid and irreproachable whole: a frequent and gratifying result, which, Dr. Krokowski almost contemptuously added, was, as such, of no further concern to the thinker and the physician. But on the other hand, there were cases where this result was not obtained, could not and should not be obtained; and who, Dr. Krokowski asked, would dare to say that these cases did not, psychically considered, form a higher, more exclusive type? For in these cases the two opposing groups of instincts—-the compulsive force of love, and the sum of the impulses urging in the other direction, among which he would particularly mention shame and disgust—-both exhibited an extraordinary and abnormal height and intensity when measured by the ordinary bourgeois standards; and the conflict between them which took place in the abysses of the soul prevented the erring instinct from attaining to that safe, sheltered, and civilized state which alone could resolve its difficulties in the prescribed harmonies of the love--life as experienced by the average

human being. This conflict between the powers of love and chastity—
-for that was what it really amounted to—-what was its issue? It
ended, apparently, in the triumph of chastity. Love was suppressed,
held in darkness and chains, by fear, conventionality, aversion, or a
tremulous yearning to be pure. Her confused and tumultuous claims
were never allowed to rise to consciousness or to come to proof in
anything like their entire strength or multiformity. But this triumph of
chastity was only an apparent, a pyrrhic victory; for the claims of love
could not be crippled or enforced by any such means. The love thus
suppressed was not dead; it lived, it laboured after fulfilment in the
darkest and secretest depths of the being. It would break through the
ban of chastity, it would emerge—-if in a form so altered as to be
unrecognizable. But what then was this form, this mask, in which
suppressed, unchartered love would reappear?

Dr. Krokowski asked the question, and looked along the listening
rows as though in all seriousness expecting an answer. But he had to
say it himself, who had said so much else already. No one knew save
him, but it was plain that he did. Indeed, with his ardent eyes, his
black beard setting off the waxen pallor of his face, his monkish
sandals and grey woollen socks, he seemed to symbolize in his own
person that conflict between passion and chastity which was his
theme. At least so thought Hans Castorp, as with the others he
waited in the greatest suspense to hear in what form love driven
below the surface would reappear. The ladies barely breathed.
Lawyer Paravant rattled his ear anew, that the critical moment might
find it open and receptive. And Dr. Krokowski answered his own
question, and said: "In the form of illness. Symptoms of disease are
nothing but a disguised manifestation of the power of love; and all
disease is only love transformed."

So now they knew—though very probably not all of them were
capable of an opinion on what they heard. A sigh passed through the
assemblage, and Lawyer Paravant weightily nodded approbation as
Krokowski proceeded to develop his theme. Hans Castorp for his part
sat with bowed head, trying to reflect on what had been said and test

his own understanding of it. But he was unpractised in such exercises, and rendered still further incapable of mental exertion by the unhappy effect of the walk he had taken. His thoughts were soon drawn off again by the sight of Frau Chauchat's back, and the arm appertaining, which was lifting and bending itself, close before Hans Castorp's eyes, so that the hand could hold the braids of hair. It made him uncomfortable to have the hand so close beneath his eye, to be forced to look at it whether he wished or no, to study it in all its human blemishes and imperfections, as though under a magnifying--glass. No, there was nothing aristocratic about this stubby schoolgirl hand, with the badly cut nails. He was even not quite sure that the ends of the fingers were perfectly clean; and the skin round the nails was distinctly bitten. Hans Castorp made a face; but his eyes remained fixed on Madame Chauchat's back, as he vaguely recalled what Dr. Krokowski had been saying, about counteracting influences of a bourgeois kind, which set themselves up against the power of love.——The arm, in its gentle upward curve, was better than the hand; it was scarcely clothed, for the material of the sleeve was thinner than that of the blouse, being the lightest gauze, which had the effect of lending the arm a sort of shadowed radiance, making it prettier than it might otherwise have been. It was at once both full and slender——in all probability cool to the touch. No, so far as the arm went, the idea about counteracting bourgeois influences did not apply.

Hans Castorp mused, his gaze still bent on Frau Chauchat's arm. The way women dressed! They showed their necks and bosoms, they transfigured their arms by veiling them in "illusion"; they did so, the world over, to arouse our desire. O God, how beautiful life was! And it was just such accepted commonplaces as this that made it beautiful——for it was a commonplace that women dressed themselves alluringly, it was so well known and recognized a fact that we never consciously realized it, but merely enjoyed it without a thought. And yet he had an inward conviction that we ought to think about it, ought to realize what a blessed, what a well--nigh miraculous arrangement it was. For of course it all had a certain end and aim; it was by a definite design that women were permitted to array themselves with irresistible allure: it was for the sake of posterity, for the perpetuation of the species. Of course. But suppose a woman were inwardly diseased, unfit for motherhood—-what then? What was the sense of her wearing gauze sleeves and attracting male attention to her physical parts if these were actually unsound? Obviously there was no sense; it ought to be considered immoral, and forbidden as such. For a man to take an interest in a woman inwardly diseased had no more sense than—-well, than the interest Hans Castorp had once taken in Pribislav Hippe. The comparison was a stupid one; it roused memories better forgotten; he had not meant to make it, it came into his head unbidden. But at this point his musings broke off, largely because Dr. Krokowski had raised his voice and so drawn attention once more upon himself. He was standing there behind his table, with his arms outstretched and his head on one side—-almost, despite the frockcoat, he looked like Christ on the cross. It seemed that at the end of his lecture Dr. Krokowski was making propaganda for psycho--analysis; with open arms he summoned all and sundry to come unto him.

"Come unto me," he was saying, though not in those words, "come unto me, all ye who are weary and heavy--laden." And he left no doubt of his conviction that all those present *were* weary and heavy--laden. He spoke of secret suffering, of shame and sorrow, of the redeeming power of the analytic. He advocated the bringing of light into the unconscious mind and explained how the abnormality was metamorphosed into the conscious emotion; he urged them to have confidence; he promised relief. Then he let fall his arms, raised his head, gathered up his notes and went out by the corridor door, with his head in the air, and the bundle of papers held schoolmaster fashion, in his left hand, against his shoulder.

His audience rose, pushed back its chairs, and slowly began to move towards the same door, as though converging upon him from all sides, without volition, hesitatingly, yet with one accord, like the throng after the Pied Piper. Hans Castorp stood in the stream without moving, his hand on the back of his chair. I am only a guest up here, he thought. Thank God I am healthy, that business has nothing to do with me; I shan't even be here for the next lecture. He watched Frau Chauchat going out, gliding along with her head thrust forward. Did she have herself psycho--analysed, he wondered. And his heart began to thump. He did not notice Joachim, coming toward him among the chairs, and started when his cousin spoke.

"You got here at the last minute," Joachim said. "Did you go very far? How was it?"

"Oh, very nice," Hans Castorp answered. "Yes, I went rather a long way. But I must confess, it did me less good than I thought it would. I won't repeat it for the present."

Joachim did not ask how he liked the lecture; neither did Hans Castorp express an opinion. By common consent they let the subject rest, both then and thereafter.

Doubts and Considerations

Tuesday was the last day of our hero's week up here, and accordingly he found his weekly bill in his room on his return from the morning walk. It was a clear and businesslike document, in a green envelope, with a picture of the Berghof building at the top, and extracts from the prospectus carried in a narrow column down the lefthand side of the sheet. "Psycho--analytic treatment, by the most modern methods" was called attention to by means of spaced type. The items, set down in a calligraphic hand, came to one hundred and eighty francs almost exactly: eight francs a day for his chamber, twelve for board and medical attendance, entrance fee twenty, disinfection of room ten, while small charges for laundry, beer, and the late dinner of the first evening made up the sum.

Hans Castorp went over the bill with Joachim and found naught to object to. "Of course I made no use of the medical attendance," he said, "but that was my own affair. It is included in the price of pension, and I couldn't expect them to make any deduction; how could they? As regards the disinfection, they must show a neat profit there, they never could have used ten francs' worth of H₂CO to smoke the American woman out. But on the whole I must say I find it cheap rather than dear, considering what they offer," And before second breakfast they went down to the management in order that Hans Castorp might acquit himself of his debt.

The management was on the ground--floor. You reached it after passing the hall, the garderobe, the kitchens and domestic offices; you could not miss the door, it had a porcelain shield. Hans Castorp took an interest in this glimpse into the business side of the enterprise. There was a neat little office, with a typist busy at her machine and three clerks bending over desks. In an adjoining office a man who looked like a head or director was working at a desk in the middle of the room; he flung a cool and calculating glance at the clients over the top of his glasses. Their affair was dispatched at the cashier's window, a note changed, money received, the bill receipted; the cousins preserving throughout these transactions the solemn, discreet, almost overawed bearing which the young German's respect for authority leads him to assume in the presence of pens, ink, and paper, or anything else which bears to his mind an official stamp. But on the way to breakfast, and later in the course of the day, they talked about the direction of the Berghof sanatorium, and Joachim, in his character as inmate, answered his cousin's questions.

Hofrat Behrens was not—-though he gave the impression of being—-owner and proprietor of the establishment. Above and behind him stood invisible powers, which to a certain extent manifested their existence in the office they had just visited. They consisted of a supervisory head and a stock company—-in which it was not a bad thing to hold shares, according to Joachim, since the members of it divided a fat dividend each year. The Hofrat was a dependent, he was merely an agent, a functionary, an associate of higher powers; the first and highest, of course, and the soul of the enterprise, with a well--defined influence upon it and upon the management itself—-though of course as directing physician he was relieved of all preoccupation with the business side. He was a native of north--western Germany, and it was common knowledge that when he took the position, years ago, he had done so contrary to his previous intention and plans. He had come here on account of his wife—-whose remains had long reposed in the village churchyard, that picturesque churchyard of Dorf Davos, which lay high up on the right--hand slope, nearer the entrance of the valley. She had been a charming person, to judge from her likenesses, though too large--eyed and asthenic--looking. Photographs of her stood about everywhere in the Hofrat's house; even oil portraits by his own amateur hand hung on the walls. Two children, a son and a daughter, had been born; then they had brought her up here, the fragile body already fever--smitten; a few months had seen the completion of the wasting--away process. Behrens, they said, had adored her. He was brought so low by the blow that he got very odd and melancholy; people saw him gesturing, sniggering, and talking to himself, on the street. He did not go back to his original place, but remained where he was—-in part, no doubt, because he could not tear himself away from her grave, but also for the less sentimental reason that he was himself in poor health and, in his own professional opinion, actually *belonged* here. He had settled down as one of the physicians who are companions in suffering to the patients in their care; who do not stand above disease, fighting her in the armour of personal security, but who themselves bear her mark—-an odd, but by no means isolated, case, and one which has its good as well as its bad side. Sympathy between doctor and patient is surely desirable, and a case might be made out for the view that only he who suffers can be the guide and healer of the suffering. And yet—-can true spiritual mastery over a power be won by him who is counted among her slaves? Can he free others who himself is not free? The ailing physician remains a paradox to the average mind, a questionable phenomenon. May not his scientific knowledge tend to be clouded and confused by his own participation, rather than enriched and morally reinforced? He cannot face disease in clear--eyed hostility to her; he is a prejudiced party, his position is

[169]

equivocal. With all due reserve it must be asked whether a man who himself belongs among the ailing can give himself to the cure or care of others as can a man who is himself entirely sound.

Hans Castorp expressed some of these doubts and speculations, as he and Joachim gossiped about the Berghof and its professional head. But Joachim answered that nobody knew whether the Hofrat was still a patient——he was probably long since cured. It was ages ago that he had first begun to practise here; independently at first, and early winning a name for himself as an extraordinarily gifted auscultator and skilful surgeon. Then the Berghof had secured him; it would soon be ten years that he had been in intimate association with it. His private residence was in the end of the north--west wing of the building (Dr. Krokowski's was not far off), and that lady of the lofty lineage, the nursing sister and directress of the establishment, of whom Settembrini had made such utter fun, and whom thus far Hans Castorp had scarcely seen, presided over the small household. The Hofrat was otherwise alone, for his son was at the university and his daughter already married, to a lawyer in one of the French cantons. Young Behrens sometimes visited his father in the holidays; he had done so once during Joachim's time up here. The ladies, he related, had been quite thrilled; their temperatures had gone up, petty jealousies had led to bickering and quarrels in the rest--hall and an increase of visits to Dr. Krokowski's private office. The assistant had his own office hours, in a special room, which, together with the large examination--rooms, the laboratory, the operating--rooms and x--ray studio, was in the well--lighted basement of the building. We call it the basement, for the stone steps leading down to it from the ground--floor created the impression that it was such——an erroneous impression, for not only was the ground--floor somewhat elevated, but the entire building stood on a sidehill, part way up the mountain, and these "basement" rooms faced the front, with a view of the gardens and valley, a circumstance negatived to some extent by the fact of the steps leading down to them. One descended, as one supposed, from the ground--floor, only to find oneself at the bottom still on it, or practically so. Hans Castorp amused himself with this illusion when he accompanied his cousin one afternoon down to the "bathing--master," that Joachim might get himself weighed. A clinical brilliance and spotlessness reigned in this sphere. Everything was as white as white; the doors gleamed with white enamel; the one leading to Dr. Krokowski's receiving--room, with the doctor's visiting--card tacked on it, was reached by two more steps down from the corridor, which gave the room behind it an air of being more spacious and withdrawn than the rest. This door was at the end of the corridor, on your right as you came downstairs. Hans Castorp kept his eye on it as he walked up and down waiting for his cousin. He saw a lady come out, a recent arrival, whose name he did not know: a small, dainty person, with curls on her forehead, and gold ear--rings. She bent over as she mounted the stairs, and held up her frock with one beringed hand, while with the other she pressed her tiny handkerchief to her lips and, all stooped as she was, stared up over it into nothing, with great blue, distracted eyes. She hurried with small tripping steps, her petticoat rustling, to the stairs, paused suddenly as though something had occurred to her, then went on tripping upward, and disappeared, still bending over and holding her handkerchief to her mouth.

Behind her, when she opened the office door, it had been much darker than in the white corridor. Obviously the brilliant lighting of these lower regions did hot extend so far; Hans Castorp remarked that a shadowed dusk, a profound twilight, prevailed in Dr. Krokowski's private sanctum.

Table--Talk

Young Hans Castorp noticed that the ancestral tremor brought on by his ill--advised walk continued to trouble him—-he found it rather an embarrassment when in the dining--room. Almost as a regular thing now, his head would begin shaking at table; he found this impossible to prevent and hard to dissemble. He tried various devices to disguise the weakness, for he could not continually support his chin on his collar; he would keep his head in action, turning it to the right and left in conversation, or bear hard against the table with the left forearm when he carried a spoonful of soup to his mouth, and support his head with his hand. In the pauses he even rested his elbow on the table, this although it was in his own eyes a piece of ill breeding, which would not pass in any society save the lax abnormal one where he now found himself. But the weakness was burdensome too and went far to spoil the meal hours for him, which he had otherwise continued to find diverting and full of interesting episode.

But the truth was—-and Hans Castorp was entirely aware of it—-that the absurd manifestation against which he struggled was not solely physical in its origin, not wholly to be accounted for by the air up here and the efforts his system made to adjust itself. Rather was it the outward expression of his inner stimulation, and bore directly upon those very episodes and diversions.

Madame Chauchat almost invariably came late to meals. Until she came, Hans Castorp could not sit and keep his feet still, but must wait in suspense for the crashing of the glass door; he knew it would make him start and that his face would feel cold all over, and this was what regularly happened. At first he had jerked round his head infuriated and followed the offender with angry eyes to her seat at the "good" Russian table. He may even have muttered some abusive epithet between his teeth, some outraged cry of protest. But now he only bent over his plate, bit his lips, or deliberately turned his head away. It seemed to him that anger was no longer in place; he even had an obscure feeling that he was partly responsible, that he shared the blame with her before the others. In short, it would be no longer so true to say he was ashamed of Frau Chauchat as that he was ashamed for her—-a feeling he might well have spared himself, for not a soul in the room troubled either over Frau Chauchat's misconduct or Hans Castorp's sensitiveness to it—-with the possible exception of the schoolmistress, Fräulein Engelhart, on his right.

This poor creature had perceived that, thanks to his sensibility in the matter of slamming doors, a certain emotional attitude toward the

Russian lady was come to subsist in her young neighbour's mind. Further, that the grounds of the attitude were of little moment compared to the fact of its existence; and, finally, that his assumed indifference—very poorly assumed, for Hans Castorp had neither talent nor training as an actor—did not mean a decrease of interest, but on the contrary indicated that the affair was passing into a higher phase. Fräulein Engelhart was for her own person quite without hopes or pretensions. She therefore launched out into extravagant enthusiasm over Frau Chauchat—about which quite the most extraordinary thing was that Hans Castorp saw perfectly how she was egging him on—not all at once, perhaps, but in the course of time—saw through it and even felt disgusted at it, yet without being the less willingly led on by her and made a fool of.

"Slam—bang!" the old spinster said. "That was *she*. No need to look up to tell who just came in. Of course, there she goes—like a kitten to a saucer of milk—how pretty it is! I wish we might change places, so you could look at her as much as you liked. Naturally you don't care to keep turning your head—that would flatter her far too much. She is greeting her table—you really ought to look, it is so refreshing to see her! When she smiles and talks as she is doing now, a dimple comes in one cheek, but not always, only when she likes. What a love of a woman! A spoilt child, that is why she is so heedless. Creatures like that one has to love, whether one will or no; they vex you with their heedlessness, but that is only one reason the more for loving them; it makes you so happy to have to care for them in spite of yourself."

She whispered on, behind her hand, for his ear alone; the flush that mantled on her downy old cheek bespoke a rising temperature, and the suggestiveness of her talk pierced Hans Castorp to the very marrow. It did him good to hear someone else confirm his view that Madame Chauchat was an enchanting creature. He was a young man of not very independent judgments, and glad to be encouraged in certain feelings he had, upon which both reason and conscience united to frown.

[173]

But Fräulein Engelhart, however much she would have liked to, could tell him practically nothing about Frau Chauchat. She knew no more than the whole sanatorium knew, and his conversations with her bore little practical fruit. She did not even know the lady to speak to, nor could she boast a single common acquaintance. Her only title to importance was that she lived in Königsberg, not very far from the Russian border; also that she knew a few scraps of Russian. These were but meagre distinctions; yet Hans Castorp was prepared to see in them something resembling an extensive personal connexion with Frau Chauchat.

"I see that she wears no ring, no wedding--ring," he said. "Why is that? She is a married woman, I think you told me?"

The schoolmistress was quite perturbed; she seemed to feel driven into a corner and sought for words to talk herself out again, so very responsible did she feel for Frau Chauchat.

"You must not attach importance to that," she finally said. "I'm positive she is married. There is no doubt of it. Of course I know some foreigners do use the Madame when they are getting a little on in years, for the sake of the greater respect people pay a married woman. But it is not the case here. Everyone knows she really has a husband, somewhere in Russia. Her maiden name was not French but Russian, something in *anow* or *ukov*—- I did know it, but I have forgotten. I will ask if you like; there must be several people here who know it. No, she wears no ring, I have noticed it myself. Dear me, perhaps she finds it makes her hand look too broad. Or she thinks it is too bourgeois and domestic to wear a plain gold wedding--ring. She might as well carry a key basket. No, she is built on broader lines than that—-Russian women all have something free and large about them. And then, a wedding--ring seems so prosaic, it is almost repellent! It is a symbol of possession; it is always saying 'Hands off'; it turns every woman into a nun. I should not be at all surprised if that is what Frau Chauchat thinks. A charming woman like her, in the bloom of youth—-why should she, every time she gives a man her hand to kiss, tell him straightway that she is bound in wedlock?"

"Good Lord," thought Hans Castorp, "how she does run on!" He looked into her face, quite alarmed. But she countered his gaze with her embarrassed, half--frightened one. They were both silent awhile and sought to recover themselves. Hans Castorp ate his luncheon and supported his chin.

At length he said: "And her husband? He doesn't trouble himself about her? Does he never visit her up here? Do you know what he does?"

"Official. Russian government official, in some distant province, Daghestan, you know, out beyond the Caucasus, he was ordered there. No, as I tell you, no one has ever seen him up here. And this time she has been here going on three months."

"She was here before, then?"

"This is the third time. And between times she goes to other places—-other sanatoriums. But it is she who sometimes visits him; not often, once in the year for a little while. One may say they live separated, and she visits him now and again."

"Well, of course, she is ill—-"

"Yes, of course—-but not *so* ill. Not so ill as to have to live all her life in sanatoriums and apart from her husband. There must be other reasons for that. Everyone up here thinks there must be other reasons. Perhaps she does not like to live out there in Daghestan, the other side of the Caucasus; it would not be strange—-such a wild, remote place! But there must be something about the man too, if she can't bear to be with him. He has a French name, but after all he is a Russian official, and that is a very rough type, I do assure you. I once saw one of them, with an iron--grey beard and a red face—-they are all frightfully corrupt too, and drink quantities of vodka, you know. They will eat a little something, for the look of the thing, a mushroom *mariné*, some caviar, and then drink out of all measure and call it a light lunch."

"You are putting everything off on him," Hans Castorp said "But we can't know if the responsibility is not hers, of their not living together. One ought to be just. When I look at her and see the unmannerly way she behaves about the door—-I assure you she's no angel; excuse me for saying so. I wouldn't trust her across the street. But you are so partial. You are blinded by prejudice in her favour."

This was the line he sometimes took. With a cunning otherwise foreign to his nature he would make out that the schoolmistress's ravings over Madame Chauchat were not what he very well knew them to be, but an independent phenomenon, of a quaint and amusing kind; about which he, Hans Castorp, made free to tease the old spinster, feeling his own withers unwrung. He risked nothing by this attitude, being confident that his accomplice would agree to anything he said, no matter how wide of the mark.

"Good--morning," he greeted her, "I hope you slept well and dreamed of your charmer? Mistress Mary, quite contrary—-or whatever her name is! Upon my word, one has only to speak of her to make you blush! You have completely lost your head over her—-you can't deny it."

And the schoolmistress, who really had blushed and tucked her head down over her cup, would mumble out of the left--hand corner of her mouth: "Shame on you, Herr Castorp! It really is too bad of you to embarrass me like this. Everyone can see we are talking about her and that you have said something to make me get red."

It was an extraordinary game the two of them were playing; each perfectly aware that they lied and double--lied, each knowing that Hans Castorp teased the schoolmistress only in order to be able to talk about Frau Chauchat. He took a morbid and extravagant pleasure in thus trifling with Fräulein Engelhart, and she on her side reciprocated; first out of a natural instinct to be the go--between in a love--affair, secondly because to oblige Hans Castorp she had actually contrived to fall victim to Frau Chauchat's charms; and finally because she felt a pathetic joy in having him tease her and make her blush. He well knew, and she well knew, all this about each other and themselves; each knew that the other knew and that the whole situation was equivocal and almost questionable. Equivocal and questionable situations were, in general, repugnant to Hans Castorp's taste, and the present one was no exception. He felt disgusted, yet for all that he went on fishing in these troubled waters, quieting his conscience with the assurance that he was only up here on a visit and would soon be leaving. He pronounced upon the young woman's charms with the air of a connoisseur; said she was "sloppy," that she looked younger and prettier full face than profile; that her eyes were too far apart; that she carried herself in a way that left much to be desired; that her arms, on the other hand, were pretty and soft-looking. He felt his head shaking as he talked; he tried to suppress the trembling, and realized not only that the schoolmistress must see his efforts, but, with profound disgust, that her head was actually shaking too! But he went on—-he had purposely called Frau Chauchat Mistress Mary, in order that he might put the question of her name; so now he said: "I suppose her name is not Mary at all; do you know what it is? I mean her given name. You must know it, being as much smitten as you are!"

The schoolmistress reflected. "Wait half a minute," she said. "I knew it, once. Was it Tatiana? No—-nor Natascha. Natascha Chauchat? No, that was not it. Wait, I have it—-it was Avdotia. Or at least something very like that. It was not Katienka or Ninotschka, of that I am certain. I can't quite get it, for the moment. But I can surely recall it if you would like to know."

And next day she actually did know the name, and uttered it the moment the glass door slammed. Frau Chauchat's name was Clavdia.

Hans Castorp did not grasp it at first. He had to have her repeat the name, even to spell it, before he understood. Then he pronounced it twice or thrice, turning his bloodshot eyes in Frau Chauchat's direction, in order, as it were, to try if it suited.

"Clavdia," he said. "Yes, that is probably it; it fits her quite well." He could not hide his pleasure in the degree of intimacy thus achieved, and from now on referred always to Frau Chauchat as Clavdia. "Your Clavdia appears to be making bread pills. That's not very elegant, I should think."

"It depends on who does it," the schoolmistress would answer. "Clavdia it becomes."

Yes, unquestionably the meal--times in the hall with the seven tables had great charm for Hans Castorp. He hated to have one come to an end, and his consolation was that soon, in two or three hours, he would be back again. While he was sitting there, it was as though he had never risen. And for the time in between? It was nothing. A short turn as far as the watercourse or the Platz, a little rest on his balcony: no great burden, no serious interruption. Not as though he had to look forward to some interest or effort, which would not have been so easy to overleap in spirit. Effort was not the rule in the well--regulated Berghof life. Hans Castorp, when he rose from one meal, could straightway by anticipation begin to rejoice in the next——if, indeed, rejoicing is not too facile, too pleasant and unequivocal a word for the sentiments with which he looked forward to another meeting with the afflicted fair one. The reader, on the other hand, may very likely find such adjectives the only ones suitable to describe Hans Castorp's personality or emotions. But we suggest that a young man with a wellregulated conscience and sense of fitness could not, whatever else he did, simply "rejoice in" Frau Chauchat's proximity. In fact, we——who must surely know——are willing to assert that he himself would have repudiated any such expression if it had been suggested to him.

It is a small detail, yet worthy of mention, that he was growing to have a contempt for certain ways of expressing himself. He went about with that dry flush on his face and hummed continually under his breath——being in a state of mind when music particularly appeals. He hummed a ditty heard he knew not where——in some evening

company or charity concert—-sung by some thread of a soprano
voice; it turned up now in his memory, a soft nothing, that went:

One word from thy sweet lips

Can strangely thrill me.

He was about to go on:

Within my heart it slips

And raptures fill me—-

but broke off instead, with a disdainful shrug. "Idiotic!" he said,
suddenly finding the tender ditty altogether tasteless, wishy--washy,
and sentimental. He put it from him with manly sobriety, almost with
regret. It was the sort of thing to satisfy a young man who had "given
his heart," as we say, given it wholly, legitimately, and with quite
definite intentions, to some healthy little goose in the flat--land and
thus might be justified in abandoning himself to his orthodox and
gratifying sensations, with all the consequences they entailed. But for
him and for his relations with Madame Chauchat (we are not
responsible for the word relations; it was the word Hans Castorp
used, not we), such songs had nothing to do with them. "Silly!" he
said sententiously, and put his nose in the air. But after pronouncing
this aesthetic judgment he lay silent in his deck--chair, not thinking of
anything more suitable to sing in its place.

One thing there was which pleased him: when he lay listening to
the beating of his heart—-his corporeal organ—-so plainly audible in
the ordered silence of the rest period, throbbing loud and
peremptorily, as it had done almost ever since he came, the sound no
longer annoyed him. For now he need not feel that it so beat of its
own accord, without sense or reason or any reference to his non-
-corporeal part. He could say, without stretching the truth, that such a
connexion now existed, or was easily induced: he was aware that he
felt an emotion to correspond with the action of his heart. He needed
only to think of Madame Chauchat—-and he did think of her—-and
lo, he felt within himself the emotion proper to the heart--beats.

Mounting Misgivings. Of the Two Grandfathers, and the Boat--ride in the Twilight

The weather was vile. In this respect Hans Castorp had no luck during the brief term of his visit. It did not snow, but rained all day long, a hateful downpour; thick mist wrapped the valley, while electric storms—an absurd and uncalled--for phenomenon, considering it was so cold that the heat had been turned on—-rolled and reverberated disagreeably through the valley.

"Too bad," Joachim said. "I thought we might take our luncheons and climb up to the Schatzalp, or something like that. But it seems it is not to happen. Let us hope the last week will be better."

But Hans Castorp answered: "Let be. I am not so anxious to undertake anything for the moment. My first excursion was no great success. I find it does me more good just to take the day as it comes, without too much variation. I leave that sort of thing to people who have been up here for years. What do I want of variety in my three weeks' time?"

He did, indeed, find his time well taken up, just as he was. Whatever his hopes, they would come to fruition—-or else they would not—-here on the spot and not on any Schatzalp. Time did not hang heavy on his hands—-rather he began to feel the end of his stay approach all too near. The second week was passing; soon two--thirds of his holiday would be gone; the third week would no sooner begin than it would be time to think of packing. The refreshment of his sense of time was long since a thing of the past; the days rushed on—-yes, in the mass they rushed on, though at the same time each single day stretched out long and longer to hold the crowded, secret hopes and fears that filled it to overflowing. Ah, time is a riddling thing, and hard it is to expound its essence!

Must we put plainer name to those inward experiences which at once both weighted and gave wings to Hans Castorp's days? We all know them; their emotional inanity ran true to type. They would have taken no different course even had their origin been such as to make applicable the silly song on which he had pronounced his severe aesthetic judgment.

Impossible that Madame Chauchat should know nothing of the threads that were weaving between her and a certain table. Indeed, Hans Castorp definitely, wilfully purposed that she should know something, or even a good deal. We say wilfully because his eyes were open, he was aware that reason and good sense were against it. But when a man is in Hans Castorp's state—-or the state he was beginning to be in—-he longs, above all, to have her of whom he dreams aware that he dreams, let reason and common sense say what they like to the contrary. Thus are we made.

So, after it had happened twice or thrice that Madame Chauchat, impelled by chance or magnetic attraction, had turned and looked in the direction of Hans Castorp's table and met each time his eyes fixed upon her, she turned the fourth time with intent—-and met them again. On the fifth occasion she did not catch him *in flagrante;* he was not at his post. Yet he straightway felt her eyes upon him, turned, and gazed so ardently that she smiled and looked away. Rapture—-and misgiving—-filled him at sight of that smile. Did she take him for a child? Very well, she should see. He cast about for means to refine upon the position. On the sixth occasion, when he felt, he divined, an inner voice whispered him, that she was looking, he pretended to be absorbed in disgusted contemplation of a pimply dame who had stopped to talk with the great--aunt. He stuck to his guns for a space of two or three minutes, until he was certain the "Kirghiz" eyes had been withdrawn—-a marvellous piece of playacting, which Frau Chauchat not only might, but was expressly intended to see through, to the end that she be impressed with Hans Castorp's subtlety and self--control. Then came the following episode. Frau Chauchat, between courses, turned carelessly about and surveyed the dining--room. Hans Castorp was on guard; their glances met, she peering at him with a vaguely mocking look on her face, he with a determination that made him clench his teeth. And as they looked, her serviette slipped down from her lap and was about to fall to the floor. She reached after it nervously and he felt the motion in all his limbs, so that he half rose from his chair and was about to spring wildly to her aid across eight yards of space and an intervening table——as though some dire catastrophe must ensue if the serviette were to touch the floor. She possessed herself of it just in time; then, still stooping, holding it by the corner, and frowning in evident vexation at the contretemps, for which she seemed to hold him responsible, she looked back once more and saw him with lifted brows, sitting there poised for a spring! Again she smiled and turned away. Hans Castorp was in the seventh heaven over this occurrence. True, he had to pay for it: for full two days—that is to say, for the space of ten meal--times, Madame Chauchat never looked his way. She even intermitted her habit of pausing on her entrance, to survey the room and, as it were, present herself to it. That was hard to bear; yet, since it undoubtedly happened on his account, it preserved the relation between them, if only on its negative side. That was something.

He saw how right Joachim had been in saying that it was hard to get acquainted here, except with one's table companions. For one brief hour after the evening meal social relations of a sort did obtain. But they often shrank to twenty minutes' length; and always Madame Chauchat spent the time, whether longer or shorter, with her own uncle, in the small salon. Her friends were the hollow--chested man, the whimsical girl with the fuzzy hair, the silent Dr. Blumenkohl, and the youth with the drooping shoulders—the "good" Russian table had, it seemed, pre--empted the room for its own use. Furthermore, Joachim was always urging an early withdrawal. He said it was in order to spend full time in the evening cure——but there were perhaps other disciplinary reasons left unspecified, which his cousin surmised and respected. We have reproached Hans Castorp with being "willful"; but certainly, whatever the goal toward which his wishes led, it was not that of social intercourse with Madame Chauchat. He concurred, generally speaking, in the circumstances that militated against it. The relation between him and the young Russian, a tense though tenuous bond, the product of his assiduous glances, was of an extra--social sort. It entailed, and could entail, no obligations. It could subsist, in his mind, along with a degree of distaste for any social approach. It was one thing for our young friend to call "Clavdia" to account for the beatings of his heart; but quite another for him, the grandson of Hans Lorenz Castorp, to be shaken in the smallest degree in the sure inward conviction that this door--slamming, finger--gnawing, bread--pill--making foreigner——who carried herself so badly, who lived apart from her husband, and without a ring on her finger careered from one resort to another——that this foreigner was indubitably not a person for him to cultivate; not, that is, over and above the secret relation we have indicated. A deep gulf divided their two existences; he felt, he knew, that he was not up to defending her in the face of any recognized social authority. Hans Castorp was, for his own person, quite without arrogance; yet a larger arrogance, the pride of caste and tradition, stood written on his brow and in his sleepy--looking eyes, and voiced itself in the conviction of his own superiority, which came over him when he measured Frau Chauchat for what she was. It was this which he neither could, nor wished to, shake off. Strangely enough, he first became vividly conscious of his conviction on a day when he heard Frau Chauchat speaking in his native tongue. She stood in the dining--room after a meal, her hands in the pockets of her sweater, and charmingly struggled to converse in German with another patient, probably a rest--hall acquaintance. Hans Castorp felt an unwonted thrill——never before had he been so proud of his mother--tongue——yet at the same time experienced a temptation to offer up his pride on the altar of quite a different feeling——the rapture which filled him at the sound of her pretty stammerings and manglings of his speech.

In a word, Hans Castorp envisaged in this opening affair between him and the heedless creature who was a member of the Berghof society no more than a holiday adventure. Before the tribunal of reason, conscience, and common sense it could make no claims to be heard; principally, of course, because when all was said and done, Frau Chauchat was an ailing woman, feeble, fevered, and tainted within; her physical condition had much to do with the questionable life she led, as also with Hans Castorp's instinctive reservations. No, it simply did not occur to him to seek her society; while as for the rest—-well, however the thing turned out, it would be over in one way or another inside ten days, when he would enter upon his apprenticeship at Tunder and Wilms's.

For the moment, however, he had begun to live in and for the emotions roused in him by the pretty patient: the up and down of suspense, fulfilment or disappointment, characteristic of such a state. He came to regard these feelings as the real meaning and content of his stay; his mood depended wholly upon their event. All the circumstances of life up here favoured their development. For the inviolably daily programme brought the two constantly together. True, Frau Chauchat's chamber was on a different storey from his own, and she performed her cure, so the schoolmistress said, in the general rest--hall on the roof (the same in which Captain Miklosich had lately turned off the light). But there were the five meal--times; and besides them, innumerable occasions in the daily goings and comings when not only might they meet, but it was practically unavoidable they should. And that, Hans Castorp thought, was all to the good. So was the fact that he had little to do between one occasion and the next, except think about them. He found, indeed, something almost breathless about being thus, as it were, immured with opportunity.

Which did not prevent him from employing all manner of devices to improve the position. His charmer came regularly late to meals; he did the same, with intent to waylay her. He dallied over his toilet, was not ready when Joachim knocked, and let his cousin go on before—-he would catch up with him. He would wait until the intuition proper to his state warned him of the right moment; then he would hurry down, not by his own stair, but by the one at the end of the corridor, which would take him past a certain door—-number seven——in the first storey. Every moment of the way, every step of the stair, offered a chance; any instant the door might open——and in practice it often did. Out she would slip, noiselessly, the door would slam behind her, she would glide to the stairs, she would pass down ahead of him, with her hand up to her braids of hair——or else he would be in front of her, feel her gaze in his back, and experience a thrill as from an ant crawling down it. His bearing, of course, was that of a person unaware of her presence, leading a free and independent existence of his own: he would bury his hands in his pockets, walk with a swagger, cough an entirely unnecessary cough, and strike himself on the chest——anything to manifest his utter unconcern.

On two occasions he refined yet further. Already seated at the table, he felt himself with both hands, and said with a fine show of irritation: "There, I've forgotten my handkerchief. That means I must trot back again to fetch it." And went back, to the end that he and she might meet on the way, since that afforded a keener throb than when she merely walked in front of or behind him. The first time he executed this manœuvre, she measured him with her eyes from a distance, swept him from head to foot, quite bold and unblushing. Then approaching nearer, turned away indifferently and passed him by. So that he got but little out of the *démarche*. The second time she stared him in the face without flinching, almost forbiddingly, even turning her head as they crossed, to follow him with her look——it went through our poor young friend like a knife. We need not pity him, for was it not all his own doing? But the encounter was gripping at the moment and even more afterwards——for only in retrospect was he clear as to what had actually happened. He had never seen Frau Chauchat's face so close, so clear in all its details. He could have counted the tiny hairs that stood up from the braid she wore wreathed round her head——they were reddish--blond, with a metallic sheen. No more than a hands--breadth or so of space had been between his face and hers, whose outline and features, peculiar though they were, had been familiar to him as long as he could remember, and spoke to

[185]

his very soul as nothing else could in all the world. It was an unusual face, and full of character (for only the unusual seems to us to have character); its mystery and strangeness spoke of the unknown north, and it teased the curiosity because its proportions and characteristics were somehow not very easy to determine. Its keynote, probably, was the high, bony structure of the prominent cheek--bones; they seemed to compress the eyes—-which were unusually far apart and unusually level with the face—-and squeeze them into a slightly oblique position; while at the same time they appeared responsible for the soft concavity of the cheek, and this, in turn, to result in the full curve of the slightly pouting lips. Then there were the eyes themselves: the narrow "Kirghiz" eyes, whose shape was yet to Hans Castorp a simple enchantment and whose colour was the grey--blue or blue--grey of distant mountains; they had the trick of sidewise, unseeing glance, which could sometimes melt them into the very hue of mystery and darkness—-these eyes of Clavdia, which had gazed so forbiddingly into his very face, and which so awfully resembled Pribislav Hippe's in shape, expression, and colour that they fairly frightened him. Resembled was not the word: they were the same eyes. The breadth, too, of the upper part of the face, the flattened nose, everything, even to the flush in the white skin, the healthy colour of the cheek—-which in Frau Chauchat's case, as in so many others, merely counterfeited health and was a superficial effect of the openair cure—-everything was precisely Pribislav, and no differently would he have looked at Hans Castorp were they to meet again as of old in the school court--yard. It had been staggering in the extreme. Hans Castorp thrilled at the encounter, yet experienced a mounting uneasiness like that he felt when he realized how narrow was the proximity that enclosed him and the fair Russian. That the long--forgotten Pribislav Hippe should appear to him in the guise of Frau Chauchat and look at him with those "Kirghiz" eyes—-this was to be immured, not with opportunity, but with the inevitable, the unescapable, to such an extent as to fill him with conflicting emotions. It was a situation rich in hope, yet heavy with dread—-it gave our young friend a feeling of helplessness, and set in motion a vague instinct to cast about, to grope and feel for help or counsel. One after another he mentally summoned up various people, the thought of whom might serve him as some sort of mental support.

There was the good, the upright Joachim, firm as a rock—yet whose eyes in these past months had come to hold such a tragic shadow, and who had never used to shrug his shoulders, as he did so often now. Joachim, with the "Blue Peter" in his pocket, as Frau Stöhr called the receptacle. When Hans Castorp thought of her hard, crabbed face it made him shiver. Yes, there was Joachim—who kept constantly at Hofrat Behrens to let him get away and go down to the longed--for service in the "plain"—the"flat--land," as the healthy, normal world was called up here, with a faint yet perceptible nuance of contempt. Joachim served the cure single--mindedly, to the end that he might arrive sooner at his goal and save some of the time which "those up here" so wantonly flung away; served it unquestioningly for the sake of speedy recovery—but also, Hans Castorp detected, for the sake of the cure itself, which, after all, was a service, like another; and was not duty duty, wherever performed? Joachim invariably went upstairs after only a quarter--hour in the drawing--rooms; and this military precision of his was a prop to the civilian laxity of his cousin, who would otherwise be likely to loiter unprofitably below, with his eye on the company in the small salon. But Hans Castorp was convinced there was another and private reason why Joachim withdrew so early; he had known it since the time he saw his cousin's face take on the mottled pallor, and his mouth assume the pathetic twist. He perfectly understood. For Marusja was almost always there in the evening—laughter--loving Marusja, with the little ruby on her charming hand, the handkerchief with the orange scent, and the swelling bosom, tainted within—Hans Castorp comprehended that it was her presence which drove Joachim away, precisely because it so strongly, so fearfully drew him toward her. Was Joachim too "immured"—and even worse off than himself, in that he had five times a day to sit at the same table with Marusja and her orange--scented handkerchief? However that might be, it was clear that Joachim was preoccupied with his own troubles; the thought of him could afford his cousin no mental support. That he took refuge in daily flight was a credit to him; but that he had to flee was anything but reassuring to Hans Castorp, who even began to feel that Joachim's good example of faithful service of the cure and the initiation which he owed to his cousin's experience might have also their bad side.

Hans Castorp had not been up here three weeks. But it seemed longer; and the daily routine which Joachim so piously observed had begun to take on, in his eyes, a character of sanctity. When, from the point of view of "those up here," he considered life as lived down in the flat--land, it seemed somehow queer and unnatural. He had grown skilled in the handling of his rugs and the art of making a proper bundle, a sort of mummy, of himself, when lying on his balcony on cold days. He was almost as skilful as Joachim—-and yet, down below, there was no soul who knew aught of such an art or the practice of it! How strange, he thought; yet at the same moment wondered at himself for finding it strange—-and there surged up again that uneasy sensation of groping for support.

He thought of Hofrat Behrens and his professional advice, bestowed *"sine pecunia,"* that he should, while he was up here, order his life like the other patients, even to the taking of his temperature. He thought of Settembrini, and of how he had laughed at that same advice, and quoted something out of *The Magic Flute*, Did thinking of either of these two afford him any moral support? Hofrat Behrens was a white--haired man, old enough to be Hans Castorp's father. He was the head of the establishment, the highest authority. And it was of fatherly authority that the young man now felt an uneasy need. But no, it would not do: he could not think with childlike confidingness of the Hofrat. The physician had buried his wife up here, and been brought so low by grief as almost to lose his mind; then he had stopped on, to be near her grave and because he himself was somewhat infected. Was he sound again?

Was he single--mindedly bent on making his patients whole, so they could go back to service in the world below? His cheeks had a purple hue, he looked fevered. That might be only the effect of the air up here; Hans Castorp, without fever, so far as he could judge without a thermometer, felt the same dry heat in his face, day in, day out. Of course, when one heard the Hofrat talk, one might easily conclude he had fever. There was something not quite right about it; it all sounded very jovial and lively, but on the whole forced, particularly when one thought of the purple cheeks and the watery eyes, which seemed to be still weeping for his wife. Hans Castorp recalled what Settembrini had said about the Hofrat's vices and chronic depression——that might have been malicious; it might have been sheer windiness. But he did not find it sustained or fortified him to think of Hofrat Behrens.

Then there was Settembrini himself, of course——the chronic oppositionist, the windbag, the "*homo humanus*," as he styled himself. Hans Castorp thought him well over, with his gift of the gab, his florid harangue on the combination of dullness and disease, and how he, Hans Castorp, had been taken to task for calling it a "dilemma for the human intelligence." What about him? Would the thought of him be anyway efficacious? Hans Castorp recalled how several times, in the extraordinarily vivid dreams that visited his sleep in this place, he had taken umbrage at the dry and subtle smile curling the Italian's lip beneath the flowing moustache; how he had railed at him for a hand--organ man, and tried to shove him away because he was a disturbing influence. But that was in his dreams--the waking Hans Castorp was no such matter, but a much less untrammelled person; not disinclined, either, on the whole, to try out the influence upon himself of this novel human type, with its critical animus and acumen, despite the fact that he found the Italian both carping and garrulous. After all, Settembrini had called himself a pedagogue; obviously he was anxious to exercise influence; and Hans Castorp, for his part, fairly yearned to be influenced——though of course, not to an extent which should cause him to pack his trunk and leave before his time, as Settembrini had in all seriousness proposed.

"*Placet experiri*," he thought to himself, with a smile. So much Latin he had, without calling himself a *homo humanus*. The upshot was that he kept his eye on Settembrini, listened keenly and critically to what he had to say when they met on their prescribed walks to the bench on the mountain--side, or down to the Platz, or wherever and whenever opportunity offered. Other occasions there were, too: for instance, at the end of a meal Settembrini would rise from table before anyone else and saunter across among the seven tables, in his check trousers, a toothpick between his lips, to where the cousins sat. He did this in defiance of law and custom, standing there in a graceful attitude, with his legs crossed, talking and gesticulating with the toothpick. Or he would draw up a chair and sit down at the corner of the table, between Hans Castorp and the schoolmistress, or between Hans Castorp and Miss Robinson, and look on while they ate their pudding, which he seemed to have forgone.

"May I beg for admission into this charmed circle?" he would say, shaking hands with the cousins, and comprehending the rest of the table in a sweeping bow. "My brewer over there——not to mention the despairing gaze of the breweress!——But, really, this Herr Magnus! Just now he has been delivering a discourse on folk--psychology. Shall I tell you what he said? 'The Fatherland, it is true, is one enormous barracks. But all the same it's got a lot of solid capacity, it's genuine. I wouldn't change it for the fine manners of the rest of them. What good are fine manners to me if I'm cheated right and left?' And more of the same kind. I am at the end of my patience. And opposite me I have a poor creature, with churchyard roses blooming in her cheeks, an old maid from Siebenbürgen, who never stops talking about her brother--in--law, a man we none of us either know or wish to know. I could stand it no longer, I shook their dust from my feet, I bolted."

"You raised your flag and took to your heels," Frau Stöhr stated.

"Pre--cisely," shouted Settembrini. "I fled with my flag. Ah, what an apt phrase! I see I have come to the right place; nobody else here knows how to coin phrases like that.——May I be permitted to inquire after the state of your health, Frau Stöhr?"

It was frightful to see Frau Stöhr preen herself.

"Good land!" she said. "It is always the same, you know yourself: two steps forward and three back. When you have been sitting here five months, along comes the old man and tucks on another six. It is like the torment of Tantalus: you shove and shove, and think you are getting to the top——"

"Ah, how delightful of you, to give poor old Tantalus a new job, and let him roll the stone uphill for a change! I call that true benevolence.——But what are these mysterious reports I have been hearing of you, Frau Stöhr? There are tales going about——tales about doubles, astral bodies, and the like. Up to now I have lent them no credence—— but this latest story puzzles me, I confess."

"I know you are poking fun at me."

"Not for an instant. I beg you to set my mind at rest about this dark side of your life; after that it will be time to jest. Last night, between half past nine and ten, I was taking a little exercise in the garden; I looked up at the row of balconies; there was your light gleaming through the dark; you were performing your cure, led by the dictates of duty and reason. 'Ah,' thought I, 'there lies our charming invalid, obeying the rules of the house, for the sake of an early return to the arms of her waiting husband.'——And now what do I hear? That you were seen at that very hour at the Kurhaus, in the *cinematógrafo*" (Herr Settembrini gave the word the Italian pronunciation, with the accent on the fourth syllable) "and afterwards in the café, enjoying punch and kisses, and——"

Frau Stöhr wriggled and giggled into her serviette, nudged Joachim and the silent Dr. Blumenkohl in the ribs, winked with coy confidingness, and altogether gave a perfect exhibition of fatuous complacency. She was in the habit of leaving the light burning on her balcony and stealing off to seek distraction in the quarter below. Her husband, meanwhile, in Cannstadt, awaited her return. She was not the only patient who practised this duplicity.

"And," went on Settembrini, "that you were enjoying those kisses in the company of—-whom, do you think? In the company of Captain Miklosich from Bucharest. They say he wears a corset—-but that is little to the point. I conjure you, madame, to tell me!

Have you a double? Was it your earthly part which lay there alone on your balcony, while your spirit revelled below, with Captain Miklosich and his kisses?"

Frau Stöhr wreathed and bridled as though she were being tickled.

"One asks oneself, had it not been better the other way about," Settembrini went on; "you enjoying the kisses by yourself, and the rest--cure with Captain Miklosich—-"

"Tehee!" tittered Frau Stöhr.

"Have the ladies and gentlemen heard the latest?" the Italian went on, without pausing for breath. "Somebody has been flown away with—-by the devil. Or, to speak literally, by his mama—-a very determined lady, I quite took to her. It was young Schneermann, Anton Schneermann, who sat at Mademoiselle Kleefeld's table. You see, his place is empty. It will soon be filled up again, I am not worried about that—-but Anton is off, on the wings of the wind, in the twinkling of an eye, rapt away before he knew where he was. Sixteen years old, and had been up here a year and a half, with six months to go. But how did it happen? Who knows? Perhaps somebody dropped a little word to Madame his mother; anyhow, she got wind of his goings--on, *in Baccho et ceteris*. She appears unannounced on the scene, some three heads taller than I am, white--haired and exceeding wroth; fetches Herr Anton a couple of boxes on the ear, takes him by the collar, and puts him on the train. 'If he is going to the dogs,' she says, 'he can do it just as well down below.' And off they go."

"Everybody within ear--shot laughed; Herr Settembrini had such a droll way of telling a story. Despite his contemptuous attitude toward the society of the place, he always knew everything that went on. He knew the name and circumstances of each patient. He knew that such and such a person had been operated on for rib resection; had it on the best authority that from the autumn onward no one with a temperature of more than 101.3° would be admitted into the establishment. He told them how last night the little dog belonging to Madame Capatsoulias from Mitylene stepped on the button of the electric signal on his mistress's night--table and occasioned much commotion and running hither and yon—-particularly because Madame Capatsoulias had been found not alone, but in the society of Assessor Düstmund from Friedrichshagen. Even Dr. Blumenkohl had to laugh at that. Pretty Marusja well--nigh choked in her orange--scented handkerchief, and Frau Stöhr yelled with laughter, holding her breast with both hands.

But to the cousins Ludovico Settembrini talked of himself and his early life; whether on the walks they took together, or during the evening in the salon, or perhaps, in the dining--room itself, after a meal, when most of the patients had left and the three sat together at their end of the table, while the waitresses cleared away and Hans Castorp smoked his Maria Mancini, which in the third week had regained a little of its savour. He was critical of what he heard, and often he felt put off; yet he listened receptively to the Italian's talk, for it opened to his understanding a world utterly new and strange.

Settembrini spoke of his grandfather, a Milanese lawyer, but even more a patriot; with something of the political agitator, and orator and journalist to boot. He too, like his grandson, had always been in the opposition; though he had been able to perform his rôle upon a larger stage than had Ludovico. The latter remarked with some bitterness that his own activities had been confined to heckling and castigating the follies and frailties of the guests at the International

Sanatorium Berghof, and to protesting against them in the name of the free and joyous human spirit. But his grandfather had had his finger in the forming of governments; he had conspired against Austria and the Holy Alliance, which had dismembered his native land and then held it in the heavy bond of servitude; he had been a zealous member of certain secret societies that had spread over Italy—a *carbonaro*, Settembrini explained, suddenly dropping his voice, as though it might still be dangerous to utter the word. In fact, from his grandson's narrative, the two hearers got a picture of a dark and tempest--tossed figure, a ringleader, political agitator, and conspirator; despite all their pains, they did not quite succeed in hiding a feeling of mistrust, even repulsion. True, the circumstances had been extraordinary. What they heard had happened long ago, almost a hundred years. It was history; and they were familiar in theory—particularly from ancient history—with the traditional figure of the tyrant--hater and liberator, such as they now heard of—-though they had never dreamed of being brought into actual human contact with him, like this! Settembrini's grandfather, so they were told, united with his conspiratorial zeal a profound love for his native land, which it was his dream to see free and united; indeed, it was out of this very combination, as a natural consequence, that his revolutionary activities flowed—and how strange this mingling of rebellion and patriotism seemed to the cousins, in whose minds an abiding sense of order was on an equal footing with their love of country! But they privately admitted, none the less, that at that time, and in that situation, it might have been conceivably possible that rebellion should go paired with civic virtue, and law--abiding--ness lie down with lazy indifference to the public weal.

But Grandfather Giuseppe had been not only an Italian patriot. He had been fellow citizen and brother--in--arms to any people struggling for its liberties. Thus after the shipwreck of a certain plot hatched in Turin for the overthrow of the military and civil government, a plot in which he had been deeply involved, he had escaped by a hair's breadth the clutches of Metternich's hirelings, and spent the time of his exile fighting and bleeding, first in Spain for the cause of constitutionalism, then in Greece for the independence of the Hellenic peoples. It was in Greece that Settembrini's father had seen the light—-which probably accounted for his being a humanist and lover of classical antiquity. His mother had been of German stock; Settembrini had married her in Switzerland and taken her about with him in his further adventurous career. He had been allowed, after ten years of exile, to return to Milan, where he had practised his profession, without for a moment ceasing to labour, with voice and pen, in verse and prose, for the establishment of a united republic, and to draw up subversive programmes characterized by dictatorial ardour, in which were promulgated in the clearest style the unification of the liberated people and the attainment of general felicity. One detail mentioned by the grandson made a profound impression upon Hans Castorp: Grandfather Giuseppe, to the day of his death, wore black—-in token, he said, of his mourning for the state of the fatherland, languishing in misery and servitude. Hans Castorp, at this piece of information, thought of his own grandfather, as he had once or twice before during Settembrini's narrative. He too, for as long as his grandson had known him, wore black clothes. But for how different a reason!

Hans Lorenz Castorp had worn the quaint old fashion to indicate his oneness with a bygone time and his essential lack of sympathy with the present; worn it up to the end of his days, when he had returned in death to his true and adequate presentment—-with the starched ruff. Certainly these were two strikingly different kinds of grandfather!

Hans Castorp pondered, his eyes fixed in a stare, cautiously shaking his head in a way that might as well be taken for a sign of admiration for Giuseppe Settembrini as for the opposite. He honourably refrained from judging what he did not understand, but simply made mental note of the contrast and let it go at that. He could see the narrow head of old Hans Lorenz, as it bent musing over the pale gold rim of the christening basin, that symbol of the passing and the abiding, of continuity through change. He had his mouth open; Hans Castorp knew the words great--great--great were about to issue from it, the sombre syllables which always reminded him of places where one walked with bent head and reverent gait. And then he saw Giuseppe Settembrini, with the tricolour on his arm, waving his sabre and breathing a vow to Heaven with dark gaze flung aloft, as he stormed the heights of despotism at the head of a liberty--loving host. Well, he thought, each of them had his fine and splendid side---he made the greater effort to be fair, because he knew himself to be partisan, on personal or partly personal grounds. For Grandfather Settembrini had fought to obtain political rights; whereas the other grandfather----or his ancestors----had originally had all the rights, and the scoundrels had taken them away from him, in the course of the centuries, by violence or pettifoggery. So both grandfathers had worn mourning, the one in the north and the one in the south, and both in the same idea; namely, to put a great gulf between them and the evil present. But whereas the one had assumed it in token of his pious reverence for the past and the dead, to whom he felt himself with his whole being to belong, the other had worn it as a sign of rebellion, in the name of progress, and in a spirit of hostility toward the past. Yes, these were two different worlds. As Herr Settembrini talked, and Hans Castorp stood, as it were, between them and cast his critical eye upon one and upon the other, they called back to his conscious mind a scene from his own past life. He saw himself rowing on a lake in Holstein, one late summer evening; the sun was down, the almost full moon rising above the bushes that bordered the lake. He rowed alone and slowly over the quiet waters, gazing to right and left at a scene fantastic as any dream. In the west it was still broad day, with a fixed and glassy air; but in the east he looked into a moonlit landscape, wreathed in the magic of rising mists and equally convincing to his bewildered sense. The strange combination lasted some brief quarter--hour before the balance finally settled in favour of night and the moon; all that time Hans Castorp's dazzled eyes went shifting in lively amazement from one scene to the other: from day to night and back again to day. The picture returned to him now.

At the same time the thought crossed his mind that Lawyer Settembrini could scarcely have been much of a jurist, considering his other occupations and the extended sphere of his activities. His grandson asseverated, however, and Hans Castorp found it credible, that the grandfather had been from early childhood down to the last day of his life inspired by the fundamental principle of justice. Our hero, all heavy--headed as he was and organically preoccupied by the six--course Berghof meal he had just eaten, made an effort to understand what Settembrini meant when he called this principle "the source and fount of liberty and progress." Progress, up to now, had had to do, in Hans Castorp's mind, with such things as the nineteenthcentury development of cranes and lifting--tackle. He was accordingly gratified to learn that Grandfather Settembrini had not underestimated the importance of such matters. Of course, his own grandfather hadn't either. The Italian paid a tribute to the native land of his two listeners, for the inventions of gunpowder—-whereby the armour of feudalism had been thrown on the scrap--heap—-and the printing--press, which had made possible the democratic propagation of ideas, and the propagation of democratic ideas, which were one and the same. For these good gifts he praised Germany; praised her for her past, but awarded his own country the palm, because she had been the first to unfurl the banner of freedom, culture, and enlightenment, at a time when all other lands were wrapped in the darkness of superstition and slavery. Yet in paying due honour, as upon their first meeting, at the bench by the watercourse, to commerce and technology (Hans Castorp's own field), Settembrini apparently did so not for the sake of these forces themselves, but purely with reference to their significance for the ethical development of mankind. For such a significance, he declared, he joyfully ascribed to them. Technical progress, he said, gradually subjugated nature, by developing roads and telegraphs, minimizing climatic differences; and by the means of communication which it created proved itself the most reliable agent in the task of drawing together the peoples of the earth, of making them acquainted with each other, of building bridges to compromise, of destroying prejudice; of, actually, bringing about the universal brotherhood of man. Humanity had sprung from the depths of fear, darkness, and hatred; but it was emerging, it was moving onward and upward, toward a goal of fellow--feeling and enlightenment, of goodness and joyousness; and upon this path, he said, the industrial arts were the vehicle conducive to the greatest progress. But all this made a confused impression on Hans Castorp. Herr Settembrini seemed to bring together in a single breath categories which in the young man's mind had heretofore been as the poles asunder——for example, technology and morals! Positively, he made the statement that Christ had been the first to proclaim the principle of equality and union, that the printing--press had propagated the doctrine, and that finally the French Revolution had elevated it into a law! All which our poor young friend found very muddling, he scarce knew why—- though the feeling was definite enough in all conscience, and though Herr Settembrini had couched his thought in the clearest and roundest of periods. Once, the Italian went on, once only in his life, and that in his early manhood, had his grandfather known what it was to feel profound joy. That was at the time of the Paris July Revolution. He had gone about proclaiming to all and sundry that some day men would place those three days alongside the six days of creation, and reverence them alike. Hans Castorp felt utterly dumbfounded——involuntarily he slapped the table with his hand. To compare those three summer days of the year 1830 when the Parisians had taken unto themselves a new constitution, to the six in which God had divided the land from the water and created the lights in the firmament of heaven, as well as flowers, trees, birds, and fishes, and all other living things——that seemed to him to be going too far. He talked it over later with Cousin Joachim, and gave clear expression to his opinion that it really was pretty thick, that he, Hans Castorp, for his part, found it positively offensive.

But still open--minded—-at least in the sense that he enjoyed the experiment he was making——he restrained the objections which his sense of fitness would have raised against the Settembrinian scheme of things. Restrained them on the theory that what seemed sedition to him might to another seem dauntless courage; and what he called bad taste might have been, in that far--off time and circumstance, but a display of the noble excesses of a high--hearted nature——for instance, when Grandfather Settembrini called the barricades "the people's throne," and talked about "dedicating the burgher's pike on the altar of humanity."

Hans Castorp knew——without putting it into so many words——why he lent an ear to Herr Settembrini. Partly it was out of a sense of duty; though also out of that holiday mood of taking everything as it came, rejecting nothing, in the knowledge that in another day or so he would spread his wings and fly back to the wonted order of things. Yes, he knew it was largely the promptings of conscience to which he hearkened; to be precise, the promptings of a conscience not altogether easy——as he sat listening to the Italian, one leg crossed over the other, drawing at his Maria Mancini; or when the three of them climbed the hill from the English quarter. Two principles, according to the Settembrinian cosmogony, were in perpetual conflict for possession of the world: force and justice, tyranny and freedom, superstition and knowledge; the law of permanence and the law of change, of ceaseless fermentation issuing in progress. One might call the first the Asiatic, the second the European principle; for Europe was the theatre of rebellion, the sphere of intellectual discrimination and transforming activity, whereas the East embodied the conception of quiesence and immobility. There was no doubt as to which of the two would finally triumph: it would be the power of enlightenment, the power that made for rational advance and development. For human progress snatched up ever more peoples with it on its brilliant course; it conquered more and more territory in Europe itself and was already pressing Asia--wards. Much still remained to be done, sublime exertions were still demanded from those spirits who had received the light. Then only the day would come when thrones would crash and outworn religions crumble, in those remaining countries of Europe which had not already enjoyed the blessings of eighteenth--century enlightenment, nor yet of an upheaval like 1789.

But the day would come, Settembrini said, with his suave smile; it would come, he repeated, if not on the wings of doves, then on the pinions of eagles; and dawn would break over Europe, the dawn of universal brotherhood, in the name of justice, science, and human reason. It would bring in its train a new Holy Alliance, the alliance of the democratic peoples of Europe, in opposition to that other Holy Alliance, the thrice--infamous organ of princes and cabinets, which Grandfather Giuseppe had personally regarded as his deadly foe; in a word, it would bring in its train the republic of the world. But before that could happen, the Asiatic principle must be met and crushed in its very stronghold and vital centre; that was to say, in Vienna. Austria must be crushed, crushed and dismembered, first to take vengeance for the past, and second to lead in the new law of justice with truth on earth.

Hans Castorp did not care for this last drift in Herr Settembrini's sonorous flow of words. He mistrusted it; it sounded too much like a personal or national animus. As for Joachim Ziemssen, whenever the Italian fell into this vein, he scowled and turned away his head, or sought to create a diversion by saying it was time for the rest--cure. Neither did Hans Castorp feel obliged to listen when the conversation took these devious paths; they clearly fell outside the limits within which his conscience prompted him to profit by Herr Settembrini's words. Yet conscience still urged him to continue in the effort; so clearly that often, as opportunity arose, he would even invite the Italian to discourse on the subject of his ideas.

Those ideas, ideals, and efforts of the aspiring will were, Settembrini said, traditional in his family. He inherited them. Grandfather, son, and grandson, each in his turn, had dedicated to them their entire lives and all their spiritual energy. The father in his own way had done so no less than Grandfather Giuseppe. True, he had not been a political agitator or active combatant in the cause of freedom, but a quiet and sensitive scholar, a humanist sitting at his writing--desk. But what, after all, was humanism if not love of human kind, and by that token also political activity, rebellion against all that tended to defile or degrade our conception of humanity? He had been accused of exaggerating the importance of form. But he who cherished beauty of form did so because it enhanced human dignity; whereas the Middle Ages, in striking contrast, had been sunk not only in superstitious hostility to the human spirit, but also in a shameful formlessness. From the very beginning he had defended the right of the human being to his earthly interests, to liberty of thought and joy in life, and insisted that we could safely leave heaven to take care of itself. Humanism—-had not Prometheus been the earliest humanist, and was he not identical with the Satan hymned by Carducci? Ah, if the cousins had only heard that arch--enemy of the Church, at Bologna, pouring the vials of his sarcasm upon the Christian sentimentalism of the *Romanticismo!* Upon Manzoni's *Inni Sacri!* Upon the shadowsand--moonlight poetry of the romantic movement, which he had compared to "Luna, Heaven's pallid nun"! *Per Bacco*, this was a joy to listen to! And they ought to have heard Carducci interpret Dante, celebrating him as the citizen of a great city--state, who had spoken out against asceticism and the negation of life, and on the side of the world--transforming and reforming deed! It was not the sickly and mystagogic figure of Beatrice which the poet had celebrated under the name of *"donna gentil e pietosa"*; rather it had been his wife, who represented in the poem the principle of worldly knowledge and practical workaday life.

Thus Hans Castorp came to hear something about Dante, and certainly from the lips of authority. He was not too much inclined to believe implicitly all Settembrini said; he considered him too much of a windbag for that. Still it was an interesting conception, this of Dante as the wide--awake citizen of a great metropolis. And now Settembrini went on to speak of himself, and to explain how the tendencies of his immediate forbears, the political from his grandfather, the humanistic from his father, had united in his own person to produce the writer and independent man of letters. For literature was after all nothing else than the combination of humanism and politics; a conjunction the more immediate in that humanism itself was politics and politics humanism. Hans Castorp did his best at this point to listen and comprehend, in the hope of finally learning wherein had consisted the crass ignorance of Magnus the brewer, and finding out what else literature actually was, above and beyond "beautiful characters." Settembrini asked his audience whether they had ever heard of Brunetto, Brunetto Latini, a Florentine notary, who about the year 1250 had written a book on the subject of the virtues and the vices. He it was who had sharpened the wits of the Florentines, taught them the art of language, and how to guide their state according to the rules of politics.

"There you have it, gentlemen, there you have it!" Settembrini cried with ardour, and enlarged upon the cult of the "word," the art of eloquence, which he called the triumph of the human genius. For the word was the glory of mankind, it alone imparted dignity to life. Not only was humanism bound up with the word, and with literature, but so also was humanity itself, man's ancient dignity and manly selfrespect ("You heard, didn't you," Hans Castorp said later to his cousin, "you heard him say that literature is a question of beautiful words? I spotted it directly"), from which it followed that politics too is bound up with the word. Or, rather, it followed directly from the union, the unity that subsisted between humanity and literature, for the beautiful word begets the beautiful deed.

"Two hundred years ago," Settembrini said, "you had a poet in your country, a magnificent old chatterbox who set great store in good handwriting because he thought it must induce a good style. He should have gone a step further and said that a good style would lead to good deeds," Settembrini added. For writing well was almost the same as thinking well, and thinking well was the next thing to acting well. All moral discipline, all moral perfection derived from the soul of literature, from the soul of human dignity, which was the moving spirit of both humanity and politics. Yes, they were all one, one and the same force, one and the same idea, and all of them could be comprehended in one single word. This word? Ah, it was already familiar to their ears; yet he would wager the cousins had never

before rightly grasped its meaning and its majesty: the word was—
-civilization! And as Settembrini brought it out, he flung his small,
yellow--skinned right hand in the air, as though proposing a toast.

Well, all that young Hans Castorp found worth listening to; not
precisely overwhelming, of a value largely experimental, but still
worth listening to. He said as much to Joachim Ziemssen later; but
Joachim had his thermometer in his mouth and could not reply to his
cousin; nor had he afterwards leisure, when, on taking it out, he read
the figure and entered it in his note--book. But Hans Castorp good-
-naturedly took cognizance of Settembrini's point of view and tested
by it his own inner experiences; from which self--examination it
principally appeared that the waking man has an advantage over the
sleeping and dreaming one. For whereas the sleeping Hans Castorp
had more than once upbraided the organ--grinder to his face and
done his utmost to drive him away because he felt him a disturbing
influence, the waking one lent him an attentive ear and made an
honest effort to minimize the opposition which his mentor's ideas
and conceptions persistently aroused in him. For it cannot be denied
that there was such opposition; some of it such as he must always
have felt from the very beginning, the rest arising from the particular
situation and his partly vicarious, partly secret and personal
experiences among "those up here."

What a creature is man, how widely his conscience betrays him!
How easy it is for him to think he hears, even in the voice of duty, a
licence to passion! Hans Castorp listened to Herr Settembrini out of a
sense of duty and fairness, in the idea of hearing both sides; with the
best of intentions he tested the latter's views on the subject of the
republic, reason and the *bello stile*. He was entirely receptive. And all
the while he was finding it more and more permissible to give his
thoughts and dreams free rein in another and quite opposite
direction. Indeed, to give expression to all that we suspect or divine,
we think it not unlikely that Hans Castorp hearkened to Herr
Settembrini's discourse in order to get from his own conscience an
indulgence which otherwise might not have been forthcoming. But

what—-or who—-was it that drew down the other side of the scales, when weighed over against patriotism, belles--lettres, and the dignity of man? It was—-Clavdia Chauchat, "Kirghiz"--eyed, "relaxed," and tainted within; when he thought of her (though thinking is far too tame a word to characterize the impulse that turned all his being in her direction), it was as though he were sitting again in his boat on the lake in Holstein, looking with dazzled eyes from the glassy daylight of the western shore to the mist and moonbeams that wrapped the eastern heavens.

The Thermometer

Hans Castorp's week here ran from Tuesday to Tuesday, for on a Tuesday he had arrived. Two or three days before, he had gone down to the office and paid his second weekly bill, a modest account of a round one hundred and sixty francs, modest and cheap enough, even without taking into consideration the nature of some of the advantages of a stay up here—advantages priceless in themselves, though for that very reason they could not be included in the bill—-and even without counting extras like the fortnightly concert and Dr. Krokowski's lectures, which might conceivably have been included. The sum of one hundred and sixty francs represented simply and solely the actual hospitality extended by the Berghof to Hans Castorp: his comfortable lodgment and his five stupendous meals.

"It isn't much, it is rather cheap than otherwise," remarked the guest to the old inhabitant. "You cannot complain of being overcharged up here. You need a round six hundred and fifty francs a month for board and lodging, treatment included. Let us assume that you spend another thirty francs for tips, if you are decent and like to have friendly faces about you. That makes six hundred and eighty. Good. Of course I know there are fixed fees and other sorts of small expenses: toilet articles, tobacco, drives, and excursions, now and then a bill for shoes or clothing. Very good. But all that won't bring it up to a thousand francs, say what you like. Not eight hundred even.

That isn't ten thousand francs a year. Certainly not more. That is what it costs you."

"Mental arithmetic very fair," Joachim said. "I never knew you were such a shot at doing sums in your head. And how broad--minded of you to calculate it by the year like that! You've learned something since you've been up here. But your figure is too high. I don't smoke, and I certainly don't expect to buy any suits while I am here, thank you."

"Then it would be lower still," Hans Castorp answered, rather confused. Why, indeed, he should have included tobacco and a new wardrobe in his calculation of Joachim's expenses is a puzzle. But for the rest, his brilliant display of arithmetic had simply been so much dust thrown in his cousin's eyes; for here, as elsewhere, his mental processes were rather slow than fast, and the truth is that a previous calculation with pencil and paper underlay his present facility. One night on his balcony (for he even took the evening cure out of doors now, like the rest) a sudden thought had struck him and he had got out of his comfortable chair to fetch pencil and paper. As the result of some simple figuring, he concluded that his cousin—-or, speaking generally, a patient at the Berghof—would need twelve thousand francs a year to cover the sum total of his expenses. Thus he amused himself by establishing the fact that he, Hans Castorp, could amply afford to live up here, if he chose, being a man of eighteen or nineteen thousand francs yearly income.

He had, as we have said, paid his second weekly bill three days before, and accordingly found himself in the middle of the third and last week of his appointed stay. The coming Sunday, as he remarked to himself and to his cousin, would see the performance of another of the fortnightly concerts, and the Monday another lecture by Dr. Krokowski; then, on Tuesday or Wednesday, he would be off, and Joachim would be left up here alone—-poor Joachim, for whom Rhadamanthus would prescribe God knew how many more months! Already there came a shade over his gentle black eyes whenever Hans Castorp's swiftly approaching departure was spoken of. Where, in

Heaven's name, had the holiday gone? It had rushed past, it had flown---and left one wondering how. For, after all, three weeks, twenty--one days, is a considerable stretch of time, too long, at least, for one to see the end at the beginning. And now, on a sudden, there remained of it no more than a miserable three or four days, nothing worth mentioning. They would, it was true, comprehend the lecture and the concert, those two recurrent variations in the weekly programme, and, thus weighted, might move a little more slowly. But on the other hand, they would be taken up with packing and leave--taking. Three weeks up here was as good as nothing at all; they had all told him so in the beginning. The smallest unit of time was the month, Settembrini had said; and as Hans Castorp's stay was less than that, it amounted to nothing; it was a "week--end visit," as Hofrat Behrens put it. Had the swift flight of time up here anything to do with the uniformly accelerated rate of organic combustion? At any rate, here was a consoling thought for Joachim during his five remaining months---in case he really got off with five. But Hans Castorp felt that during these three weeks they ought to have paid more attention, to have kept better watch, as Joachim did in his daily measurings, during which the seven minutes seemed like a quite considerable stretch of time. Hans Castorp grieved for his cousin, reading in his eyes his pain at the approaching parting. He felt the strongest possible sympathy at the thought of the poor chap's having to stop on up here when he himself was down in the flat--land, helping bring the nations together through the development of commerce and communications. His own regret was at times so lively as to burn in his breast and cause him to doubt whether he would have the heart, when the time came, to leave Joachim alone; and this vicarious suffering was probably the reason why he himself referred less and less to his impending departure. It was Joachim who came back to it; for Hans Castorp, moved by native tact and delicacy, seemed to wish to forget it up to the last moment.

"At least." Joachim said more than once in these days, "let us hope it has done you good to be up here, and that you will feel the benefit when you are at home again."

"I'll remember you to everybody," Hans Castorp responded, "and say you are coming back in five months at the outside. Done me good? If it has done me good to be up here? I should like to think so; some improvement must surely have taken place, even in this short time. I have received a great many new impressions, new in every sense of the word; very stimulating, but a good deal of strain too, physically and mentally. I have not at all the feeling of having really got acclimatized—which would certainly be the first necessary step toward improvement. Maria, thank goodness, is her old self; for several days now, I have been able to get the aroma. But my handkerchief still becomes red from time to time when I use it—and this damned heat in my face, and these idiotic palpitations, I shall apparently have them up to the last minute. No, it seems I can't talk about being acclimatized—how could I, either, in so short a time? It would take longer than this to overcome the change of atmosphere and adjust oneself perfectly to the unusual conditions, so that a real recovery could begin and I should commence to put on flesh. It is too bad. It was certainly a mistake not to have given myself more time—-for of course I could have had it. I have the feeling that once I am at home again I shall need to sleep three weeks on end to get rested from the rest I've had! That shows you how tired I sometimes feel. And now, to cap the climax, I get this catarrh—-"

It looked, in fact, as though Hans Castorp would return home in possession of a first--class cold. He had caught it, probably, in the rest--cure, and, again probably, in the evening rest--cure—which for almost a week now he had been taking in the balcony, despite the long spell of cold, wet weather. He was aware that weather of this kind was not recognized as bad; such a conception hardly existed up here, where the most inclement conceivable went unheeded and had no terrors for anyone. With the easy adaptability of youth, which suits itself to any environment, Hans Castorp had begun to imitate this indifference. It might rain in bucketfuls, but the air was not supposed to be the more damp for that——nor was it, in all probability, for the dry heat in the face persisted, as though after drinking wine, or sitting in an overheated room. And however cold it got, the radiators were never heated unless it snowed, so it was of no avail to take refuge in one's chamber, since it was quite as comfortable on the balcony, when one lay in one's excellent chair, wrapped in a paletot and two good camel's--hair rugs put on according to the ritual. As comfortable? It was incomparably more so. It was, in Hans Castorp's reasoned judgment, a state of life which more appealed to him than any in all his previous experience, so far as he could remember. He did not propose to be shaken in this view for any *carbonaro* or quill--driver in existence, no matter how many malicious and equivocal jokes he made on the subject of the "horizontal." Especially he liked it in the evening, when with his little lamp on the stand beside him and his long--lost and now restored Maria alight between his lips he enjoyed the ineffable excellencies of his reclining--chair. True, his nose felt frozen, and the hands that held his book——he was still reading *Ocean Steamships*—— were red and cramped from the cold. He looked through the arch of his loggia over the darkening valley, jewelled with clustered or scattering lights, and listened to the music that drifted up nearly every evening for almost an hour. There was a concert below, and he could hear, pleasantly subdued by the distance, familiar operatic selections, snatches from *Carmen, Il Trovatore, Freischütz;* or well--built, facile waltzes, marches so spirited that he could not help keeping time with his head, and gay mazurkas. Mazurka? No, Marusja was her name, Marusja of the little ruby. And in the next loggia, behind the thick wall of milky glass, lay Joachim, with whom Hans Castorp exchanged a word now and then, low--toned, out of consideration for the other horizontallers. Joachim was as well off in his loggia as Hans Castorp in his, though, being entirely unmusical, he could not take the same pleasure in the concerts. Too bad! He was probably studying his Russian primer instead. But Hans Castorp let *Ocean Steam-- ships* fall on the coverlet and gave himself up to the music; he contemplated with such inward gratification the translucent depth of a musical invention full of individuality and charm that he thought with nothing but hostility of Settembrini and the irritating things he had said about music——that it was politically suspect was the worst, and little better than the remark of Grandfather Giuseppe about the July Revolution and the six days of creation.

Joachim, though he could not partake of Hans Castorp's pleasure in the music, nor the pungent gratification purveyed by Maria, lay as snugly ensconced as his cousin. The day was at an end. For the time everything was at an end; there would be no more emotional alarums, no more strain on the heart--muscles. But equally there was the assurance that to--morrow it would begin all over again, all the favouring probabilities afforded by propinquity and the household regimen. And this pleasing combination of snugness and confident hope, together with the music and the restored charms of Maria, made the evening cure a state almost amounting to beatification for young Hans Castorp.

All which had not prevented the guest and novice from catching a magnificent cold, either in the evening rest--cure or elsewhere. He felt the onset of catarrh, with oppression in the frontal sinus, and inflamed uvula; he could not breathe easily through the passage provided by nature; the air struck cold and painfully as it struggled through, and caused constant coughing. His voice took on overnight the tonal quality of a hollow bass the worse for strong drink. According to him, he had not closed an eye, his parched throat making him start up every five minutes from his pillow.

"Very vexatious," Joachim said, "and most unfortunate. Colds, you know, are not the thing at all, up here; they are not *reçus*. The authorities don't admit their existence; the official attitude is that the dryness of the air entirely prevents them. If you were a patient, you would certainly fall foul of Behrens, if you went to him and said you had a cold. But it is a little different with a guest,——you have a right to have a cold if you want to. It would be good if we could check the catarrh. There are things to do, down below, but here——I doubt if anyone would take enough interest in it. It is not advisable to fall ill up here; you aren't taken any notice of. It's an old story——but you are coming to hear it at the end. When I was new up here, there was a lady who complained of her ear for a whole week and told everybody how she suffered. Behrens finally looked at it. 'Make yourself quite easy, madame,' he said; 'it is not tubercular.' That was an end of the matter! Well, we must see what can be done. I will speak to the bathing--master early to--morrow morning, when he comes to my room. Then it will go through the regular channels, and perhaps something will come of it."

Thus Joachim and the regular channels proved reliable. On Friday, after Hans Castorp returned from the morning round, there was a knock at his door, and he was vouchsafed the pleasure of personal acquaintance with Fräulein von Mylendonk——

Frau Director, as she was called. Up to now he had seen this over--occupied person only from a distance, crossing the corridor from one patient's room to another, or when she had popped up for a moment in the dining--room and he had been aware of her raucous voice. But now he himself was the object of her visit. His catarrh had fetched her. She knocked a short, bony knock, entered almost before he had said come in, and then, upon the threshold, bent round to make sure of the number of the room.

"Thirty--four," she croaked briskly. "Right. Well, young 'un, *on me dit, que vous avez pris froid. Wy, kaschetsja, prostudilisj, Lei è raffreddato*, I hear you have caught a cold. What language do you speak? Oh, I see, you are young Ziemssen's guest. I am due in the operating--room. Somebody there to be chloroformed, and he has just been eating bean salad. I have to have my eyes everywhere. Well, young 'un, so you have a cold?"

Hans Castorp was taken aback by this mode of address, in the mouth of a dame of ancient lineage. In her rapid speech she slurred over her words, all the time restlessly moving her head about with a circular action, the nose sniffingly in the air—the motion of a caged beast of prey. Her freckled right hand, loosely closed with the thumb uppermost, she held in front of her and waved it to and fro on the wrist, as though to say: "Come, make haste, don't attend to what I say, but say what you have to and let me be off!" She was in the forties, of stunted growth, without form or comeliness, clad in a belted pinaforish garment of clinical white, with a garnet cross on her breast. Sparse, reddish hair showed beneath the white coif of her profession; her eyes were a waterly blue, with inflamed lids, and one of them, as a finishing touch, had a stye in a well--advanced stage of development in the corner. Their glance was unsteady and flickering. Her nose was turned up, her mouth like a frog's, and furnished to boot with a wry and protruding lower lip, which she used like a shovel to get her words out. Hans Castorp looked at her, and all the modest and confiding friendliness native to him spoke in his eyes.

"What sort of cold is it, eh?" repeated the Directress. She seemed to try to concentrate her gaze and make it penetrate; but it slipped aside. "We don't care for such colds. Are you subject to them? Your cousin has been too, hasn't he? How old are you? Twenty--four? Yes, it's the age. And so you come up here and get a cold?

There ought not to be any talk about colds up here; that sort of twaddle belongs down below." It was fearsome to see how she shovelled out this word with her lower lip.

"You have a beautiful bronchial catarrh, that is plain"—again she made that curious effort to pierce him with her gaze, and again she could not hold it steady. "But catarrhs are not caused by cold; they come from an infection, which one takes from being in a receptive state. So the question is, are we dealing with a harmless infection or with something more serious? Everything else is twaddle. It is possible that your receptivity inclines to the harmless kind," she went on, and looked at him with her over--ripe stye, he knew not how. "Here, I will give you a simple antiseptic—-it may do you good," and she took a small packet out of the leather bag that hung from her girdle. It was formamint. "But you look flushed—as though you had fever." She never stopped trying to fix him with her gaze, and always the eyes glided off to one side.

"Have you measured?"

He answered in the negative.

"Why not?" she asked, and her protruding lower lip hung in the air after she spoke. He made no answer. The poor youth was still young; he had never got over his schoolboy shyness. He sat, so to speak, on his bench, did not know the answer and took refuge in dumbness.

"Perhaps you never do take your temperature?"

"Oh, yes, Frau Director, when I have fever."

"My dear child, one takes it in the first instance to see whether one has fever. According to you, you have none now?"

"I can't tell, Frau Director. I cannot really tell the difference. Ever since I came up here, I have been a little hot and shivery."

"Aha! And where is your thermometer?"

"I haven't one with me, Frau Director. Why should I, I am not ill; I am only up here on a visit."

"Rubbish! Did you send for me because you weren't ill?"

"No," he laughed politely, "it was because I caught a little——"

"Cold. We've often seen such colds. Here, young 'un," she said, and rummaged again in her bag. She brought out two longish leather cases, one red and one black, and put them on the table. "This one is three francs fifty, the other five. The five-franc one is better, of course. It will last you a lifetime if you take care of it."

Smiling he took up the red case and opened it. The glass instrument lay like a jewel within, fitted neatly into its red velvet groove. The degrees were marked by red strokes, the tenths by black ones; the figures were in red and the tapering end was full of glittering quicksilver. The column stood below blood-heat.

Hans Castorp knew what was due to himself and his upbringing. "I will take this one," he said, not even looking at the other. "The one at five francs. May I——"

"Then that's settled," croaked the Directress. "I see you don't niggle over important purchases. No hurry, it will come on the bill. Give him to me. We'll drive him right down"——She took the thermometer out of his hand and plunged it several times through the air, until the mercury stood below 95°. "He'll soon climb up again!" she said. "Here is your new acquisition. You know how we do it up here? Straight under the tongue, seven minutes, four times a day, and shut the lips well over it. Well, young 'un, I must get on. Good luck!" And she was out at the door.

Hans Castorp bowed her out, then stood by the table, staring from the door through which she had disappeared to the instrument she had left behind. "So that," he thought, "was Directress von Mylendonk. Settembrini doesn't care for her, and certainly she has her unpleasant side. The stye isn't pretty——but of course she does not have it all the time. But why does she call me 'young 'un,' like that? Rather rude and familiar, seems to me. So she has sold me a thermometer——I suppose she always has one or two in her pocket. They are to be had everywhere here, Joachim said, even in shops where you would least expect it. But I didn't need to take the trouble to buy it; it just fell into my lap." He took the article out of its case, looked at it, and walked restlessly up and down the room. His heart beat strong and rapidly. He looked toward the open balcony door, and considered seeking counsel of Joachim, but thought better of it and paused again by the table. He cleared his throat by way of testing his voice; then he coughed.

"Yes," he said. "I must see if I have the fever that goes with the cold." Quickly he put the thermometer in his mouth, the mercury beneath the tongue, so that the instrument stuck slantingly upwards from his lips. He closed them firmly, that no air might get in. Then he looked at his wrist-watch. It was six minutes after the half-hour. And he began to wait for the seven minutes to pass.

"Not a second too long," he thought, "and not one too short. They can depend on me, in both directions. They needn't give me a 'silent sister,' like that Ottilie Kneifer Settembrini told us of." He walked about, pressing down the thermometer with his tongue.

The time crept on; the term seemed unending. When he looked at his watch, two and a half minutes had passed—-and he had feared the seven minutes were already more than up. He did a thousand things: picked up objects about the room and set them down again, walked out on the balcony—-taking care that his cousin should not notice his presence—-and looked at the landscape of this high valley, now so familiar to him in all its phases; with its horns, its crests and walls, with the projecting wing of the "Brembühl," the ridge of which sloped steeply down to the valley, its flanks covered with rugged undergrowth, with its formations on the right side of the valley, whose names were no less familiar than the others, and the Alteinwand, which from this point appeared to close in the valley on the south. He looked down on the garden beds and paths, the grotto and the silver fir; he listened to the murmur that rose from the rest--hall; and he returned to his room, settling the thermometer under his tongue. Then, with a motion of the arm which drew away the sleeve from his wrist, he brought the forearm before his eyes and found that by dint of pushing and shoving, pulling and hauling, he had managed to get rid of full six minutes. The last one he spent standing in the middle of the room—-but then, unfortunately, he let his thoughts wander and fell into a "doze," so that the sixty seconds flew by on the wings of the wind; and, when he looked again, the eighth minute was already past its first quarter.

"It doesn't really matter, so far as the result is concerned," he thought, and tearing the instrument out of his mouth, he stared at it in confusion.

He was not immediately the wiser. The gleam of the quicksilver fell with the reflection of the glass case where the light struck it, and he could not tell whether the mercury had ascended the whole length of the column, or whether it was not there at all. He brought the instrument close to his eyes, turned it hither and thither——all to no purpose. But at last a lucky turn gave him a clearer view; he hastily arrested his hand and brought his intelligence to bear. Mercurius, in fact, had climbed up again, just as the Frau Directress said. The column was perceptibly lengthened; it stood several of the black strokes above normal. Hans Castorp had 99.6°.

Ninety--nine and six tenths degrees in broad daylight, between ten and half past in the morning. That was too much; it was "temperature." It was fever consequent on an infection, for which his system had been eager. The question was now, what kind of infection? 99.6°——why, Joachim had no more, nor anyone else up here, except the moribund and bedridden. Not Fräulein Kleefeld with her pneumothorax, nor——nor Madame Chauchat. Naturally, in his case it was not the same kind, certainly not; he had what would have been called at home a feverish cold. But the distinction was not such a simple one to make. Hans Castorp doubted whether the fever had only come on when the cold did, and he regretted not having consulted a thermometer at the outset, when the Hofrat suggested it. He could see now that this had been very reasonable advice; Settembrini had been wrong to sneer at it as he had——Settembrini, with his republic and his *bello stile*. Hans Castorp loathed and contemned the republic and the *bello stile* as he stood there consulting his thermometer; he kept on losing the mark and turning the instrument this way and that to find it again. Yes, it registered 99.6°——and this in the early part of the day!

He was thoroughly upset. He walked the length of the room twice or thrice, the thermometer held horizontally in his hand, so as not to jiggle it and make it read differently. Then he carefully deposited it on the wash--hand--stand, and went with his overcoat and rugs into the balcony. Sitting down, he threw the covers about him, with practised hand, first from one side, then from the other, and lay still, waiting until it should be time for Joachim to fetch him for second breakfast. Now and then he smiled——it was precisely as though he smiled *at* somebody. And now and then his breast heaved as he caught his breath and was seized with his bronchial cough. Joachim found him still lying when he entered at eleven o'clock at sound of the gong for second breakfast.

"Well?" he asked in surprise, coming up to his cousin's chair.

Hans Castorp sat awhile without answering, looking in front of him. Then he said: "Well, the latest is that I have some fever."

"What do you mean?" Joachim asked. "Do you feel feverish?"

Again Hans Castorp let him wait a little for the answer, then delivered himself airily as follows: "Feverish, my dear fellow, I have felt for a long time——all the time I have been up here, in fact. But at the moment it is not a matter of subjective emotion, but of fact. I have taken my temperature."

"You've taken your temperature? What with?" Joachim cried, startled.

"With a thermometer, naturally," answered Hans Castorp, not without a caustic tinge to his voice. "Frau Director sold me one. Why she should call me young 'un I can't imagine. It is distinctly not *comme il faut*. But she lost no time in selling me an excellent thermometer; if you would like to convince yourself, you can; it is there on the wash--hand--stand. It is only slight fever."

Joachim turned on his heel and went into the bedroom. When he came back, he said hesitatingly: "Yes, it is 99.5½°."

"Then it has gone down a little," his cousin responded hastily. "It was six."

"But you can't call that slight fever," Joachim said. "Certainly not for the forenoon. This is a pretty how--d'ye--do!" And he stood by his cousin's side as one stands before a how--d'ye--do, arms akimbo and head dropped. "You'll have to go to bed."

Hans Castorp had his answer ready. "I can't see," he remarked, "why I should go to bed with a temperature of 99.6° when the rest of you, who haven't any less, can run about as you like."

"But that is different," Joachim said. "Your fever is acute and harmless, the result of a cold."

"In the first place," said Hans Castorp, speaking with dignity and dividing his remarks into categories, "I cannot comprehend why, with a harmless fever——assuming for the moment, that there is such a thing——one must keep one's bed, while with one that is not harmless you needn't. And secondly, I tell you the fever has not made me hotter than I was before. My position is that 99.6° is 99.6°. If you can run about with it, so can I."

"But I had to lie for four weeks when I first came," objected Joachim, "and they only let me get up when it was clear that the fever persisted even after I had lain in bed."

Hans Castorp smiled. "Well, and——?" he asked. "I thought it was different with you. It seems to me you are contradicting yourself; first you say our cases are different; then you say they are alike. That seems sheer twaddle to me."

Joachim made a right--about turn. When he turned round again, his sun--tanned visage showed an even darker shade.

"No," he said, "I am not saying they are alike; you're getting muddled. I only mean that you've a very nasty cold. I can hear it in your voice, and you ought to go to bed, to cut it short, if you mean to go home next week. But if you don't want to——I mean go to bed——why, don't. I am not prescribing for you. Anyhow, let's go to breakfast. Make haste, we are late already."

"Right--oh!" said Hans Castorp, and flung off his covers. He went into his room to run the brush over his hair, and Joachim looked again at the thermometer on the washhand--stand. Hans Castorp watched him. They went down, silently, and took their places in the dining--room, which, as always at this hour, shimmered white with milk. The dwarf waitress brought Hans Castorp his Kulmbacher beer, as usual, but he put on a long face and waved it away. He would drink no beer to--day; he would drink nothing at all, or at most a swallow of water. The attention of his table--mates was attracted: they wanted to know the cause of his caprice. Hans Castorp said carelessly that he had a little fever—-really minimal: 99.6°.

Then how altogether ludicrous it was to see them! They shook their fingers at him, they winked maliciously, they put their heads on one side, crooked their forefingers beside their ears and waggled them in a pantomime suggestive of their delight at having found him out, who had played the innocent so long.

"Aha," said the schoolmistress, the flush mounting in her ancient cheek, "what sort of scandal is this?"

And "Aha, aha!" went Frau Stöhr too, holding her stumpy finger next her stumpy nose. "So our respected guest has some temperament too! Foxy--loxy is in the same boat with the rest of us after all!"

Even the great--aunt, when the news travelled up to her end of the table, gave him a meaningful glance and smile; pretty Marusja, who had barely looked at him up to now, leaned over and stared, with her round brown eyes, her handkerchief to her lips—-and shook her finger too. Frau Stöhr whispered the news to Dr. Blumenkohl, who could hardly do otherwise than join in the game, though without looking at Hans Castorp. Only Miss Robinson sat as she always did and took no share in what was going on. Joachim kept his eyes on the table--cloth.

It flattered Hans Castorp's vanity to be taken so much notice of; but he felt that modesty required him to disclaim their attentions. "No, no," he said. "You are all mistaken, my fever is the most harmless thing in the world; I simply have a cold, my eyes run, and my chest is stopped up. I have coughed half the night; it is thoroughly unpleasant of course."—-But they would not listen; they laughed and flapped their hands at him.

"Yes, of course, we know all about it—-we know these colds; they are all gammon—-you can't fool us!" and with one accord they challenged Hans Castorp to an examination on the spot. The news excited them. Throughout the meal their table was the liveliest among the seven. Frau Stöhr became almost hysterical. Her peevish face looked scarlet above her neck--ruche, and tiny purple veins showed in the cheeks. She began to talk about how fascinating it was to cough. It was a solid satisfaction, when you felt a tickling come in your chest, deep down, and grow and grow, to reach down after it, and get at it, so to say. Sneezing was much the same thing. You kept on wanting to sneeze until you simply couldn't stand it any longer; you looked as if you were tipsy; you drew a couple of breaths; then out it came, and you forgot everything else in the bliss of the sensation. Sometimes the explosion repeated itself two or three times. That was the sort of pleasure life gave you free of charge. Another one was the joy of scratching your chilblains in the spring, when they itched so gorgeously; you took a furious pleasure in scratching till the blood came; and if you happened to look in the glass you would be astonished to see the ghastly face you made.

The coarse creature regaled the table with these repulsive details throughout the brief but hearty meal. When it was over, the cousins walked down to the Platz; Joachim seemed preoccupied; Hans Castorp was in an agony of snuffles and cleared his rasping throat continually.

On the way home Joachim said: "I'll make you a suggestion. To--morrow, after midday meal, I have my regular monthly examination. It is not the general; Behrens just auscultates a little and has Krokowski make some notes. You might come along and ask them to listen to you a bit. It is too absurd——if you were at home, you would send for Heidekind, and up here, with two specialists in the house, you run about and don't know where you are, nor how serious it is, and if it would not be better for you to go to bed."

"Very good," said Hans Castorp. "It's as you say, of course. I can do that. And it will be interesting to see an examination."

Thus it was settled between them, and it fell out that as they arrived before the sanatorium, they met the Hofrat himself, and took the occasion to put their request at once.

Behrens came out of the vestibule, tall and stooped, a bowler hat on the back of his head, a cigar in his mouth; purple--cheeked, watery--eyed, in the full flow of his professional activities. He had just come from the operating--room, so he said, and was on his way to private practice in the village.

"Morning, gentlemen, morning," he said. "Always on the jump, eh? How's everything in the big world? I've just come from an unequal duel with saw and scalpel—great thing, you know, resection of ribs. Fifty per cent of the cases used to be left on the table. Nowadays we have it down finer than that; but even so it's a good plan to get the *mortis causa* fixed up beforehand. The chap to--day knew how to take the joke—put up a good fight for a minute or so.—-Crazy thing, a human thorax that's all gone; pulpy, you know, nothing to catch hold of—slight confusion of ideas, so to speak. Well, well—-and how are your constitutionalities? Sanctified metabolisms functioning O.K., doing their duty in the sight of the Lord? The walks go better in company, Ziemssen, old fellow, what? Hello, what are you crying about, Mr. Tripper?" He suddenly turned on Hans Castorp. "It's against the rules to cry in public—-they might all start!"

"It's only my cold, Herr Hofrat," answered Hans Castorp. "I don't know how I did it, but I've a simply priceless catarrh. It's right down on my chest, and I cough a good deal too."

"Indeed!" Behrens remarked. "You ought to consult a reliable physician."

Both cousins laughed, and Joachim answered, heels together: "We were just going to, Herr Hofrat. I have my examination to--morrow, and we wanted to ask if you would be so kind as to look my cousin over as well. The question is whether he will be well enough to travel on Tuesday."

"A. Y. S.," said Behrens. "At your service. With all the pleasure in life. Ought to have done it long ago. Once you are up here, why not? But one doesn't like to seem forth--putting. Very good then, to--morrow at two—-directly after grub."

"I have a little fever too." Hans Castorp further observed.

"You don't say!" Behrens cried out. "I suppose you think you are telling me news?

Do you think I've no eyes in my head?" He pointed with his great index finger to his goggling, bloodshot, watery eyes. "Well, and how much?"

Hans Castorp modestly mentioned the figure.

"Forenoon, eh? H'm, that's not so bad. Not bad at all, for a beginner—-shows talent. Very good then, the two of you, tomorrow at two. Very much honoured. Well, so long—-enjoy yourselves!" He paddled away downhill, his knees bent, leaving a long streamer of cigar smoke behind him.

"Well, that came out just as you wanted it to," Hans Castorp said. "We couldn't have struck it luckier, and now I am in for it. He won't be able to do much, of course—-he may prescribe some sort of pectoral syrup or some cough lozenges. However, it is good to have a little encouragement when you feel the way I do. But for heaven's sake what makes him rattle on so? It struck me as funny at first, but in the long run I can't say I like it. 'Sanctified metabolism'—-what sort of gibberish is that?

If I understand what he means by metabolism, it is nothing but physiology, and to talk about its being sanctified—-irreverent, I call it. I don't enjoy seeing him smoke, either; it distresses me, because I know it is not good for him and gives him melancholia. Settembrini said his joviality is forced, and one must admit that Settembrini has his own views and knows whereof he speaks. I probably ought to have more opinions of my own, as he says, and not take everything as it comes, the way I do. But sometimes one starts out with having

[221]

an opinion and feeling righteous indignation and all that, and then something comes up that has nothing to do with judgments and criticism, and then it is all up with your severity, and you feel disgusted with the republic and the *bello stile*——"

He rambled on incoherently, not clear himself as to what he wanted to say. His cousin merely gave him a side glance, then turned away with an *au revoir*, and each betook him to his own balcony.

"How much?" asked Joachim softly, after a while——as though he had seen Hans Castorp consult his thermometer.

And the latter answered indifferently: "Nothing new."

He had in fact, directly he entered, taken up his new acquisition from the washhand--stand and plunged it repeatedly through the air, to obliterate the morning's record. Then he went into the balcony with the glass cigar in his mouth, like an old hand. But contrary to some rather exaggerated expectations, Mercurius climbed no further than before——though Hans Castorp kept the instrument under his tongue eight minutes for good measure. But after all, 99.6° was unquestionably fever, even though no higher than the earlier record. In the afternoon the gleaming column mounted up as far as 99.7°, but declined to 99.5° by evening, when the patient was weary with the excitement of the day. Next morning it showed 99.6°, climbing during the morning to the same level as before. And so arrived the hour for the main meal of the day, bringing the examination in its wake.

Hans Castorp later recalled that Madame Chauchat was wearing that day a goldenyellow sweater, with large buttons and embroidered pockets. It was a new sweater, at least new to Hans Castorp, and when she made her entrance, tardily as usual, she had paused an instant and, in the way he knew so well, presented herself to the room. Then she had glided to her place at the table, slipped softly into it, and begun to eat and chatter to her table--mates. All this was as it happened every day, five times a day; Hans Castorp observed it as usual, or perhaps even more poignantly than usual, looking over at the "good" Russian table past Settembrini's back, as he sat at the crosswise table between. He saw the turn of her head in conversation, the rounded neck, the stooping back. Frau Chauchat, for her part, never once turned round during the whole meal. But when the sweet had been handed, and the great clock on the wall above the "bad" Russian table struck two, it actually happened, to Hans Castorp's amazement and mystification, that precisely as the hour struck, one, two, the fair patient turned her head and a little twisted her body and looked over her shoulder quite openly and pointedly at Hans Castorp's table. And not only at his table. No, she looked at himself, unmistakably and personally, with a smile about the closed lips and the narrow, Pribislav eyes, as though to say: "Well, it is time: are you going?" And the eyes said thou, for that is the language of the eyes, even when the tongue uses a more formal address. This episode shook and bewildered Hans Castorp to the depths of his being. He hardly trusted his senses, and at first gazed enraptured in Frau Chauchat's face, then, lifting his eyes, stared into vacancy over the top of her head. Was it possible she knew he was to be examined at two o'clock? It looked like it; but that was as impossible as that she should be aware of the thought that had visited his mind in the last minute; namely, that he might as well send word to the Hofrat, through Joachim, that his cold was better, and he considered an examination superfluous. This idea had presented itself to him in an advantageous light, but now withered away under that searching smile, transmuted into a hideous sense of futility. The second after, Joachim had laid his rolled-up serviette beside his plate, signalled to his cousin by raising his eyebrows, and with a bow to the company risen from the table. Whereat Hans Castorp, inwardly reeling, though outwardly firm in step and bearing, rose too, and feeling that look and smile upon his back, followed Cousin Joachim out of the room.

Since the previous morning they had not spoken of what lay before them, and silently now they moved down the corridor together. Joachim hastened his steps, for it was already past the appointed hour, and Hofrat Behrens laid stress on punctuality. They passed the door of the office and went down the clean linoleum--covered stairs to the "basement." Joachim knocked at the door facing them; it bore a porcelain shield with the word *Consulting--room.*

"Come in," called Behrens, stressing the first word. He was standing in the middle of the room, in his white smock, holding the black stethoscope in his hand and tapping his thigh with it.

"*Tempo, tempo,*" said he, directing his goggling gaze to the clock on the wall. "*Un poco piu presto, signori!* We are not here simply and solely for the honourable gentlemen's convenience."

Dr. Krokowski was sitting at the double--barrelled writing--table by the window. He wore his usual black alpaca shirt, setting off the pallor of his face; his elbows rested on the table, in one hand a pen, the other fingering his beard; while before him lay various papers, probably the documents in reference to the patients to be examined. He looked at the cousins as they entered, but it was with the idle glance of a person who is present only in an auxiliary capacity.

"Well, give us your report card," the Hofrat answered to Joachim's apologies, and took the fever chart out of his hand. He looked it over, while the patient made haste to lay off his upper garments down to the waist and hang them on the rack by the door. No one troubled about Hans Castorp. He looked on awhile standing, then let himself down in a little old--fashioned easy--chair with bob--tassels on the arms, beside a small table with a carafe on it. Bookcases lined the walls, full of pamphlets and broadbacked medical works. Other furniture there was none, except an adjustable chaiselongue covered with oilcloth. It had a paper serviette spread over the pillow.

"Point 7, point 9, point 8," Behrens said running through the weekly card, whereon were entered the results of Joachim's five daily "measurings." "Still a little too much lighted up, my dear Ziemssen. Can't exactly say you've got more robust just lately"——by the lately he meant during the past four weeks.——"Not free from infection," he said. "Well, that doesn't happen between one day and the next; we're not magicians."

Joachim nodded and shrugged his bare shoulders. He refrained from saying that he had been up here since a good deal longer than yesterday.

"How about the stitches in the right hilum, where it always sounded so sharp?

Better? eh? Well, come along, let me thump you about a bit." And the auscultation began.

The Hofrat stood leaning backwards, feet wide apart, his stethoscope under his arm, and tapped from the wrist, using the powerful middle finger of his right hand as a hammer, and the left as a support. He tapped first high up on Joachim's shoulderblade at the side of the back, above and below—-the well--trained Joachim lifting his arm to let himself be tapped under the arm--pit. Then the process was repeated on the left side; then the Hofrat commanded: "Turn!" and began tapping the chest; first next the collar--bone, then above and below the breast, right and left. When he had tapped to his satisfaction, he began to listen, setting his stethoscope on Joachim's chest and back, and putting his ear to the ear--piece. Then Joachim had to breathe deeply and cough—-which seemed to strain him, for he got out of breath, and tears came in his eyes. And everything that the Hofrat heard he announced in curt, technical phrases to his assistant over at the writing--table, in such a way that Hans Castorp was forcibly reminded of the proceedings at the tailor's when a very correctly groomed gentleman measures you for a suit, laying the tape about your trunk and limbs and calling off the figures in the order hallowed by tradition for the assistant to take them down in his book. "Faint," "diminished," dictated Hofrat Behrens. "Vesicular," and then again "vesicular" (that was good, apparently). "Rough," he said, and made a face. "Very rough." "Rhonchi." And Dr. Krokowski entered it all in his book, just like the tailor's assistant.

Hans Castorp followed the proceedings with his head on one side, absorbed in contemplation of his cousin's torso. The ribs—-thank Heaven, he had them all!—-rose under the taut skin as he took deep inhalations, and the stomach fell away. Hans Castorp studied that youthful figure, slender, yellowish--bronze, with a black fell along the breastbone and the powerful arms. On one wrist Joachim wore a gold chainbracelet. "Those are the arms of an athlete," thought Hans Castorp. "I never made much of gymnastics, but he always liked them, and that is partly the reason why he wanted to be a soldier. He has always been more inclined than I to the things of the body——or inclined in a different way. I've always been a civilian and cared more about warm baths and good eating and drinking, whereas he has gone in for manly exertion. And now his body has come into the foreground in another sense and made itself important and independent of the rest of him——namely, through illness. He is all 'lit up' within and can't get rid of the infection and become healthy, poor Joachim, no matter how much he wants to get down to the valley and be a soldier. And yet look how he is developed, like a picture in a book, a regular Apollo Belvedere, except for the hair. But the disease makes him ailing within and fevered without; disease makes men more physical, it leaves them nothing but body"——his own thought startled him, and he looked quickly at Joachim with a questioning glance, that travelled from the bared body up to the large, gentle black eyes. Tears stood out in them, from the effort of the forced breathing and coughing and they gazed into space with a pathetic expression as the examination went on.

But at last Hofrat Behrens had come to an end. "Very good, Ziemssen," he said.

"Everything in order, so far as possible. Next time" (that would be in four weeks) "it is bound to show further improvement."

"And Herr Hofrat, how much longer do you think——"

"So you are going to pester me again? How do you expect to give your lads the devil down below, in the lit--up state you are in? I told you the other day to call it half a year; you can reckon from then if you like, but you must regard it as minimal. Have a little ordinary politeness! It's a decent enough life up here, after all; it's not a convict prison, nor a Siberian penal settlement! Or perhaps you think it is? Very good, Ziemssen, be off with you! Next! Step lively!" He stretched out his arm and handed the stethoscope to Dr. Krokowski, who got up and began some supernumerary tapping on Joachim's person.

Hans Castorp had sprung up. With his eyes fixed on the Hofrat, standing there with his legs apart and his mouth open, lost in thought, the young man began in all haste to make ready, with the result that he defeated his own purpose and fumbled in getting out of his shirt. But finally he stood there, blond, white--skinned, and narrow--chested, before Hofrat Behrens. Compared with Joachim, he looked distinctly the civilian type. The Hofrat, still lost in thought, let him stand. Dr. Krokowski had finished and sat down, and Joachim was dressing before Behrens finally decided to take notice.

"Oh--ho!" he said, "so that's you, is it?" He gripped Hans Castorp on the upper arm with his mighty hand, pushed him away, and looked at him sharply——not in the face, as one man looks at another, but at his body; turned him round, as one would turn an inanimate object, and looked at his back. "H'm," he said. "Well, we shall see." And began tapping as before.

He tapped all over, as he had with Joachim, and several times went back and tapped again. For some while, for purposes of comparison, he tapped by turns on the lefthand side near the collar--bone, and then somewhat lower down.

"Hear that?" he asked Dr. Krokowski. And the other, sitting at the table five paces off, nodded to signify that he did. He sunk his head on his chest with a serious mien, and the points of his whiskers stuck out.

"Breathe deep! Cough!" commanded the Hofrat, who had taken up the stethoscope again; and Hans Castorp worked hard for eight or ten minutes, while the Hofrat listened. He uttered no word, simply set the instrument here or there and listened with particular care at the places he had tapped so long. Then he stuck the stethoscope under his arm, put his hands on his back, and looked at the floor between himself and Hans Castorp.

"Yes, Castorp," he said—-this was the first time he had called the young man simply by his last name—-"the thing works out *præter propter* as I thought it would. I had my suspicions—-I can tell you now—-from the first day I had the undeserved honour of making your acquaintance; I made a pretty shrewd guess that you were one of us and that you would find it out, like many another who has come up here on a lark and gone about with his nose in the air, only to discover, one fine day, that it would be as well for him—-and not only *as* well, mark that—-to make a more extended stay, quite without reference to the beauties of the scenery."

Hans Castorp had flushed; Joachim, in act to button his braces, paused as he stood, and listened.

"You have such a kind, sympathetic cousin over there," went on the Hofrat, motioning with his head in Joachim's direction and balancing himself on his heels.

"Very soon, we hope, we will be able to say that he *has been* ill; but even when he gets that far, it will still be true that he *has been* ill—-and the fact—- *a priori*, as the philosophers say—-casts a certain light upon yourself, my dear Castorp.

"But he is only my step--cousin, Herr Hofrat."

"Tut! You won't disown him, will you? Even a step--cousin is a blood relation. On which side?"

"The mother's, Herr Hofrat. He is the son of a step—-"

"And your mother—-she's pretty jolly?"

"No, she is dead. She died when I was little."

"And of what?"

"Of a blood--clot, Herr Hofrat."

"A blood--clot, eh? Well, that's a long time ago. And your father?"

"He died of pneumonia," Hans Castorp said; "and my grandfather too," he added.

"Both of them, eh? Good. So much for your ancestors. Now about yourself—-you have always been rather chlorotic, haven't you? But you didn't tire easily at physical or mental work. Or did you—-what? A good deal of palpitation? Only of late? Good. And a strong inclination to catarrhal and bronchial trouble?—-Did you know you have been infected before now?"

"I?"

"Yes, you—-I have you personally in mind. Can you hear any difference?" The Hofrat tapped by turns on Hans Castorp's left side, first above and then lower down.

"It sounds rather duller there," said Hans Castorp.

"Capital. You ought to be a specialist. Well, that is a dullness, and such dullnesses are caused by the old places, where fibrosis has supervened. Scars, you know. You are an old patient, Castorp, but we won't lay it up against anybody that you weren't found out. The early diagnosis is very difficult—particularly for my colleagues down below; I won't say we have better ears—-though the regular practice does do something. But the air helps us, helps us hear, if you understand what I mean, this thin, dry air up here."

"Certainly, of course," Hans Castorp said.

"Very good, Castorp. And now listen, young man, to my words of wisdom. If that were all the trouble with you, if it was a case of nothing but the dullness and the scars on your bagpipe in there, I should send you back to your lares and penates and not trouble my head further about you. But as things stand, and according to what we find, and since you are already up here—well, there is no use in your going down, for you'd only have to come up again."

Hans Castorp felt the blood rush back to his heart; it hammered violently; and Joachim still stood with his hands on his back buttons, his eyes on the floor.

"For besides the dullness," said the Hofrat, "you have on the upper left side a rough breathing that is almost bronchial and undoubtedly comes from a fresh place. I won't call it a focus of softening, but it is certainly a moist spot, and if you go down below and begin to carry on, why, you'll have the whole lobe at the devil before you can say Jack Robinson."

Hans Castorp stood motionless. His mouth twitched fearfully, and the hammering of his heart against his ribs was plain to see. He looked across at Joachim, but could not meet his cousin's eye; then again in the Hofrat's face, with its blue cheeks, blue, goggling eyes, and little, crooked moustache.

"For independent confirmation," Behrens continued, "we have your temperature of 99.6° at ten o'clock in the morning, which corresponds pretty well to the indications given by the auscultation."

"I thought," Hans Castorp said, "that the fever came from my cold."

"And the cold," rejoined the Hofrat, "where does that come from? Listen, Castorp, let me tell you something, and mark my words—-for so far as I can tell, you've all the cerebral convolutions a body needs. Now: our air up here is good for the disease—-I mean good *against* the disease, you understand—-you think so, don't you? Well, it is true. But also it is good *for* the disease; it begins by speeding it up, in that it revolutionizes the whole body; it brings the latent weakness to the surface and makes it break out. Your catarrh, fortunately for you, is a breaking--out of that kind. I can't tell if you were febrile down below; but it is certainly my opinion that you have been from your first day up here, and not merely since you had your catarrh."

"Yes," Hans Castorp said, "I think so too."

"You were probably fuddled right from the start, in my opinion," the Hofrat confirmed him. "Those were the soluble toxins thrown off by the bacteria; they act like an intoxicant upon the central nervous system and give you a hectic flush. Now, Castorp, we'll stick you into bed and see if a couple of weeks' rest will sober you up. What follows will follow. We'll take a handsome x--ray of you——you'll enjoy seeing what goes on in your own inside. But I tell you straightaway, a case like yours doesn't get well from one day to the next: it isn't a question of the miracle cures you read about in advertisements. I thought when I first clapped eyes on you that you would be a better patient than your cousin, with more talent for illness than our brigadiergeneral here, who wants to clear out directly he has a couple of points less fever. As if 'lie down' isn't just as good a word of command as 'stand up'! It is the citizen's first duty to be calm, and impatience never did any good to anyone. Now, Castorp, watch out you don't disappoint me and give the lie to my knowledge of human nature! Get along now, into the caboose with you——march!"

With that Hofrat Behrens closed the interview and sat down at the writing--table; this man of many occupations began to fill in his time with writing until the advent of the next patient. But Dr. Krokowski arose from his place and strode up to Hans Castorp. With his head tipped back sideways, and one hand on the young man's shoulder, smiling so heartily that the yellowish teeth showed in his beard, he shook him warmly by the hand.

CHAPTER V

Soup--Everlasting

And now we are confronted by a phenomenon upon

which the author himself may well comment, lest the reader do so in his stead. Our account of the first three weeks of Hans Castorp's stay with "those up here"—-twenty--one midsummer days, to which his visit, so far as human eye could see, should have been confined—-has consumed in the telling an amount of time and space only too well confirming the author's halfconfessed expectations; while our narrative of his next three weeks will scarcely cost as many lines, or even words and minutes, as the earlier three did pages, quires, hours, and working--days. We apprehend that these next three weeks will be over and done with in the twinkling of an eye.

Which is perhaps surprising; yet quite in order, and conformable to the laws that govern the telling of stories and the listening to them. For it is in accordance with these laws that time seems to us just as long, or just as short, that it expands or contracts precisely in the way, and to the extent, that it did for young Hans Castorp, our hero, whom our narrative now finds visited with such an unexpected blow from the hand of fate. It may even be well at this point to prepare the reader for still other surprises, still other phenomena, bearing on the mysterious element of time, which will confront us if we continue in our hero's company.

For the moment we need only recall the swift flight of time—-even of a quite considerable period of time—-which we spend in bed when we are ill. All the days are nothing but the same day repeating itself—-or rather, since it is always the same day, it is incorrect to speak of

repetition; a continuous present, an identity, an everlastingness—
-such words as these would better convey the idea. They bring you
your midday broth, as they brought it yesterday and will bring it to-
-morrow; and it comes over you—but whence or how you do not
know, it makes you quite giddy to see the broth coming in—that you
are losing a sense of the demarcation of time, that its units are
running together, disappearing; and what is being revealed to you as
the true content of time is merely a dimensionless present in which
they eternally bring you the broth. But in such a connexion it would
be paradoxical to speak of time as passing slowly; and paradox, with
reference to such a hero, we would avoid. Hans Castorp, then, went
to bed on the Saturday afternoon, as it had been ordained by Hofrat
Behrens, the highest authority in our little world. There he lay, in his
nightshirt with the embroidered monogram on the pocket, his hands
clasped at the back of his head, in his cleanly white bed, the death-
-bed of the American woman and in all probability of many another
person; lay there with his confiding blue eyes, somewhat glassy with
his cold, directed toward the ceiling, and contemplated the singularity
of his fate. This is not to say that, if he had not had a cold, his gaze
would have been any clearer or more single--minded. No, just as it
was, it accurately mirrored his inner state, and that, whatever its
simplicity, was full of troubled, involved, dubious, not quite
ingenuous thoughts. For as he lay, he would be shaken from deep
within him by a frantic burst of triumphant laughter, while his heart
stood still with an anguish of extravagant anticipation like nothing he
had ever known before; again, he would feel such a shudder of
apprehension as sent the colour from his cheek, and then it was
conscience itself that knocked, in the very throbs of his heart as it
pulsed against his ribs.

On that first day Joachim left him to his rest, avoiding all
discussion. He went two or three times tactfully into the sickroom,
nodded to the patient, and inquired if he could do anything. It was
easy for him to understand and respect Hans Castorp's reserve—the

more in that he shared it, even feeling his own position to be more difficult than the other's.

But on Sunday forenoon, when he came back from the walk which for the first time in weeks had been solitary, there was no putting it off any longer; they must take counsel together over the necessary next step.

He sat down by the bed and said, with a sigh: "Yes, it's no good; we must act—they are expecting you down home."

"Not yet," Hans Castorp answered.

"No, but inside the next few days, Wednesday or Thursday."

"Oh, they aren't expecting me so precisely on a particular day," Hans Castorp said.

"They have other things to do besides counting the days until I get back. I'll be there when I get there and Uncle Tienappel will say: 'Oh, there you are again,' and Uncle James: 'Well, had a good time?' And if I don't arrive, it will be some time before they notice it, you may be sure of that. Of course, after a while we'd have to let them know."

"You can see how unpleasant the thing is for me," Joachim said, sighing again.

"What is to happen now? I feel in a way responsible. You come up here to pay me a visit, I take you in, and here you are, and who knows when you can get away and go into your position down below? You must see how extremely painful that is to me."

"Just a moment," said Hans Castorp, without removing his hands from their clasped position behind his neck. "Surely it is unreasonable for you to break your head over it. Did I come up here to visit you? Well, of course in a way I did; but after all, the principal reason was to get the rest Heidekind prescribed. Well, and now it appears I need more of a rest than he or any of us dreamed. I am not the first who thought of making a flying visit up here for whom it fell out differently. Remember about Tousles--deux's second son, and how it turned out with him—-I don't know whether he is still alive or not; perhaps they have fetched him away already, while we were sitting at our meal. That I am somewhat infected is naturally a great surprise to me; I must get used to the idea of being a patient and one of you, instead of just a guest. And yet in a way I am scarcely surprised, for I never have been in such blooming health, and when I think how young both my parents were when they died, I realize that it was natural I shouldn't be particularly robust! We can't deny that you had a weakness that way; we make no bones of it, even if it is as good as cured now, and it may easily be that it runs a little in the family, as Behrens suggested. Anyhow, I have been lying here since yesterday thinking it all over, considering what my attitude has been, how I felt toward the whole thing, to life, you know, and the demands it makes on you. A certain seriousness, a sort of disinclination to rough and noisy ways, has always been a part of my nature; we were talking about that lately, and I said I sometimes should have liked to be a clergyman, because I took such an interest in mournful and edifying things—-a black pall, you know, with a silver cross on it, or R. I. P.—- *requiescat in pace*, you know. That seems to me the most beautiful expression—-I like it much better than 'He's a jolly good fellow,' which is simply rowdy. I think all that comes from the fact that I have a weakness myself, and always felt at home with illness—-the way I do now. But things being as they are, I find it very lucky that I came here, and that I was examined. Certainly you have no call to reproach yourself. You heard what he said: if I were to go down and continue as I have been, I should have the whole lobe at the devil before I could say Jack Robinson."

"You can't tell," Joachim said. "That is just what you never can tell. They said you had already had places, of which nobody took any notice and they healed of themselves, and left nothing but a few trifling dullnesses. It might have been the same way with the moist spot you are supposed to have now, if you hadn't come up here at all. One can never know."

"No, as far as knowing goes, we never can. But just for that reason, we have no right to assume the worst—-for instance with regard to how long I shall be obliged to stop here. You say nobody knows when I shall be free to go into the ship--yard; but you say it in a pessimistic sense, and that I find premature, since we cannot know. Behrens did not set a limit; he is a long--headed man, and doesn't play the prophet. There are the x--ray and the photographic plate yet to come before we can definitely know the facts; who knows whether they will show anything worth talking about, and whether I shall not be free of fever before that, and can say good--bye to you. I am all for our not striking before the time and crying wolf to the family down below. It is quite enough for the present if we write and say—-I can do it myself with the fountainpen if I sit up a little—-that I have a severe cold and am febrile, that I am stopping in bed, and shall not travel for the present. The rest will follow."

"Good," said Joachim. "We can do that for the present. And for the other matters we can wait and see."

"What other matters?"

"Don't be so irresponsible! You only came for three weeks, and brought a steamer trunk. You will need underwear and linen, and winter clothes—-and more footwear. And anyhow, you will want money sent."

"If," said Hans Castorp, "*if* I need it."

"Very well, we'll wait and see. But we ought not"—-Joachim paced up and down the room as he spoke, "we ought not to behave like ostriches. I have been up here too long not to know how things go. When Behrens says there is a rough place, almost rhonchi—-oh well, of course, we can wait and see."

There, for the time, the matter rested; and the weekly and fortnightly variations of the normal day set in. Hans Castorp could partake of them even in his present state, if not at first hand, then through the reports Joachim gave when he came and sat by the bedside for fifteen minutes.

His Sunday morning breakfast--tray was adorned with a vase of flowers; and they did not fail to send him his share of the Sunday pastries. After luncheon the sounds of social intercourse floated up from the terrace below, and with tantara and squealing of clarinets the fortnightly concert began. During its progress Joachim entered, and sat down by the open balcony door; his cousin half reclined in his bed, with his head on one side, and his eyes swimming with pious enjoyment as he listened to the mounting harmonies, and bestowed a momentary metaphorical shoulder--shrug upon Settembrini's twaddle about music being "politically suspect."

And, as we have said, he had Joachim post him upon the sights and events of the sanatorium life. Had there, he asked, been any toilets made in honour of the day, lace matinées or that sort of thing?—-though for lace matinées the weather was too cold. Whether there were people going driving (certain expeditions had in fact been undertaken, among others by the Half--Lung Club, which had gone in a body to Clavadel). On the next day, Monday, he demanded to hear all about Dr. Krokowski's lecture, when Joachim came from it and looked in upon his cousin on his way to the rest--cure. Joachim did not feel like talking, he appeared disinclined to make a report. He would have let the subject drop, as it had after the previous lecture, had not Hans Castorp persisted, and demanded to hear details.

"I am lying up here," he said, "paying full pension. I am entitled to have all that is going." He recalled the Monday of two weeks ago, and his solitary walk, which had done him so little good; and committed himself to the view that it was that walk which had revolutionized his system and brought to the surface the latent infection.

"But what a stately and solemn way the people hereabout have of talking," he said, "I mean the common people; almost like poetry. 'Then thank ye kindly and God be with ye,' " he repeated, giving the words the woodman's intonation. "I heard that up in the woods, and I shall remember it all my life. You get to associate a thing like that with other memories and impressions, you know, and you never forget it as long as you live.——Well, so Krokowski held forth again on the subject of love, did he? What did he say about it to--day?"

"Oh, nothing in particular. You know from the other time how he talks."

"But what did he offer that was new?"

"Nothing different.——Oh, well, the stuff to--day was pure chemistry," Joachim unwillingly condescended to enlighten his cousin. It seemed there was a sort of poisoning, an auto--infection of the organisms, so Dr. Krokowski said; it was caused by the disintegration of a substance, of the nature of which we were still ignorant, but which was present everywhere in the body; and the products of this disintegration operated like an intoxicant upon the nerve--centres of the spinal cord, with an effect similar to that of certain poisons, such as morphia, or cocaine, when introduced in the usual way from outside.

"And so you get the hectic flush," said Hans Castorp. "But that's all worth hearing. What doesn't the man know! He must have simply lapped it up. You just wait, one of these days he will discover what that substance is that exists everywhere in the body and sets free the soluble toxins that act like a narcotic on the nervous system; then he will be able to fuddle us all more than ever. Perhaps in the past they were able to do that very thing. When I listen to him, I could almost think there is some truth in the old legends about love potions and the like.——Are you going?"

"Yes," Joachim said, "I must go lie down. My curve has been rising since yesterday. This affair of yours has had its effect on me."

That was the Sunday, and the Monday. The evening and the morning made the third day of Hans Castorp's sojourn in the "caboose." It was a day without distinction, an ordinary weekday, that Tuesday——but after all, it was the day of his arrival in this place, he had been here a round three weeks, and time pressed; he would have to send a letter home and inform his uncle of the state of affairs, even though cursorily and without reference to their true inwardness. He stuffed his down quilt behind his back, and wrote upon the note--paper of the establishment, to the effect that his departure was being delayed beyond the appointed time. He was in bed with a feverish cold, which Hofrat Behrens——over--conscientious as he probably was——refused to take lightly; insisting on regarding it as immediately connected with his (Hans Castorp's) constitution and general state of health. The physician had perceived directly he saw him that he was decidedly anæmic; and take it all in all, it seemed as though the limit he had originally set for his stay was not regarded by the authorities as long enough for a full recovery. He would write again as soon as he could.——That's the idea, thought Hans Castorp; not too much or too little; and whatever the issue, it will satisfy them for a while. The letter was given to the servant, with instructions that it be taken direct to the station and sent off by the earliest possible train, instead of being posted in the usual way in the house letter--box, with consequent delays.

Our adventurous youth felt much relieved to have set affairs in such good train——if likewise a good deal plagued by his cough and the heavy--headedness caused by his catarrh——and now he began to live each day as it came——a day which never varied, which was always broken up into a number of sections, and which, in its abiding uniformity, could not be said either to pass too fast or to hang too heavy on the hands. In the morning the bathing--master would give a mighty thump on the door and enter——a nervous individual named Turnherr, who wore his sleeves rolled up, and had great standing veins upon his forearms, and a gurgling, impeded speech. He addressed Hans Castorp, as he did all the patients, by the number of his room, and rubbed him with alcohol. Not long after he left, Joachim would appear ready dressed, to greet his cousin, inquire after his seven o'clock temperature, and communicate his own.

While he breakfasted below, Hans Castorp did the same above, his down quilt tucked behind his back, in enjoyment of the good appetite a change engenders. He was scarcely disturbed by the bustling and businesslike entrance of the two physicians, who at this hour made a hurried round of the dining--hall and the rooms of the bedridden and moribund. Hans Castorp, with his mouth full of jam, announced himself to have slept "splendidly" and looked over the rim of his cup at the Hofrat, who leaned with his fists on the centre table, and hastily scanned the fever chart. Both physicians wished him good--morning, and he responded in an unconcerned drawl as they went out. Then he lighted a cigarette, and beheld Joachim returning from the morning walk, almost before he realized his departure. Again they chatted of this and that; Joachim went to lie down until second breakfast, and the interval seemed so short that even the emptiest--headed could hardly have felt bored. Hans Castorp, indeed, had so much food for thought in the events of the past three weeks, so much to ponder in his present state and what might come of it, that although two bound volumes of an illustrated periodical from the Berghof library lay upon his night--table, he had no need to resort to them.

It was no different with the brief hour during which Joachim took his regular walk down to the Platz. He came in to Hans Castorp afterwards, told him whatever of interest he had seen, and sat or stood a few minutes by the sick--bed before he withdrew to his own balcony for the midday rest. And how long did that last? Again, only a brief hour. It seemed to Hans Castorp he had barely settled to commune a little with his own thoughts, hands folded behind his head and eyes directed upon the ceiling, before the gong droned through the house, summoning all those not bedridden or moribund to prepare for the principal meal of the day.

Joachim went down, and the "midday broth" was brought---"broth" in a symbolic sense merely, considering in what it consisted. Hans Castorp was not on sick--diet. He lay there and paid full pension, and what they brought him in the abiding present of that midday hour was by no means broth, it was the full six--course Berghof dinner, in all its amplitude, with nothing left out. Even on week--days this was a sumptuous meal; on Sundays it was a gala banquet and "gaudy," prepared by a cosmopolitan chef in the kitchens of the establishment, which were precisely those of a European hotel *de luxe*. The "dining--room girl" whose duty it was to serve the bedridden brought it to him in dainty cook--pots under nickel--plated dish--covers. She produced an invalid--table, a marvel of one--legged equilibrium, adjusted it across his bed, and Hans Castorp banqueted like the tailor's son in the fairy--story.

As he finished, Joachim would return, and it might be as late as half past two before the latter went into his loggia, and the hush of the main rest period fell upon the Berghof. Not quite, perhaps; perhaps it would be nearer the truth to call it a quarter after, but these odd quarter--hours outside the round figures do not count, they are swallowed up unregarded, in places where one reckons time in large units—on long train journeys of many hours on end, or wherever one is in a state of vacant suspense, with all one's being concentrated on pulling the time behind one. A quarter past two will pass for half past, will even pass for three, on the theory that it is already well on the way toward it. The thirty minutes are taken as a sort of onset to the full hour from three to four, and inwardly discounted. In this wise the duration of the main rest period was finally reduced to no more than an hour; and even this hour was lopped off at its latter end, elided, as it were. Dr. Krokowski played the part of apostrophe. Yes, nowadays when Dr. Krokowski went his independent afternoon round, he no longer made a circle round Hans Castorp; our young man was no longer an interval and hiatus, he counted as much as the others, he too was a patient. He was questioned, not ignored, as had so long been the case, to his slight and concealed but daily recurring annoyance. It was on Monday that Dr. Krokowski for the first time manifested himself in the room—manifested being the only proper word for the phenomenon as Hans Castorp, with an involuntary start, perceived it. He lay in half— or quarter—slumber, and became aware that the Assistant was beside him, having entered not through the door, but approaching from outside. His round at this time lay not through the corridor, but along the balconies, and he had come through the open door of the loggia with an effect of having flown through the air. There he stood at Hans Castorp's bedside, in all his pallor and blackness, broad--shouldered and squat, his lips parted in a manly smile that showed the yellowish teeth through his beard—-the apostrophe!

"You seem surprised to see me, Herr Castorp," he said, mildly baritone, drawling, unquestionably rather affected: he gave the *r* a foreign, palatal sound, not rolled, but pronounced with a single impact of the tongue against the upper front teeth. "But I am only performing my pleasant duty, in seeing after your welfare. Your relations with us have entered upon a new phase. Overnight the guest has become the comrade." His patient was rather alarmed by the word comrade.—-"Who would have thought it?" he jested fraternally. "Who would have thought it on that evening when I had the honour of making your acquaintance, and you replied to my mistaken supposition—-at that time mistaken—-with the explanation that you were perfectly healthy? I believe I expressed some doubt, but I assure you I did not mean it in that sense. I will not pretend to being more sharp--sighted than I am. I was not thinking of a moist spot. My remark was meant only in the general, philosophical sense, as a doubt whether the two conceptions, man and perfect health, were after all consistent one with the other. Even to--day, after the examination, I confess that I personally, as distinguished from my honoured chief, cannot regard the moist spot as the most important factor in the situation. It is, for me, a secondary phenomenon—-the organic is always secondary—-" Hans Castorp drew a short breath.

"—-and thus your catarrh is, in my view, a third--line phenomenon," Dr. Krokowski concluded, very softly. "How is it? The rest in bed will undoubtedly be efficacious, in this respect. What have you measured to--day?" And from then on the Assistant's visit was in the key of an ordinary professional call, to which it kept

[243]

during the following days and weeks. Dr. Krokowski would enter by the open balcony door at a quarter to four or earlier, greet the patient with manly readiness, put the usual professional questions, with perhaps a little personal touch as well, a jest or two——and if all this had a slight aura of the questionable about it, yet one can get used even to the questionable, provided it keeps within bounds. It was not long before Hans Castorp forgot any feeling he may have had about Dr. Krokowski's visits. They took their place in the programme of the normal day, and performed, as it were, an elision in the latter end of the main rest period.

The Assistant would return along the balconies at four o'clock or thereabouts, that is to say mid--afternoon. Yes, thus suddenly, before one realized it, there one was, in the very deep of the afternoon, and steadily still deepening on toward twilight. Before tea was finished drinking, up above and down below, it was well on the way toward five o'clock; and by the time Joachim returned from his third daily round and looked in on his cousin, it would be near enough to six to reduce the remaining rest period to no more than a single hour—-reckoned always in round numbers. It was an easy matter to kill that much time, if one had ideas in one's head, and a whole *orbis pictus* on the table to boot.

Joachim, on his way to the evening meal, stopped to say goodbye. Hans Castorp's tray was brought. The valley had long since filled with shadow, and darkened apace as he ate. When he had done, he leaned back against his down quilt, with the magic table cleared before him, and looked into the growing dusk, to--day's dusk, yet scarcely distinguishable from the dusk of yesterday or last week. It was evening——and had just been morning. The day, artificially shortened, broken into small bits, had literally crumbled in his hands and was reduced to nothing: he remarked it to himself with a start—-or, at any rate, he did at least remark; for to shudder at it was foreign to his years. It seemed to him that from the beginning of time he had been lying and looking thus.

One day——some ten or twelve had passed since Hans Castorp retired to bed——there was a knock on his door at about this hour, before Joachim had returned from dinner and the social half--hour. Upon Hans Castorp's inquiring "Come in," it opened, and Ludovico Settembrini appeared——and lo, on the instant the room was flooded with light. For the visitor's first motion, while still on the threshold, had been to turn on the electric light, which filled the room in a trice with vibrating brilliance, and reverberated from the gleaming white ceiling and furniture.

The Italian had been the only one of the guests after whom Hans Castorp had expressly asked in these days. Joachim indeed, when he stood or sat by his cousin for ten or fifteen minutes——and that happened ten times in the course of the day——would relate whatever there was of interest or variation in the daily life of the community; and Hans Castorp's questions, whenever he put any, had been of a general nature. The exile wished to know whether there were new guests, or if any of the familiar faces were absent; it seemed to gratify him that only the former was the case. There was one new--comer, a hollow--cheeked, green--complexioned young man, who had been given a place at the next table on the right with Frau Iltis and the ivory--skinned Levi. Hans Castorp might look forward to the pleasure of seeing him. So no one had left?

Joachim answered in a curt negative, his eyes on the ground. But he had to reply to this question every day or so, until at last he became restive and sought to answer once for all by saying that, so far as he knew, no one was purposing to leave——nobody did leave very much, up here, as a matter of fact.

But Hans Castorp had asked after Settembrini by name, and desired to hear what he had "said to it." To what? "Why, that I am in bed and supposed to be ill." Settembrini, it seemed, had expressed himself on the subject, though briefly. On the very day of Hans Castorp's disappearance he had come to find out his whereabouts of Joachim, obviously prepared to hear that the guest had departed; and on learning the explanation had responded only in Italian: first

"*Ecco!*" and then "*Poveretto!*"—-as much as to say: "There you are, poor chap!"—-It needed no more Italian than the cousins could boast to understand the sense in which he uttered the words. "Why '*poveretto*'?" Hans Castorp inquired. "He sits up here with his literature made of politics and humanism and he is very little good for the ordinary interests of life. He needn't look down his nose and pity me like that, I shall get down to the flat--land before he does."

And now Herr Settembrini stood here in the suddenly illuminated room—-Hans Castorp, who had raised himself on his elbow and turned blinking toward the door, recognized him and flushed. Settembrini wore, as usual, his thick coat with the wide lapels, a frayed turnover collar, and the check trousers. As he came from supper, he was armed with the usual wooden toothpick. The corner of his mouth, beneath the beautiful curve of his moustache, displayed the familiar fine, dry, critical smile.

"Good--evening, Engineer! May I be permitted to look in on you? If so, I need light—-you will pardon my taking it upon myself"—-and he waved his small hand toward the lamp in the ceiling. "You were absorbed in contemplation, I should not wish to disturb you. A tendency to meditate is surely natural under the circumstances, and if you want to talk, you have your cousin. You see, I am well aware that I am superfluous. But even so—-we live here close together, a sympathy springs up between man and man, intellectual and emotional sympathy.—-It has been a full week that we have not seen you. I began to think you had left, as I saw your place empty down in the refectory. The Lieutenant told me better—-or should we say worse, if that would not sound impolite? Well, and how are you? How do you feel? Not too much cast down, I hope?"

"Ah, that is you, Herr Settembrini! How friendly of you! Refectory—-oh, I say, that is good! Always at your jokes—-but do sit down. You are not disturbing me in the least. I was lying there musing—-no, musing is too much to say. I was simply too lazy to turn on the light. Thanks very much, I am subjectively as good as normal, and my cold is much better from lying in bed. But it was a secondary phenomenon, so everybody tells me. My temperature is still not what it should be, I have 99.5° to 99.7°, all the time."

"You take your temperature regularly?"

"Yes, six times a day, like the rest of you. Pardon me, I am still laughing at your calling our dining--hall a refectory. That is what they are called in a cloister, isn't it?

After all, there is some resemblance—-not that I have been in a cloister, but I imagine they are something like this. And I have the 'Rule' at my fingers' ends, and observe it faithfully."

"As a pious brother should. One might say that your novitiate is at an end and you have made your profession. My formal congratulations. You even say 'our' dininghall. But, without meaning to affront your manly dignity, you remind me more of a young nun than a monk, a regular new--shorn, innocent bride of Christ, with great martyrlike eyes. I have seen such lambs, here and there about the world; never without a certain—-a certain access of sensibility. Yes, your cousin has told me about it. So you had yourself examined after all, at the eleventh hour."

"Since I was febrile—-of course, Herr Settembrini. What do you want? If I had been at home, I should have consulted a physician. And here, at the source and fount so to speak, with two specialists in the house—-it would have been very strange—-"

"Of course, of course. And you took your temperature, too, before they told you to. But they did recommend it, from the beginning. And the Mylendonk slipped you the thermometer?"

"Slipped me—-? Since the occasion arose, I bought one from her."

"I understand. An irreproachable transaction. And how many months did the chief knock you down for? Good heavens, I have asked you that before! Do you remember?

You had just come. You answered with such assurance—-"

"Of course I remember. I have had many new experiences since that time, but that I remember as though it were yesterday. You were so amusing, and spoke of Behrens as the judge of the lower regions—-Radames, was it? No, wait, that is something else."

"Rhadamanthus? Yes, I may have called him that. I am afraid I do not remember every phrase that happens to well up to my lips."

"Rhadamanthus, of course. Minos and Rhadamanthus. And you spoke to us of Carducci at the same time—-"

"Pardon me, my dear young friend, we will, if you please, leave him out. The name, at this moment, sounds too strange upon your tongue."

"That's good too," laughed Hans Castorp. "But I have learned a good deal about him through you.—-Yes, at that time I had not the faintest suspicion, I answered you that I was here for three weeks, I did not know any different. The Kleefeld girl had just been whistling at me with her pneumothorax, I hardly knew where I was. But I was feeling febrile even then—-for the air up here is not only good *against* the illness, you know, it is also good *for* it, it sometimes brings it to the surface—-which is of course a necessary step in the cure."

"An alluring hypothesis. And has Hofrat Behrens also told you about the GermanRussian woman we had here last year—no, year before last—-for five months? He did not? He should have. A charming woman, of Russo--German origin, married, a young mother. She came from the Baltic provinces somewhere—-lymphatic, anæmic, but probably some more serious trouble as well. She spent a month here and complained that she felt ill all the time. They told her to be patient. Another month passes, she continues to assert that she is actually worse instead of better. They point out to her that only the physician can judge how she is—-she herself only knows how she feels; which does not signify. They are satisfied with the condition of her lung. Good. She says no more, she goes on with the cure, and loses weight by the week. The fourth month she faints during the examination. That is nothing, says Behrens, her lung is perfectly satisfactory. But by the fifth month she cannot get about, she goes to bed and writes to her husband, out in the Baltic provinces; Behrens gets a letter from him marked 'personal' and 'urgent' in a very firm hand—-I saw it myself. Yes, says Behrens, and shrugs his shoulders, it seems to be indicated that she certainly cannot stand the climate up here. The woman was beside herself. He ought to have said that before, she had felt it from the beginning, she declared—-they had killed her among them. Let us hope she recovered her strength when she went back to her husband."

"Oh, that's good, that's very good! You do tell stories capitally, Herr Settembrini; every word is so plastic. And that story about the girl that went bathing in the lake, the one they gave the 'silent sister' to take her temperature with—-I have often laughed at it, all by myself. Yes, what strange things do happen. One lives and learns. But my own case is still quite uncertain. The Hofrat is supposed to have discovered a trifling weakness, places where I was infected long ago, I heard them myself when, he tapped me, and some fresh places he can hear now—-what a funny word fresh is to use in such a connexion! But so far there are only the acoustic indications; real diagnostic certainty we shall only arrive at when I am about again, and the x--ray and photography have taken place. Then we shall have positive knowledge."

"You think so? You know that the photographic plate often shows spots that are taken for cavities when there are none there? And that, sometimes, it shows no spots although there is something there? *Madonna*—-the photographic plate! There was a young numismatician up here, with fever; and since he had fever, there were cavitiesplain to be seen on the plate. They could even hear them. They treated him for phthisis, and he died. The postmortem showed his lung to be sound; the cause of his death was some coccus or other."

"Oh, come, Herr Settembrini. Talking about post--mortems already. I haven't got that far yet, I assure you."

"Engineer, you are a wag."

"And you are an out--and--out critic and sceptic, I must say. You do not even believe in science. Can you see spots on your plate, Herr Settembrini?"

"Yes, it shows some spots."

"And you really are ill too?"

"Yes, I am unfortunately rather ill," replied Settembrini, and his head drooped. There was a pause, in which he gave a little cough. Hans Castorp, from his bed, regarded his guest, whom he had reduced to silence. It seemed to him that with his two simple inquiries he had refuted Settembrini's whole position, even the republic and the *bello stile*. And he did nothing on his side to resume the conversation. After a while Herr Settembrini straightened himself, with a smile.

"Tell me, Engineer," he said, "how have your family taken the news?"

"What news do you mean? Of my delayed return? Oh, my family, you know, consists of three uncles, a great--uncle and his two sons, who are more like my cousins. Other family I have none, I was doubly orphaned when I was very small. As to how they took it---they know as much, and as little, as I myself. At first, when I had to go to bed, I wrote that I had a severe cold, and could not travel. Yesterday, as it seemed rather long after all, I wrote again, saying that my catarrh had drawn Hofrat Behren's attention to the condition or my chest, and that he insisted I should remain until he is clear what the condition is. You may be perfectly sure they took it calmly---it didn't upset them."

"And your position? You spoke of a sphere of practical activity, where you were intending to enter shortly on certain duties."

"Yes, as volunteer apprentice. I have asked them to excuse me for the present. You must not imagine they are in despair over my defection. They can carry on indefinitely without an assistant."

"Good. Everything is in order, then, in that direction. Perfect equanimity all along the line. It is a phlegmatic race of people in your part of the country, is it not? But energetic, certainly?"

"Oh, yes, very energetic," said Hans Castorp. He mentally assayed the temper of his native city, and found that his interlocuter had characterized it justly. "Phlegmatic and energetic, yes, I should say they are."

"I assume," continued Herr Settembrini, "in case your stay is prolonged, we shall make the acquaintance of your uncle—-I mean your great--uncle—-shall we not? He will undoubtedly come up to ascertain your condition."

"Out of the question," cried Hans Castorp. "Under no conceivable circumstances. Wild horses could not drag him up here. My uncle is apoplectic, you understand; he has almost no neck at all. No, he has to have a reasonable atmospheric pressure; it would be worse for him up here than it was for your lady from the Baltic provinces—he would be in a dreadful way."

"I am disappointed. And apoplectic? Energy and phlegm are not much use under those circumstances.—-Your uncle is rich, I suppose? You are all rich down your way?"

Hans Castorp smiled at Herr Settembrini's literary generalizations. And again, from his distant couch, he cast a metaphorical eye upon the sphere from which he had been snatched. He called up memories, he made an effort to judge objectively, and found that distance enabled him to do so.

He answered: "One is rich—-or else one isn't. And if not, so much the worse. I myself am no millionaire, but what I have is secured to me, I have enough to live on and be independent. But personalities aside—-well, if you had said one must be rich, I should have agreed with you. If you aren't rich, or if you leave off being, then woe be unto you. 'Oh, *he*?' they will say about this or that person. 'He hasn't any money, has he?' Literally that, and making just such a face; I

have often heard them, and I see now it made an impression on me—
-which it would not have done, of course, unless it had struck me as
strange. Or don't you think that follows? No, I don't think you, for
instance, as *homo humanus*, would feel very comfortable down there;
it often struck me that it was pretty strong, as I can see now, though I
am a native of the place and for myself have never had to suffer from
it. If a man does not serve the best and dearest wines at his dinners,
people don't go, and his daughters are left on his hands. That is what
they are like. Lying here and looking at it from this distance, I find it
pretty gross. What were the words you used—phlegmatic and—and
energetic. That's very good. But what does it mean? It means hard,
cold. And what do hard and cold mean? They mean cruel. It is a
cruel atmosphere down there, cruel and ruthless. When you lie here
and look at it, from a distance, it makes you shudder."

Settembrini listened, and nodded; nodded after Hans Castorp had
come to an end, for the present, of his pronouncement and fallen
silent.

Then he took a breath and said: "I will not seek to extenuate the
specific forms which life's normal cruelty assumes in your native
sphere. It is all one—for the reproach of cruelty rests upon somewhat
sentimental grounds. You would scarcely even have levelled it, while
you were in that atmosphere, for fear of being ridiculous in your own
eyes. You left it to the drones to make, and rightly. That you make it
now bears witness to a certain estrangement, which I should be sorry
to see increase; since he who falls in the habit of making it is in
danger of being lost to life, to the manner of life to which he was
born. Do you know, Engineer, what I mean by being lost to life?

I, I know it, I see it here every day. Six months at most after they
get here, these young people—and they are mostly young who
come—have lost every idea they had, except flirtation and
temperature. And if they remain a year, they will have lost the power
of grasping any other; they will find any other 'cruel'—or, more
precisely, ignorant and inadequate. You are fond of anecdote—I
could serve your turn. I could tell you of a young man I know, a

husband and son, who was up here for eleven months. He was a little older than you, yes, rather older. They let him go home, provisionally, as much improved; he returned to the bosom of his family——not uncles, you understand, but his wife and his mother. The whole day he lay with the thermometer in his mouth, he took no interest in anything else. 'You don't understand,' he said. 'No one understands who has not lived up there. Down here the fundamental conception is lacking.' In the end it was the mother who settled it. 'Go back,' she said. 'There is nothing to be done with you any more.' He went back, went back 'home'——you know, don't you, that they call this home when they have once lived here? He was entirely estranged from his young wife, she lacked the fundamental conception, and she gave up trying to get it. It was borne in upon her that he would find a mate up here who had it, and that he would stop with her."

Hans Castorp seemed to be only half listening. He went on staring into the incandescent brilliance of his white room, as into far space.

He laughed belatedly, and said: "He called it home? That is sentimental, as you say. You know no end of stories. I was still thinking of what we said about hardness and cruelty; the same idea has gone through my head a number of times in these days. You see, a person has to have a rather thick skin to find it natural, the way they have of thinking and talking down there, the 'has he got any money?' and the face they make when they say it. It never came quite natural to me, though I am no *homo humanus*. I can see, now I look back, that I was always struck by it. Perhaps that had to do with my tendency to illness, though I did not know about it at the time—-those old places which I heard myself the other day. And now Behrens has found a fresh place. That, I must say, was a surprise to me——and yet, in a way, I don't know that it was, after all. I never have felt myself as firm as a rock, and my parents, both of them, dying so young——for I have been doubly orphaned from youth up, you know——"

Herr Settembrini described a single gesture, with head, hand, and shoulders. Pleasantly, courteously, it put the question: "Well, and what of it?"

"You are an author," Hans Castorp said, "a literary man. It must be easy for you to understand a thing like that; you can feel how under those circumstances a man might not be of tough enough fibre to find that sort of cruelty quite natural, the cruelty of ordinary people, who go about joking and making money and filling their bellies.—-I don't know if I am expressing myself"—-

Settembrini bowed. "You mean," he interrupted, "that the early and repeated contact with death developed in you a tendency which made you sensitive to the harshness and crudity, let us say the cynicism, of our everyday, worldly existence."

"Precisely!" cried Hans Castorp, in honest enthusiasm. "You have expressed it to a T, Herr Settembrini. Contact with death! I was sure that you, as a literary man—-"

Settembrini put out his hand, laid his head on one side, and closed his eyes. It was a mild and beautiful gesture, a plea for silence and further hearing. He held it some seconds, even after Hans Castorp had ceased to speak and was waiting in suspense for what was to come. But at length he opened his black eyes, organ--grinder eyes, and spoke: "Permit me. Permit me, Engineer, to say to you, and to bring it home to you, that the only sane, noble—-and I will expressly add, the only religious way to think of death is as part and parcel of life; to regard it, with the understanding and with the emotions, as the inviolable condition of life. It is the very opposite of sane, noble, reasonable, or religious to divorce it in any way from life, or to play it off against it. The ancients adorned their sarcophagi with the emblems of life and procreation, and even with obscene symbols; in the religions of antiquity the sacred and the obscene often lay very close together. These men knew how to pay homage to death. For death is worthy of homage, as the cradle of life, as the womb of palingenesis. Severed from life, it becomes a spectre, a distortion, and worse. For death, as an independent power, is a lustful power, whose vicious attraction is strong indeed; to feel drawn to it, to feel sympathy with it, is without any doubt at all the most ghastly aberration to which the spirit of man is prone."

Herr Settembrini left off speaking. He finished with this generalization, and made it the definite period of his discourse. He had spoken in a very serious vein and by no means with conversational intent; he even refrained from giving Hans Castorp the opportunity for a rejoinder; but simply dropped his voice at this point and concluded his remarks. He sat now with his lips closed, his hands folded in his lap, one leg in its check trouser flung over the other, slightly swinging the foot, which he regarded with an austere expression.

Hans Castorp too preserved silence. He leaned back in his *plumeau*, turned his head to the wall, and drummed with his finger-
-ends on the coverlet. He felt set to rights, chidden, corrected; in his silence there was no little childish obstinacy. The pause lasted some time.

At length Herr Settembrini lifted his head, and said with a smile: "You very likely recall, Engineer, that we have had a similar discussion once before——one might say the same discussion. We were talking about disease and dullness——I think we were taking a walk——and you found the combination a paradox, on the ground of your reverence for ill health. I called that reverence a dismal fancy which dishonoured human thought; and I was gratified to find you not disinclined to entertain my plea. We spoke of the neutrality and the intellectual indecision of youth, of its liberty of choice, of its inclination to play with all possible points of view, and that one should not——or need not——regard these experimentations as final and definite elections. Will you permit me"——Herr Settembrini smiled and bent forward as he sat, his feet close together on the floor, his hands between his knees, his head stretched out and a little on one side——"will you permit me"——and his voice had the faintest tremor in it——"to be beside you in your essays and experiments, and to exercise a corrective influence when there appears to be danger of your taking up a destructive position?"

"Why, certainly, Herr Settembrini"—-Hans Castorp hastened to abandon his forced and even peevish attitude, stop drumming on the bed--cover, and turn to his guest with friendliness, even with contrition. "It is uncommonly kind of you—-I must ask myself if I really—-that is, if there is anything—-"

"*Sine pecunia*, of course," quoted Herr Settembrini, as he rose. "I can't let myself be outdone!" They both laughed. The outer door opened, next moment the inner one as well. It was Joachim, returned from "society." When he saw the Italian he flushed, as Hans Castorp had done; the deep bronze of his face deepened by another shade.

"Oh, you have company," he said. "How nice for you! I was detained, they made me make one of a table of bridge. They call it bridge," he said, shaking his head, "as they do outside, but it was really something else entirely. I won five marks—-"

"Only so it doesn't become a vice with you," Hans Castorp laughed. "Ahem! Herr Settembrini has beguiled the time for me—-no, that is not the proper expression, though it may be all right for your mock bridge. Herr Settembrini has filled the time for me, and given it content, whereas when mock bridge breaks out in our midst, a respectable man feels he has to fight his way through. And yet to have the privilege of listening to Herr Settembrini, to get the benefit of his good counsel, I could almost wish to keep my fever, and stop up here with you indefinitely. They would have to give me a 'silent sister' to measure with."

"I repeat, Engineer, you are a wag," said the Italian. He took leave gracefully and went. Alone with his cousin, Hans Castorp heaved a sigh.

"Oh, what a schoolmaster!" he said. "A humanistic one, of course. He never leaves off setting you right—-first by means of anecdote, then by abstractions. And the things one gets to talk about with him, things you would never have thought you could talk about, or even understand! And if I had met him down below," he added, "I never should have understood."

At this hour Joachim would remain with him for a while, sacrificing a half or threequarters of an hour of the evening cure. Sometimes they played chess on Hans Castorp's magic table; Joachim had brought a set of chess--men from below. Then he would take his wrappings and go into the balcony, thermometer in mouth, and Hans Castorp too took his temperature for the last time, while soft music, near or far, stole up from the dark valley. The cure ended at ten. He heard Joachim, he heard the pair from the "bad" Russian table; he turned on his side and invited slumber.

The night was the harder half of the day, for Hans Castorp woke often, and lay not seldom hours awake; either because his slightly abnormal temperature kept him stimulated, or because his horizontal manner of life, detracted from the power, or the desire, to sleep. To make up for their briefness, his hours of slumber were animated by extremely lively and varied dreams, which he could ponder on awaking. And if the hours of the day were shortened by their frequent division into small sections, it was the blurred monotony of the marching hours of the night which operated with the like effect. Then as dawn came on, he found it diverting to watch the gradual grey, the slow emergence of the room and the objects in it, as though by the drawing of veils; to see day kindling outside, with smouldering or with lively glow; and it was always a surprise when the moment came round again and the thump of the bathing--master on his door announced to Hans Castorp that the daily programme was again in force. He had brought no calendar with him on his holiday, and did not always find himself sure of the date. Now and then he asked his cousin; who, in turn, was not always quite sure either. True, the Sundays, particularly the fortnightly one with the concert——it was the second Hans Castorp had spent in this situation——gave him a fixed point. So much was certain, that by little and little they had now got well on in September, close on to the middle. Since he went to bed, the cold and cloudy weather had given place to a succession of wonderful midsummer days. Every morning Joachim appeared arrayed in white flannel trousers, to greet his cousin, and Hans Castorp felt a pang of regret, in which both heart and youthful muscles joined, at the loss of all this splendid weather. He murmured that it was "a shame," but added to console himself that even if he were up and about he would hardly know how to take advantage of it, since it seemed it did not answer for him to exert himself much. And the wide--open balcony door did afford him some share of the warm shimmer outside. But toward the end of his prescribed term of lying, the weather veered again. It grew misty and cold overnight, the valley was hid by gusts of wet snow, and the dry heat of the radiator filled the room. Such was the day on which Hans Castorp reminded the doctor, on his morning round, that the three weeks were out, and asked leave to get up.

"What the deuce—-you don't say!" said Behrens. "Time's up, is it? Let's see: yes, you're right—-good Lord, how fast we grow old! Things haven't changed much with you, in the mean time. Normal yesterday? Yes, up to six o'clock in the afternoon. Well, Castorp, I won't grudge you human society any longer. Up with you, man, and get on with your walks—-within the prescribed limits, of course. We'll take a picture of the inside of you—-make a note of it," he said as he went out, jerking his great thumb over his shoulder at Hans Castorp, and looking at the pallid assistant with his bloodshot, watery blue eyes. Hans Castorp left the "caboose."

In galoshes, with his collar turned up, he accompanied his cousin once more to the bench by the watercourse and back. On the way he raised the question of how long the Hofrat might have let him lie had he not been reminded. And Joachim, looking worried, opened his mouth to emit a single pessimistic syllable, spread out his hands in an expressive gesture, and gave it up.

Sudden Enlightenment

A week passed before Hans Castorp received, through the Directress von Mylendonk, the summons to present himself in the x--ray laboratory. He had not liked to press matters. The Berghof was a busy place, doctors and assistants had their hands full. New guests had recently come in: two Russian students with shocks of hair and black blouses closed to the throat, showing not a vestige of linen; a Dutch married couple, who were given places at Settembrini's table; and a hunch--backed Mexican, who frightened his table by fearful attacks of asthma, when he would clutch his neighbour, whether man or woman, in an iron grip like a vice, and draw him, as it were, struggling and crying for help, into the circle of his own extremity. The dining--room was nearly full, though the winter season did not actually begin until October. And Hans Castorp's case was scarcely of such severity as to give him any special claim to attention. Frau Stöhr, for all her stupidity and ill breeding, was unquestionably worse off than he—-not to mention Dr. Blumenkohl. One must have lacked all discrimination not to have behaved retiringly, in Hans Castorp's place—-particularly since discrimination was in the atmosphere of the house. The mild cases were of no great account, that he had often heard. They were slightingly spoken of, looked at askance, not only by the more serious and the very serious cases, but even by each other. Logically, of course, each mild case was thus driven to think slightingly of itself; yet preserved its individual self--respect by merging it with the general, as was natural and human.

"Oh," they would say, of this or that patient, "there's not much amiss with him. He hardly even ought to be up here, he has no cavities at all." Such was the spirit—-it was aristocratic in its own special sense, and Hans Castorp deferred to it, out of an inborn respect for law and order of every sort. It was natural to him to conform to the proverb which bids us, when in Rome, do as the Romans do. And indeed travellers show small breeding when they jeer at the customs and standards of their hosts, for of characteristics that do honour to their possessors there are all sorts and kinds. Even toward Joachim Hans Castorp felt a certain deference—-not so much because he was the older inhabitant, his guide and cicerone in these new surroundings, as because he was unquestionably the more serious case of the two. Such being the attitude, it was easy to understand that each patient inclined to make the most he could of his individual case, even exaggerating its seriousness, so as to belong to the aristocracy, or come as close to it as possible. So Hans Castorp, when asked at table, might add a couple of tenths to his temperature, and could never help feeling flattered when they shook their fingers at him and called him an artful dodger. But even when he laid it on a little, he still remained a member of the lower orders, in whom an attitude of unassuming diffidence was only right and proper.

He took up the life of his first three weeks, that familiar, regular, well--regulated life with Joachim, and it went as pat as though he had never left it off. The interruption, indeed, had been insignificant, as he saw when he resumed his seat at table. Joachim, who laid deliberate stress on such occasions, had decorated his place with a few flowers; but there was no great ceremony about the greetings of the other guests, these were almost what they would have been after a separation of three hours instead of three weeks. This was not due to indifference toward his simple and sympathetic personality, nor to preoccupation with their own absorbing physical state; but merely because they had actually not been conscious of the interval. And Hans Castorp could readily follow them in this; since sitting there in his place at the end of the table, between the schoolmistress and Miss Robinson, it was as though he had sat here no longer ago than yesterday at the furthest.

If, even at his own table, the end of his retirement caused no stir, how should it have been remarked in the rest of the dining--room? And literally no soul had taken notice of it save Settembrini, who strolled over at the end of the meal to exchange a lively greeting. Hans Castorp, indeed, would have made a mental reservation, in which he may or may not have been justified: he told himself that Clavdia Chauchat had noticed his return, that she had no sooner made her tardy entrance, and let the glass door slam behind her, than she rested her narrow gaze upon him—-which he had met with his own—-and that even after she sat down, she had turned and looked toward him, smiling over her shoulder, as she had three weeks before, on the day of his examination. The movement had been so open, so regardless—-regardless of both himself and the other guests—-that he did not know whether to be in ecstasies over it or to take it as a mark of contempt and feel angry. At all events, his heart had contracted beneath this glance, which so markedly and intoxicatingly gave the lie to the lack of social relations subsisting between him and the fair patient. It had contracted almost painfully at the moment when the glass door slammed, for to that moment he had looked forward with his breath coming thick and fast.

It must be said that Hans Castorp's sentiments toward the patient of the "good" Russian table had made distinct progress during his retirement. The sympathy he entertained in his mind and his simple heart for this medium--sized person with the gliding gait and the "Kirghiz" eyes, as good as amounted to being "in love"—-we shall let the word stand, although in strictness it is a conception of "down below," a word of the plains, capable of giving rise to a misconception: namely, that the tender ditty beginning "One word from thy sweet lips" was to some extent applicable to his state. Her picture had hovered before him in those early hours when he had lain awake and watched the dawn unveil his chamber; or at evening when the twilight thickened. It had been vividly present the night Settembrini had suddenly entered his room and turned on the light; was the reason why he had coloured under the humanistic eye. In each hour of his diminished day he had thought of her: her mouth, her cheek--bones, her eyes, whose colour, shape, and position bit into his very soul; her drooping back, the posture of her head, her cervical vertebra above the rounding of her blouse, her arms enhanced by their thin gauze covering. Possessed of these thoughts, his hours had sped on soundless feet; if we have concealed the fact, we did so out of sympathy for the turmoil of his conscience, which mingled with the terrifying joy his visions imparted. Yes, he felt both terror and dread; he felt a vague and boundless, utterly mad and extravagant anticipation, a nameless anguish of joy which at times so oppressed the young man's heart, his actual and corporeal heart, that he would lay one hand in the neighbourhood of that organ, while he carried the other to his brow and held it like a shield before his eyes, whispering: "Oh, my God!"

For behind that brow were thoughts—or half--thoughts—which imparted to the visions their perilous sweetness. Thoughts that had to do with Madame Chauchat's recklessness and abandon, her ailing state, the heightening and accentuation of her physical parts by disease, the corporealization, so to speak, of all her being as an effect of disease—an effect in which he, Hans Castorp, by the physician's verdict, was now to share. He comprehended the grounds of her audacity, her total disregard in smile and glance of the fact that no social relation existed between them, that they did not even know each other; it was as though they belonged to no social system, as though it were not even necessary that they should speak to each other! Precisely this it was that frightened Hans Castorp; for frightened he was, in the same sense as when, in the consulting--room, he had looked from Joachim's nude body with panic--stricken searching up to his eyes—only that then the grounds of his fear had been pity and concern, whereas here something quite different was in play.

But now the Berghof life, that wonderfully favoured and well--regulated existence, was once more in full swing on its narrow stage. Hans Castorp, whilst awaiting his xray examination, continued to enjoy its measured course, together with good Cousin Joachim, and to do, hour for hour, precisely as he did. No question but his cousin's society was beneficial to our young man. For though Joachim's were but a companionship in suffering, yet he suffered, as it were, conformably with military etiquette; even, though unconsciously, to the point of finding satisfaction in the service of the cure, of substituting it for the service down below and making of it an interim profession. Hans Castorp was not so dull as not to perceive all this, yet at the same time he was aware of its corrective and restraining influence upon his more civilian temper. It may have been this companionship, its example and the control it exercised, which held him back from overt steps and rash undertakings. For he saw all that Joachim had to endure from the daily assaults of an orange--scented atmosphere, commingled of such elements as round brown eyes, a little ruby, a great deal of unwarranted laughter, and a bosom fair to outward eyes. The honour and good sense which made Joachim flee these enticements gripped Hans Castorp, kept him under control, and prevented him from "borrowing a lead--pencil" so to speak——from the narrow--eyed one, a thing which he otherwise, from what we know of him, might well have been ready to do.

Joachim never spoke of the laughter--loving Marusja, and thus Hans Castorp could not mention Clavdia Chauchat. He made up for this by his stolen commerce with the schoolmistress at table, when he would sit supporting his chin after the manner of old Hans Lorenz, and tax the spinster with her weakness for the charming invalid, until her face positively flamed. He pressed her to find out new and interesting facts about Madame Chauchat's personal affairs, her origin, her husband, her age, the particulars of her illness. He wanted to know if she had children. Oh, no, she had none; what should a woman like her do with children? Probably she was strictly forbidden to have any, and if she did, what kind of children would they be? Hans Castorp was forced to acquiesce. And now it was probably late in the day, he threw out, with prodigious objectivity. Madame Chauchat's profile, at times, seemed to him already a little sharp. She must be over thirty. Fräulein Engelhart rejected the idea with scorn. Thirty? At worst not more than twenty--eight. She forbade her neighbour to use such words about Clavdia's profile. It was the softest, sweetest, most youthful profile in the world, and at the same time interesting——of course it was not the profile of any ordinary healthy bread--and--butter miss. To punish him, she went on to say that she knew Frau Chauchat entertained a male visitor, a certain fellow--countryman who lived down in the Platz. She received him afternoons in her chamber.

It was a good shot. Hans Castorp's face changed in spite of himself; he tried to react, saying: "Well, well! You don't say so!" but the words sounded strained. He was incapable of treating lightly the existence of this fellow--countryman of Frau Chauchat, much as he wished to appear to do so, and came back to it again and again, his lips twitching. A young man? Young and good--looking, according to all accounts, the schoolmistress answered; she could not say from her own observation. Was he ill?

Only a light case, at most. "Let us hope," Hans Castorp remarked with scorn, "that he displays more linen than the other two, at the 'bad' Russian table." Fräulein Engelhart, on punishment intent, said she could vouch for that. He gave in, and admitted that it was a matter for concern. He earnestly charged her to find out all she could about this young man who came and went between the Platz and Frau Chauchat's room. A few days later she brought him, not information about the young Russian, but a fresh and startling piece of news. She knew that Clavdia Chauchat was having her portrait painted, and asked Hans Castorp if he knew it too. If not, he might be assured she had it on the best authority. She had been sitting for some time, to a person here in the house, and the person was——the Hofrat! Yes, Herr Hofrat Behrens, no less, and he received her for the purpose almost daily in his private dwelling. This intelligence affected Hans Castorp even more than the other. He made several forced jokes about it. Why, certainly, the Hofrat was known to occupy himself with oil--painting. Why not? It wasn't a crime, anybody was free to paint. And the sittings took place in the widower's own house——he hoped, at least, that Fräulein von Mylendonk was present! The schoolmistress objected that the Directress was probably too busy. No busier than the doctor ought to be, Hans Castorp severely rejoined. The remark sounded final; but he was far from letting the subject drop. He exhausted himself in questions: about the picture, what size it was, and whether it was a head or a knee--length;

about the hours of the sitting—-but Fräulein Engelhart could not gratify him with these particulars, and had to put him off until she could make further inquiry.

Hans Castorp measured 99.7° as a result of this communication. The visits Frau Chauchat received upset him far less than these she made. Her personal and private life—-quite aside from what went on in it—-had begun to be a source of anguish and unrest; how much keener, then, were his feelings when he heard such questionable things about the way she spent her time! Speaking generally, it was altogether possible that her relations with the Russian visitor had a disinterested and harmless character. But Hans Castorp had been for some time now inclined to reject harmless and disinterested explanations as being in the nature of "twaddle"; nor could he regard in any other light this oil--painting, considered as a bond of interest between a widower with a robust vocabulary and a narrow--eyed, soft--stepping young female. The taste displayed by the Hofrat in his choice of a model was too like Hans Castorp's own for him to put great faith in the disinterested character of the affair, and the thought of the Hofrat's purple cheeks and bloodshot, goggling eyes only strengthened his scepticism. An observation which he made in these days, of his own accord and quite by chance, had a different effect upon him, though here again what he saw confirmed his own taste. There sat, at the same table with Frau Salomon and the greedy schoolboy with the glasses, at the cousins' left, near the side door, a patient who was, so Hans Castorp had heard, a native of Mannheim. He was some thirty years old; his hair was thin, his teeth poor, and he had a self--depreciating manner of speech. He it was who played the piano evenings, usually the wedding march from *Midsummer Night's Dream*. He was said to be very religious—-as "those up here" naturally often were. Every Sunday he went to service down in the Platz, and in the rest--cure he read devotional books with a chalice or palm branch on the front cover. This man's eyes, so Hans Castorp one day observed, travelled the same road as his own: they hung upon Madame Chauchat's lissom person with timid, doglike devotion. Once Hans Castorp had remarked this, he could not forbear corroborating it again and again. He saw him stand, of an evening, in the card--room, among the other guests, quite lost in gazing at the lovely, contaminate creature on the sofa in the small salon, in talk with the whimsical, fuzzy--haired Tamara, Dr. Blumenkohl, and the hollow--chested, stooping young men who were her table--mates. He saw him turn away, then twist his head, with a piteous expression of the upper lip, and roll his eyes back over his shoulder in her direction. He saw him colour and *not* look up, but then gaze avidly as with a crash the glass door fell to, and Frau Chauchat slipped to her place. And more than once he saw how the poor soul would place himself, after the meal, between the "good" Russian table and the exit, in order that she might pass close by him; she gave him neither glance nor thought, while he devoured her at close range with eyes full of sadness to their very depths.

This discovery of his affected young Hans Castorp no little, though the plaintive, devouring gaze of the Mannheimer did not trouble his rest like the thought of Clavdia Chauchat's private relations with Hofrat Behrens, a man so much his superior in age, person, and position. Clavdia took no interest in the Mannheimer——had she done so, it would not have escaped Hans Castorp's perception; in this case it was not the dart of jealousy he felt pierce his soul. But he did have all the sensations which the drunkenness of passion knows, when it sees its own case duplicated in the outer world, and which form a most fantastic mixture of disgust and fellow--feeling. To explore and lay open all the windings of his emotions would keep us far too long; suffice it to say that his observation of the Mannheimer gave our poor young friend enough to think on and to suffer.

In this wise passed the week before his x--ray examination. He had not known it was so long. But one morning at early breakfast he received the order through the Directress (she had a fresh stye, so this harmless though disfiguring ailment was clearly constitutional) to present himself in the laboratory that afternoon; and behold, when he came to think of it, a week had passed. He and his cousin were to go together, a half--hour before tea; the occasion would serve for Joachim to have another x--ray taken, as the old one was by now out of date.

They shortened the main rest period by thirty minutes and, promptly as the clock struck half past three, descended the stairs to the so--called basement, and sat down in the small antechamber between the consulting--room and the laboratory. Joachim was quite cool, this being for him no new experience, Hans Castorp rather feverishly expectant, as no one, up to the present, had ever had a view into his organic interior. They were not alone. Several other patients were already sitting when they entered, with tattered illustrated magazines on their laps, and they all waited together: a young Swede, of heroic proportions, who sat at Settembrini's table; of whom one heard that, when he entered, the previous April, he had been so ill they had almost refused to take him, but he had put on nearly six stone, and was about to be discharged cured. There was also a mother from the "bad" Russian table, herself a lamentable case, with her long--nosed, ugly boy, named Sascha, whose case was more lamentable still. These three had been waiting longer than the cousins and would therefore go in before them——evidently there had been some sort of hitch in the laboratory, and a cold tea was on the cards.

They were busy in there. The voice of the Hofrat could be heard, giving directions. It was somewhat past the half--hour when the door was opened by the technical assistant to admit the Swedish giant and fortune's minion. His predecessor had evidently gone out by another door. But now matters moved more rapidly. After no more than ten minutes they heard the Scandinavian stride off down the corridor, a walking testimonial to the establishment and the health resort; and the Russian mother was admitted with her Sascha. Both times, as the door opened, Hans Castorp observed that it was half dark in the x--ray room; an artificial twilight prevailed there, as in Dr. Krokowski's analytic cabinet. The windows were shrouded, daylight shut out, and two electric lights were burning. But as Sascha and his mother went in, and Hans Castorp gazed after them, the corridor door opened, and the next patient entered the waiting--room——she was, of course, too early, on account of the delay in the laboratory. It was Madame Chauchat.

It was Clavdia Chauchat who appeared thus suddenly in the little waiting--room. Hans Castorp recognized her, staring--eyed, and distinctly felt the blood leave his cheeks. His jaw relaxed, his mouth was on the point of falling open. Her entrance had taken place so casually, so unforeseen, she had not been there, and then, all at once, there she was, and sharing these narrow quarters with the cousins. Joachim flung a quick glance at Hans Castorp, afterwards not only casting down his eyes, but taking up again the illustrated sheet he had laid aside, and burying his face in it. Hans Castorp could not summon resolution to do the same. He grew very red, after his sudden pallor, and his heart pounded.

Frau Chauchat seated herself by the laboratory door, in a little round easy--chair with stumpy, as it were rudimentary arms. She leaned back, crossed one leg lightly over the other, and stared into space. She knew she was being looked at, and her Pribislav eyes shifted their gaze nervously, almost squinting. She wore a white sweater and blue skirt, and had a book from the lending--library in her lap. She tapped softly with the sole of the foot that rested on the floor.

After a minute and a half she changed her position; looked round, stood up, with an air of not knowing what she was to do or where to go——and began to speak. She was asking something, she addressed a question to Joachim, though he sat there apparently deep in his magazine, while Hans Castorp was doing nothing at all. She shaped the words with her lips and gave them voice out of her white throat; it was the voice, not deep, but with the slightest edge, and pleasantly husky, that Hans Castorp knew——had known so long ago and yet heard so lately, swing: "With pleasure, only you must be sure to give it me back after the lesson." Those words had been uttered clearly and fluently; these came rather hesitatingly and brokenly, the speaker had no native right to them, she only borrowed them, as Hans Castorp had heard her do before, when he experienced the mingled feeling of superiority and ecstasy we have described. One hand in her sweater pocket, the other at the back of her head, Frau Chauchat asked: "May I ask for what time you had an appointment?"

And Joachim, with a quick look at his cousin, answered, drawing his heels together as he sat: "For half past three."

She spoke again: "Mine was for a quarter to four. What is it then—-it is nearly four. Some people just entered, did they not?"

"Yes, two people. They were ahead of us. There seems to be some delay, everything is a half--hour late."

"It is disagreeable," she said, nervously touching her hair.

"Rather," responded Joachim. "We have been waiting nearly half an hour already."

Thus they conversed, and Hans Castorp listened as in a dream. For his cousin to speak to Frau Chauchat was almost the same as his doing it himself—-and yet how altogether different! That "Rather" had affronted him, it sounded odd and brusque, if not worse, in view of the circumstances. To think that Joachim could speak to her like that—-to think that he could speak to her at all!—-and very likely he prided himself on his pert "Rather"—-much as Hans Castorp had played up before Joachim and Settembrini when he was asked how long he meant to stay, and answered: "Three weeks." It was to Joachim, though he had the paper in front of his nose, that she had turned with her question; because he was the older inhabitant of course, whom she had known longer by sight; but perhaps for another reason as well, because they two might meet on a conventional footing and carry on an ordinary conversation in articulate words; because nothing wild and deep, mysterious and terrifying, held sway between them. Had it been somebody brown--eyed, with a ruby ring and orange perfume, who sat here waiting with them, it would have been his, Hans Castorp's, part to lead the conversation and say: "Rather" in the purity and detachment of his sentiments. "Yes, madame, certainly rather unpleasant," he would have said; and might have taken his handkerchief out of his breast pocket with a flourish, and blown his nose. "Have patience, our case is no better than yours." How surprised Joachim would have been at his fluency—-but without seriously wishing himself in Hans Castorp's place. No, and Hans Castorp was not jealous of Joachim for being able to talk to Frau Chauchat. He was satisfied that she should have addressed herself to his cousin; it showed that she recognized the situation for what it was.—-His heart pounded.

After Joachim's cavalier treatment of Madame Chauchat—-in which Hans Castorp seemed to savour something almost like faint hostility on his cousin's part toward their fair fellow--patient, a hostility at which he could not help smiling, despite the commotion in his mind—"Clavdia" tried a turn up and down the room. Then, finding the space too confined, she too took up an illustrated paper, and returned to the easychair with the rudimentary arms. Hans Castorp looked at her, with his chin in his collar, like his grandfather—it was laughable to see how like the old man he looked. Frau Chauchat had crossed one leg over the other again, and her knee, even the whole slender line of the thigh, showed beneath the blue skirt. She was only of middle height—-a thoroughly proper and delightful height, in Hans Castorp's eyes—-but relatively long--legged, and narrow in the hips. She sat leaning forward, with her crossed forearms supported on her knee, her shoulders drooping, and her back rounded, so that the neck--bone stuck out prominently, and nearly the whole spine was marked out under the close--fitting sweater. Her breasts, which were not high and voluptuous like Marusja's, but small and maidenly, were pressed together from both sides. Hans Castorp recalled, suddenly, that she too was sitting here waiting to be x--rayed. The Hofrat painted her, he reproduced her outward form with oil and colours upon the canvas. And now, in the twilighted room, he would direct upon her the rays which would reveal to him the inside of her body. When this idea occurred to Hans

Castorp, he turned away his head and put on a primly detached air; a sort of seemly obscurantism presented itself to him as the only correct attitude in the presence of such a thought.

The waiting together in the little room did not last for long. They evidently gave rather short shrift to Sascha and his mother in there, in their effort to make up for lost time. The technician in his white smock once more appeared, Joachim stood up and tossed his paper back on to the table, and Hans Castorp, not without inward hesitation, followed him to the open door. He was struggling with chivalrous scruples, also with the temptation to put himself, after all, upon conventional terms with Frau Chauchat, to speak to her and offer her precedence—-in French, if he could manage. Hastily he sought to muster the words, the sentence structure. But he did not know if such courtesies were practised up here; probably the established order was more powerful than the rules of chivalry. Joachim must know, and as he made no motion to defer to sex, even though Hans Castorp looked at him imploringly, the latter followed his cousin past Frau Chauchat, who merely glanced up from her stooping posture as they went through the door into the laboratory.

He was too much possessed by the events of the last ten minutes, and by what he left behind, for his mind to pass immediately with his body over the threshold of the x--ray laboratory. He saw nothing, or only vaguely, in the artificially lighted room; he still heard Frau Chauchat's pleasantly veiled voice, with which she had said: "What is it, then? ... Some people have just gone in ... It is disagreeable"—-the sound of it still shivered sweetly down his back. He saw the shape of her knee under the cloth skirt, saw the bone of her neck, under the short reddish--blond hairs that were not gathered up into the braids—-and again the shiver ran down his back. Then he saw Hofrat Behrens, with his back to them, standing before a sort of built--in recess, looking at a black plate which he held at arm's length toward the dim light in the ceiling. They passed him and went on into the room, followed by the assistant, who made preparations to dispatch their affair. It smelled very odd in here, the air was filled with a sort of stale ozone. The built--in structure, projecting between the two black--hung windows, divided the room into two unequal parts. Hans Castorp could distinguish physical apparatus. Lenses, switch--boards, towering measuring--instruments, a box like a camera on a rolling stand, glass diapositives in rows set in the walls. Hard to say whether this was a photographic studio, a dark--room, or an inventor's workshop and technological witches' kitchen.

Joachim had begun, without more ado, to lay bare the upper half of his body. The helper, a square--built, rosy--cheeked young native in a white smock, motioned Hans Castorp to do the same. It went fast, and he was next in turn. As Hans Castorp took off his waistcoat, Behrens came out of the smaller recess where he had been standing into the larger one.

"Hallo," said he. "Here are our Dioscuri, Castor and Pollux. If you feel any inclination to blub, kindly suppress it. Just wait, we shall soon see through you both. I expect, Castorp, you feel a little nervous about exposing your inner self to our gaze?

Don't be alarmed, we preserve all the amenities. Look here, have you seen my picture--gallery?" He led Hans Castorp by the arm before the rows of dark plates on the wall, and turned on a light behind them. Hans Castorp saw various members: hands, feet, knee--pans, thigh--and leg--bones, arms, and pelvises. But the rounded living form of these portions of the human body was vague and shadowy, like a pale and misty envelope, within which stood out the clear, sharp nucleus——the skeleton.

"Very interesting," said Hans Castorp.

"Interesting sure enough," responded the Hofrat. "Useful object--lesson for the young. X--ray anatomy, you know, triumph of the age. There is a female arm, you can tell by its delicacy. That's what they put around you when they make love, you know." He laughed, and his upper lip with the close--cropped moustache went up still more on one side. The pictures faded. Hans Castorp turned his attention to the preparations for taking Joachim's x--ray.

It was done in front of that structure on the other side of which Hofrat Behrens had been standing when they entered. Joachim had taken his place on a sort of shoemaker's bench, in front of a board, which he embraced with his arms and pressed his breast against it, while the assistant improved the position, massaging his back with kneading motions, and putting his arms further forward. Then he went behind the camera, and stood just as a photographer would, legs apart and stooped over, to look inside. He expressed his satisfaction and, going back to Joachim, warned him to draw in his breath and hold it until all was over. Joachim's rounded back expanded and so remained; the assistant, at the switch--board, pulled the handle. Now, for the space of two seconds, fearful powers were in play——streams of thousands, of a hundred thousand of volts, Hans Castorp seemed to recall——which were necessary to pierce through solid matter. They could hardly be confined to their office, they tried to escape through other outlets: there were explosions like pistol--shots, blue sparks on the measuring apparatus; long lightnings crackled along the walls. Somewhere in the room appeared a red light, like a threatening eye, and a phial in Joachim's rear filled with green. Then everything grew quiet, the phenomena disappeared, and Joachim let out his breath with a sigh. It was over.

"Next delinquent," said the Hofrat, and nudged Hans Castorp with his elbow.

"Don't pretend you're too tired. You will get a free copy, Castorp; then you can project the secrets of your bosom on the wall for your children and grandchildren to see!"

Joachim had stepped down; the technician changed the plate. Hofrat Behrens personally instructed the novice how to sit and hold himself.

"Put your arms about it," he said. "Embrace the board——pretend it's something else, if you like. Press your breast against it, as though it filled you with rapture. Like that. Draw a deep breath. Hold it!" he commanded. "Now, please!" Hans Castorp waited, blinking, his lungs distended. Behind him the storm broke loose: it crackled, lightened, detonated——and grew still. The lens had looked into his inside.

He got down, dazed and bewildered, notwithstanding he had not been physically sensible of the penetration in the slightest degree.

"Good lad," said the Hofrat. "Now we shall see." The experienced Joachim had already moved over toward the entrance door and taken position at a stand; at his back was the lofty structure of the apparatus, with a bulb half full of water, and distillation tubes; in front of him, breast--high, hung a framed screen on pulleys. On his left, between switch--board and instrumentarium, was a red globe. The Hofrat, bestriding a stool in front of the screen, lighted the light. The ceiling light went out, and only the red glow illumined the scene. Then the master turned this too off, with a quick motion, and thick darkness enveloped the laboratory.

"We must first accustom the eyes," the Hofrat was heard to say, in the darkness.

"We must get big pupils, like a cat's, to see what we want to see. You understand, our everyday eyesight would not be good enough for our purposes. We have to banish the bright daylight and its pretty pictures out of our minds."

"Naturally," said Hans Castorp. He stood at the Hofrat's shoulder, and closed his eyes, since the darkness was so profound that it did not matter whether he had them open or shut. "First we must wash our eyes with darkness to see what we want to see. That is plain. I find it quite right and proper, as a matter of fact, that we should collect ourselves a little, beforehand——in silent prayer, as it were. I am standing here with my eyes shut, and have quite a pleasant sleepy feeling. But what is it I smell?"

"Oxygen," said the Hofrat. "What you notice in the air is oxygen. Atmospheric product of our little private thunderstorm, you know. Eyes open!" he commanded.

"The magicking is about to begin." Hans Castorp hastened to obey.

They heard a switch go on. A motor started up, and sang furiously higher and higher, until another switch controlled and steadied it. The floor shook with an even vibration. The little red light, at right angles to the ceiling, looked threateningly across at them. Somewhere lightening flashed. And with a milky gleam a window of light emerged from the darkness: it was the square hanging screen, before which Hofrat Behrens bestrode his stool, his legs sprawled apart with his fists supported on them, his blunt nose close to the pane, which gave him a view of a man's interior organism.

"Do you see it, young man?" he asked. Hans Castorp leaned over his shoulder, but then raised his head again to look toward the spot where Joachim's eyes were presumably gazing in the darkness, with the gentle, sad expression they had worn during the other examination. "May I?" he asked.

"Of course," Joachim replied magnanimously, out of the dark. And to the pulsation of the floor, and the snapping and cracking of the forces at play, Hans Castorp peered through the lighted window, peered into Joachim Ziemssen's empty skeleton. The breastbone and spine fell together in a single dark column. The frontal structure of the ribs was cut across by the paler structure of the back. Above, the collar--bones branched off on both sides, and the framework of the shoulder, with the joint and the beginning of Joachim's arm, showed sharp and bare through the soft envelope of flesh. The thoracic cavity was light, but blood--vessels were to be seen, some dark spots, a blackish shadow.

"Clear picture," said the Hofrat, "quite a decent leanness—-that's the military youth. I've had paunches here—-you couldn't see through them, hardly recognize a thing. The rays are yet to be discovered that will go through such layers of fat. This is nice clean work. Do you see the diaphragm?" he asked, and indicated with his finger the dark arch in the window, that rose and fell. "Do you see the bulges here on the left side, the little protuberances? That was the inflammation of the pleura he had when he was fifteen years old. Breathe deep," he commanded. "Deeper! Deep, I tell you!" And Joachim's diaphragm rose quivering, as high as it could; the upper pans of the lungs could be seen to clear up, but the Hofrat was not satisfied. "Not good enough," he said. "Can you see the hilus glands? Can you see the adhesions? Look at the cavities here, that is where the toxins come from that fuddle him." But Hans Castorp's attention was taken up by something like a bag, a strange, animal shape, darkly visible behind the middle column, or more on the right side of it—-the spectator's right. It expanded and contracted regularly, a little after the fashion of a swimming jelly--fish.

"Look at his heart," and the Hofrat lifted his huge hand again from his thigh and pointed with his forefinger at the pulsating shadow. Good God, it was the heart, it was Joachim's honour--loving heart, that Hans Castorp saw!"

"I am looking at your heart," he said in a suppressed voice.

"Go ahead," answered Joachim again; probably he smiled politely up there in the darkness. But the Hofrat told him to be quiet and not betray any sensibility. Behrens studied the spots and the lines, the black festoon in the intercostal space; while Hans Castorp gazed without wearying at Joachim's graveyard shape and bony tenement, this lean *memento mori*, this scaffolding for mortal flesh to hang on. "Yes, yes! I see, I see!" he said, several times over. "My God, I see!" He had heard of a woman, a longdead member of the Tienappel connexion, who had been endowed or afflicted with a heavy gift, which she bore in all humility: namely, that the skeletons of persons about to die would appear before her. Thus now Hans Castorp was privileged to behold the good Joachim—-but with the aid and under the auspices of physical science; and by his cousin's express permission, so that it was quite legitimate and without gruesome significance. Yet a certain sympathy came over him with the melancholy destiny of his clairvoyant relative. He was strongly moved by what he saw—or more precisely, by the fact that he saw it—-and felt stirrings of uneasy doubt, as to whether it was really permissible and innocent to stand here in the quaking, crackling darkness and gaze like this; his itch to commit the indiscretion conflicted in his bosom with religious emotion and feelings of concern.

But a few minutes later he himself stood in the pillory, in the midst of the electrical storm, while Joachim, his body closed up again, put on his clothes. Again the Hofrat peered through the milky glass, this time into Hans Castorp's own inside; and from his half--utterances, his broken phrases and bursts of scolding, the young man gathered that what he saw corresponded to his expectations. He was so kind as to permit the patient, at his request, to look at his own hand through the screen. And Hans Castorp saw, precisely what he must have expected, but what it is hardly permitted man to see, and what he had never thought it would be vouchsafed him to see: he looked into his own grave. The process of decay was forestalled by the powers of the light--ray, the flesh in which he walked disintegrated, annihilated, dissolved in vacant mist, and there within it was the finely turned skeleton of his own hand, the seal ring he had inherited from his grandfather hanging loose and black on the joint of his ringfinger——a hard, material object, with which man adorns the body that is fated to melt away beneath it, when it passes on to another flesh that can wear it for yet a little while. With the eyes of his Tienappel ancestress, penetrating, prophetic eyes, he gazed at this familiar part of his own body, and for the first time in his life he understood that he would die. At the thought there came over his face the expression it usually wore when he listened to music: a little dull, sleepy, and pious, his mouth half open, his head inclined toward the shoulder.

The Hofrat said: "Spooky, what? Yes, there's something distinctly spooky about it."

He closed off the current. The floor ceased to vibrate, the lightnings to play, the magic window was quenched in darkness. The ceiling light came on. As Hans Castorp flung on his clothes, the Hofrat gave the two young men the results of his observations, in non--technical language, out of regard for their lay minds. It seemed that in Hans

Castorp's case, the test of the eye confirmed that of the ear in a way to add lustre to science. The Hofrat had seen the old as well as the fresh spots, and "strands" ran from the bronchial tubes rather far into the organ itself—-"strands" with "nodules."

Hans Castorp would be able to see for himself later, in the diapositive which they would give him for his very own. The word of command was calm, patience, manly self--discipline; measure, eat, lie down, wake, and drink tea. They left; Hans Castorp, going out behind Joachim, looked over his shoulder. Ushered in by the technician, Frau Chauchat was entering the laboratory.

Freedom

How did it seem now to our young Hans Castorp? Was it as though the seven weeks which, demonstrably and without the shadow of a doubt, he had spent with them up here, were only seven days? Or, on the contrary, did they seem much longer than had actually been the case? He asked himself, inwardly, and also by way of asking Joachim; but he could not decide. Both were probably true: when he looked back, the time seemed both unnaturally long and unnaturally short, or rather it seemed anything but what it actually was—in saying which we assume that time is a natural phenomenon, and that it is admissible to associate with it the conception of actuality. At all events October was before the door, it might enter any day. The calculation was an easy one for Hans Castorp to make, and he gathered the same result from the conversation of his fellow--patients. "Do you know that in five days it will be the first again?" he heard Hermine Kleefeld say to two of her familiars, the student Rasmussen and the thick--lipped young man, whose name was Gänser. It was after luncheon, and the guests lingered chatting in the dining--room, though the air was heavy with the odours of the meal just served, instead of going into the afternoon rest--cure. "The first of October, I saw it on the calendar in the office. That makes the second of its kind I've spent in the pleasure resort. Well, summer is over, in so far as there has been a summer, that is—-it has really been a sell, like life in general." She shook her head, fetched a sigh from her one lung, and rolled up to the ceiling her dull and stolid eyes.

"Cheer up, Rasmussen," she said, and slapped her comrade on the drooping shoulder.

"Make a few jokes!"

"I don't know many," he responded, letting his hands flap finlike before his breast,

"and those I do I can't tell, I'm so tired all the time."

" 'Not even a dog,' " Gänser said through his teeth, " 'would want to live longer'——if he had to live like this."

They laughed and shrugged their shoulders.

Settembrini had been standing near them, his toothpick between his lips. As they went out he said to Hans Castorp: "Don't you believe them, Engineer, never believe them when they grumble. They all do it, without exception, and all of them are only too much at home up here. They lead a loose and idle life, and imagine themselves entitled to pity, and justified of their bitterness, irony, and cynicism. 'This pleasure resort,' she said. Well, isn't it a pleasure resort, then? In my humble opinion it is, and in a very questionable sense too. So life is a 'sell,' up here at this pleasure resort! But once let them go down below and their manner of life will be such as to leave no doubt that they mean to come back again. Irony, forsooth! Guard yourself, Engineer, from the sort of irony that thrives up here; guard yourself altogether from taking on their mental attitude! Where irony is not a direct and classic device of oratory, not for a moment equivocal to a healthy mind, it makes for depravity, it becomes a drawback to civilization, an unclean traffic with the forces of reaction, vice, and materialism. As the atmosphere in which we live is obviously very favourable to such miasmic growths, I may hope, or rather, I must fear, that you understand my meaning."

Truly the Italian's words were of the sort that seven weeks ago, down in the flatland, would have been empty sound to Hans

Castorp's ears. But his stay up here had made his mind receptive to them: receptive in the sense that he comprehended them with his mind, if not with his sympathies, which would have meant even more. For although he was at bottom glad that Settembrini, after all that had passed, continued, as he did, still to talk to him, admonishing, instructing, seeking to establish an influence upon his mind, yet his understanding had reached the point where he was critical of the Italian's words, and at times, up to a point, withheld his assent.

"Imagine," he said to himself, "he talks about irony just as he does about music, he'll soon be telling us that it is politically suspect——that is, from the moment it ceases to be a 'direct and classic device of oratory.' But irony that is 'not for a moment equivocal' —-what kind of irony would that be, I should like to ask, if I may make so bold as to put in my oar? It would be a piece of dried--up pedantry!" Thus ungrateful is immature youth! It takes all that is offered, and bites the hand that feeds it. But it would have seemed too risky to put his opposition into words. He confined himself to commenting upon what Herr Settembrini had said about Hermine Kleefeld, which he found ungenerous——or rather, had his reasons for wishing to find it so.

"But the girl is ill," he said. "She is seriously ill, without the shadow of a doubt——she has every reason for pessimism. What do you expect of her?"

"Disease and despair," Settembrini said, "are often only forms of depravity."

"And Leopardi," thought Hans Castorp, "who definitely despaired of science and progress? And our schoolmaster himself? He is infected too and keeps coming back here, and Carducci would have had small joy of him."

Aloud he said: "You *are* good! Why, the girl may lie down and die any day, and you call it depravity! You'll have to make that a little clearer. If you said that illness is sometimes a consequence of depravity, that would at least be sensible."

"Very sensible indeed!" Settembrini put in. "My word! So if I stopped at that, you would be satisfied?"

"Or if you said that illness may serve as a pretext for depravity—-that would be all right, too."

"*Grazie tanto!*"

" But illness a *form* of depravity? That is to say, not originating in depravity, but itself depravity? That seems to me a paradox."

"I beg of you, Engineer, not to impute to me anything of the sort. I despise paradoxes, I hate them. All that I said to you about irony I would say over again about paradoxes, and more besides. Paradox is the poisonous flower of quietism, the iridescent surface of the rotting mind, the greatest depravity of all! Moreover, I note that you are once more defending disease—-"

"No; what you are saying interests me. It reminds me of things Dr. Krokowski says in his Monday lectures. He too explains organic disease as a secondary phenomenon."

"Scarcely the pure idealist."

"What have you against him?"

"Just that."

"You are down on analysis?"

"Not always—-I am for it and against it, both by turns."

"How am I to understand that?"

"Analysis as an instrument of enlightenment and civilization is good, in so far as it shatters absurd convictions, acts as a solvent upon natural prejudices, and undermines authority; good, in other words, in that it sets free, refines, humanizes, makes slaves ripe for freedom. But it is bad, very bad, in so far as it stands in the way of action, cannot shape the vital forces, maims life at its roots. Analysis can be a

[281]

very unappetizing affair, as much so as death, with which it may well belong—-allied to the grave and its unsavory anatomy."

"Well roared, lion," Herr Castorp could not help thinking, as he often did when Herr Settembrini delivered himself of something pedagogic. Aloud he only said: "We've been having to do with x--ray anatomy in these days, down on the lower--floor. Behrens called it that, when he x--rayed us."

"Oh, so you have made that stage too? Well?"

"I saw the skeleton of my hand," Hans Castorp said, and sought to call up the feeling that had mounted in him at the sight. "Did you get them to show you yours?"

"No, I don't take the faintest interest in my skeleton. But what was the physician's verdict?"

"He saw 'strands '—-strands with nodules.'"

"The scoundrel!"

"I have heard you call Hofrat Behrens that before, Herr Settembrini. What do you mean by it?"

"I assure you the epithet was deliberately chosen."

"No, Herr Settembrini, there I find you are unjust. I admit the man has his faults; his manner of speech becomes disagreeable in the long run, there is something forced about it, especially when one remembers he had the great sorrow of losing his wife up here. But what an estimable and meritorious man he is, after all, a benefactor to suffering humanity! I met him the other day coming from an operation, resection of ribs, a matter of life and death, you know. It made a great impression on me, to see him fresh from such exacting and splendid work, in which he is so much the master. He was still warm from it, and had lighted a cigar by way of reward. I envied him."

"That was commendable of you. Well, and your sentence?"

"He has not set any definite time."

"That is good too. And now let us betake us to our cure, Engineer. Each to his own place."

They parted at the door of number thirty--four.

"You are going up to the roof now, Herr Settembrini? It must be more fun to lie in company than alone. Do you talk? Are they pleasant people?"

"Oh, they are nothing but Parthians and Scythians."

"You mean Russians?"

"Russians, male and female," said Settembrini, and the corner of his mouth spanned a little. "Good--bye, Engineer."

He had said that of malice aforethought, undoubtedly. Hans Castorp walked into his own room in confusion. Was Settembrini aware of his state? Very likely, like the schoolmaster he was, he had been spying on him, and seen which way his eyes were going. Hans Castorp was angry with the Italian and also with himself, for having by his lack of self--control invited the thrust. He took up his writing materials to carry them with him into the balcony——for now it was no more use; the letter home, the third letter, must be written——and as he did so he went on whipping up his anger, muttering to himself about this windbag and logic chopper, who meddled with matters that were no concern of his, and chirruped to the girls in the street. He felt quite disinclined to the effort of writing, the organ--grinder had put him off it altogether, with his innuendo. But no matter what his feelings, he must have winter clothing, money, footwear, linen—-in brief, everything he might have brought with him had he known he was coming, not for three short summer weeks, but for an indefinite stay which was certain to last for a piece into the winter—-or rather, considering the notions about time current up here, was quite likely to last all the winter. It was this he must let them know at home, even if only as a possibility; he must tell the whole story, and not put them, or himself, off any longer with pretexts.

In this spirit, then, he wrote, practising the technique he had so often seen Joachim practise; with a fountain--pen, in his deck--chair, with his knees drawn up and the portfolio laid upon them. He wrote upon the letter--paper of the establishment, of which he kept a supply in his table drawer, to James Tienappel, who stood closest to him among the three uncles, and asked him to pass the news on to the Consul. He spoke of an unfortunate occurrence, of suspicions that had proved justified, of the medical opinion that it would be best for him to remain where he was for a part, perhaps for all of the winter, since cases like his often proved more obstinate than those that began more alarmingly and it was clearly advisable to go after the infection energetically and root it out once for all. From this point of view, he considered, it had been a most fortunate circumstance that he had chanced to come here, and been induced to submit to an examination, for otherwise he might have remained for some time in ignorance of his condition, and been apprised of it later and more alarmingly. As for the length of time which would probably be required for the cure, they must not be surprised to hear the whole winter might easily slip away before his return——in short, that he might come down hardly earlier than Joachim. Ideas about time were different up here from those ordinarily held about the length of stay at the baths, or at an ordinary cure. The smallest unit of time, so to speak, was the month, and a single month was almost no time at all.

The weather was cool, he sat in his overcoat, with a rug about him, and his hands were cold. At times he looked up from the paper which he was covering with these reasonable and sensible phrases, at the landscape now so familiar he scarcely saw it any more: this extended valley with its retreating succession of peaks at the entrance——they looked pale and glassy to--day——with its bright and populous floor, which glistened when the sun shone full upon it, and its forest--clad or meadowy slopes, whence came the sound of cow--bells. He wrote with growing ease, and wondered why he had dreaded to write. For as he wrote he felt that nothing could be clearer than his presentation of the matter, and that there was no doubt it would meet with perfect comprehension at home. A young man of his class and circumstances acted for himself when it seemed advisable; he took advantage of the facilities which existed expressly for him and his like. So it was fitting. If he had taken the journey home, they would have made him come back again on hearing his report. He asked them to send what things he needed. And at the end he asked to have money sent: a monthly cheque of eight hundred marks would cover everything.

He signed his name. It was done. This last letter was exhaustive, it covered the case; not according to the time--conceptions of down below, but according to those obtaining up here; it asserted Hans Castorp's *freedom*. This was his own word, albeit not expressed; he would hardly have shaped the syllables even in his mind; but he felt the full sense of its meaning, as he had come to know it during his stay up here——a sense which had little to do with the Settembrinian significance——and his breast was shaken with that excited alarm, which swept over him in a wave, as it had done before.

His head was hot with the blood that had gone to it as he wrote, his cheeks burned. He took the thermometer from his lamp--stand and "measured," as though to make use of an opportunity. Mercurius had gone up to 100°.

"Look at that," he thought; and added a postscript to his letter: "It did strain me rather, after all, to write this. My temperature is 100°. I see that I must be very quiet, for the present. You must excuse me if I don't write often." Then he lay back, and held up his hand toward the light, palm outward, as he had held it behind the lightscreen. But the light of day did not encroach upon its living outline; rather it looked more substantial and opaque for its background of bright air, only its outer edges were rosily illuminated. This was his living hand, that he was used to see, to use, to wash——not that uncanny scaffolding which he had beheld through the screen. The analytic grave then opened was closed again.

Whims of Mercurius

October began as months do: their entrance is, in itself, an unostentatious and soundless affair, without outward signs and tokens; they, as it were, steal in softly and, unless you are keeping close watch, escape your notice altogether. Time has no divisions to mark its passage, there is never a thunder--storm or blare of trumpets to announce the beginning of a new month or year. Even when a new century begins it is only we mortals who ring bells and fire off pistols.

To Hans Castorp the first day of October and the last day of September were as like as two peas; both were equally cold and unfriendly, and those that followed were the same. In the rest--cure one used one's overcoat and both camel's--hair rugs, not only in the evening, but in the day--time. The fingers that held the book were stiff and clammy, however the cheeks burned; and Joachim was strongly tempted to resort to his fur sack, but resisted, in order not to pamper himself thus early in the season. Some days later, however—that is, between the beginning and middle of the month—there came another change: a latter summer set in, with amazing splendour. The praises of this mountain October, which Hans Castorp had heard, were not idly sung. For some two and a half weeks all the glories of heaven reigned over valley and mountain, one day outvied another in blueness and clarity, and the sun burned down with such immediate power that everyone felt impelled to don the lightest of wear, muslin frocks and linen trousers already put aside. The adjustable canvas parasol without a handle was called into requisition, and fitted by its cunning device of holes and pegs on to the arm of the reclining--chair; and even its shelter was felt to be insufficient against the midday glare.

"I'm glad I'm here still, for this," said Hans Castorp to his cousin. "It has been so wretched at times, and now it is as though we had the winter behind us, and only good weather to look forward to." He was quite right. There were indeed not many signs that pointed to the true state of the calendar; and even those there were did not strike the eye.

Aside from the few oak--trees that had been set out down in the Platz, where they had just managed to survive, and long before now had despondently shed their leaves, the whole region held no deciduous trees to give the landscape an autumnal cast; only the hybrid Alpine alder, which renews its soft needles as though they were leaves, showed a wintry baldness. The other trees of the region, whether towering or stunted, were evergreen pines and firs, invincible against the assaults of this irregular winter, which might scatter its snow--storms through all the months of the year: only the many--shaded, rust--red tone that lay over the forest gave notice, despite the glowing sunshine, of a declining year. Yet, looking closer, there were the wild flowers, speaking, though softly, yet to the same effect; the meadow orchis, the bushy aquilegia were no longer in bloom, only the gentian and the lowly autumn crocus, bearing witness to the inner sharpness of the superficially heated air, that could pierce one to the bone as one sat, like a chill in fever, though one glowed outwardly from the ardour of the sun.

Hans Castorp did not keep inward count of the time, as does the man who husbands it, notes its passing, divides and tells and labels its units. He had not heeded the silent entry of the tenth month, but he was arrested by its appeal to the senses, this glowing heat that concealed the frost within and beneath it. It was a sensation which, to anything like this degree, he had never before experienced, and it aroused him to the culinary comparison which he made to Joachim, of an *omelette en surprise*, holding an ice concealed within the hot froth of the beaten egg. He often made such comments, talking headlong and volubly, as a man does in a feverish chill. But between whiles he was silent; we shall not say self--absorbed, for his attention was presumably directed outwards, though upon a single point. All else, whether of the animate or the inanimate world, swam about him in a mist——a mist of his own making, which Hofrat Behrens and Dr. Krokowski would doubtless have explained as the product of soluble toxins, as the befuddled one himself did also, though without having the slightest power or even desire to rid himself of the state they induced. For that is an intoxication, by which one is possessed, under the influence of which one abhors nothing more than the thought of sobriety. It asserts itself against impressions that would weaken its force, it will not admit them, it wards them off. Hans Castorp was aware, and had even spoken of the fact, that Madame Chauchat's profile was not her strong point, that it was no longer quite youthful, was even a little sharp. And the consequence? He avoided looking at her in profile, he literally closed his eyes when he caught that view of her, even at a distance; it pained him. Why?

Should not reason have leaped to take advantage of the favourable moment to reasert itself? But what do we ask? He grew pale with rapture when, tempted by the brilliant weather, she appeared at second breakfast in the white lace matinée which made her look so ravishing——appeared late, accompanied by the banging of the door, smiling, her arms raised in a pretty posture, and presented herself thus to the dining--room before she glided to her seat. But he was enraptured not so much because she looked so charming, as because her charm added strength to the sweet intoxication in his brain, the intoxication that willed to be, that cared only to be justified and nourished. An authority of Ludovico Settembrini's way of thinking might have characterized as depravity, as a "form of depravity," such a lack of good intention. Hans Castorp sometimes pondered over the literary things the Italian had said about illness and despair——which he had found incomprehensible, or at least pretended to himself to find them so. He looked at Clavdia Chauchat——at the flaccidity of her back, the posture of her head; he saw her come habitually late to table, without reason or excuse, solely out of a lack of order and disciplined energy. He saw the same lack when she let slam every door through which she passed, when she moulded bread pellets at the table, when she gnawed her fingers; and he had a suspicion, which he did not put into words, that if she was ill——and that she was, probably incurably, since she had been up here so often and so long——her illness was in good part, if not entirely, a moral one: as Settembrini had said, neither the ground nor the consequence of her "slackness," but precisely one and the same thing. He recalled the contemptuous gesture of the humanist when he spoke of the "Parthians and Scythians" in whose company he was forced to take the rest--cure. It had been a gesture not only of deliberate, but also of natural and instinctive disdain; and that feeling was quite comprehensible to Hans Castorp. Had he not once, who always sat so erect at table, loathed and despised the banging of doors, and never, never was tempted to gnaw his fingers, because to that end Maria had been given him instead, had he not once taken deep offence at the unmannerly behaviour of Frau Chauchat, and felt an unconquerable sense of superiority when he heard the narrow--eyed one essay to speak his mother--tongue?

The present state of his feelings, however, had put on one side any such sentiments as these; it was now the Italian who was the object of his irritation, because he, in his benightedness, had spoken of Parthians and Scythians and had *not* meant thereby the persons at the "bad" Russian table, the shock--headed, linenless students, who sat there disputing endlessly in their outlandish tongue, which was obviously the only one they knew, and which, in its soft, spineless character reminded Hans Castorp of the thorax without ribs Hofrat Behrens had described to him. True, the manners and customs of such people might readily awaken feelings of disgust in the breast of a humanist. They ate with their knives, and unmentionably messed the front of their blouses. Settembrini asserted that one of them, a medical student well on in his training, was so ignorant of Latin, as not to know, for example, what the word vacuum meant. As for the married couple in number thirty--two, Hans Castorp's own daily experience of them was such as to render quite credible Frau Stöhr's report, that when the bathingmaster entered their room in the morning for the usual massage, they received him lying in bed together.

All this might well be true. But after all, the distinction between "good" and "bad" was a plain one, it did not exist for nothing. Hans Castorp assured himself that he felt only contempt for any propagandist of the republic and the *bello stile* who went about with his nose in the air, and calmly——with particular calm, although at the same time both febrile and fuddled——lumped the members of both tables together under the title of Parthians and Scythians. Hans Castorp understood only too well the sense in which he used it, since he had begun to understand the connexion between Frau Chauchat's illness and her "slackness." But as he had one day put it to Joachim: one begins by being angry and disgusted, and then all at once "something quite different enters in," that has "nothing to do with moral judgment," and it is all up with your severity; you are simply not at home to pedagogic influences, however republican, however eloquent. But, we are impelled to ask, probably again in the spirit of Ludovico Settembrini, what sort of questionable experience is this, which palsies a man's judgment, robs him of all claim to it, or even makes him waive that claim, and experience in so doing the abandonment of ecstasy? We do not ask its name——for that everyone knows. Our question rather refers to its moral quality; and we confess that we do not anticipate any very self--confident reply. In Hans Castorp's case its nature was evident in the extent to which he not only ceased to exercise his judgment, but even began to experiment for his own part and upon his own mortal vesture. He tried, for instance, how it would feel to sit at table with his back all relaxed, and discovered that it afforded sensible relief to the pelvic muscles. Again, one day, instead of punctiliously closing a door behind him, he let it slam; and this too he found both fitting and agreeable. It corresponded to the shoulder--shrug with which Joachim had greeted him at the station, and which was so habitual among those up here.

In brief, our traveller was now over head and ears in love with Clavdia Chauchat——we may still use the phrase, since we have already obviated any possible misunderstanding on the score of it. We have seen that the essence of his passion was something quite other than the tender and pensive mood of that oft--quoted ditty: rather it was a wild and vagrant variation upon the lovesick lute, it was mingled frost and fire, like the state of a fever patient, or the

October air in these high altitudes. What he actually lacked, in fact, was an emotional bridge between two extremes. On the one hand his passion dwelt, with an immediacy that left the young man pale and staring, upon Frau Chauchat's knee, the line of her thigh, her back, her neck--bone, her arms that pressed together her little breasts——in a word, it dwelt upon her body, her idle, accentuated body, exaggerated by disease and rendered twice over body. And, on the other hand, it was something in the highest degree fleeting and tenuous; a thought, nay, a dream, the frightful, infinitely alluring dream of a young man whose unspoken, unconscious questioning of the universe has received no answer save a hollow silence. We have as much right as the next person to our private thoughts about the story we are relating; and we would here hazard the surmise that young Hans Castorp would never have overstepped so far the limits originally fixed for his stay if to his simple soul there might have been vouchsafed, out of the depth of his time, any reasonably satisfying explanation of the meaning and purpose of man's life.

For the rest, his lovesick state afforded him all the joy and all the anguish proper to it the world over. The anguish is acute, it has, like all anguish, a mortifying element; it shatters the nervous system to an extent that takes the breath away, and can wring tears from the eyes of a grown man. As for the joys, to do them justice, they were manifold, and no less piercing than the anguish, though their occasion might be trifling indeed. Almost any moment of the Berghof day might bring one forth. For example, about to enter the dining--room, Hans Castorp would perceive the object of his dreams behind him——an experience clear and simple in anticipation, but inwardly ravishing to the point of tears. Their eyes meet at close range, his own and her greygreen ones, whose slightly oriental shape and position pierce him to the very marrow. He is incapable of connected thought, but unconsciously steps back to give her precedence through the door. With a half--smile, a half--audible "*Merci,*" she accepts his conventional courtesy and, passing him by, enters the room. He stands there, within the aura of her personality as it sweeps past, idiotic with happiness at the encounter, and at the word which has been uttered by her mouth directly for his ear. He follows her, he moves unsteadily to his own table and, sinking into his chair, becomes aware that Clavdia, as she too takes her place, has turned to look at him. He thinks she wears an expression as though musing on their encounter at the door. Oh, unbelievable adventure! Oh, joy, rapture, and boundless exaltation! Ah, no, this drunkenness of fantastic bliss Hans Castorp could never have experienced at the glance of any healthy little goose down in the flat--land, to whom he might have, calmly, correctly, and with most definite intentions, "given his heart," and devoted the sentiments described in the song. He greets the schoolmistress with feverish sprightliness——she has seen the whole thing, and her downy old cheek wears its dusky signal——and then bombards Miss Robinson with English conversation, so absurdly that she, not versed in the ecstatic, fairly recoils, and measures him with mistrustful eyes.

Another time, as they sit at the evening meal, the serene rays of the setting sun fall upon the "good" Russian table. The curtains have been drawn over the window and the verandah door, but somewhere there is a little crack, and through it the red gleam finds its way, not hot, but dazzling, and falls upon Frau Chauchat's face, so that she shields it with her hand as she sits talking with the concave countryman on her right. It is annoying but not serious, nobody troubles about it, probably not even the fair one herself. But across the dining--room Hans Castorp sees it——quiescent awhile, like the others. He examines the situation, follows the course of the ray of light, makes up his mind where it enters. It comes from the bay--window in the right--hand corner, between the verandah door and the "bad" Russian table, at a goodish distance from Frau Chauchat's place, and almost equally far from Hans Castorp's. Without a word he gets up and, serviette in hand, crosses over among the tables, draws the creamcoloured curtains so that they lap well over one another, convinces himself by a glance over his shoulder that the ray from the setting sun is shut out and Frau Chauchat relieved, and with an air of perfect equanimity goes back to his place. An observant young man, who takes it upon himself to perform a needful courtesy neglected by others. But few of them even noticed his act; Frau Chauchat, however, instantly felt the relief, and turned round, remaining in that position until Hans Castorp had resumed his place and, sitting down, looked over at her, when she thanked him, with a friendly, rather surprised smile, and a bow that was less an inclination than a shoving forward of the head. He acknowledged by a bow in his turn. His heart stood stock--still, it seemed not to beat. Only after the whole thing was over did it begin again, and hammered, and only then did he become conscious that Joachim had kept his eyes directed upon his plate. Afterwards, too, he realized that Frau Stöhr had nudged Dr. Blumenkohl in the side, and then looked about at their own and other tables, trying to catch people's eyes.

All this is the sheerest commonplace; but the commonplace becomes remarkable when it springs from remarkable soil. There were periods of strain and periods when the tension between them beneficently relaxed—-though perhaps the tension existed less between them than it did in Hans Castorp's fevered imagination, for how far Madame Chauchat was affected we can only guess. In these days of fine weather the majority of the guests betook themselves to the verandah, after the midday meal, and stood about in groups, sunning themselves, for a quarter--hour or so, in a scene much like that on the Sunday afternoons of the fortnightly concerts. All these young people, absolutely idle, overfed on a meat and sweet diet, and without exception feverish—-chattered and laughed, philandered, made eyes. Frau Salomon from Amsterdam would perch on the balustrade, hard pressed on the right by the knees of the thicklipped Gänser, on the left by the Swedish minion—-who, it appeared, was quite recovered, but extending his cure for a little space before going home. Frau Iltis was apparently a widow; for she had rejoiced only lately in the visit of a "fiancé"—-a melancholy, inferior--looking person, whose presence had not in the least prevented her from accepting the attentions of the hook--nosed, fiery--eyed Captain

Miklosich, him of the waxed mustachios and swelling chest. New figures turned up on the terrace: ladies of various nationalities from the general rest--halls, and new arrivals since the first of October, whom Hans Castorp barely knew by name. Then there were cavaliers of Herr Albin's kidney, monocled youths of seventeen, a spectacled, rosyfaced young Dutchman with a mania for collecting postage stamps; certain Greeks, with pomaded hair and almond--shaped eyes, inclined to overreach at table; and a pair of young dandies who were nicknamed Max and Moritz, and bore a great reputation for breaking out of bounds. The humpbacked Mexican, whose ignorance of any language save his own lent him the facial expression of a deaf person, took endless photographs, dragging his tripod from one point to another on the terrace. Sometimes the Hofrat would appear, and perform his "stunt" with the bootlaces. And somewhere in the thick of the crowd would lurk solitary the religious devotee from Mannheim; Hans Castorp would watch disgustedly to see his great sad eyes take their secret way. But to return, by way of example, to some of those strains and stresses to which Hans Castorp's state was prone. Our young man was sitting on a painted garden chair, with his back against the wall, talking with his cousin, whom he had forced, against his will, to come outside; in front of him; by the balustrade, Frau Chauchat stood smoking with her table--mates. He talked for her benefit; she turned her back. His thirst for conversation was not satisfied by Joachim; he must needs make an acquaintance—-and whose? No other than Hermine Kleefeld's. He directed a casual word toward that young lady, then presented himself and his cousin by name, and drew up another chair, in order to carry on the game. Did she know, he asked, what a deuce of a fright she had put him in, at their first encounter, when she had whistled him such an inspiriting welcome? He did not mind owning that she had accomplished her purpose; he had felt as though someone had hit him on the head—-she might ask his cousin! He called it an outrage, frightening harmless strangers like that, piping at them with her pneumothorax! And so forth and so on. Joachim, quite aware of the rôle that was being forced upon him, sat with his eyes on the ground; even

Fräulein Kleefeld gradually perceived, from Hans Castorp's distraught and wandering eye, that she was being made a tool of, and felt piqued accordingly. And still the poor youth went on smirking and turning phrases and modulating his voice, until at last he actually succeeded in making Frau Chauchat turn round and look him in the face. But only for a moment. Her Pribislav eyes glided rapidly down his figure, as he sat there one knee over the other, with a deliberate insouciance which had all the effect of scorn; they paused for a space upon his yellow boots, and then carelessly, with perhaps a smile in their depths, withdrew.

It was a bitter, bitter blow. Hans Castorp talked on awhile, feverishly. Then, inwardly smitten by the power of that gaze upon his boots, he fell silent almost in the middle of a word, and lapsed into deep dejection. Fräulein Kleefeld, bored and offended, went her way. Joachim remarked, not without irritation, that perhaps they might go up to the rest--cure now. And a broken spirit answered feebly that they might. Hans Castorp anguished piteously for two days. Nothing occurred in that time to be balsam for his smarting wound. What had she meant by her look? Why, in the name of reason, had she visited him with her scorn? Did she regard him merely as a healthy young noodle from down in the flat--land, whose receptivity was sure to be of the harmless sort; as a guileless, ordinary chap, who went about laughing and earning his daily bread and filling his belly full; as a model pupil in the school of life, with no comprehension of anything but the tedious advantages of a respectable career? Was he, he asked himself, a mere feckless tourist and three--weeks' guest, or was he a man who had made his profession on the score of a moist spot, a member of the order, one of those up here, with a good two months to his credit——and had not Mercurius only yesterday evening climbed up to 100°? Ah, here, even here, lay the bitter drop that overflowed his cup: Mercurius had ceased to mount! The fearful depression of these days had a chilling, sobering, relaxing effect upon Hans Castorp's system, which, to his profound chagrin, displayed itself in a reduced degree of fever, scarcely higher than normal. He had the cruel experience of proving to himself that all his anguish, all his dejection, had no other result than to separate him still further from Clavdia, and from that which was significant in her existence.

The third day brought the blessed release. It was early upon a magnificent October morning, sunny and fresh. The meadows were covered with silvery--grey webs. The sun and the waning moon both hung high up in a lucent heaven. The cousins were abroad earlier than usual, meaning to honour the fine weather by extending their morning walk a little further than the prescribed limits, and continuing the forest path beyond the bench by the watercourse. Joachim's curve, too, had lately shown a gratifying decrease; he had accordingly suggested this refreshing irregularity, and Hans Castorp had not said no.

"We seem to be cured," he said, "no fever, free of infection, as good as ripe for the world again. Why shouldn't we have our fling?" They set out with walking--sticks, and hatless——for since his "profession" Hans Castorp had resigned himself to the prevailing custom, despite the original assertion of his own contrary--minded conventions. But they had not yet covered the initial ascent of the reddish path, had arrived only at about that point where the novice had once encountered the pneumatic crew, when they saw at some distance ahead of them, slowly mounting, Frau Chauchat; Frau Chauchat in white, a white sweater and white flannel skirt, even white shoes. Her redblond hair gleamed in the morning sun. To be precise, Hans Castorp saw her; Joachim was made aware of her presence by an unpleasant sensation of being dragged and pulled along by his cousin, who had started up at a great pace, after having suddenly checked and almost stood still on the path. Joachim found the compulsion exceedingly annoying. His breath came shorter, he began to cough, Hans Castorp, with his eyes on his goal, and his breathing apparatus apparently in splendid trim, gave little heed; and Joachim, having recognized the situation for what it was, drew his brows together and kept step for step, feeling it out of the question to let his cousin go on alone. The lovely morning made Hans Castorp sprightly. And his soul, in that period of black depression, had secretly assembled its powers. He felt a sure intuition that the moment was come to break the ban. He strode on, dragging the panting and reluctant Joachim in his train, and they had as good as overtaken Frau Chauchat, at the point where the path grew level and turned to the right along the wooded hillock. Here the young man slackened his pace, not to be breathless with exertion in the moment of carrying out his purpose. And just beyond the bend in the path, between mountain and precipice, where the sunlight slipped athwart the boughs of the rust--coloured firs, it actually fell out, the wonder came to pass, that Hans Castorp, on Joachim's left, overtook the fragile fair one, he went by her with a manly stride, and then, at the moment when he was beside her, on her right, greeted her with a profoundly respectful, hatless inclination of the head, and a murmured "good--morning," to which she answered by a friendly bow, that showed no trace of surprise, and a good--morning in her turn. She said it in Hans Castorp's mother--tongue, and smiled with her eyes. And all that was something different, something fundamentally and blessedly other than that look she had bent upon his boots—it was a gift of fortune, an unexampled turn in affairs, a joy well--nigh beyond comprehending, it was the blessed release. Transported by that word, look, and smile, half blinded by his senseless joy, Hans Castorp trod on winged feet, hurrying the misused Joachim with him, who uttered not a word, and gazed away down the steep. It had been a manœuvre of a rather unscrupulous sort; in Joachim's eyes, as Hans Castorp well knew, it looked very like treachery. Yet it was not the same thing as borrowing a lead--pencil of a perfect stranger; one might even say it would have been ill--bred to pass by a lady with whom one had been for months under the same roof and not salute her. They had even been in conversation with her, that time in the waiting--room. That was why Joachim could say nothing; but Hans Castorp well knew another reason that made his honour--loving cousin walk on in silence with averted head, while he himself was so supremely happy, so glad all over, at the success of his manœuvre. Never a man down in the flatland who had "given his heart" to some healthy, commonplace little goose, been successful in his suit, and experienced all the orthodox and anticipatory gratifications proper to his state, never could such a man be blissfuller, no, not half so blissful, as Hans Castorp now over this momentary joy which he had snatched.—-And so, after a while, he clapped his cousin heartily on the shoulder and said: "Hullo, what's the matter with you? Isn't it magnificent to--day? Let's go down to the Kurhaus afterwards, there will probably be music. Perhaps they'll play that thing from *Carmen*.—- What's the matter? Has anything got under your skin?"

"No," Joachim answered. "But you look so hot, I'm afraid your curve has gone up again."

It had. The greeting he had exchanged with Clavdia Chauchat had overcome the mortifying depression; it was at bottom the consciousness of this which had lain at the root of Hans Castorp's gratification. Yes, yes, Joachim was right, Mercurius was mounting again: when Hans Castorp consulted him, on their return from their walk, he had climbed up to 100.4°.

Encyclopædic

If certain insinuations on Herr Settembrini's part had angered Hans Castorp, the annoyance was quite unjustified, as also his feeling that the schoolmaster had been spying on him. A blind man must have seen how it stood with the youth; he himself did nothing to conceal his state, being prevented by a certain native and lofty simplicity. He inclined rather to wear his heart upon his sleeve, in contrast—if you like, favourable contrast—-to the devotee from Mannheim, with his thin hair and furtive mien. But in general we would emphasize the fact that people in Hans Castorp's state regularly feel a craving for self--revelation, an impulse to confess themselves, a blind preoccupation with self, and a thirst to possess the world of their own emotions, which is the more offensive to the sober onlooker, the less sense, reasonableness, or hope there lies in the whole affair.

How people in this state go about to betray themselves is hard to define; but it seems they can neither do nor leave undone anything which would not have that effect——doubly so, then, in a society like that of the Berghof, where, as the critically minded Herr Settembrini once expressed it, people were possessed of two ideas, and only two: temperature——and then again temperature. By the second temperature he meant preoccupation with such questions as, for instance, with whom Frau CónsulGeneral Wurmbrandt from Vienna consoled herself for the defection of Captain Miklosich——whether with the Swedish minion, or Lawyer Paravant from Dortmund, or both. Everybody knew that the bond between the lawyer and Frau Salomon from Amsterdam, after subsisting for several months, had been broken by common consent, and that Frau Salomon had followed the leanings of her time of life and taken up with callow youth. The thick--lipped Gänser from Hermine Kleefeld's table was for the present under her wing; she had taken him "to have and to hold," as Frau Stöhr, in legal parlance, yet not without perspicuity, had put it——and thus Lawyer Paravant was free either to quarrel or to compound with the Swede over the favours of the Frau Consul--General, as seemed to him advisable.

These affairs then——in which, of course, the passage along the balconies, at the end of the glass partitions, played a considerable rôle——were rife in Berghof society, particularly among the fevered youth. They occupied people's minds, they were a salient feature of life up here——and even in saying thus much we are far from having precisely defined the position with regard to them. Hans Castorp, on this subject, received a singular impression: it was that a certain fundamental fact of life, which is conceded the world over to be of great importance, and is the fertile theme of constant allusion, both in jest and earnest, that this fundamental fact of life bore up here an entirely altered emphasis. It was weighty with a new weight; it had an accent, a value, and a significance which were utterly novel——and which set the fact itself in a light to make it look much more alarming than it had been before. Thus far, whenever we have referred to any questionable performances at the Berghof, we have done so in what may have seemed a light and jesting tone; this without prejudice to our real opinion as to the levity, or otherwise, of the performances, and solely for the usual obscure reasons which prompt other people to adopt the same. But as a matter of fact, that tone was far less usual in our present sphere than it is elsewhere in the world. Hans Castorp had considered himself pretty well--informed on the subject of the above--named "fact of life" which has always and everywhere been such a favourite target for shafts of wit. And he may have been right in so considering. But now he found that the knowledge he had had down in the flat--land had been most inadequate, that he had actually been in a state of simple ignorance. For his personal emotions in the time of his stay up here——upon the nature of which we have been at some pains to enlighten the reader, and which had been at moments so acute as to wring from the young man that cry of "Oh, my God!"——had opened his eyes, had made him capable of hearing and comprehending the wild, the overstrained, the namelessly extravagant key in which all the "affairs" up here were set. Not that, even up here, they did not make jests on the subject. But up here, far more than down below, jests seemed out of place. They made one's teeth to chatter, and took away one's breath, they betrayed themselves too plainly for what they were, a thin and obvious disguise for a hidden extremity——or rather, an extremity impossible to hide. Hans Castorp well remembered the mottled pallor of Joachim's skin when, for the first and only time, he had innocently alluded to Marusja's physical charms in the light tone he might have assumed at home. He remembered the chill withdrawal of the blood from his own face, the time he had drawn the curtain to shield Madame Chauchat from the sun; he knew that he had seen the same look on other faces up here, both before and since——he usually remarked it in pairs, as, for example, on the faces of Frau Salomon and young Gänser, in the beginning of that relation between them so happily described by Frau Stöhr. Hans Castorp, we say, recalled all this, and realized that under such circumstances it would not only have been very hard for him not to "betray himself," but that the effort would not have been worth his pains. In other words, not alone the noble simplicity which did him honour, but also a certain sympathetic something in the air urged him not to do violence to his feelings or make any secret of his condition.

Joachim had, as we know, early spoken of the difficulty of forming acquaintances up here. In reality this arose chiefly from the fact that the cousins formed a miniature group by themselves in the society of the cure; but also because the soldierly Joachim was bent on nothing else but speedy recovery, and hence objected on principle to any closer contact or more social relations with his fellow sufferers. It was a good deal this attitude of his that prevented his cousin from exposing his feelings more freely to the world at large. Even so, there came an evening when Joachim might behold his cousin the centre of a group composed of Hermine Kleefeld, Gänser, Rasmussen, and the youth of the monocle and the finger--nail, making an impromptu speech on the subject of Frau Chauchat's peculiar and exotic facial structure, and betraying himself by his unsteady voice and the excited glitter of his eyes, until his listeners exchanged glances, nudged each other, and tittered.

This was painful for Joachim; but the object of their mirth seemed insensible to his own self--betrayal; perhaps he felt that his state, if concealed and unregarded, would never come to any proof. He might count, however, on a general understanding of it, and as for the inevitable malice that went with it, he took that for granted. People, not only at his own table, but at neighbouring ones as well, enjoyed seeing him flush and pale when the glass door slammed. And even this gratified him; it was like an outward confirmation and assertion of his inner frenzy, which seemed to him calculated to forward his affair, and encourage his vague and senseless hopes. And so it too made him happy. It came to this: that people actually stood about in groups to observe the infatuated youth——after dinner, on the terrace, or on a Sunday afternoon before the porter's lodge, when the letters were distributed, for on that day they were not carried to the patients' rooms. He was quite generally known to be very far gone, drunk as a lord and not caring who knew it. Frau Stöhr, Fräulein Engelhart, Hermine Kleefeld and her friend the tapir--faced girl, Herr Albin, the young man with the finger--nail, and perhaps others among the guests—-would stand together and watch him, with the corners of their mouths drawn down, fairly chortling, whilst he, poor wight, his face aglow with the heat that from the first had never left him, with the glittering eye the gentleman rider's cough had kindled, would gaze, forlornly and frantically smiling, in one certain direction.

It was really splendid of Herr Settembrini, under these circumstances, to go up to Hans Castorp, engage him in conversation, and ask him how he did. But it is doubtful whether the young man knew how to value and to be grateful for such benevolence and freedom from prejudice. One Sunday afternoon the guests were thronging about the porter's lodge, stretching out their hands for letters. Joachim was among the foremost; but Hans Castorp had stopped in the rear, angling, in the fashion we have described, for a look from Clavdia Chauchat. She was standing near by, among a group of her table--mates, waiting until the press about the lodge should be lightened. It was an hour when all the patients mingled, an hour rich in opportunity, and for that reason beloved of our young man. The week before, he had stood at the window so close to Madame Chauchat that she had in fact jostled him, and then, with a little bow, had said: *"Pardon."* Whereat he, with a feverish presence of mind for which he thanked his stars, had responded: *"Pas de quoi, madame."*

What a blessed dispensation of providence, he thought, that there should be a regular Sunday afternoon distribution of letters! One might say that he spent the week in waiting for the next week's delivery. And waiting means hurrying on ahead, it means regarding time and the present moment not as a boon, but an obstruction; it means making their actual content null and void, by mentally overleaping them. Waking, we say, is long. We might just as well—-or more accurately—say it is short, since it consumes whole spaces of time without our living them or making any use of them as such.

We may compare him who lives on expectation to a greedy man, whose digestive apparatus works through quantities of food without converting it into anything of value or nourishment to his system. We might almost go so far as to say that, as undigested food makes man no stronger, so time spent in waiting makes him no older. But in practice, of course, there is hardly such a thing as pure and unadulterated waiting.

Well, the week had been somehow devoured, and the hour for the Sunday afternoon post came round again, so like the other it seemed never to have changed. Like to that other, what thrilling opportunities it offered, what prospects lay concealed within it of coming into social relations with Frau Chauchat! Prospects that made the heart of young Hans Castorp leap and contract, yet without actually issuing in action; for against their doing so lay certain obstacles of a nature partly military, partly civil. In other words, they were in part the fruit of Joachim's presence, in part the result of Hans Castorp's own moral compunctions; but also, in part, they rested upon his sure intuition that social relations with Frau Chauchat, conventional relations, in which one made bows and addressed her as madame, and spoke French as far as possible, were not the thing at all, were neither necessary nor desirable. He stood and watched her laugh as she spoke, precisely as Pribislav Hippe had laughed as he spoke, that time in the school yard: she opened her mouth rather wide, and her slanting, grey--green eyes narrowed themselves to slits above the cheek--bones. That was, to be sure, not "beautiful"; but when one is in love, the aesthetic judgment counts for as little as the moral.

"You are expecting dispatches, Engineer?"

Only one person could talk like that—-and he a disturber of Hans Castorp's peace. The young man started and turned toward Herr Settembrini, who stood there smiling the same fine, humanistic smile that had sat upon his features when he greeted the newcomer, at the bench by the watercourse. Now, as then, it mortified Hans Castorp. We know how often, in his dreams, he had sought to drive away the organ--grinder as an element offensive to his peace; but the waking man is more moral than the sleeping, and, as before, the sight of that smile not only had a sobering effect upon Hans Castorp, but gave him a sense of gratitude, as though it had responded to his need.

"Dispatches, Herr Settembrini? Good Lord, I'm no ambassador! There might be a postcard there for one of us. My cousin is just asking."

"That devil on two sticks in there has handed mine out to me already," Herr Settembrini said, and carried his hand to the side pocket of the inevitable pilot coat.

"Interesting matter, I must confess, of literary and social import. It is about an encyclopædic publication, to which a philanthropic institution has considered me worthy to contribute. Beautiful work, in short——" Herr Settembrini interrupted himself. "But how about you?" he asked. "How are your affairs going? For instance, how far has the process of acclimatization gone? You have not been so long among us but that one may still put the question."

"Thanks, Herr Settembrini. It still has its difficulties it seems. It very likely will have, up to the last day. My cousin told me when I came that many people never got used to it. But one gets used in time to not getting used."

"A complicated process," laughed the Italian. "An odd way of settling down in a place. But of course youth is capable of anything. It doesn't get used to things, but it strikes roots."

"And after all, this isn't a Siberian penal settlement."

"No. Ah, you have a fancy for oriental simile. Natural enough. Asia surrounds us——wherever one's glance rests, a Tartar physiognomy." Herr Settembrini gave a discreet glance over his shoulder. "Genghis Khan," he said. "Wolves of the steppes, snow, vodka, the knout, Schlüsselburg, Holy Russia. They ought to set up an altar to Pallas Athene, here in the vestibule——to ward off the evil spell. Look yonder——there is a species of Ivan Ivanovitch without a shirt--front, having a disagreement with Lawyer Paravant. Both of them want to be in the front rank to receive their letters. I can't tell which of them is in the right, but, for my part, Lawyer Paravant fights under the ægis of the goddess. He is an ass, of course; but at least he knows some Latin."

Hans Castorp laughed——a thing Herr Settembrini never did. One could not imagine him laughing heartily; he never got further than the fine, dry crisping of the corner of his mouth. He looked at the laughing young man, and presently asked: "Have you received your diapositive?"

"I have received it," Hans Castorp weightily affirmed. "Just the other day. Here it is," and he felt for it in his inner breast pocket.

"Ah, you carry it in a case. Like a certificate, as it were——a sort of membership card. Very good. Let me see it." And Herr Settembrini held it against the light, between the thumb and forefinger of his left hand; a little glass plate framed in strips of black paper. The gesture was a common one up here, one often saw it. His face, with the black almond--shaped eyes, displayed a slight grimace as he did so, but whether this happened in the effort to see more clearly or for other causes, he did not permit it to appear.

"Yes, yes," he said, after a while. "Here is your identity card. Thanks very much," and he handed the plate back to Hans Castorp over his shoulder, without looking.

"Did you see the strands?" asked Hans Castorp. "And the nodules?"

"You know," Herr Settembrini answered him very deliberately, "my opinion of these productions. You know too that those spots and shadows there are very largely of physiological origin. I have seen a hundred such pictures, looking very like this of yours; the decision as to whether they offered definite proof or not was left more or less to the discretion of the person looking at them. I speak as a layman, but a layman of a good many years' experience."

"Does your own look much worse than this one?"

"Rather worse. I am aware, however, that our lords and masters do not base any diagnosis on the evidence of these toys alone. Then you purpose stopping the winter up here with us?"

"Yes—-Lord knows—-I am beginning to get used to the idea of not going back until my cousin does."

"Getting used, that is, to not getting used—-you put that very wittily. I hope you have received supplies from home—-winter clothing, stout foot--gear?"

"Everything—-all in the proper order. I informed my relatives, and our housekeeper sent me everything by express delivery. I shall do nicely now."

"I am relieved. But hold—-you need a bag, a fur sack! What are we thinking of? This late summer is treacherous—-it can turn to winter inside an hour. You will be spending the coldest months up here."

"Yes, the sleeping--sack," Hans Castorp said. "That is a requisite, I suppose. It had crossed my mind that we must be going down to the Platz one of these days soon to buy one. One never needs the thing again, of course—-but even for the five or six months it is worth while. '

"It is, it is.—-Engineer," said Herr Settembrini in a low voice, coming close to the young man as he addressed him, "don't you know there is something frightful in the way you fling the months about? Frightful because unnatural, inconsistent with your character; it is due solely to the facility of your time of life. Ah, the fatal facility of youth! It is the despair of the teacher, for its proneness to display itself in the wrong direction. I beg you, my young friend, not to adopt the phrases current up here, but to speak the language of the European culture native to you. Up here there is too much Asia. It is not without significance that the place is full of Muscovite and Mongolian types. These people—-" Herr Settembrini motioned with his chin over his shoulder—-

"do not put yourself in tune with them, do not be infected with their ideas; rather set yourself against them, oppose your nature, your higher nature against them; cling to everything which to you is by nature and tradition holy, as a son of the godlike West, a son of civilization: and, for example, time. This barbaric lavishness with time is in the Asiatic style; it may be a reason why the children of the East feel so much at home up here. Have you never remarked that when a Russian says four hours, he means what we do when we say one? It is easy to see that the recklessness of these people where time is concerned may have to do with the space conceptions proper to people of such endless territory. Great space, much time—they say, in fact, that they are the nation that has time and can wait. We Europeans, we cannot. We have as little time as our great and finely articulated continent has space, we must be as economical of the one as of the other, we must husband them, Engineer! Take our great cities, the centres and foci of civilization, the crucibles of thought! Just as the soil there increases in value, and space becomes more and more precious, so, in the same measure, does time. *Carpe diem!* That was the song of a dweller in a great city. Time is a gift of God, given to man that he might use it—use it, Engineer, to serve the advancement of humanity."

Whatever difficulty, if any, his phrases offered Herr Setternbrini's Mediterranean palate, he brought them out with a clarity, a euphony, one might almost say a plasticity, that was truly refreshing. Hans Castorp made no answer save the short, stiff, embarrassed bow of a pupil receiving a reprimand. What could he have said?

Herr Settembrini had delivered a private lecture, almost whispered it into his ear, with his back to the rest of the people in the room; it had been so pointed, so unsocial, so little conversable in its nature, that merely to commend its eloquence seemed lacking in tact. One does not tell a schoolmaster that he has expressed himself well. Hans Castorp, indeed, had done so once or twice in the early days of their acquaintance, probably from an instinct to preserve the social equilibrium; but the humanist's utterances had never before reached quite such a didactic pitch. There was nothing for it but to pocket the admonition, feeling as embarrassed as a schoolboy at so much moralizing. Moreover, one could see by Herr Settembrini's expression that he had not finished his train of thought. He still stood so close to Hans Castorp that the young man was constrained to bend a little backwards; and his black eyes gazed fixedly into the other's face.

"You suffer, Engineer," he went on. "You are like one distraught—-who could help seeing it? But your attitude toward suffering can be a European attitude; it should not be the oriental, which in its soft abandonment inclines so readily to seek this spot. The oriental attitude toward suffering is one of pity and a boundless patience—-that cannot, it ought not to be ours, to be yours!—-Look—-we were speaking of what the post had brought us, look at these! Or better, come with me, it is impossible here—-let us withdraw, and I will disclose to you certain matters. Come with me!" And turning, he drew Hans Castorp away, and they entered one of the small reception--rooms, the first on the right next the vestibule, which stood empty. It was furnished as a reading--and writing--room, with oak panelling and a light, vaulted ceiling, bookcases, a centre table covered with news-papers in holders and surrounded with seats, and writing appurtenances arranged in the bay--windows. Herr Settembrini advanced as far as the neighbourhood of one of the windows, Hans Castorp followed. The door remained open.

The Italian sought the baggy side pocket of his pilot coat, and drew thence with impetuous hand a bundle of papers in a large, already opened envelope. Its contents—-various printed matter, and a sheet of writing—-he ran through his fingers under Hans Castorp's eye.

"These papers," he said, "bear the stamp, in French, of the International League for the Organization of Progress. I have them from Lugano, where there is an office of a branch of the League. You inquire after its principles, its scope? I will define them for you, in two words. The League for the Organization of Progress deduces from Darwinian theory the philosophic concept that man's profoundest natural impulse is in the direction of self--realization. From this it follows that all those who seek satisfaction of this impulse must become co--labourers in the cause of human progress. Many are those who have responded to the call; there is a considerable membership, in France, Italy, Spain, Turkey, and in Germany itself. I myself have the honour or having my name inscribed on the roll. A comprehensive and scientifically executed programme has been drawn up, embracing all the projects for human improvement conceivable at the moment. We are studying the problem of our health as a race, and the means for combating the degeneration which is a regrettable accompanying phenomenon of our increasing industrialization. The League envisages the founding of universities for the people, the resolution of the class conflict by means of all the social ameliorations which recommend themselves for the purpose, and finally the doing away with national conflicts, the abolition of war through the development of international law. You perceive that the objects toward which the League directs its efforts are ambitious and broad in their scope. Several international periodicals are evidence of its activities—-monthly reviews, which contain articles in three or four languages on the subject of the progressive evolution of civilized humanity. Numerous local groups have been established in the various countries; it is expected that they will exert an edifying and enlightening influence by means of discussion evenings and appropriate Sunday observances. Above all, the League will strive its utmost to aid with the material at its disposal the political party of progress in every country. You follow me, Engineer?"

"Absolutely," Hans Castorp replied, with precipitation. He had, as he spoke, the feeling of a man who finds himself slipping, but for the moment contrives to keep his feet.

Herr Settembrini appeared satisfied. "I assume that these are new and surprising ideas to you?"

"Yes, I confess this is the first time I have heard of these—-these endeavours."

"Ah," Settembrini murmured, "ah, if you had only heard of them earlier! But perhaps it is not yet too late. These circulars——you would like to know what they say?

Listen. Last spring a formal meeting of the League was called, at Barcelona. You are aware that that city can boast of a quite special affinity with progressive political ideas. The congress sat for a week, with banquets and festivities. I wanted to go——good God, I yearned to be there and take part in the deliberations. But that scurvy rascal of a Hofrat forbade me on pain of death, so——well, I was afraid I should die, and I didn't go. I was in despair, as you may imagine, over the trick my unreliable health had played me. Nothing is more painful than to be prevented by our physical, our animal nature from being of service to reason. My satisfaction, therefore, over this communication from Lugano is the more lively. You are curious to know what it says? I can imagine. But first, a few brief explanations: the League for the Organization of Progress, mindful of its task of furthering human happiness——in other words, of combating human suffering by the available social methods, to the end of finally eliminating it altogether; mindful also of the fact that this lofty task can only be accomplished by the aid of sociology, the end and aim of which is the perfect State, the League, in session at Barcelona, determined upon the publication of a series of volumes bearing the general title: *The Sociology of Suffering*. It should be the aim of the series to classify human suffering according to classes and categories, and to treat it systematically and exhaustively. You ask what is the use of classification, arrangement, systematization? I answer you: order and simplification are the first steps toward the mastery of a subject——the actual enemy is the unknown. We must lead the human race up out of the primitive stages of fear and patient stupidity, and set its feet on the path of conscious activity. We must enlighten it upon two points: first, that given effects become void when one first recognizes and then removes their causes; and second, that almost all individual suffering is due to disease of the social organism. Very well; this is the object of the *Sociological Pathology*. It will be issued in some twenty folio volumes, treating every species of human suffering, from the most personal and intimate to the great collective struggles arising from the conflicting interests of classes and nations; it will, in short, exhibit the chemical elements whose combination in various proportions results in all the ills to which our human flesh is heir. The publication will in every case take as its norm the dignity and happiness of mankind, and seek to indicate the measures and remedies calculated to remove the cause of each deviation. Famous European specialists, physicians, psychologists, and economists will share in the composition of this encyclopædia of suffering, and the general editorial bureau at Lugano will act as the reservoir to collect all the articles which shall flow into it. I can read in your eyes the question as to what my share is to be in all these activities. Hear me to the end. This great work will not neglect the belletrist in so far as he deals with human suffering: a volume is projected which shall contain a compilation and brief analysis of such masterpieces of the world's literature as come into question by depicting one or other kind of conflict—for the consolation and instruction of the suffering. This, then, is the task entrusted to your humble servant, in the letter you see here."

"You don't say, Herr Settembrini! Allow me to offer you my heartiest congratulations! That is a magnificent commission, just in your line, I should think. No wonder the League thought of you! And what joy you must feel to aid in the elimination of human suffering!"

"It is a work very broad in its scope," Herr Settembrini said thoughtfully, "and will require much consideration and wide reading. Especially," he added, and his gaze seemed to lose itself in the immensity of his task, "since literature has regularly chosen to depict suffering, and even second--and third--rate masterpieces treat of it in one form or another. But what of that? So much the better! However comprehensive the work may be, it is at least of a nature that will permit me to carry it on, if needs must, even in this accursed place—-though I hope I need not be here long enough to bring it to a conclusion. That is something," he said, moving closer to Hans

[311]

Castorp, and subduing his voice nearly to a whisper, "that is something which can hardly be said of the duties nature lays upon you, Engineer! This is what I wanted to bring out, this is the word of warning I have been trying to utter. You know what admiration I feel for your profession. But as it is a practical, not an intellectual calling, you are differently situated from myself, in that you can only pursue it down in the world——only there can you be a true European, only there can you actively fight suffering, improve the time, further progress, with your own weapons and in your own way. If I have told you of the task that has fallen to my lot, it was only to remind you, only to recall you to yourself, only to clarify certain conceptions of yours which the atmospheric conditions up here were obviously beginning to becloud. I would urge it upon you: hold yourself upright, preserve your self--respect, do not give ground to the unknown. Flee from this sink of iniquity, this island of Circe, whereon you are not Odysseus enough to dwell in safety. You will be going on all fours——already you are inclining toward your forward extremities, and presently you will begin to grunt——have a care!"

The humanist had uttered these admonitions in the same low voice, shaking his head impressively. He finished with drawn brows and eyes directed toward the ground. To answer him slightly or jestingly, as Hans Castorp would once have done, was out of the question. The young man weighed that possibility for a second, standing with lowered lids. Then he lifted his shoulders and spoke, no louder than Herr Settembrini: "What shall I do?"

"What I told you."

"You mean——go away?"

Herr Settembrini was silent.

"What you mean to say is that I should leave for home?"

"It was the advice I gave you on the first evening, Engineer."

"Yes——and then I was free to do so, though it seemed to me silly to throw up the sponge just because the air up here put me about a bit. But now it is a rather different state of affairs: I have been examined, and Hofrat Behrens told me in so many words that it would be no good my going home, I should only have to come back again; and that if I stopped down there, the whole lobe would be at the devil before you could say Jack Robinson."

"I know; and now you have the evidence in your pocket."

"You say that so ironically—-with the right kind of irony, of course, that cannot for a moment be misunderstood, the direct and classic device of oratory—-you see, I remember the things you say. But do you mean that after you have seen this photograph, after the x--ray and Behrens's diagnosis, you take it upon yourself to advise me to go home?"

Settembrini hesitated for a second. Then he drew himself up, and directed the gaze of his black eyes full upon Hans Castorp's face. He answered, with an emphasis not quite without theatrical effect: "Yes, Engineer, I take it upon myself."

But Hans Castorp's bearing too had stiffened. He stood with his heels together, and looked straight at Herr Settembrini in his turn. This time it was a duel. Hans Castorp stood his ground. Influences from not far off gave him strength. Here was a schoolmaster—-but yonder was a woman with narrow eyes. He made no apologies for his words, he did not beg Herr Settembrini not to take offence; he answered: "Then you are more prudent for yourself than for others. You did not go to Barcelona in the face of the doctor's orders. You were afraid of death, and you stopped up here."

To a certain point Herr Settembrini's pose was undeniably shaken; his smile, as he answered, was slightly forced.

"I know how to value a ready answer—-even though your logic smacks of sophistry. It would disgust me to enter the lists in the sort of rivalry that is too current up here; otherwise I might reply that my case is far more serious than yours—-so much more, in fact, that it is only by artificial means, almost by deliberate self--deception, that I can keep alive the hope of leaving this place and having sight of the world below before I die. In the moment when that hope can no longer be decently sustained, in that moment I shall turn my back on this establishment, and take private lodgings somewhere in the valley. That will be sad; but as the sphere of my labours is the freest, the least material in the world, the change cannot prevent me from resisting the forces of disease and serving the cause of humanity, up to my latest breath. The difference between us, in this respect, I have already pointed out to you. Engineer, you are not the man to assert your better self in these surroundings. I saw it at our first meeting. You reproach me with not having gone to Barcelona. I submitted to the prohibition, not to destroy myself untimely. But I did so with the most stringent reservations; my spirit protested in pride and anguish against the dictates of my wretched body. Whether that protest survives in you, as you comply with the behests of our powers that be——whether it is not rather the body, the body and its evil propensities, to which you lend a ready ear——"

"What have you against the body?" interrupted Hans Castorp suddenly, and looked at him with wide blue eyes, the whites of which were veined with blood. He was giddy with his own temerity and showed as much.——Whatever am I saying? he thought. I'm getting out of my depth. But *I* won't give way; now I have begun, I won't give him the last word if I can help it. Of course he will have it anyhow, but never mind, I will make the most of it while I can.——He enlarged upon his objection: "But you are a humanist, are you not? What can you have to say against the body?"

Settembrini's smile this time was unforced and confident. " 'What have you against analysis?' " he quoted, with his head on one side. " 'Are you down on analysis?' You will always find me ready to answer you, Engineer," he said, with a bow and a sweeping downward motion of the hand, "particularly when your opposition is spirited; and you parry not without elegance. Humanist——yes, certainly, I am a humanist. You could never convict me of ascetic inclinations. I affirm, honour, and love the body, as I protest I affirm, honour, and love form, beauty, freedom, gaiety, the enjoyment of life. I represent the world, the interest of this life, against a sentimental withdrawal and negation, classicism against romanticism. I think my position is unequivocal. But there is one power, one principle, which commands my deepest assent, my highest and fullest allegiance and love; and this power, this principle, is the intellect. However much I dislike hearing that conception of moonshine and cobwebs people call 'the soul' played off against the body, yet, within the antithesis of body and mind, the body is the evil, the devilish principle, for the body is nature, and nature—-within the sphere, I repeat, of her antagonism to the mind, and to reason—-is evil, mystical and evil. 'You are a humanist?' By all means I am a humanist, because I am a friend of mankind, like Prometheus, a lover of humanity and human nobility. That nobility is comprehended in the mind, in the reason, and therefore you will level against me in vain the reproach of Christian obscurantism—-"

Hans Castorp demurred.

"You will," Herr Settembrini persisted, "level this reproach in vain, if humanistic pride one day learns to feel as a debasement and disgrace the fact that the intellect is bound up with the body and with nature. Did you know that the great Plotinus is said to have made the remark that he was ashamed to have a body?" asked Settembrini. He seemed eager for a reply, and Hans Castorp was constrained to confess that this was the first he had heard of it.

"We have it from Porphyrius. An absurd remark, if you like. But the absurd is the intellectually honourable; and nothing can be more pitiable than the reproach of absurdity, levelled against the mind as it asserts its dignity against nature, and refuses to abdicate before her.—-Have you heard of the Lisbon earthquake, Engineer?"

"An earthquake? No—-I see no newspapers up here—-"

"You misunderstand me. *En passant*, let me say it is a pity, and very indicative of the spirit of this place, that you neglect to read the papers. But you misunderstand me, the convulsion of nature to which

I refer is not modern. It took place some hundred and fifty years ago."

"I see. Oh, wait––I have it. I have read that Goethe said to his servant, that night in his bedchamber––"

"No, it was not of that I was speaking," Settembrini interrupted him, closing his eyes, and shaking his small sallow hand in the air. "Besides, you are confusing two catastrophes. You are thinking of the earthquake of Messina. I have in mind the one that visited Lisbon in the year 1755."

"Pardon."

"Well, Voltaire was outraged by it."

"Outraged? That is––how do you mean?"

"He rebelled. Yes. He declined to accept that brutal *fatum et factum*. His spirit refused to abdicate before it. He protested in the name of reason and the intellect against that scandalous dereliction of nature, to which were sacrificed thousands of human lives, and three--quarters of a flourishing city. You are astonished? You smile?

You may well be astonished; but as for smiling, give me leave to tell you it is out of place. Voltaire's attitude was that of a worthy descendant of those old Gauls that shot their arrows against the heavens. There, Engineer, you have the hostility the intellect feels against nature, its proud mistrust, its high--hearted insistence upon the right to criticize her and her evil, reason--denying power. Nature is force; and it is slavish to suffer force, to abdicate before it––to abdicate, that is, inwardly. And there too you have the humanistic position which runs not the slightest risk of involving itself in contradictions, or of relapsing into churchly hypocrisy, when it sees in the body the antagonist, the representative of the evil principle. The contradiction you imagine you see is at bottom always the same. 'What have you against analysis?' Nothing––when it serves the cause of enlightenment, freedom, progress. Everything when it is pervaded by the horrible *haut goût* of the grave. And thus too with the body. We are to honour and uphold the body when it is a question of emancipation, of beauty, of freedom of thought, of joy, of desire. We must despise it in so far as it sets itself up as the principle of gravity and inertia, when it obstructs the movement toward light; we must despise it in so far as it represents the principle of disease and death, in so far as its specific essence is the essence of perversity, of decay, sensuality, and shame."

These last words Settembrini had uttered standing close to Hans Castorp, very rapidly and tonelessly, as though to make an end of the subject. Succour was nigh for the youth: Joachim entered the reading--room, with two postcards in his hand. The Italian broke off; and the dexterity with which he altered his tone for one in a lighter and fitting social key was not lost upon his pupil—-if so Hans Castorp may be called.

"There you are, Lieutenant! Have you been looking for your cousin? I must apologize; we had fallen into conversation—-if I am not mistaken, we have even had a slight disagreement. He is not a bad reasoner, your cousin, a by no means contemptible antagonist in an argument—-when he takes the notion."

Humaniora

Hans Castorp and Joachim Ziemssen, arrayed in white trousers and blue blazers, were sitting in the garden after dinner. It was another of those much--lauded October days: bright without being heavy, hot and yet with a tang in the air. The sky above the valley was a deep southern blue and the pastures beneath, with the cattle tracks running across and across them, still a lively green. From the rugged slopes came the sound of cowbells; the peaceful, simple, melodious tintinnabulation came floating unbroken through the quiet, thin, empty air, enhancing the mood of solemnity that broods over the valley heights.

The cousins were sitting on a bench at the end of the garden, in front of a semicircle of young firs. The small open space lay at the north--west of the hedged--in platform, which rose some fifty yards above the valley, and formed the foundations of the Berghof building. They were silent. Hans Castorp was smoking. He was also wrangling inwardly with Joachim, who had not wanted to join the society on the verandah after luncheon, and had drawn his cousin against his will into the stillness and seclusion of the garden, until such time as they should go up to their balconies. That was behaving like a tyrant—when it came to that, they were not Siamese twins, it was possible for them to separate, if their inclinations took them in opposite directions. Hans Castorp was not up here to be company for Joachim, he was a patient himself. Thus he grumbled on, and could endure to grumble, for had he not Maria? He sat, his hands in his blazer pockets, his feet in brown shoes stretched out before him, and held the long, greyish cigar between his lips, precisely in the centre of his mouth, and drooping a little. It was in the first stages of consumption, he had not yet knocked off the ash from its blunt tip; its aroma was peculiarly grateful after the heavy meal just enjoyed. It might be true that in other respects getting used to life up here had mainly consisted in getting used to not getting used to it. But for the chemistry of his digestion, the nerves of his mucous membrane, which had been parched and tender, inclined to bleeding, it seemed that the process of adjustment had completed itself. For imperceptibly, in the course of these nine or ten weeks, his organic satisfaction in that excellent brand of vegetable stimulant or narcotic had been entirely restored. He rejoiced in a faculty regained, his mental satisfaction heightened the physical. During his time in bed he had saved on the supply of two hundred cigars which he had brought with him, and some of these were still left; but at the same time with his winter clothing from below, there had arrived another five hundred of the Bremen make, which he had ordered through Schalleen to make quite sure of not running out. They came in beautiful little varnished boxes, ornamented in gilt with a globe, several medals, and an exhibition building with a flag floating above it.

As they sat, behold, there came Hofrat Behrens through the garden. He had taken his midday meal in the dining--hall to--day, folding his gigantic hands before his place at Frau Salomon's table. After that he had probably been on the terrace, making the suitable personal remark to each and everybody, very likely displaying his trick with the bootlaces for such of the guests as had not seen it. Now he came lounging through the garden, wearing a check tail--coat, instead of his smock, and his stiff hat on the back of his head. He too had a cigar in his mouth, a very black one, from which he was puffing great white clouds of smoke. His head and face, with the over--heated purple cheeks, the snub nose, watery blue eyes, and little clipped moustache, looked small in proportion to the lank, rather warped and stooping figure, and the enormous hands and feet. He was nervous; visibly started when he saw the cousins, and seemed embarrassed over the necessity of passing them. But he greeted them in his usual picturesque and expansive fashion, with "Behold, behold, Timotheus!" going on to invoke the usual blessings on their metabolisms, while he prevented their rising from their seats, as they would have done in his honour.

"Sit down, sit down. No formalities with a simple man like me. Out of place too, you being my patients, both of you. Not necessary. No objection to the *status quo*," and he remained standing before them, holding the cigar between the index and middle fingers of his great right hand.

"How's your cabbage--leaf, Castorp? Let me see, I'm a connoisseur. That's a good ash——what sort of brown beauty have you there?"

"Maria Mancini, *Postre de Banquett*, Bremen, Herr Hofrat. Costs little or nothing, nineteen pfennigs in plain colours——but a bouquet you don't often come across at the price. Sumatra--Havana wrapper, as you see. I am very wedded to them. It is a medium mixture, very fragrant, but cool on the tongue. Suits it to leave the ash long, I don't knock it off more than a couple of times. She has her whims, of course, has Maria; but the inspection must be very thorough, for she doesn't vary much, and draws perfectly even. May I offer you one?"

"Thanks, we can exchange." And they drew out their cases.

"There's a thorough--bred for you," the Hofrat said, as he displayed his brand.

"Temperament, you know, juicy, got some guts to it. St. Felix, Brazil——I've always stuck to this sort. Regular 'begone, dull care,' burns like brandy, has something fulminating toward the end. But you need to exercise a little caution——can't light one from the other, you know——more than a fellow can stand. However, better one good mouthful than any amount of nibbles."

They twirled their respective offerings between their fingers, felt connoisseur--like the slender shapes that possessed, or so one might think, some organic quality of life, with their ribs formed by the diagonal parallel edges of the raised, here and there porous wrapper, the exposed veins that seemed to pulsate, the small inequalities of the skin, the play of light on planes and edges.

Hans Castorp expressed it: "A cigar like that is alive——it breathes. Fact. Once, at home, I had the idea of keeping Maria in an air--tight tin box, to protect her from damp. Would you believe it, she died! Inside of a week she perished——nothing but leathery corpses left."

They exchanged experiences upon the best way to keep cigars——particularly imported ones. The Hofrat loved them, he would have smoked nothing but heavy Havanas, but they did not suit him. He told Hans Castorp about two little Henry Clays he had once taken to his heart, in an evening company, which had come within an ace of putting him under the sod.

"I smoked them with my coffee," he said, "and thought no more of it. But after a while it struck me to wonder how I felt——and I discovered it was like nothing on earth. I don't know how I got home——and once there, well, this time, my son, I said to myself, you're a goner. Feet and legs like ice, you know, reeking with cold sweat, white as a table--cloth, heart going all ways for Sunday—-sometimes just a thread of a pulse, sometimes pounding like a trip--hammer. Cerebration phenomenal. I made sure I was going to toddle off—-that is the very expression that occurred to me, because at the time I was feeling as jolly as a sand--boy. Not that I wasn't in a funk as well, because I was—-I was just one large blue funk all over. Still, funk and felicity aren't mutually exclusive, everybody knows that. Take a chap who's going to have a girl for the first time in his life; he is in a funk too, and so is she, and yet both of them are simply dissolving with felicity. I was nearly dissolving too—-my bosom swelled with pride, and there I was, on the point of toddling off; but the Mylendonk got hold of me and persuaded me it was a poor idea. She gave me a camphor injection, applied icecompresses and friction—-and here I am, saved for humanity."

The Hofrat's large, goggling blue eyes watered as he told this story. Hans Castorp, seated in his capacity of patient, looked up at him with an expression that betrayed mental activity.

"You paint sometimes, don't you, Herr Hofrat?" he asked suddenly.

The Hofrat pretended to stagger backwards. "What the deuce! What do you take me for, youngster?"

"I beg your pardon. I happened to hear somebody say so, and it just crossed my mind."

"Well, then, I won't trouble to lie about it. We're all poor creatures. I admit such a thing has happened. *Anch' io sono pittore*, as the Spaniard used to say."

"Landscape?" Hans Castorp asked him succinctly, with the air of a connoisseur, circumstances betraying him to this tone.

"As much as you like," the Hofrat answered, swaggering out of sheer selfconsciousness. "Landscape, still life, animals—-chap like me shrinks from nothing."

"No portraits?"

"I've even thrown in a portrait or so. Want to give me an order?"

"Ha ha! No, but it would be very kind of you to show us your pictures some time——we should enjoy it."

Joachim looked blankly at his cousin, but then hastened to add his assurances that it would be very kind indeed of the Hofrat.

Behrens was enchanted at the flattery. He grew red with pleasure, his tears seemed this time actually on the point of falling.

"With the greatest pleasure," he cried. "On the spot if you like. Come on, come along with me, I'll brew us a Turkish coffee in my den."

He pulled both young men from the bench and walked between them arm in arm, down the gravel path which led, as they knew, to his private quarters in the north--west wing of the building.

"I've dabbled a little in that sort of thing myself," Hans Castorp explained.

"You don't say! Gone in for it properly——oils?"

"Oh, no, I never went further than a water--colour or so. A ship, a sea--piece, childish efforts. But I'm fond of painting, and so I took the liberty——"

Joachim in particular felt relieved and enlightened by this explanation of his cousin's startling curiosity; it was in fact more on his account than on the Hofrat's that Hans Castorp had offered it. They reached the entrance, a much simpler one than the impressive portal on the drive, with its flanking lanterns. A pair of curving steps led up to the oaken house door, which the Hofrat opened with a latch--key from his heavy bunch. His hand trembled, he was plainly in a nervous state. They entered an antechamber with clothes--racks, where Behrens hung his bowler on a hook, and thence passed into a short corridor, which was separated by a glass door from that of the main building. On both sides of this corridor lay the rooms of the small private dwelling. Behrens called a servant and gave an order;

[322]

then to a running accompaniment of whimsical remarks ushered them through a door on the right. They saw a couple of rooms furnished in banal middle--class taste, facing the valley and opening one into another through a doorway hung with portières. One was an "old--German" dining--room, the other a living--and working--room, with woollen carpets, bookshelves and sofa, and a writing--table above which hung a pair of crossed swords and a student's cap. Beyond was a Turkish smoking--cabinet. Everywhere were paintings, the work of the Hofrat. The guests went up to them at once on entering, courteously ready to praise. There were several portraits of his departed wife, in oil; also, standing on the writing--table, photographs of her. She was a thin, enigmatic blonde, portrayed in flowing garments, with her hands, their finger--tips just lightly enlaced, against her left shoulder, and her eyes either directed toward heaven or else cast upon the ground, shaded by long, thick, obliquely outstanding eyelashes. Never once was the departed one shown looking directly ahead of her toward the observer. The other pictures were chiefly mountain landscapes, mountains in snow and mountains in summer green, mist--wreathed mountains, mountains whose dry, sharp outline was cut out against a deep--blue sky——these apparently under the influence of Segantini. Then there were cowherds' huts, and dewlapped cattle standing or lying in sun--drenched high pastures. There was a plucked fowl, with its long writhen neck hanging down from a table among a setting of vegetables. There were flower--pieces, types of mountain peasantry, and so on——-all painted with a certain brisk dilettantism, the colours boldly dashed on to the canvas, and often looking as though they had been squeezed on out of the tube. They must have taken a long time to dry——-but were sometimes effective by way of helping out the other shortcomings.

They passed as they would along the walls of an exhibition, accompanied by the master of the house, who now and then gave a name to some subject or other, but was chiefly silent, with the proud embarrassment of the artist, tasting the enjoyment of looking on his own works with the eyes of strangers. The portrait of Clavdia Chauchat hung on the window wall of the living--room—-Hans Castorp spied it out with a quick glance as he entered, though the likeness was but a distant one. Purposely he avoided the spot, detaining his companions in the dining--room, where he affected to admire a fresh green glimpse into the valley of the Serbi, with ice--blue glaciers in the background. Next he passed of his own accord into the Turkish cabinet, and looked at all it had to show, with praises on his lips; thence back to the living--room, beginning with the entrance wall, and calling upon Joachim to second his encomiums. But at last he turned, with a measured start, and said: "But surely that is a familiar face?"

"You recognize her?" the Hofrat wanted to know.

"It is not possible I am mistaken. The lady at the 'good' Russian table, with the French name—-"

"Right! Chauchat. Glad you think it's like her."

"Speaking," Hans Castorp lied. He did so less from insincerity than in the consciousness that, on the face of things, he ought not to have been able to recognize her. Joachim could never have done so—-good Joachim, who saw the whole affair now in its true light, after the false one Hans Castorp had first cast upon it; saw how the wool had been pulled over his eyes; and with a murmured recognition applied himself to help look at the painting. His cousin had paid him out for not going into society after luncheon.

It was a bust--length, in half profile, rather under life--size, in a wide, bevelled frame, black, with an inner beading of gilt. Neck and bosom were bare or veiled with a soft drapery laid about the shoulders. Frau Chauchat appeared ten years older than her age, as often happens in amateur portraiture where the artist is bent on making a character study. There was too much red all over the face, the nose was badly out of drawing, the colour of the hair badly hit off, too straw--colour; the mouth was distorted, the peculiar charm of the features ungrasped or at least not brought out, spoiled by the exaggeration of their single elements. The whole was a rather botched performance, and only distantly related to its original. But Hans Castorp was not particular about the degree of likeness, the relation of this canvas to Frau Chauchat's person was close enough for him. It purported to represent her, in these very rooms she had sat for it, that was all he needed; much moved he reiterated: "The very image of her!"

"Oh, no," the Hofrat demurred. "It was a pretty clumsy piece of work, I don't flatter myself I hit her off very well, though we had, I suppose, twenty sittings. What can you do with a rum sort of face like that? You might think she would be easy to capture, with those hyperborean cheek--bones, and eyes like cracks in a loaf of bread. Yes, there's something about her—-if you get the detail right, you botch the ensemble. Riddle of the sphinx. Do you know her? It would probably be better to paint her from memory, instead of having her sit. Did you say you knew her?"

"No; that is, only superficially, the way one knows people up here."

"Well, I know her under her skin—-subcutaneously, you see: blood pressure, tissue tension, lymphatic circulation, all that sort of thing. I've good reason to. It's the superficies makes the difficulty. Have you ever noticed her walk? She slinks. It's characteristic, shows in her face—-take the eyes, for example, not to mention the complexion, though that is tricky too. I don't mean their colour, I am speaking of the cut, and the way they sit in the face. You'd say the eye slit was cut obliquely, but it only looks so. What deceives you is the epicanthus, a racial variation, consisting in a sort of ridge of integument that runs from the bridge of the nose to the eyelid, and comes down over the inside corner of the eye. If you take your finger and stretch the skin at the base of the nose, the eye looks as straight as any of ours. Quite a taking little dodge—-but as a matter of fact, the epicanthus can be traced back to an atavistic vestige—-it's a developmental arrest."

"So that's it." Hans Castorp said. "I never knew that—-but I've wondered for a long time what it is about eyes like that."

"Vanity," said the Hofrat, "and vexation of spirit. If you simply draw them in slanting, you are lost. You must bring about the obliquity the same way nature does, you must add illusion to illusion—-and for that you have to know about the epicanthus. What a man knows always comes in handy. Now look at the skin—-the epidermis. Do you find I've managed to make it lifelike, or not?"

"Enormously," said Hans Castorp. "Simply enormously. I've never seen skin painted anything like so well. You can fairly see the pores." And he ran the edge of his hand lightly over the bare neck and shoulders, the skin of which, especially by contrast with the exaggerated red of the face, was very white, as though seldom exposed. Whether this effect was premeditated or not, it was rather suggestive. And still Hans Castorp's praise was deserved. The pale shimmer of this tender, though not emaciated, bosom, losing itself in the bluish shadows of the drapery, was very like life. It was obviously painted with feeling; a sort of sweetness emanated from it, yet the artist had been successful in giving it a scientific realism and precision as well. The roughness of the canvas texture, showing through the paint, had been dexterously employed to suggest the natural unevennesses of the skin—-this especially in the neighbourhood of the delicate collar--bones. A tiny mole, at the point where the breasts began to divide, had been done with care, and on their rounding surfaces one thought to trace the delicate blue veins. It was as though a scarcely perceptible shiver of sensibility beneath the eye of the beholder were passing over this nude flesh, as though one might see the perspiration, the invisible vapour which the life beneath threw off; as though, were one to press one's lips upon this surface, one might perceive, not the smell of paint and fixative, but the odour of the human body. Such, at least, were Hans Castorp's impressions, which we here reproduce—-and he, of course, was in a peculiarly susceptible state. But it is none the less true that Frau Chauchat's portrait was by far the most telling piece of painting in the room.

Hofrat Behrens rocked back and forth on his heels and the balls of his feet, his hands in this trouser pockets, as he gazed at his work in company with the cousins.

"Delighted," he said. "Delighted to find favour in the eyes of a colleague. If a man knows a bit about what goes on under the epidermis, that does no harm either. In other words, if he can paint a little below the surface, and stands in another relation to nature than just the lyrical, so to say. An artist who is a doctor, physiologist, and anatomist on the side, and has his own little way of thinking about the under sides of things——it all comes in handy too, it gives you the *pas*, say what you like. That birthday suit there is painted with science, it is organically correct, you can examine it under the microscope. You can see not only the horny and mucous strata of the epidermis, but I've suggested the texture of the corium underneath, with the oil--and sweat--glands, the blood--vessels and tubercles--—and then under that still the layer of fat, the upholstering, you know, full of oil ducts, the underpinning of the lovely female form. What is in your mind as you work runs into your hand and has its influence--—it isn't really there, and yet somehow or other it is, and that is what gives the lifelike effect."

All this was fuel to Hans Castorp's fire. His brow was flushed, his eyes fairly sparkled, he had so much to say he knew not where to begin. In the first place, he had it in mind to remove the picture of Frau Chauchat from the window wall, where it hung somewhat in shadow, and place it to better advantage; next, he was eager to take up the Hofrat's remarks about the constitution of the skin, which had keenly interested him; and finally, he wanted to make some remarks of his own, of a general and philosophical nature, which interested him no less mightily.

Laying his hands upon the painting to unhook it, he eagerly began: "Yes, yes indeed, that is all very important. What I'd like to say is——I mean, you said, Herr Hofrat, if I understood rightly, you said: 'In another relation.' You said it was good when there was some other relation besides the lyric——I think that was the word you used——the artistic, that is; in short, when one looked at the thing from another point of view——the medical, for example. That's all so enormously to the point, you know——I do beg your pardon, Herr Hofrat, but what I mean is that it is so exactly and precisely right, because after all it is not a question of any fundamentally different relations or points of view, but at bottom just variations of one and the same, just shadings of it, so to speak, I mean: variations of one and the same universal interest, the artistic impulse itself being a part and a manifestation of it too, if I may say so. Yes, if you will pardon me, I will take down this picture, there's positively no light here where it hangs, permit me to carry it over to the sofa, we shall see if it won't look entirely——what I meant to say was: what is the main concern of the study of medicine? I know nothing about it, of course——but after all isn't its main concern with human beings?

And jurisprudence——making laws, pronouncing judgment——its main concern is with human beings too. And philology, which is nearly always bound up with the profession of pedagogy? And theology, with the care of souls, the office of spiritual shepherd? All of them have to do with human beings, all of them are degrees of one and the same important, the same fundamental interest, the interest in humanity. In other words, they are the humanistic callings, and if you go in for them you have to study the ancient languages by way of foundation, for the sake of formal training, as they say. Perhaps you are surprised at my talking about them like that, being only a practical man and on the technical side. But I have been thinking about these questions lately, in the rest--cure; and I find it wonderful, I find it a simply priceless arrangement of things, that the formal, the idea of form, of beautiful form, lies at the bottom of every sort of humanistic calling. It gives it such nobility, I think, such a sort of disinterestedness, and feeling, too, and——and——courtliness——it makes a kind of chivalrous adventure out of it. That is to say——I suppose I am expressing myself very ridiculously, but——you can see how the things of the mind and the love of beauty come together, and that they always really have been one and the same——in other words, science and art; and that the calling of being an artist surely belongs with the others, as a sort of fifth faculty, because it too is a humanistic calling, a variety of humanistic interest, in so far as its most important theme or concern is with man—-you will agree with me on that point. When I experimented in that line in my youth, I never painted anything but ships and water, of course. But notwithstanding, in my eyes the most interesting branch of painting is and remains portraiture, because it has man for its immediate object—-that was why I asked at once if you had done anything in that field.—-Wouldn't this be a far more favourable place for it to hang?"

Both of them, Behrens no less than Joachim, looked at him amazed—-was he not ashamed of this confused, impromptu harangue? But no, Hans Castorp was far too preoccupied to feel self--conscious. He held the painting against the sofa wall, and demanded to know if it did not get a much better light. Just then the servant brought a tray, with hot water, a spirit--lamp, and coffee--cups.

Behrens motioned them into the cabinet, saying: "Then you must have been more interested in sculpture, originally, than in painting, I should think. Yes, of course, it gets more light there; if you think it can stand it. I should suppose so, because sculpture concerns itself more purely and exclusively with the human form. But we mustn't let the water boil away."

"Quite right, sculpture," Hans Castorp said, as they went. He forgot either to hang up or put down the picture he had been holding, but tugged it with him into the neighbouring room. "Certainly a Greek Venus or athlete is more humanistic, it is probably at bottom the most humanistic of all the arts, when one comes to think about it!"

"Well, as far as little Chauchat goes, she is a better subject for painting than sculpture. Phidias, or that other chap with the Mosaic ending to his name, would have stuck up their noses at her style of physiognomy.—-Hullo, where are you going with the ham?"

"Pardon me, I'll just lean it here against the leg of my chair, that will do very well for the moment. The Greek sculptors did not trouble themselves about the head and face, their interest was more with the body, I suppose that was their humanism.——And the plasticity of the female form——so that is fat, is it?"

"That is fat," the Hofrat said concisely. He had opened a hanging cabinet, and taken thence the requisites for his coffee--making: a cylindrical Turkish mill, a long--handled pot, a double receptacle for sugar and ground coffee, all in brass. "Palmitin, stearin, olein," he went on, shaking the coffee berries from a tin box into the mill, which he began to turn. "You see I make it all myself, it tastes twice as good.——Did you think it was ambrosia?"

"No, of course I knew. Only it sounds strange to hear it like that," Hans Castorp said.

They were seated in the corner between door and window, at a bamboo tabouret which held an oriental brass tray, upon which Behrens had set the coffee--machine, among the smoking utensils. Joachim was next Behrens on the Ottoman, overflowing with cushions; Hans Castorp sat in a leather arm--chair on castors, against which he had leaned Frau Chauchat's picture. A gaily--coloured carpet was beneath their feet. The Hofrat ladled coffee and sugar into the long--handled pot, added water, and let the brew boil up over the flame of the lamp. It foamed brownly in the little onion--pattern cups, and proved on tasting both strong and sweet.

"Your own as well," Behrens said. "Your 'plasticity'——so far as you have any——is fat too, though of course not to the same extent as with a woman. With us fat is only about five per cent of the body weight, in females it is one sixteenth of the whole. Without that subcutaneous cell structure of ours, we should all be nothing but fungoid growths. It disappears, with time, and then come the unæsthetic wrinkles in the drapery. The layer is thickest on the female breast and belly, on the front of the thighs, everywhere, in short, where there is a little something for heart and hand to take hold of. The soles of the feet are fat and ticklish."

Hans Castorp turned the cylindrical coffee--mill about in his hands. It was, like the rest of the set, Indian or Persian rather than Turkish; the style of the engraving showed that, with the bright surface of the pattern standing out against the purposely dulled background. He looked at the design, without immediately seeing what it was. When he did, he blushed unawares.

"Yes, that is a set for single gentlemen," Behrens said. "I keep it locked up, you see, my kitchen queen might hurt her eyes looking at it. It won't do you gentlemen any harm, I take it. It was given to me by a patient, an Egyptian princess who once honoured us with a year or so of her presence. You see, the pattern repeats itself on the whole set. Pretty roguish, what?"

"Yes, it is quite unusual," Hans Castorp answered. "Ha ha! No, it doesn't trouble me. But one can take it perfectly seriously; solemnly, in fact——only then it is rather out of place on a coffee--machine. The ancients are said to have used such motifs on their sarcophagi. The sacred and the obscene were more or less the same thing to them."

"I should say the princess was more for the second," Behrens said. "Anyhow she still sends me the most wonderful cigarettes, superfinissimos, you know, only sported on "first--class occasions." He fetched the garish--coloured box from the cupboard and offered them. Joachim drew his heels together as he received his cigarette. Hans Castorp helped himself to his; it was unusually large and thick, and had a gilt sphinx on it. He began to smoke——it was wonderful, as Behrens had said.

"Tell us some more about the skin," he begged the Hofrat; "that is, if you will be so kind." He had taken Frau Chauchat's portrait on his knee, and was gazing at it, leaning back in his chair, the cigarette between his lips. "Not about the fat--layer, we know about that now. About the human skin in general, that you know so well how to paint."

"About the skin. You are interested in physiology?"

"Very much. Yes, I've always felt a good deal of interest in it. The human body——yes, I've always had an uncommon turn for it. I've sometimes asked myself whether I ought not to have been a physician——it wouldn't have been a bad idea, in a way. Because if you are interested in the body, you must be interested in disease——specially interested, isn't that so? But it doesn't signify, I might have been such a lot of things——for example, a clergyman."

"Indeed?"

"Yes, I've sometimes had the idea I should have been decidedly in my element there."

"How did you come to be an engineer, then?"

"I just happened to——it was more or less outward circumstances that decided the matter."

"Well, about the skin. What do you want to hear about your sensory sheath? You know, don't you, that it is your outside brain——ontogenetically the same as that apparatus of the so--called higher centres up there in your cranium? The central nervous system is nothing but a modification of the outer skin--layer; among the lower animals the distinction between central and peripheral doesn't exist, they smell and taste with their skin, it is the only sensory organ they have. Must be rather nice——if you can put yourself in their place. On the other hand, in such highly differentiated forms of life as you and I are, the skin has fallen from its high estate; it has to confine itself to feeling ticklish; that is to say, to being simply a protective and registering apparatus——but devilishly on the qui vive for anything that tries to come too close about the body. It even puts out feelers——the body hairs, which are nothing but hardened skin cells——and they get wind of the approach of whatever it is, before the skin itself is touched. Just between ourselves, it is quite possible that this protecting and defending function of the skin extends beyond the physical. Do you know what makes you go red and pale?"

"Not very precisely."

"Well, neither do we, 'very precisely,' to be frank—-at least, as far as blushing is concerned. The situation is not quite clear; for the dilatory muscles which are presumably set in action by the vasomotor nerves haven't yet been demonstrated in relation to the blood--vessels. How the cock really swells his comb, or any of the other well--known instances come about, is still a mystery, particularly where it is a question of emotional influences in play. We assume that a connexion subsists between the outer rind of the cerebrum and the vascular centre in the medulla. Certain stimuli—-for instance, let us say, like your being powerfully embarrassed, set up the connexion, and the nerves that control the blood--vessels function toward the face, and they expand and fill, and you get a face like a turkey--cock, all swelled up with blood so you can't see out of your eyes. On the other hand, suppose you are in suspense, something is going to happen—-it may be something tremendously beautiful, for aught I care—-the blood--vessels that--feed the skin contract, it gets pale and cold and sunken, you look like a dead man, with big, lead--coloured eye--sockets and a peaked nose. But the *Sympathicus* makes your heart thump away like a good fellow."

"So that is how it happens," Hans Castorp said. '

"Something like that. Those are reactions, you know. But it is the nature of reactions and reflexes to have a reason for happening; we are beginning to suspect, we physiologists, that the phenomena accompanying emotion are really defence mechanisms, protective reflexes of the system. Goose--flesh, now. Do you know how you come to have goose--flesh?"

"Not very clearly either, I'm afraid."

"That is a little contrivance of the sebaceous glands, which secrete the fatty, albuminous substance that oils your skin and keeps it supple, and pleasant to feel of. Not very appetizing, maybe, but without it the skin would be all withered and cracked. Without the cholesterin, it is hard to imagine touching the human skin at all.

[333]

These sebaceous glands have little erector--muscles that act upon them, and when they do so, then you are like the lad when the princess poured the pail of minnows over him. Your skin gets like a file, and if the stimulus is very powerful, the hair ducts are erected too, the hair on your head bristles up and the little hairs on your body, like quills upon the fretful porcupine—-and you can say, like the youth in the story, that now you know how to shiver and shake."

"Oh," said Hans Castorp, "I know how already. I shiver rather easily, on all sorts of provocation. Only what surprises me is that the glands are erected for such different reasons. It gives one goose--flesh to hear a slate--pencil run across a pane of glass; but when you hear particularly beautiful music you suddenly find you have it too, and when I was confirmed and took my first communion, I had one shiver after another, it seemed as though the prickling and stickling would never leave off. Imagine those little muscles acting for such different reasons!"

"Oh," Behrens said, "tickling's tickling. The body doesn't give a hang for the content of the stimulus. It may be minnows, it may be the Holy Ghost, the sebaceous glands are erected just the same."

Hans Castorp regarded the picture on his knee.

"Herr Hofrat," he said, "I wanted to come back to something you said a moment ago, about internal processes, lymphatic action, and that sort of thing. Tell us about it—-particularly about the lymphatic system, it interests me tremendously."

"I believe you," Behrens responded. "The lyrnph is the most refined, the most rarefied, the most intimate of the body juices. I dare say you had an inkling of the fact in your mind when you asked. People talk about the blood, and the mysteries of its composition, and what an extraordinary fluid it is. But it is the lymph that is the juice of juices, the very essence, you understand, ichor, blood--milk, *crème de la crème;* as a matter of fact, after a fatty diet it does look like milk." And he went on, in his lively and whimsical phraseology, to gratify Hans Castorp's desire. And first he characterized the blood, a serum composed of fat, albumen, iron, sugar and salt, crimson as an opera--cloak, the product of respiration and digestion, saturated with gases, laden with waste products, which was pumped at 98.4° of heat from the heart through the blood--vessels, and kept up metabolism and animal warmth throughout the body——in other words, sweet life itself. But, he said, the blood did not come into immediate contact with the body cells. What happened was that the pressure at which it was pumped caused a milky extract of it to sweat through the walls of the bloodvessels, and so into the tissues, so that it filled every tiny interstice and cranny, and caused the elastic cell--tissue to distend. This distension of the tissues, or *turgor*, pressed the lymph, after it had nicely swilled out the cells and exchanged matter with them, into the *vasa lymphatica*, the lymphatic vessels, and so back into the blood again, at the rate of a litre and a half a day. He went on to speak of the lymphatic tubes and absorbent vessels; described the secretion of the breast milk, which collected lymph from legs, abdomen, and breast, one arm, and one side of the head; described the very delicately constructed filters called lymphatic glands which were placed at certain points in the lymphatic system, in the neck, the arm--pit, and the elbow--joint, the hollow under the knee, and other soft and intimate parts of the body.

"Swellings may occur in these places," Behrens explained. "Indurations of the lymphatic glands, let us say, in the knee--pan or the arm--joint, dropsical tumours here and there, and we base our diagnosis on them——they always have a reason, though not always a very pretty one. Under such circumstances there is more than a suspicion of tubercular congestion of the lymphatic vessels."

Hans Castorp was silent a little space.

"Yes," he said, then, in a low voice, "it is true, I might very well have been a doctor. The flow of the breast milk——the lymph of the legs——all that interests me very, very much. What is the body?" he rhapsodically burst forth. "What is the flesh? What is the physical being of man? What is he made of? Tell us this afternoon, Herr Hofrat, tell us exactly, and once and for all, so that we may know!"

"Of water," answered Behrens. "So you are interested in organic chemistry too?

The human body consists, much the larger part of it, of water. No more and no less than water, and nothing to get wrought up about. The solid parts are only twenty--five per cent of the whole, and of that twenty are ordinary white of egg, protein, if you want to use a handsomer word. Besides that, a little fat and a little salt, that's about all."

"But the white of egg—-what is that?"

"Various primary substances: carbon, hydrogen, nitrogen, oxygen, sulphur. Sometimes phosphorus. Your scientific curiosity is running away with itself. Some albumens are in composition with carbohydrates; that is to say, grape--sugar and starch. In old age the flesh becomes tough, that is because the collagen increases in the connective tissue—-the lime, you know, the most important constituent of the bones and cartilage. What else shall I tell you? In the muscle plasma we have an albumen called fibrin; when death occurs, it coagulates in the muscular tissue, and causes the *rigor mortis.*"

"Right--oh, I see, the *rigor mortis*," Hans Castorp said blithely. "Very good, very good. And then comes the general analysis—-the anatomy of the grave."

"Yes, of course. But how well you put it! Yes, the movement becomes general, you flow away, so to speak—-remember all that water! The remaining constituents are very unstable; without life, they are resolved by putrefaction into simpler combinations, anorganic."

"Dissolution, putrefaction," said Hans Castorp. "They are the same thing as combustion: combination with oxygen—-am I right?"

"To a T. Oxidization."

"And life?"

"Oxidization too. The same. Yes, young man, life too is principally oxidization of the cellular albumen, which gives us that beautiful animal warmth, of which we sometimes have more than we need. Tut, living consists in dying, no use mincing the matter— *une destruction organique*, as some Frenchman with his native levity has called it. It smells like that, too. If we don't think so, our judgment is corrupted."

"And if one is interested in life, one must be particularly interested in death, mustn't one?"

"Oh, well, after all, there is some sort of difference. Life is life which keeps the form through change of substance."

"Why should the form remain?" said Hans Castorp.

"Why? Young man, what you are saying now sounds far from humanistic."

"Form is folderol."

"Well, you are certainly in great form to-day—-you're regularly kicking over the traces. But I must drop out now," said the Hofrat. "I am beginning to feel melancholy," and he laid his huge hand over his eyes. "I can feel it coming on. You see, I've drunk coffee with you, and it tasted good to me, and all of a sudden it comes over me that I am going to be melancholy. You gentlemen must excuse me. It was an extra occasion, I enjoyed it no end—-"

The cousins had sprung up. They reproached themselves for having taxed the Hofrat's patience so long. He made proper protest. Hans Castorp hastened to carry Frau Chauchat's portrait into the next room and hang it once more on the wall. They did not need to re--traverse the garden to arrive at their own quarters; Behrens directed them through the building, and accompanied them to the dividing glass door. In the mood that had come over him so unexpectedly, his goggling eyes blinked, and the bone of his neck stuck out, both more than ever; his upper lip, with the clipped, onesided moustache, had taken on a querulous expression. As they went along the corridors Hans Castorp said to his cousin: "Confess that it was a good idea of mine."

"It was a change, at least," responded Joachim. "And you certainly took occasion to air your views on a good many subjects. It was a bit complicated for me. It is high time now that we went in to the rest--cure, we shall have at least twenty minutes before tea. You probably think it is folderol to pay so much attention to it, now you've taken to kicking over the traces. But you don't need it so much as I do, after all."

Research

And now came on, as come it must, what Hans Castorp had never thought to experience: the winter of the place, the winter of these high altitudes. Joachim knew it already: it had been in full blast when he arrived the year before—-but Hans Castorp rather dreaded it, however well he felt himself equipped. Joachim sought to reassure him.

"You must not imagine it grimmer than it is," he said, "not really arctic. You will feel the cold less on account of the dryness of the air and the absence of wind. It's the thing about the change of temperature above the fog line; they've found out lately that it gets warmer in the upper reaches, something they did not know before. I should say it is actually colder when it rains. But you have your sleeping--bag, and they turn on the heat when they absolutely must."

And in fact there could be no talk of violence or surprises; the winter came mildly on, at first no different from many a day they had seen in the height of summer. The wind had been two days in the south, the sun bore down, the valley seemed shrunken, the side walls at its mouth looked near and bald. Clouds came up, behind Piz Michel and Tinzenhorn, and drove north--eastwards. It rained heavily. Then the rain turned foul, a whitish--grey, mingled with

snow--flakes---soon it was all snow, the valley was full of flurry; it
kept on and on, the temperature fell appreciably, so that the fallen
snow could not quite melt, but lay covering the valley with a wet and
threadbare white garment, against which showed black the pines on
the slopes. In the dining--room the radiators were lukewarm. That
was at the beginning of November---All Souls'---and there was no
novelty about it. In August it had been even so; they had long left off
regarding snow as a prerogative of winter. White traces lingered after
every storm in the crannies of the rocky Rhätikon, the chain that
seemed to guard the end of the valley, and the distant monarchs to
the south were always in snow. But the storm and the fall in the
temperature both continued. A pale grey sky hung low over the
valley; it seemed to dissolve in flakes and fall soundlessly and
ceaselessly, until one almost felt uneasy. It turned colder by the hour.
A morning came when the thermometer in Hans Castorp's room
registered 44°, the next morning it was only 40°. That was cold. It
kept within bounds, but it persisted. It had frozen at night; now it
froze in the day--time as well, and all day long; and it snowed, with
brief intervals, through the fourth, the fifth, and the seventh days. The
snow mounted apace, it became a nuisance. Paths had been shovelled
as far as the bench by the watercourse, and on the drive down to the
valley; but these were so narrow that you could only walk single file,
and if you met anyone, you must step off the pavement and at once
sink knee--deep in snow. A stoneroller drawn by a horse, with a man
at his halter, rolled all day long up and down the streets of the cure,
while a yellow diligence on runners, looking like an old--fashioned
post--coach, plied between village and cure, with a snow--plough
attached in front, shovelling the white masses aside. The world, this
narrow, lofty, isolated world up here, looked now well wadded and
upholstered indeed: no pillar or post but wore its white cap; the steps
up to the entrance of the Berghof had turned into an inclined plane;
heavy cushions, in the drollest shapes, weighed down the branches of
the Scotch firs---now and then one slid off and raised up a cloud of
powdery white dust in its fall. Round about, the heights lay
smothered in snow; their lower regions rugged with the evergreen

growth, their upper parts, beyond the timber line, softly covered up to their many--shaped summits. The air was dark, the sun but a pallid apparition behind a veil. Yet a mild reflected brightness came from the snow, a milky gleam whose light became both landscape and human beings, even though these latter did show red noses under their white or gaily--coloured woollen caps.

In the dining--room the onset of winter—-the "season" of the region—-was the subject of conversation at all seven tables. Many tourists and sportsmen were said to have arrived and taken up residence at the hotels in the Dorf and the Platz. The height of the piled--up snow was estimated at two feet; its consistency was said to be ideal for skiing. The bob--run, which led down from the north--western slope of the Schatzalp into the valley, was zealously worked on, it would be possible to open it in the next few days, unless a thaw put out all calculations. Everyone looked forward eagerly to the activities of these sound people down below—-to the sports and races, which it was forbidden to attend, but which numbers of the patients resolved to see, by cutting the rest--cure and slipping out of the Berghof. Hans Castorp heard of a new sport that had come from Scandinavia, "ski--jöring": it consisted in races in which the participants were drawn by horses while standing in their skis. It was to see this that so many of the patients had resolved to slip out.—-There was talk too of Christmas.

Christmas! Hans Castorp had never once thought of it. To be sure, he had blithely said, and written, that he must spend the winter up here with Joachim, because of what the doctors had discovered to be the state of his health. But now he was startled to realize that Christmas would be included in the programme—-perhaps because (and yet not entirely because) he had never spent the Christmas season anywhere but in the bosom of the family. Well, if he must he must; he would have to put up with it. He was no longer a child; Joachim seemed not to mind, or else to have adjusted himself uncomplainingly to the prospect; and, after all, he said to himself, think of all the places and all the conditions in which Christmas has been celebrated before now!

Yet it did seem to him rather premature to begin thinking about Christmas even before the Advent season, six weeks at least before the holiday! True, such an interval was easily overleaped by the guests in the dining--hall: it was a mental process in which Hans Castorp had already some facility, though he had not yet learned to practise it in the grand style, as the older inhabitants did. Christmas, like other holidays in the course of the year, served them for a fulcrum, or a vaulting--pole, with which to leap over empty intervening spaces. They all had fever, their metabolism was accelerated, their bodily processes accentuated, keyed up——all this perhaps accounted for the wholesale way they could put time behind them. It would not have greatly surprised him to hear them discount the Christmas holiday as well, and go on at once to speak of the New Year and Carnival. But no——so capricious and unstable as this they were not, in the Berghof dining--room. Christmas gave them pause, it gave them even matter for concern and brain--racking. It was customary to present Hofrat Behrens with a gift on Christmas eve, for which a collection was taken up among the guests——and this gift was the subject of much deliberation. A meeting was called. Last year, so the old inhabitants said, they had given him a travelling--trunk; this time a new operating--table had been considered, an easel, a fur coat, a rocking--chair, an inlaid ivory stethoscope. Settembrini, asked for suggestions, proposed that they give the Hofrat a newly projected encyclopædic work called *The Sociology of Suffering;* but he found only one person to agree with him, a book--dealer who sat at Hermine Kleefeld's table. In short, no decision had been reached. There was difficulty about coming to an agreement with the Russian guests; a divergence of views arose. The Muscovites declared their preference for making an independent gift. Frau Stöhr went about for days quite outraged on account of a loan of ten francs which she inadvisedly laid out for Frau Iltis at the meeting, and which the latter had "forgotten" to return. She "forgot" it. The shades of meaning

Frau Stöhr contrived to convey in this word were many and varied, but one and all expressive of an entire disbelief in Frau Iltis's lack of memory, which, it appeared, had been proof against the hints and proddings Frau Stöhr freely admitted having administered. Several times she declared she would resign herself, make Frau Iltis a present of the sum. "I'll pay for both of us," she said.

"Then *my* skirts will be cleared!" But in the end she hit upon another plan and communicated it to her table--mates, to their great delight: she had the "management" refund her the ten francs and insert it in Frau Iltis's weekly bill. Thus was the reluctant debtor outwitted, and at least this phase of the matter settled.

It had stopped snowing, the sky began to clear. The blue--grey cloud--masses parted to admit glimpses of the sun, whose rays gave a bluish cast to the scene. Then it grew altogether fair; a bright hard frost and settled winter splendour reigned in the middle of November. The arch of the loggia framed a glorious panorama of snow--powdered forest, softly filled passes and ravines, white, sunlit valleys, and radiant blue heavens above all. In the evening, when the almost full moon appeared, the world lay in enchanted splendour, marvellous. Crystal and diamond it glittered far and wide, the forest stood up very black and white, the quarter of the heavens where the moon was not showed deeply dark, embroidered with stars. On the flashing surface of the snow, shadows, so strong, so sharp and clearly outlined that they seemed almost more real than the objects themselves, fell from houses, trees, and telegraph--poles. An hour or so after sunset there would be some fourteen degrees of frost. The world seemed spellbound in icy purity, its earthly blemishes veiled; it lay fixed in a deathlike, enchanted trance.

Hans Castorp stopped until far into the night in his balcony above the ensorcelled winter scene—-much longer than Joachim, who retired at ten or a little later. His excellent chair, with the sectional mattress and the neck--roll, he pulled close to the snow--cushioned balustrade; at his hand was the white table with the lighted readinglamp, a stack of books, and a glass of creamy milk, the "evening milk" which was brought to each of the guests' rooms at nine o'clock. Hans Castorp put a dash of cognac in his, to make it more palatable. Already he had availed himself of all his means of protection against the cold, the entire outfit: lay ensconced well up to his chest in the buttoned--up sleeping--sack he had acquired in one of the well--furnished shops in the Platz, with the two camel's--hair rugs folded over it in accordance with the ritual. He wore his winter suit, with a short fur jacket atop, a woollen cap, felt boots, and heavily lined gloves, which, however, could not prevent the stiffening of his fingers.

What held him so late——often until midnight and beyond, long after the "bad" Russian pair had left their loge——was partly the magic of the winter night, into which, until eleven, were woven the mounting strains of music from near and far. But even more it was inertia and excitement, both of these at once, and in combination: bodily inertia, the physical fatigue which hated any idea of moving; and mental excitement, the busy preoccupation of his thoughts with certain new and fascinating studies upon which the young man had embarked, and which left his brain no rest. The weather affected him, his organism was stimulated by the cold; he ate enormously, attacking the mighty Berghof meals, where the roast goose followed upon the roast beef, with the usual Berghof appetite, which was always even larger in winter than in summer. At the same time he had a perpetual craving for sleep; in the daytime, as well as on the moonlit evenings, he would drop off over his books, and then, after a few minutes' unconsciousness, betake himself again to research. Talk fatigued him. He was more inclined than had been his habit to rapid, unrestrained, even reckless speech; but if he talked with Joachim, as they went on their snowy walks, he was liable to be overtaken by giddiness and trembling, would feel dazed and tipsy, and the blood would mount to his head. His curve had gone up since the oncoming of winter, and Hofrat Behrens had let fall something about injections; these were usually given in cases of obstinate high temperature, and Joachim and at least two--thirds of the guests had them. But he himself felt sure that the increase in his bodily heat had to do with the mental activity and excitation which kept him in his chair on the balcony until deep into the glittering, frosty night. The reading which held him so late suggested such an explanation to his mind.

No little reading was done, in the rest--halls and private loggias of the International Sanatorium Berghof; largely, however, by the new--comers and "short--timers," for the patients of many months' or years' standing had long learned to kill time without mental effort or means of distraction, by dint of a certain inner virtuosity they came to possess. They even considered it beginners' awkwardness to glue yourself to a book. It was enough to have one lying in your lap or on your little table, in case of need. The collection of the establishment was an amplification of the literature found in a dentist's waiting--room—in many languages, profusely illustrated, and offered free of charge. The guests exchanged volumes from the loan--library down in the Platz; now and again there would be a book for which everybody scrambled, even the condescending old inhabitants reaching out their hands with ill--concealed eagerness. At the moment it was a cheap paper--backed volume, introduced by Herr Albin, and entitled *The Art of Seduction:* a very literal translation from the French, preserving even the syntax of that language, and thus gaining in elegance and pungency of presentation. In matter it was an exposition of the philosophy of sensual passion, developed in a spirit of debonair and man--of--the--worldly paganism. Frau Stöhr had read it early, and pronounced it simply ravishing. Frau Magnus, the same who had lost her albumen tolerance, agreed unreservedly. Her husband the brewer purported to have profited personally by a perusal, but regretted that his wife should have taken up that sort of thing, because such reading spoiled the women and gave them immodest ideas. His remarks not a little increased the circulation of the volume. Two ladies of the lower rest--hall, Frau Redisch, the wife of a Polish industrial magnate, and Frau Hessenfeld, a widow from Berlin, both of these new arrivals since October, claimed the book at the same time, and a regrettable incident arose after dinner, yes, more than regrettable, for there was a violent scene, overheard by Hans Castorp, in his loggia above. It ended in spasms of hysteria on the part of one of the women—it might have been Frau Redisch, but equally well it might have been Frau Hessenfeld—and she was borne away beside herself to her own room. The youth of the place had got hold of the treatise before those of riper years; studying it in part in groups, after supper, in their various rooms. Hans Castorp himself saw the youth with the finger--nail hand it to Fränzchen Oberdank in the dining--room—she was a new arrival and a light case, a flaxen--haired young thing whose mother had just brought her to the sanatorium. There may have been exceptions; there may have been those who employed the hours of the rest--cure with some serious intellectual occupation, some conceivably profitable study, either by way of keeping in touch with life in the lowlands, or in order to give weight and depth to the passing hour, that it might not be pure time and nothing else besides. Perhaps here and there was one—not, of course, to mention Herr Settembrini, with his zeal for eliminating human suffering, or Joachim with his Russian primer yes, there might be one, or two, thus occupied; if not among the guests in the dining--room, which seemed not very likely, then among the bedridden and moribund. Hans Castorp inclined to believe it. He himself, after imbibing all that *Ocean Steamships* had to offer him, had ordered certain books from home, some of them bearing on his profession, and they had arrived with his winter clothing: scientific engineering, technique of ship--building, and the like. But these volumes lay now neglected in favour of other textbooks belonging to quite a different field, an interest in which had seized upon the young man: anatomy, physiology, biology, works in German, French and English, sent up to the Berghof by the book--dealer in the village, obviously because Hans Castorp had ordered them, as was indeed the case. He had done so of his own motion, without telling anyone, on a solitary walk he took down to the Platz while Joachim was occupied with the weekly weighing or injection. His cousin was surprised when he saw the books in Hans Castorp's hands. They were expensive, as scientific works always are: the prices were marked on the wrappers and inside the front covers. Joachim asked why, if his cousin wanted to read such books, he had not borrowed them of the Hofrat, who surely possessed a wellchosen stock. The young man answered that it was quite a different thing to read when the book was one's own; for his part, he loved to mark them and underline passages in pencil. Joachim could hear, hours on end, the noise made by the paperknife going through the uncut leaves. The volumes were heavy, unhandy. Hans Castorp propped them against his chest or stomach as he lay; they were heavy, but he did not mind. Lying there, his mouth half open, he let his eye glide down the learned page, upon which fell the light from his red--shaded lamp, though he might have read, if need were, by the brilliance of the moonlight alone. He read, following the lines down the page with his head, until at the bottom his chin lay sunk upon his breast——and in this position the reader would pause perhaps for reflection, dozing a little or musing in half--slumber, before lifting his eyes to the next page. He probed profoundly. While the moon took its appointed way above the crystalline splendours of the mountain valley, he read of organized matter, of the properties of protoplasm, that sensitive substance maintaining itself in extraordinary fluctuation between building up and breaking down; of form developing out of rudimentary, but always present, primordia; read with compelling interest of life, and its sacred, impure mysteries.

What was life? No one knew. It was undoubtedly aware of itself, so soon as it was life; but it did not know what it was. Consciousness, as exhibited by susceptibility to stimulus, was undoubtedly, to a certain degree, present in the lowest, most undeveloped stages of life; it was impossible to fix the first appearance of conscious processes at any point in the history of the individual or the race; impossible to make consciousness contingent upon, say, the presence of a nervous system. The lowest animal forms had no nervous systems, still less a cerebrum; yet no one would venture to deny them the capacity for responding to stimuli. One could suspend life; not merely particular sense--organs, not only nervous reactions, but life itself. One could temporarily suspend the irritability to sensation of every form of living matter in the plant as well as in the animal kingdom; one could narcotize ova and spermatozoa with chloroform, chloral hydrate, or morphine. Consciousness, then, was simply a function of matter organized into life; a function that in higher manifestations turned upon its avatar and became an effort to explore and explain the phenomenon it displayed——a hopeful--hopeless project of life to achieve self--knowledge, nature in recoil——and vainly, in the event, since she cannot be resolved in knowledge, nor life, when all is said, listen to itself.

What was life? No one knew. No one knew the actual point whence it sprang, where it kindled itself. Nothing in the domain of life seemed uncausated, or insufficiently causated, from that point on; but life itself seemed without antecedent. If there was anything that might be said about it, it was this: it must be so highly developed, structurally, that nothing even distantly related to it was present in the inorganic world. Between the protean amœba and the vertebrate the difference was slight, unessential, as compared to that between the simplest living organism and that nature which did not even deserve to be called dead, because it was inorganic. For death was only the logical negation of life; but between life and inanimate nature yawned a gulf which research strove in vain to bridge. They tried to close it with hypotheses, which it swallowed down without becoming any the less deep or broad. Seeking for a connecting link, they had condescended to the preposterous assumption of structureless living matter, unorganized organisms, which darted together of themselves in the albumen solution, like crystals in the mother--liquor; yet organic differentiation still remained at once condition and expression of all life. One could point to no form of life that did not owe its existence to procreation by parents. They had fished the primeval slime out of the depth of the sea, and great had been the jubilation——but the end of it all had been shame and confusion. For it turned out that they had mistaken a precipitate of sulphate of lime for protoplasm. But then, to avoid giving pause before a miracle——for life that built itself up out of, and fell in decay into, the same sort of matter as inorganic nature, would have been, happening of itself, miraculous—-they were driven to believe in a spontaneous generation—-that is, in the emergence of the organic from the inorganic—-which was just as much of a miracle. Thus they went on, devising intermediate stages and transitions, assuming the existence of organisms which stood lower down than any yet known, but themselves had as forerunners still more primitive efforts of nature to achieve life: primitive forms of which no one would ever catch sight, for they were all of less than microscopic size, and previous to whose hypothetic existence the synthesis of protein compounds must already have taken place.

What then was life? It was warmth, the warmth generated by a form--preserving instability, a fever of matter, which accompanied the process of ceaseless decay and repair of albumen molecules that were too impossibly complicated, too impossibly ingenious in structure. It was the existence of the actually impossible--to--exist, of a half--sweet, half--painful balancing, or scarcely balancing, in this restricted and feverish process of decay and renewal, upon the point of existence. It was not matter and it was not spirit, but something between the two, a phenomenon conveyed by matter, like the rainbow on the waterfall, and like the flame. Yet why not material—-it was sentient to the point of desire and disgust, the shamelessness of matter become sensible of itself, the incontinent form of being. It was a secret and ardent stirring in the frozen chastity of the universal; it was a stolen and voluptuous impurity of sucking and secreting; an exhalation of carbonic acid gas and material impurities of mysterious origin and composition. It was a pullulation, an unfolding, a form--building (made possible by the overbalancing of its instability, yet controlled by the laws of growth inherent within it), of something brewed out of water, albumen, salt and fats, which was called flesh, and which became form, beauty, a lofty image, and yet all the time the essence of sensuality and desire. For this form and beauty were not spiritborne; nor, like the form and beauty of sculpture, conveyed by a neutral and spiritconsumed substance, which could in all purity make beauty perceptible to the senses. Rather was it conveyed and shaped by the somehow awakened voluptuousness of matter, of the organic, dying--living substance itself, the reeking flesh.

As he lay there above the glittering valley, lapped in the bodily warmth preserved to him by fur and wool, in the frosty night illumined by the brilliance from a lifeless star, the image of life displayed itself to young Hans Castorp. It hovered before him, somewhere in space, remote from his grasp, yet near his sense; this body, this opaquely whitish form, giving out exhalations, moist, clammy; the skin with all its blemishes and native impurities, with its spots, pimples, discolorations, irregularities; its horny, scalelike regions, covered over by soft streams and whorls of rudimentary lanugo. It leaned there, set off against the cold lifelessness of the inanimate world, in its own vaporous sphere, relaxed, the head crowned with something cool, horny, and pigmented, which was an outgrowth of its skin; the hands clasped at the back of the neck. It looked down at him beneath drooping lids, out of eyes made to appear slanting by a racial variation in the lid--formation. Its lips were half open, even a little curled. It rested its weight on one leg, the hip--bone stood out sharply under the flesh, while the other, relaxed, nestled its slightly bent knee against the inside of the supporting leg, and poised the foot only upon the toes. It leaned thus, turning to smile, the gleaming elbows akimbo, in the paired symmetry of its limbs and trunk. The acrid, steaming shadows of the arm--pits corresponded in a mystic triangle to the pubic darkness, just as the eyes did to the red, epithelial mouth--opening, and the red blossoms of the breast to the navel lying perpendicularly below. Under the impulsion of a central organ and of the motor nerves originating in the spinal marrow, chest and abdomen functioned, the peritoneal cavity expanded and contracted, the breath, warmed and moistened by the mucous membrane of the respiratory canal, saturated with secretions, streamed out between the lips, after it had joined its oxygen to the hæmoglobin of the blood in the air--cells of the lungs. For Hans Castorp understood that this living body, in the mysterious symmetry of its blood--nourished structure, penetrated throughout by nerves, veins, arteries, and capillaries; with its inner framework of bones—-marrow--filled tubular bones, blade--bones, vertebræ—-which with the addition of lime had developed out of the original gelatinous tissue and grown strong enough to support the body weight; with the capsules and well--oiled cavities, ligaments and cartilages of its joints, its more than two hundred muscles, its central organs that served for nutrition and respiration, for registering and transmitting stimuli, its protective membranes, serous cavities, its glands rich in secretions; with the system of vessels and fissures of its highly complicated interior surface, communicating through the body--openings with the outer world—-he understood that this ego was a living unit of a very high order, remote indeed from those very simple forms of life which breathed, took in nourishment, even thought, with the entire surface of their bodies. He knew it was built up out of myriads of such small organisms, which had had their origin in a single one; which had multiplied by recurrent division, adapted themselves to the most varied uses and functions, separated, differentiated themselves, thrown out forms which were the condition and result of their growth.

This body, then, which hovered before him, this individual and living I, was a monstrous multiplicity of breathing and self--nourishing individuals, which, through organic conformation and adaptation to special ends, had parted to such an extent with their essential individuality, their freedom and living immediacy, had so much become anatomic elements that the functions of some had become limited to sensibility toward light, sound, contact, warmth; others only understood how to change their shape or produce digestive secretions through contraction; others, again, were developed and functional to no other end than protection, support, the conveyance of the body juices, or reproduction. There were modifications of this organic plurality united to form the higher ego: cases where the multitude of subordinate entities were only grouped in a loose and doubtful way to form a higher living unit. The student buried himself in the phenomenon of cell colonies; he read about half--organisms, algæ, whose single cells, enveloped in a mantle of gelatine, often lay apart from one another, yet were multiple--cell formations, which, if they had been asked, would not have known whether to be rated as a settlement of single--celled individuals, or as an individual single unit, and, in bearing witness, would have vacillated quaintly between the I and the we. Nature here presented a middle stage, between the highly social union of countless elementary individuals to form the tissues and organs of a superior I, and the free individual existence of these simpler forms; the multiple--celled organism was only a stage in the cyclic process, which was the course of life itself, a periodic revolution from procreation to procreation. The act of fructification, the sexual merging of two cell--bodies, stood at the beginning of the upbuilding of every multiple--celled individual, as it did at the beginning of every row of generations of single elementary forms, and led back to itself. For this act was carried through many species which had no need of it to multiply by means of proliferation; until a moment came when the non--sexually produced offspring found themselves once more constrained to a renewal of the copulative function, and the circle came full. Such was the multiple state of life, sprung from the union of two parent cells, the association of many non--sexually originated generations of cell units; its growth meant their increase, and the generative circle came full again when sexcells, specially developed elements for the purpose of reproduction, had established themselves and found the way to a new mingling that drove life on afresh.

Our young adventurer, supporting a volume of embryology on the pit of his stomach, followed the development of the organism from the moment when the spermatozoon, first among a host of its fellows, forced itself forward by a lashing motion of its hinder part, struck with its forepart against the gelatine mantle of the egg, and bored its way into the mount of conception, which the protoplasm of the outside of the ovum arched against its approach. There was no conceivable trick or absurdity it would not have pleased nature to commit by way of variation upon this fixed procedure. In some animals, the male was a parasite in the intestine of the female. In others, the male parent reached with his arm down the gullet of the female to deposit the semen within her; after which, bitten off and spat out, it ran away by itself upon its fingers, to the confusion of scientists, who for long had given it Greek and Latin names as an independent form of life. Hans Castorp lent an ear to the learned strife between ovists and animalculists: the first of whom asserted that the egg was in itself the complete little frog, dog, or human being, the male element being only the incitement to its growth; while the second saw in a spermatozoon, possessing head, arms, and legs, the perfected form of life shadowed forth, to which the egg performed only the office of "nourisher in life's feast." In the end they agreed to concede equal meritoriousness to ovum and semen, both of which, after all, sprang from originally indistinguishable procreative cells. He saw the single--celled organism of the fructified egg on the point of being transformed into a multiple--celled organism, by striation and division; saw the cell--bodies attach themselves to the lamellæ of the mucous membrane; saw the germinal vesicle, the blastula, close itself in to form a cup or basin--shaped cavity, and begin the functions of receiving and digesting food. That was the gastrula, the protozoon, primeval form of all animal life, primeval form of flesh--borne beauty. Its two epithelia, the outer and the inner, the ectoderm and the entoderm, proved to be primitive organs out of whose foldings--in and --out, were developed the glands, the tissues, the sensory organs, the body processes. A strip of the outer germinal layer, the ectoderm, thickened, folded into a groove, closed itself into a nerve canal, became a spinal column, became the brain. And as the fœtal slime condensed into fibrous connective tissue, into cartilage, the colloidal cells beginning to show gelatinous substance instead of mucin, he saw in certain places the connective tissue take lime and fat to itself out of the sera that washed it, and begin to form bone. Embryonic man squatted in a stooping posture, tailed, indistinguishable from embryonic pig; with enormous abdomen and stumpy, formless extremities, the facial mask bowed over the swollen paunch; the story of his growth seemed a grim, unflattering science, like the cursory record of a zoological family tree. For a while he had gill--pockets like a roach. It seemed permissible, or rather unavoidable, contemplating the various stages of development through which he passed, to infer the very little humanistic aspect presented by primitive man in his mature state. His skin was furnished with twitching muscles to keep off insects; it was thickly covered with hair; there was a tremendous development of the mucous membrane of the olfactory organs; his ears protruded, were movable, took a lively part in the play of the features, and were much better adapted than ours for catching sounds. His eyes were protected by a third, nictating lid; they were placed sidewise, excepting the third, of which the pineal gland was the rudimentary trace, and which was able, looking upwards, to guard him from dangers from the upper air. Primitive man had a very long intestine, many molars, and sound--pouches on the larnyx the better to roar with, also he carried his sex--glands on the inside of the intestinal cavity. Anatomy presented our investigator with charts of human limbs, skinned and prepared for his inspection; he saw their superficial and their buried muscles, sinews, and tendons: those of the thighs, the foot, and especially of the arm, the upper and the forearm. He learned the Latin names with which medicine, that subdivision of the humanities, had gallantly equipped them. He passed on to the skeleton, the development of which presented new points of view——among them a clear perception of the essential unity of all that pertains to man, the correlation of all branches of learning. For here, strangely enough, he found himself reminded of his own field——or shall we say his former field?——the scientific calling which he had announced himself as having embraced, introducing himself thus to Dr. Krokowski and Herr Settembrini on his arrival up here. In order to learn something——it had not much mattered what——he had learned in his technical school about statics, about supports capable or flexion, about loads, about construction as the advantageous utilization of mechanical material. It would of course be childish to think that the science of engineering, the rules of mechanics, had found application to organic nature; but

[353]

just as little might one say that they had been derived from organic nature. It was simply that the mechanical laws found themselves repeated and corroborated in nature. The principle of the hollow cylinder was illustrated in the structure of the tubular bones, in such a way that the static demands were satisfied with the precise minimum of solid structure. Hans Castorp had learned that a body which is put together out of staves and bands of mechanically utilizable matter, conformably to the demands made by draught and pressure upon it, can withstand the same weight as a solid column of the same material. Thus in the development of the tubular bones, it was comprehensible that, step for step with the formation of the solid exterior, the inner parts, which were mechanically superfluous, changed to a fatty tissue, the marrow. The thigh--bone was a crane, in the construction of which organic nature, by the direction she had given the shaft, carried out, to a hair, the same draught--and pressure--curves which Hans Castorp had had to plot in drawing an instrument serving a similar purpose. He contemplated this fact with pleasure; he enjoyed the reflection that his relation to the femur, or to organic nature generally was now threefold: it was lyrical, it was medical, it was technological; and all of these, he felt, were one in being human, they were variations of one and the same pressing human concern, they were schools of humanistic thought.

But with all this the achievements of the protoplasm remained unaccountable: it seemed forbidden to life that it should understand itself. Most of the bio--chemical processes were not only unknown, it lay in their very nature that they should escape attention. Almost nothing was known of the structure or composition of the living unit called the "cell." What use was there in establishing the components of lifeless muscle, when the living did not let itself be chemically examined? The changes that took place when the *rigor mortis* set in were enough to make worthless all investigation. Nobody understood metabolism, nobody understood the true inwardness of the functioning of the nervous system. To what properties did the taste corpuscles owe their reaction? In what consisted the various kinds of excitation of certain sensory nerves by odour--possessing substances? In what, indeed, the property of smell itself? The specific odours of man and beast consisted in the vaporization of certain unknown substances. The composition of the secretion called sweat was little understood. The glands that secreted it produced aromata which among mammals undoubtedly played an important rôle, but whose significance for the human species we were not in a position to explain. The physiological significance of important regions of the body was shrouded in darkness. No need to mention the vermiform appendix, which was a mystery; in rabbits it was regularly found full of a pulpy substance, of which there was nothing to say as to how it got in or renewed itself. But what about the white and grey substance which composed the medulla, what of the optic thalamus and the grey inlay of the *pans Varolii?* The substance composing the brain and marrow was so subject to disintegration, there was no hope whatever of determining its structure. What was it relieved the cortex of activity during slumber?

What prevented the stomach from digesting itself——as sometimes, in fact, did happen after death? One might answer, life: a special power of resistance of the living protoplasm; but this would be not to recognize the mystical character of such an explanation. The theory of such an everyday phenomenon as fever was full of contradictions. Heightened oxidization resulted in increased warmth, but why was there not an increased expenditure of warmth to correspond? Did the paralysis of the sweat--secretions depend upon contraction of the skin? But such contraction took place only in the case of "chills and fever," for otherwise, in fever, the skin was more likely to be hot. Prickly heat indicated the central nervous system as the seat of the causes of heightened catabolism as well as the source of that condition of the skin which we were content to call abnormal, because we did not know how to define it.

But what was all this ignorance, compared with our utter helplessness in the presence of such a phenomenon as memory, or of that other more prolonged and astounding memory which we called the inheritance of acquired characteristics? Out of the question to get even a glimpse of any mechanical possibility of explication of such performances on the part of the cell--substance. The spermatozoon that conveyed to the egg countless complicated individual and racial characteristics of the father was visible only through a microscope; even the most powerful magnification was not enough to show it as other than a homogeneous body, or to determine its origin; it looked the same in one animal as in another. These factors forced one to the assumption that the cell was in the same case as with the higher form it went to build up: that it too was already a higher form, composed in its turn by the division of living bodies, individual living units. Thus one passed from the supposed smallest unit to a still smaller one; one was driven to separate the elementary into its elements. No doubt at all but just as the animal kingdom was composed of various species of animals, as the human--animal organism was composed of a whole animal kingdom of cell species, so the cell organism was composed of a new and varied animal kingdom of elementary units, far below microscopic size, which grew spontaneously, increased spontaneously according to the law that each could bring forth only after its kind, and, acting on the principle of a division of labour, served together the next higher order of existence.

Those were the genes, the living germs, bioblasts, biophores--lying there in the frosty night, Hans Castorp rejoiced to make acquaintance with them by name. Yet how, he asked himself excitedly, even after more light on the subject was forthcoming, how could their elementary nature be established? If they were living, they must be organic, since life depended upon organization. But if they were organized, then they could not be elementary, since an organism is not single but multiple. They were units within the organic unit of the cell they built up. But if they were, then, however impossibly small they were, they must themselves be built up, organically built up, as a law of their existence; for the conception of a living unit meant by definition that it was built up out of smaller units which were subordinate; that is, organized with reference to a higher form. As long as division yielded organic units possessing the properties of life—-assimilation and reproduction—-no limits were set to it. As long as one spoke of living units, one could not correctly speak of elementary units, for the concept of unity carried with it in perpetuity the concept of subordinated, upbuilding unity; and there was no such thing as elementary life, in the sense of something that was already life, and yet elementary.

And still, though without logical existence, something of the kind must be eventually the case; for it was not possible to brush aside like that the idea of the original procreation, the rise of life out of what was not life. That gap which in exterior nature we vainly sought to close, that between living and dead matter, had its counterpart in nature's organic existence, and must somehow either be closed up or bridged over. Soon or late, division must yield "units" which, even though in composition, were not organized, and which mediated between life and absence of life; molecular groups, which represented the transition between vitalized organization and mere chemistry. But then, arrived at the molecule, one stood on the brink of another abyss, which yawned yet more mysteriously than that between organic and inorganic nature: the gulf between the material and the immaterial. For the molecule was composed of atoms, and the atom was nowhere near large enough even to be spoken of as extraordinarily small. It was so small, such a tiny, early, transitional mass, a coagulation of the unsubstantial, of the not--yet--substantial and yet substance--like, of energy, that it was scarcely possible yet—-or, if it had been, was now no longer possible—-to think of it as material, but rather as mean and border--line between material and immaterial. The problem of another original procreation arose, far more wild and mysterious than the organic: the primeval birth of matter out of the immaterial. In fact the abyss between material and immaterial yawned as widely, pressed as importunately—-yes, more importunately—-to be closed, as that between organic and inorganic nature. There must be a chemistry of the immaterial, there must be combinations of the insubstantial, out of which sprang the material—-

-the atoms might represent protozoa of material, by their nature substance and still not yet quite substance. Yet arrived at the "not even small," the measure slipped out of the hands; for "not even small" meant much the same as "enormously large"; and the step to the atom proved to be without exaggeration portentous in the highest degree. For at the very moment when one had assisted at the final division of matter, when one had divided it into the impossibly small, at that moment there suddenly appeared upon the horizon the astronomical cosmos!

The atom was a cosmic system, laden with energy; in which heavenly bodies rioted rotating about a centre like a sun; through whose ethereal space comets drove with the speed of light years, kept in their eccentric orbits by the power of the central body. And that was as little a mere comparison as it would be were one to call the body of any multiple--celled organism a "cell state." The city, the state, the social community regulated according to the principle of division of labour, not only might be compared to organic life, it actually reproduced its conditions. Thus in the inmost recesses of nature, as in an endless succession of mirrors, was reflected the macrocosm of the heavens, whose clusters, throngs, groups, and figures, paled by the brilliant moon, hung over the dazzling, frost--bound valley, above the head of our muffled adept. Was it too bold a thought that among the planets of the atomic solar system—-those myriads and milky ways of solar systems which constituted matter—-one or other of these inner--worldly heavenly bodies might find itself in a condition corresponding to that which made it possible for our earth to become the abode of life? For a young man already rather befuddled inwardly, suffering from abnormal skin--conditions, who was not without all and any experience in the realm of the illicit, it was a speculation which, far from being absurd, appeared so obvious as to leap to the eyes, highly evident, and bearing the stamp of logical truth. The "smallness" of these innerworldly heavenly bodies would have been an objection irrelevant to the hypothesis; since the conception of large or small had ceased to be pertinent at the moment when the cosmic character of the "smallest" particle of matter had been revealed; while at the same time, the conceptions of "outside" and "inside" had also been shaken. The atom--world was an "outside," as, very probably, the earthly star on which we dwelt was, organically regarded, deeply "inside." Had not a researcher once, audaciously fanciful, referred to the "beasts of the Milky Way," cosmic monsters whose flesh, bone, and brain were built up out of solar systems? But in that case, Hans Castorp mused, then in the moment when one thought to have come to the end, it all began over again from the beginning! For then, in the very innermost of his nature, and in the inmost of that innermost, perhaps there was just himself, just Hans Castorp, again and a hundred times Hans Castorp, with burning face and stiffening fingers, lying muffled on a balcony, with a view across the moonlit, frost--nighted high valley, and probing, with an interest both humanistic and medical, into the life of the body!

He held a volume of pathological anatomy in the red ray from his table--lamp, and conned its text and numerous reproductions. He read of the existence of parasitic celljuncture and of infectious tumours. These were forms of tissue——and very luxuriant forms too——produced by foreign cell--bodies in an organism which had proved receptive to them, and in some way or other——one must probably say perversely——had offered them peculiarly favourable conditions. It was not so much that the parasite took away nourishment from the surrounding tissues, as that, in the process of building up and breaking down which went on in it as in every other cell, it produced organic combinations which were extraordinarily toxic——undeniably destructive——to the cells where it had been entertained. They had found out how to isolate the toxin from a number of micro--organisms and produce it in concentrated form; and it was amazing to see what small doses of this substance, which simply belonged to a group of protein combinations, could, when introduced into the circulation of an animal, produce symptoms of acute poisoning and rapid degeneration. The outward sign of this inward decay was a growth of tissue, the pathological tumour, which was the reaction of the cells to the stimulus of the foreign bacilli. Tubercles developed, the size of a millet--seed, composed of cells resembling mucous membrane, among or within which the bacilli lodged; some of these were extraordinarily rich in protoplasm, very large, and full of nuclei. However, all this good living soon led to ruin; for the nuclei of these monster cells began to break down, the protoplasm they contained to be destroyed by coagulation, and further areas of tissue to be involved. They were attacked by inflammation, the neighbouring blood--vessels suffered by contagion. White blood--corpuscles were attracted to the seat of the evil; the breakingdown proceeded apace; and meanwhile the soluble toxins released by the bacteria had already poisoned the nerve--centres, the entire organization was in a state of high fever, and staggered——so to speak with heaving bosom——-toward dissolution.

Thus far pathology, the theory of disease, the accentuation of the physical through pain; yet, in so far as it was the accentuation of the physical, at the same time accentuation through desire. Disease was a perverse, a dissolute form of life. And life? Life itself? Was it perhaps only an infection, a sickening of matter? Was that which one might call the original procreation of matter only a disease, a growth produced by morbid stimulation of the immaterial? The first step toward evil, toward desire and death, was taken precisely then, when there took place that first increase in the density of the spiritual, that pathologically luxuriant morbid growth, produced by the irritant of some unknown infiltration; this, in part pleasurable, in part a motion of self--defence, was the primeval stage of matter, the transition from the insubstantial to the substance. This was the Fall. The second creation, the birth of the organic out of the inorganic, was only another fatal stage in the progress of the corporeal toward consciousness, just as disease in the organism was an intoxication, a heightening and unlicensed accentuation of its physical state; and life, life was nothing but the next step on the reckless path of the spirit dishonoured; nothing but the automatic blush of matter roused to sensation and become receptive for that which awaked it.

The books lay piled upon the table, one lay on the matting next his chair; that which he had latest read rested upon Hans Castorp's stomach and oppressed his breath; yet no order went from the cortex to the muscles in charge to take it away. He had read down the page, his chin had sunk upon his chest, over his innocent blue eyes the lids had fallen. He beheld the image of life in flower, its structure, its flesh--borne loveliness. She had lifted her hands from behind her head, she opened her arms. On their inner side, particularly beneath the tender skin of the elbow--points, he saw the blue branchings of the larger veins. These arms were of unspeakable sweetness. She leaned above him, she inclined unto him and bent down over him, he was conscious of her organic fragrance and the mild pulsation of her heart. Something warm and tender clasped him round the neck; melted with desire and awe, he laid his hands upon the flesh of her upper arms, where the fine--grained skin over the triceps came to his sense so heavenly cool; and upon his lips he felt the moist clinging of her kiss.

The Dance of Death

Not long after Christmas, the gentleman rider died.——But before that event the Christmas holidays came and went, the two, or if you reckoned Holy Night the three feast--days, to which Hans Castorp had looked forward with some alarm and headshaking dubiety, as to what they would really be like, up here. In the event, they came on and passed like other days, with a morning, an afternoon, and an evening; only moderately unreasonable in respect of weather——it thawed a little——and not greatly different from others of their kind. Outwardly, they had been somewhat garnished and set off; inwardly they had held sway in the heads and hearts of men for their appointed time; then, leaving behind them some deposit of impressions out of the common run, they slipped away into the recent, then into the distant past.

The Hofrat's son, Knut by name, came for the holidays and lived with his father in the wing of the building; a good--looking young man, save that his cervical vertebra was already too prominent. The presence of young Behrens could be felt in the air: the ladies showed a proneness to laugh, to bicker, and to adorn their persons. They boasted in conversation of having met Knut in the garden, the wood, or the English quarter. He himself had guests: a number of his fellow students came up to the valley, six or seven young men who lodged in the village but ate at the Hofrat's table, and with others of their corps scoured the region in a body. Hans Castorp avoided them. He gave them a wide berth with Joachim whenever necessary; he felt no least desire to meet them. A whole world divided those up here from these singing, roving, staffbrandishing youths—-he wished neither to see nor to hear anything of them. They looked, most of them, like northerners, there might be Hamburgers among them; and Hans Castorp felt very shy of meeting his fellow townsmen. He had often uncomfortably considered the possibility that somebody or other from home might arrive at the Berghof—-had not the Hofrat said that Hamburg always furnished a handsome contingent to the establishment? There might be some among the bedridden and moribund; but the only one visible was a hollow--cheeked business man, said to come from Cuxhaven, who had been sitting for two weeks at Frau Iltis's table. Hans Castorp, seeing him, rejoiced in the knowledge that one came little into touch with guests at other tables than one's own; and further, that his native sphere was an extended one. He saw that the presence of the man from Cuxhaven made no difference to his happiness, and this went far to relieve his fears about the arrival of other Hamburgers.

Christmas eve came on apace, one day it was at hand, the next it was here. When first it had been talked of at table—-to Hans Castorp's great surprise—-it had been yet a good six weeks away, as much time as his original term up here, plus the three weeks in bed. But those first six weeks, as he thought of them in retrospect, seemed a very long time, while the six just passed had been insignificant. His fellow--guests were right to make light of them. Six weeks, why, that was not so many as the week had days; little indeed, when one considered what a small affair a week was, from Monday to Sunday and then Monday again. One needed only to see how valueless the next smaller time--unit was to realize that not much could come even of a whole row of them put together. Rather the total effect was to intensify the process of contraction, shrinkage, blurring, and effacement. What was one day, taken for instance from the moment one sat down to the midday meal to the same moment fourand--twenty hours afterwards? It was, to be sure, four--and--twenty hours——but equally it was the simple sum of nothings. Or take an hour spent in the rest--cure, at the dinnertable, or on the daily walk——and these ways of employing the time--unit practically exhausted its possibilities——what was an hour? Again, nothing. And nothing were all these nothings, they were not serious in the nature of them, taken together. The only unit it was possible to regard with seriousness was the smallest one of all: those seven times sixty seconds during which one held the thermometer between one's lips and continued one's curve——they, indeed, were full of matter and tenacious of life; they could expand into a little eternity; they formed small concretions of high density within the scurrying shadows of time's general course.

The holidays disturbed but little the even tenor of the Berghof ways. A well--grown fir--tree had been set up a few days beforehand on the right--hand wall of the diningroom, the side wall next the "bad" Russian table; a waft of its fragrance came to the noses of the diners now and then, above the heavy odours of the food, and wakened something like pensiveness in the eyes of a few among the guests seated at the seven tables. When they came to supper on the twenty--fourth, they found the tree gaily decked with tinsel, little glass balls, gilded pine--cones, tiny apples in nets, and varied confections. The coloured wax tapers burned throughout the meal and afterwards. And a tiny, taper--decked tree burned likewise, it was said, in the rooms of the bedridden and moribund——each had his own. The parcel post in the last few days had been very heavy. Joachim

Ziemssen and Hans Castorp received carefully packed remembrances from their far--away home, and spread them out in their rooms: judicious gifts of cravats and other articles of clothing, expensive trifles in leather and nickel, and quantities of Christmas cakes, nuts, apples and marzipan——the cousins looked doubtfully at these last supplies, wondering whenever they should have occasion to consume them. Schalleen, as Hans Castorp knew, had not only packed his presents, but bought them, after consultation with the uncles. There was a letter too from James Tienappel, typescript to be sure, but upon heavy paper with his private letterhead, communicating his own and his father's best wishes for the holidays and for a speedy recovery, and including at once greetings for the oncoming New Year as well--a sensible and practical procedure, which followed Hans Castorp's own: he having sent his Christmas messages betimes, under cover with the monthly clinical report.

The tree in the dining--room burned, crackled, and dispensed its fragrance, waking the minds and hearts of the guests to a realization of the day. People had dressed for dinner, the men wore evening clothes and the women jewels, mayhap presents from loving husbands down below. Clavdia Chauchat had exchanged the customary sweater for a frock with a hint of the fanciful about it, suggesting a national costume——Russian peasant, or Balkan, perhaps Bulgarian; a light--coloured, flowing, and girdled arrangement, embroidered, and set with tiny tinsel ornaments. Such a garment gave her figure an unwonted softness and fullness, and suited what Settembrini called her "Tartar physiognomy," particularly the "prairie--wolf's eyes."

They were gay at the "good" Russian table; there the first champagne cork was heard to pop. It set the example, which was followed by nearly all the others. At the cousins' table it was the great--aunt who dispensed champagne for her niece and Marusja, and treated the others as well. The menu was choice. It finished with cheese straws and bon--bons, to which the guests added coffee and liqueurs. Now and then a twig would flare up on the Christmas--tree;

there would be work to put it out, and shrill, immoderate panic among the ladies. Toward the end of the meal Settembrini came to sit for a while at the end of the cousins' table; he wore his everyday clothes, and sported his toothpick. He quizzed Frau Stöhr with spirit, and made a few remarks about the carpenter's son and rabbi of humanity, whose birthday they fancied they were celebrating to--day. Whether he had actually lived, Settembrini said, was uncertain; yet his time had given birth to an idea, which had continued its triumphant course even up to to--day: the idea of the dignity of the human spirit, the idea of equality---in a word, they were celebrating the birth of individualistic democracy, and to it he would empty the glass they gave him. Frau Stöhr found his remarks *équivoque* and unfeeling: she rose under protest to the toast, and as the other tables were being emptied, they followed the general movement toward the drawing--rooms.

Hofrat Behrens, with Knut and Fräulein von Mylendonk, attended the social evening for half an hour. The occasion was to be signalized by the presentation of the gift to the head of the establishment, which accordingly took place, in the room with the optical apparatus. The Russians presented their gift, a large round silver plate, with the Hofrat's monogram engraved in the middle; its utter inutility was plain to every eye. He might at least lie on the chaise--longue which was the gift of the rest of the guests---though it was at present without cover or cushions, having merely a cloth drawn over it. The head end was adjustable; Behrens stretched out full length, with his silver plate under his arm, closed his eyes, and began to snore like a saw--mill, giving out that he was Fafnir with the treasure hoard. Much laughter and applause ensued; Frau Chauchat laughed so hard that her eyes became two cracks, and her mouth stood open---precisely, Hans Castorp remarked, as had been the case with Pribislav Hippe when he laughed.

Directly the head went out, the guests sat down to cards, the Russians occupying, as usual, the small salon. Some of the patients still stood about the room where the Christmas--tree was, watching the candle stumps die down in their sockets, and munching the goodies hanging from the boughs. Here and there at the tables, which were already laid for breakfast, sat a solitary person, with his head on his hand, silently brooding.

Christmas--day was damp and misty. These were clouds they were among, Behrens asserted; mist there was none, up here. But mist or clouds, the damp was perceptible. The surface of the lying snow began to thaw, grew soft and porous. In the rest--cure, one's face and hands were stiff and red—-one suffered far more than in colder, sunny weather.

The feast--day was marked by an evening concert, a real concert with rows of chairs and printed programmes, offered to the guests by House Berghof; consisting of songs by a professional singer who lived up here and gave lessons. She wore two medals pinned side by side on her corsage, had arms like sticks, and a voice whose peculiar toneless quality cast a saddening light upon the grounds for her stay in these regions. She sang:

Ich trage meine Minne

Mit mir herum.

Her accompanist was likewise a resident. Frau Chauchat sat in the first row, but took advantage of the intermission to go out, leaving Hans Castorp free to enjoy the music in peace—-after all, it *was* music—and to read the text of the songs, as printed upon the programme. Herr Settembrini sat awhile beside him, and made a few plastic and resilient phrases upon the dull quality of the singer's *bel canto*, expressing also ironic satisfaction over the home talent displayed in the entertainment. It was so charming, he said, that they were just among themselves. Then he too went away—-to tell truth, Hans Castorp was not sorry to see the backs of them both, the narrow--eyed one and the pedagogue; he could the better devote himself to the singing, and draw comfort from the reflection that all over the world, even in the most extraordinary places, music was made—-very likely even on polar expeditions.

One had a slight differentiating consciousness of the day after Christmas, something that just made it not quite the same as an ordinary Sunday or week--day. Then it was over, and the whole holiday lay in the past—-or, equally, it lay in the distant future, a year away: twelve months would bring it round again, seven more than the time Hans Castorp had spent up here.

But just after the Christmas season, and before the New Year broke, the gentleman rider died. The cousins learnt of the death from Fritz Rotbein's nurse, Alfreda Schildknecht, called Sister Berta, who met them in the corridor and discreetly communicated the sad event. Hans Castorp felt a profound interest; partly because the signs of life he had heard from the gentleman rider were among the earliest impressions of his stay up here, those which had first, or so it seemed to him, called up the flush to his face which since had never left it; but partly also upon moral, one might almost say upon spiritual grounds. He detained Joachim long in talk with the deaconess, who hung with the extreme of pleasure upon their conversation. It was a wonder, she said, that the gentleman rider had lived over the holidays. He had long since shown himself a doughty cavalier, but what it was he breathed with, at the end, nobody could tell. For days and days he had lived only by the aid of enormous quantities of oxygen. Yesterday alone he had consumed forty containers, at six francs apiece—-that mounted up, the gentlemen could reckon the cost themselves; and his wife, in whose arms he had died, was left wholly penniless. Joachim expressed disapproval of the expenditure. Why delay by these torturing and costly artificial expedients a death absolutely certain to supervene? One could not blame the man for blindly consuming the precious gas they urged upon him. But those in charge should have behaved with more reason, they should have let him go his way, in God's name, quite aside from the circumstances, more so when taking them into consideration. The living, after all, had their rights—-and so on. Hans Castorp disagreed emphatically. His cousin, he said, talked almost like Settembrini, without any regard or reverence for suffering. The man had died in the end, that finished it; there was no more to be done to show one's concern, and it had been due to the dying to spend what one could. Thus Hans Castorp. He only hoped the Hofrat had not showed a lack of decent feeling by railing at the poor man at the end. There had been no need, Fräulein Schildknecht said. Only one little thoughtless effort he had made to escape, to spring out of bed; but the merest hint of the futility of such a proceeding had been enough to make him desist once and for all.

Hans Castorp went to view the gentleman rider's mortal remains. He did this of set purpose, to show his contempt for the prevailing system of secrecy, to protest against the egotistic policy of seeing and hearing nothing of such events; to register by his act his disapproval of the others' practice. He had tried to introduce the subject of the death at table, but was met with such a flat and callous rebuff on all sides as both to anger and embarrass him. Frau Stöhr had been downright gruff. What did he mean by introducing such a subject—-what kind of upbringing had he had? The house regulations protected the patients from having such things come to their knowledge; and now here was a young whipper--snapper bringing it up at table, and even in the presence of Dr. Blumenkohl, whom the same fate might any day overtake (this behind her hand). If it happened again, she would complain. Then it was that, thus reproved, Hans Castorp had taken—-and expressed—-a resolve: he would visit their departed comrade, and discharge the last duty of silent respect toward his remains. He persuaded Joachim to do the same.

Sister Berta arranged that they be admitted to the gentleman rider's room, which lay in the first storey beneath their own. The widow received them—-a small, distracted blonde, much reduced by night watching, with a red nose, her handkerchief before her mouth, and wearing a plaid cloak, with the collar turned up, as it was very cold in the room. The heat was turned off, the balcony door stood open. The young people said what was fitting to say, in voices respectfully subdued; then, upon a woeful gesture from the widow, they passed through the room to the bed, walking on their tiptoes and weaving reverently forward. They stood by the dead, each after his fashion: Joachim with heels together, half inclined in a salute, Hans Castorp relaxed and pensive, with hands clasped before him and head on one side, much as he often stood to listen to music. The gentleman rider lay with his head pillowed high, so that his body, that elongated structure, the outgrowth of life's manifold processes, with the elevation of the feet at the end beneath the sheet, looked very flat, almost like a board. A garland of flowers lay at about the knees; a palm--leaf outstanding from it touched the great, yellow, bony hands resting crossed upon the sunken breast. Yellow and bony was the face too, with its bald skull and hooked nose, its angular cheek--bones and bushy, reddish--yellow moustaches, whose full curve gave the grey and stubbly hollows of the cheeks a yet hollower look. The eyes were closed, with a certain unnatural definiteness—-pressed down, not shut, thought Hans Castorp. That was what they called the last service of love; but it happened rather as a service to the survivors than to the dead. And it must be done betimes too, soon after death; for if the myosin process went far in the muscles, it would be too late, he would lie there and stare and one could no longer sustain the illusion of his slumber.

Perfectly at home, in more than one respect in his element, Hans Castorp stood at the bier, expertly reverential. "He seems to sleep," said he, humanely; though such was far from being the case. Then, in a voice appropriately subdued, he began a conversation with the widow, eliciting information about the sufferings, the last days and moments of her departed husband, and the arrangements for transporting the body to Carinthia; displaying a sympathy and conversance that was in part physicianly, in part priestly and moralizing. The widow, speaking in her drawling, nasal, Austrian accent, with now and then a sob, found it remarkable that young folk should so occupy themselves with a stranger's pain. Hans Castorp answered that he and his cousin were themselves ill; that he, when still very young, had stood at the deathbed of near relatives; he was a double orphan, and, if he might say so, long familiar with the sight of death. She asked what profession he had chosen; he replied that he "had been" an engineer.

"Had been?" she queried.

"Had been," he replied, in the sense that his illness and a stay up here of still undetermined length had come between him and his work; that might mean a considerable interruption, even a turning--point in his career, he could not tell. Joachim, at this, searched his face in some alarm. And his cousin? He was a soldier, was at present in training for an officer.

"Ah," she said, "the trade of a soldier is another serious calling, one must be prepared to come into close touch with death, it is well to accustom oneself to the sight beforehand." She dismissed the cousins with thanks and expressions of friendliness, which could not but touch them, considering her distressed state, and the bill for oxygen her departed husband had left behind him.

They returned to their own storey, Hans Castorp greatly pleased and edified by the visit.

"*Requiescat in pace,*" he said. "*Sit tibi terra levis. Requiem æternam dona ei, Domine.* You see, when death is in question, when one speaks to or of the dead, then the Latin comes in force; it is, so to say, the official language. So then you see that death is a thing apart. But it isn't a humanistic gesture, speaking Latin in honour of death; and the Latin isn't what you learn at school, either——the spirit of it is quite different, one might almost say hostile. It is ecclesiastical Latin, monkish Latin, mediæval dialect, a sort of dull, monotonous, underground chanting. Settembrini has no use for it, it is nothing for humanists and republicans and suchlike pedagogues, it comes from quite another point of the compass. I find one ought to be clear about these two intellectual trends, or perhaps it would be better to say states of mind: I mean the devout and the free--thinking. They both

have their good sides; what I have against Settembrini's——the free-
-thinking line——is that he seems to imagine it has a corner in human
dignity. That's exaggerated, I consider, because the other has its own
kind of dignity too, and makes for a tremendous lot of decorum and
correct bearing and uplifting ceremony; more, in fact, than the free-
-thinking, when you remember it has our human infirmity and
proneness to err directly in mind, and thoughts of death and decay
play such an important rôle in it. Have you seen *Don Carlos* given at
the theatre? Do you remember at the Spanish court, when King
Philip comes in, all in black, with the Garter and the Golden Fleece,
and takes off his hat——it looks pretty much like one of our melons—
-he lifts it from the top, and says: 'Cover, my lords,' or something like
that? That is the last degree of formality, I should think; no talk of
any free--and--easy manners there! The Queen herself says: 'In my
own France how different!' Of course it is too precise for her, too
fussy, she would like it a little gayer and more human. But what is
human? Everything is human. I find all that strict punctilio and God-
-fearing solemnity of the Spanish is a very dignified kind of humanity;
while on the other hand the word human can be used to cover up
God knows what loose and slovenly ways——you know that
yourself."

"I do indeed," Joachim said. "Naturally, I can't abide any kind of
looseness or slovenliness. There must be discipline."

"Yes, you say that as a soldier; and I must admit the military has
an understanding of these matters. The widow was right when she
said your trade is a solemn one, that has to reckon on coming to grips
with death. You have your tight--fitting, immaculate uniform, with a
stiff collar——there's your *bienséance* for you; then your regulations of
rank, and military obedience, and all the forms you preserve toward
each other——quite in the Spanish spirit, there is something reverent
about it, I can do with it very well, at bottom. We civilians ought to
show more of the same spirit in our customs and manners, I should
really like it, and find it fitting. I think the world, and life generally, is
such as to make it appropriate for us all to wear black, with a starched

ruff instead of your stand--up collar; and for all our intercourse with each other to be subdued and ceremonial, and mindful of death. That would seem right and moral to me. There is another of Settembrini's arrogant ideas; I may tell him so, some time: he thinks he has a monopoly of morals as well as of human dignity—-with his talk about 'practical lifework' and Sunday services in the name of 'progress'—-as though one hadn't something else to think about, on Sundays, besides progress!—-and his 'systematic elimination of suffering'; you have not heard anything about that, but he has instructed me on the subject, and it is to be systematically eliminated by means of a lexicon. I may find all that positively immoral—-but what of it? I don't tell him so, naturally. He fairly goes for me, you know, of course in his plastic way, and says: 'I warn you, Engineer.' But a person can take leave to think what he pleases, at least: 'Sire, grant freedom of thought.' Let me tell you something," he went on—-they had by now arrived in Joachim's room, and Joachim was making ready for the rest--cure—-" let me tell you something I propose to do. We live up here, next door to the dying, close to misery and suffering; and not only we act as though we had nothing to do with it, but it is all carefully arranged in order to spare us and prevent our coming into contact with it, or seeing anything at all—-they will take away the gentleman rider while we are at breakfast or tea—-and that I find immoral. The Stöhr woman was furious, simply because I mentioned his death. That's too absurd for words. She is ignorant, to be sure, and thinks that '*Leise, leise, fromme Weise*' comes out of *Tannhäuser*, she said so the other day. But even so, she might have a little human feeling, and the rest of them too. Well, I have made up my mind to concern myself a bit in future with the severe cases and the moribund. It will do me good—-I feel our visit just now has done me good already. That poor chap Reuter in number twentyfive, whom I saw through the door when I first came, he has most likely long ago been gathered to his fathers, and been spirited away on the quiet. His eyes were so enormous even then. But there are more of them, the house is full, and they keep coming. Sister Alfreda or the Directress, or even Behrens himself, would most likely be glad to put us in the way of it. Say that one of the moribund was having a birthday, and we hear of it——that could easily be brought about. Good. We send him, or her, whichever it is, a pot of flowers, an attention from two fellow--guests, who prefer to remain anonymous, with best wishes for recovery; it is always polite to say that. Then afterwards, of course, it is found out who sent it, and he——or she——in her infirmity, lets us greet her, in a friendly way, through the door--way; she may even ask us in for a minute, and we have a little human intercourse with him, before he sinks away. That's how I imagine it. Are you agreed? For my part, my mind is made up."

Joachim had not much to bring up against the plan. "It is against the rules of the house," he said. "In a certain way you would be transgressing them. But Behrens would probably be willing to make an exception, and give permission, if you wanted it, I should think. You might refer to your interest in the medical side."

"Yes, among other things," Hans Castorp answered: for in truth somewhat involved motives lay at the bottom of his desire. His protest against the prevailing egotism was only one of these: there was also and in particular a spiritual craving to take suffering and death seriously, and pay them the respect that was their due. Contact with the suffering and dying would, or so he hoped, feed and strengthen this craving of the spirit, by counteracting the manifold woundings to which it was daily and hourly subjected, and which he felt the more keenly on account of the Settembrinian critique. Instances there were only too many: if one had asked Hans Castorp for them, he would probably have mentioned certain persons who were admittedly not much ailing, and not under the smallest compulsion, but who made a pretext of slight illness to live up here, for their own pleasure, and because the life suited them. Such was the Widow Hessenfeld, whom we have mentioned in passing. Her passion was betting; she staked against the gentlemen every conceivable object upon every conceivable subject: the weather, the dishes at dinner, the result of the monthly examination, the prescribed length of stay of this or that person, the champions in the skating, sleighing, bob--racing, and skiing competitions, the duration of this or that amour among the guests of the cure, and a hundred other, often quite indifferent or trifling subjects. Staked chocolate, champagne, and caviar, which were then ceremonially partaken of in the restaurant; or money, or cinematograph tickets, or even kisses, given and received——in brief, she brought with her passion for betting much life and excitement into the dining--room; though her proceedings were not such as could be taken seriously by Hans Castorp, who even felt that her mere presence was prejudicial to the dignity of a serious cure.

For he was inwardly concerned to protect that dignity and uphold it in his own eyes——though now, after nearly half a year among those up here, it cost him something to do so. The insight he gradually won into their lives and activities, their practices and points of view, was not encouraging. We have mentioned the two slim young elegants, seventeen and eighteen years old, nicknamed Max and Moritz, whose exploits were the talk of the cure, and who were in the habit of climbing out of the window at night in order to play poker and dissipate down below in female society. Only lately——that is to say, perhaps a week after the New Year, for we must bear in mind that while we tell the story, time streams silently and ceaselessly on——it had been spread abroad at breakfast that the bathing--master had just caught the pair, in crumpled evening clothes, lying on their beds. Even Hans Castorp laughed; but this, however humiliating it was to his better feelings, was nothing compared to the tales that circulated about a certain lawyer from Jüterbog, Einhuf by name; a man perhaps forty years old, with a pointed beard and very hairy hands, who had taken the Swede's place at Herr Settembrini's table. It was reported of him not only that he came home drunk every night, but that recently he had failed to do even that, having been discovered lying in the meadow. He passed for a Don Juan: Frau Stöhr could point out the damsel——of whom it was also known that she had an affianced lover down in the flat--land——who was seen at a certain hour coming our of Lawyer Einhuf's room, clad in a fur coat with combinations underneath, and nothing more. That was a scandal; not only to the general, but even more to Hans Castorp's private sense, and derogatory to his spiritual endeavours. It even came to this: that the thought of Lawyer Einhuf could not enter his mind without calling up there, by an association of ideas, the thought of Fränzchen Oberdank, the little creature with the sleek blond head, whose mamma, a worthy dame from the provinces, had brought her up to the Berghof a few weeks before. Fränzchen's case, on her arrival, and even after the examination, had been thought a light one. But perhaps she had failed in the service of the cure, perhaps hers was one of those cases in which the air proved in the first instance to be good not against but for the disease. Or perhaps the child may have become involved in some intrigue, the excitement of which was seriously bad for her. Four weeks after her arrival she entered the dining--room fresh from a second examination, tossing her little hand--bag in the air, and crying out in her fresh young voice: "Hurrah, hurrah! I shall have to stop a year!"—-at which the whole room resounded with Homeric laughter. But two weeks later the whisper went round that Lawyer Einhuf had behaved like a blackguard to Fränzchen Oberdank. The expression is ours, or, rather, Hans Castorp's; for those who spread the news found it too old a story to be moved to the use of strong language. They shrugged their shoulders and gave it out as their view that it took two to play at such games, and that it was unlikely anything had happened against the will of either participant. This, at least, was Frau Stöhr's demeanour, her ethical reaction to the affair in question.

Caroline Stöhr was dreadful. If anything had power to distract our young Hans Castorp, in the course of his sincerely felt spiritual strivings, it was the personality, the very existence of this woman. Her perpetual malapropisms were quite enough. She said insolvent when she meant insolent, and uttered the most amazing rubbish by way of explaining the astronomical phenomena involved in an eclipse of the sun. One day she almost reduced Herr Settembrini to permanent stupefaction by telling him that she was reading a book from the library which would interest him; namely, "Schiller's translation of Benedetto Cenelli." She adored expressions of a cheap and common stamp, worn threadbare by over--use, which got on Hans Castorp's nerves—as, for example, "you haven't the faintest idea!" or "how utterly too--too!" It had for long been the fashionable jargon to say "simply gorgeous" to express the idea of brilliant, or excellent; this phrase now proved to have outlived its usefulness. It was entirely prostituted, the juice quite sucked out of it; and Frau Stöhr clutched eagerly at the newest currency: everything, whether in jest or earnest, was "devastating," the bobrun, the sweet for dinner, her own temperature—and this sounded equally offensive in her mouth. She had a boundless appetite for gossip. One day she might relate that Frau Salomon was wearing the most costly lace underwear in preparation for her examination, and prided herself very much upon her appearance before the physicians on these occasions. There was probably more truth than poetry in the statement. Hans Castorp himself had the impression that the examinations, quite aside from their result, had their pleasurable side for the ladies, and that they adorned themselves accordingly. But what should one say to Frau Stöhr's assertion that Frau Redisch, from Posen, who, it was feared, suffered from tuberculosis of the spine, had to walk up and down entirely naked before Hofrat Behrens, for ten minutes once a week? This statement was almost as improbable as it was objectionable; but Frau Stöhr swore to it by all that was holy—though it was hard to understand how the poor creature could expend so much zeal and energy, and be so dogmatic, upon matters like these, when her own personal condition gave so much cause for concern. She was sometimes seized by attacks of panic and whimpering, caused by the lassitude which seemed to be constantly on the increase, or by her rising curve; when she would come sobbing to table, the chapped red cheeks streaming with tears, and wail into her handkerchief: Behrens wanted to send her to bed, she would like to know what he had said behind her back was the matter with her, she wanted to look the truth in the face. One day she had remarked to her horror that her bed had been placed with the foot in the direction of the entrance door; the discovery nearly sent her into spasms. It was not easy to understand her rage and terror; Hans Castorp did not see at once what she meant, and inquired: "Well? And what then? What was there about the bed standing like that?"

For God's sake, couldn't he understand? Feet first! She had made desperate outcry, and the position of the bed had to be altered at once, though it caused her to lie with her face to the light, and thus disturbed her sleep.

But none of this was really serious; it could not meet Hans Castorp's spiritual needs. A frightful occurrence, which happened at about this time, during a meal, made a profound impression upon him. Among the newer patients was a schoolmaster named Popoff, a lean and silent man, with his equally lean and silent wife. They sat together at the "good" Russian table; and one day, while the meal was in full swing, the man was seized with a violent epileptic fit, and with that oft--described demoniac unearthly shriek fell to the floor, where he lay beside his chair, striking about him with dreadfully distorted arms and legs. To make matters worse, it was a fish dish that had just been handed, and there was ground for fear that Popoff, in his spasm, might choke on a bone. The uproar was indescribable. The ladies, Frau Stöhr in the lead, with Mesdames Salomon, Redisch, Hessenfeld, Magnus, Iltis, Levi, and the rest following hard upon, were taken in a variety of ways, some of them almost as badly as Popoff. Their yells resounded. Everywhere were twitching eyelids, gaping mouths, writhing torsos. One of them elected to faint, silently. There were cases of choking, some of them having been in the act of chewing and swallowing when the excitement began. Many of the guests at the various tables fled, through any available exit, even actually seeking the open, though the weather was very cold and damp. The whole occurrence, however, took a peculiar cast, offensive even beyond the horror of it, through an association of ideas due to Dr. Krokowski's latest lecture. In the course of his exposition of love as a power making for disease, the psycho--analyst had touched upon the "falling sickness." This affliction, which, in pre-

-analytic times, he said, men had by turns interpreted as a holy, even a prophetic visitation, and as a devilish possession, he went on to treat of, half poetically, half in ruthlessly scientific terminology, as the equivalent of love and an orgasm of the brain. In brief, he had cast such an equivocal light upon the disease that his hearers were bound to see, in Popoff's seizure, an illustration of the lecture, an awful manifestation and mysterious scandal. The flight on the part of the ladies was, accordingly, a disguised expression of modesty. The Hofrat himself had been present at the meal; he, with Fräulein von Mylendonk and one or two more robust guests, carried the ecstatic from the room, blue, rigid, twisted, and foaming at the mouth as he was; they put him down in the hall, where the doctors, the Directress, and other people could be seen hovering over the unconscious man, whom they afterwards bore away on a stretcher. But a short time thereafter Herr Popoff, quite happy and serene, with his equally serene and happy wife, was to be seen sitting at the "good" Russian table, finishing his meal as though nothing had happened.

Hans Castorp was present at this episode, and evinced all the outward signs of concern and alarm, but at bottom he was not edified, God help him! True, Popoff might have choked on his mouthful of fish; but he had not. Perhaps, in all his unconscious mouthings and goings--on, he had all the while somehow taken jolly good care not to. Now he was sitting there, eating blithely away, as though he had never been behaving like a drunken berserk—very probably he remembered nothing at all about it. But in his person he was not a man to strengthen Hans Castorp's respect for suffering; his wife, too, after her fashion, only added to those impressions of frivolous irregularity against which Hans Castorp wrestled and which he sought to counteract by coming into closer touch, despite the prevailing attitude, with the suffering and dying in the establishment.

In the same storey with the cousins, not far from their rooms, lay a young girl named Leila Gerngross. According to Sister Berta, she was about to die. Inside ten days she had had four violent hemorrhages, and her parents had come, in the hope to take her home while she still lived. But it was impossible; the Hofrat said poor little Gerngross could not stand the journey. She was sixteen or seventeen years old. Hans Castorp saw here the opportunity to carry out his plan with the pot of flowers and the good wishes for speedy recovery. There was, it is true, no birthday feast to celebrate, in all human probability little Leila would never see another—-it came in the spring, Hans Castorp learned. But he felt the fact need not prevent his offering his respectful sympathy. When he went down with his cousin for their morning walk, he entered a flower--shop near the Kurhaus; and breathing in agreeably the moist, earthy, scentladen air, he chose with care from the array a charming hortensia, and ordered it conveyed to the little sufferer's room, with a card, upon which he wrote no names, but simply "From two house--mates, with best wishes for recovery." All this was an exquisite activity to Hans Castorp; he enjoyed the fragrant breath of the plants; the soft warmth of the shop, after the cold outside, made his eyes fill with tears. His heart beat with a feeling of adventure and audacity, a conviction of the good sense of his modest enterprise, to which, privately, he ascribed a certain symbolic value.

Leila Gerngross had no private nursing, she was under the immediate supervision of Fräulein von Mylendonk and the physicians. Sister Berta too went in and out of her room, and it was she who gave the young people news of the result of their attention. The little one, in her hopeless and circumscribed state, was as pleased as a child with the strangers' greeting. The pot stood at her bedside, she caressed it with eyes and hands, saw that it was kept watered, and even in her severest fits of coughing rested her tortured gaze upon it. Likewise the parents, retired Major Gerngross and wife, were touched and pleased; and since it was impossible, for them, as complete strangers, to guess the givers, Fräulein Schildknecht could not—-she confessed it—-refrain from revealing the cousins' identity. She transmitted the desire of the whole family that they should come and receive the thanks due their gift; and thus, on the next day but one, the deaconess ushered the two on tiptoe into Leila's apartment.

The dying girl was indeed a charming blond creature, with eyes of true forget--menot blue. Despite great loss of blood, and the effort to breathe with an utterly insufficient remnant of sound lung--tissue, she looked fragile indeed, yet not too distressing. She thanked them, and talked a little, in a pleasant, though toneless voice, while a faint rosy glow overspread her cheeks and lingered there. Hans Castorp suitably explained and excused his seeming intrusion, speaking in a low, moved voice, with delicate reverence. He did not lack much—-the impulse was present in him—-of falling upon his knees by the bedside; and he clasped the patient's hot little hand long and closely in his, despite its being not moist but actually wet, for the child's sweat secretion was so great, she perspired so much, that the flesh must have been shrivelled, if the transudation had not been counteracted by copious draughts of lemonade, a carafe of which stood on the bedside table. The parents, afflicted as they were, sustained the brief colloquy with courteous inquiries as to the state of the cousins' health, and other conversational devices. The Major was a broad--shouldered man, with a low forehead and bristling moustaches, a tower of strength; his organic innocence of his little daughter's phthisical tendency was plain to any eye. It was rather the mother who was responsible for the inherited taint; she was small, and of a distinctly consumptive type, and her conscience seemed burdened with the knowledge of her fatal bequest. Leila, after ten minutes' talk, gave signs of fatigue, or rather of over--excitement; the flush deepened in her cheek, and her forget--me--not eyes glittering disquietingly. The cousins, on a sign from the nurse, made their adieux; and then the poor mother followed them into the corridor, and broke out into selfreproachings, which affected Hans Castorp very painfully. From her, from her alone it came, she said remorsefully, again and again. Her husband had nothing whatever to do with it. Even she, she assured them, had been only temporarily affected, only a slight and superficial case, when she was quite a young girl. She had outgrown it entirely, had been sure that she was quite cured. For she had wished to marry, she had so longed to marry and live, and she had done it: healed and sound she had wedded her dear husband, himself as sound as a berry, who on his side had no notion at all of such things. But sound and strong as he was, that had not helped: the dreadful, hidden, and forgotten thing had come to light in the child, it would end by destroying her; she, the mother, had escaped and was entering into a healthy old age, but the poor, lovely darling would die, the physicians gave them no hope——and she, she alone was to blame, with her buried past.

The young people sought to console her, to say something about the possibility of a turn for the better. But the Major's wife only sobbed and thanked them for all they had done, for the gift of the plant, and the diversion and pleasure their visit had brought her child. She lay there, poor little one, lonely and suffering upon her bed, while other young creatures were glad of life, and could dance with fine young men to their heart's desire——and even the disease could not kill the desire to dance. They had brought her a ray of sunshine——my God, it would be the last. The hortensia had been like homage at a ball, the brief chat with the two fine young cavaliers a tiny *affaire de cœur;* she, the mother, had seen it.

All this impressed Hans Castorp rather painfully——and she had pronounced the French badly too, which irritated him beyond words. He was no fine cavalier, he had visited little Leila only as a protest against the ruling spirit of egotism in the place, and in a physicianly and priestly capacity. He was rather put out over the turn the affair had taken, and the interpretation the mother had put upon it. But on the other hand, he felt a lively pleasure at having actually carried out his undertaking. Two impressions in particular lingered from the enterprise: one, the earthy odours of the flower--shop; the other, Leila's wet little hand——they had sunk into his mind and soul. And as thus a beginning had been made, he arranged on the same day with Alfreda Schildknecht a visit to her patient, Fritz Rotbein, who was as bored with life as his nurse, though to him, unless all signs failed, only a short term still remained.

Nothing for it but that the good Joachim must go along. Hans Castorp's charitable impulse was stronger than his cousin's distaste; which the latter, moreover, could only manifest by silence and averted eyes, since he could not stand for it except by betraying a lack of Christian feeling. Hans Castorp saw that very well, and drew advantage from it. Equally he perceived the military grounds for the distaste; but if he himself felt the happier and stronger for such undertakings, if they seemed to him conducive to good ends? In that case, he must simply override Joachim's silent disapproval. He deliberated with his cousin whether they might send or bring flowers to Fritz Rotbein, he being a man. He desired to do so. Flowers, he felt, were proper to the occasion, and the purchase of the pretty, well--shaped purple hortensia had greatly pleased him. He came to the conclusion that Fritz Rotbein's sex was, so to speak, neutralized by his mortal state; also that there was no need of a birthday to serve as excuse, since the dying are to be treated as though in enjoyment of a permanent birthday. Thus minded, he sought once more with his cousin the warm, earthy, scentladen air of the flower--shop, and brought back a dewy fragrant bunch of roses, wallflowers, and carnations, with which they entered Herr Rotbein's room, ushered by Alfreda Schildknecht.

The sufferer was not more than twenty years old, if so much, but rather bald and grey. He looked waxen and wasted, with large hands, nose, and ears; showed himself glad unto tears for the kindness of the visit, and the diversion it afforded him, and indeed, out of weakness, did weep a little as he greeted the two and received the bouquet. His first words, uttered almost in a whisper, were with reference to the flowers, and he went on to talk about the European flower trade, and its everincreasing proportions—-about the enormous exportation from the nurseries of Nice and Cannes, the shipments by train--load and post that went off daily from these places all over Europe; about the wholesale markets of Paris and Berlin, and the supplies for Russia. For he was a business man; his point of view was the commercial one, and would be so long as life remained to him. His father, a doll--manufacturer in Coburg, had sent him to England to be educated, he told them in a whisper, and there he had fallen ill. They had taken his fever for typhoid, and treated it accordingly, with liquid diet, which had much reduced him. Up here they had let him eat, and eat he had; in the sweat of his brow he had sat in his bed and tried to build himself up. But it was all too late, the intestinal tract was already involved. In vain they sent him tongue and spiced eel from home——he could not digest it. His father, whom Behrens summoned by telegraph, was now on the way from Coburg; for decisive action was to be taken, they would try at least what they could do with rib resection, though the chances of success diminished daily. Rotbein conveyed all this in a whisper, and with great objectivity. Even in the matter of the operation he took a business view, for, so long as he lived, that would be his angle of approach. The expense, he whispered, was fixed at a thousand francs, including the anesthesia of the spinal cord; practically the whole thoracic cavity was involved, six or eight ribs, and the question was whether it would pay. Behrens would like to persuade him; but the doctor's interest in the matter was single, whereas his own seemed equivocal; he was not at all clear that he would not do better just to die in peace, with his ribs intact.

It was hard to advise him. The cousins thought the Hofrat's brilliant reputation as a surgeon should be considered. It was agreed at length to leave the decision to the elder Rotbein, soon to arrive. Young Fritz wept again a little as they took their leave; his tears fell in strange contrast to the dry matter--of--factness of his thought and speech. He begged the gentlemen to repeat their visit, and they willingly promised to do so, but it did not come about. The doll--manufacturer arrived in the evening, next morning they proceeded to operate, and after that young Fritz was in no condition to receive callers. Two days later, passing the room with Joachim, Hans Castorp saw that it was being turned out. Sister Alfreda had already packed her little trunk and left the Berghof, to go to another *moribundus* in another establishment. Heaving a sigh, her eye--glass ribbon behind her ear, she had betaken herself thither, since such and only such was the prospect life held out to her.

An empty room, a room that had been "vacated"—with its furniture turned topsyturvy, and both doors standing wide, as one saw it in passing, on the way to the dining-room or one's daily walks—was a most significant, and yet withal such an accustomed sight that one thought little of it, especially when one had, in one's time, taken possession of just such a "vacated" room, and settled down to feel at home in it. Sometimes you knew whose room it had been, and that indeed gave you to think. Thus a week later Hans Castorp passed by and saw Leila Gerngross's room in just that condition; and in this instance his understanding rebelled for the moment against what he saw. He stood and looked, perplexed and startled, and the Hofrat came that way, to whom he spoke.

"I see it is being turned out here. Good-morning, Herr Hofrat. Then little Leila—"

"Ay," answered Behrens, and shrugged his shoulders. After a pause for the meaning of the gesture to take effect, he added: "So you paid court to her in form, just before the doors were shut? Decent of you, to take an interest in my lungers, considering you are relatively sound yourself. Shows a pretty trait of character—no, no, don't be shy, quite a pretty trait. Shall I introduce you a bit here and there, what? I have all sorts of jail-birds in their little cells, if you want to see them. Just now, for instance, I am on my way to visit my 'Overfilled.' Want to come? I'll introduce you as a sympathetic fellow sufferer."

Hans Castorp replied that the Hofrat had taken the words out of his mouth, and offered him what he was on the point of asking. He would gratefully accept the permission to accompany him; but who was the 'Overfilled' and how did Hofrat Behrens mean him to understand the title?

"Quite literally," said the Hofrat. "Quite exactly, no metaphors. She'll tell you about herself." A few paces brought them before the room, and the Hofrat entered, bidding his companion wait.

As the double doors opened, the visitor heard the sound of clear and hearty laughter, which yet sounded short--winded, as though the person within were gasping for breath. Then it was shut away; but he heard it again when, a few minutes later, he was bidden to enter, and Behrens presented him to the blonde lady lying there in bed and looking at him with curiosity out of her blue eyes. She lay half sitting, supported by pillows, and seemed very restless; she laughed incessantly, struggling the while for breath: a high, purling, silver laughter, as though her plight excited or amused her. She was amused too, very likely, by the Hofrat's turns of phrase in introducing the visitor, and called out repeated thanks and good--byes as he went off; waved her hand at his departing back; sighed melodiously, with runs of silver merriment, and pressed her hand against her heaving breast under the batiste night--gown. Her legs, it seemed, were never still.

The lady's name was Frau Zimmermann. Hans Castorp knew her by sight; she had sat for some weeks at the table with Frau Salomon and the lad who bolted his food; then she had disappeared, and so far as Hans Castorp may have troubled about it, he supposed that she had gone home. Now he found her again, under the name of the "Overfilled," and awaited an explanation.

"Ha ha, ha ha!" she carolled, in high glee, holding her fluttering bosom.

"Frightfully funny man, is Behrens; killingly funny, makes you die of laughing. But sit down, Herr Kasten, or Garsten, or whatever your name is; you have such a funny name----ha ha, ha ha! You must please excuse me; do sit down on that chair near my feet, but please don't mind if I thrash about with my legs, I cannot help it."

She was almost pretty, with clear--cut, rather too well--defined though agreeable features, and a tiny double chin. Her lips and even the tip of her nose were blue, probably from lack of air. Her hands had an appealing thinness; the laces of the nightdress set them off; but she could keep them quiet no more than her feet. Her throat was like a girl's, with "salt--cellars" above the delicate collar--bones; and her breast, heaving and struggling under the night--gown with her laughter and gasping breaths, looked tender and young. Hans Castorp decided to send or bring her flowers, a bouquet from the nurseries of Nice and Cannes, dewy and fragrant. With some misgiving he joined in her breathless and volatile mirth.

"And so you go round visiting the fever cases?" she asked. "That's very amusing and friendly of you! But I'm not a fever case; that is, I wasn't in the least, until just now—-until this business—-listen, and tell me if it isn't just the funniest thing you ever heard in all your life!" And wrestling for air, amid trills and roulades of laughter, she related her story.

She had come up a little ill—-well, ill, of course, for otherwise she would not have come; perhaps not quite a slight case, but rather slight than grave. The pneumothorax, that newest triumph of modern surgical technique, so rapidly become popular, had been brilliantly successful in her case. She made most gratifying progress, her condition was entirely satisfactory. Her husband—-for she was married, though childless—-might hope to have her home again in three or four months. Then, to divert herself, she made a trip to Zürich—-there had been no other reason for her going, save simply to amuse herself—-she had amused herself to her heart's content, but found herself overtaken by the need to be "filled up" again and entrusted the business to a physician where she was. A nice, amusing young man—-but what was the result? Here she was overtaken by a perfect paroxysm of laughter. He had filled her too full! There were no other words to describe it, that said it all. He had meant too well by her, he had probably not too well understood the technique; the long and short of it was, in that condition, not able to breathe, suffering from cardiac depression, she had come back—-ah, ha, ha, ha! and Behrens, cursing and storming with a vengeance, had stuck her into bed. For now she was ill indeed, not actually in high fever, but finished, done, made a mess of—-oh, what a face he was making, how funny he looked, ha, ha, ha!

She pointed at Hans Castorp and laughed so hard that even her brow grew blue. The funniest thing of all, she said, was the way Behrens raved and reviled—-it had made her laugh, at first, when she discovered that she was overfilled.

"You are in absolute danger of your life," he had bellowed at her, just like that, without making any bones of it. "What a bear—ah, ha, ha, ha!—-you really must please forgive me."

It remained unclear what aspect of Behrens's outburst had made her laugh; whether his brusqueness, and because she did not believe what he said, or whether she did believe it—-as indeed she must, it would seem—-and quite simply found the fact of her imminent danger "too funny for words." Hans Castorp got the impression that it was the latter; and that she was pealing, trilling, and cascading with laughter only out of childish irresponsibility and the incomprehension of her birdlike brain. He disapproved. He sent her some flowers, but never again beheld the laughter-loving lady—-who, indeed, after she had sustained life upon oxygen for some days, expired in the arms of her hurriedly summoned husband. "As big a goose as they make them," the Hofrat called her, in telling Hans Castorp of her death.

But the young man had by then made further connexions among the serious cases, thanks to the Hofrat and the house nurses; and Joachim had to accompany him on the visits he made; for instance to the son of Tous--les--deux—-the second, for the room of the first had long since been swept and garnished and fumigated with H_2CO. They paid visits as well to Teddy, a boy who had lately been sent up from the "Fridericianum"—-as the school below was called—-because his case proved too severe for the life there; to Anton Farlowitsch Ferge, the Russo--German insurance agent, a good--natured martyr; and to that unhappy, and yet so coquettish creature, Frau von Mallinckrodt. She, like all the foregoing, received flowers, and was even fed more than once from the hands of Hans Castorp, in the presence of Joachim. They gradually acquired the name of good Samaritans and Brothers of Charity; Settembrini thus referred to their activities one day to Hans Castorp.

"*Sapperlot*, Engineer! What is this I am hearing of your activities? So you have thrown yourself into a career of benevolence? You are seeking justification through good works?"

"Nothing worth mentioning, Herr Settembrini. Nothing to make a fuss about. My cousin and I—-"

"Don't talk to me about your cousin. When the two of you make yourselves talked about, it is you we are dealing with. Your cousin's is a good and simple nature, most worthy of respect; exposed to no intellectual perils, the sort that gives a schoolmaster not one anxious moment. You'll not make me believe he is the moving spirit. No; yours is the more gifted, if also the more exposed nature. You are, if I may so express myself, life's delicate child, one has to trouble about you. And moreover you have given me permission to trouble about you."

"Certainly, Herr Settembrini—-once and for all. Very kind of you. 'Life's delicate child,' why, that's very pretty—-only an author would think of it. I don't know if I've to flatter myself over the title, but I like the sound of it at least, I must say that. Yes, I do occupy myself rather with the 'children of death,' if that is what you refer to. I look in here and there among the serious cases and the dying when I have time, the service of the cure doesn't suffer from it. I visit the ones who aren't here for the fun of the thing, leading a disorderly life—-the ones who are busy dying."

"And yet it is written: 'Let the dead bury their dead,' " said the Italian. Hans Castorp raised his arms, to signify that there was so much written, on both sides, it was hard to know the rights of it. Of course, the organ--grinder had voiced a disturbing point of view, that was to be expected. Hans Castorp was ready, now as ever, of his own free will to lend an ear to Settembrini's teachings, and by way of experiment to be influenced by them. But he was far from being prepared to give up, for the sake of a pedagogic point of view, enterprises which he vaguely, despite Mother Gerngross and her phrases, despite the uninspiring young Rotbein and the cachinnations of the "Overfilled," found somehow helpful and significant.

Tous--les--deux's son was named Lauro. He too received flowers, earthy, heavenlysmelling violets from Nice, "from two sympathetic housemates, with best wishes for recovery"; and as this anonymity had by now become purely formal, since everyone knew the source whence such attentions came, Tous--les--deux herself thanked the cousins when they chanced to meet in the corridor. The pale, dark Mexican mother begged them, with a few incoherent words, and chiefly by means of a pathetic gesture of invitation, to come and receive in person the thanks of her son— *son seul et dernier fils, qui allait mourir aussi*. They went at once. Lauro proved to be an astonishingly handsome young man, with great glowing eyes, a nose like an eagle's beak, quivering nostrils, and beautiful lips, with a small black moustache sprouting above them. But his bearing was so theatrical and swaggering that Hans Castorp, this time no less than Joachim Ziemssen, was glad when they closed the invalid's door behind them. Tousles--deux had ranged forlornly up and down the room, with her long, bent--kneed stride, in her black cashmere shawl, with the black scarf knotted beneath her chin, her forehead crossed with wrinkles, great pouches of skin under the jet--black eyes, and one corner of her large mouth pathetically drooping. Sometimes she approached them as they sat by the bed, to reiterate her parrotlike speech: "*Tous les dé, vous comprenez, messiés—premièrement l'un et maintenant l'autre.*" And the handsome Lauro delivered himself of rolling, ranting, intolerably bombastic phrases, also in French, to the effect that he knew how a hero should die and meant to do it: *comme heros, à l'espagnol*, like his young brother, *de même quo son fier jeune frère* Fernando, who likewise had died like a Spanish hero. He gesticulated, he tore open his shirt to offer his yellow breast to the stroke of fate; and continued thus, until an attack of coughing, which

[389]

forced a thread of red foam to his lips, quenched his harangue and gave the cousins an excuse to go out, on tiptoe.

They did not mention the visit to Lauro's bedside; even to themselves they refrained from comment on his behaviour. But both were better pleased with their call upon Anton Karlowitsch Ferge from St. Petersburg, who lay in bed, with his great good--natured beard and his just as good--natured--looking great Adam's apple, recovering slowly from the unsuccessful attempt which had been made to install the pneumothorax in his interior economy, and which had been within a hair's breadth of costing Herr Ferge his life on the spot. He had suffered a frightful shock, the pleurashock—a quite frequent occurrence in cases where this fashionable technique was applied. But Herr Ferge's shock had been exceptionally dangerous, a total collapse and critical loss of consciousness, in a word so severe an attack that the operation had been broken off at once, and was indefinitely postponed.

Herr Ferge's good--natured grey eyes grew large and round, his face went ashen--coloured, when he came to speak of the operation, which must have been horrible indeed. "No anesthesia, my dear sir. In this case it doesn't do, a sensible man understands that and accepts the situation as it is. But the local doesn't reach very far down, it only benumbs the surface flesh, you feel it when they lay you open, like a pinching and squeezing. I lie there with my face covered, so I can't see anything: the assistant holds me on one side and the Directress on the other. I feel myself being pinched and squeezed, that is the flesh they are laying back and pegging down. Then I hear the Hofrat say: 'Very good'; and then he begins, with a blunt instrument—it must be blunt, not to pierce through too soon—to go over the pleura and find the place where he can make an incision and let the gas in; and when he begins moving about over my pleura with his instrument—oh, Lord, oh, Lord! I felt like—I felt it was all up with me—it was something perfectly indescribable. The pleura, my friends, is not anything that should be felt of; it does not want to be felt of and it ought not to be. It is taboo. It is covered up with flesh and put away once and for all; nobody and nothing ought to come near it. And now he uncovers it and feels all over it. My God, I was sick at my stomach. Horrible, awful; never in my life have I imagined there could be such a sickening feeling, outside hell and its torments. I fainted; I had three faintingfits one after the other, a green, a brown, and a violet. And there was a stink—-the shock went to my sense of smell and I got an awful stench of hydrogen sulphide, the way it must smell in the bad place; with all that I heard myself laughing as I went off—-not the way a human being laughs—-it was the most indecent, ghastly kind of laughing I ever heard. Because, when they go over your pleura like that, I tell you what it is: it is as though you were being tickled—-horribly, disgustingly tickled—-that is just what the infernal torment of the pleura--shock is like, and may God keep you from it!"

Often, and never without blanching and shuddering, did Anton Karlowitsch Ferge come back to this infernal experience of his, and torture himself with it in retrospect. He had from the first professed himself a simple man; the "higher things" of this life, he said, were utterly beyond him, he expressly stipulated that no intellectual or emotional demands be made upon him; he, for his part, made none upon anybody else. This bargain once struck, he turned out to talk not unentertainingly of his experiences in the life from which his illness had withdrawn him. He had been in the employ of a fire--insurance company, and made constant extended journeys from St. Petersburg up and down the whole of Russia, visiting insured factory buildings and spying out those which were financially suspect; for it was a fact supported by statistics that the larger percentage of fires occurred in just those factories where business was not going too well. Thus he was sent out to study a plant, under this or that pretext, and render an account to his company, so that serious loss could be provided against betimes, by increased counter--insurance or dividing the risk. He told of winter journeys through the length and breadth of Russia, of night travel in extreme cold, in sledges that you lay down in, under sheepskin covers, and when you roused you could see the eyes of wolves gleaming like stars across the snow. He carried his provisions frozen, cabbage soup and white bread, in boxes; when they stopped to change horses, at a station, these could be thawed out, as required, and the bread would be as fresh as on the day it was baked. But when there came a sudden mild spell, he would find that the soup he had brought with him in chunks had melted and run away.

Thus Herr Ferge; now and then interrupting his narrative with a sigh, and the remark that it was all very well——if only they did not try the pneumothorax again. His talk was devoid of the "higher things," but it was full of facts, and interesting to listen to, particularly for Hans Castorp, who found it profited him to hear about Russia and life as it was lived there: about samovars and pirogues, Cossacks, and wooden churches with so many towers shaped like onion--tops as to look like a whole colony of mushrooms. He led Herr Ferge to talk about the people, the strange and exotic northern types, with their Asiatic tincture, the prominent cheek--bones and FinnishMongolian slant to the eye; listening with anthropological interest to all that he heard. At his request, Herr Ferge spoke Russian to him; the outlandish, spineless, washed--out idiom came pouring from under the good--natured moustaches, out of the goodnatured Adam's apple; and Hans Castorp enjoyed it the more, youthlike, because all this was, pedagogically considered, forbidden fruit he was tasting.

He and Joachim spent many a quarter--hour with Anton Karlowitsch. Also they visited the lad Teddy from the Fridericianum, a young exquisite of fourteen years, blond and elegant, with a private nurse, and arrayed in white silk corded pyjamas. He was rich, he told them, and an orphan. He was here awaiting the moment for a serious operation they intended to try, for the removal of certain infected parts. Now and again, when he had a good day, he would leave his bed and dress in his neat sports attire to mingle for an hour in the company below. The ladies liked to dally with him, and he listened to their talk, for example to that concerning Lawyer Einhuf, the young lady in the combinations, and Fränzchen Oberdank. Then he would return to his bed. Thus idly and elegantly passed the time for the lad Teddy; and it was very plain that he expected nothing more from life than just this which he had.

Then there was Frau Mallinckrodt in number fifty, Natalie by name, with the black eyes and the gold rings in her ears; coquettish, fond of dress, but a perfect Lazarus and Job in female form, whom God had been pleased to afflict with every kind of infirmity. Her entire organism seemed infected, and she suffered from all possible complaints by turns and simultaneously. The skin was sympathetically involved, being covered in large tracts by an itching eczema, with open sores here and there, even on the mouth, which made feeding difficult. Then she suffered from internal inflammations of various kinds—of the pleura, the kidneys, the lungs, the periosteum, even of the brain, so that she was subject to loss of consciousness; finally cardiac weakness, the result of constant pain and fever, gave her the greatest distress and even made it, at times, impossible for her to swallow, so that a mouthful of food would remain stuck in her throat. The woman's state was truly pitiable, and she was alone in the world; for she had left home and children for the sake of a lover, a mere youth, only to be forsaken in her turn—all this she herself related to the cousins—and now was without a home, if not without means, since her husband saw that she should not want. She accepted with no false pride the fruits of his charity or his unquenched love, whichever it was, seeing herself quite humbly as a dishonoured and sinful creature; and so bore all the plagues of Job with astounding patience and resilience, with the elementary powers of resistance of her sex, which triumphed over all the misery of her tawny body, and even made of the gauze dressings which she had to wear about her head a becoming personal adornment. She changed her jewels many times in the day, began with corals in the morning and ended at night with pearls. Hans Castorp's flowers greatly delighted her; she obviously regarded them as the expression of gallant rather than charitable sentiments, and invited both young men to tea in her room. She drank from an invalid cup, all her fingers

[393]

decked to the joint with opals, amethysts, and emeralds; in no long time she had told her guests her story, the golden ear--rings swaying as she talked. Told of her respectable, tiresome husband, her no less respectable and tiresome children, who were precisely like their father, and for whom she had not been able to feel great warmth of affection; of the half boy, half man with whom she had fled, whose poetic tenderness she never tired of describing. But his family had taken him away from her, by guile and force commingled——and perhaps he too had been revolted by her illness, which had then suddenly and violently broken out. Perhaps the gentlemen were revolted too, she asked coquettishly, and her inborn femininity triumphed even over the eczema that covered half her face.

Hans Castorp felt only contempt for the revolted lover and expressed it by a shoulder--shrug. The poetic youth's defection was as a spur to himself and he began to take occasion to perform what services he could for the unhappy woman, in the repeated visits he made to her room: services that required no nursing skill, as, for instance, feeding her the midday broth after his own meal, giving her to drink when the food stuck in her throat, helping her to change her position in bed——for to add to everything else she had a wound from an operation, which made lying difficult. He practised himself in these acts of benevolence, looking in on her on his way to the dining--hall, or when returning from a walk, and telling Joachim to go on ahead, he would stop for a moment in number fifty, to see after a case; he experienced a pleasing sense of expanding being, the fruit of his conviction that what he did was both useful in itself and possessed of a secret significance. There was also a malicious satisfaction he had in the blamelessly Christian stamp his activities bore——it was so clear that on no ground whatever, either the military or the humanistic and pedagogic, were they open to any serious reproach.

It was some time after this that they took up Karen Karstedt; and both Hans Castorp and Joachim felt peculiarly drawn to her. She had been up here for years and was an out--patient of the Hofrat, who had commended her to the cousins' benevolence. She was entirely without private means and dependent upon unfeeling relatives--once, in fact, they had taken her away, since she was sure to die in any case; and only at the Hofrat's intercession did they send her back. She lived in a modest pension in the village; a nineteen--year--old, undersized little person, with sleek, oily hair, and eyes for ever timidly trying to hide a brilliance that accorded only too well with the hectic flush on her cheek. Her voice had the characteristic huskiness, but was sympathetic. She coughed almost constantly; and all her finger--ends were plastered up, as they had running sores.

The Hofrat, then, had appealed to the cousins in Karen's behalf--they were such kind--hearted chaps---and they made her their especial ward; beginning with the gift of flowers, following on with a visit to the poor child upon her little balcony in the village; and continuing with various outings which the three took together, to see a skating race or a bob--sleigh competition. For the winter sport season was now at its height, there was a special week overcrowded with "events"---those feats and displays to which the cousins had previously paid only cursory attention. Joachim was averse from every kind of distraction up here. He was not here, he said, on their account; he was not here to enjoy life, and to put up with his sojourn in the measure in which it furnished him agreeable change and diversion. He was here solely and simply to get well as quickly as he could, in order to join the service below, real service, not the service of the cure, which was but a substitute---though to be sure he grudged any falling off in the duty he owed it. He was forbidden to join in the sports, to go and gape at them he did not like. As for Hans Castorp, he took too seriously, in too stern an inward a sense, his own share in the life of those up here to have a thought or a glance for the doings of people who made a sports station of the valley.

But now his benevolent preoccupation with poor Fräulein Karstedt made some change in these views---and Joachim could hardly dissent without seeming unChristian. They fetched the patient at her humble lodging, in glorious, frosty--sunny weather, and escorted her through the English quarter, so named after the Hotel d'Angleterre, and along the main street, lined with luxurious shops. Sleighs were jingling up and down; there were hosts of people, the idle rich and pleasure--loving from all over the world, who filled the Kurhaus and the other hotels of the place; all hat--less, all clad in sports costumes which were the last word in elegance and beauty of fabric, all bronzed with winter sunburn and the glaring reflections from snowy slopes. All this world, including the cousins and their protegée, were betaking themselves to the rink, which lay in the depth of the valley not far from the Kurhaus; in summer it was a meadow, used for football. Music was playing, the Kurhaus band, stationed in the gallery of the wooden pavilion, above the four--cornered racecourse. Beyond all lay the mountains, in deep snow, against a dark--blue sky. Our young people passed through the entrance and the crowd that, seated in ascending tiers, surrounded the course on three sides; they found places for themselves, and sat down to look on. The professional skaters, in close--fitting costumes of black *tricot* with furred and braided jackets, cut figures, hovered and balanced, leaped and spun. A pair of virtuosi, male and female, professionals and *hors concours*, performed feats which they alone in all the world could perform, and evoked storms of applause and fanfares of trumpets. Six young men of various nationalities competed for the speed prize, and laboured six times round the four--sided course, bent over, with their hands behind their backs, some with handkerchiefs tied round their mouths. A bell rang in the midst of the music, and the crowd would burst out now and again with shouts of encouragement and applause.

It was a gay company, in which the three invalids, the cousins and their protegee, sat and looked about them. There were white--teethed Englishmen in Scotch caps, talking in French to highly--scented ladies dressed from head to foot in bright--coloured woollens——some of them even wore knickerbockers; Americans with small, neat heads, on which the hair "was plastered down, pipe in mouth, and wearing shaggy furs the skin--side out; bearded, elegant Russians, looking barbarically rich, and Malayan Dutchmen, all these sitting among the German and Swiss population, as well as a sprinkling of indeterminate types——all speaking French——perhaps from the Balkans or the Levant. Hans Castorp showed certain weakness for this motley semibarbarous world; but Joachim put it aside as mongrel and questionable. At intervals there were events for children, who staggered over the course with a snow--shoe on one foot and a ski on the other. In one race each boy pushed a girl before him on a shovel; in another the winner carried a lighted taper, and must arrive at the goal with it still burning; or must climb over obstacles in his path, or pick up potatoes with a tin spoon and deposit them in watering--pots placed along the course. Everybody was in extravagant spirits. The richest children were pointed out, the prettiest and those from well--known families: there were the little daughter of a Dutch multi--millionaire, the son of a Prussian prince, and a twelve--year--old lad who bore the name of a champagne known the world over. Young Karen was gay with the rest, and coughed persistently as she laughed; clapping for joy and very gratitude her poor hands with the running finger--ends.

The cousins took her to see the bob--sleigh races as well. It was no distance to the terminus, either from Karen's lodging or from the Berghof; for the track came down from the Schatzalp and ended in the village, among the houses on the western slope. At that point a hut had been erected, where word was received by telephone of the departures up above.

Then the low sleds would come singly, with long intervals between, around the curves of the white course, that shone metallic between frozen barriers of snow. The riders were men and women, in white woollens, with gay--coloured scarves of all nationalities wound about them. They were all red and lusty, and it snowed into their faces as they came on. Sledges would skid and upset, rolling their riders into the snow——and the onlookers would take photographs of the scene. Here too music played. The spectators sat in small tribunes, or pressed upon the narrow path that had been shovelled alongside the course; or thronged the wooden bridges which spanned it, watching the sleds that from time to time whizzed beneath. This was the path taken by the corpses from the sanatorium above, Hans Castorp thought: round these curves, under these bridges they came, down, down, to the valley below. He spoke of it to the others.

They even took Karen, one afternoon, to the Bioscope Theatre in the Platz—-she loved it all so very much. The bad air they sat in was offensive to the three, used as they were to breathing the purest; it oppressed their breathing and made their heads feel heavy and dull. Life flitted across the screen before their smarting eyes: life chopped into small sections, fleeting, accelerated; a restless, jerky fluctuation of appearing and disappearing, performed to a thin accompaniment of music, which set its actual *tempo* to the phantasmagoria of the past, and with the narrowest of means at its command, yet managed to evoke a whole gamut of pomp and solemnity, passion, abandon, and gurgling sensuality. It was a thrilling drama of love and death they saw silently reeled off; the scenes, laid at the court of an oriental despot, galloped past, full of gorgeousness and naked bodies, thirst of power and raving religious selfabnegation; full of cruelty, appetite, and deathly lust, and slowing down to give a full view of the muscular development of the executioner's arms. Constructed, in short, to cater to the innermost desires of an onlooking international civilization. Settembrini, as critic, Hans Castorp thought, and whispered as much to his cousin, would doubtless have sharply characterized what they saw as repugnant to a humanistic sense, and have scarified with direct and classic irony the prostitution of technical skill to such a humanly contemptible performance. On the other hand, Frau Stöhr, who was sitting not far from our three friends, seemed utterly absorbed; her ignorant red face was twisted into an expression of the hugest enjoyment.

And so were the other faces about them. But when the last flicker of the last picture in a reel had faded away, when the lights in the auditorium went up, and the field of vision stood revealed as an empty sheet of canvas, there was not even applause. Nobody was there to be applauded, to be called before the curtain and thanked for the rendition. The actors who had assembled to present the scenes they had just enjoyed were scattered to the winds; only their shadows had been here, their activity had been split up into millions of pictures, each with the shortest possible period of focus, in order to give it back to the present and reel it off again at will. The silence of the crowd, as the illusion passed, had about it something nerveless and repellent. Their hands lay powerless in face of the nothing that confronted them. They rubbed their eyes, stared vacantly before them, blinking in the brilliant light and wishing themselves back in the darkness, looking at sights which had had their day and then, as it were, had been transplanted into fresh time, and bedizened up with music. The despot died beneath the knife, with a soundless shriek. Then came scenes from all parts of the world: the President of the French Republic, in top--hat and cordon, sitting in a landau and replying to a speech of welcome; the Viceroy of India, at the wedding of a rajah; the German Crown Prince in the courtyard of a Potsdam garrison. There was a picture of life in a New Mecklenburg village; a cock--fight in Borneo, naked savages blowing on nose--horns, a wild elephant hunt, a ceremony at the court of the King of Siam, a courtesans' street in Japan, with geishas sitting behind wooden lattices; Samoyeds bundled in furs, driving sledges drawn by reindeer through the snowy wastes of Siberia; Russian pilgrims praying at Hebron; a Persian criminal under the knout. They were present at all these scenes; space was annihilated, the clock put back, the then and there played on by music and transformed into a juggling, scurrying now and here. A young Moroccan woman, in a costume of striped silk, with trappings in the shape of chains, bracelets, and rings, her swelling breasts half bared, was suddenly brought so close to the camera as to be life--sized; one could see the dilated nostrils, the eyes full of animal life, the features in play as she showed her white teeth in a laugh, and held one of her hands, with its blanched nails, for a shade to her eyes, while with the other she waved to the audience, who stared, taken aback, into the face of the charming apparition. It seemed to see and saw not, it was not moved by the glances bent upon it, its smile and nod were not of the present but of the past, so that the impulse to respond was baffled, and lost in a feeling of impotence. Then the phantom vanished. The screen glared white and empty, with the one word *Finis* written across it. The entertainment was over, in silence the theatre was emptied, a new audience took the place of that going out, and before their eager eyes the cycle would presently unroll itself again.

Incited by Frau Stöhr, who joined them at the exit, they paid a visit to the café at the Kurhaus, Karen clapping her hands in delighted gratitude. Here too there was music, a small, red--uniformed orchestra, conducted by a Bohemian or Hungarian first violin, who stood apart from the others, among the dancing couples, and belaboured his instrument with frantic wreathings of his body. Life here was *mondaine*: strange drinks were handed at the tables. The cousins ordered orangeade for the refreshment of their charge and themselves, while Frau Stöhr took a brandy and sugar. The room was hot and dusty. At this hour, she said, the café life was not yet in full swing, the dancing became much livelier as the evening advanced, and numerous patients from the sanatoria, as well as dissipated folk from the hotels and the Kurhaus, many more than were here as yet, came later to join the fun. More than one serious case had here danced himself into eternity, tipping up the beaker of life to drain the last drop, and *in dulci jubilo* suffering his final hæmorrhage. The *dulci jubilo* became, on her unlettered lips, something extraordinary. The first word she pronounced *dolce*, with some reminiscence of her musical husband's Italian vocabulary; but the second suggested *jubilee*, or an attempt to yodel, or goodness alone knew what. The cousins both devoted themselves assiduously to the straws in their glasses, when this Latin was given out—-but Frau Stöhr took no offence. She began, drawing back her lips and showing her rodent--like teeth, to drop hints and make insinuations on the subject of the relations of the three young people. As far as poor Karen was concerned, it was all pretty obvious, and, as Frau Stöhr said, she could not but enjoy being chaperoned, on her little outings, by such fine cavaliers. But the other side was not so easy to come at. However, ignorance and stupidity notwithstanding, the creature's feminine intuition helped her to a glimpse, even though a partial and vulgarized one, of the truth. For she saw, and even teasingly aimed at the fact, that Hans Castorp was the cavalier, and young Ziemssen merely in attendance; further—-for she was aware of the state of Hans Castorp's feeling toward Madame Chauchat—-that he was playing the gallant to poor little Karstedt because he did not know how to approach the other. It was a simple guess, lacking profundity and not actually covering all the facts of the case—-in short, it was only too worthy of Frau Stöhr, and when she came out with it, flat--footed, he did not even answer, save by a faint smile and an impenetrable stare. So much was true, after all, that poor Karen did afford him a substitute, an intangible yet real support, as did the rest of his charitable activities. But at the same time they were an end in themselves too. The inward satisfaction he experienced whenever he fed the afflicted Frau Mallinckrodt her broth, or suffered Herr Ferge to tell him once more the tale of the infernal pleura--shock, or saw poor Karen clapping her ravaged and mortifying hands in grateful joy, was perhaps of a vicarious and relative kind; yet it was none the less pure and immediate. It was rooted in a tradition diametrically opposed to the one Herr Settembrini, as pedagogue, represented—-yet seemed to him, young Hans Castorp, for all that, not unworthy of having applied to it the *placet experiri*.

The little house where Karen Karstedt lived lay near the railway track and the watercourse, on the way to the Dorf, quite conveniently for the cousins to fetch her after breakfast for the morning walk. Going thence toward the village, to arrive upon the main street, one had before one the little Schiahorn, and on its right three peaks which were called the Green Towers, but were now covered like the rest with snow that gleamed blindingly in the sun. Still further to the right came the round summit of the Dorfberg, and a quarter of the way up its slope was visible the cemetery of the Dorf, surrounded by a wall, obviously commanding a fine view, very likely of the distant lake, and thus suggesting itself naturally as the goal of a promenade. Thither they went, one lovely morning—-indeed, all the days now were lovely; with a hot sun, a sparkling frost, a deep--blue, windless air, and a scene that glittered whitely all abroad. The cousins, one of them brick--red in the face, the other bronzed, walked without overcoats, which would have been intolerable in this sunshine: young Ziemssen in sports clothes, with "arctics," Hans Castorp in arctics as well, but with long trousers, not feeling worldly enough to don short ones. This was the new year, between the beginning and middle of February——yes, the last figure in the date had changed since Hans Castorp came up here, it was written now with the next higher digit. The minute--hand on time's clock had moved one space further on: not one of the large spaces, not one which measured the centuries or the decades; it was only the year that had been shoved forward by one figure; though Hans Castorp had been up here not a whole year yet, but scarcely more than half a one, it had jerked itself on, as does the minute--hand of certain large clocks, which only register by five minutes at a time; and was now pointing motionless, awaiting the moment to move forward again. But the hand that marked the months would have to move on for ten spaces more, only two more, in fact, than it had moved since he came up here; for February did not count, being once begun——as money changed counts as money spent.

To the graveyard then, on the slope of the Dorfberg, the three wended their way——we tell it to complete the tale of their excursions. It was Hans Castorp's idea; Joachim probably had scruples at first, on the score of poor Karen, but in the end agreed that it was useless to pretend with her, or to carry out Frau Stöhr's cowardly policy of shielding her from all that could remind her of her end. Karen Karstedt was not yet so far on as to display the self--deception that marks the last stage. She knew quite well how it stood with her, and what the necrosis of her finger--tips meant: knew too that her unfeeling relatives would not hear of the unnecessary expense of having her sent back home, and that it would be her lot, after her exit, to fill a modest space up yonder. In short, it might even be said that such an excursion was more fitting, morally spoken, than many another, than the cinematograph or the bob--sleigh races, for example——and surely it was no more than proper to make those lying up there a visit once in a way, as a comradely attention, provided one did not regard it as in the same class with an ordinary walk or excursion to a point of interest.

Slowly they went, in single file, up the narrow path that had been made in the snow, leaving the highest villas behind and below them, and watching the familiar scene unroll in its winter splendour, a little altered in perspective, and opening out to the north--west, toward the entrance of the valley. There was the hoped--for view of the lake, now a frozen and snow--covered round, bordered with trees; the mountains seemed to slope directly down to its farther shore, while beyond these again showed unfamiliar peaks, all in full snow, overtopping each other against the blue sky. The young folk looked at the view, standing in the snow before the stone gateway to the cemetery; then they entered through the ironwork grille, which was on the latch. Here too they found paths shovelled between the small enclosures, each of which was surrounded with its railing, each containing a number of graves. The snow rounded over and built up each smooth and even elevation, with its cross of stone or metal, its small monument adorned with medallions and inscriptions. No soul was to be seen or heard, the quiet remoteness and peace of the spot seemed deep and unbroken in more than one sense. A little stone angel or cupid, finger on lip, a cap of snow askew on its head, stood among the bushes, and might have passed for the genius of the place——the genius of a silence so definite that it was less a negation than a refutation of speech. The silence it guarded was far from being empty of content or character. Here it would have been in place for our two male visitors to take off their hats, had they had any on. But they were, even Hans Castorp, bare--headed; and could only walk reverently, their weight on the balls of their feet, making instinctive inclinations on one side and the other, single file in the wake of Karen Karstedt, as she led the way.

The cemetery was irregular in shape, having begun as a narrow rectangle facing the south, and then thrown out other rectangles on both sides. Successive increases in size had evidently been necessary, and ploughed land had been taken in. Even so, the present enclosure seemed fairly full, both along the wall and in the less desirable inner plots; one could hardly see or say just where another interment was to take place. The three wandered for some time discreetly along the paths, among the enclosures, stopping to decipher a name or date here or there. The tablets and crosses were modest affairs, that must have cost but little. The inscriptions bore names from every quarter of the earth, they were in English or Russian—-or other Slavic tongues—-also German, Portuguese, and more. The dates told their own sad story, for the time they covered was generally a short span indeed, the age between birth and death averaging not much more than twenty years. Not crabbed age, but youth peopled the spot; folk not yet settled in life, who from all corners of the earth had come together here to take up the horizontal for good and all.

Somewhere in the thick of the graves, near the heart of the acre, lay a small, flat, levelled place, the length of a man, between two rounded mounds with wreaths of everlasting hanging on their headstones. Involuntarily the three paused here, the young girl first, to read the mournful inscriptions; Hans Castorp stood relaxed, his hands clasped before him, his eyes veiled and his mouth somewhat open, young Ziemssen very self--controlled, and not only erect, but even bending a thought backward; and both the cousins stole a glance at Karen's face. She stood there, aware of their glance, with modest and shamefaced mien, her head bent on her shoulder, blinking her eyes and smiling a strained little smile.

Walpurgis--Night

Within the next few days it would be seven months since Hans Castorp's advent among those up here; while Cousin Joachim, who had already had five to his credit, would soon be able to look back upon twelve; that is to say, upon a whole round year. Round, indeed, in a cosmic sense; for since the doughty little locomotive had set him down at these heights, the earth had completed one full course round the sun, and was returned to the point whence it had then set out. The carnival season was at hand, and Hans Castorp inquired among the old inhabitants of the Berghof what it would be like.

"*Magnifique*," answered Settembrini, whom the cousins had again encountered on the morning walk. "Gorgeous," he said. "Every bit as lively as it is in the Prater. You shall see, Engineer, 'the gayest gallants of the night, in brilliant rows advancing,' " he quoted, and went on in his most mocking vein, couching his gibes in sounding phrases, with a telling accompaniment of arm, shoulder, and head movements. "What do you expect? Even in *maisons de santé* they have their balls for the fools and idiots, I've read; why not up here as well? The programme includes various *danses macabres*, as you may imagine; but unfortunately some of last year's guests will not be here—the party being over at half past nine, you perceive—"

"Do you mean—oh, capital!" laughed Hans Castorp. "Herr Settembrini, you are a wretch! Half past nine—I say, did you get that?" he turned to his cousin. "Herr Settembrini means it would be too early for some of last year's guests to take part. Ha ha—spooky! He means the ones that have taken leave of the flesh and the things of the flesh in the mean time. But I am all excitement," he said. "I think it's quite proper to celebrate the feasts up here as they come, and mark off the time in the usual way. Just a dead level of monotony, without any breaks at all, would be too awful for words. We have had Christmas already, we took notice of the beginning of the New Year; and now comes Shrove Tuesday; after that, Palm Sunday, Holy Week, Easter; then six weeks after that, Whitsunday; then it is almost midsummer, the solstice, and we begin to go toward autumn—"

"Stop, stop, stop!" Settembrini cried, lifting his face to heaven and pressing his temples with the palms of his hands. "Be quiet, I cannot listen to you letting go the reins like that!"

[405]

"Pardon me, I mean it just the other way. Behrens will finally have to make up his mind to the injections, to get rid of my infection; my temperature sticks at 99.3° to four, five, six, and even seven. I am, and I continue to be, life's delicate child! I don't mean I am a long--termer, Rhadamanthus hasn't let me in for any definite number of months; but he did say it would be nonsense to interrupt the cure, when I've been up here so long already, and invested so much time, so to speak. Even if he did set a term, what good would it do me? When he says, for instance, half a year, that is to be taken as the minimum, it is always more. Look at my cousin; he was to have finished the beginning of the month—-finished in the sense of being healed, cured—-and the last time Behrens saw him, he stuck on four more to make sure he is entirely sound—-well, then, where are we? Why, at the summer solstice, just as I said, without the faintest notion of offending you, and on the way to winter. Well, well, for the present what we have before us is Fasching, and as I say, I consider it fit and proper to celebrate it in the usual way, just as it comes in the calender. Frau Stöhr tells me the concierge sells tin horns in his lodge, did you know that?"

And so it fell out. Shrove Tuesday came on apace; before one had actually seen it on the way, it arrived. All sorts of absurd instruments were snarling and squealing in the dining--hall, even at early breakfast; at midday, paper snakes were launched from the table where Gänser, Rasmussen, and Fräulein Kleefeld sat. Paper caps were mounted; they, like the trumpets, were to be had of the concierge. The round--eyed Marusja was among the first to appear in one. But in the evening—-ah, in the evening there were festivities in the hall and the reception--rooms, in the course of which—-but we alone know to what, thanks to Hans Castorp's enterprising spirit, these carnival gaieties led up in their course; and we do not mean to let our knowledge betray us into indiscretion. We shall pay time all the honour due it, and precipitate nothing. Nay, rather, we shall incline to protract the tale, out of feeling for young Hans Castorp's moral compunctions, which have so long prevented him from crossing his Rubicon. Everybody went down to the Platz in the afternoon, to see the streets in carnival mood, with harlequins and columbines shaking their rattles, with maskers on foot and in jingling, decorated sleighs, among whom went forward lively skirmishes, and much confetti was flung. Spirits were very high at all seven tables when the guests assembled for the evening meal; there was every indication that the fun begun abroad would continue in the same key within doors. The concierge had done a thriving trade in rattles and tin trumpets; Lawyer Paravant had been the first to go further in the same line, putting on a lady's kimono and a braid of false hair belonging to Frau Consul--General Wurmbrandt; he wore his moustaches drawn down on each side of his mouth with the tongs, and looked the very picture of a Chinaman, evoking loud applause from all quarters. The management had done its share. Each of the seven tables was decked with a paper lantern, a coloured moon with a lighted candle inside; when Settembrini entered, and passed by Hans Castorp's, he quoted:

"See the gorgeous tongues of fire—-

Club as gay as heart's desire—-"

He brought out the words with his fine, dry smile, and sauntered to his place, where he was greeted with a rain of missiles like tiny pellets, that broke and scattered a spray of perfume where they fell. Yes, from the first moment the key was high. The bursts of laughter were unintermitted; paper snakes hung down from the chandeliers, swaying to and fro; confetti swam in the sauces; very early the dwarf waitress brought in the first ice--pail, the first bottle of champagne. Inspired by Lawyer Einhuf, the guests drank it mixed with burgundy. Toward the end of the meal the ceiling light went out, and only the colourful twilight of the paper lanterns illumined the room, making of the scene an Italian night, and setting the crown upon the mood of the evening. Settembrini passed over a paper to Hans Castorp's table, by the hand of Marusja, who sat nearest him, with a green tissue--paper jockey cap on her head; on it he had written with a pencil:

"But mind, the mountain's magic--mad to--night,

And if you choose a will--o'--the--wisp to light

Your path, take care, 'twill lead you all astray."

This was received with enthusiasm, though Dr. Blumenkohl, whose state had now much altered for the worse, muttered something to himself, with the expression peculiar to him upon his face, or rather upon his lips; he seemed to be asking what sort of verses were these. But Hans Castorp considered that an answer was due, he felt it incumbent on him to cap the quotation, though it was unlikely he would have produced anything very striking. He searched his pockets for a pencil, but found none, nor could Joachim or the schoolmistress supply his need; and his bloodshot eyes looked to the east for aid, to the farther left--hand corner of the room——it was plain that his fleeting purpose was dissipated in a widening circle of associations. He paled a little, and entirely lost sight of his original intention.

Other good ground there was for paling. Frau Chauchat had made special toilet for carnival, she wore a new gown, or at least one new to our hero, of thin, dark silk, probably black, or at most shot with a golden brown. It was cut with a modest little round neck like a schoolgirl's frock, hardly so much as to show the base of the throat, or the collar--bones, or the slightly prominent bone at the back of the neck, beneath the soft fringes or her hair. But it left free to the shoulder Clavdia's arms, so tender and yet so full, so cool, so amazingly white, set off against the dark silk of her frock, with such ravishing effect that it made Hans Castorp close his eyes, and murmur within himself: "O my God!" He had never seen such a mode before. Ball gowns he had seen, stately and ceremonial, cut in conformity with a fashion that exposed far more of the person than this one did, without achieving a jot of its sensational effect. Poor Hans Castorp! He was reminded of a theory he had once held about these arms, on making their acquaintance for the first time, veiled in diaphanous gauze: that it was the gauze itself, the "illusion" as he called it, which had lent them their indescribable, unreasonable seductiveness. Folly! The utter, accentuated, blinding nudity of these arms, these splendid members of an infected organism, was an experience so intoxicating, compared with that earlier one, as to leave our young man no other recourse than again, with drooping head, to whisper, soundlessly: "O my God!"

Later on, another paper was handed over, on which was written:

"Society to heart's desire—-

In faith, of brides, a party,

And jolly bachelors on fire

With forward hopes and hearty."

"Bravo, bravo!" they shouted. They were drinking coffee by now, served in little brown earthenware jugs, and some of them liqueurs as well, for instance Frau Stöhr, who adored the sweet and spirituous. The company began to rise from table, to move about, to pay visits. Part of the guests had already moved into the reception--rooms, others remained seated, still faithful to the drink they had mingled. Settembrini, coffee--cup in hand, sporting his toothpick, crossed over and sat down between Hans Castorp and the schoolmistress.

" 'The Harz,' " he said. " 'Near Schierke and Elend.' Did I exaggerate, Engineer?

Here's a bedlam for you! But wait, the fun is not over so soon; far from leaving off, it has not even reached its height. From what I hear, there will be more masquerading; certain people have left the room, we are justified in anticipating almost anything."

Even as he spoke, new maskers entered: women dressed as men, with beards and moustaches of burnt cork, betraying themselves by their figures and looking like characters in comic opera; men in women's clothes, tripping over their skirts. Here was the student Rasmussen in a black jet--trimmed toilet, displaying a pimpled *décolleté* and fanning himself front and back with a paper fan; there was a Pierrot, costumed in white underwear, with a lady's felt hat, a powdered face that gave his eyes an unnatural expression, and lips garish with blood--red pomade—-the youth with the fingernail. A Greek from the "bad" Russian table, who rejoiced in beautiful legs, strutted in tights, with short cloak, paper ruff, and dagger, personating a fairy prince, or a Spanish grandee. All these costumes had been improvised since the end of the meal. Frau Stöhr could sit still no longer. She too disappeared, and presently returned dressed as a charwoman, with skirt looped up and sleeves rolled back; a paper cap tied under her chin, armed with pail and brush; she began scrubbing about under the tables, among the feet of those still sitting.

" 'See beldam Baubo riding now,' " quoted Settembrini, as she appeared; and gave the next line too, in his clear and "plastic" delivery. She heard it, and retorted by calling him a turkey--cock and bidding him keep his filthy jokes to himself. With the licence of the season she addressed him, Herr Settembrini, with the thou. But indeed this familiarity had become quite general during the meal. He girded himself to reply, when a fresh stir and laughter in the hall interrupted him, and those in the dining--room looked up expectantly.

Followed by a troop of guests, two singular figures entered. One was dressed like a nurse; but her black uniform was marked off from head to foot by short white strips close under each other, with a longer one at regular intervals, like degrees on a thermometer. She had one finger laid to her pallid lips, and in her other hand a fever chart. Her companion was all in blue, with blue paint on lips, brows, throat, cheeks, and chin, and a blue woollen cap wry over one ear. He was dressed in a "pull--over" of glazed blue linen, tied round the ankles, and stuffed out into a great paunch round the middle. These were Frau Iltis and Herr Albin; they wore cardboard placards, on which were written "The Silent Sister" and "The Blue Peter"; together, with sidling gait they moved through the room.

What applause there was! What ringing shouts! Frau Stöhr, her broom under her arm and her hands on her knees, laughed like the charwoman she impersonated. Only Settembrini was unmoved. He cast one glance at the successful maskers and his lips became a fine thin line beneath the waving moustaches.

Among the troop streaming in the rear of the blue and silent ones, came Clavdia Chauchat, together with the woolly--haired Tamara and the man with the hollow chest, named Buligin, who was dressed in evening clothes. Clavdia brushed Hans Castorp's table with the folds of her new gown, and crossed the room to where young Gänser and the Kleefeld were sitting. Her companions followed the rout out of the dining--hall after the two allegorical maskers, but she stood there, her hands behind her back, laughing and chatting, her eyes like narrow slits. She too had mounted a cap——it was not a bought one, but the kind one makes for children, a simple cocked hat of white paper, set rakishily on her head, and suiting her, of course, to a marvel. Her feet showed beneath the dark golden--brown silk of her frock, whose skirt was somewhat draped. Of her arms we shall say no more in this place. They were bare to the shoulder.

" 'Look at her well,' " Hans Castorp heard Herr Settembrini say, as though from a distance, following her with his glance as she presently left the room. " 'The fair one, see! 'Tis Lilith!' "

"Who?" asked Hans Castorp.

Herr Settembrini's literary soul was pleased. He answered: " 'Adam's first wife is she.' "

Besides themselves there was only Dr. Blumenkohl at the table, sitting in his place at the other end. Everyone else, even Joachim, was now in the drawing--rooms. Hans Castorp said——and he too addressed his companion with the licence of the season, and said thou to him: "Dear me, you're full of poetry to--night. What Lily do you mean?

Did Adam marry more than once? I didn't know it."

"According to the Hebraic mythus, Lilith became a night--tripping fairy, a *'belle dame sans merci'*, dangerous to young men especially, on account of her beautiful tresses."

"What the deuce! A hobgoblin with beautiful tresses! You couldn't stand that, could you? You would come along and turn on the

[411]

electric light and bring the young men back to the path of virtue—
-that's what you do, isn't it?" Hans Castorp said whimsically. He had
drunk rather freely of the mixed burgundy and champagne.

"Hark ye, Engineer—-and take heed what I say," Settembrini
answered frowning.

"You will kindly address me with the accepted form employed in
the educated countries of the West, the third person *pluralis*, if I may
make bold to suggest it."

"Why? Isn't this carnival? The other is the accepted form
everywhere to--night."

"Yes, it is—-and its charm lies in its very abandon. When
strangers, who would regularly use the third person, speak to each
other in the second, it is an objectionable freedom, it is wantonly
playing with the roots of things, and I despise and condemn it,
because at the bottom the usage is audaciously and shamelessly
levelled against our civilization and our enlightened humanity. Do
not, for one moment, imagine I addressed you with this form just
now. I was quoting from the masterpiece of your national literature—
-I used poetic licence."

"So did I. I am using a sort of poetic licence now, because it seems
to me to suit the occasion, and that is why I do it. I don't say I find it
perfectly natural and easy to say thou to you, on the contrary it costs
me an effort, I have to poke myself up to it; but I do so freely, gladly,
and with all my heart—-"

"With all your—-"

"Yes, quite sincerely, with all my heart. We have been up here for
some time together—-do you realize it is seven months? That is not
much, perhaps, as they reckon time here; but in the ordinary way it is
a good deal, after all. Well, we have spent it with each other, because
life brought us together. We have met almost daily, and had
interesting conversations, in part upon subjects of which, down
below, I should not have had the faintest understanding. But up here

I have, they seem to me very real and pertinent; and I was always very keen, in our discussions, or rather, when you explained things to me, as a *homo humanus*, for of course I was too inexperienced to contribute anything, and could only feel that all you said was highly worth listening to. It is through you I have learned to understand such a lot—-that about Carducci was the least part of it—take the republic and the *bello stile* and how they hang together, or time with human progress, and how if there was no time there could be no human progress, and the world would be only a standing drain and stagnant puddle—-what should I have known of all that if it weren't for you? So I simply address you as though we were old and close friends, without further ceremony, and you must excuse me, because I don't know any other way. You sit there, and I speak to you like this, and it is all that's necessary. For you are not, to me, just any man, with a name, like another; you are a representative, Herr Settembrini, an ambassador to this place and to me. Yes, that is what you are," Hans Castorp asserted, and struck the table with the flat of his hand. "So now I will thank you," he went on, and shoved his champagne and burgundy along the table toward Herr Settembrini's coffee--cup, as though to touch glasses with him. "I thank you for having taken trouble for me in these seven months, for having lent a hand to a young donkey in all the new experiences that came to him, and tried to influence him for his good—- *sine pecunia*, of course—-partly by means of anecdote and partly in abstractions. I distinctly feel the moment has come to thank you for all you have done, and to beg your pardon for being a troublesome pupil—-a 'difficult,' no, a 'delicate child of life'—-that was what you called me. It touched me very much to have you say that; and I feel touched every time I think of it. The troublesome child—-that I have been for you, in your capacity as pedagogue—-you remember, you came to speak of that on the first day we met, it is one of the associations you have taught me, the relation between humanism and pedagogy; and there are many others I shall think of as time goes on. You must forgive me, then, and not think too hardly of me. I drink your health, Herr Settembrini; I drink to those literary endeavours of yours for the

[413]

elimination of human suffering." He ceased speaking, bent over and drained his glass, hiccupped twice, and stood up. "Now let us join the others."

"Why, Engineer, what has come over you?" the Italian asked in surprise, rising in his turn. "That sounds like a parting."

"A parting? No—why?" Hans Castorp evaded him—not only in words, but in action, for he turned as he spoke, describing a curve with the upper part of his body, and came to a stop before Fräulein Engelhart, who had just entered to fetch them. She said that a carnival punch, contributed by the management, was being dispensed by no less a person than the Hofrat himself, and bade them come if they cared for a glass. So they went together.

The little round white--covered table, with Hofrat Behrens behind it, stood the centre of a press of guests, each holding out a sherbet cup to be filled, into which the dispenser ladled the steaming drink out of a tureen. He too had made concessions to the carnival spirit: he wore his usual white surgeon's coat, for even to--day his professional activity must go on; but he had added a genuine Turkish fez, crimson, with a black tassel dangling over one ear. His appearance, of itself sufficiently striking, needed no more than this to render it quite outlandish. The long white smock exaggerated his height; one felt that if he were to stand erect and hold up his head, he would be more than life--size; and atop was the small head, with its high colour and unique cast of feature. Never before had Hans Castorp been so impressed with its oddity as when he saw it to--day under this absurd head--gear: the flat, snub--nosed, purple--flushed physiognomy, the watery, goggling blue eyes beneath tow--coloured brows, and the blond, close--trimmed moustache mounted crookedly above the full, bow--shaped lips. Turned away from the steam that wreathed upwards from the bowl, he held the ladle high and let the sweet arrack punch run in a brown, flowing stream into the glasses they held toward him, rattling on the while with his usual flow of whimsical jargon.

"Herr Urian sits up above," Settembrini interpreted in a low voice with a wave of the hand.

Dr. Krokowski was there too, short, stout, solid, with his black alpaca shirt fastened like a domino on his shoulders, the sleeves dangling. He was holding his punch--glass with his hand at the level of his eyes and twisting the wrist round as he talked and jested with a group of masqueraders. Music was heard; the tapir--faced lady was playing Handel's *Largo* on the violin, and then a drawing--room sonata by Grieg, characteristically northern in mood. The Mannheimer accompanied her on the piano. There was good--natured applause, even from the bridge--tables, which had been set up and occupied by maskers, with bottles in coolers at their sides. The doors were all open, and some of the guests stood in the hall as well. A group about the punch--table watched the Hofrat, who was introducing a new diversion. Bent over the table with his eyes closed and his head thrown back in evidence of good faith, he was sketching with his mighty hand a figure on the back of a visiting--card, the outline of a pig. It was rather more fanciful than realistic, yet undoubtably the lineaments of a pig, which under these difficult conditions, without the help of his eyes, he had managed to trace. It was a feat, and he could perform it. The little eyes were almost in the right place, so was the pointed ear, and the tiny legs under the rounded little belly; the curving line of the back ended in a small neat ringlet of tail. There was a general "Ah!" as he finished; then everyone was fired with an ambition to emulate the master. What abortions were brought forth! They lacked all coherence. The eyes were outside the head, the legs inside the paunch, the line of the latter came nowhere near joining, the little tail curled away by itself without organic connexion with the figure, an independent arabesque. They nearly split with laughing; the group increased. The notice of the bridge party was attracted, the players were drawn by curiosity and came up holding their cards fan--shaped in their hands. The bystanders watched the performer to see that he did not wink---which his feeling of powerlessness made him sometimes do; they

[415]

giggled and guffawed while he committed his frantic blunders, and burst out in extravagant mirth when he at last opened his eyes and looked down upon his ridiculous handiwork. Blatant self--confidence lured everyone on to try his hand. The card, a large one, was soon filled on both sides with overlapping failures. The Hofrat contributed a second from his case; whereon Lawyer Paravant, after taking thought, essayed to draw a pig without lifting the pencil—and lo, the measure of his unsuccess led all the rest: his creation had no faintest likeness either to a pig or to anything else on the broad earth. It was greeted with hilarity and boisterous congratulations. Menu cards were fetched from the dining--room, and now several people could draw at the same time; each performer having his own circle of onlookers and aspirants, waiting for the pencil he was using. There were three pencils, they snatched them out of each other's hands. The Hofrat, having set the sport afoot, and seen it thriving, withdrew with his adjutants.

Hans Castorp stood in the thick of the crowd, at Joachim's back, watching. He rested his elbow on his cousin's shoulder and supported his chin with all five fingers of that hand, his other arm set akimbo on his hip. He was talking and laughing, anxious to try his skill; asked on all sides for a pencil, and at length received a stump of a thing, hardly to be held between thumb and forefinger. Then he shut his eyes, lifted his face to the ceiling, and drew, all the time uttering objurgations against the pencil, some horrible inanity upon the paper, in his haste spoiling even this, and running off the paper on to the tablecloth. "That doesn't count!" he cried as his audience burst out in well--merited jeers. "What can you do with a pencil like that—-deuce take it!" and he flung the offending morsel into the punch--bowl. "Has anybody a decent one? Who will lend me a pencil? I must have another try. A pencil, a pencil, who has a pencil?" he shouted, leaning with his left hand on the table, and shaking the other high in the air. There was no answer. Then he turned and, passing through the room, went straight up to Clavdia Chauchat, who, as he was well aware, was standing near the door of the little salon, watching with a smile the throng round the punchtable. Behind him he heard someone calling—-euphonious words, in a foreign tongue: *"Eh, Ingegnere! Aspetti! Che cosa fa, Ingegnere! Un po' di ragione sa! Ma è matto questo ragazzo!"* But he drowned out the voice with his own, and Herr Settembrini, flinging up his hand with a swing of the arm—-a gesture common in his own country, whose meaning it would be hard to put into words—and giving vent to a long--drawn "Eh—-h!" turned his back on the room and the carnival gaieties.—-But Hans Castorp was standing on the tiled court of the school yard, gazing at close quarters into these blue--grey--green epicanthus eyes, above the prominent cheekbones, and saying: "Do *you* happen to have a pencil?"

He was deadly pale, as pale as when he had come back blood--spattered to the lecture, from that walk of his. The nerves controlling the blood--vessels that supplied his face functioned so well that the skin, robbed of all its blood, went quite cold, the nose looked peaked, and the hollows beneath the young eyes were lead--coloured as any corpse's. And the *Sympathicus* caused his heart, Hans Castorp's heart, to thump, in such a way that it was impossible to breathe except in gasps; and shivers ran over him, due to the functioning of the sebaceous glands, which, with the hair follicles, erected themselves.

She stood there, in her paper cap, and looked him up and down, with a smile that betrayed no trace of pity, nor any concern for the ravages written on his brow. The sex knows no such compassion, no mercy for the pangs that passion brings; in that element the woman is far more at home than the man, to whom, by his very nature, it is foreign. Nor does she ever encounter him in it save with mocking and malignant joy—-compassion, indeed, he would have none of.

He had used the second person singular. She answered: "I? Perhaps I have, let me see." Her voice and smile did betray an excitement, a consciousness—-such as comes when the first word is uttered in a relationship long secretly sustained—-a subtle consciousness, which concentrates all the past in a single moment of the present. "You are so eager——you are very ambitious"——she continued thus to mock him, in her slightly veiled, pleasantly husky voice, with her quaint pronunciation, giving a foreign sound to the *r* and making the vowels too open, even accenting the word ambitious on the first syllable, with exotic effect; rummaging and peering the while in her leather bag, whence she fetched out, first a handkerchief, and then a little silver pencil, slender and fragile, a pretty trinket scarcely meant for use——the other, the first one, had been something more to take hold of.

"*Voilà*," she said, and held the toy by its end before his eyes, between thumb and forefinger, and lightly turned it to and fro.

Since she thus both gave and withheld it, he took it, so to speak, without receiving it: that is, he held out his hand, with the fingers ready to grasp the delicate thing, but not actually touching it. His eyes——in their leaden sockets——went from the little object to Clavdia's Tartar physiognomy. His bloodless lips were open, and so remained, he did not use them to utter the words, as he said: "You see, I knew you would have one."

"*Prenez garde, il est un peu fragile*" she said. "*C'est à visser, tu sais.*"

Their heads bent over it together, and she showed him the mechanism——it was quite ordinary, the little needle of hard, probably worthless lead came down as one loosened the screw.

They stood bent toward each other. The stiff collar of his evening dress served him to support his chin.

"A poor thing——but *yours*," he said, brow to brow with her, speaking down upon the pencil, stiff--lipped, so that most of the labials went unsounded.

"Ah, so you are even witty," she answered him, with a short laugh. She straightened up, and surrendered the pencil. It is a question by what means he was witty, since it was plain there was not a drop of blood in his head. "Well, away with you, go and draw, draw yourself out!" And wittily in her turn, she seemed to drive him away.

"But you have not drawn yet, you must draw too," he said, without managing the *m* in must, and drew a step backwards, invitingly.

"I?" she said again, with an inflection of surprise which seemed to have reference to something else than his invitation. She stood a moment in smiling confusion, then as if magnetized followed him a few steps toward the punch--table.

But interest in the activity there seemed to have fallen away. Someone was still drawing, but without an audience. The cards were covered with futilities, they had all done their worst, and now the current had set in another direction. Directly the doctors had left the scene, the word had gone round for a dance, already the tables were being pushed back; spies were posted at the doors of the writing--and music--rooms, with orders to give the sign in case the "old man," Krokowski, or the Oberin should show themselves. A young Slavic youth attacked *con espressione* the keyboard of the little nut--wood piano, and the first couple began to turn about within an irregular circle of chairs and tables, on which the spectators perched themselves.

Hans Castorp dismissed the departing punch--table with a wave of the hand, and indicated with his chin two empty seats in a sheltered corner of the small salon, near the portières. He did not speak, perhaps because the music was too loud. He drew up a seat—it was a reclining--chair with plush upholstery—for Frau Chauchat, in the corner he had indicated, and took for himself a creaking, crackling basket--chair with curling arms, in which he sat down, bent forward toward her, his own arms on the arms of the chair, her pencil in his hand and his feet drawn back under his seat. She lay buried in the plushy slope, her knees brought high; notwithstanding which, she crossed one leg over the other, and swung her foot in the air, in its black patent--leather shoe and black silk stocking spanned over the anklebone. There was a coming and going in the room, some of the guests standing up to dance, while others took their places to rest.

"You've a new frock on," he said, as an excuse for looking at her; and heard her answer.

"New? So you are acquainted with my wardrobe?"

"Am I right?"

"Yes—-I had it made here lately; the tailor down in the village, Lukaçek, did it. He does work for several of the ladies up here. Do you like it?"

"Very much," he said, surveying her once more and then casting down his eyes.

"Would you like to dance?" he added.

"Would you like to?" she asked, with lifted brows, yet smiling, and he answered: "I would, if you wished."

"That is not so brave as I thought you were," she said, and when he laughed deprecatingly, she went on: "Your cousin has gone up already."

"Yes, he is my cousin," he confirmed her, unnecessarily. "I noticed he had gone, he is probably in the rest--cure by now."

"*C'est un jeune homme très étroit, très honnête, très allemand.*"

"*Étroit? Honnête?*" he repeated. "I understand French better than I speak it. You mean he is pedantic. You think we are pedantic, we Germans—- *nous autres allemands ?*"

"*Nous causons de votre cousin. Mais c'est vrai*, you are a little bourgeois. *Vous aimez l'ordre mieux que la liberté, toute l'Europe le sait.*"

"*Aimer, aimer—-qu'est--ce que c'est? Ça manque de définition, ce mot là.* We love what we have not—-that is proverbial," Hans Castorp asserted. "Lately," he went on,

"I've thought very much about liberty. That is, I've heard the word so often, I've begun to think about it. *Je te le dirai en français*, what I have been thinking. *Ce que toute l'Europe nomme la liberté, c'est peut--être une chose assez pédante et assez bourgeoise en comparaison de notre besoin d'ordre—c'est ça!*"

"*Tiens! C'est amusant! C'est ton cousin à qui tu penses en disant des choses étranges comme ça?*"

"No, *c'est vraiment une bonne âme*, a simple nature, not exposed to intellectual dangers, *tu sais. Mais il n'est pas bourgeois, il est militaire.*"

"Not exposed?" she repeated his word, not without difficulty. "*Tu veux dire une nature tout à fait ferme, sûr d'elle--même? Mais il est sérieusement malade, ton pauvre cousin.*"

"Who told you so?"

"We all know about each other, up here."

"Was it Hofrat Behrens?"

"*Peut--être en me faisant voir ces tableaux.*"

"*C'est à dire: en faisant ton portrait!*"

"*Pourquoi pas? Tu l'as trouvé réussi, mon portrait?*"

"*Mais oui, extrêmement. Behrens a très exactement rendu ta peau, oh, vraiment très fidèlement. J'aimerais beaucoup être portraitiste, moi aussi, pour avoir l'occasion d'étudier ta peau comme lui.*"

"*Parlez allemand, s'il vous plaît!*"

"Oh, I speak German, even in French. *C'est une sorte d'étude artistique et médicale—-en un mot: il s'agit des lettres humaines, tu comprends.—* What do you say, shall we dance?"

"Oh, no, it would be childish—-behind their backs! *Aussitôt que Behrens reviendra, tout le monde va se précipiter sur les chaises. Ce sera fort ridicule.*"

"Have you such respect for him as that?"

"For whom?" she said, giving her query a curt, foreign intonation.

"For Behrens."

"*Mais va donc avec ton Behrens!* But there really is not room to dance. *Et puis sur le tapis*—- Let us look on."

"Yes, let's," he assented, and gazed beyond her, with his blue eyes, his grandfather's musing eyes, in his pale young face, at the antics of the masked patients in salon and writing--room. There was the Silent Sister capering with the Blue Peter, there was Frau Salomon as master of ceremonies, dressed in evening clothes with a white waistcoat and swelling shirt--front; she wore a monocle and a tiny painted moustache, and twirled upon tiny, high--heeled patent--leather shoes, that came out oddly beneath her black trousers, as she danced with the Pierrot, whose blood--red lips stared from his ghastly white face, with the eyes of an albino rabbit. The Greek flourished his symmetrical legs in their lavender tights alongside the darkly glittering Rasmussen in his low--cut gown. Lawyer Paravant in his kimono, Frau ConsulGeneral Wurmbrandt, and young Gänser danced all three together, with their arms round each other. As for Frau Stöhr, she danced with her broom, pressing it to her heart and caressing the bristles as though they were a man's hair.

"Yes, let's," Hans Castorp repeated, mechanically. They spoke in low tones, covered by the music. "Let us sit here, and look on, as though in a dream. For it is like a dream to me, that we are sitting like this—- *comme un rêve singulièrement profond, car il faut dormir très profondément pour rêver comme cela. Je veux dire—c'est un rêve bien connu, rêvé de tout temps, long, éternel, oui, être assis près de toi comme à présent, voilà l'éternité.*"

"*Poète!*" she said. "*Bourgeois, humaniste, et poète—voilà l'allemand au complet, comme il faut!*"

"*Je crains que nous ne soyons pas du tout et nullement comme il faut,*" he answered. "*Sous aucun égard. Nous sommes peut--être des* delicate children of life, *tout simplement.*"

"*Joli mot. Dis--moi donc.—Il n'aurait pas été fort difficile de rêver ce rêve--là plus tôt. C'est un peu tard, que monsieur se résout d'adresser la parole à son humble servante.*"

"*Pourquoi des paroles?*" he said. "*Pourquoi parler? Parler, discourir, c'est une chose bien républicaine, je le concède. Mais je doute, que ce soit poétique au même degré. Un de nos pensionnaires, qui est un peu devenu mon ami, M. Settembrini—*"

"*Il vient de te lancer quelques paroles.*"

"*Eh bien, c'est un grand parleur sans doute, il aime même beaucoup à réciter de beaux vers—mais est--ce un poète, cet homme--là?*"

"*Je regrette sincèrement de n'avoir jamais eu le plaisir de faire la connaissance de ce chevalier.*"

"*Je le crois bien.*"

"*Ah, tu le crois?*"

"*Comment? C'était une phrase tout--à--fait indifférente, ce que j'ai dit là. Moi, tu le remarques bien, je ne parle guère le français. Pourtant, avec toi je préfère cette langue à la mienne, car pour moi, parler français, c'est parler sans parler, en quelque manière—sans responsabilité, ou comme nous parlons en rêve. Tu comprends?*"

"*A peu près.*"

"*Ça suffit.—Parler,*" went on Hans Castorp, "*pauvre affaire! Dans l'éternité, on ne parle point. Dans l'éternité, tu sais, on fait comme en dessinant un petit cochon: on penche la tête en arrière et on ferme les yeux."*

"Pas mal, ça! Tu es chez toi dans l'éternité, sans aucun doute, tu le connais à fond. Il faut avouer, que tu es un petit rêveur assez curieux.'"

"Et puis," said Hans Castorp , *"si je t'avais parlé plus tôt, il m'aurait fallu te dire 'vous'."*

"Eh bien, est--ce que tu as l'intention de me tutoyer pour toujours?"

"Mais oui. Je t'ai tutoyé de tout temps et je te tutoierai éternellement."

"C'est un peu fort, par exemple. En tout cas, tu n'auras pas trop longtemps l'occasion de me dire 'tu'. Je vais partir."

It took time for the words to penetrate his consciousness. Then he started up, staring about him as though roused out of a dream. The conversation had proceeded rather slowly, for Hans Castorp spoke French uneasily, feeling for the sense. The piano had been silent awhile, now it sounded again, under the hands of the man from Mannheim, who had relieved the Slavic youth. He put some music in place, and Fräulein Engelhart sat down beside him to turn the leaves. The party was thinning out; many of the guests had presumably taken up the horizontal. From where they sat they could see no one; but there were players at the card--tables in the writing--room.

"You are going to—-what?" Hans Castorp asked, quite dashed.

"I am going away," she repeated, smiling with pretended surprise at his discomfiture.

"Impossible," he said. "You are jesting."

"Not at all. I am perfectly serious. I am leaving."

"When?"

"To--morrow. *Après dîner.*"

There took place within him a feeling of general collapse. He said: "Where?"

"Far away."

"To Daghestan?"

"*Tu n'es pas mal instruit. Peut--être, pour le moment—-*"

"Are you cured, then?"

"*Quant à ça—-non.* But Behrens thinks there is not greatly more to be gained here, for the present. *C'est pourquoi je vais risquer un petit changement d'air.*"

"Then you are coming back!"

"That is the question. Or, rather, the question is when. *Quant à moi, tu sais, j'aime la liberté avant tout et notamment celle de choisir mon domicile. Tu ne comprends guère ce que c'est: d'être obsédé d'indépendance. C'est de ma race, peut--être.*"

"*Et ton mari au Daghestan te l'accorde—-ta liberté?*"

"*C'est la maladie qui me la rend. Me voilà à cet endroit pour la troisième fois. J'ai passé un an ici, cette fois. Possible que je revienne. Mais alors tu seras bien loin depuis longtemps.*"

"You think so, Clavdia?"

"*Mon prénom aussi! Vraiment tu les prends bien au sérieux, les coutumes du carnaval!*"

"Then you know about my case too?"

"*Oui—-non—-comme on sait ces choses ici. Tu as une petite tache humide là dedans et un peu de fièvre, n'est--ce pas?*"

"*Trente--sept et huit ou neuf l'après--midi*" said Hans Castorp. "And you?"

"Oh, mon cas, tu sais, c'est un peu plus compliqué——pas tout--à--fait simple."

"Il y a quelque chose dans cette branche de lettres humaines dite la médecine," Hans Castorp said, *"qu'on appelle bouchement tuberculeux des vases de lymphe."*

"Ah! Tu as mouchardé, mon cher, on le voit bien."

"Et toi—— forgive me! Let me ask you a question——ask it in all earnestness: six months ago, when I left the table for my first examination——you looked round after me—-do you remember?"

"Quelle question! Il y a six mois!"

"Did you know where I was going?"

"Certes, c'était tout--à--fait par hasard——"

"Behrens had told you?"

"Toujours ce Behrens!"

"Oh, il a représenté ta peau d'une façon tellement exacte——D'ailleurs, c'est un veuf aux joues ardentes et qui possède un service à café très remarquable. Je crois bien qu'il connaît ton corps non seulement comme médecin, mais aussi comme adepte d'une autre discipline de lettres humaines."

"Tu as décidément raison de dire, que tu parles en rêve, mon ami."

"Soit. Laisse--moi rêver de nouveau, après m'avoir réveillé si cruellement par cette cloche d'alarme de ton départ. Sept mois sous tes yeux——et à présent, où en réalité j'ai fait ta connaissançe, tu me parles de départ!"

"Je te répète, que nous aurions pu causer plus tôt."

"You would have liked it?"

"Moi? Tu ne m'échapperas pas, mon petit. Il s'agit de tes intérêts, à toi. Est--ce que tu étais trop timide pour t'approcher d'une femme à qui tu parles en rêve maintenant, ou est--ce qu'il y avait quelqu'un qui t'en a empêché?"

"Je te l'ai dit. Je ne voulais pas te dire 'vous.'"

"Farceur! Réponds donc——ce monsieur beau parleur, cet italien--là qui a quitté la soirée——qu'est--ce qu'il t'a lancé tantôt?"

"Je n'en ai entendu absolument rien. Je me soucie très peu de ce monsieur, quand mes yeux te voient. Mais tu oublies——il n'aurait pas été si facile du tout de faire ta connaissance dans le monde. Il y avait encore mon cousin, avec qui j'étais lié et qui incline très peu à s'amuser ici; il ne pense à rien qu'à son retour dans les plaines, pour se faire soldat."

"Pauvre diable! Il est, en effet, plus malade qu'il ne sait. Ton ami italien du reste ne va pas trop bien non plus."

"Il le dit lui--même. Mais mon cousin——est--ce vrai? Tu m'effraies."

"Fort possible qu'il va mourir, s'il essaye d'être soldat dans les plaines."

"Qu'il va mourir. La mort. Terrible mot, n'est--ce pas? Mais c'est étrange, il ne m'impressionne pas tellement aujourd'hui, ce mot. C'était une façon de parler bien conventionnelle, lorsque je disais: 'Tu m'effraies.' L'idée de la mort ne m'effraie pas. Elle me laisse tranquille. Je n'ai pas pitié——ni de mon bon Joachim ni de moi--même, en entendant qu'il va peut--être mourir. Si c'est vrai, son état ressemble beaucoup au mien et je ne le trouve pas particulièrement imposant. Il est moribond, et moi, je suis amoureux, eh bien!——Tu as parlé à mon cousin à l'atelier de photographie intime, dans l'antichambre, tu te souviens."

"Je me souviens un peu."

"Donc ce jour--là Behrens a fait ton portrait transparent!"

"Mais oui."

"Mon dieu! Et l'as--tu sur toi?"

"Non, je l'ai dans ma chambre."

"Ah—-dans ta chambre. Quant au mien, je l'ai toujours dans mon portefeuille. Veux--tu que je te le fasse voir?"

"Mille remerciements. Ma curiosité n'est pas invincible. Ce sera un aspect très innocent."

"Moi, j'ai vu ton portrait extérieur. J'aimerais beaucoup mieux voir ton portrait intérieur qui est enfermé dans ta chambre. Laisse--moi demander autre chose! Parfois un monsieur russe qui loge en ville vient te voir. Qui est--ce? Dans quel but vient--il, cet homme?"

"Tu es joliment fort en espionnage, je l'avoue. Eh bien, je réponds. Oui, c'est un compatriote souffrant, un ami. J'ai fait sa connaissance à une autre station balnéaire, il y a quelques années déjà. Nos relations? Les voilà: nous prenons notre thé ensemble, nous fumons deux ou trois papiros, et nous bavardons, nous philosophons, nous parlons de l'homme, de Dieu, de la vie, de la morale, de mille choses. Voilà mon compte rendu. Es--tu satisfait?"

"De la morale aussi! Et qu'est--ce que vous avez trouvé en fait de morale, par exemple?"

"La morale? Cela t'intéresse? Eh bien, il nous semble, qu'il faudrait chercher la morale non dans la vertu, c'est--à--dire dans la raison, la discipline, les bonnes mœurs, l'honnêteté, mais plutôt dans le contraire, je veux dire dans le péché, en s'abandonnant au danger, à ce qui est nuisible, à ce qui nous consume. Il nous semble qu'il est plus moral de se perdre et même de se laisser dépérir, que de se conserver. Les grands moralistes n'étaient point de vertueux, mais des aventuriers dans le mal, des vicieux, des grands pécheurs qui nous enseignent à nous

*incliner chrétiennement devant la misère. Tout ça doit te déplaire
beaucoup, n'est--ce pas?"*

He was silent; sitting as before, with his feet twined together, thrust
back beneath the creaking wicker chair, leaning toward the figure
opposite, in its cocked hat; her pencil between his fingers. With Hans
Lorenz Castorp's blue eyes he looked out into the room. It was
empty, the company dispersed. The piano, in the corner diagonally
opposite, was being touched softly and lightly with one hand, by the
Mannheimer, by whose side sat Fräulein Engelhart, turning the
leaves of a music--book she held on her knee. At this pause which
had ensued in the conversation between Hans Castorp and Clavdia
Chauchat, the pianist left off playing, and sat with his hand in his lap,
while Fräulein Engelhart continued to turn the pages of her music-
-book. These four alone remained, from all the carnival merry-
-makers; they sat here motionless. The silence lasted several minutes.
Deeper and deeper, under its weight, sank the heads of the pair at the
piano: his toward his keyboard, hers toward her book; but at last the
two as by common consent stood up cautiously, and carefully
refraining from any glance in the direction of the opposite corner,
their heads drawn down in their shoulders, their arms hanging stiffly
at their sides, disappeared together, on tiptoe, through the
writingroom.

"Everyone is going," said Frau Chauchat. *"C'étaient les derniers. Il
se fait tard. Eh bien, la fête de carnaval est finie."* She raised her arms
to remove the paper cap from her head, with its reddish braid wound
round it like a wreath. *"Vous connaissez les conséquences, monsieur."*

But Hans Castorp gainsaid them, closing his eyes, and not
otherwise changing his position. He answered: *"Jamais, Clavdia.
Jamais je te dirai 'vous,' jamais de la vie ni de la mort,* if one may say
that——one should be able to. *Cette forme de s'adresser à une personne,
qui est cette de l'Occident cultivé et de la civilisation humanitaire, me
semble fort bourgeoise et pédante. Pourquoi, au fond, de la forme? La
forme, c'est la pédanterie elle--même! Tout ce que vous avez fixé à*

l'égard de la morale, toi et ton compatriote souffrant—tu veux sérieusement que ça me surprenne? Pour quel sot me prends-tu? Dis donc, qu'est-ce que tu penses de moi?"

"C'est un sujet qui ne donne pas beaucoup à penser. Tu es un petit bonhomme convenable, de bonne famille, d'une tenue appétissante, disciple docile de ses précepteurs et qui retournera bientôt dans les plaines, pour oublier complètement qu'il a jamais parlé en rêve ici et pour aider à rendre son pays grand et puissant par son travail honnête sur le chantier. Voilà ta photographie intime, faite sans appareil. Tu la trouves exacte, j'espère?"

"Il y manque quelques détails que Behrens y a trouvés."

"Ah, les médecins en trouvent toujours, ils s'y connaissent."

"Tu parles comme M. Settembrini. Et ma fièvre? D'où vient-elle?"

"Allons donc, c'est un incident sans conséquence qui passera vite."

"Non, Clavdia, tu sais bien que ce que tu dis là n'est pas vrai et tu le dis sans conviction, j'en suis sûr. La fièvre de mon corps et le battement de mon cœur harassé et le frissonement de mes membres, c'est le contraire d'un incident, car ce n'est rien d'autre" —and his pale face with the twitching lips bent closer over hers— *"rien d'autre que mon amour pour toi, oui, cet amour qui m'a saisi à l'instant, où mes yeux t'ont vue, ou, plutôt, que j'ai reconnu quand je t'ai reconnue toi—et c'était lui, évidemment, qui m'a mené à cet endroit—-"*

"Quelle folie!"

"Oh, l'amour n'est rien, s'il n'est pas de la folie, une chose insensée, défendue et une aventure dans le mal. Autrement, c'est une banalité agréable, bonne pour en faire de petites chansons paisibles dans les plaines. Mais quant à ce que je t'ai reconnue et que j'ai reconnu mon amour pour toi—oui, c'est vrai, je t'ai déjà connue, anciennement, toi et tes yeux merveilleusement obliques et ta bouche et ta voix, avec

laquelle tu parles——une fois déjà, lorsque j'étais collégien, je fea demandé ton crayon, pour faire enfin ta connaissance mondaine, parceque je t'aimais irraisonablement, et c'est de là, sans doute, c'est de mon ancien amour pour toi, que ces marques me restent que Behrens a trouvées dans mon corps, et qui indiquent que jadis aussi j'étais malade——"

His teeth struck together. As he raved, he had drawn one foot from under his chair, and moved it forward, so that the other knee touched the floor, there he knelt before her, his head bent, his whole body quivering. "*Je t'aime,* " he babbled, "*je t'ai aimée de tout temps, car tu es le Toi de ma vie, mon rêve, mon sort, mon envie, mon éternel désir——*"

"*Allons, allons!*" she said. "*Si tes précepteurs te voyaient——*"

But he shook his head, violently, bowed as it was toward the carpet, and replied: "*Je m'en ficherais, je me fiche de tous ces Carducci et de la République éloquente et du progrès humain dans le temps, car je t'aime!*"

She caressed softly the close--cropped hair at the back of his head.

"*Petit bourgeois!*" she said. "*Joli bourgeois à la petite tache humide. Est--ce vrai que tu m'aimes tant?*"

And beside himself at her touch, now on both his knees, with bowed head and closed eyes, he went on: "*Oh, l'amour, tu sais——Le corps, l'amour, la mort, ces trois ne font qu'un. Car le corps, c'est la maladie et la volupté, et c'est lui qui fait la mort, oui, ils sont charnels tous deux, l'amour et la mort, et voilà leur terreur et leur grande magie! Mais la mort, tu comprends, c'est d'une part une chose mal famée, impudente, qui fait rougir de honte; et d'autre part c'est une puissance très solennelle et très majestueuse——beaucoup plus haute que la vie riante gagnant de la monnaie et farcis-- sant sa panse——beaucoup plus vénérable que le progrès qui bavarde par les temps——parcequ'elle est l'histoire et la noblesse et la piété et l'éternel et le sacré qui nous fait tirer le chapeau et marcher sur la pointe des pieds.—Or, de même, le corps, lui aussi, et l'amour du corps, sont une affaire indécente et fâcheuse, et le corps rougit et pâlit à sa surface par frayeur et honte de lui--même. Mais aussi il est une grande gloire adorable, image miraculeuse de la vie organique, sainte merveille de la forme et de la beauté, et l'amour pour lui, pour le corps humain, c'est de même un intérêt extrêmement humanitaire et une puissance plus éducative que toute la pédagogie du monde! Oh, enchantante beauté organique qui ne se compose ni de teinture à l'huile ni de pierre, mais de matière vivante et corruptible, pleine du secret fébrile de la vie et de la pourriture! Regarde la symétrie merveilleuse de l'édifice humain, les épaules et les hanches et les mamelons fleurissants de part et d'autre sur la poitrine, et les côtes arrangées par paires, et le nombril au milieu dans la mollesse du ventre, et le sexe obscur entre les cuisses! Regarde les omoplates se remuer sous la peau soyeuse du dos, et l'échine qui descend vers la luxuriance double et fraîche des fesses, et les grandes branches des vases et des nerfs qui passent du tronc aux rameaux par les aisselles, et comme la structure des bras correspond à celle des jambes. Oh, les douces régions de la jointure intérieure du coude et du jarret, avec leur abondance de délicatesses organiques sous leurs coussins de chair! Quelle fête immense de les caresser, ces endroits délicieux du corps humain! Fête à mourir sans plainte après!*

Oui, mon dieu, laisse--moi sentir l'odeur de la peau de ta rotule, sous laquelle l'ingénieuse capsule articulaire sécrète son huile glissante! Laisse--moi toucher dévotement de ma bouche l'Arteria femoralis qui bat au front de ta cuisse et qui se divise plus bas en les deux artères du tibia! Laisse--moi ressentir l'exhalation de tes pores et tâter ton duvet, image humaine d'eau et d'albumine, destinée pour l'anatomie du tombeau, et laisse--moi périr, mes lèvres aux tiennes!"

He did not stir, or open his eyes; on his knees with bowed head, his hands holding the silver pencil outstretched before him, he remained, swaying and quivering. She said: *"Tu es en effet un galant qui sait solliciter d'une manière profonde, à l'allemande."* And she set the paper cap on his head.

"Adieu, mon prince Carnaval! Vous aurez une mauvaise ligne de fièvre ce soir, je vous le prédis."

She slipped from her chair, and glided over the carpet to the door, where she paused an instant, framed in the doorway; half turned toward him, with one bare arm lifted high, her hand upon the hinge. Over her shoulder she said softly: *"N'oubliez pas de me rendre mon crayon."*

And went out.

CHAPTER VI

Changes

*W*hat is time? A mystery, a figment—and all--powerful. It

conditions the exterior world, it is motion married to and mingled with the existence of bodies in space, and with the motion of these. Would there then be no time if there were no motion? No motion if no time? We fondly ask. Is time a function of Space? Or space of time? Or are they identical? Echo answers. Time is functional, it can be referred to as action; we say a thing's "brought about" by time. What sort of thing? Change! Now is not then, here not there, for between them lies motion. But the motion by which one measures time is circular, is in a closed circle; and might almost equally well be described as rest, as cessation of movement—for the there repeats itself constantly in the here, the past in the present. Furthermore, as our utmost effort cannot conceive a final limit either to time or in space, we have settled to think of them as eternal and infinite—-apparently in the hope that if this is not very successful, at least it will be more so than the other. But is not this affirmation of the eternal and the infinite the logical--mathematical destruction of every and any limit in time or space, and the reduction of them, more or less, to zero? Is it possible, in eternity, to conceive of a sequence of events, or in the infinite of a succession of space--occupying bodies?

Conceptions of distance, movement, change, even of the existence of finite bodies in the universe—-how do these fare? Are they consistent with the hypothesis of eternity and infinity we have been driven to adopt? Again we ask, and again echo answers. Hans Castorp revolved these queries and their like in his brain. We know that from the very first day of his arrival up here his mind had been much disposed to such sleeveless speculation. Later, perhaps, a certain sinister but strong desire of his, since gratified, had sharpened it the more and confirmed it in its general tendency to question and to carp. He put these queries to himself, he put them to good cousin Joachim, he put them to the valley at large, lying there, as it had these months on end, deep in snow; though from none of these quarters could he expect anything like an answer, from which the least would be hard to say. For himself, it was precisely because he did not know the answers that he put the questions. For Joachim, it was hardly possible to get him even to consider them, he having, as Hans Castorp had said, in French, on a certain evening, nothing else in his head but the idea of being a soldier down below. Joachim wrestled with these hopes of his, that now seemed almost within his grasp, now receded into the distance and mocked him there; the struggle grew daily more embittered, he even threatened to end it once for all by a single bold bid for liberty. Yes, the good, the patient, the upright Joachim, so affected to discipline and the service, had been attacked by fits of rebellion, he even questioned the authority of the "Gaffky scale": the method employed in the laboratory——the lab, as one called it——to ascertain the degree of a patient's infection. Whether only a few isolated bacilli, or a whole host of them, were found in the sputum analysed, determined his "Gaffky number," upon which everything depended. It infallibly reflected the chances of recovery with which the patient had to reckon; the number of months or years he must still remain could with ease be deduced from it, beginning with the six months that Hofrat Behrens called a "week--end," and ending with the "life sentence," which, taken literally, often enough meant very little indeed. Joachim, then, inveighed against the Gaffky scale, openly giving notice that he questioned its authority——or perhaps not *quite* openly, he did not say so to the authorities, but expressed his views to his cousin, and even in the dining--room. "I'm fed up with it, I won't be made a fool of any longer," he said, the blood mounting to his bronzed face. "Two weeks ago I had Gaffky two, a mere nothing, my prospects were the best. And to--day I am regularly infested---number nine, if you please. No talk of getting away. How the devil can a man know where he is? Up on the Schatzalp there is a man, a Greek peasant, an agent had him sent here from Arcadia, he has galloping consumption, there isn't the dimmest hope for him. He may die any day---and yet they've never found even the ghost of a bacillus in his sputum. On the other hand, that Belgian captain that was discharged cured the other day, he was simply alive with them, Gaffky ten---and only the very tiniest cavity. The devil fly away with Gaffky! I'm done, I'm going home, if it kills me!" Thus Joachim; and all his company were pained to see the gentle, serious youth so overwrought. Hans Castorp, when he heard the threat, could scarcely refrain from quoting a certain opinion he had heard expressed in French, by a third party. But he was silent. Was he to set himself up to his cousin for a model of patience, as did Frau Stöhr, who actually admonished Joachim not to be blasphemous, but to humble his pride, and take pattern by her, Caroline Stöhr, and the faithfulness and firm resolve which made her hold out up here, instead of returning to queen it in her Cannstadt home---to the end that when she did go back it would be as a sound and healthy wife to the arms of her impatient husband? No, such language was not for Hans Castorp---since Carnival he had had a bad conscience towards his cousin. Conscience told him Joachim must surely be aware of a certain matter never referred to between them; must see in it something very like disloyalty and desertion---taken in connexion with a pair of brown eyes we know, an unwarranted tendency to laughter, and an orange--scented handkerchief, to whose influence Joachim was daily five times exposed, yet gave no ground to evil, but steadfastly fixed his eyes upon his plate. Yes, even the silent hostility which Joachim opposed to his cousin's problems and speculations on the subject of time, Hans Castorp felt as an expression of the military decorum which reproached himself. While as for the valley, that snowed--in winter valley, when Hans Castorp, lying in his excellent chair, directed upon it his inquiring metaphysical gaze, it was silent too. Its peaked summits, its domes and crests and brown--green--reddish forests stood there silent, and mortal time flowed over and about them: sometimes luminous against a deep--blue sky, sometimes shrouded in vapours, sometimes glowing rosy in the parting sun, sometimes glittering with hard, diamondlike brilliance in the magic moonlight---but always, always in snow, for six long, incredible, though scurrying months. All the guests declared they could not bear to look any more at the snow, they were sick of it; they had had their fill in the summer--time, and now these masses and heaps and slopes and cushions of snow, day in and day out, were more than they could stand, their spirits sank under the weight of it. And they took to coloured glasses, green, yellow, and red, to save their eyes, but still more their feelings.

Mountain and valley, then, had been lying in deep snow for six months; nay, seven, for as we talk, time strides on—-not only present time, taken up with the tale we are telling, but also past time, the bygone time of Hans Castorp and the companions of his destiny, up among the snows—-time strides on, and brings changes with it. The prophecy which so glibly, so much to Herr Settembrini's disgust, Hans Castorp had made on the eve of Carnival, was in a fair way to be fulfilled. True, the solstice was not immediately at hand; yet Easter had passed over the valley, April advanced, with Whitsuntide in plain view; spring, with the melting of the snows, would soon be here. Not all the snow would melt: on the heights to the south, and on the north in the rocky ravines of the Rhatikon, some would still remain, and through the summer months more was sure to fall, though it would scarcely lie. Yet the year revolved, and promised changes in its course; for since that night of Carnival when Hans Castorp had borrowed a lead--pencil of Frau Chauchat and afterwards returned it to her again, receiving in its stead a remembrance which he carried about with him in his pocket, since that night six weeks had passed, twice as many as made up the original term of Hans Castorp's sojourn among those up here.

Yes, six weeks had gone by, since that evening when Hans Castorp made the acquaintance of Clavdia Chauchat, and then returned so much later to his chamber than the duty--loving Joachim to his. Six weeks since the day after, bringing her departure, her departure for the present, her temporary departure, for Daghestan, far away eastwards beyond the Caucasus. That her absence would be only temporary, that she intended to return, that she would or must return, at some date yet unspecified, of this Hans Castorp possessed direct and verbal assurances, given, not during that reported conversation in the French tongue, but in a later interval, wordless to our ears, during which we have elected to intermit the flow of our story along the stream of time, and let time flow on pure and free of any content whatever. Yes, such consolatory promises must have been vouchsafed our young man before he returned to number thirty--four; for he had had no word with Frau Chauchat on the day following, had not seen her indeed, save twice at some distance: once when the glass door slammed, and she had slipped for the last time to her place at table, clad in her blue cloth skirt and white sweater. The young man's heart had been in his throat—-only the sharp regard Fräulein Engelhart bent upon him had hindered him from burying his face in his hands. The other time had been at three o'clock, when he stood at a corridor window giving on the drive, a witness to her departure.

It took place just as other such which Hans Castorp had witnessed during his stay up here. The sleigh or carriage halted before the door, coachman and porter strapped fast the trunks, while friends gathered about to say good--bye to the departing one, who, cured or not, and whether for life or death, was off for the flat--land. Others besides friends gathered round as well, curious on--lookers, who cut the rest--cure for the sake of the diversion thus afforded. There would be a frock--coated official representing the management, perhaps even the physicians themselves; then out came the gracious recipient of the attentions paid by this little world to a departing guest; generally with a beaming face, and a bearing which the excitement of the moment rendered far more animated than usual. To--day it was Frau Chauchat who issued from the portal, in company with her concave fellow--countryman, Herr Buligin, who was to accompany her for part of the way. She wore a long, shaggy, fur--trimmed travellingcloak, and a large hat; she was all smiles, her arms were full of flowers, she too seemed possessed by the pleasurable excitement due to the prospect of change, if to nothing else, which was common to all those who left, whatever the circumstances of their leaving, and whether with the consent of the physicans, or in sheer desperation and at their own risk. Her cheeks were flushed, and she chattered without stopping, probably in Russian, while the rug was being arranged over her knees. People presented farewell bouquets, the great--aunt gave a box of Russian sweetmeats. Numerous other guests besides Frau Chauchat's Russian companions and table--mates, stood there to see her off; among them Dr. Krokowski, showing his yellow teeth through his beard in a hearty smile, the schoolmistress, and the man from Mannheim, who gazed gloomily and furtively from a distance, and whose eyes found out Hans Castorp as he stood at his corridor window looking down upon the scene. Hofrat Behrens did not show himself—he had probably ere now taken private leave of the traveller. The horses started up, amid farewells and hand--wavings from the bystanders; and then, as Frau Chauchat sank smilingly back against the cushions of the sleigh, her eyes swept the façade of the Berghof, and rested for the fraction of a second upon Hans Castorp's face. In pallid haste he sought his loggia, thence to get a last glimpse of the sleigh as it went jingling down the drive toward the Dorf. Then he flung himself into his chair, and drew out his keepsake, his treasure, that consisted, this time, not of a few reddish--brown shavings, but a thin glass plate, which must be held toward the light to see anything on it. It was Clavdia's x--ray portrait, showing not her face, but the delicate bony structure of the upper half of her body, and the organs of the thoracic cavity, surrounded by the pale, ghostlike envelope of flesh. How often had he looked at it, how often pressed it to his lips, in the time which since then had passed and brought its changes with it—such changes as, for instance, getting used to life up here without Clavdia Chauchat, getting used, that is, to her remoteness in space! Yet after all, this adaptation took place more rapidly than one might have thought possible; for was not time up here at the Berghof arranged and organized to the end that one should get very rapidly used to things, even if the getting used consisted chiefly in getting used to not getting used? No longer might he expect that rattle and crash at the beginning of each of the five mighty Berghof meals. Somewhere else, in some far--off clime, Clavdia was letting doors slam behind her, somewhere else she was expressing herself by that act, as intimately bound up with her very being and its state of disease as time is bound up with the motion of bodies in space. Perhaps, indeed, her whole disease consisted in that, and in nothing else.——But though lost to view, she was none the less invisibly present to Hans Castorp; she was the genius of the place, whom, in an evil hour, an hour unattuned to any simple little ditty of the flat--land, yet one of passing sweetness, he had known and possessed, whose shadowy presentment he now wore next his months--long--labouring heart. At that hour his twitching lips had stammered and babbled, in his own and foreign tongues, for the most part without his own volition, the maddest things: pleas, prayers, proposals, frantic projects, to which all consent was denied, and rightly: as, that he might be permitted to accompany the genius beyond the Caucasus; that he might follow after it; that he might await it at the next spot which its free and untrammelled spirit should select as a domicile; and thereafter never be parted from it more—-these and other such rash, irresponsible utterances. No, all that our simple young adventurer carried away from that hour was his ghostly treasure trove, and the possibility, perhaps the probability, of Frau Chauchat's return for a fourth sojourn at the Berghof——sooner or later, as the state of her health might decree. But whether sooner or later——as she had said again at parting——Hans Castorp would by that time be "long since far away." It was a prophecy whose slighting note would have been harder to bear had he not known that prophecies are sometimes made in order that they may *not* come to pass——as a spell, indeed, against their fulfilment. Prophecies of this kind mock the future: saying to it how it should shape itself, to the end that it shall shame to be so shaped. The genius, in the course of the conversation we have repeated, and elsewhere, called Hans

Castorp a *"joli bourgeois au petit endroit humide,"* which might in some sense be considered a translation of the Settembrinian epithet "life's delicate child"; and the question thus was, which constitutes of the mingled essence of his being would prove the stronger, the bourgeois or the other. The genius, though, had failed to take into consideration the fact that Hans Castorp too had come about a good deal in the world, and might easily return hither at a fitting moment—though, in all soberness, was he not sitting up here entirely in order that he might not need to return. Precisely and explicitly that was with him, as with so many others, the very ground of his continued presence.

One prophecy, indeed, made on that carnival evening, made in mockery, was fulfilled: Hans Castorp's fever chart did display a sharply rising curve. He marked it down with a feeling of solemnity. Thereafter it fell a trifle, and then ran on, unchanged save for slight undulations, well above its accustomed level. It was fever, the degree and persistency of which, according to the Hofrat, was out of all proportion to the condition of his lung. "H'm, young fellow me lad, you're more infected than one would take you for," he said. "We'll have to come on to the hypos. They'll serve your turn, or I'm a Dutchman. In three or four months you ought to be as fit as a fiddle." Thus it came about that Hans Castorp had to produce himself, twice in the week, Monday and Saturday after the morning exercise, down in the "lab," where he was given his injections.

These were given by either physician indifferently; but the Hofrat performed the operation like a virtuoso, with a fine sweep, squeezing the little syringe at the very moment he pressed the point home. And he cared not a doit where he thrust his needle, so that the pain was often acute, and the spot hard and inflamed long afterwards. The effect of the inoculations on the entire organism was very noticeable, the nervous system reacted as after hard muscular exertion; and their strength was displayed in the heightened fever which was their immediate result. The Hofrat had said they would have this effect, and so it fell out. The whole affair, each time, took but a second; one after another, the row of patients received their dosage, in thigh or arm, and turned away. But once or twice, when the Hofrat was in a more lively mood, not depressed by the tobacco he had smoked, Hans Castorp came to speech with him, and conducted the brief conversation somewhat as follows: "I still remember the coffee and the pleasant talk we had last autumn, Herr Hofrat," he would say. "Only yesterday, or perhaps the day before, was it, I was reminding my cousin of how we happened to—-"

"Gaffky seven," said the Hofrat. "Last examination. The chap simply can't part with his bacilli. And yet he keeps at me worse than ever, to let him get away so he can wear a sword tied round his middle. What a child it is! Makes me a scene over a month or so of time, as though it were aeons passing over our heads. Means to leave, whether or no—-does he say the same to you? You ought to give him a pretty straight talking--to. Take it from me, you'll have him hopping the twig if he is too previous about going down and breathing the nice damp air into his weak spot. A swordswallower like that doesn't necessarily possess so much grey matter; but you, as the steady civilian, you ought to see to it he doesn't make an ass of himself."

"I do talk to him, Herr Hofrat," Hans Castorp responded, taking the reins again into his hands. "I do, often, when he begins to kick against the pricks—-and I think he will listen to reason. But the examples he has before his eyes are all the wrong kind. He is always seeing people going off on their own, without authority from you; it looks mighty gay, as though they were really leaving for good, and that is a temptation to all but the strongest characters. For instance, lately—-who was it went off? A lady, from the 'good' Russian table, that Frau Chauchat. She's gone to Daghestan, they say. Well, Daghestan—-I don't know the climate, it is probably better, when all is said and done, than being right down on the water. But after all, it is the flat--land, according to our ideas up here—-though for aught I know it may be mountainous, geographically speaking; I am not much up on the subject. But how can a person who isn't sound live out there, where all the proper ideas are totally lacking, and nobody has a notion of the regimen, the rest--cure, and measuring, and all that? Anyhow, she will be coming back, she told me so herself--happened to. How did we come to speak of her?---Yes, Herr Hofrat, I remember as thought it was yesterday, how we met you in the garden, or, rather, you met us, for we were sitting on a bench---I could show you the very bench, to--day, that we were sitting on---we were sitting and smoking. Or, rather, I was smoking, for my cousin doesn't smoke, oddly enough. You were smoking too, and we exchanged our brands, I recall. Your Brazil I found excellent; but I suspect one has to go about them a little gingerly, or something may happen as it happened to you that time with the two little imported--when your bosom swelled with pride, and you nearly toddled off, you know. I may joke about it, since it turned out all right. I've ordered another couple of hundred of my Maria lately. I'm very dependent on her, she suits me in every respect. But the carriage and customs make the cost rather mount up---so if you have anything good to suggest, Herr Hofrat, I'm ready to have a go at the domestic product---I see some attractive weeds in the windows. Yes, we were privileged to look at your paintings, I remember the whole thing so well. And I was perfectly amazed at your oil technique, I'd never venture anything like it. You showed us the portrait you made of Frau Chauchat, simply first--class treatment of the skin---I must say I was very much struck by it. At that time I was not personally acquainted with the sitter, only by sight. But just before she went off, I got to know her."

"You don't say!" answered the Hofrat---a little as he had that time when Hans Castorp told him, shortly before the first examination, that he had fever. He said no more.

"Yes," went on the youth, "I made her acquaintance---a thing that isn't so easy, hereabouts, you know. But Frau Chauchat and I, we managed, at the eleventh hour, we had some conversation---Ff---fl!" went Hans Castorp, and drew his breath sharply through his teeth. The needle had gone in. "That was certainly a very important nerve you happened to hit on, Herr Hofrat," he said. "I do assure you, it hurt like the devil. Thanks, a little massage does it good … Yes, we came a little closer to each other, in conversation."

"Ah? Well?" the Hofrat said. His manner was as one expecting from his own experience a very favouring reply, and expressing his agreement in anticipation by the way he puts the question.

"I'm afraid my French was rather lame," Hans Castorp answered evasively. "I haven't had much occasion to use it. But the words somehow come into one's mind when one needs them—so we understood each other tolerably well."

"I believe you," said the Hofrat. "Well?" he repeated his inquisition; and even added, of his own motion: "Pretty nice, what?"

Hans Castorp stood, legs and elbows extended, his face turned up, buttoning his shirt--collar.

"It's the old story," he said. "At a place like this, two people, or two families, can live weeks on end under one roof, without speaking. But some day they get acquainted, and take to each other, only to find that one of the parties is on the point of leaving. Regrettable incidents like that happen, I suppose. In such cases, one feels like keeping in touch by post, at least. But Frau Chauchat—"

"Tut, she won't, won't she?" the Hofrat laughed.

"No, she wouldn't hear of it. Does she write to you, now and again, from where she is staying?"

"Lord bless you!" Behrens answered, "she'd never think of it. In the first place, she's too lazy, and in the second—how could she? I can't read Russian, though I can jabber it, after a fashion, when I have to, but I can't read a word—nor you either, I should suppose. And the puss can purr fast enough in French or in book German, but writing—it would floor her altogether. Think of the spelling! No, my poor young friend, we'll have to console each other. She always comes back again, sooner or later. Different people take it differently—it's a question of procedure, or of temperament. One goes off and keeps coming back, another stops long enough that he doesn't need to come back. Just put it to your cousin that if he goes off now, you're likely to be still here to see him return in state."

"But Herr Hofrat, how long do you mean that I——?"

"That you? You mean that he, don't you? That he won't stop as long a time below as he has been up here, that is what I mean, and so I tell you. That's my humble opinion, and I lay it on you to tell him so from me, if you will be so kind as to undertake the commission."

Such, more or less, would be the trend of their conversation, artfully conducted by Hans Castorp, who, however, reaped nothing or less than nothing for his pains. How long one must remain in order to see the return of a person departed before her time——on that point the result was equivocal; while as for direct news of the departed fair one, he got simply none at all. No, he would have no news of her, so long as they were separated by the mystery of time and space. She would never write, and no opportunity would be afforded him to do so. And when he came to think of it, how should it be otherwise? Was it not very bourgeois, even pedantic, of him, to imagine they ought to write, when he himself had been of opinion that it was neither necessary nor desirable for them to speak? Had he even spoken with her, that carnival evening——anything that might be called speaking, and not rather the utterance of a dream, couched in a foreign tongue, and very little "civilized" in its drift? Why should he write to her, on letter--paper or on postcards, setting down for her edification, as he did for that of his people at home, the fluctuations of his curve? Clavdia had been right in feeling herself dispensed from writing by virtue of the freedom her illness gave her. Speaking and writing were of course the first concern of a humanistic and republican spirit; they were the proper affair of Brunetto Latini, the same who wrote the book about the virtues and the vices, and taught the Florentines the art of language and how to guide their state according to the rules of politics.

And here Hans Castorp was reminded of Ludovico Settembrini, and flushed, as once he had when the Italian entered his sick--room and turned on the light. Hans Castorp might have applied to him with his metaphysical puzzles, if only by way of challenge or in a carping spirit, without any serious expectation of an answer from the humanist, whose concerns and interests, of course, were all of this earth. But since the carnival gaieties, and Settembrini's impassioned exit from the music--room, there had been a coolness between them, due on Hans Castorp's side to a bad conscience, on the other's to the deep wound dealt his pedagogic pride. They avoided each other, and for weeks exchanged not a single word. In the eyes of one whose view it was that all moral sanctions resided in the reason and the virtue, Hans Castorp must have ceased to be "a delicate child of life"; Herr Settembrini must by now have given him up for lost. The youth hardened his heart, he scowled and stuck out his lips when they met, and the Italian's darkly ardent gaze rested upon him in silent reproach. But his resentment dissolved on the instant, the first time Herr Settembrini spoke to him, which, as we have said, happened after weeks of silence. Even so, it was in passing, and in the form of a classical allusion, for the understanding of which some training in occidental culture was required. They met, after dinner, in the glass door——that door which nowadays was never guilty of banging. Settembrini overtook the young man, and in the act to pass him, said: "Well, Engineer, and how have you enjoyed the pomegranate?"

Hans Castorp smiled, overjoyed, but in confusion. He answered: "I don't quite understand, Herr Settembrini. Did we have any pomegranates? I don't recall having tasted——oh, yes, once in my life I had pomegranate juice and soda; it was too sweet."

The Italian, already in front of him, turned his head to say: "Gods and mortals have been known to visit the nether world and find their way back again. But in that kingdom they know that he who tastes even once of its fruits belongs to them."

He passed on, in his everlasting check trousers, and left Hans Castorp behind, presumably, and to a certain extent actually, staggered by so much allusiveness; though he was stirred to irritation at its being taken for granted, and muttered through his teeth after the

[447]

departing back: "*Carducci--Latini--humani--spagheti*— get along, do, and leave me in peace!"

Yet he was at bottom sincerely glad to have the silence broken. For despite his keepsake, the macabre trophy he wore next his heart, he leaned upon Herr Settembrini, set great store by his character and opinions; and the thought of being cast off would have weighed upon his spirit more heavily than that remembered boyish feeling of being left behind at school and not counting any more, of enjoying, like Herr Albin, the boundless advantages of his shameful state. He did not venture, however, himself to address his mentor; who, for his part, let weeks elapse before he again approached his "delicate child."

The ocean of time, rolling onwards in monotonous rhythm, bore the Easter--tide on its billows. And they observed the season at the Berghof, as they did consistently all the recurrent feasts of the year, by way of breaking up and articulating the long stretches of time. At early breakfast there was a nosegay of violets at each place; at second breakfast each guest had a coloured egg; while sugar and chocolate hares adorned and made festive the midday table.

"Have you ever made a voyage by steamship, Tenente? Or you, Engineer?" asked Herr Settembrini, strolling up to the cousins' table, toothpick in mouth. Most of the guests were shortening the main rest--cure in honour of the day, and devoting a quarter--hour to coffee and cognac. "These rabbits and coloured eggs somehow remind me of the life on board a great oceangoing boat, where you stare at a briny waste and a bare horizon for weeks on end, and even the exaggerated ease of the life scarcely avails to make you forget its precariousness, the submerged consciousness of which continues to gnaw at the depths of your being. I still recall the spirit in which the passengers in such an ark piously observe the feasts of terra firma: they have thoughts of the outer world, they are sensitive to the calendar. On shore it would be Easter today, they say; or, to--day they are celebrating the King's birthday——and we will celebrate too, as best we may. We are human beings too. Isn't that the idea?"

The cousins acquiesced. It was precisely that. Hans Castorp, touched by being once more addressed, and pricked by his conscience, praised Herr Settembrini's words in sounding tones; pronounced them capital; said how spirited they were, how much the language of a literary man. He could not say too much. Undoubtedly, though only superficially, as Herr Settembrini, in his plastic way, had remarked, the comfort on board an ocean steamer did make one forget the element of risk in the circumstances. If he might venture to add anything, he would say it even induced a sort of light--headedness, a tempting of fate, which the ancients——in his desire to please he quoted the classics!——had called *hubris*. Belshazzar, King of Babylon, and that sort of thing. In short, it came close to being blasphemous. Yet, on the other hand, the luxury of an ocean--going vessel connoted (!) a majestic triumph of the human spirit, it was an honour to human kind, to launch all this comfort and luxury upon the salt sea foam and there sustain it——man thus boldly set his foot, as it were, upon the forces of nature, controlled the wild elements; and that connoted (!) the victory of civilization over chaos——if he might make so free as to employ the phrase.

Herr Settembrini listened attentively, legs and arms crossed, daintily stroking with the toothpick his flowing moustaches.

"It is remarkable," he said. "A man cannot make general observations to any extent, on any subject, without betraying himself, without introducing his entire individuality, and presenting, as in an allegory, the fundamental theme and problem of his own existence. This, Engineer, is what you have just done. All you have just now said came from the very depths of your personality; even the present stage you have arrived at found there poetic expression, and showed itself to be still the experimental——"

"*Placet experiri*," Hans Castorp said, with the Italian *c*, laughed and nodded.

"*Sicuro*—— if what is involved is not recklessness and loose living, but an honourable passion to explore the universe. You spoke of

[449]

hubris, that was the word you employed. The *hubris* which the reason opposes to the powers of darkness is the highest human expression, and calls down "upon it the swift revenge of envious gods—-as when, *per esempio*, such an ark *de luxe* gets shipwrecked and goes gallantly beneath the waves. That is defeat with honour. Prometheus too was guilty of *hubris*—-and his torture on the Scythian cliffs was from our point of view a holy martyrdom. But what about that other kind of *hubris*, which perishes in a wanton trifling with the forces of unreason and hostility to the human race? Is that—-can that—-be honourable?

Si, o no?"

Hans Castorp stirred his coffee--cup, though there was nothing in it.

"Engineer, Engineer," said the Italian, and nodded musingly, his black eyes fixed on space, "are you not afraid of the hurricane which is the second circle of the Inferno, and which whirls and whips the offenders after the flesh, those lost unhappy ones who sacrificed their reason to their desire? *Gran dio!* When I picture you, flapping about in the gale, heels over head—-I could almost swoon out of sheer pity, and fall 'as a dead body falls.' "

They laughed, glad that he should be pleased to jest and talk poetry. But Settembrini added: "You remember, Engineer, on the evening of *mardi gras*, as you sat over your wine, you took your leave of me—-yes, in a way, it amounted to that. Well, to--day it is my turn. You see me, gentlemen, in act to bid you farewell. I am leaving House Berghof."

The cousins were aghast.

"Impossible! You are joking," Hans Castorp cried, as he had cried once before, on a like occasion. He was nearly as much startled now as then.

Settembrini answered, in his turn: "Not at all. It is as I tell you. More than that, the news should be to you no news. I once explained to you that in the moment when I became aware that my hope of looking forward to a return to my work within any reasonable time was no longer tenable, in that moment I was settled to strike my tent, so far as this establishment is concerned, and seek in the village a permanent *logis*. Well——the moment has arrived. I cannot recover, that is settled. I can prolong my days, but only up here. My final sentence is for life——Hofrat Behrens with his customary vivacity has pronounced my doom. Very well, I have drawn the inevitable inference. I have taken new quarters, and am about to remove thither my small earthly possessions, and the tools of my literary craft. It is not far from here, in the Dorf; we shall surely see each other, surely I will not lose sight of you; but as a fellow--guest of this establishment I have the honour to take my leave."

Such was the announcement Settembrini had made, that Easter Sunday. Both cousins had shown themselves exceedingly upset. They had talked at length and repeatedly with him, on the subject of his resolve; also about how he could carry on the service of the cure even after he left the Berghof; about his taking with him and continuing the great encyclopædic task he had set himself, that survey of the masterpieces of belles--lettres, from the point of view of human suffering and its elimination; finally, about Herr Settembrini's future lodging, in the house of a "petty chandler," as the Italian called him. The chandler, it appeared, let his upper storeys to a Bohemian ladies'--tailor, who in his turn let out lodgings. And now all these arrangements lay in the past. Time had moved steadily on, and brought more than one change in its train. Settembrini had ceased to have residence at the Berghof, he had taken up his abode with Lukaçek, the ladies' tailor——and that indeed some weeks back. He had not made his exit in a sleigh, but on foot, wearing a short yellow coat, garnished sparsely with fur at the collar and wrists, and accompanied by a man who trundled the earthly and literary baggage of the humanist on a hand--lorry. He pinched one of the dining--room girls in the cheek with the back of two fingers, and went off down the drive, swinging his stick——they watched him go. This, as we said, was well on in April, three--quarters of the month lay in the past. It was still the depth of winter——in their chambers the thermometer registered scarcely more than forty degrees; outside there were fifteen degrees of frost, and if one left one's ink--well in the loggia, it froze overnight into an icy lump, like a piece of coal. Yet one knew that spring was nigh. There were days when the sun shone, on which one felt in the air its delicate presence. The melting of the snows was at hand, and brought with it certain changes to the Berghof——despite the authority of Hofrat Behrens, despite all he could say, in dining--hall and bed--chamber, at every meal, at every visit, at every examination, to combat the prevailing prejudice against the season.

Were they, he asked, up here for the winter sports, or were they patients? And if the latter, what good on earth were snow and ice to them? Had they the notion in their heads that the melting snow was a bad time for them to be here? Nonsense!——it was the best time of all. He could show them that there were relatively fewer bedridden, in the whole valley, at this time than at any other in the year. And there was not a spot in the world that was not less favourable to lung--patients at this season than the one they were in. Anybody with a spark of common sense would stop on, and give himself the benefit of the hardening process which this sort of weather afforded. Then, provided they remained for their appointed time, they would be fully healed, staunch against any rigours of any climate in the world. And so forth. But the prejudice stuck, let him say what he would. The Berghof emptied. Perhaps it was the oncoming spring that got in their bones and upset even the steadiest--going; but at all events, the number of "wild," unauthorized departures from House Berghof increased until the situation verged upon the critical. For instance, Frau Salomon from Amsterdam, despite the pleasure she got from displaying her lace underwear at examinations, despite the fact that she was not improving, but getting steadily worse, took an entirely mad and illegitimate leave for the flat--land. Her sojourn in the valley extended much further back than Hans Castorp's; she had entered more than a year ago, with only a slight weakness, for which a three months' stay had been prescribed. Four months later the word was that she would be perfectly sound inside another six weeks. But at the end of that time there was heard no talk of a cure; she must stop for at least another four months. Thus it had gone on: certainly this was no bagnio, no Siberian penal settlement; Frau Salomon had remained, and displayed her beauteous underwear. But now, when the snows were melting, and she was prescribed, at her examination, another six months, on account of whistling sounds in the upper left lung, and unmistakable discords under the left shoulder--blade, her patience suddenly came to an end, and she left for her wet and windy Amsterdam, uttering invectives against Dorf and Platz, the far--famed climate, the doctors, and the International Sanatorium Berghof. Was that well done?

Hofrat Behrens raised shoulders and arms, and let the latter fall with a clap against his sides. At latest, he said, Frau Salomon would be back in the autumn—-and for good and all. We shall be able to test the truth of his prophecy, for we are destined to spend yet much earthly time at this pleasure resort. But the Salomon case was far from being the only one of its kind. Time brought about many changes. Time always did—-but more gradually, in the rule, not so strikingly. There were gaps at the tables, all seven of them, at the "good" as well as at the "bad" Russian table, and at those that stood transversely to the room. Not that this alone would have given an exact or fair picture of the situation; for there were always arrivals, as well as leave--takings, the bedrooms might be full—-though there one dealt with patients whose condition had finally put an end to their exercising any choice in the matter. The gaps in the diningroom were partly due to the exercise of choice; but some of them yawned in a particularly hollow manner—as, for instance, at Dr. Blumenkohl's place—-he being dead. That expression he wore, as of something bad--tasting in the mouth, had grown more and more pronounced. Then he became permanently bedridden, and then he died—-no one knew precisely when, his affair being disposed of with the usual tact and delicacy. A gap. Frau Stöhr sat next it—-it made her shudder, so she

[453]

moved over to Joachim Ziemssen's other side, in the room of Miss Robinson, discharged cured, and opposite the schoolmistress, Hans Castorp's neighbour, still faithful to her post. The latter was sitting, for the time, alone on her side of the table, for the other three places were free. The student Rasmussen had grown daily thinner and weaker, he was now bedridden, probably moribund. The great--aunt, with her niece and the fullbreasted Marusja, had gone a journey---that was the usual way to put it, because everybody knew they would be back again. They would certainly be back by autumn, so you could hardly say they had left. The summer solstice----once Whitsuntide was past----stood immediately before them; and after the longest day in the year they would go downhill with a rush, toward winter. At that rate the great--aunt and Marusja were as good as back again----which was as it should be, for the lively Marusja was very far from being cured, and the schoolmistress knew positively that the brown--eyed one had tuberculous ulcers on her swelling bosom, which had more than once already necessitated an operation. Hans Castorp, as Fräulein Engelhart said this, gave a hasty glance at Joachim bending sedulously over his plate a face gone all mottled. The lively great--aunt had given her table--mates a farewell supper in the restaurant, to which were bidden the cousins, Frau Stöhr and Fräulein Engelhart----a proper banquet, with caviar, champagne, and liqueurs. Joachim had been very silent, in fact had spoken only once or twice, and then hardly above a whisper; so that the old lady, in a burst of good feeling, had sought to cheer him up, even going so far as to set aside accepted forms and address him with the thou. "Never mind, *Väterchen*, cheer up, eat, drink, and be merry, we'll be coming back again," she said. "Let's all eat, drink, and be merry, and begone, dull care! God will send the autumn in His own good time, before we know it----so why be sad?" Next morning she presented half the diningroom with gay boxes of confits and left, with her two charges, on their little outing. And Joachim? Did he find things easier, for that? Or did he suffer an agony of inward emptiness in view of the vacant places at table? Had his unwonted irritability, his threats of taking un--sanctified leave, anything to do with Marusja's departure?

Or, on the other hand, that he had after all *not* left, but lent an ear to the Hofrat's gospel of the melting snows—-was that fact any way connected with the circumstance that the full--bosomed Marusja was not gone for good but only on a journey, and would be back again in five of the smallest time--units known to House Berghof? Ah, yes, they were both true, this and the other, as Hans Castorp was well aware, without ever having exchanged a syllable with Joachim on the subject—-which he was as careful to refrain from doing as his cousin was, on his side, to avoid mention of another person also lately gone off for a little trip.

In the mean time, who was sitting at Settembrini's table, in the place vacated by the Italian and in the company of certain Dutchmen who were possessed of such mighty appetites that every day, before the five--course Berghof dinner, even before the soup, each one of them ordered and ate three fried eggs? Who, we say, but Anton Karlowitsch Ferge, the same who had experienced the hellish torment of the pleurashock! Yes, Herr Ferge was out of bed. Without the aid of the pneumothorax he had so improved as to be able to spend most of the day up and dressed, and even to assist at the Berghof meals, with his bushy, good--natured moustaches, and his exaggerated Adam's apple, just as good--natured. The cousins chatted with him sometimes, in dining--room or salon, or even inclined their hearts unto that simple sufferer, and took him with them on the daily walks. Elevated discourse was beyond him; but within his limits he could talk very acceptably about the manufacture of galoshes, and about distant parts of the Russian empire, Samara, Georgia and so on, as they plodded through slush and fog.

For the roads were really hardly passable. They streamed with water and reeked with mist. The Hofrat, indeed, said it was not mist, only cloud; but in Hans Castorp's judgment this was quibbling. The spring fought out a bitter struggle, with a hundred setbacks into the depth of winter; the battle lasted months long, well into June. There were times in March when the heat was almost unendurable, as one lay, in the lightest of clothing, in the reclining--chair on the balcony, with the little parasol erected against the sun. In those days some of the ladies plumped for summer, and arrayed themselves in muslins for early breakfast—-excusably, perhaps, in view of the singularity of the climate up here, which was favourable to illusion on the score of weather, jumbling, as it did, all the seasons together. Yet their forehandedness was but short--sightedness after all, showing paucity of imagination, the stupidity which cannot conceive anything beyond the present moment; even more was it an avidity for change, a time--devouring restlessness and impatience. It was March by the calendar, therefore it was spring, which meant as good as summer; and they pulled out their summer clothes, to appear in them before autumn should overtake them. Which, in fact, it did. With April, cold, wet, cloudy weather set in. A long spell of rain turned at length into flurries of fresh snow. Fingers were stiff in the loggia, both camel's--hair rugs were called into service, it did not lack much of putting the fur sleeping--sack in requisition anew; the management brought itself to turn on the heat, and on all hands were heard bitter complainings—-the spring had betrayed them. Toward the end of the month the valley lay deep in snow; but then it thawed, just as certain experienced or weather--sensitive among the guests had prophesied it would: Frau Stöhr, the ivory Levi, but equally the Widow Hessenfeld, smelt and felt it simultaneously, before ever the smallest little cloud showed itself over the top of the granite formation to the south. Frau Hessenfeld got colic, Fräulein Levi became bedridden, and Frau Stöhr, drawing back her lips from her ratlike teeth with the churlish expression she had, daily and hourly gave utterance to her superstitious fear of a hæmorrhage—-for it was common talk that the thaw brought them about, or at least favoured them. It became unbelievably warm. The heat was turned off, balcony doors were left open all night, and still it was over fifty degrees in the morning. The snow melted apace, it turned grey, became porous and saturated; the drifts shrank together, and seemed to sink into the earth. There was a gurgling, a trickling and oozing, all abroad. The trees dripped, their masses of snow slid off; the shovelled--up barricades in the streets, the pallid layers carpeting the meadows, disappeared alike, though not all at once, they had lain too heavy for that. Then what lovely apparitions of the springtime revealed themselves! It was unheard--of, fairylike. There lay the broad meadows, with the coneshaped summit of the Schwarzhorn towering in the background, still in snow, and close in on the right the snow--buried Skaletta glacier. The common scene of pasture and hayrick was still snow--clad, though with a thin and scanty coat, that everywhere showed bare patches of dark earth or dry grass sucking through. Yet after all, the cousins found, what a curious sort of snow it was! Thick in the distance, next the wooded slopes, but in the foreground a mere sprinkling at most; the stretches of discoloured and winter--killed grass were dappled or sprigged with white. They looked closer, they bent down surprised——it was not snow, it was flowers: snow--flowers, a snow of flowers, short--stemmed chalices of white and palest blue. They were crocuses, no less; sprung by millions from the soggy meadow--bottom, and so thick that one actually confused them with the snow into which they merged.

The cousins smiled at the deception, and for joy at the wonder before their eyes——at this timorous and lovely assumption of protective coloration, as it were, on the part of these first shy returning motions of organic life. They picked some of the flowers, studied the structure of their charming cups, and stuck them in their buttonholes; wore them home and put them in glasses on their stands; for the deathly torpor of the winter had lasted long indeed——however short it had seemed.

But that flowery snow was soon covered with real; even the blue soldanellas and red and yellow primroses that followed on suffered the same fate. What a fight that was, spring had to wage up here, before it finally conquered! It was flung back ten times before it could get a foothold——back to the next onset of winter, with icy wind, flurries of snow, and a heated house. At the beginning of May——for while we have been talking of crocuses, April has merged into May——it was real torture to write even so much as a postcard while sitting in the loggia, the fingers so stiffened in the raw, Novemberish air.

The four or five shade--trees in the Platz were as bare as they would be in a valley January. It rained days on end, a whole week. Only the compensating excellence of the type of reclining--chair in use up here could render tolerable the ordeal of lying hours with wet and stiffened face, out here in the reeking mist. Yet all the while, in secret, it was a spring rain that fell; and more and more, the longer it lasted, did it betray itself as such. Under it the snow melted quite away, there was no more white, only here and there a vestige of dirty grey——and now, at long last, the meadows began to green!

What a joy that was, what a boon to the eyes, after so much white! But there was another green, surpassing in its tender softness even the hue of the new grass, and that was the green of young larch buds. Hans Castorp could seldom refrain from caressing them with his hand, or stroking his cheeks with them as he went on his walks—-their softness and freshness were irresistible. "It almost tempts one to be a botanist," he said to his companion. "It's a fact, I could almost wish to be a natural scientist, out of sheer joy at the reawakening of nature, after a winter like this up here. That's gentian, man, that you see up there on the cliffs; and this is a sort of little yellow violet——something I'm not familiar with. And this is ranunculus, they look just the same down below, the natural order *Ranunculaceæ*: compound, I remember, a particularly charming plant, androgynous, you can see a lot of stamens and pistils, an androecium and a gynaeceum, if I remember rightly. I really must root out some old volume of botany or other, and polish up my knowledge in this field.——My hat, how gay it's getting to look in the world!"

"It will be even more so in June," Joachim said. "The flowering--time in these parts is famous. But I hardly think I'll be here for it.—-That's probably from Krokowski, that you get the idea of studying botany?"

Krokowski? What made him say that? Oh, very likely because Dr. Krokowski had been uttering himself botanically in one of his lectures of late. Yes, we shall be in error if we assume that because time has brought about many changes at the Berghof, Dr. Krokowski no longer delivers his lectures. He delivers them as before, one every two weeks, in a frock--coat, though no longer in sandals, for those he wears only in the summer, and soon will be donning them again: delivers them every second Monday, in the dining--room, as on that far--off day when Hans Castorp returned late and bloodbespattered from his walk. For three--quarters of a year now had the analyst held forth on the subject of love and disease. Never much at one time, in little chats, from half to three--quarters of an hour long, he had dealt out the treasures of his intellect; and one received the impression that he need never leave off, that he could as well go on for ever. It was a sort of half--monthly Thousand and One Nights' Entertainment, spinning itself out at will, calculated, like the stories of Scheherazade, to gratify the curiosity of a prince, and turn away his wrath. Dr. Krokowski's theme, in its untrammelled scope, reminded one, indeed, of the undertaking to which Settembrini had vowed himself, the Encyclopædia of Suffering. And the extent to which it offered points of departure could be seen from the circumstance that the lecturer had lately talked about botany——to be precise, about mushrooms. But he had perhaps slightly changed his theme by now. He was at present discussing love and death; finding occasion for observations in part subtly poetic in their nature, in part ruthlessly scientific. And thus it was, in this connexion, that the learned gentlemen, speaking with his drawling, typically Eastern cadence, and his softly mouthed *r*, came upon the subject of botany; that is to say, upon the subject of mushrooms. These creatures of the shade, luxuriant and anomalous forms of organic life, were fleshly by nature, and closely related to the animal kingdom. The products of animal metabolism, such as albumen, glycogen, animal starch, in short, were present in them. And Dr. Krokowski went on to speak of a mushroom, famous in classical antiquity and since, on account of its form and the powers ascribed to it——a fungus in whose Latin name the epithet *impudicus* occurred; and which in its form was suggestive of love, in its odour of death. For it was a striking fact that the odour of the *Impudicus* was that of animal decay: it gave out that odour when the viscous, greenish, spore--bearing fluid dripped from its bell-

-shaped top. Yet even to--day, among the ignorant, the mushroom passed for an aphrodisiac. All that, Lawyer Paravant found, had been a bit strong for the ladies. He was still here, having hearkened to the Hofrat's propaganda, and stuck out the melting season. Likewise Frau Stöhr, who had shown strength of character and set her face against every temptation to unlawful departure, expressed herself at table to the effect that Krokowski had been positively "obscure" to--day, with his classical mushroom. She had actually said obscure, the poor creature, and gone on making one howler after another.

But what surprised Hans Castorp was that his cousin should have mentioned Dr. Krokowski and his botanical allusions; for the psycho--analyst had been as little referred to between them as Clavdia Chauchat or Marusja. By common consent they had passed over his ways and works in silence. But now Joachim had mentioned him---though in an irritable tone. His saying, too, that he would not be here for the flowering season had sounded very much out of sorts. Good Cousin Joachim seemed on the way to losing his equilibrium. His voice vibrated with irritation when he talked, and the old gentleness and moderation were of the past. Was it that he missed the orange perfume? Did the way they put him off with his Gaffky number drive him to the verge of despair? Or was he of more than one mind whether he should await the autumn up here or resolve on unlawful departure?

In reality it was something besides all these that had given the shade of vexation to Joachim's voice and made him mention the recent botanical lecture with contempt. Hans Castorp did not know this---or rather, he did not know that Joachim knew it; as for himself, he knew it well enough, did this venturesome spirit, this delicate nursling of life, this schoolmaster's plague! In a word, Joachim had caught his cousin at his tricks again, had found him out in another species of disloyalty, not so unlike the one he had been guilty of on the evening of carnival, only possessed of a still keener point in the circumstance that of this one he made a practice. In the rhythmic monotony of time's flow, in the well--nigh minute articulation of the normal day—-that day which was ever, even unto confusion and distraction, the same day, an abiding eternity, so that it was hard to say how it ever managed to bring forth any change—-in the inviolable, unbreachable regimen, we say, of that normal day, Dr. Krokowski's routine of visits took him, as of yore, through all the rooms, or rather through all the balconies, from chair to reclining--chair, between half past three and four in the afternoon. How often had the normal day of the Berghof renewed itself, since the faroff time when Hans Castorp lay and grumbled within himself because Dr. Krokowski described an arc about him and left him on one side! The guest of that day had long become the comrade—-Dr. Krokowski often thus addressed him when he made his rounds; and if, as Hans Castorp said to Joachim, the military associations of the word, with the exotic pronunciation of the *r*, sounded singularly inappropriate in his mouth, yet the word itself did not go so badly with his robust and hearty, confidence--inviting manner. But that again, in its turn, was belied by his blackness and pallor, so that some aura of the questionable always hung about the man.

"Well, comrade, and how goes it?" the doctor said, as, coming from the barbarian Russians, he approached the head end of Hans Castorp's reclining--chair. The patient, hands folded on his chest, smiled daily at the blithe address, smiled with a friendly, albeit rather harassed mien, watching the doctor's yellow teeth, that were visible through his beard. "Slept right well, did you?" Dr. Krokowski would go on. "Curve going down? Up, eh? Never mind, it will be all right before you come to get married. Good day to you." And he would go on into Joachim's balcony. For these afternoon rounds were merely a *coup d'œil*, no more.

But once in a way he would stop rather longer, standing there broad--shouldered and sturdy, ever with his manly smile, chatting with the comrade of this and that: the weather, the various departures and new arrivals, the mood the patient was in, whether good or bad; sometimes about his personal affairs, origin and prospects—-before he uttered the formula: "Good day to you" and passed on. Hans

Castorp would shift his hands to behind his head, and reply to all he was asked, smiling in his turn. He experienced a penetrating sense of uncanniness, yes, but he answered. They spoke in low tones, so that Joachim, despite the fact that the glass partition only half separated them, could not make out what they said—indeed, made not the slightest effort to do so. He heard his cousin get up from his chair and go indoors, probably to show the doctor his curve; and the conversation seemed to be further prolonged inside the chamber, to judge from the length of time before the Assistant appeared, this time from the inside, through his room.

What did the comrades talk about? Joachim never put the question. But if one of us were to do so, an answer in general terms might be forthcoming, as that there is much matter for an exchange of views, between two comrades and fellow--men when they possess ideas in common, and one of them has arrived at the point of conceiving the material universe in the light of a downfall of the spirit, a morbid growth upon it, while the other, as physician, is wont to treat of the secondary character of organic disease. Yes, there was, we should say, much to talk about, much to say on the subject of the material as the dishonourable decay of the immaterial, of life as the impudicity of substance, or disease as an impure manifestation of life. With the current lectures for background, the conversation might swing from the subject of love as a force making for disease, from the supersensory nature of the indications, to "old" and "fresh" infected areas, to soluble toxins and love potions, to the illumination of the unconscious, to the blessings of psycho--analysis, the transference of symptoms—in short, how can we know what all they talked about, Dr. Krokowski and young Castorp, when all these are merely guesses and suppositions thrown out in response to a hypothetic question!

In any case, they talked no longer; it had lasted only a few weeks. Of late the Assistant spent no more time with this particular patient than with the others, but confined himself chiefly to the "Well, comrade?" and "Good day to you," on his rounds. But now Joachim had made another discovery, he had fathomed the duplicity of his cousin—without, be it said, any faintest intention of so doing, without having bent his military honour to the office of spy. It happened quite simply that he had been summoned, one Wednesday, from the first rest period, to go down to the basement and be weighed by the bathing--master. He came down the clean linoleum--covered steps that faced the consulting--room door, with the x--ray cabinets on either side: on the left the organic, on the right, round the corner and one step lower down, the analytic, with Dr. Krokowski's visiting--card tacked on the door. Joachim paused halfway down the stair, as he saw his cousin coming from the consulting--room, where he had just had an injection. He stepped hastily through the door, closed it with both hands, and without looking round, turned toward the door which had the card fastened on it with drawing--pins. He reached it with a few noiseless, crouching steps, knocked, bent to listen, with his head close to the tapping finger. And as the "Come in" in an exotic baritone sounded on the other side, Joachim saw his cousin disappear into the half--darkness of Dr. Krokowski's analytic lair.

A New--Comer

Long days—-the longest, objectively speaking, and with reference to the hours of daylight they contained; since their astronomical length could not affect the swift passage of them, either taken singly or in their monotonous general flow. The vernal equinox lay three months back, the solstice was at hand. But the seasons up here followed the calendar with halting steps, and only within the last few days had spring fairly arrived: a spring still without hint of summer's denser air, rarefied, ethereal, and balmy, with the sun sending silvery gleams from a blue heaven, and the meadows blithe with parti--coloured flowers.

Hans Castorp found bluebells and yarrow on the hill--side, like the ones Joachim had put in his room to greet him when he came; and seeing them, realized how the year was rounding out. Those others had been the late blossoms of the declining summer; whereas now the tender emerald grass of the sloping meadows was thick--starred with

every sort of bloom, cup--shaped, bell--shaped, star--shaped, any-
-shaped, filling the sunny air with warm spice and scent: quantities of
wild pansies and fly--bane, daisies, red and yellow primulas, larger
and finer than any Hans Castorp had ever seen down below, so far as
he could recall noticing, and the nodding soldanella, peculiar to the
region, with its little eye--lashed bells of rose--colour, purple, and
blue.

Hans Castorp gathered a bunch of all this loveliness and took it to
his room; by no means with the idea of decoration, but of set and
serious scientific intent. He had assembled an apparatus to serve his
need: a botanical text--book, a handy little trowel to take up roots, a
herbarium, a powerful pocket--lens. The young man set to work in his
loggia, clad in one of the light summer suits he had brought up with
him when he came—-another sign that his first year was rounding
out its course.

Fresh--cut flowers stood about in glasses within his room, and on
the lamp--stand beside his highly superior chair. Flowers half faded,
wilted but not dry, lay scattered on the floor of the loggia and on the
balustrade; others, between sheets of blottingpaper, were giving out
their moisture under pressure from heavy stones. When they were
quite dry and flat, he would stick them with strips of paper into his
album. He lay with his knees up, one crossed over the other, the
manual open face down upon his chest like a little gabled roof;
holding the thick bevelled lens between his honest blue eyes and a
blossom in his other hand, from which he had cut away with his
pocketknife a part of the corolla, in order the better to examine the
thalamus—-what a great fleshy lump it looked through the powerful
lens! The anthers shook out their yellow pollen on the thalamus from
the tips of their filaments, the pitted pistil stood stiffly up from the
ovaries; when Hans Castorp cut through it longitudinally, he could
see the narrow channel through which the pollen grains and utricles
were floated by the nectar secretion into the ovarian cavity. Hans
Castorp counted, tested, compared; he studied the structure and
grouping of calyx and petals as well as the male and female organs;

compared what he found with the sketches and diagrams in his book; and saw with satisfaction that these were accurate when tested by the structure of such plants as were known to him. Then he went on to those he had not known the names of, and by the help of his Linnæus established their class, group, order, species, family, and genus. As he had time at his disposal, he actually made some progress in botanical systematization on the basis of comparative morphology. Beneath each dried specimen in his herbarium he carefully inscribed in ornamental lettering the Latin name which a humanistic science had gallantly bestowed on it; added its distinguishing characteristics, and submitted the whole to the approval of the good Joachim, who was all admiration.

Evenings he gazed at the stars. He was seized with an interest in the passing year—he who had already spent some twenty--odd cycles upon this earth without ever troubling his head about it. If the writer has been driven to talk about the vernal equinox and suchlike, it is because these terms formed the present mental furniture of our hero, which he now loved to set out on all occasions, here too surprising his cousin by the fund of information at his command.

"The sun," he might begin, as they took their walks together, "will soon be entering the sign of the Crab. Do you know what that means? It is the first summer sign of the zodiac, you know. Then come Leo and Virgo, and then the autumn, the equinox, toward the end of September, when the rays of the sun fall vertically upon the equator again, as they did in March, when the sun was in the sign of the Ram."

"I regret to say it escaped my attention," Joachim said grumpily. "What is all that you are reeling off so glibly about the Ram and the zodiac?"

"Why, you know what the zodiac is—the primitive heavenly signs: Scorpio,

Sagittarius, Capricorn, Aquarius, and the rest. How can you help being interested in them? At least, you must know there are twelve of them, three for each season, the ascending and the declining year, the circle of constellations through which the sun passes. I think it's great. Imagine, they have been found employed as ceiling decoration in an Egyptian temple——and a temple of Aphrodite, to boot——not far from Thebes. They were known to the Chaldeans too, the Chaldeans, if you please, those Arabic--Semitic old necromancers, who were so well versed in astrology and soothsaying. They knew and studied the zone in the heavens through which the planets revolve; and they divided it into twelve signs by constellations, the *dodecatemoria*, just as they have been handed down to us. Magnificent, isn't it?

There's humanity for you!"

"You talk about humanity just like Settembrini."

"Yes——and yet not just the same either. You have to take humanity as it is; but even so I find it magnificent. I like to think about the Chaldeans when I lie and look at the planets they were familiar with——for, clever as they were, they did not know them all. But the ones they did not know I cannot see either. Uranus was only recently discovered, by means of the telescope——a hundred and twenty years ago."

"You call that recently?"

"I call it recently——with your kind permission——in comparison with the three thousand years since their time. But when I lie and look at the planets, even the three thousand years get to seem 'recently,' and I begin to think quite intimately of the Chaldeans, and how in their time they gazed at the stars and made verses on them——and all that is humanity too."

"I must say, you have very tall ideas in your head."

"You call them tall, and I call them intimate——it's all the same, whatever you like to call it. But when the sun enters Libra again, in about three months from now, the days will have shortened so much that day and night will be equal. The days keep on getting shorter until about Christmas--time, as you know. But now you must please bear in mind that, while the sun goes through the winter signs—-Capricorn, Aquarius, and Pisces—-the days are already getting longer! For then spring is on the way again—-the three--thousandth spring since the Chaldeans; and the days go on lengthening until we have come round the year, and summer begins again."

"Of course."

"No, not of course at all—-it is really all hocus--pocus. The days lengthen in the winter--time, and when the longest comes, the twenty--first of June, the beginning of summer, they begin to go downhill again, toward winter. You call that 'of course'; but if one once loses hold of the fact that it *is* of course, it is quite frightening, you feel like hanging on to something. It seems like a practical joke—-that spring begins at the beginning of winter, and autumn at the beginning of summer. You feel you're being fooled, led about in a circle, with your eye fixed on something that turns out to be a moving point. A moving point in a circle. For the circle consists of nothing but such transitional points without any extent whatever; the curvature is incommensurable, there is no duration of motion, and eternity turns out to be not 'straight ahead' but 'merry--go--round'!"

"For goodness' sake, stop!"

"The feast of the solstice—-midsummer night! Fires on the mountain--top, and ring--around--a--rosy about the leaping flames! I have never seen it; but they say our rude forefathers used thus to celebrate the first summer night, the night with which autumn begins, the very midday and zenith of the year, the point from which it goes downhill again: they danced and whirled and shouted and exulted—-and why, really, all that primitive exultation? Can you make it out? What were they so jolly about? Was it because from then on the world went down into the dark—-or perhaps because it had up till then gone uphill, and now the turning--point was reached, the fleeting moment of midsummer night and midsummer madness, the meeting--place of tears and laughter? I express it as it is, in the words that come to me. Tragic joy, triumphant sadness that was what made our ancestors leap and exult around the leaping flames: they did so as an act of homage to the madness of the circle, to an eternity without duration, in which everything recurs—-in sheer despair, if you like."

"But I don't like," growled Joachim. "Pray don't put it off on me. Pretty large concerns you occupy yourself with, nights when you do your cure."

"Yes, I'll admit you are more practically occupied with your Russian grammar. Why, man, you're bound to have perfect command of the language before long; and that will be a great advantage to you if there should be a war—-which God forbid."

"God forbid? You talk like a civilian. War is necessary. Without it, Moltke said, the world would soon go to pieces altogether it would rot."

"Yes, it has a tendency that way, I admit. And I'll go so far as to say," began Hans Castorp, and was about to return to the Chaldeans, who had carried on wars too, and conquered Babylonia, even if they were a Semitic people, which was almost the same as saying they were Jews—-when the cousins became simultaneously aware that two gentlemen, walking close in front of them, had been attracted by what they were saying and interrupted their own conversation to look around.

They were on the main street, between the Kurhaus and Hotel Belvedere, on their way back to the village. The valley was gay in its new spring dress, all bright and delicate colour. The air was superb. A symphony of scents from meadows full of flowers filled the pure, dry, lucent, sun--drenched air. They recognized Ludovico Settembrini, with a stranger; but it seemed as though he for his part either did not recognize them or did not care for a meeting, for he turned round again, quickened his step, and plunged into conversation, accompanied by his usual lively gestures. When the cousins came up on his right and gaily greeted him, he exclaimed: "*Sapristi!*" and "Well, well, well!" with every mark of delighted surprise; yet would have held back and let them pass on, but that they failed to grasp his intention——or else saw no sense in it. For Hans Castorp was genuinely pleased to see him thus, after a lapse of time: he stopped and warmly shook hands, asked how he did, and looked in polite expectation at his companion. Settembrini was thus driven to do what he obviously preferred not to do, but what seemed the only natural thing, under the circumstances: namely, to present them to each other, which he accordingly did, with much appropriate gesticulation, and the gentlemen shook hands, half standing, half walking on. It appeared that the stranger, who might be about Settembrini's age, was a housemate of his, the other tenant of Lukaçek the ladies' tailor. His name, so the young people understood, was Naphta. He was small and thin, clean--shaven, and of such piercing, one might almost say corrosive ugliness as fairly to astonish the cousins. Everything about him was sharp: the hooked nose dominating his face, the narrow, pursed mouth, the thick, bevelled lenses of his glasses in their light frame, behind which were a pair of pale--grey eyes——even the silence he preserved, which suggested that when he broke it, his speech would be incisive and logical. According to custom he was bare--headed and overcoatless—--and moreover very well dressed, in a dark--blue flannel suit with white stripes. Its quiet but modish cut was at once marked down by the cousins, whose worldly glances were met by their counterpart, only quicker and keener, from the little man's own side. Had Ludovico Settembrini not known how to wear with such easy dignity his threadbare pilot coat and check trousers, he must have suffered by contrast with his company. This happened the less in that the checks had been freshly pressed, doubtless by the hands of his landlord, and might, at a little distance, have been taken for new. The worldly and superior quality of the ugly stranger's tailoring made him stand nearer to the cousins than to Settembrini; yet it was not only his age which ranged him rather with the latter, but also a quite pronounced something else, most conveniently exemplified by the complexion of the four. For the two younger were brown and burnt, the two elder pale: Joachim's face had in the course of the winter turned an even deeper bronze, and Hans Castorp's glowed rosy red under his blond poll. But over Herr Settembrini's southern pallor, so well set off by his dark moustache, the sun's rays had no power; while his companion, though blond--haired——his hair was a metallic, colourless ashenblond, and he wore it smoothed back from a lofty brow straight over his whole head——also showed the dead--white complexion of the brunette races. Two out of the four——

Hans Castorp and Settembrini——carried walking--sticks; Joachim, as a military man, had none, and Naphta, after the introductions, clasped his hands again behind him. They, and his feet as well, were small and delicate, as befitted his build. He had a slight cold, and coughed unobtrusively.

Herr Settembrini at once and elegantly overcame the hint of embarrassment or vexation he had betrayed at first sight of the young people. He was in his gayest mood, and made all sorts of jesting allusions as he performed the introductions——for example, he called Naphta *"princeps scholasticorum."* Joy, he said, quoting Aretine, held brilliant court within his, Settembrini's, breast; a joy due to the blessing of the springtime——to which commend him. The gentlemen knew he had a certain grudge against life up here often enough he had railed against it!——All honour, then, to the mountain spring! It was enough of itself to atone for all the horrors of the place. All the disquieting, provocative elements of spring in the valley were here lacking: here were no seething depths, no steaming air, no oppressive humidity! Only dryness, clarity, a serene and piercing charm. It was after his own heart, it was superb. They were walking in an uneven row, four abreast whenever possible; when people came towards or passed them, Settembrini, on the right wing, had to walk in the road, or else their front for the moment broke up, and one or the other stepped back——either Hans Castorp, between the humanist and Cousin Joachim, or little Naphta on the left side. Naphta would give a short laugh, in a voice dulled by his cold: its quality in speaking was reminiscent of a cracked plate tapped on by the knuckle.

Indicating the Italian by a sidewise nod, he said, with a deliberate enunciation: "Hark to the Voltairian, the rationalist! He praises nature, because even when she has the chance she doesn't befog us with mystic vapours, but preserves a dry and classic clarity. And yet—-what is the Latin for humidity?"

"*Humor*," cried Settembrini, over his shoulder. "And the humour in the professor's nature--observations lies in the fact that like Saint Catherine of Siena he thinks of the wounds of Christ when he sees a red primula in the spring."

"That would be witty, rather than humorous," Naphta retorted. "But in either case a good spirit to import into nature; and one of which she stands in need."

"Nature," said Settembrini, in a lower voice, not so much over as along his shoulder, "needs no importations of yours. She is Spirit herself."

"Doesn't your monism rather bore you?"

"Ah, you confess, then, that it is simply to divert yourself that you wrench God and nature apart, and divide the world into two hostile camps?"

"I find it most interesting to hear you characterize as love of diversion what I mean when I say Passion and Spirit."

"And you, who put such large words to such empty uses, don't forget that you sometimes reproach me for being rhetorical."

"You will stick to it that Spirit implies frivolity. But it cannot help being what it is: dualistic. Dualism, antithesis, is the moving, the passionate, the dialectic principle of all Spirit. To see the world as cleft into two opposing poles—that is Spirit. All monism is tedious. *Solet Aristoteles quærere pugnam.*"

"Aristotle? Didn't Aristotle place in the individual the reality of universal ideas?

That is pantheism."

"Wrong. When you postulate independent being for individuals, when you transfer the essence of things from the universal to the particular phenomenon, which Thomas Aquinas and Bonaventura, as good Aristotelians, did, then you destroy all unity between the world and the Highest Idea; you place the world outside of God and make God transcendent. That, my dear sir, is classic mediævalism."

"Classic medievalism! What a phrase!"

"Pardon me, I merely apply the concept of the classic where it is in place: that is to say, wherever an idea reaches its culmination. Antiquity was not always classic. And I note in you a general repugnance to the Absolute; to the broader application of categories. You don't even want absolute Spirit. You only want to have Spirit synonymous with democratic progress."

"I should hope we are at one in the conviction that Spirit, however absolute, ought never to become the advocate of reaction."

"Yet you are always claiming it as the advocate of freedom!"

"Why do you say 'yet'? Is it freedom that is the law of love of one's kind, or is it nihilism and all uncharitableness?"

"At any rate, it is the last two of which you are so obviously afraid."

Settembrini flung up his arm. The skirmish broke off. Joachim looked bewildered from one to the other, and Hans Castorp with lifted brows stared at the path before him. Naphta had spoken sharply and apodictically; yet he had been the one to defend the broader conception of freedom. He had a way of saying "Wrong!" with a ringing nasal sound, and then clipping his lips tightly together over it—the effect was not ingratiating. Settembrini had countered for the most part lightly, yet with a fine warmth in his tone, as when he urged their essential agreement upon certain fundamental points. He now began, as Naphta did not speak again, to gratify the natural curiosity of the young people about the new-comer—some sort of explanation being obviously their due after the dialogue just ended.

[472]

Naphta passively let him go on, without heeding. He was, so Settembrini said, professor of ancient languages in the Fridericianum—-bringing out the title with pompous emphasis, as Italians do. His lot was the same as the speaker's own: that is, he had been driven to the conclusion that his stay would be a long one, and had left the sanatorium for private quarters under the roof of Lukaçek the ladies' tailor. The high school of the resort had cannily secured the services of this distinguished Latinist—the pupil of a religious house, as Settembrini father vaguely expressed it—-and it went without saying that he was an adornment to his position. In short, Settembrini extolled the ugly Naphta not a little, regardless of the abstract disputation they had just had, which now, it seemed, was to be resumed.

Settembrini went on to explain the cousins to Herr Naphta, whereby it came out that he had already spoken of them. Here, he said, was the young engineer who had come up on three weeks' leave, only to have Herr Hofrat Behrens find a moist place in his lung; and here was that hope of the Prussian army organization, Lieutenant Ziemssen. He spoke of Joachim's revolt and intended departure, and added that one must not insult the Engineer by imputing to him any less zealous desire to return to his interrupted labours.

Naphta made a wry face.

"The gentlemen have an eloquent advocate. Far be it from me to question the accuracy of his interpretation of your thoughts and wishes. Work, work—why, he would call me nothing less than an enemy of mankind— *inimicus humanæ naturæ*— if I dared suggest that there have been times when talk in that vein would utterly fail to produce the desired effect: times when the precise opposite to his ideal was held in incomparably higher esteem. Bernard of Clairvaux, for instance, preached an order of progress towards perfection quite different from any Signor Ludovico ever dreamed of. Would you like to hear what it was? His lowest stage was in the 'mill,' the second on the 'ploughed field,' the third, and most commendable—-don't listen,

Settembrini!—-was upon 'the bed of repose.' The mill was the symbol of earthly life—-not a bad figure. The ploughed field represented the soul of the layman, the scene of the labours of priest and teacher. This was a stage higher than the mill. But the bed—-"

"That will do, we understand," cried Settembrini. "Sirs, is he going to expatiate now upon the purpose and uses of the 'lewd day--bed'?"

"I did not know, Ludovico, that you were a prude. To see you looking at the girls ... What has become of your pagan single--mindedness? I continue: the bed is the place of intercourse between the wooing and the wooed: symbolically, it typifies devotional retirement from the world for the purpose of contact with God."

"Fie! *Andate, andate!*" the Italian fended him off, in a voice almost tearful. They all laughed. But Settembrini went on, with dignity: "No, no, I am a European, an Occidental, whereas the order of progress you describe is purely Eastern. The Orient abhors activity. Lao--Tse taught that inaction is more profitable than anything else between heaven and earth. When all mankind shall have ceased to do anything whatever, then only will perfect repose and bliss reign upon this earth. There you have your intercourse with God."

"Oh, indeed! And what about Western mysticism—-and what about quietism, a religion that numbers Fénelon among its disciples? Fénelon taught that every action is faulty, since every will to act is an insult to God, who wills to act alone. I cite the propositions of Molinos. There is no doubt that the spiritual possibility of finding salvation in repose has been disseminated pretty generally all over the world."

Here Hans Castorp put in his word. With the courage of simplicity he mixed in the debate, and, gazing into space, delivered himself thus: "Devotion, retirement—-there is something in it, it sounds reasonable. We practise a pretty high degree of retirement from the world, we up here. No doubt about it. Five thousand feet up, we lie in these excellent chairs of ours, contemplating the world and all that therein is, and having our thoughts about it. The more I think of it, the surer I am that the bed of repose——by which I mean my deck--chair, of course——has given me more food for thought in these ten months than the mill down in the flat--land in all the years before. There's simply no denying it."

Settembrini looked at him, a melancholy gleam in his dark eye. "Engineer!" he said, restrainingly. He took Hans Castorp's arm and drew him a little aside, as though to speak to him in private "How often have I told you that one must realize what one is and think accordingly! Never mind the propositions. Our Western heritage is reason——reason, analysis, action, progress: these, and not the slothful bed of monkish tradition!"

Naphta had been listening. He turned his head to say, "Monkish tradition! As if we did not owe to the monks the culture of the soil of all Europe! As if it were not due to them that Germany, France and Italy yield us corn and wine and fruit to--day, instead of being covered with primeval forest and swamp! The monks, my dear sir were hard workers——"

"*Ebbè!* Well, then!"

"Certainly against his intentions, at least. What I am calling your attention to is nothing less than the distinction between the utilitarian and the humane."

"And what I am calling your attention to is the fact, which I observe with indignation, that you are still dividing the world up into opposing factions."

"I grieve to have incurred your displeasure. Yet it is needful to make distinctions, and to preserve the conception of the *Homo Dei*, free from contaminating constituents. It was you Italians that invented banking and exchange, which may God forgive you! But the English invented the economic social theory, and the genius of humanity can never forgive them that."

"Ah, the genius of humanity was alive in that island's great economic thinkers too!——You wanted to say something Engineer?"

Hans Castorp demurred—-yet said something anyhow, Naphta as well as Settembrini listening with a certain suspense: "From what you say, Herr Naphta, you must sympathize with my cousin's profession, and understand his impatience to be at it. As for me I am an out--and--out civilian, my cousin often reproaches me with it. I have never seen service; I am a child of peace, pure and simple, and have even sometimes thought of becoming a clergyman—-ask my cousin if I haven't said as much to him many a time! But for all that, and aside from my personal inclinations—-or even, perhaps, not altogether aside from them—-I have some understanding and sympathy for a military life. It has such an infernally serious side to it, sort of ascetic, as you say—-that was the expression you used, wasn't it? The military always has to reckon on coming to grip with death, just as the clergy has. That is why there is so much discipline and decorum and regularity in the army, so much 'Spanish etiquette,' if I may say so; and it makes no great difference whether one wears a uniform collar or a starched ruff, the main thing is the asceticism, as you so beautifully said.—-I don't know if I've succeeded in making my train of thought quite—-"

"Oh, quite," said Naphta, and flung a glance at Settembrini, who was twirling his cane and looking up at the sky.

"And that," went on Hans Castorp, "is why I thought you must have great sympathy with the feelings of my cousin Ziemssen. I am not thinking of 'Church and King' and suchlike associations of ideas, that a lot of perfectly well--meaning and conventional people stand for. What I mean is that service in the army—-service is the right word—-isn't performed for commercial advantage, nor for the sake of the economic doctrine of society, as you call it—-and that must be the reason why the English have such a small army, a few for India, and a few at home for reviews—-"

"It is useless for you to go on, Engineer," Settembrini interrupted him. "The soldier's existence—-I say this without intending the slightest offence to Lieutenant Ziemssen—-cannot be cited in the argument, for the reason that, as an existence, it is purely formal—-in and for itself entirely without content. Its typical representative is the infantry soldier, who hires himself out for this or that campaign. Take the soldiers of the Spanish Counter--Reformation, for instance, or of the various revolutionary armies, the Napoleonic or Garibaldian—-or take the Prussian. I will be ready to talk about the soldier when I know what he is fighting *for*."

"But that he does fight," rejoined Naphta, "remains the distinctive feature of his existence as a soldier. Let us agree so far. It may not be enough of a distinction to permit of his being 'cited in the argument'; but even so, it puts him in a sphere remote from the comprehension of your civilian, with his bourgeois acceptation of life."

"What you are pleased to call the bourgeois acceptation of life," retorted Settembrini, speaking rather tight--lipped, with the corners of his mouth drawn back beneath the waving moustache, while his neck screwed up and around out of his collar with fantastic effect, "will always be ready to enter the lists on any terms you like, for reason and morality, and for their legitimate influence upon young and wavering minds."

A silence followed. The young people stared ahead of them, embarrassed. After a few paces, Settembrini said—-having brought his head and neck to a natural posture once more: "You must not be surprised to hear this gentleman and me indulging in long disputations. We do it in all friendliness, and on a basis of considerable mutual understanding."

That had a good effect—it was human and gallant of Herr Settembrini. But then Joachim, meaning well in his turn, and thinking to carry forward the conversation within harmless channels, was fated to say: "We happened to be talking about war, my cousin and I, as we came up behind you."

"I heard you," Naphta answered. "I caught your words and turned round. Were you talking politics, discussing the world situation?"

"Oh, no," laughed Hans Castorp. "How should we come to be doing that? For my cousin here, it would be unprofessional to discuss politics; and as for me, I willingly forgo the privilege. I don't know anything about it——I haven't had a newspaper in my hand since I came."

Settembrini, as once before, found this reprehensible. He proceeded to show himself immensely well informed upon current events, and gave his approval to the state of world affairs, in so far as they were running a course favourable to the progress of civilization. The European atmosphere was full of pacific thought and plans for disarmament. The democratic idea was on the march. He said he had it on reliable authority that the "Young Turks" were about to abandon their revolutionary undertakings. Turkey as a national, constitutional state——what a triumph for humanity!

"Liberalization of Islam," Naphta scoffed. "Capital! enlightened fanaticism——oh, very good indeed! And of interest to you too," he said, turning to Joachim. "Because when Abdul Hamid falls, then there will be an end of your influence in Turkey, and England will set herself up as protector.——You must always give full weight to the information you get from our friend Settembrini," he said to both cousins——and this too sounded almost insolent: as though he thought they would be inclined to take Settembrini lightly. "On national--revolutionary matters he is very well informed. In his country they cultivate good relations with the English Balkan Committee. But what is to become of the Reval agreement, Ludovico, if your progressive Turks are successful? Edward VII will no longer be able to give the Russians free access to the Dardanelles; and if Austria pulls herself together to pursue an active policy in the Balkans, why——-"

"Oh, you, with your Cassandra prophecies!" Settembrini parried. "Nicholas is a lover of peace. We owe him the Hague conferences, which will always be moral events of the first order."

"Yes, Russia must give herself time to recover from her little mishap in the East."

"Fie, sir! Why should you scoff at human nature's yearning for social amelioration?

A people that thwarts such aspirations exposes itself to moral obloquy. '

"But what is politics for, then, if not to give both sides a chance to compromise themselves in turn?"

"Are you espousing the cause of Pan--Germanism?"

Naphta shrugged his shoulders, which were not quite even—-in fact, to add to his ugliness, he was probably a little warped. He disdained to reply, and Settembrini pronounced judgment: "At all events, what you say is cynical. You see nothing but political trickery in the lofty exertions of democracy to fulfil itself internationally—-"

"Where you would like me to see idealism or even religiosity. What I *do* see is the last feeble stirrings of the instinct of self--preservation, the last remnant at the command of a condemned world--system. The catastrophe will and must come—-it advances on every hand and in every way. Take the British policy. England's need to secure the Indian glacis is legitimate. But what will be the consequences of it? Edward knows as well as you and I that Russia has to make good her losses in Manchuria, and that internal peace is as necessary to her as daily bread. Yet—-he probably can't help himself—-he forces her to look westward for expansion, stirs up slumbering rivalries between St. Petersburg and Vienna—-"

"Oh, Vienna! Your interest in that ancient obstruction is due, I presume, to the fact that her decaying empire is a sort of mummy, as it were, of the Holy Roman Empire of the German people."

"While you, I suppose, are Russophil out of humanistic affinity with Cæsaropapism.

"Democracy, my friend, has more to hope from the Kremlin than she has from the Hofburg; and it is disgraceful for the country of Luther and Gutenberg——"

"It is probably not only disgraceful, but stupid into the bargain. But even this stupidity is an instrument of fate——"

"Oh, spare me your talk about fate! Human reason needs only to will more strongly than fate, and she *is* fate!"

"One always wills one's fate. Capitalistic Europe is willing hers."

"One believes in the coming of war if one does not sufficiently abhor it."

"Your abhorrence of war is logically disjointed if you do not make the state itself your point of departure."

"The national state is the temporal principle, which you would like to ascribe to the evil one. But when nations are free and equal, when the small and weak are safeguarded from aggression, when there is justice in the world, and national boundaries——"

"Yes, I know, the Brenner frontier. The liquidation of Austria. If I only knew how you expect to bring that about without war!"

"And I should like to know when I ever condemned a war for the purpose of realizing national aspirations!"

"But you say——"

"No, here I must really corroborate Herr Settembrini," Hans Castorp mixed in the dispute, which he had been following as they went, regarding attentively each speaker in turn, with his head on one side. "My cousin and I have had the privilege of frequent conversations with him on this and kindred subjects——what it amounted to, of course, was that we listened while he explained and developed his views——so I can vouch for the fact, and my cousin here will confirm me, that Herr Settembrini spoke more than once, with great enthusiasm, of the revolutionary principle, and about rebellion and reform——which is no very peaceful principle, I should think——

-and of the mighty efforts still to be made before it triumphs everywhere, and the great universal worldrepublic can come into being. Those were his words, though of course it sounded much more plastic and literary as he said it. But the part I have the most exact memory of, and have retained quite literally, because being a thorough--going civilian I found it quite alarming, was that he said the day would come, if not on the wings of doves, then on the pinions of eagles——it was the eagles' pinions I was startled at——and that Vienna must be brought low before peace and prosperity could ensue. So it is not possible to say that Herr Settembrini condemned war as such. Am I right, Herr Settembrini?"

"More or less," said the Italian shortly, twirling his cane, with averted head.

"Too bad," Naphta smiled maliciously. "There you are, convicted of warlike inclinations out of the mouth of your own pupil. '*Assument pennas ut aqailæ*' ——"

"Voltaire himself approved of a war for civilization, and advised Frederick to fight Turkey."

"Instead of which, he allied himself with her——he he! And then the world--republic!

I refrain from asking what becomes of the principle of revolt when peace and prosperity have once been brought about. For it is plain that from that moment rebellion becomes a crime——"

"You know quite well, as do these young men here, that we are dealing with a progress in human affairs conceived of as endless."

"But all motion is in circles," said Hans Castorp. "In space and time, as we learn from the law of periodicity and the conservation of mass. My cousin and I were talking about it lately. How then can progress be conceived of, in closed motion without constant direction? When I lie in the evening and look at the zodiac—that is, the half of it that is visible to us——and think about the wise men of antiquity——"

"You ought not to brood and dream, Engineer," Settembrini interrupted him. "You must resolve to trust to the instincts of your youth and your blood, urging you in the direction of action. And also your training in natural science is bound to link you to progressive ideas. You see, through the space of countless ages, life developing from infusorium up to man: how can you doubt, then, that man has yet before him endless possibilities of development? And in the sphere of the higher mathematics, if you would rest your case thereon, then follow your cycle from perfection to perfection, and, from the teaching of our eighteenth century, learn that man was originally good, happy, and without sin, that social errors have corrupted and perverted him, and that he can and will once more become good, happy, and sinless, by dint of labour upon his social structure—-"

"Herr Settembrini has omitted to add," broke in Naphta, "that the Rousseauian idyll is a sophisticated transmogrification of the Church's doctrine of man's original free and sinless state, his primal nearness and filial relation to God; to which state he must finally return. But the re--establishment of the City of God, after the dissolution of all earthly forms, lies at the meeting--place of the earthly and the heavenly, the material and the spiritual; redemption is transcendental—-and as for your capitalistic worldrepublic, my dear Doctor, it is odd in this connexion to hear you talking about instinct. The instinctive is entirely on the side of the national. God Himself has implanted in men's breasts the instinct which bids them separate into states. War—-"

"War," echoed Settembrini, "war, my dear sir, has been forced before now to serve the cause of progress; as you will grant if you will recall certain events in the history of your favourite epoch—-I mean the period of the Crusades. These wars for civilization stimulated economic and commercial relations between peoples, and united Western humanity in the name of an idea."

"And how tolerant you always are towards an idea! I would the more courteously remind you that the effect of the Crusades and the economic relations they stimulated was anything but favourable to internationalism. On the contrary, they taught the peoples to become conscious of themselves, and thus furthered the development of the national idea."

"Right; that is to say, right in so far as it was a question of the relation between the peoples and the priesthood; for it was indeed at that time that the mounting consciousness of national honour began to harden itself against hieratical presumption—-"

"Though what you call hieratical presumption is nothing else than the conception of human unity in the name of the Spirit!"

"We are familiar with that spirit—-and we have no great love for it."

"Your mania for nationalism obviously shrinks from the world--conquering cosmopolitanism of the Church. Still, I cannot see how you reconcile your nationalism with your horror of war. Because your obsolescent cult of the State must make you a champion of a positive conception of law, and as such—-"

"Oh, if we are talking about law—-the conceptions of natural law and universal human reason have survived, my dear sir, in inter-national law."

"Pshaw, your international law is only another Rousseauian transmogrification of the *ius divinum*, which has nothing in common with either nature or human reason, resting as it does upon revelation—-"

"Let us not quarrel over names, Professor! What I call natural and international law, you are free to call the *ius divinum*. The important thing is that above the explicit jurisprudence of national states there rises a higher jurisdiction, empowered to decide between conflicting interests by means of courts of arbitration."

"Courts of arbitration! The very name is idiotic! In a civil court, to pronounce upon matters of life and death, communicate the will of God to man, and decide the course of history!—-Well, so much for the 'wings of doves.' Now for the 'eagles' pinions'——what about them?"

"Civilian society——"

"Oh, society doesn't know what it wants. It shouts for a campaign against the fall in the birth--rate, it demands a reduction in the cost of bringing up children and training them to a profession——and meanwhile men are herded like cattle, and all the trades and professions are so overcrowded that the fight round the feeding--trough puts in the shade the horrors of past wars. Open spaces, garden cities! Strengthening the stock!

But why strengthen it, if civilization and progress have decided there shall be no more war? Whereas war would cure everything——it would 'strengthen the stock' and at the same time stop the decline in the birth--rate."

"You are joking, of course——you can't mean what you say. And our discussion comes to an end at the right moment, for here we are," Settembrini said, and pointed out to the cousins with his stick the cottage before whose gate they had paused. It stood near the beginning of the village: a modest structure, separated from the street by a narrow front garden. A wild grape--vine, springing from bare roots at the door, flung an arm along the ground--floor wall towards the display window of a tiny shop. The ground--floor, Settembrini explained, belonged to the chandler; Naphta was domiciled a floor higher up, with the tailor's shop, and his own quarters were in the roof, where he had a peaceful little study.

Naphta, with unexpectedly spontaneous cordiality, expressed the hope that he might have the pleasure of meeting them again. "Come and see us," he said. "I would say: 'Come and see me,' if Dr. Settembrini here had not prior claims upon your friendship. Come, however, as often as you like, whenever you feel you would like a talk. I prize highly an interchange of ideas with youth, and am perhaps not entirely without pedagogic tradition. Our Master of the Lodge here"——he nodded toward Settembrini——"would have it that the bourgeois humanism of the day has a monopoly of the pedagogic gift; but we must take issue with him. Until another time, then!"

Settembrini made difficulties——there *were* difficulties, he said. The days of the Lieutenant's sojourn up here were numbered; and as for the Engineer, he would doubtless redouble his zeal in the service of the cure, in order to follow his cousin down to the valley with all the speed he might.

Both young men assented in turn. They had bowed their acceptance of Herr Naphta's invitation, and next minute they also bowed their acknowledgment of the justice of Herr Settembrini's remarks. So everything was left open.

"What did he call him?" asked Joachim, as they climbed the winding path to the Berghof.

"I understood him to say 'Master of the Lodge,' " answered Hans Castorp. "I was just wondering about it. It was probably some joke or other, they have such odd names for each other. Settembrini called Naphta *'princeps scholasticorum'*—— not so bad, either. The schoolmen were the theologians of the Middle Ages, the dogmatic philosophers, if you like. They spoke several times of the Middle Ages; it reminded me of the first day I came, when Settembrini said there was a good deal up here that was mediæval—it was Adriatica von Mylendonk, her name, I mean, made him say so.——How did you like him?"

"Who? The little man? Not very much. Though he said some things I liked. That about courts of arbitration——they *are* nothing but canting hypocrisy, of course. But I did not care much for the man himself——a person may say as many good things as he likes, it doesn't matter to me, if he himself is a queer fish. And queer he is, you can't deny it. That stuff about the 'place of intercourse' was distinctly shady, not to mention anything else. And did you see the big Jewish nose he had? Nobody but Jews have such puny figures. Are you really thinking of visiting the man?"

"Visit him—of course we'll visit him," declared Hans Castorp. "When you talk about his being puny, that's only the military in you speaking. And as for his nose, the Chaldeans had the same kind, and they knew devilish well what they were about, on more subjects than alchemy. Naphta has something of the mystagogue about him, he interests me a good deal. I won't say that I make him out altogether, yet, but if we meet him often perhaps we shall; I don't think it at all unlikely we may learn something from the acquaintance with him."

"Oh, you, with your learning! Getting wiser all the time, with your biology, and your botany, and your continual changing from one idea to another! You began philosophizing about time the first day you came. But we didn't come up here to acquire wisdom. We came to acquire health, to get healthier and healthier until we are entirely well, and are free to quit, and go down below where we belong!"

" 'Of old sat Freedom on the heights,' " quoted Hans Castorp airily. "Tell me first what freedom is," he went on. "Naphta and Settembrini disputed over it a good deal without coming to any conclusion. Settembrini says it is the law of love of one's kind; that sounds like his ancestor, the Carbonaro. But however valiant he was, and however valiant our Settembrini himself is—-"

"Yes, he got uncomfortable when we talked about physical courage."

"I can't help thinking he would be afraid of things little Naphta wouldn't be, and that his freedom and his bravery are more or less folderol. Do you think he would have the courage '*de se perdre ou même se laisser dépérir*'?"

"Why do you suddenly begin talking French?"

"Oh, I don't know. The atmosphere up here is so international. I don't know which would find more pleasure in it—-Settembrini for the sake of his bourgeois worldrepublic, or Naphta for his hierarchical cosmopolis. As you see, I kept my ears open; but even so

I found it far from clear. On the contrary, the result was more confusion than anything else."

"It always is. You will find that when people discuss and express their views nothing ever comes of it but confusion worse confounded. I tell you, it doesn't matter in the least what a man's views are, so long as he is a decent chap. The best thing is to have no opinions, and just do one's duty."

"Yes, you can say that because you are a soldier, and your existence is purely formal. But it's different with me, I am a civilian, and more or less responsible. And I must say it's rather upsetting to have on the one hand a man preaching an international world--republic, and absolutely barring war, and yet so patriotic that he is for ever demanding the rectification of the Brenner frontier, to the point of fighting a war for civilization over it; and then on the other a little chap contending that every national state is an invention of the devil, and hurrahing for some universal unification he sees on the far horizon—-yet in the next minute justifying our national instincts and making awful fun of peace conferences. What a mix--up! By all means we must go visit him, and try to understand what it is all about. You say we did not come up here to get wiser, but healthier, and that is true. But all this confusion must be reconciled; and if you don't think so, why then you are dividing the world up into two hostile camps, which, I may tell you, is a grievous error, most reprehensible."

Of the City of God, and Deliverance by Evil

Hans Castorp was in his loggia, studying a plant which, now that the astronomical summer had begun, and the days were shortening, flourished luxuriantly in many places: the columbine or aquilegia, of the ranunculus family, which grew in clumps, with long stalks bearing the blue, violet, or reddish--brown blossoms, and spreading herbaceous foliage. They grew everywhere, but most profusely in that quiet bottom where, nearly a year ago, he had first seen them: that remote and wooded ravine, filled with the sound of rushing water, where on the bench above the footbridge, that ill--risked, ill--timed, ill--fated walk of his had ended. He revisited it now and again.

It was, if one began it a little less rashly than he had, no great distance thither. If you mounted the slope from the end of the sledge--run in the village, you could reach in some twenty minutes the picturesque spot where the wooden bridge of the path through the forest crossed above the run as it came down from the Schatzalp, provided you kept to the shortest route, did not loiter about, nor pause too long to get your breath. Hans Castorp, when Joachim was detained at home in the service of the cure, for some examination, blood--test, x--ray photography, weighing, or injection, would stroll thither in good weather, after second breakfast, or even after first; or he would employ the hours between tea and dinner in a visit to his favourite spot, to sit on the bench where once the violent nose--bleeding had overtaken him, to listen with bent head to the sound of the torrent and gaze at the secluded scene, with the hosts of blue aquilegias blooming in its depths.

Was it only for this he came? No, he sat there to be alone: to recall and go over in his mind the events and impressions of the past months. They were many, varied, and hard to classify; so interwoven and mingled they seemed, as almost to obscure any clear distinction between the concrete fact and the dreamed or imagined. But one and all, they had in their essence something fantastic, something which made his heart, unreliable as it had been from his first day up here, stand still when he thought of them, and then wildly flutter. Or could its flutterings be sufficiently accounted for by the reflection that a round year had gone by since first he sat here, that on this very spot whither once he had come in a condition of lowered vitality and seen the apparition of Pribislav Hippe, the aquilegias were blossoming anew?

Now, at least, on his bench by the rushing water, he had no more nose--bleeding——that was a thing of the past. Joachim had said from the very first that it was not easy to get acclimatized, and at the time of that earlier visit he was still finding it difficult. But he had made progress; and now, after eleven months, the process must be regarded as finished. More, in that direction, could not be expected. The chemistry of his digestion had adjusted itself, Maria had her ancient relish, his parched mucous membranes having sufficiently recovered to let him savour again the bouquet of that estimable brand of cigars. He still loyally ordered them from Bremen whenever his stock ran low, although the shop--windows of the international resort displayed attractive wares. Maria, he felt, made a sort of bond between him, the exile, and his home in the "flat--land"——a bond more effectual than the postcards he now and then sent to his uncle, the intervals between which grew longer in proportion as he imbibed the more spacious time conceptions prevalent "up here." He mostly sent picture postcards, as being pleasanter to receive, with charming views of the valley in winter and in summer dress. They gave precisely the room he needed to tell his kinsmen the latest news of his state, whatever had been let fall by the doctors after the monthly or general examination: such as that, both to sight and hearing, he had unmistakably improved, but was still not entirely free from infection; that his continued slight excess of temperature came from small infected areas which were certain to disappear without a trace if he had patience, and then he would never need to return hither. He well knew that long letters were neither asked nor expected, it being no humanistic or literary circle to which he addressed himself down there, and the replies he received were equally lacking in expansiveness. They merely accompanied the means of subsistence which came to him from home, the income from his paternal inheritance. Turned into Swiss currency, this was so advantageous that he had never spent one instalment when the next arrived, enclosed in a letter of a few typed lines signed "James Tienappel," conveying his greetings and best wishes for recovery, together with the same from Grand--uncle Tienappel and sometimes from the seafaring Peter as well.

The Hofrat, so Hans Castorp told his people, had latterly given up the injections: they did not suit the young patient. They gave him headache and fatigue, caused loss of appetite, reduced his weight, and, while making his temperature go up at first, had not succeeded in reducing it in the long run. His face glowed rosy--red with dry, internal heat, a sign that for this child of the lowland, bred in an atmosphere that rejoiced in a high degree of humidity, acclimatization could only consist in "getting used to not getting used to it"—-which, in fact, Rhadamanthus himself never did, being perpetually purple--cheeked. "Some people can't get used to it," Joachim had said; and this seemed to be Hans Castorp's case. For even that trembling of the neck, which had come upon him soon after his arrival here, had never quite passed off, but would attack him as he walked or talked—-yes, even up here in his blue--blossoming retreat, while he sat pondering the whole complex of his adventures; so that the dignified chin--support of Hans Lorenz Castorp had become almost fixed habit with him. He himself would all at once be conscious of using it and have a swift memory of the old man's choker collar, the provisional form of the ruff; the pale gold round of the christening basin; the ineffably solemn sound of the "great--great- -great." These and suchlike associations would gradually in their turn lead him back to reflect upon the whole mass of his adventures in life.

Pribislav Hippe never again appeared to him in bodily form, as once eleven months before. The progress of acclimatization was over, there were no more visions. No more did his body lie supine while his ego roved back to a far--off present. No more of such incidents. The vividness and clarity of that memory--picture, if it returned to hover before his eyes, yet kept within sane and normal bounds—-but might move Hans Castorp to draw out of his breast pocket the glass plate which he had received as a gift, and kept there in an envelope enclosed in a letter--case. It was a small negative. Held in the same plane with the ground, it was black and opaque; but lifted against the light, it revealed matter for a humanistic eye: the transparent reproduction of the human form, the bony framework of the ribs, the outline of the heart, the arch of the diaphragm, the bellows that were the lungs; together with the shoulder and upper--armbones, all shrouded in a dim and vaporous envelope of flesh—-that flesh which once, in Carnival week, Hans Castorp had so madly tasted. What wonder his unstable heart stood still or wildly throbbed when he gazed at it, and then, to the sound of the rushing waters, leaning with crossed arms against the smooth back of his bench, his head inclined upon one shoulder, among the blossoming aquilegias, began to turn over everything in his mind!

It hovered before his eyes—-the image of the human form divine, the masterpiece of organic life—-as once upon that frosty, starry night when he had plunged so profoundly into the study of it. His contemplation of its inner aspect was bound up in the young man's mind with a host of problems and discriminations, not of a kind the good Joachim had need to concern himself with, but for which Hans Castorp had come to feel as a civilian responsible. True, down in the plain he had never been aware of them, nor probably ever would have been. It was up here that the thing came about, where one sat piously withdrawn, looking down from a height of five thousand feet or so upon the earth and all that therein was—-and it might be, also, by virtue of one's physical condition, with one's body brought, as it were, into higher relief by the toxins that were released by the localized inner infection to burn, a dry heat, in the face. His musings brought him upon Settembrini, organ--grinder and pedagogue, whose father had seen the light of day in Hellas, who chose to define love of the image as comprehending politics, eloquence, and rebellion, and who would consecrate the burgher's pike upon the altar of humanity. He thought of Comrade Krokowski, and the traffic they two had been having in the twilighted room below stairs. He thought of the twofold nature of analysis, and questioned how far it was applicable to realities and conducive to progress, how far related to the grave and its noisome anatomy. He called up the figures of the two grandfathers, the rebel and the loyalist, both, for reasons diametrically opposed, black--clad; confronted them with each other, and tried their worth. He went further, and took counsel with himself over such vast problems as form and freedom, body and spirit, honour and shame, time and eternity—-and succumbed to a brief but violent spell of giddiness, on a sudden thought that all about him the columbines were in blossom once more, and his year here rounding to its close.

He had an odd name for the serious mental preoccupations which absorbed him in his picturesque retreat; he called them "taking stock"; the expression, crude as it was, defined for him an employment which he loved, even though it was bound up in his mind with the phenomena of fear and giddiness and palpitation, and made his face burn even more than its wont. Yet there seemed a peculiar fitness in the fact that the mental strain involved obliged him to make use of the ancestral chin--support; that way of holding his head lent him an outward dignity in keeping with thoughts which passed through his brain as he contemplated the image.

"*Homo dei*" —- that was what the ugly Naphta had called the image, when he was defending it against the English doctrine of an economic society. And, by a natural association, Hans Castorp decided that in the interest of these mental activities of his, and his responsible position as a civilian member of society, he must really—-and Joachim must too—pay that little man the honour of a visit. Settembrini did not like the idea, as Hans Castorp was shrewd and thin--skinned enough to know. Even the first meeting had displeased the humanist, who had obviously tried to prevent it and protect his pupils from intercourse with Naphta, notwithstanding that he personally associated and discussed with him. His "pupils"—-thus life's delicate child disingenuously put it, knowing all the time that it was himself alone who was the object of Settembrini's solicitude. So it is with schoolmasters. They permit themselves relaxations, saying that they are "grown up," and refuse the same to their pupils, saying that they are not "grown up." It was a good thing, then, that the hand--organ man was not actually in a position to deny young Hans Castorp anything—-nor had even tried to do so. It was only necessary that the delicate child should conceal his thin--skinned perceptions and assume an air of unconsciousness; when there was nothing to prevent his taking friendly advantage of Naphta's invitation. Which, accordingly, he did, Joachim going along with him, willy--nilly, on a Sunday afternoon after the main rest--cure, not many days later than their first meeting.

It was but a few minutes' walk from the Berghof down to the vine--wreathed cottage door. They went in, passing on their right the entrance to the little shop, and climbed the narrow brown stairs to the door of the first storey. Near the bell was a small plate, with the name of Lukaçek, Ladies' Tailor. The door was opened by a half--grown boy, in a sort of livery of gaiters and striped jacket, a little page, with shaven poll and rosy cheeks. Him they asked for Professor Naphta, impressing their names on his mind, as they had brought no cards; he said he would go and deliver them to Herr Naphta——whom he named without a title. The door opposite the entrance stood open, and gave a view of the shop, where, regardless of the holiday, Lukaçek the tailor sat crosslegged on a table and stitched. He was sallow and bald--headed, with a large, drooping nose, beneath which his black moustaches hung down on both sides his mouth and gave him a surly look.

"Good--afternoon," Hans Castorp greeted him.

"*Grütsi,*" answered the tailor, in the Swiss dialect, which fitted neither his name nor his looks and sounded queer and unsuitable.

"Working hard?" went on Hans Castorp, motioning with his head. "Isn't to--day Sunday?"

"Something pressing," the tailor said curtly, stitching.

"Is it pretty? Are you making it in a hurry for a party?" Hans Castorp guessed. The tailor let this question hang, for a little; bit off his cotton and threaded his needle afresh. After a while he nodded.

"Will it be pretty?" persisted Hans Castorp. "Will it have sleeves?"

"Yes, sleeves; it's for an old 'un," answered Lukaçek, with a strong Bohemian accent. The return of the lad interrupted this parley, which had been carried on through the doorway. Herr Naphta begged the gentlemen to come in, he announced, and opened a door a few steps further on in the passage, lifting the portière that hung over it to let them enter. Herr Naphta, in slippers, stood on a mossy green carpet just within, and received his guests.

Both cousins were surprised by the luxury of the two-windowed study. They were even astonished; for the poverty of the cottage, the mean stair and wretched corridor, led one to expect nothing of the kind. The contrast lent to Naphta's elegant furnishings a note of the fabulous, which of themselves they scarcely possessed, and would not otherwise have had in the eyes of Hans Castorp and Joachim Ziemssen. Yet they were elegant too, even strikingly so; indeed, despite writing-table and bookshelves the room hardly had a masculine look. There was too much silk about—-wine-coloured, purplish silk; silken window-hangings, silken portières, and silken coverings to the furniture arranged on the narrow side of the room in front of a wall almost entirely covered with a Gobelin tapestry. Baroque easy-chairs with little pads on the arms were, grouped about a small metal-bound table, and behind it stood a baroque sofa with velvet cushions. Bookcases lined the entrance wall on both sides of the door. They and the writing-table or, rather, roll-top desk, which stood between the windows, were of carved mahogany; the glass doors of the bookcases were lined with green silk. But in the corner to the left of the sofa-group stood a work of art, a large painted wood--carving, mounted on a red-covered dais: a *pietà*, profoundly startling, artlessly effective to the point of being grotesque. The Madonna, in a cap, with gathered brows and wry, wailing mouth, with the Man of Sorrows on her lap—-considered as a work of art it was primitive and faulty, with crudely emphasized and ignorant anatomy, the hanging head bristling with thorns, face and limbs bloodbesprinkled, great blobs of blood welling from the wound in the side and from the nail-prints in hands and feet. This show-piece did indeed give a singular tone to the silken chamber. The wall-paper, on the window wall and above the bookcases, had obviously been supplied by the tenant: the green stripe in it matched the soft velvet carpet spread over the red drugget. The windows had cream--coloured blinds down to the floor. Only the ceiling had been impossible to treat: it was bare and full of cracks; but a small Venetian lustre hung down from it.

"We've come for a little visit," said Hans Castorp, with his eyes more on the pious horror in the corner than on the owner of the surprising room, who was expressing his gratification that the cousins had kept their word. With a hospitable motion of his small right hand he would have ushered them to the satin chairs. But Hans Castorp went as if spellbound straight up to the wooden group, and stood before it, arms akimbo and head on one side.

"What is this you have here?" he asked, in a low voice. "It's frightfully good. What depiction of suffering! It's old, of course?"

"Fourteenth century," answered Naphta. "Probably comes from the Rhine. Does it impress you?"

"Enormously," said Hans Castorp. "It would impress anybody—-couldn't help it. I should never have thought there could be anything in the world at once so—-forgive me—-so ugly, and so beautiful."

"All works of art whose function it is to express the soul and the emotions," Naphta responded, "are always so ugly as to be beautiful, and so beautiful as to be ugly. That is a law. Their beauty is not fleshly beauty, which is merely insipid—-but the beauty of the spirit. Moreover, physical beauty is an abstraction," he added; "only the inner beauty, the beauty of religious expression, has any actuality."

"We are most grateful to you for making these distinctions clear," Hans Castorp said. "Fourteenth century?" he inquired of himself; "that means thirteen hundred soand--so? Yes, that is the Middle Ages, the way the books say; and I can more or less recognize in this thing the conception I have been getting of them lately. I never knew anything about the Middle Ages before, myself, being on the technical side. But up here they have been brought home to me in various ways. There was no economic doctrine of society then, that's plain enough. What is the name of the artist?"

Naphta shrugged his shoulders.

"What does it matter?" he said. "We should not ask—for in the time when it was made they never did. It was not created by some wonderful and well--advertised single genius. It is an anonymous product, anonymous and communal. Moreover, it is very advanced Middle Ages—-Gothic, *signum mortificationis*. No more of the palliating and beautifying that the Roman epoch thought proper to a depiction of the Crucifixion: here you have no royal crown, no majestic triumph over martyrdom and the world. It is the most utter and radical declaration of submission to suffering and the weakness of the flesh. Pessimistic and ascetic—-it is Gothic art alone which is truly that. You are probably not familiar with the work of Innocent III, *De miseria humanæ conditionis*: an exceedingly witty piece of writing—-it was written at the end of the twelfth century, but this was the earliest art to furnish an illustration to it."

Hans Castorp heaved a deep sigh. "Herr Naphta," he said, "every word you say interests me enormously. '*Signum mortificationis*'— is that right? I'll remember it.

'Anonymous and communal'—-and that will take some thinking about too. You are quite right in assuming I don't know the work of that pope—-I take it Innocent III *was* a pope? Did I understand you to say it is witty and ascetic? I must confess I should never have thought the two things went hand in hand; but when I put my mind to it, of course it is obvious that a discourse on human misery gives one a good chance to poke fun at the things of the flesh. Is the work obtainable? Perhaps if I got up my Latin I could read it."

"I have it here," Naphta said, motioning with his head toward one of the bookcases.

"It is at your service. But, shall we not sit down? You can look at the *pietà* from the sofa. Tea is just coming in."

The little servant was fetching the tea, also a charming silver--bound basket containing slices of layer cake. And behind him, on the threshold, who should stand, on winged feet, wreathed in his subtle smile, and exclaiming: *"Sapperlot!"* and *"Accidente"*—-who, indeed, but the lodger from upstairs, Herr Settembrini, dropped in to keep them company? From his little window, he said, he had seen the cousins enter, and made haste to finish the page of the encyclopædia which he had at the moment in hand, in order to beg an invitation. Nothing more natural than his coming: it was justified by his old acquaintance with the Berghof guests, no less than by his relations with Naphta, which, despite deep--seated divergences of opinion, were lively on both sides, the host accepting his presence as a thing of course. All this did not prevent Hans Castorp from getting two impressions from his advent, one as clearly as the other: first, that Herr Settembrini had come to prevent them—-or rather him—-from being alone with little Naphta, and to establish, as it were, a pedagogic equilibrium; second, that Herr Settembrini did not object the least in the world, but rather the contrary, to exchanging his room in the loft for a sojourn in Naphta's fine and silken chamber, nor to taking a good and proper tea. He rubbed together his small yellow hands, with their line of hair running down the back from the little finger, before he fell to, with unmistakable and outspoken relish upon the layer cake, which had a chocolate filling.

The conversation continued on the subject of the *pietà*, Hans Castorp holding it to the point with look and word, and turning to the humanist as though to put him in critical rapport with the work of art. Herr Settembrini's aversion was obvious in the very air with which he turned towards it—-for he had originally sat down with his back to that corner of the room. He was too polite to express all he felt, and confined himself to pointing out certain defects in the physical proportions of the work, offences against nature, which were far from working upon his emotions, because they did not spring from archaic ineptitude, but from deliberate bad intent—-a fundamentally opposed principle.—-In which latter statement Naphta maliciously concurred. Certainly, there was no question of technical lack of skill. What we had here was conscious emancipation from the natural, a contempt for nature manifested by a pious refusal to pay her any homage whatever. Whereupon Settembrini declared that disregard of nature and neglect of her study only led men into error. He characterized as absurd the formlessness to which the Middle Ages and all periods like them had been a prey, and began, in sounding words, to exalt the Graeco--Roman heritage, classicism, form, and beauty, reason, the pagan joy of life. To these things and these alone, he said, was it given to ameliorate man's lot on earth. Hans Castorp broke in here. What, he asked, about Plotinus, then, who was known to have said that he was ashamed of having a body? Or Voltaire, who, in the name of reason, protested against the scandalous Lisbon earthquake? Were they absurd? Perhaps. Yet it seemed to him, as he thought about it, that what one characterized as absurd might also be thought of as intellectually honourable; from which it would follow that the absurd hostility to nature evinced by Gothic art, when all was said and done, was as fine in its way as the gestures of Plotinus or Voltaire, since it testified to the selfsame emancipation, the same indomitable pride, which refused to abdicate in favour of blind natural forces—-

Naphta burst out laughing. He sounded more than ever like a cracked plate and ended in a fit of coughing.

Settembrini said floridly to Hans Castorp: "Your brilliance is almost a discourtesy to our host, since it makes you appear ungrateful for this delicious cake. But I don't know that gratitude is your strong point. The kind I mean consists in making a good use of favours received."

As Hans Castorp looked rather mortified, he added in his most charming manner: "We all know you for a wag, Engineer: but your sly quips at the expense of the true, the good, and the beautiful will never make me doubt your fundamental love of them. You are aware, of course, that there is only one sort of revolt against nature which may be called honourable; that which revolts in the name of human beauty and human dignity. All others bring debasement and degradation in their train, even when not directed to that end. And you know, too, what inhuman atrocities, what murderous intolerance were displayed by the century to which the production behind me owes its birth. Look at that monstrous type, the inquisitor—for instance, the sanguinary figure of Conrad von Marburg—and his infamous zeal in the persecution of everything that stood in the way of supernatural domination! You are in no danger of acclaiming the sword and the stake as instruments of human benevolence!"

"Yet in its service," countered Naphta, "laboured the whole machinery by means of which the Holy Office freed the world of undesirable citizens. All the pains of the Church, even the stake, even excommunication, were inflicted to save the soul from everlasting damnation—which cannot be said of the mania for destruction displayed by the Jacobins. Permit me to remark that any system of pains and penalties which is not based upon belief in a hereafter is simply a bestial stupidity. And as for the degradation of humanity, the history of its course is precisely synchronous with the growth of the bourgeois spirit. Renaissance, age of enlightenment, the natural sciences and economics of the nineteenth century, have left nothing undone or untaught which could forward this degradation. Modern astronomy, for example, has converted the earth, the centre of the All, the lofty theatre of the struggle between God and the Devil for the possession of a creature burningly coveted by each, into an indifferent little planet, and thus—at least for the present—put an end to the majestic cosmic position of man—upon which, moreover, all astrology bases itself."

"For the present?" Herr Settembrini asked, threateningly. His own manner of speaking had something in it of the inquisitor waiting to pounce upon the witness so soon as he shall have involved himself in an admission of guilt.

"Certainly. For a few hundred years, that is," assented Naphta, coldly. "A vindication, in this respect, of scholasticism is on the way, is even well under way, unless all signs fail. Copernicus will go down before Ptolemy. The heliocentric thesis is meeting by degrees with an intellectual opposition which will end by achieving its purpose. Science will see itself philosophically enforced to put back the earth in the position of supremacy in which she was installed by the dogma of the Church."

"What? What? Intellectual opposition? Science philosophically enforced? What sort of voluntarism is this you are giving vent to? And what about pure knowledge, what about science? What about the unfettered quest for truth? Truth, my dear sir, so indissolubly bound up with freedom, the martyrs in whose cause you would like us to regard as criminals upon this planet but who are rather the brightest jewels in her crown?"

Herr Settembrini's question, and its delivery, were prodigious. He sat very erect, his righteous words rolled down upon little Naphta, and he let his voice swell out at the end, so that one could tell how sure he was his opponent could only reply with shamefaced silence. He had been holding a piece of layer cake between his fingers, but now he laid it back on his plate, as if loath to bite into it after launching his question. Naphta responded, with disagreeable composure: "My good sir, there is no such thing as pure knowledge. The validity of the Church's teaching on the subject of science, which can be summed up in the phrase of Saint Augustine: *Credo, ut intellegam:* I believe, in order that I may understand, is absolutely incontrovertible. Faith is the vehicle of knowledge, intellect secondary. Your pure science is a myth. A belief, a given conception of the universe, an idea——in short, a will, is always in existence; which it is the task of the intellect to expound and demonstrate. It comes down every time to the *quod erat demonstrandum*. Even the conception of evidence itself, psychologically speaking, contains a strong element of voluntarism. The great schoolmen of the twelfth and thirteenth centuries were agreed that what is false in theology cannot be true in philosophy. We can, if you like, leave theology out of the argument; but a humanity, a cultural conception, which refuses to recognize that what is philosophically false cannot be scientifically true, is not worthy the name. The accusation of the Holy Office against Galileo stated that his thesis was philosophically absurd. A more crushing arraignment could not well be."

"Aha! The reasoning of our great genius turned out in the long run to have the greater validity! No, let us be serious, *Professore!* Answer me this, answer me in the presence of these two young listeners: Do you believe in truth, in objective, scientific truth, to strive after the attainment of which is the highest law of all morality, and whose triumphs over authority form the most glorious page in the history of the human spirit?"

Hans Castorp and Joachim—-the first faster than the second—-turned their heads from Settembrini to Naphta.

Naphta replied: "There can be no such triumphs as those you speak of; for the authority is man himself—-his interests, his worth, his salvation—-and thus between it and truth no conflict is possible. They coincide."

"Then truth, according to you—-"

"Whatever profits man, that is the truth. In him all nature is comprehended, in all nature only he is created, and all nature only for him. He is the measure of all things, and his welfare is the sole and single criterion of truth. Any theoretic science which is without practical application to man's salvation is as such without significance, we are commanded to reject it. Throughout the Christian centuries it was accepted fact that the natural sciences afforded man no edification. Lactantius, who was chosen by Constantine the Great as tutor to his son, put the position very clearly when he asked in so many words what heavenly bliss he could attain by knowing the sources of the Nile, or the twaddle of the physicists anent the heavenly bodies. Answer him if you can! Why have we given the Platonic philosophy the preference over every other, if not because it has to do with knowledge of God, and not knowledge of nature? Let me assure you that mankind is about to find its way back to this point of view. Mankind will soon perceive that it is not the task of true science to run after godless understanding; but to reject utterly all that is harmful, yes, even all that ideally speaking is without significance, in favour of instinct, measure, choice. It is childish to accuse the Church of having defended darkness rather than light. She did well, and thrice well, to chastise as unlawful all unconditioned striving after the 'pure' knowledge of things—-such striving, that is, as is without reference to the spiritual, without bearing on man's salvation; for it is this unconditioned, this a--philosophical natural science that always has led and ever will lead men into darkness."

"Your pragmatism," Settembrini responded, "needs only to be translated into terms of politics for it to display its pernicious character in full force. The good, the true, and the just, is that which advantages the State: its safety, its honour, its power form the sole criterion of morality. Well and good. But mark that herewith you fling open the door for every sort of crime to enter; while as for human truth, individual justice, democracy, you can see what will become of them—-"

"If I might be permitted," Naphta interpolated, "to introduce a little logic into the premises, I should state the question thus: either Ptolemy and the schoolmen were right, and the world is finite in time and space, the deity is transcendent, the antithesis between God and man is sustained, and man's being is dual; from which it follows that the problem of his soul consists in the conflict between the spiritual and the material, to which all social problems are entirely secondary—-and this is the only sort of individualism I can recognize as consistent—-or else, on the other hand, your Renaissance astronomers hit upon the truth, and the cosmos is infinite. Then there exists no suprasensible world, no dualism; the Beyond is absorbed into the Here, the antithesis between God and nature falls; man ceases to be the theatre of a struggle between two hostile principles, and becomes harmonious and unitary, the conflict subsists merely between his individual and his collective interest; and the will of the

State becomes, in good pagan wise, the law of morality. Either one thing or the other."

"I protest!" cried Settembrini, holding his tea--cup outstretched at arm's length toward his host. "I protest against the imputation that the modern State means the subjugation of the individual to evil ends! I protest against the dilemma in which you seek to place us, between Prussianism and Gothic reaction! Democracy has no meaning whatever if not that of an individualistic corrective to State absolutism of every kind. Truth and justice are the immediate jewels of personal morality. If, at times, they may appear to stand counter, even to be hostile, to the interests of the State, they may do so while all the time holding before their eyes her higher, yes, let us boldly say, her spiritual weal. To find in the Renaissance the origin of Stateworship—-what bastard logic! The achievements wrung from the past—I use the word literally, my dear sir—-wrung from the past by the Renaissance and the intellectual revival are personality, freedom, and the rights of man."

The listeners heaved each a deep sigh—-they had been holding their breaths during Herr Settembrini's great replication. Hans Castorp did not let himself go altogether, yet could not refrain from slapping the edge of the table with his hand. "Magnificent," he said, between clenched teeth. Joachim too evinced lively approval, despite the word Herr Settembrini had let fall about Prussianism. Both of them turned toward the antagonist who had just suffered this crushing rebuff—- Hans Castorp with such eagerness that he fell unconsciously into the very posture he had taken at the pigdrawing, his elbows on the table and his chin in his palm, and peered in suspense into Herr Naphta's face.

And Naphta sat there, tense and motionless, his lean hands in his lap. He said: "I try to introduce a little logic into the debate, and you answer me with lofty sentiments. I was already tolerably well aware that what is called liberalism—-individualism the humanistic conception of citizenship—-was the product of the Renaissance. But the fact leaves me entirely cold, realizing as I do that your great heroic age is a thing of the past its ideals defunct, or at least lying at their latest gasp, while the feet of those who will deal them the *coup de grâce* are already before the door. You call yourself, if I am not mistaken, a revolutionist. But you err in holding that future revolutions will issue in freedom. In the past five hundred years, the principle of freedom has outlived its usefulness. An educational system which still conceives itself as a child of the age of enlightenment, with criticism as its chosen medium of instruction, the liberation and cult of the ego the solvent of forms of life which are absolutely fixed—such a system may still, for a time, reap an empty rhetorical advantage; but its reactionary character is, to the initiated, clear beyond any doubt All educational organizations worthy of the name have always recognized what must be the ultimate and significant principle of pedagogy: namely the absolute mandate, the iron bond, discipline, sacrifice, the renunciation of the ego, the curbing of the personality. And lastly, it is an unloving miscomprehension of youth to believe that it finds its pleasure in freedom: its deepest pleasure lies in obedience."

Joachim sat up straight. Hans Castorp reddened. Herr Settembrini excitedly twisted his fine moustache.

"No," Naphta went on. "Liberation and development of the individual are not the key to our age, they are not what our age demands. What it needs, what it wrestles after, what it will create—-is Terror."

He uttered the last word lower than the rest; without a motion of his body. Only his eye--glasses suddenly flashed. All three of them, as they heard it, jumped, even Herr Settembrini, who, however, promptly collected himself and smiled.

"And may one ask," he queried, "whom, or what—-you see I am all question, I ask even how to ask—-whom, or what you envisage as the bringer of this—-this—-I repeat the word with some unwillingness—-this Terror?"

Naphta sat motionless, flashing like a drawn blade. He said: "I am at your service. I believe I do not err in assuming our agreement in the conception of an original ideal state of man, a condition without government and without force, an unmediated condition as the child of God, in which there was neither lordship nor service, neither law nor penalty, nor sin nor relation after the flesh; no distinction of classes, no work, no property: nothing but equality, brotherhood, and moral perfectitude."

"Very good. I agree," declared Settembrini. "I agree with everything except the relations after the flesh, which obviously must at all times have subsisted, since man is a highly developed vertebrate, and, like other creatures of his kind——"

"As you like. I am merely stating our fundamental agreement with respect to the original, paradisial state of man, his freedom from law, and his unmediated relation with God, which state was lost to him by his fall. I believe we may go side by side for another few steps of the way: in that we both explain the State as a social contract, taking account of the Fall and entered into as a safeguard against evil, and that we both see in it the origin of sovereign power——"

"*Benissimo!*" cried Settembrini. "Social contract——why, that is Enlightenment, that is Rousseau. I had no idea——"

"One moment, pray. We part company here. All power and all control was originally vested in the people, who made it over, together with the right to make laws, to their princes. But from this your school deduces in the first instance the right of the people to revolt from the monarchy. Whereas we, on the contrary——"

"We?" thought Hans Castorp, breathlessly. "Who are 'we'? I must certainly ask Settembrini afterwards, whom he means by 'we.' "

"We, for our part," Naphta was saying, "perhaps no less revolutionary than you, have consistently deduced the supremacy of the Church over the secular power. The temporal nature of the power of the State is, as it were, written on its forehead; but even if it were not, it would be enough to point to the historical fact that its authority goes back to the will of the people, whereas that of the Church rests upon the divine sanction, to establish its character as a device which, if not precisely contrived by the power of evil, is nevertheless a faulty and inadequate makeshift."

"The State, my dear sir——"

"I am acquainted with your views on the subject of the national State. As your Virgil has it: 'Fatherland--love conquers all, and hunger unsated for glory.' You add the corrective of a somewhat liberal individualism——that is democracy, but it leaves quite untouched your fundamental relation to the State. That the soul of democracy is the power of money, apparently does not impugn it—-or would you deny the fact?

Antiquity was capitalistic, because of its State cult. The Christian Middle Ages clearly recognized the inherent capitalism of the secular State: 'Money will be emperor' is a prophecy made in the eleventh century. Would you deny that it has now literally come to pass, and with it the utter bedevilment of life in general?"

"My dear friend, you have the floor. I am only eager to make the acquaintance of the Great Unknown, the bringer of the Terror."

"A perilous curiosity on your part, as the spokesman of a class of society which has acted as the standard--bearer of freedom—-considering it is that very freedom that has dragged the world to the brink of destruction. Your goal is the democratic Imperium, the apotheosis of the principle of the national State in that of the universal, the WorldState. And the emperor of this World--State? Your Utopia is monstrous——and yet, at this point, we find ourselves to a certain extent again on common ground. For your capitalistic world--republic is, in truth, transcendental in character; the World--State is the secular State transcended; and we unite in the faith that the final, perfected State, lying dim upon the far horizon, should correspond to man's original, primitive perfection. Since the time of Gregory the Great, the founder of the State of God, the Church has always regarded it as her task to bring mankind back under the divine guidance. Gregory's claim to temporal power was put forward not for its own sake, but rather because his delegated dictatorship was to be the means and the way to the goal of redemption——a transitional stage between the pagan State and the heavenly kingdom. You have spoken to your pupils here of the bloody deeds of the Church, her chastisements and her intolerance; very foolishly so, for it stands to reason that the zeal of the godly cannot be pacifistic in character——Gregory himself said: 'Cursed be the man who holds back his sword from the shedding of blood.' That power is evil we know. But if the kingdom is to come, then it is necessary that the dualism between good and evil, between power and the spirit, here and hereafter, must be for the time abrogated to make way for a single principle, which shall unify asceticism and domination. This is what I mean by the necessity for the Terror."

"But the standard--bearer, the standard--bearer?"

"Do you still ask? Is your Manchester liberalism unaware of the existence of a school of economic thought which means the triumph of man over economics, and whose principles and aims precisely coincide with those of the kingdom of God? The Fathers of the Church called mine and thine pernicious words, and private property usurpation and robbery. They repudiated the idea of personal possessions, because, according to divine and natural law, the earth is common to all men, and brings forth her fruits for the common good. They taught that avarice, a consequence of the Fall, represents the rights of property and is the source of private ownership. They were humane enough, anti--commercial enough, to feel that all commercial activity was a danger to the soul of man and its salvation. They hated money and finance, and called the empire of capital fuel for the fires of hell. The fundamental economic principle that price is regulated by the operation of the law of supply and demand, they have always despised from the bottom of their hearts; and condemned taking advantage of chance as a cynical exploitation of a neighbour's need. Even more nefarious, in their eyes, was the exploitation of time; the montrousness of receiving a premium for the passage of time—interest, in other words—and misusing to one's own advantage and another's disadvantage a universal and God--given dispensation."

"*Benissimo!*" cried Hans Castorp, in his excitement availing himself of Herr Settembrini's formula of assent. "The time—a universal, God--given dispensation!

That is highly important."

"Quite," said Naphta. "Indeed, these humane spirits were revolted by the idea of the automatic increase of money; they regarded as usury every kind of interest--taking and speculation, and declared that every rich man was either a thief or the heir of a thief. They went further. Like Thomas Aquinas, they considered trade, pure and simple, buying and selling for profit, without altering or improving the product, a contemptible occupation. They were not inclined to place a very high value on labour in and for itself, as being an ethical, not a religious concern, and performed not in the service of God, but as a part of the business of living. This being the case, they demanded that the measure of profit or of public esteem should be in proportion to the actual labour expended, and accordingly it was not the tradesman or the industrialist, but the labourer and the tiller of the soil, who were honourable in their eyes. For they were in favour of making production dependent upon necessity, and held mass production in abhorrence. Now, then: after centuries of disfavour these principles and standards are being resurrected by the modern movement of communism. The similarity is complete, even to the claim for world--domination made by international labour as against international industry and finance; the world--proletariat, which is today asserting the ideals of the *Civitas Dei* in opposition to the discredited and decadent standards of the capitalistic bourgeoisie. The dictatorship of the proletariat, the politico--economic means of salvation demanded by our age, does not mean domination for its own sake and in perpetuity; but rather in the sense of a temporary abrogation, in the Sign of the Cross, of the contradiction between spirit and force; in the sense of overcoming the world by mastering it; in a transcendental, a transitional sense, in the sense of the Kingdom. The proletariat has taken up the task of Gregory the Great, his religious zeal burns within it, and as little as he may it withhold its hand from the shedding of blood. Its task is to strike terror into the world for the healing of the world, that man may finally achieve salvation and deliverance, and win back at length to freedom from law and from distinction of classes, to his original status as child of God."

Thus Naphta. The little group was silent. The young men looked to Herr Settembrini. It was, they felt, his affair.

He said: "Astounding. I am staggered——I admit it. I had not expected this. *Roma locuta.* Rome has spoken, and how——how has she spoken! Herr Naphta has before our eyes performed a hieratic *salto mortale*—— if the epithet is inconsistent, the inconsistency has been 'temporarily abrogated'——oh, yes! I repeat, it is astounding. Could you conceive, Professor, of any possible criticism, if only on the score of consistency?

A few minutes ago you were at pains to make comprehensible to us a Christian individualism based on the dualism of God and the world, and to prove its pre--eminence over all politically determined morality. And now you profess a socialism pushed to the point of dictatorship and terrorism. How do you reconcile the two things?"

"Opposites," said Naphta, "may be consistent with each other. It is the middling, the neither--one--thing--nor--the--other that is preposterous. Your individualism, as I have already taken the liberty of remarking, is defective. It is a confession of weakness. It corrects its pagan State morality by the admixture of a little Christianity, a little 'rights of man,' a little so--called liberty——but that is all. An individualism that springs from the cosmic, the astrological importance of the individual soul, an individualism not social but religious, that conceives of humanity not as a conflict between the ego and society, but as a conflict between the ego and God, between the flesh and the spirit—-a genuine individualism like that sorts very well with the most binding communism."

"Anonymous and communal," said Hans Castorp.

Settembrini glared at him. "Be quiet, Engineer," he said, with a severity probably due to nervous irritation. "Inform yourself, but don't try to express your views. That is an answer, at least," he said, turning to Naphta again. "It gives me cold comfort, but it is an answer. Let us examine all the consequences flowing from it. Along with industry, your Christian communism would reject machinery, technique, material progress. Along with what you call trade—-money and finance, which in antiquity ranked higher than agriculture and manual labour—-you reject freedom. For it is clear, so clear as to be evident to the meanest intelligence, that all social relations, public and private, would be attached to the soil, as in the Middle Ages; even—-I feel some reluctance to say it—-even the person of the individual. If only the soil can maintain life, then only the possession of it can confer freedom. Manual labourers and peasants, however honourable their position, if they possess no real property, can only be the property of those who do. As a matter of fact, until well on in the Middle Ages the great mass of the population, even the town--dwellers, were serfs. In the course of our discussion you have let fall various allusions to the dignity of the human being. Yet you are defending the morality of an economic system which deprives the individual of liberty and self--respect."

"About self--respect and the lack of it," responded Naphta, "there is a good deal to be said. For the moment, I should be glad if the association were to make you conceive of liberty less as a beautiful gesture and more as a serious problem. You assert that Christian morality, with all its beauty and benignity, makes for servitude. And I, on the other hand, assert that the question of freedom—-the question of cities, to put it more concretely—-has always been a highly ethical question, and is historically bound up with the inhuman degeneration of commercial morality, with all the horrors of modern industrialism and speculation, and with the devilish domination of money and finance."

"I must insist that you do not take refuge behind scruples and antinomies, but come out squarely where you belong, in favour of the blackest sort of reaction."

"It would be the first step toward true liberty and love of humanity to free one's mind of the flabby fear engendered by the very mention of the word reaction."

"Well, that is enough," declared Herr Settembrini, in a voice that trembled slightly, pushing away his cup and plate——they were empty by now——and rising from the satin sofa. "Enough for to--day, enough for a whole day, I should think. Our thanks, Professor, for the delicious entertainment, and for the very *spirituel* discourse. My young friends here from the Berghof are summoned by the service of the cure, and I should like, before they go, to show them my cell up above. Come, gentlemen. *Addio, Padre!"*

Hans Castorp marked the appellation with lifted brows. So now it was *padre!* They submitted to Herr Settembrini's breaking up the little party and disposing of themselves without giving Naphta the chance to come along supposing he had been inclined. The young men in their turn thanked their host and took their leave, urged by Naphta to come again. They went with Herr Settembrini, Hans Castorp bearing with him the crumbling pasteboard volume containing *De miseria humanæ conditionis*, which his host put into his hands. The surly Lukaçek still sat on his table and sewed at the sleeved garment for the old woman. They had to pass his open door to mount the ladderlike stair to the top storey. It was, properly speaking, scarcely a storey at all, being simply a loft with naked rafters and beams inside the roof; it had the close air of a garret and smelt of warm shingles. But it was divided into two rooms, which served the republican capitalist and belletristic collaborator on the *Sociology of Suffering* as study and sleeping--cabinet. These he blithely displayed to his young friends, characterizing them as retired and cosy, in order to supply them with suitable adjectives in which to praise them, which they accordingly did. They both found his quarters charmingly cosy and retired, just as he said. They had a glimpse into the tiny sleeping--chamber, merely a short and narrow bedstead in the corner under the sloping roof, and a small drugget on the floor beside it; then they turned again to the study, which was no less sparsely furnished, but orderly to the point of formality, or even frigid. Heavy old--fashioned chairs, four in number, with rush seats, were symmetrically placed on either side the door, the divan was pushed against the wall, and a round table with a green cover held the centre of the room, upon which for all ornament---or, possibly, for refreshment, but in any case with an effect of chaste sobriety---there stood a water--bottle with a glass turned upside--down over it. Books and pamphlets leaned against each other in a little hanging shelf, and at the open window stood a high--legged, flimsy folding desk, with a small, thick felt mat on the floor beneath it, just large enough to afford standing--room. Hans Castorp took up position here for a minute to try what it was like. This was Herr Settembrini's workshop, where he wrote articles in belles--lettres to contribute to the encyclopædia of human suffering. The young man rested his elbows on the slanting surface of the desk, and announced that he found the little apartment very retired and cosy. Thus, he presumed, aloud, might Ludovico's father, with his long, aristocratic nose, have bent over his work at Padua---and learned that he was standing, indeed, at the very desk of the deceased scholar; nay, more, that the chairs, the table, even the water--bottle, had been his, and that the chairs had come down from the Carbonaro grandfather, the walls of whose law office at Milan they once had graced. That made a great impression on the young people; the chairs straightway began in their eyes to betray affinity with political agitation---Joachim, who had been sitting all unconscious on one, with his legs crossed, got up at once, looked at it mistrustfully, and did not sit down again. But Hans Castorp, at the elder Settembrini's desk, thought how the younger now laboured here, to mingle the politics of the grandfather and the father's humanism in a blend of literary beauty. At length they all went off together, the author having offered to see his friends to their door.

They were silent for some way; but the silence spoke of Naphta, and Hans Castorp could wait. He felt sure Herr Settembrini would mention his house--mate, had come out with them for that very purpose. He was not mistaken.

Drawing a long breath, as if to get a good start, the Italian began: "My friends, I should like to warn you."

As he paused, after that, Hans Castorp asked, affecting surprise: "Against what?"

He might as well have said against whom, but expressed himself impersonally to show how completely unconscious he was of Herr Settembrini's meaning——a meaning which even Joachim perfectly comprehended.

"Against the personage whose guest we have just been," answered Settembrini, "and whose acquaintance I have unwillingly been the means of your making. Chance willed it, as you saw, I could not prevent it. But the responsibility is mine, and as such I feel it. It is my duty to point out to your tender years the intellectual perils of intercourse with this man, and to beg you to keep your acquaintance with him within safe limits. His form is logic, but his essence is confusion."

"He does seem rather weird," was Hans Castorp's view. "Some of the things he said were very queer: it sounded as if he meant to say that the sun revolves round the earth." But how could they, he went on, have suspected that a friend of his, Herr Settembrini's, was an unsuitable person for them to associate with? As he himself admitted, they had made the acquaintance through him, had met the man first in his company, and seen that the two walked and took tea together. Surely that must mean——

"Of course, Engineer, of course." Herr Settembrini's voice was full of mild resignation, it even trembled. "I am open to this rejoinder, and so you make it. Good. I am quite ready to accept the responsibility. I live under the same roof as this man, our meetings are unavoidable, one word leads on to another, an acquaintance is formed. Herr Naphta is a person of most unusual mental powers. He is by nature discursive, and so am I. Condemn me if you will——I avail myself of the opportunity to cross swords with an antagonist who is after all my equal. I have no one else——anywhere.——

In short, it is true that I visit him and he me, we take walks together. We dispute. We quarrel, nearly every day, till we draw blood; but I confess the contrariness and mischievousness of his ideas but render our acquaintance the more attractive. I need the friction. Opinions cannot survive if one has no chance to fight for them——and I am only confirmed in mine. How could you assert so much of yours, Lieutenant, or you, Engineer? You are defenceless against intellectual sophistry, you are exposed to danger from the influence of this half fanatical, half pernicious quackery——danger to the intellect and to the soul."

Hans Castorp rejoined that it was probably all true; he and his cousin were naturally more or less prone to such dangers——it was the same old story about the delicate child of life, he understood perfectly. But on the other hand, one might cite Petrarch and his maxim, which was familiar to Herr Settembrini. And after all it was worth listening to, all that Naphta had to say. One must admit that that about the communistic period, when no one would be allowed to receive interest, was first--rate; also some of the things he said about education which he, Hans Castorp, would probably never otherwise have got to hear.

Settembrini compressed his lips, and Hans Castorp hastened to say that, as for his own attitude, it was of course entirely non--partisan; he only meant that he had enjoyed hearing what Naphta had to say about the deepest desire of youth. "But do explain this one thing to me," he went on. "This person——I call him that by way of showing my detachment, and that I don't by any means altogether agree with all he says, but am inclined to make important reservations——"

"And very rightly so," cried Settembrini gratefully. "——He had a great deal to say against money, the soul of the State, as he expressed himself, and against propertyholding, which he considers thievery; in short, against the capitalistic system, which he called, if I remember rightly, fuel for the fires of hell, or something like that. He sang the praises of the Middle Ages for forbidding the taking of interest. And all the time the man himself must have, if I may say so——you get such a surprise when you first enter his room and see all that silk——"

"Ah, yes," smiled Settembrini, "the taste is very characteristic of him."

"——the beautiful old furniture," Hans Castorp went on, "the *pieta* out of the fourteenth century, the Venetian lustre, the little page in livery——and such a lot of chocolate layer cake, too——he must personally be pretty well off, I should think——"

"Herr Naphta," Settembrini answered, "is, personally, as little of a capitalist as I am."

"But?" queried Hans Castorp. "There is a but in your tone, Herr Settembrini."

"Well, those people never let anyone lack who belongs to them."

"Those people?"

"The Fathers."

"Fathers? What Fathers?"

"Why, Engineer, I mean the Jesuits."

A pause ensued. The cousins displayed the greatest astonishment. Hans Castorp cried out: "What! Good Lord!——you can't mean it! You don't mean to say the man is a Jesuit!"

"You have guessed aright," Herr Settembrini said with punctilio.

"I never in all my life——who would ever think of such a thing? So that is why you called him *padre!*"

"That was a polite exaggeration," Settembrini answered. "Herr Naphta is not a Father. His illness is to blame for his not having got that far. But he has finished his noviciate and taken his first vows. The state of his health obliged him to give up his theological studies, after which he spent some years in a school belonging to the Society, where he acted as prefect and preceptor of the younger pupils. That was in sympathy with his pedagogic leanings, and he continues in the same line up here, by teaching Latin at the Fridericianum. He has been here five years. When, or if, he can leave this place, remains in doubt. But he belongs to the Society, and even if the bond were a looser one than it is, he would never want for anything. As I told you, he is personally poor; that is to say, without possessions. That is the rule of the Society; which, however, commands immense riches, and, as you saw, looks well after its own."

"Thunder and lightning!" Hans Castorp said. "And I never even knew that such things existed any more! A Jesuit! Well, well! But do tell me——if he is so well looked after by those people, why in the world does he live——I don't mean to say a word about your lodgings, Herr Settembrini, and you are certainly charmingly fixed, at Lukaçek's, it is so retired and cosy there; but I mean, if Naphta really has such a pile as that, to speak vulgarly, why doesn't he take another apartment, in a better house, more stately, with a proper entrance and large rooms? There is something secret and suspicious--looking about him, there in that hole, with all that silk——"

Settembrini shrugged his shoulders.

"He is probably guided by considerations of taste and tact," he said "I imagine he salves his anti--capitalistic conscience by living in a poor house, and indemnifies himself by living in the style he keeps. And I should say that discretion plays some role in the affair too. No use advertising to all the world how well the Devil takes care of his own. He shows an unpretentious façade, and behind it gives free rein to tastes——such as a prince of the Church——"

"Extraordinary!" Hans Castorp said. "It is all perfectly new and astonishing to me—-I am free to confess. Why, Herr Settembrini we are really very much indebted to you for this new acquaintance. Many a time and oft we shall be going down to pay him a visit—-I am sure of that. Such discourse does wonders in the way of enlarging the horizon—-it gives one glimpses into a world the existence of which one never dreamed. A proper Jesuit! When I say proper the adjective stands for all that passes through my mind ss I say it. I mean, is he a real, actual Jesuit? I know you mean a person can't be proper with the Devil supporting him from behind—-but what *I* mean is, is he proper *as a Jesuit*? That is what I am thinking. He said certain things—-you know the ones I mean—-about modern communism, and the religious zeal of the proletariat, and not withholding its hand from bloodshed—-I wont discuss them further, but surely your grandfather, with his citizen's pike, was a perfect ewe lamb by comparison—-please forgive my language. Is that allowed? Do his authorities stand for it? Is that the doctrine of the Roman Church, which all the religious societies all over the world propagate by means of intrigue, or so they say? Isn't it—-what is the word? —-heretical, abnormal, incorrect? Those are the things I am thinking about Herr Naphta—-and I should be pleased to have your opinion on them."

Settembrini smiled. "Very simple. Herr Naphta is, of course, first of all a Jesuit. He is that always, and before everything else. But he is also a man of intellect—-or I should not be seeking his society—-and as such he is always searching for new combinations, new associations and adaptations, new shades of meaning proper to the time. You saw how he surprised even me by his theories. He had never gone so far with me before. I made use of the very evident stimulus of your presence to stir him up to the point of saying his last word on a certain subject. It sounded ridiculous enough, monstrous enough—-"

"Yes, yes; but tell me, why did he never become a Father? He was old enough, wasn't he?"

"I did tell you——it was his illness prevented him."

"Well, but don't you think——if he is first a Jesuit and second a man of intellect, always making new combinations——don't you think this second, added characteristic has to do with his illness?"

"What do you mean by that?"

"I only mean——look: he has a moist spot, and that hinders him from becoming a Father. But his combinations would probably have hindered him anyhow, and so, in a certain way, the spot and the combinations hang together. In his way he too is a sort of delicate child——a *joli jésuite* with a *petite tache humide.*"

They had reached the sanatorium, but stood in a little group on the terrace before the house talking still awhile before parting, and watched by a few guests who happened to be lounging there. Herr Setrembrini said: "I repeat, my young friends——I warn you. I cannot prevent you from cultivating the acquaintance now it is made, if curiosity leads you to do so. But arm yourselves, arm your hearts and minds with suspicion, oppose him with a critical spirit. I will characterize this man for you with a single word. He is a voluptuary."

The cousins made astonished faces. Hans Castorp asked: "A——-what? But he is a member of a Society. They have to take certain vows, I have always supposed——-and then he is such a poor creature physically, so——-"

"You are talking rubbish, Engineer," Settembrini interposed. "It has nothing to do with physical insufficiency; while as for the vows you speak of, there are always reservations. I was speaking in a broader, more intellectual sense, your comprehension of which I felt I might presume upon, by now. You probably remember my visiting you one day in your room——it was long ago, frightfully long ago——-you had just finished your three weeks in bed, after being received into the sanatorium."

"Of course. You came in at dusk, and turned on the light——I remember it as if it were yesterday——-"

"Good. We fell into talk, as we have often done, I rejoice to say, and upon somewhat elevated subjects. We spoke, I believe, of life and death: of the dignity of death in so far as it is the condition and appurtenance of life, and the grotesqueness into which it declines so soon as the mind erects it into an independent principle. Young men," went on Herr Settembrini, standing close to the two, with the thumb and middle finger of his left hand splayed out like a fork, as if to collect their attention, while he raised the forefinger of his right in warning, "imprint it upon your minds: the mind is sovereign. Its will is free, it conditions the moral world. Let it once dualistically isolate death, and death will become, in actual fact, *actu*, by this mental act of will, you understand me, a power in itself, the power opposed to life, the inimical principle, the great temptation; whose kingdom is the kingdom of the flesh. You ask me why of the flesh? I answer you: because it unlooses and delivers, because it is deliverance—-yet not deliverance from evil, but deliverance by evil. It relaxes manners and morals, it frees man from discipline and restraint, it abandons him to lust. If I warn you against this man, whose acquaintance with you I have unwillingly brought about, if I exhort you to go thrice--armed with a critical spirit in all your dealings with him, it is because all his thoughts are voluptuous, and stand under the ægis of death—-and death is the most dissolute of powers, as I told you then, Engineer—-I well remember my words, for I never fail to retain in my mind any good and telling phrase I may have chanced to avail myself of—-a power hostile to civilization and progress, to work and to life, against whose mephitic breath it is the noblest task of the teacher to shield the mind of youth."

Who could talk more beautifully than Herr Settembrini, who clearer, or in betterrounded periods? Hans Castorp and Joachim Ziemssen thanked him most warmly for all he had said, and mounted the Berghof steps, while Herr Settembrini betook himself once more to his humanistic writing--desk, in the storey above Naphta's silken cell. This first visit of the cousins to Naphta, whose course we have described, was followed by two or three others; one, even, in the absence of Herr Settembrini. All of them afforded young Hans Castorp much food for thought, when, in his blueblossoming retreat, with the image of the human form divine, called *Homo Dei*, hovering before his mind's eye, he sat and "took stock."

Choler. And Worse

August arrived, and with its entry slipped past the anniversary of our hero's arrival in these parts. So much the better when it was gone—-young Hans Castorp had scarcely looked forward to it with pleasure. And that was the rule. The anniversary was not popular. The old inhabitants passed it by without thought; and—-though in general they seized on every pretext for jollification, and took occasion to celebrate their own private anniversaries in addition to these that accented the recurrent rhythm of the year; making merry with popping of corks in the restaurant, over birthdays, general examinations, imminent departures whether "wild" or sanctioned, and the like—-they accorded to the anniversary of arrival no other attention than that of a profound silence. They let it slip past, perhaps they actually managed to forget it, and they might be confident that no one else would remember. They set store by a proper articulation of the time, they gave heed to the calendar, observed the turning--points of the year, its recurrent limits. But to measure one's own private time, that time which for the individual in these parts was so closely bound up with space—-that was held to be an occupation only fit for new arrivals and short--termers. The settled citizens preferred the unmeasured, the eternal, the day that was for ever the same; and delicately each respected in others the sentiment he so warmly cherished himself. To say to anybody that this day three years ago was the day of his arrival, that would have been considered brutal, in consummately bad taste—-it simply never happened. Even Frau Stöhr, whatever her lacks in other respects, was far too tactful and well disciplined to let it slip out. Certainly she united great ignorance with her infected and feverish physical state. Recently at table she had alluded to the "affectation" of the tip of her lung; and the conversation having taken a historical turn, she explained that dates were her "ring of Polycrates"—-a remark which made her hearers stare. But it was unthinkable that she should remind young Ziemssen his year would be up in February—-though she had very likely thought of it. For the unhappy creature's head was full of useless baggage, and she loved to keep track of other people's affairs. But the tradition of the place held her in check.

Thus also on Hans Castorp's anniversary. She may have even tried to nod at him meaningfully, at table; but encountering a vacant stare dexterously withdrew. Joachim too had kept silence, though he probably had clearly in mind the date on which he had fetched the guest from the Dorf station. Joachim was ever by nature taciturn; had always talked less than his cousin, even before they came up here—-there had never been any comparison between him and the humanists and controversialists of their acquaintance—-and in these days his silence had assumed heroic proportions, only monosyllables passed his lips. His manner, however, spoke volumes. It was plain that in his mind the Dorf station was associated with another order of ideas than those of arrival or meeting people. He was conducting a lively correspondence with the flatland; his resolve was ripening, his preparations drawing to a head. July had been warm and bright. But with August bad weather set in, cloudy and damp; with first a sleety drizzle and then actual snow. And it lasted—-with interludes of single resplendent days—-all through the month, and on into September. At first the rooms held the warmth of the summery period just past: they stood at fifty degrees, which passed for comfortable. But it grew rapidly colder; there were rejoicings when the snowfall whitened the valley, for the sight of it—-the sight alone, for the mere drop of the temperature would not have sufficed—-compelled the management to heat, first the dining--room, then the chambers as well; so that when one rolled out of the rugs, at the end of a rest period, and re--entered one's chamber, one might warm one's stiffened fingers against the hot pipes, though the dry air these gave out did accentuate the burning in the cheeks.

Was it winter again? Almost the senses thought so. On every hand were loud complaints, that they had been cheated out of their summer; though they had really cheated themselves, abetted by conditions both natural and artificial, and by a consumption of time--units reckless alike within and without. Reason was aware that fine autumnal weather was certain to follow, there would be a succession of brilliant days each outvying the other, and so fine that one might still honour them with the name of summer, save for the flatter arc the sun made in its course, and its earlier setting. But the effect of the winter landscape on the spirit was stronger than the power of such consolatory thoughts. The cousins would stand at the closed door into the balcony, and look out with loathing into the whirl of flakes--it was Joachim who stood thus, and in a suppressed voice he said: "So that's to begin all over again, is it?"

From behind him in the room Hans Castorp responded: "That would be rather early--surely it can't be settling down to winter already--but it has a terribly final look. If winter consists in darkness and cold, snow and hot pipes, then there's no denying it's winter again. And when you think we'd just finished with it and that the snow only just melted--at least, it seems that way, doesn't it, as though spring were only just over--well, it gives one a turn, I will say. It is actually a blow to one's love of life--let me explain to you how I mean. I mean the world as normally arranged is conducive to man's needs and his pleasure in life--isn't that so? I won't go so far as to say that the whole natural order of things, for instance the size of the earth, the time it takes to revolve on its axis and about the sun, the division between day and night, summer and winter--in short, the whole cosmic rhythm, if you like to call it that--was especially arranged for our use and behoof; that would be cheek, I suppose, and simple--minded into the bargain. It would be teleological reasoning, as the philosophers express it. No, it would be truer to say that our needs are--thank God that it should be so--in harmony with the larger, the fundamental facts of nature. I say thank God, for it is really ground for praising Him. Now, when summer or winter comes along down below, the past summer or winter is far enough in the past to make one glad to see it again—-and therein lies some of the joy we have in life. But up here this order and harmony are destroyed: first because there are no proper seasons, as you yourself said when I first came, but only summer days and winter days all mixed up together; and secondly, because what we spend up here isn't time at all, and the new winter, when it comes, isn't new, but the same old winter all the time. All that explains perfectly the disgust you feel when you look out at the window."

"Thanks," Joachim said. "And now that you have explained it, you feel so satisfied that you are even satisfied with the situation itself—-although in all human—-no!" said he. "I'm done. Fed up. It's beastly. The whole thing is just one tremendous, rotten, beastly sell; and I, for my part—-" He went with hasty steps through the room, and shut the door angrily behind him. Unless Hans Castorp was much mistaken, there had been tears in the mild, beautiful eyes.

He left the other staggered. So long as Joachim had confined himself to putting his determination into words, his cousin had not taken it too seriously. But now that silence spoke for him, and his behaviour too, Hans Castorp was alarmed, for he saw that the military Joachim was the man to translate words into deeds—-he was so alarmed that he grew pale, and his pallor was for them both. *"Fort possible qu'il va mourir,"* he thought. And that piece of third--hand information mingled itself with an old, painful, never--quite--to--be--suppressed fear, which made him say to himself: "Is it possible he could leave me alone up here—-me, who only came on a visit to him? That would be crazy, horrible; at the bare thought of it I can feel my heart flutter and my cheek pale. Because *if* I am left up here—-as I shall be, if he goes down, for it is out of the question for me to go with him—- *if* I am left up here, it is for ever; alone I should never find my way back. Never back down to the world again. And at the thought my heart stands still."

Such the course of Hans Castorp's fearful musings. But that very afternoon, certitude was vouchsafed. Joachim declared himself, the die was cast, the bridges burnt.

They went down after tea to the basement for the monthly examination. This was the beginning of September. On entering the warm air of the consulting--room, they saw Dr. Krokowski sitting at his table, and the Hofrat, very blue in the face, leaning against the wall with his arms crossed, tapping his shoulder with the stethoscope, and yawning at the ceiling. "*Mahlzeit*, children," said he, languidly. His mood was lax, resigned and melancholic, and he had probably been smoking. There were also, however, some objective grounds for his state, as the cousins had heard: international scandal of a kind only too familiar in the establishment. A certain young girl called Emmy Nolting had entered House Berghof two years before in the autumn, and after a stay of some nine months departed cured. But before September was out she had returned, saying she did not "feel well" at home. In February, with lungs from which all vestige of rhonchi had disappeared, she was sent home again——but by the middle of July was back in her place at Frau Iltis's table. This Emmy, then, had been discovered in her room at one o'clock at night in company with another sufferer, a Greek named Polypraxios, the same whose shapely legs had attracted favourable attention the night of *mardi gras*—— a young chemist whose father owned dye--works in the Piraeus. The discovery had been made through the jealousy of another young girl, a friend of Emmy, who had found her way to Emmy's room by the same route the Greek had taken——namely, across the balconies; and, distracted by her jealous rage, had made great outcry, so that everybody came running, and the scandal became known to the sparrows on the house--tops. Behrens had to send all three of them away; and had been at the moment going over the whole unsavoury affair with Krokowski, who had had both girls under private treatment. The Hofrat, as he examined, continued to let fall remarks, in resigned and dreary tones——for he was such a master of auscultation that he could listen to a man's inside, dictate what he heard to his assistant, and talk about something else all the time.

"Ah, yes, gentlemen," he said, "this cursed *libido.* You can get some fun out of the thing, it's all right for you.—-Vesicular.—-But a man in my position, verily I say unto you—-dullness here—-he hath his belly full. Is it my fault that phthisis and concupiscence go together—-slight harshness here? I didn't arrange it that way; but before you know where you are you find yourself the keeper of a stew—-restricted here under the left shoulder. We have psycho--analysis, we give the noodles every chance to talk themselves out—-much good it does them! The more they talk the more lecherous they get. I preach mathematics.—-Better here, the rhonchi are gone.—-I tell them that if they will occupy themselves with the study of mathematics they will find in it the best remedy against the lusts of the flesh. Lawyer Paravant was a bad case; he took my advice, he is now busy squaring the circle, and gets great relief. But most of them are too witless and lazy, God help them!—-Vesicular.—-You see, I know it's only too easy for young folk to go to the bad up here—-I used to try to do something about these debauches. But it happened a few times that some brother or bridegroom asked me to my face what affair it was of mine—-and since then I've stuck to my last.—-Slight rales up on the right."

He finished with Joachim, thrust his stethoscope in the pocket of his smock, and rubbed his eyes with both huge hands, as was his habit when he had "backslidden" and become melancholy. Half mechanically, between yawns, he reeled off his patter: "Well, Ziemssen, just keep your pecker up, you'll be all right yet. You aren't like a picture in a physiology--book, there's a hitch here and there, and you haven't cleaned up your Gaffky, you've even gone up a peg or so, it's six this time—-but never mind, don't pull a long face, you are better than you were when you came, I can hand it to you in writing. Just another five or six months—- *monaths*, I mean. Did you know that is the earlier form of the word? I mean to say *monath*, after this—-"

"Herr Hofrat," Joachim began. He stood bare to the waist, heels together and chest out, with a determined bearing, and as mottled in the face as ever he had been that time when Hans Castorp first made observations on the pallor of the deeply tanned. Behrens ran on without noticing: "—-and if you stop another round half year and do particular pipe--clay, why, you'll be a made man, you can take Constantinople singlehanded; you'll be strong enough to command a regiment of Samsons—-" Who knows how much more nonsense he might have uttered if Joachim's unflinching determination to make himself heard had not brought him to a stand.

"Herr Hofrat," the young man said, "I should like to tell you, if you will pardon me, that I have decided to leave."

"What's that? So you want to leave? I thought you wanted to go down later as a sound man, to be a soldier."

"No, I must leave now, Herr Hofrat, in a week, that is."

"Do you mean what you say? You want to hop out of the frying--pan into the fire?

You're going to hook it? Don't you call that desertion?"

"No, Herr Hofrat, I don't look at it in that light. I must join my regiment."

"Even though I tell you I can surely discharge you in half a year, but not before?"

Joachim's bearing became even more correct. He took in his stomach, and replied, repressed and curt: "I have been here a year and a half, Herr Hofrat. I cannot wait any longer. Originally it was to have been three months. Since then it has been increased, first another three, then another six, and so on, and still I am not cured."

"Is that my fault?"

"No, Herr Hofrat. But I cannot wait any longer. If I don't want to miss my opportunity, I cannot wait to make my full cure up here. I must go down now. I need a little time for my equipment and other arrangements."

"Your family knows what you are doing——do they consent?"

"My mother——-yes. It is all arranged. The first of October I join the seventy--sixth regiment as cornet."

"At all hazards?" Behrens asked, and fixed him with his bloodshot eyes.

"I have the honour," Joachim answered, his lips twitching.

"Very good, Ziemssen." The Hofrat's tone changed; he abandoned his position, he relaxed in every way. "Very well, then. Stir your stumps, go on, and God be with you. I see you know your own mind, and so much is certainly true, that it is your affair and not mine. Every pot stands on its own bottom. You go at your own risk, I take no responsibility. But good Lord, it may turn out all right. Soldiering is an out--of--doors job. It may do you good, you may come through all right."

"Yes, Herr Hofrat."

"Well, and what about your cousin, the peaceful citizen over there? He wants to go along with you, does he?" This was Hans Castorp, who was supposed to answer. He stood there as pale as at that first examination, which had ended by his being admitted as a patient. Now, as then, his heart could be seen hammering against his side. He said: "I should like to be guided by your opinion, Herr Hofrat."

"My opinion. Good." He drew him to him by the arm and began to tap and listen. He did not dictate. It went rather fast. When he finished, he said: "You may go."

Hans Castorp stammered: "You——-you mean——-I am cured?"

"Yes, you are cured. The place above in the left lobe is no longer worth talking about. Your temperature doesn't go with it. Why you have it, I don't know. I assume it is of no further importance. So far as I am concerned, you can go "

"But—-Herr Hofrat—-may I ask—-that is—-you are perhaps not altogether serious?"

"Not serious? Why not? What do you suppose? And incidentally, what do you think of me, might I be allowed to ask? What do you take me for? A bawdy--house keeper?"

He was in a towering passion. The blood flared up in his cheeks and turned their blue to violet, his one--sided lip was wrenched so high that the canines of the upper jaw were visible. He advanced his head like a steer, with staring, bloodshot watery eyes "I won't have it," he bellowed. "In the first place, I'm not the proprietor here!

I'm on hire. I'm a doctor! I'm nothing but a doctor, I would give you to understand. I'm not a pimp. I'm no Signor Amoroso on the Toledo, in *Napoti bella*. I am a servant of suffering humanity! And if either one of you should perchance have conceived a different opinion of me and my character then you can both go to the devil with my compliments—-you can go to the dogs or you can turn up your toes, whichever you like, and a pleasant journey to you!"

He strode across the room and was out of the door that led to the x--ray waitingroom. It crashed behind him. The cousins looked imploringly at Dr. Krokowski, who buried his nose in his papers. They hurried into their clothes. On the stair Hans Castorp said: "That was awful. Have you ever seen him like that before?"

"No, not like that. But the authorities sometimes get these attacks. The important thing is to behave with dignity and let them pass over. He was irritated about the business with Polypraxios and Emmy Nolting. But did you see," Joachim went on, and the joy of having fought and won his battle mounted in him and almost took away his breath, "did you see how he gave in and showed no more fight, directly he saw I was in earnest? All one has to do is to show some pluck, and not let oneself be shouted down. Now I've even got a sort of leave—-at least, he said himself I'll probably pull out of it—-and I'm travelling in a week—-in three weeks I'll be with the colours," he finished, altering his phrase, and confining the joy that trembled in his voice to his own affairs, without reference to Hans Castorp's.

The latter was silent. He spoke no word, either of Joachim's "leave" or his own—- which might equally well have been mentioned. He made his preparations for the restcure, put the thermometer in his mouth, flung the camel's--hair rugs about him with swift, practised hand, the perfected technique of that consecrated art the flat--land knows not of; then he lay still, neat as a sausage--roll, in his excellent chair, in the chill dampness of the early autumn afternoon.

The rain--clouds hung low. Remnants of snow rested on the boughs of the silver fir. The banner of the establishment was furled round its staff. A low murmur of voices rose from the rest--hall, whence last year, at much about this time, the voice of Herr Albin had risen to Hans Castorp's ear. The cure was going on, the patients sat there with soon--chilled faces and fingertips. To him all this was long--established habit, the inevitable course of life; he knew the gratitude of the settled patient for the blessing of being able to lie, snugly ensconced, and think everything over at leisure.

So it was settled, Joachim was to go. Rhadamanthus had released him; not *rite*, not with a clean bill of health, yet half approvingly, on the ground, and in recognition, of his constant spirit. He would go down: first with the narrow--gauge road as far as Landquart, then to Romanshorn, then across the wide, bottomless lake, over which in the legend the rider rode, across all Germany, and home. He would stop there, in the valley world, among men with no notion of the way to live, ignorant of "measuring" and of the whole ritual of rug--wrapping, of fur sleeping--sacks, of the three daily walks, of—-it was hard to say, hard to count all the things of which those down below stood in blank ignorance; but the mere picture of Joachim, after a year and a half up here, living in the darkness of that flat--landish incomprehension—-a picture only of Joachim, with hardly the faintest hypothetical reference to Hans Castorp himself—-so bewildered the young man that he closed his eyes and waved it away with a motion of the hand, murmuring: "Impossible!"

And since it was impossible, he would live on up here, alone, without Joachim?

Yes, it came to that. How long? Until Behrens discharged him cured—-in earnest, that is, not as he had to--day. But that was so indefinite a time--limit that he could no more prophesy it than could Joachim, on a like occasion long ago. Again, would the impossible by then have become any more possible? On the contrary, Joachim's rash departure did—-in honesty—-offer his cousin a support, now, before the impossible should become utterly so, a guide and companion on a path which of himself he would never, never find again. Ah, if one consulted humanistic pedagogy, how humanistic pedagogy would adjure him to take the hand and accept the offered guidance! But Herr Settembrini was only a representative—-of things and forces worth hearing about, it was true, but not the only forces there were. And with Joachim it was the same. He was a soldier. He was leaving—-almost at the very time set for the return of the high--breasted one, for it was known that she would return in October. While the departure of the civilian Hans Castorp became impossible precisely because he had to wait for Clavdia Chauchat, whose return, as yet, was not even thought of. "I don't look at it in that light," Joachim had answered when Rhadamanthus talked about desertion—-though as far as Joachim was concerned that had probably only been some of the Hofrat's melancholic maundering. But for him, the civilian, the thing was different. For him—-ah, here was the right idea, the thought which he had set himself to evolve, as he lay out in the cold and damp—-for him the real desertion would lie in his taking advantage of the occasion to dash off unlawfully—-or half unlawfully—-to the flat--land. It would be the abandonment of certain comprehensive responsibilities which had grown up out of his contemplation of the image called *Homo Dei;* it would be the betrayal of that appointed task of "stock--taking," that hard and harassing task, which was really beyond the powers native to him, but yet afforded his spirit such nameless and adventurous joys; that task it was his duty to perform, here in his chair, and up there in his blue--blossoming retreat.

He tore the thermometer out of his mouth, violently as never before save when the Oberin had sold him the toy and he had first used it. He looked at it with the same avid curiosity now as then. Ah, Mercurius had indeed bounded upwards: he stood at 100.5°, almost .6°.

Hans Castorp threw off his covers, sprang up and strode to the corridor door and back. Then he lay down again, called softly to Joachim, and asked him what he measured. "I'm not measuring any more," replied his cousin.

"Well, I've some temperament," Hans Castorp said, emulating Frau Stöhr; Joachim, behind the glass pane, answered never a word.

He said no more, on that day or the following; made no effort to find out his cousin's plans—-which would, indeed, be driven to declare themselves in no long time, by his either taking certain steps or refraining from them. They did so—-by the latter. Hans Castorp seemed to hold with that quietism in whose view all action was an insult to God, who prefers to act by Himself. At all events, the young man's activity during these days confined itself to a visit to Behrens; a consultation of which Joachim was aware, the result of which he could have accurately predicted beforehand. His cousin had explained that he took the liberty of placing more reliance upon the Hofrat's oft--repeated exhortations to stop up here long enough to perfect his cure than he did upon an ill--considered verdict pronounced in the heat of the moment. His temperature was 100.5°, one could not regard himself as discharged in form; and unless the Hofrat's recent statement was to be regarded in the light of an expulsion, to which he, the speaker, was not aware he had laid himself open, he wished to say that upon mature consideration he had decided to remain and await the event of a complete cure. To all which the Hofrat had merely responded: "*Bon!* Werry good—-no offence intended, none taken," or words to that effect. That was talking like a sensible man; hadn't he seen first off that Hans Castorp had more talent as a patient than that fire--eater his cousin? And so on.

All of this corresponded pretty accurately to Joachim's guess. He said nothing, only noting in silence that Hans Castorp made no move to join in his preparations for departure. But the good Joachim was busy enough, in all conscience, with his own affairs. He had no more time to concern himself with his cousin's fate or further sojourn. Within his own bosom the tempest raged. It was as well he no longer took his temperature——he had, so he said, let his instrument fall, and broken it——for the thermometer might have given contrary counsel: so fearfully wrought up was he, now darkly glowing, now pale with joyful agitation. He could no longer lie still in the cure; Hans Castorp heard how he went up and down all day in his room, throughout those hours, four times each day, when all over House Berghof the horizontal obtained. A year and a half it had been. And now at last, at last, he was off for the flat--land, for home and his regiment! Even though with only half a discharge. It was no trifling event——Hans Castorp's heart went out to his cousin as he heard his restless pacing. Eighteen months, the wheel full circle and halfway round again, he had lived up here, deep, deep into the life of the place, the inviolable ebb and flow of it, for seven times seventy days; and now he would go down to live among strangers and the uninitiate. What difficulties would he not have, to acclimatize himself? Would it be surprising if Joachim's agitation consisted only in part of joyful emotion, and also in part of dread——if it was not also the pang of parting with all this familiar life that made him stride thus up and down his room? We leave Marusja out of account.

But joy weighed down the scale. The good Joachim's heart overflowed at his lips. He spoke always of himself, he made no reference to Hans Castorp's future. He said how fresh and new the world would seem, himself, all life, and every day, every hour of the time. Once more he would rejoice in real, solid time, the long, vital years of youth. He spoke of his mother, Hans Castorp's step--aunt Ziemssen, who had the same gentle black eyes as her son. She had never visited him up here in all this time; put off like him from month to month, from half--year to half--year, she had delayed for the entire term of his stay in the mountains. He spoke of the oath of fidelity to the colours, which he would soon be taking—-spoke ardently, with a smile on his face. It was a solemn ceremony: in the presence of the standard he would be sworn to it, literally, to the standard—-" You don't say! Seriously?" Hans Castorp asked. "To the flag--pole?

To that scrap of bunting?" Even so! It was symbolic; in the artillery they were sworn to the gun. What fanatical customs, the civilian remarked; extravagantly emotional he found them. Joachim nodded, full of pride and joy.

He spent his time in preparations; settled his last account with the management, and days ahead of time began to pack. He packed his summer and winter clothing, and had the sleeping--bag and camel's--hair rugs sewed up in sacking by one of the servants. They might be useful at manœuvres. He began to make his farewells; paid visits to Naphta and Settembrini—-alone, for his cousin did not offer to go with him, nor did he ask what Settembrini had said to Joachim's imminent departure and to Hans Castorp's imminent stopping--behind. Whether Settembrini had remarked "Yes, yes," or "I see, I see," or both, or merely *"Poveretto!"* To Hans Castorp it was evidently all one. Came the eve of departure. Joachim performed for the last time each act of the daily round: each meal, each rest period, each walk; he took leave of the physicians and the Oberin. The morning dawned. He came to table with cold hands and burning eyes; he had not closed them all night. He ate scarce a mouthful; and when the dwarf waitress came to say that his trunks had been strapped, he started up from his chair to take leave of his table--mates. Frau Stöhr wept, the easy, brineless tears of the simpleminded; and after, behind Joachim's back, shook her head at the schoolmistress and turned her hand about in the air, with the fingers spread out, thus expressing a cheap and common scepticism on the score of Joachim's competence to depart, and his future welfare. Hans Castorp saw her do it, as he drank out his cup standing, in act to follow his cousin. Then came the business of tipping, and receiving the management's official farewell in the vestibule. The usual group of spectators stood about: Frau Iltis with her "steriletto," the ivory Levi, the inordinate Popoff and his wife. They waved their handkerchiefs as the wagon went down the drive with the brake on. Joachim had been presented with roses. He wore a hat, Hans Castorp none.

The morning was glorious, with the first sunshine after days of gloom. The Schiahorn, the Green Towers, the round top of the Dorfberg stood out unchangeable and unmistakable against the blue; Joachim's eyes rested on them. Hans Castorp said it was almost a pity the weather had turned so fine on the last day. There was a sort of spite about it; partings were always easier if some inhospitable impression was left at the end. To which Joachim: he didn't need anything to make it easier, and this was excellent weather for manœuvres, he could do with it down below. They said little else. Things being as they were between them, and the situation for them both, there was indeed not much to say. The lame porter sat on the box with the driver. Erect and bouncing on the hard cushions, they laid the watercourse behind them, the narrow--gauge track; drove along the irregularly built--up street beside the latter, and drew up in the paved square before the station of the Dorf, that was little more than a shell. Hans Castorp with a thrill recalled first impressions. Since his arrival, thirteen months before, in the twilight, he had not seen the station. "Here was where I arrived," he remarked superfluously, to Joachim, who only said: "So you did," and paid the coachman.

The nimble lame man attended to tickets and luggage. They stood together on the platform by the miniature train, in one of whose grey--upholstered compartments Joachim kept a place with his overcoat, travelling--rug and roses. "Well, get along, and take your fanatical oath," Hans Castorp told his cousin, and Joachim answered: "I mean to." What else was there to say? Last greetings to exchange, greetings to those down below, to those up here. Hans Castorp drew patterns on the asphalt with his cane. "Take your places!" shouted the guard. Hans Castorp started; looked at Joachim, Joachim at him. They put out their hands. Hans Castorp was vaguely smiling; the other's eyes looked sad, beseeching. "Hans!" he said——yes, incredible and painful as the thing was, it happened: he had called his cousin by his first name. Not with the thou, not "old fellow," or "man," by which forms they had addressed each other their lives long. No, in defiance of all reserve, almost gushingly, he called his cousin by his first name. "Hans!" he said, and pressed his hand imploringly——and the latter noted that the excitement of the journey, the sleepless night, the emotion, made Joachim's head tremble on his neck, as his own did when he "took stock"——"Hans," he said earnestly, "come down soon!" He swung himself up. The door banged, the train whistled, the carriages shunted together. The little engine puffed and pulled off, the train glided after. The traveller waved his hat from the window, the other, on the platform, his hand. Desolately he stood, after that, a long time, alone. Then slowly he retraced the path that more than a year ago he had first traversed with Joachim.

An Attack, and a Repulse

The wheel revolved. The hand on time's clock moved forward. Orchis and aquilegia were out of bloom, and the mountain pink. The deep--blue, star--shaped gentian and the autumn crocus, pale and poisonous, appeared again among the damp grass, and a reddish hue overspread the forests. The autumn equinox was past. All Souls' was in sight——and, for practised time--consumers, probably also the Advent season, the solstice, and Christmas. But for the moment there were lovely October days, a succession of them, like that on which the cousins had viewed the Hofrat's paintings. Since Joachim's departure Hans Castorp sat no more at Frau Stöhr's table, the one with Dr. Blumenkohl's empty place, at which the gay Marusja had been wont to smother her irresponsible mirth in her orange--scented pocket--handkerchief. New guests, strangers, sat there now. Our friend, two months deep in his second year, had been given a new place by the management at a near--by table, diagonally to his old one, between that and the "good" Russian table. In short, Settembrini's table. Yes, Hans Castorp sat in the humanist's vacated seat, again at the end, facing the "doctor's place," which at each of the seven tables was left free for the Hofrat and his famulus to use when they could. At the upper end, next the place of the medical presiding officer, the hump--backed Mexican sat, perched on many cushions; the amateur photographer, whose facial expression was that of a deaf person, because he possessed no language with which to communicate his thoughts. Beside him sat the ancient maiden lady from Siebenbürgen. She, as Herr Settembrini had said, claimed the interest of all and sundry for her brother--in--law, a man of whom nobody knew anything, or wished to know. Regularly at certain hours of the day this lady was to be seen at the balustrade of her loggia with a little Tula--silver--handled cane across the nape of her neck——it served also as a support on her walks——-expanding her flat chest by means of deep--breathing exercises. Opposite her sat a Czech, whom everybody called Herr Wenzel, as his family name was impossible to pronounce. Herr Settembrini, indeed, did once essay to utter the involved succession of consonants; less in good faith than by way of testing gaily the elegant helplessness of his Latinity in face of that matted and tangled growth of sound. Although plump as a mole, with an appetite amazing even up here, the Czech had for four years been asseverating that there was no hope for him. Of an evening, he would strum the songs of his native land upon a beribboned mandolin; or talk about his sugar--beet plantation, and the pretty girls who worked it. On Hans Castorp's either side sat the wedded pair from Halle, Magnus the brewer and his wife, about whom melancholy hung as a cloud, because they had no tolerance for certain important products of metabolism: he sugar, she albumen. Their spirits, particularly the sallow Frau Magnus's, were proof against any ray of cheer; forlornity exhaled from her like damp from a cellar; even more than Frau Stöhr she represented that unedifying union of dullness and disease, which had offended Hans Castorp's soul——-under correction from Herr Settembrini. Herr Magnus was livelier and chattier, though only in a vein intolerable to the Italian's literary sense. He was inclined to choler too, and often clashed with Herr Wenzel on political and other grounds. The nationalistic aspirations of the Czech exasperated him; again, the latter declared himself in favour of prohibition, and made moral remarks about the brewing industry, while Herr Magnus, very red in the face, defended from the hygienic viewpoint the unexceptionableness of the drink with which his interests were bound up. At such moments as these, Herr Settembrini's light and humorous touch had often preserved the amenities; but Hans Castorp, in his place, found his authority little able to cope with the situation.

With only two of his table--mates had he personal relations: Anton Karlowitsch Ferge from St. Petersburg, that good--natured sufferer, was one, on his left. He had things to tell, under his bushy, red--brown moustaches, about the manufacture of rubber shoes; about distant regions in the polar circle, about perpetual winter at the North Cape. Hans Castorp and he sometimes made their daily round together. The other, who joined them as occasion offered, and who sat next the hump--backed Mexican, at the far end of the table, was the man from Mannheim, with the thin hair and poor teeth—-Ferdinand Wehsal by name, and merchant by calling—-whose eyes had rested with such dismal longing upon Frau Chauchat's pleasing person, and who since that carnival night had sought Hans Castorp's company.

He did so with meek persistence, with a deprecating devotion which was even repugnant to Hans Castorp, understanding as he did its involved origins; but to which he felt himself humanly bound to respond. Blandly, then, and aware that even a lifting of the brows would suffice to make the poor--spirited creature cringe and shrink away, he suffered Wehsal's fawning presence, and the latter lost no chance to make himself agreeable. He suffered the man to carry his overcoat as they went on their walks together, and Wehsal did this devotedly; suffered even the conversation of the Mannheimer, which was depressing to a degree. Wehsal had an itch to raise questions like this: would there be any sense in making a declaration of love to a woman whom one adored, but who made absolutely no response—-a declaration, in other words, of hopeless love? What did his companion think? For his part, he thought well of the idea, he thought there would be boundless happiness in the experience. Even if the act of confession aroused nothing but disgust, and involved great humiliation, still it insured a moment of intimate contact with the beloved object. The confidence drew her into the circle of his passion, and if after that all was indeed over, yet the loss was paid for by the despairing bliss of the moment; for the avowal was an act of force, the more satisfying the greater the resistance it encountered. At this point a darkening of Hans Castorp's brows made Wehsal desist, though it had more reference to the presence of the good--natured Ferge, with his shrinking from the higher flights of conversation, than to any moral censorship on the part of our hero. Unwilling to make him out as either better or worse than he really was, we feel bound to mention that the wretched Wehsal, one evening when they were alone, prayed him, with pallid lips, for the love of God to tell him what had taken place after the *mardi gras* festivities, and Hans Castorp had good--naturedly complied, without, as the reader may imagine, introducing any wanton or flippant element into his recital. Still, there seems every reason, on our part and on his, not to go into it very much, and we will only add that thereafter Wehsal carried his friend's overcoat with even more self--abnegation than before.

So much of our Hans's table--mates. The seat at his right was vacant, was only occupied for a few days by a guest, such as he himself had once been, a visiting relative from below, an envoy, one might say—-no other than Hans's uncle James Tienappel.

It was uncanny, to have suddenly sitting next him a delegate and ambassador from home, exhaling from the very weave of his English suit of clothes the atmosphere of that old life in the "upper" world so far below. But it was bound to come. For a long time Hans Castorp had silently reckoned with the possibility of an advance from the flat--land, and even been fairly sure what personal shape it would take. It was, in fact, not difficult to guess who would come, for Peter, the seafaring man, was almost out of the question, while as for Great--uncle Tienappel himself, it was no less true than ever that wild horses could not drag him to a spot from the atmospheric pressure of which he had everything to fear. No, James was the man to be sent with a commission from home to search out the truant—-and his advent had been expected even earlier. After Joachim had returned alone, and told the family circle what the state of things was, the visit had been due and overdue, and thus Hans Castorp was not in the slightest degree nonplussed when, scarcely two weeks after his cousin left, the concierge handed him a telegram. He opened it with foreknowledge of its contents, and read the announcement of James Tienappel's impending arrival. He had business in Switzerland, and would take the occasion to make Hans a visit on his heights. He would be here the day after to--morrow.

"Good," thought Hans Castorp. "Excellent," he thought. And added to himself something like "Don't mention it!" "If you only knew!" he silently apostrophized the oncoming one. In a word, he took the approaching visit with utter composure; announced it to Hofrat Behrens and the management, engaged a room—-Joachim's, it being still vacant—-and on the next day but one, at the hour of his own arrival, towards eight o'clock—-it was already dark—-drove in the same uncomfortable vehicle in which he had seen Joachim off, down to station "Dorf, " to meet the envoy from the flat--land, who had come to spy out the land.

Crimson--faced, bare--headed, overcoatless, he stood at the edge of the platform as the train rolled in, beneath his relative's carriage window, and told him to come on out, for he was here. Consul Tienappel—-he was Vice--Consul, having obligingly relieved his father of that office too—-stepped out, wrapped in his winter overcoat, and half frozen, for the October evening was chill, indeed was nearly cold enough for frost, toward morning it would probably freeze; stepped out of his compartment in lively surprise, which he expressed after the elegant, somewhat rarefied manner of the

[539]

gentlemanly north--west German; greeted his nephew--cousin with repeated and emphatically uttered exclamations of satisfaction at his appearance; saw himself relieved by the lame concierge of all care for his luggage, and climbed with Hans Castorp up on the high, hard seat of the cabriolet, in the square outside. They drove under a heaven thick with stars, and Hans Castorp, his head tipped back, with pointing forefinger expounded to his uncle--cousin the starry field, named planets by name and showed off this or that constellation. The other, more observant of his companion than of the cosmos, said to himself that it was perhaps conceivable, it was at least not actually lunatic, to begin a conversation by talking about the stars, but there were other subjects that lay closer to hand. Since when, he asked, had Hans Castorp known so much about matters up aloft; and the young man replied that his knowledge was the fruit of long lying in the evening rest--cure, spring, summer, autumn, and winter. What? He lay out in a balcony at night? Oh, yes. The Consul would too. He would have nothing else to do.

"Certainly, of course," James Tienappel acquiesced, rather intimidated. His fosterbrother spoke on, equably, monotonously. He sat without hat or overcoat, in the air, fresh to frostiness, of the autumn evening. "I suppose you aren't cold?" James asked him, shivering in his inch--thick ulster. He talked fast and rather indistinctly, his teeth showing a tendency to chatter. "We don't feel the cold," Hans Castorp said, with tranquil brevity.

The Consul could not look at him enough as they sat and drove. Hans Castorp asked after relatives and friends at home. James conveyed various greetings, including Joachim's, who was already with the colours, and radiant with pride and joy. Hans Castorp received them with a quiet word of thanks, without asking more particular questions about his home. Disquieted by an indefinite something, either emanating from his nephew, or caused by his own unsettlement after the long journey, James looked about him, not able to descry much of the landscape; he drew in a deep breath of the strange air, exhaled it, and pronounced it magnificent. Of course, the other answered, not for nothing was it famous far and wide. It had great properties. It accelerated oxidization, yet at the same time one put on flesh. It was capable of healing certain diseases which were latent in every human being, though its first effects were strongly favourable to these, and by dint of a general organic compulsion, upwards and outwards, made them come to the surface, brought them, as it were, to a triumphant outburst.——Beg pardon——triumphant?——Yes; had he never felt that an outbreak of disease had something jolly about it, an outburst of physical gratification?

"Certainly, of course," the uncle hastened to say, with his lower jaw under imperfect control. And then announced that he could stop eight days—a week, that was; seven days—-or perhaps six. He said he found Hans Castorp looking very fit indeed, thanks to a stay that had been so much longer than anyone anticipated, and this being the case he supposed his nephew would travel down with him when he left.

"Oh, no, I don't quite intend to play the fool like that," Hans Castorp said. Uncle James talked like a valley man. Let him stop up here a bit, look about him and get used to things, he would change his tune. The thing was to achieve an absolute cure, and to that end Behrens had just lately socked him another six months. "Are you crazy?" the uncle asked. He addressed his relative as "young man," and asked if he was crazy. A holiday that would soon have lasted a year and a quarter, and now another half a year on top of that! Who, deuce take it, had all that time to waste? Hans Castorp laid back his head, and laughed, a quiet, brief chuckle. Time! Uncle James would have to alter his ideas about time, in the first place, before he could talk. Tienappel said he would have a serious conversation to--morrow with the Hofrat, on Hans's affair. "By all means," advised the nephew. "You'll like him. An interesting character, brusque to a degree, yet melancholy." He pointed up to the lights on the Schatzalp, and casually mentioned that they had to bring down their corpses by bobsleigh in the winter. The gentlemen supped together in the restaurant, after Hans Castorp had conducted his relative to his room and given him a chance to get a wash--up. It had been fumigated with H_2CO, he explained, quite as thoroughly as though the late tenant had not gone off without leave, but in quite a different way—--an exit instead of an exodus. The uncle inquired what he meant. "Jargon," said Hans Castorp. "A way we have in the service. Joachim deserted—--deserted to the colours—--funny, but it can be done. But make haste, or we shall get nothing hot to eat." In the warm, well--lighted restaurant they sat down facing each other at the raised table in the window. The dwarf waitress served them nimbly, and James ordered a bottle of burgundy, which was presented lying in a basket. They touched glasses, and the grateful glow ran through their veins. The younger talked of life up here, of the events the changing seasons brought in their course, of various personalities among the patients, of the pneumothorax, the functioning of which he explained at length, describing the ghastly nature of the pleura--shock, and citing the case of the good--natured Herr Ferge, with the threecoloured fainting--fits, the hallucinatory stench, and the diabolic laughing--fit when they felt over the pleura. He paid for the meal. James ate and drank heartily, as was his custom—--with an appetite still further sharpened by his journey and the change of air. But he intermitted the process several times, sat with his mouth full of food and forgot to chew, holding his knife and fork at an obtuse angle above his plate and regarding Hans Castorp with a fixed stare. He seemed unaware that he did this, nor did the other give sign of remarking it. Consul Tienappel's temples, covered with thin blond hair, showed swollen veins.

The conversation did not run upon their home below, there was no reference to family or personal, business or city affairs, nor yet to the firm of Tunder and Wilms, Ship--builders, Smelters, and Machinists, who were still waiting for their apprentice—- though it was likely they had too much else to do to be aware that they were waiting. James Tienappel had touched, of course, on these topics, during their drive and after, but they had fallen flat; no one had picked them up. They had bounded off, as it were, from Hans Castorp's serene,

unfeigned, unmistakable sangfroid, which was like a suit of armour;
like his indifference to the chill of that autumn evening, like his little
phrase "We don't feel the cold." This air of his may have been the
reason why his uncle looked at him so fixedly. They spoke of the
Oberin and the doctors, of Dr. Krokowski's lectures, at one of which
James would be present if he stopped a week. Who had told the
nephew the uncle would wish to be present? Nobody——he had
simply assumed it, with such tranquil certitude as to render absurd
the bare idea of not being present, which, accordingly, James
hastened to disclaim with a quick "Certainly, of course," as though
anxious to show he had never for a moment considered it. It was this
very power, quiet yet compelling, that caused Consul Tienappel all
unconsciously to gaze at his nephew; and now even open--mouthed,
for he found his nasal passages obstructed, though, so far as he knew,
he had no catarrh. He heard his relative hold forth upon the disease
which was the business of life up here, and upon the receptivity
commonly displayed for it; upon Hans Castorp's own simple but
tedious case, upon the attraction the bacilli had for the cellular tissue
of the air passages of the throat, bronchial tubes, and pulmonary
vesicles; upon the formation of nodules, the manifestation of soluble
toxins and their narcotic effect upon the system; of the breaking-
-down of the tissues, of caseation, and the question whether the
disease would be arrested by a chalky petrefaction and heal by means
of fibrosis, or whether it would extend the area, create still larger
cavities, and destroy the organ. He was told of the "galloping" form
the disease sometimes assumed, which made the end an affair of not
more than a few months or even weeks; of pneumotomy, of the
Hofrat's masterly surgery, of resection of the lungs, an operation
which was to be performed to--morrow or the day after upon a severe
case just brought to the sanitorium, a charming, or once--charming
Scotswoman suffering from *gangrœna pulmonum*, gangrene of the
lungs, a green and black pestilence, which obliged her to inhale all
day a vaporized solution of carbolic acid, lest she go out of her head
from sheer physical disgust. Here, suddenly, the Consul, to his own
great surprise and chagrin, burst out laughing. He fairly snorted, but

recovered himself immediately, horrified; coughed, and tried his best to disguise the senseless outbreak. He felt a relief, which however bore within it the seeds of fresh disquiet, when he saw that Hans Castorp paid no heed, though he must have noticed the incident, but passed it over with an unconcern which was not so much tact, consideration, or courtesy, as it was the purest indifference, an uncanny invulnerability or complaisance, as though he had long ceased to notice or to feel surprise at such occurrences. Perhaps the Consul wished to make his burst of hilarity appear plausible; perhaps he had some other connexion in mind; at all events, he abruptly took over the conversation and began talking like a club--man. The veins stood out on his forehead, as he described a *chansonette* by a certain café--chantant artiste, a perfectly crazy piece of goods, who was then on the boards at St. Pauli, taking away the breath of his Hamburg fellowmales by her temperamental charms, which he essayed to describe to his cousin. His tongue was a little thick, though that need not have troubled him, since his cousin's strange complaisance seemed to cover this phenomenon like the other. But his weariness became at length so overpowering that the meeting broke up at about half past ten, and he was scarcely capable of attending when he was introduced to the oftmentioned Dr. Krokowski, who sat reading a newspaper near the door of one of the salons. He responded little else than "Certainly, of course" to the doctor's blithe and hearty greeting, and was relieved when his nephew left him, passing by the balcony from Joachim's room to his own, after bidding him good--night and saying he would fetch him for eight o'clock breakfast. He was glad to relapse into the deserter's bed, with his regular good--night cigarette——with which he nearly caused a conflagration, by twice falling asleep with it alight between his lips.

James Tienappel, whom Hans Castorp addressed by turns as Uncle James and James, was a long--legged man close to the forties, dressed in good English suiting and florid linen; with thinnish canary--yellow hair, blue eyes set close together, a closeclipped, straw--coloured moustache, and carefully manicured hands. He had continued to live in the old Consul's roomy villa in Harvestehuder Way, though he had been a husband and father for some years, having taken a wife from his own social sphere, of his own highly civilized and elegant type, with the same soft, quick, pointedly polite manner of speech. In his own sphere he passed for a very energetic, cautious and—-despite his refined ways—coldly practical man of business. But outside it—-when he travelled south, for instance—-he displayed a kind of eager pliancy, a quick and friendly readiness to step outside his own personality, which was by no means a sign of the insecurity of his own culture, but rather betrayed a conviction of its sufficiency, and a desire to correct his own aristocratic limitations; it evidenced a wish not to show surprise at new ways, even when he found them extraordinary past belief. "Certainly, of course," he would hasten to remark, so that nobody might say of him that with all his elegance he was limited. He had come up here on a definite practical mission, to see how matters stood with his dilatory young kinsman, to "prize him loose," as he put it to himself, and take him back home. But he was conscious that he was operating on foreign territory; and the first few minutes up here had made him suspect that he was a guest in a sphere quite foreign to him, and more instead of less self--assured than his own. His business instincts conflicted with his good breeding—-the more keenly the more he was aware of the self--confident poise of the institutional life. All this Hans Castorp had realized when he replied to the Consul's wire with an inward "Don't mention it!" But we must not suppose that he consciously practised on his uncle with the strange properties of the place. He had been too long a part of it; it was not he who wielded them against the aggressor, but they him. Everything—-from the moment when an emanation from his nephew had first whispered to the Consul that his undertaking had small chance of success—-everything about the situation fulfilled itself, simply, inevitably, up to the end, and Hans Castorp accompanied the process with his melancholy, fatalistic smile.

On the first morning, at breakfast, the host made his guest acquainted with his circle of table--mates. Afterwards James met the Hofrat, who came paddling through the dining--room, with the black and pale assistant in his wake, strewing on all sides his regular rhetorical question: "Slept well?" He met the Hofrat, and from his lips heard that not only had it been a clipper of an idea to come on a visit to his marooned cousin, but that he served his own interest even better in so coming, for that he was totally anæmic was plain to any eye. He, Tienappel, anæmic?—-" Ray--ther so," said Behrens, and putting up a forefinger pulled down the skin under James's eye. "Rayther so!" he reiterated. The avuncular guest would be turning a clever trick to stretch himself out on his balcony for a few weeks and do his best to emulate the good example set him by his nephew. In his condition he could do nothing sharper than to act as though he had a slight case of *tuberculosis pulmonum*— it was always present anyhow. "Certainly, of course," replied the Consul hastily; and as the Hofrat paddled off, he gazed after the man and his neck--bone, with open mouth and mien sedulously polite, for quite a while, his nephew standing by, utterly unmoved, unscathed. They took the prescribed walk, as far as the watercourse and back, after which James Tienappel experienced his first rest--cure. Hans Castorp lent him one of his camel'shair rugs, in addition to James's own plaid; he himself found one cover quite enough this fine autumn weather. And instructed him step by step in the traditional art of putting on rugs; yes, after he had got the Consul all nicely mummified, deliberately undid him again, to the end that he should pack himself up alone, with Hans Castorp lending a helping hand. Then the adept taught the catechumen how to attach the linen parasol to his chair and adjust it against the sun.

The Consul was pleased to be jocose. The spirit of the flat--land was still strong within him, and he made merry over his lesson, as he had earlier over the prescribed exercise after breakfast. But when he saw the peaceful, uncomprehending smile with which his nephew met his jests, a smile in which was mirrored all the serene selfassurance of the local tradition, alarm laid hold on him. He feared, actually, the impairment of his business energy, and hastily resolved to have the decisive conversation with the Hofrat as soon as possible and get it over—-that very afternoon if it could be done, while he still possessed and could bring to bear the strength of conviction which he had brought with him from below. He distinctly felt that this was weakening, that his own good breeding had joined hands against him with the spirit of the place.

And furthermore he felt that it had been superfluous for the Hofrat to advise him, on account of his anæmia, to live during his stay here as the patients did. For, it appeared, this followed of itself; no other course seemed possible. This was perhaps partly the fruit of his nephew's calm and invulnerable self--assurance; perhaps it was not absolutely the only and inevitable course to pursue—-but how was a man of his breeding to distinguish? Nothing could be clearer than that the abundant second breakfast should follow upon the rest period, after which the stroll down to the Platz appeared the natural and inevitable sequence—-and then Hans Castorp did his uncle up again. He did him up—-the right phrase for it—-and there, in the autumn sunlight, in a chair whose qualities should be sung rather than spoken, he let him lie, until a clanging gong summoned the patients to the midday meal. So lavish was it, so altogether tiptop and first--rate, that the main rest period which ensued seemed an inward necessity rather than an outward conformity, and James participated in it with the sincerest personal conviction. And so on until the mighty supper and the social evening in the salon with the optical diversions. What objection could be brought against a daily regimen like that, which so blandly took acquiescence for granted?

None, surely, even though the Consul's critical powers had not been diminished by a physical discomfort which, while not actual illness, yet, composed of mingled fatigue and excitement, with the concomitants of chill and feverishness, was burdensome enough.

Hans Castorp had availed himself of the official channels in arranging for that ardently desired consultation with Hofrat Behrens:

he had given a message to the bathing--master, which the latter passed on to the Oberin, and Consul Tienappel had the opportunity of making the acquaintance of this peculiar personality. She appeared to him as he lay upon his balcony, and her extraordinary manner put a severe strain on the good breeding of the hapless gentleman lying there in his chair like a sausage--roll. He would be so good, he was told, to have patience for a few days; the Hofrat was busy, there were operations and general examinations, suffering humanity must take precedence, that was a sound Christian principle; and as he was ostensibly in good health, he must get used to the idea that he was not number one up here, that he must stand back and await his turn. It would be different if he wished to make an appointment for an examination——she, Adriatica, would not have been surprised if he had. When she looked him straight in the eyes——like that——she found his rather blurred and flickering; and he looked, as he lay, not as though everything were in the best of order with him, she herself would hardly give him a clean bill of health. Was it really an examination or a private interview he wanted? "The latter, of course," James assured her. Then he would be so good as to wait until she let him know. The Hofrat had not much time for private interviews.

In short, it all turned out quite otherwise than James had expected, and the conversation with the Directress no little disturbed his equanimity. A man of his breeding hesitated to say rudely to his nephew that he found her an appalling person: it would be indiscreet, considering how plainly Hans Castorp's manner revealed his acceptance of all the extraordinary phenomena up here. James merely tapped at his nephew's door, and insinuated that Fräulein Mylendonk was surely extremely original. Hans Castorp looked up inquiringly, and half assented; asking, in his turn: "Did she sell you a thermometer?" "Me——no," said his uncle. "Is that the custom up here?" The worst of it was that Hans Castorp would clearly not have been surprised if she had. It was "We don't feel the cold" all over again. And the Consul did feel the cold, felt it persistently, though his head was hot. He thought to himself that if the Oberin had offered him a thermometer, he would certainly have refused it, and thereby have committed a blunder, since he could not ask to use his nephew's—-he was too civilized for that.

Some days passed, perhaps four or five. The life of the ambassador ran on rails—-the rails laid for it to run on—-and that it should run off them was unthinkable. The Consul had his experiences, got his impressions—-in which we shall not trouble to follow him. One day, in Hans Castorp's room, he lifted from its easel on the chest of drawers a black glass plate, one of the small personal articles with which the owner adorned his cleanly quarters. He held it toward the light; it proved to be a photographic negative. He looked at it—-"What is that?" he said. He might well ask. It showed the headless skeleton of a human form—-the upper half, that is—-enveloped in misty flesh; he recognized the female torso. "That? Oh, a souvenir," the nephew answered. To which the uncle replied: "Pardon me," and hastily replaced the picture on its easel. We give this merely as example of the sort of experience the four or five days supplied him. He attended one of Dr. Krokowski's *conférences*— that he should stop away was unthinkable. On the sixth day he achieved the much--desired private talk with the Hofrat. He was sent for, and after breakfast descended the stairs to the basement, to have a serious word with the man on the subject of his nephew and the way he spent his time.

When he came up, he asked, in a still, small voice: "Did you ever hear the like of that?"

But it was plain that Hans Castorp had. It was plain that whatever James could tell him would not make him "feel the cold." So James broke off, and to his nephew's further, mildly interested query answered: "Oh, nothing." But from hour to hour he developed a new habit: of peering diagonally upwards, with drawn brows and puckered lips, then suddenly turning his head to repeat the same gaze in the opposite direction. Had the interview with the Hofrat also gone off differently from James's expectations? Had it lost its character as a private interview, had the subject shifted from Hans Castorp to James Tienappel? One might think so. The Consul showed himself in high spirits. He talked a great deal, laughed without reason, struck his nephew with his fist in the pit of the stomach, shouting: "Hullo there, old fellow!"

Between times he had that look, first here and then suddenly there. But there came to be another, more definite goal to his glances, at table, on their walks, and in the salon of an evening.

We have heard of a certain Frau Redisch, wife of a Polish industrialist, who had sat at the table with Frau Salomon, absent without leave, and the greedy schoolboy with the round spectacles. The Consul had scarcely noticed her at first, and indeed she was just a rest--hall dame, like another—-a shortish brunette of abundant forms, no longer of the youngest, even slightly grey, but with a coquettish double chin and lively brown eyes. In point of culture she was far from being able to hold her own with Frau Consul Tienappel down below. So much is certain. But the Consul, after Sunday supper, in the hall, made the discovery, thanks to the *décolleté* of Frau Redisch's spangled black frock, that her bosom was very white and voluptuous, the breasts pressed together so that the crease between them was visible for some way; and the mature and elegant gentleman was as much shaken by this discovery as though it possessed for him a new and undreamed--of significance. He sought and made acquaintance with Frau Redisch; conversed with her at length, first standing and then sitting, and went up to bed singing. Next day Frau Redisch wore no spangled frock, her bosom was shrouded; but the Consul knew what he knew, and stuck by his discovery. He sought to intercept the lady on her walks, and strolled beside her in conversation, bending towards and over her in the most gallant and pointed way; he drank to her at table and she responded, smiling so much as to show several gold fillings in her teeth; he spoke of her to his nephew, and said she was a divine creature—-whereupon he burst out in song. And all this Hans Castorp let pass, with perfect equanimity, as much as to say that it was all regular and true to form. But it could not strengthen James's authority over his junior, nor add lustre to his embassy. The meal at which he saluted Frau Redisch by lifting his glass—-twice in fact, during it, once at the fish and once at the sherbet—-was one which the Hofrat partook of at Hans Castorp's table, in the course of his turn round the seven, at each of which his place at the upper end was reserved. He sat folding his giant hands between Herr Wehsal and the hunch--backed Mexican, with whom he spoke Spanish, for he could talk in almost any language, even Turkish and Hungarian. He sat, with his little onesided moustache and his blue, goggling, bloodshot eyes, and looked on at Consul Tienappel saluting Frau Redisch with his glass of Bordeaux. Afterwards, as the meal progressed, the Hofrat made a little speech, incited thereunto by James, who unexpectedly asked him, down the whole length of the table, what was the process of physical decomposition. The Hofrat was at home in that field, the physical was so to speak his domain, he was the king of it; would he not tell them what happened when the body decomposed?

"In the first place," the Hofrat complied, putting his elbows on the table and bowing over his folded hands, "in the first place, your belly bursts. You lie there on your chips and sawdust, and you bloat; the gases swell you up, puff you all out, the way frogs do when bad little boys fill them up with air. You get to be a regular balloon; the skin of your belly can't stand it any more, it bursts. You go pop. You relieve yourself mightily, like Judas Iscariot when he fell from the bough and all his bowels gushed out. And after that you are fit for society again. If you got leave to come back, you could visit your friends without being offensive. You are thoroughly stunk out. After that you're perfectly refined, like the burghers of Palermo, hanging in the cellars of the Capucins outside Porta Nuova: quite the gentlemen they are, all dried up and elegant, everybody respects them. The main thing is to get well stunk out."

"Certainly, of course," said the Consul. "Thanks very much." The next morning he had vanished.

He was off, gone down with the first little train to the flat--land---though not without having put his affairs in order----that we would not suggest. He had paid his bill, and the fee for the fumigation of his room; then, in all haste, without a syllable to his relative, he had packed his hand--bags----probably the night before, or even in the dawning, when everybody else was asleep----and when Hans Castorp entered his uncle's room at the hour for early breakfast, he found it empty.

Arms akimbo, he stood and said: "Well, well!" And a pensive smile overspread his features. "Yes, yes," he said, and nodded. Somebody had taken to his heels. In headlong haste, breathless, as though the moment of resolution must not be let slip, he had flung his things together and made off. Not with his cousin by his side, not after fulfilment of his lofty mission, but glad to save even himself by flight, the goodman had deserted to the flat--land----well, pleasant journey to you, Uncle James!

Hans Castorp let no one suspect his ignorance of his uncle's plans. Particularly not the lame concierge who had taken his uncle to the station. From Lake Constance James sent back a card, saying that he had had a telegram requiring his immediate return for business reasons. He had not liked to disturb his cousin (a polite lie). And he wished him a continued pleasant sojourn at House Berghof. Was that said in mockery? If so, Hans Castorp found it highly disingenuous, for his uncle had been in no jesting mood when he cut short his stay. No, he had become inwardly aware----one could conceive him paling at the thought----that even as it was, after only a week up here, he would find everything down below wrong and out of place, and that the feeling would last a considerable time before readjustment set in: it would seem to him unnatural to go to his office, instead of taking a prescribed walk after breakfast, and thereafter lying ritually wrapped, horizontal in a balcony. And this dread perception had been the immediate ground of his flight.

Thus ended the campaign of the flat--land to recover its lost Hans Castorp. Our young man did not conceal from himself that the total failure of this embassy marked a crisis in the relations between himself and the world below. It meant that he gave it up, finally and with a metaphorical shrug of the shoulders; it meant, for himself, the consummation of freedom—-the thought of which had gradually ceased to make him shudder.

Operationes Spirituales

Leo Naphta came from a little place near the Galician--Volhynian border. His father, of whom he spoke with respect, obviously with the feeling that he was now remote enough from his native scene to view it with impartial benevolence, had been the village *schochet*, or slaughterer—-a calling different indeed from that of the gentile butcher, who was labourer and tradesman, whereas Leo's father was an official, and the holder of a spiritual office. Elie Naphta, after being tested by the rabbi in his pious proficiency, had been empowered by him to slaughter suitable animals after the Mosaic law and according to Talmudic prescription. The performance of his ritual task had imparted something priestly to his being; and his blue eyes, which the son described as sending out gleams like stars, had held in their depth a wealth of silent spiritual fervour. The solemnity of his bearing spoke of that early time when the killing of animals had been in actual fact a priestly office. Leo, or Leib, as he had been called in his childhood, had been allowed to watch in the court--yard while the father carried out his task, aided by his helper, a powerful youth of the athletic Jewish type, beside whom the slender Elie with his round blond beard seemed still more fragile and delicate. Standing near the victim, which was hobbled and bound indeed, but not stunned, he would lift the mighty slaughter--knife and bring it to rest in a deep gash close to the cervical vertebra; while the assistant held the quickly filling basins to receive the gushing, steaming blood, and the child looked on at the sight with that childish gaze which often pierces through the sense into the essential, and may have been in an unusual degree the gift of the starry--eyed Elie's son. He knew that Christian butchers had to stun their cattle with a blow from a club before killing them, and that this regulation was made in order to avoid unnecessary cruelty. Yet his father, so fine and so intelligent by comparison with those louts, and starry--eyed as never one of them, did his task according to the Law, striking down the creature while its senses were undimmed, and letting its life--blood well out until it sank. The boy Leib felt that the stupid *goyim* were actuated by an easy and irreverent good nature, which paid less honour to the deity than did his father's solemn mercilessness; thus the conception of piety came to be bound up in his mind with that of cruelty, and the idea of the sacred and the spiritual with the sight and smell of spurting blood. For he probably saw that his father had not chosen his bloody trade out of the same brutal tastes that moved the lusty gentile butcher or his own Jewish assistant to find gratification in it, but rather on spiritual grounds, and in a sense bespoken by the starry eyes.

Yes, Elie Naphta had been a brooding and refining spirit; a student of the *Torah*, but a critic as well, discussing the Scriptures with his rabbi—-with whom he not infrequently disagreed. In his village, and not only among those of his own creed, he had passed for something unusual, for a man of more than common knowledge—-knowledge for the most part of holy things, but possibly also of matters that might not be quite canny, and anyhow were not in the ordinary run. There was something irregular, schismatic, about him, something of the familiar of God, a Baal--Shem or Zaddik, a miracle--man. Once he had actually cured a woman of a malignant sore, and another time a boy of spasms, simply by means of blood and invocations. But it was precisely this aura of an uncanny piety, in which the odour of his blood--boltered calling played a part, that proved his destruction. There had been the unexplained death of two gentile boys, a popular uprising, a panic of rage—-and Elie had died horribly, nailed crucifix--wise on the door of his burning home. His tuberculous, bedridden wife, the boy Leo, and four brothers and sisters, all wailing and lamenting with upflung arms, had fled the country.

Not utterly and entirely penniless, thanks to the father's foresight, the little troop came to rest in a small town of the Vorarlberg. Frau

Naphta found work in a cottonspinning factory, where she laboured as long as her strength held out, while the children attended the common school. The mental pabulum purveyed by this establishment probably answered to the needs of Leo's brothers and sisters; but for him, the eldest, it was quite insufficient. From his mother he had the seeds of his lung disease; from his father, besides his slenderness of build, an extraordinary intelligence: mental gifts that were from the first bound up with instinctive aspirations, a lofty ambition, and an ardent yearning for the more refined side of life, which caused him to reach out passionately beyond the sphere of his origin. The fourteen- -and fifteen--year--old lad managed to get hold of books out of school hours, and with lawless avidity continued to educate himself and feed his growing and impatient mind. He thought and uttered things which made the failing mother draw her head down crookedly between her shoulders and look at him with both wasted hands flung out. His person and the answers he gave at religious instruction drew upon him the attention of the district rabbi, and this devout and learned man received him as a private pupil, gratifying his taste for form by instruction in Hebrew and the classics, his logical turn by mathematics. But the good man was ill paid for his pains; as time went on, it became ever clearer that he had nourished a viper in his bosom. As once between Elie Naphta and his rabbi, so it was here. They fell out, exasperation on religious and philosophical grounds ensued and grew more and more embittered; the upright cleric had everything to endure from the irritability, captiousness, scepticism, and cutting dialectic of young Leo. Added to that, the lad's turn for sophistry and his insatiable intellect had latterly taken on a revolutionary cast. An acquaintance with the son of a social- -democratic member of the Reichsrat, and with this popular hero himself, turned his thoughts on politics, and made him apply his passion for logic to the field of social criticism. He said things that made the hair stand up on the head of the good Talmudist, who in politics was entirely loyal, and gave the final blow to the relations between master and pupil. In brief it came to this: that Leo was cast out, forbidden to cross the threshold of his master's study——precisely at the time when Rahel Naphta lay dying.

And then, immediately after the mother's passing, Leo made the acquaintance of Father Unterpertinger. The sixteen--year--old lad sat lonely on a bench in the park district of the Margaretentop, as it was called, a small height on the bank of the Ill, overlooking the town, whence one had a pleasant spreading view over the valley of the Rhine. He sat there lost in troubled and bitter thoughts of his fate and his future, when a member of the teaching staff of the Morning Star, the *pensionnat* of the Society of Jesus, out for a walk, sat down near him, put down his hat on the bench, crossed one leg over the other under his cassock, and after reading his breviary awhile began a conversation which waxed very lively, and proved in the end a decisive factor in Leo's destiny. The Jesuit, a much--travelled and cultured person, a judge and fisher of men, pedagogue by passion and conviction, pricked up his ears at the scornful tone, the clearly articulated sentences, in which the poor Jewish lad answered his first questions. A keen and tortured intellect breathed in the words, and, probing further, the good father discovered a command of fact and a caustic elegance of thought made only the more surprising by the ragged exterior of the youth. They spoke of Karl Marx, whose *Capital* Leo had studied in a cheap edition; and passed from him to Hegel, of whom or about whom he had also read enough to be able to say something striking. Whether from a general tendency to paradox, or with intent to be courteous, he called Hegel a "Catholic thinker"; and on the father's laughing query how that could be substantiated, since Hegel, as Prussian State philosopher, must surely be counted definitely with the Protestants, the boy replied that precisely the phrase "State philosopher" strengthened his position, and justified his characterization in a religious, though, of course, not in a churchly--dogmatic sense. *For* (Leo loved the conjunction, it came from his mouth with a triumphant, ruthless ring, his eyes flashing behind his spectacles every time he could bring it in) politics and Catholicism were, as conceptions, psychologically akin, both of them belonging to a category which embraced all that was objective, feasible, empirical, with an issue into active life. Opposed to it stood the Protestant, the pietistic sphere, which had its origin in mysticism. Jesuitism, he added, clearly betrayed the political, the pedagogical element in Catholicism; the Society had always regarded statecraft and education as its rightful domain. And he cited Goethe, who, rooted in Protestantism and assuredly Protestant as he was, had yet, by virtue of his objectivity and his doctrine of action, possessed a strongly Catholic side. He had defended auricular confession, and as an educator had been well--nigh Jesuitical.

Naphta may have said these things out of conviction, or because they were clever, or because, being a poor lad, he knew how adroit flattery could be made to serve his ends. The Father laid less stress on their intrinsic value than upon the general ability of which they gave evidence. Their talk had been prolonged, the Father soon possessed himself of the facts of Leo's personal situation, and finished by inviting the youth to visit him at the school.

And thus it was vouchsafed to Naphta to enter the precincts of the Stella Matutina. It is quite conceivable that he had already long since coveted the scholarly and social charms of that atmosphere; and now, by this turn of affairs, he had won a new master and patron far better calculated than the old one to prize and promote his peculiar aptitudes, a master cool by nature, whose value lay in his cosmopolitanism; an entry into whose circle now became the object of the Jewish lad's desire. Like many gifted people of his race, Naphta was both natural aristocrat and natural revolutionary; a socialist, yet possessed by the dream of shining in the proudest, finest, most exclusive and conventional sphere of life. That first utterance which the society of a Catholic theologian had tempted from him was—-however comparative and analytical in form—-in substance a declaration of affection for the Roman Church, as a power at once spiritual and aristocratic (in other words anti--material), at once superior and inimical to worldly things (in other words, revolutionary). And the homage he thus paid was genuine, and

[557]

profound; for, as he himself explained, Judaism, by virtue of its secular and materialistic leanings, its socialism, its political adroitness, had actually more in common with Catholicism than the latter had with the mystic subjectivity and self--immolation of Protestantism; the conversion of a Jew to the Roman Catholic faith was accordingly a distinctly less violent spiritual rupture than was that of a Protestant. Sundered from the shepherd of his original fold, orphaned, forsaken, full of craving after freer air and forms of existence upon which his native gifts gave him a claim, Naphta, who was long past the age of consent, was so impatient for profession that he saved his patron all the trouble of winning this soul—-or rather, this extraordinary head—-for his sect. Even before Leo's baptism he had, at the Father's instigation, found temporary lodgment in the Stella Matutina, where he was given food for both body and mind; and had migrated hither with the greatest equanimity, and the callousness of the born aristocrat, leaving his brothers and sisters to the care of the Poor Guardians and a destiny suited to their lesser gifts.

The property of the establishment was extensive, comprising in its buildings space for four hundred pupils, with wood and meadow land, half a dozen playing--fields, farm buildings, and stalls for hundreds of cows. The institution was at once boardingschool, model farm, athletic training--school, foster--mother of future scholars, and temple of the muses—-for there were constant performances of plays and music. The life was both monastic and manorial. With its discipline and elegance, its quiet good cheer, its well--being, its intellectual atmosphere, and the precision of its varied daily regimen, it soothed and flattered the lad Leo's deepest instincts. He was exaggeratedly happy. He ate excellent meals in a spacious refectory where the rule of silence obtained—-as in the corridors of the establishment—-and in the centre of which a young prefect sat on a raised platform and read aloud. Leo's zeal in his classes was fiery; and despite the weakness of his chest he made every effort to hold his own in the games and sports. He went devotedly to early mass, and took part in the Sunday service with a fervour which must have been gratifying to his priestly teachers. His social bearing was no less satisfactory to them. And on high days and holy--days, after the cake and wine, he made one of the long line of pupils who, in grey and green uniform with a stripe on the trousers, high collar and kepi, went walking in the country.

He thrilled with gratitude at the consideration they showed him, in respect of his origin, his infant Christianity, and his personal fortunes. No one in the institution seemed to know that he was an object of charity. The rules of the house favoured the concealment of his homeless and family--less state. It was forbidden to send parcels of food or sweets to the pupils; if any came, they were divided and Leo received his share with the others. And the cosmopolitanism of the institution prevented his race from being perceptible. There were other young exotics among the pupils, such as the Portuguese South--Americans, who looked even more "Jewish" than he did, and thus the idea did not come up. An Ethiopian prince had been received at the same time with Naphta; he had woolly hair, and was distinctly Moorish in appearance, though most distinguished.

In class Leo expressed the desire to study theology, in order to prepare himself for membership in the Society, in case he should be found worthy. In consequence, his place was changed from the "second school," where the food and living conditions were more modest, to the first, where he was served by waiters at table, and had a cubicle between a Silesian nobleman, the Count of Harbuval and Chamaré, and the young Marquis di Rangoni--Santacroce from Modena. He passed his examinations brilliantly, and, true to his resolve, quitted the pupil--life of the school to enter upon his noviciate in near--by Tisis, where he led a life of service and humility, silent subordination and religious discipline, and imbibed therefrom a spiritual relish fully equal to the fanatical expectations of his early years.

Meanwhile, however, his health suffered; less, indeed, through the severity of the noviciate, which was not lacking in physical recreation, than from within. The subtlety and acumen characteristic of the educational system of which he was now the object met his own natural tendencies half--way. He spent all his days and a good share of his nights in intellectual exercises, in searchings of the conscience, in contemplation, in introspection, into which he flung himself with such a passion of contentiousness as to involve him in a thousand difficulties, contradictions, and controversies. He was the despair——if at the same time the greatest hope——of his tutors, whom he daily pushed to the limits of their endurance by his raging dialectic and the subtility of his mental processes. *"Ad hœc quid tu?"* he would ask, the glasses of his spectacles flashing. And the cornered Father could only admonish him to pray for a tranquil spirit——*"ut in aliquem gradum quietis in anima perveniat."* This tranquillity, when achieved, consisted of a complete atrophy of the personality, a state of insensibility in which the individual became a lifeless tool; it was a veritable "graveyard peace," the uncanny outward signs of which Brother Naphta could see on the empty, staring faces of those about him, but to which he would never attain, even by the route of physical decay.

It spoke for the intellectual fibre of those in authority over him that his delays and drawbacks had no effect on his standing. At the end of his two years' noviciate, the Pater Provincial himself sent for him, and after the interview sanctioned his admission into the Society. The young scholastic, having taken the four lowest orders of doorkeeper, acolyte, lector, and exorcizor, and also the "simple" vows, was now definitely a member of the Society, and set out for Falkenberg, the Jesuit college in Holland, to begin his theological studies.

He was then twenty years old. At the end of three years, the unfavourable climate and the continued mental strain had so combined to aggravate his hereditary complaint that a longer stay would have endangered his life. His superiors were alarmed by a hæmorrhage; he hovered for weeks between life and death, when they hurried him, barely convalescent, back whence he had come. In the institution where he had been a pupil he found occupation as prefect and supervisor of the boarders, and teacher of the humanities and philosophy. Such an interval was in any case prescribed for the students of the Society; but it usually lasted only a few years, after which one returned to the college to take up again the seven years' course of study and carry it to its conclusion. This, however, it was not granted Brother Naphta to do. He continued ailing; doctor and superior decided that it was best for him to serve his order here among the pupils, in the good country air, with plenty of outdoor occupation on the farm. He took indeed the first of the higher orders, and won therewith the right to chant the Epistle on Sundays at mass——a right, however, which he never exercised, first because he was entirely unmusical, and second because of his weak chest, which made his voice break and unfitted it for singing. He never got further than being subdeacon——not even to diaconate, much less to priesthood. The hæmorrhages recurred, the fever persisted, and he had finally come to the mountains for an extended cure at the Society's expense. This was now in its sixth year, and gradually coming to be no longer so much a cure as a fixed condition of existence, a residence for life in rarefied atmosphere, coloured by some activity as Latin master in the Davos gymnasium for slightly tubercular boys.

All this, in much greater detail, Hans Castorp learned in the course of visits to Naphta's silken cell, either alone or in company with his table-mates Ferge and Wehsal, whom he had introduced there; or else when he met Naphta out on a walk, and strolled back to the Dorf in his company. He learned it as occasion offered, bit by bit, but also in the form of continuous narrative; and found it all highly extraordinary. Not only so, but he incited Ferge and Wehsal to find it the same, which they accordingly did. The former, indeed, all the while protested that he was just a plain man, and this high-flown stuff utterly beyond him, his experience with the pleura-shock having been the sole event in his life to raise it above the most humdrum sphere. Wehsal, however, obviously enjoyed this narrative of a man's rise to success from humble and oppressed beginnings——and in any case there was no ground in it for arrogance, since the good fortune seemed dwindling away again in the prevailing fleshly infirmity. Hans Castorp, for his part, regretted the reverse in Naphta's affairs, thinking with pride and concern of the ambitious Joachim, who with a heroic effort had burst through the tough web of the Rhadamanthine rhetoric and flown to the colours, where his cousin's fancy painted him clinging to the standard with three fingers upraised in the oath of fealty. To such a standard had Naphta too sworn faith, he too had been received beneath its folds: this had been the very figure he had employed when explaining his Society to Hans Castorp. But obviously, with his deviations and combinations, he was less true to his oath than Joachim to his. Hans Castorp, listening to the future or *ci--devant* Jesuit, felt himself strengthened in his views as a civilian and child of peace, while realizing that this man and Joachim would each find something satisfying in the calling of the other and recognize its likeness with his own. For the one was as military as the other, and both in every sense of the word; both being ascetic, both hierarchical, both bound to strict obedience and "Spanish etiquette." This last in particular played a great rôle in Naphta's society, originating as it did in Spain. Its exercises, which were a sort of pendant to the army regulations issued later by the Prussian Frederick to his infantry, were first written in the Spanish language, Naphta often making use of Spanish phrases in his narrative and descriptions. Thus he would speak of the "*dos banderas*"—-the two standards—-the Satanic and the celestial, beneath which the armies gathered for the great struggle: the one near Jerusalem, where Christ was the "*capitán general*" of all the faithful, the other on the plains of Babylon, of which the "*caudillo*" or chieftain was Lucifer. And had not the establishment of the Morning Star been, precisely, a military academy, the pupils of which were drilled by divisions in military and spiritual decorum, a mingling, so to speak, of stand--up collar and Spanish ruff? And ideas of rank and preferment, which played such a brilliant part in Joachim's profession—-how plainly, Hans Castorp thought, were they visible in that other society, wherein Naphta, alas, by reason of his illness, had been prevented from making further headway! By his account, the Society was exclusively composed of officers on fire with zeal, moved by the single thought of distinguishing themselves *(insignis esse,* in Latin). And these, according to the teaching of their founder and first general, the Spanish Loyola, performed a far more splendid service than any could who were guided merely by their normal reason. For theirs was a work of supererogation *(ex supererogatione)* in that they not only combated the rebellion of the flesh *(rebellio carnis),* which after all was incumbent upon any average healthy human reason to do, but were hostile to even an inclination toward the things of the sense, toward love of self and love of worldly things, even where these had not been directly forbidden. For it was better and more honourable to assail the foe *(agere contra),* that is, to attack, than merely to defend oneself *(resistere).* To weaken and break the foe—-those were the instructions in the service--book; and here again, its author, the Spanish Loyola, was of one mind with Joachim's *capitan general,* the Prussian Frederick, with his motto of "Attack, attack! Keep on their heels! *Attaquez donc toujours!"* But what Naphta's and Joachim's worlds had most of all in common was their attitude towards the shedding of blood, their axiom that one must not hold back one's hand. Therein, as worlds, as orders, as states of society, they were in stern accord. The child of peace would listen with avidity to Naphta's stories of the warlike monks of the Middle Ages, who, ascetic to the point of physical exhaustion, and filled with a ghostly lust of power, had been unsparing in bloodshed to the end of establishing the kingdom of God and its supernal overlordship; of the warlike Templars, who had held it of far greater worth to die in battle with the infidel than in their beds, and no crime but the highest glory, to kill or be killed for Christ's sake. Luckily, Settembrini had not been present at that conversation. He continued to fill the rôle of organ--grinder, and sang the praises of peace to harp and psaltery, but there was always the holy war against Vienna, to which he never said nay, though Naphta visited his foible with scorn and contempt, and when

[563]

the Italian was glowing with passionate feeling, would lead the bourgeoisie of all Christendom into the field against him, swearing that every country, or else no country at all, was his fatherland, and repeating with cutting effect the phrase of a general of the Society, named Nickel, according to which our love of country was "a plague, and the certain death of Christian love."

It was, of course, his ascetic ideal that made Naphta call patriotism a scourge—and what all did he not comprehend under the word, what all, according to him, did not run counter to the ascetic ideal and the kingdom of God. For not alone attachment to home and family, but even clinging to life and health were so set down, he made it a reproach to the humanist that the latter sang the praises of peace and happiness quarrelsomely accused him of love of the flesh *(amor carnalis)* and dependence upon bodily comfort *(commodorum corporis)*, and told him to his face that it was the worst sort of bourgeois irreligiosity to ascribe to health or life itself any importance whatsoever.

That was in the course of the great disputation on sickness and health, which one day, close on Christmas, arose out of certain differences they had during a snowy walk to the Platz and back. They all took part Settembrini, Naphta, Hans Castorp, Ferge and Wehsal—one and all slightly feverish, at once nervously stimulated and physically lethargic from walking and talking in the severe frost, all subject to fits of shivering, and—whether principals in the argument, like Settembrini and Naphta, or for the most part receptive, like the others, contributing only short ejaculations from time to time—all, without exception, so utterly absorbed that they stopped several times by the way, in a disorderly, gesticulating knot, blocking the path of the passersby, who had to describe a circle to get round them. People even paused and listened in astonishment to their extravagance.

The discussion had grown out of a reference somebody made to Karen Karstedt, poor Karen with the open finger--ends, whose death had lately occurred. Hans Castorp had heard nothing of her sudden turn for the worse and final exit, else he would gladly have assisted at the last rites, as a comradely attention, if not simply out of his confessed liking for funerals. But the local practice of discretion had prevented him from hearing of it until too late. Karen had gone to take up the horizontal for good, in the garden of the Cupid with the crooked snow--cap. *Requiem æternam.* He dedicated a few friendly words to her memory, interrupted by Herr Settembrini, who began making game of his pupil's charitable activities, his visits to Leila Gerngross, Rotbein the business man, the "overfilled" Frau Zimmermann, the braggart son of Tous--lesdeux, and the afflicted Natalie von Mallinckrodt. He censured Hans Castorp in retrospect for paying tribute in costly flowers to that dismal, ridiculous crew; and Hans Castorp replied that with the temporary exception of Frau von Mallinckrodt and the boy Teddy, the recipients of his attentions had now in all seriousness died—-to which Herr Settembrini retorted by asking if that made them any more respectable. Well, after all, Hans Castorp responded, wasn't there such a thing as Christian reverence before suffering? Before Settembrini could put him down, Naphta interposed, and began to speak of the devout excesses manifested by pious souls in the Middle Ages, astounding cases of fanatic devotion and ecstasy in the care of the sick: kings' daughters kissing the stinking wounds of lepers, voluntarily exposing themselves to contagion and calling the ulcers they received their "roses"; or drinking the water that had been used for the cleansing of abscesses, and vowing that nothing had ever tasted so good.

Settembrini made as though he would vomit. It was not so much, he said, the physically disgusting element in these tales that turned his stomach as the monstrous lunacy which betrayed itself in such a conception of the love of humanity. Then, recovering his poise and good humour, he drew himself up and held forth upon the recent progress of humanitarian ideals, the triumphant forcing back of epidemic disease, upon hygiene and social reform; he contrasted the horrors of pestilence with the feats of modern medical science.

All these, Naphta responded, were very honest bourgeois achievements; but they would have done more harm than good in the centuries under discussion. They would have profited neither one side nor the other; the ailing and wretched as little as the strong and prosperous, these latter not having been piteous for pity's sake, but for the salvation of their own souls. Successful social reform would have robbed them of their necessary justification, as it would the wretched of their sanctified state. The persistence of poverty and sickness had been in the interest of both parties, and the position could be sustained just so long as it was possible to hold to the purely religious point of view.

"A filthy point of view," Settembrini declared. A position the stupidity of which he felt himself above combating. This talk of the sanctified lot of the poor and wretched—-yes, and what the Engineer, in his simplicity, had said about the Christian reverence due to suffering—-was simply gammon, resting as it did on a misconception, on mistaken sympathy, on erroneous psychology. The pity the well person felt for the sick—-a pity that almost amounted to awe, because the well person could not imagine how he himself could possibly bear such suffering—-was very greatly exaggerated. The sick person had no real right to it. It was, in fact, the result of an error in thinking, a sort of hallucination; in that the well man attributed to the sick his own emotional equipment, and imagined that the sick man was, as it were, a well man who had to bear the agonies of a sick one—-than which nothing was further from the truth. For the sick man was—-precisely that, a sick man: with the nature and modified reactions of his state. Illness so adjusted its man that it and he could come to terms; there were sensory appeasements, short circuits, a merciful narcosis; nature came to the rescue with measures of spiritual and moral adaptation and relief, which the sound person naïvely failed to take into account. There could be no better illustration than the case of all this tuberculous crew up here, with their reckless folly, light--headedness and loose morals, and their total lack of desire for health. In short, let the sound man with all his respect for illness once fall ill himself, and he would soon see that being ill is a state of being in itself—-no very honourable one either—-and that he had been taking it a good deal too seriously.

At this point Anton Karlowitsch Ferge girded his loins to remonstrate—-he defended the pleura--shock against sneers and contumely. So Herr Settembrini thought you could take the pleura--shock too seriously, did he? With all due respect and gratitude and all that, he, Ferge, must really beg Herr Settembrini's pardon! His great Adam's apple and his good--natured moustaches worked up and down as he repudiated any lack of respect for the sufferings he had undergone. He was just a plain man, an insurance agent, with no high--falutin ideas; even the present conversation soared far above his head. But if Herr Settembrini meant to suggest that the pleura--shock was a good example of what he was talking about—-that torture by tickling, with its stench of sulphur and its three--coloured fainting fit—-well, really he was very much obliged to Herr Settembrini, he really must thank him very kindly indeed; but there had been nothing of the sort about the pleura--shock—-not it! Talk about adjustments and "merciful narcosis"—-why, it had been the most sickening piece of business under the shining sun, and nobody who had not been through it could have the least idea—-

"Yes, yes," Herr Settembrini said. Herr Ferge's collapse got more and more remarkable as time went on, and he would presently be wearing it like a halo round his head. He, Settembrini, had no great respect for sick folk who laid claim to consideration on the score of their illness. He was ill himself, and seriously; but in all sincerity he felt inclined to be ashamed of the fact. However, his present remarks were purely abstract and impersonal; and the distinction he made between the nature and reactions of a well and a sick man was based on common sense, as the gentlemen would see if they would think about insanity—-take, for instance, hallucinations. Suppose one of his companions, the Engineer, say, or Herr Wehsal, should enter his room to--night at dusk and see his deceased father sitting there in a corner, who should look at and speak to him—-that would be absolutely monstrous, wouldn't it? A shattering experience, which would confound both sense and reason, and make him get out of the room as fast as he could and put himself in the care of a specialist in nervous ailments. Or wouldn't it? The joke of the thing was that such an experience would not be possible for any of the gentlemen present, since they were all in enjoyment of full mental health. If it did happen to any of them, it would be a sure sign that they were *not* sound, but diseased, and they would not react to the appearance with emotions of horror and by taking to their heels, but treat it as though it were entirely in order, and begin a conversation with it—-this being, in fact, the reaction of a person suffering from a hallucination. To suppose that such hallucinations affected the person subject to them with the same horror as would be felt by a sound mind was a defect of the imagination to which normal persons were often prone.

Herr Settembrini spoke with droll and plastic effect. His picture of the father in the corner made them all laugh, even Ferge, put out though he was by the slight to his pleura--shock. Herr Settembrini took advantage of their hilarity to expatiate further on the contemptibleness of people who were subject to hallucinations, and of *pazzi* in general. It was his opinion that these people gave way a great deal more than they need, and often had it in their power to control their own freakishness. He had made this observation when he had visited asylums for the insane. For in the presence of the doctor, or of a stranger, the patients would mostly intermit their jabbering, grimaces, and weaving to and fro, and behave quite sensibly, as long as they felt themselves under scrutiny, only to let themselves go again afterwards. For lunacy undoubtedly in many cases meant the kind of self--abandonment which was the refuge of a weak nature against extreme distress, a defence against such overwhelming blows of destiny as it felt itself, when in its right mind, unable to cope with. But almost anybody might get in that state; and he, Settembrini, had held more than one lunatic to temporary self--control, simply by opposing to his humbuggery an air of inexorable reason.

[568]

Naphta laughed derisively; Hans Castorp protested his readiness to believe Herr Settembrini's statement. Indeed, as he pictured him smiling beneath his moustaches and fixing the feeble--minded with the eye of remorseless reason, he could well understand how the poor fellow had had to pull himself together and behave with "temporary self--control," though probably finding Herr Settembrini's presence a most unwelcome incident.—-But Naphta too had had experience of asylums for the insane. He recalled a visit to the violent ward, where he had seen such sights as—-my God, such sights as would have been a bit too much even for Herr Settembrini's intelligent eye or disciplinary powers: Dantesque scenes, monstrous tableaux of horror and agony: naked madmen squatting in the continuous bath, in every posture of mental anguish or in the stupor of despair; some shrieking aloud, others with uplifted arms and gaping mouths whence issued laughter that mingled all the elements of hell—-

"Aha," cried Herr Ferge, and took leave to remind them of the laughter which had escaped him when they went over his pleura. In short, Herr Settembrini's inexorable pedantry would have had to confess itself beaten before these sights in the violent ward; in the face of which, the shudder of religious awe would surely have been a more human reaction than this condescending twaddle about reason, which our Worshipful Brother and Eminent Preceptor saw fit to put forward as a treatment for insanity.

Hans Castorp was too preoccupied to question the new titles Naphta was conferring on Herr Settembrini. Hastily he made a resolve to look them up the first chance he got; for the moment, he had his hands full with the present conversation. Naphta was acrimoniously debating the general tendency which led the humanist to exalt health and cry down and belittle illness. Herr Settembrini's attitude was, he thought, a remarkable, even admirable example of self--abnegation, considering he was ill himself. But the position, no matter how strikingly meritorious, was as mistaken as it could well be: resting as it did upon a respect and reverence for the human body which could only be justified if that body had remained in original sinlessness, instead of sinking to its present fallen state *(statu degradationis)*. For it had been created immortal, and by the original sins of depravity and abomination, by the degeneration of its nature, it had become mortal and corruptible, and was thus to be regarded as the prison--house and torture--chamber of the soul, or as the fit instrument for rousing the conscience to a sense of shame and confusion *(pudoris et confusionis sensum)*, as Saint Ignatius had it.

The humanist Plotinus, exclaimed Hans Castorp, was also known to have given expression to the same idea. But Herr Settembrini flung up his hands and ordered the young man not to confuse two different points of view—-and, for the rest, to be advised and maintain an attitude of receptivity.

Naphta, continuing, derived the reverence which the Christian Middle Ages paid to physical suffering from the fact that it acquiesced on religious grounds in the sight of the anguish of the flesh. For the wounds of the body not only emphasized its sunken state, they also corresponded in the most edifying manner to the envenomed corruption of the soul, and thereby gave rise to emotions of true spiritual satisfaction: whereas blooming health was a misleading phenomenon, insulting to the conscience of man and requiring to be counteracted by an attitude of debasement and humility before physical infirmity, which was infinitely beneficial to the soul. *Quis me liberabit de corpore mortis huius?* Who will deliver me from the body of this death?

There spoke the voice of the spirit, which was eternally the voice of true humanity. On the contrary—-according to Herr Settembrini's view, presented with no little heat—-it was a voice from the darkness, a voice from a world upon which the sun of reason and humanity was not yet risen. Truly, in his own physical person he was contaminate; yet what mattered that, since his mind was untainted and sound—-and quite competent to bring confusion to his priestly opponent in any discussion touching the body, or to laugh him to scorn over the soul? He took too high a flight in celebrating the human body as the true temple of the Godhead; for Naphta straightway declared that this mortal fabric was nothing more than a veil between us and eternity; whereupon Settembrini definitely forbade him the use of the word humanity—-and so it went on. Bare--headed, their faces stiff in the cold, they trod in their rubber galoshes the crisp, creaking, cinder--strewn snow, or ploughed through porous masses in the gutter: Settembrini in a winter jacket with beaver collar and cuffs—-the fur was worn to the pelt, and looked fairly mangy, but he knew how to carry it off with an air; Naphta in a long black overcoat that came down to his heels and up to his ears, and showed none of the fur with which it was lined throughout. Both speakers treated their theme as of the utmost personal concern; and both often turned, not to each other but to Hans Castorp, with argument and exposition, referring to their opponents with a jerk of the head or thumb. They had him between them, and he turned his head to assent first to one and then to the other; now and again he stood stock--still on the path, tipping his body back from the waist and gesturing with his fur--lined glove as he made some quite inadequate contribution to the talk. Ferge and Wehsal circled about, now in front and now behind, now in a single row until they had to break up their line again to let people pass.

It was due to some remark of theirs that the debate took on a less abstract tone, and all the company joined in a discussion of torture, cremation and punishment—-both capital and corporal. It was Ferdinand Wehsal who introduced the last--named; with obvious relish, Hans Castorp observed. As was to be expected, Herr Settembrini, in high--sounding words, invoked the dignity of the human race against a procedure whose results were as devastating in education as in penology. And equally to be ex--pected, though rendered startling by a certain kind of gloomy ferocity, was Naphta's approval of the bastinado. According to him, it was absurd to prate about human dignity, since true dignity indwelt not in the flesh but in the spirit. The soul of man was for ever prone to suck the joys of this earthly life from the flesh instead of the spirit; thus pain, by rendering bitter to him the things of the senses, was highly efficacious, driving him back to the spirit and giving the latter the mastery over the flesh. It was shallow to contend that the discipline of the whipping--post had anything particularly shameful about it. Saint Elizabeth had been flogged by her confessor, Conrad von Marburg, until the blood came, and by such means her soul was rapt "to the third choir of angels." She herself, moreover, had beaten with rods an old woman who was too sleepy to make her confession. The members of a certain sect, and even other persons of devout and serious character, submitted to flagellation in order that the spiritual impulse might be strengthened. Would anyone seriously contend that such a procedure was barbarous and inhuman? It was true that corporal punishment was on the decline in certain countries which considered themselves in the van of progress: but the belief that such a decline was a sign of enlightenment became only the more comic the longer it persisted.

Well, anyhow, Hans Castorp considered, so much was granted: that in the antithesis between body and soul it was undoubtedly the body which embodied——the body embodied, that wasn't so bad, was it?——the evil principle; in so far as the body was naturally nature——pretty good, too, that!——and nature, being diametrically opposed to the spirit and reason, was by that fact intrinsically evil——mystically evil, one might say, if it didn't sound like showing off! But it followed from this that the body should be treated accordingly, and made to profit from disciplinary methods, which might also be called mystically evil. Herr Settembrini, for instance, that time when the weakness of the flesh had prevented him from attending the Congress for the Advancement of Civilization at Barcelona, ought to have had a Saint Elizabeth at his side——!

Everybody laughed; but while the humanist was bringing up his guns, Hans Castorp hastily began to talk about a beating he had once received, when he was in one of the lower forms in the gymnasium, where this form of punishment still survived to some extent, and there were always switches on hand. His, Hans Castorp's social position had been too good for the masters to venture to lay hands on him; but he had once been whipped by a stronger pupil, a big lout of a fellow who had laid on with the flexible switch across Hans Castorp's thin--stockinged calves. It had hurt so confoundedly—-so "mystically"—-that he had fairly sobbed for rage, and the tears had ignominiously flowed down. And he recalled having read that in the penitentiaries, when men are flogged, the most hardened reprobates will blubber like little children. Herr Settembrini hid his face in his hands, that were clad in very shabby leather gloves; and Naphta, with statesmanlike calm, asked how else they would expect to reduce refractory criminals—-unless by putting in the stocks, which were quite the suitable furnishing for a prison. A humane penitentiary would be neither one thing nor the other, an æsthetic compromise: if Herr Settembrini did not think so, then it was clear that, though an æsthete, he had very little sense of the fitness of things. And in the field of education, a conception of human dignity which would bar corporal punishment from the schools had its roots, according to Naphta, in the liberalindividualism of our bourgeois, humanitarian age, in an enlightened absolutism of the ego, which was, indeed, now dying off, to give place to social conceptions made of sterner stuff: ideas of discipline and conformity, of coercion and compliance, to the realization of which an element of godly severity would be needful, and which, when realized, would make us alter all our ideas on the subject of the chastisement of the human carcass.

"Hence the phrase *perinde ac si cadaver*," scoffed Settembrini. Naphta suggested that since God, in punishment of our sins, had visited us with the shameful and horrible sentence of bodily corruption, after all it was not such a frightful insult to that same body that it should now and then get a flogging. And then, somehow, all at once, they came upon the subject of cremation.

Settembrini paid it homage. That indignity of corruption, he said, of which Naphta spoke, could by its means be redressed. On practical as well as on ideal grounds, mankind was now about to redress it. He explained that he was helping prepare for an international congress for the promotion of cremation, the scene of whose labours would probably be Sweden. A model crematorium would be exhibited, planned in accordance with the latest researches and experiments, with a hall of urns; they hoped to rouse widespread interest and enthusiasm. What an effete and obsolete procedure burial was, under our modern conditions——the price of land, the expansion of our cities and consequent shoving of the graveyards out on to the periphery! And the chop--fallen funeral processions, with their dignity curtailed by present--day traffic conditions! Herr Settembrini had plenty of disillusioning facts at his command. He made a droll picture of a grief--stricken widower on his daily pilgrimage to the graveside, to hold communion with the beloved departed; and said that the man must have a superfluity of that most precious of human commodities, time; and further, that the rush of business in a large modern burying--ground must surely dash his atavistic bliss. The destruction of the body by fire——what a cleanly, sanitary, dignified, yes, heroic conception that was, compared with abandoning it to the miserable processes of decay and assimilation by the lower forms of life! Yes, the newer method was more satisfying emotionally too, and kinder to the human longing after immortality. For what the fire destroyed was the more perishable part of the body, the elements which even during one's life were got rid of by metabolism; whereas those which accompanied man through life, taking least share in the process of change, those became the ashes, and with them the survivors possessed the deceased's imperishable part.

"Oh, charming," Naphta said. "Oh, really, *very* good! Man's imperishable part, his ashes!"

Naphta evidently meant to hold humanity fast to its old, irrational position in the face of established biological fact; meant to force it to remain at the stage of primitive religion, where death was a spectre surrounded by such mysterious terrors that the gaze of reason could not be focused upon it. What barbarism! The fear of death went back to a very low cultural stage, when violent death was the rule, and its horrors thus became associated with the idea of death in general. But now, thanks to the development of hygiene and the increase in personal security, a natural death was the rule, a violent one the exception; modern man had come to think of repose, after exhaustion of his powers, as not at all dreadful, but normal and even desirable. No, death was neither spectre nor mystery. It was a simple, acceptable, and physiologically necessary phenomenon; to dwell upon it longer than decency required was to rob life of its due. Accordingly, the Hall of Death (as the modern crematory and vault for the urns was to be called) would be supplemented by a Hall of Life, where architecture, painting, sculpture, music, and poetry would combine to draw the thoughts of the survivors from the contemplation of death, from weak and unavailing grief, and fix them upon the joys of life.

"On with the dance!" Naphta mocked. "Don't let them make too much of the funeral rites, don't let them pay too much respect to such a simple fact as death—but without that simple fact, there would never have been either architecture nor painting, sculpture nor music, poetry nor any other art."

"He deserts to the colours," murmured Hans Castorp dreamily.

"Your remark is incomprehensible," Settembrini answered him, "which doesn't prevent it from being at the same time silly. Either the experience of death must be the last experience of life, or else it must be a bugaboo, pure and simple."

"Will there be obscene symbols employed in the Hall of Life, like those on the ancient sarcophagi?" Hans Castorp asked with a serious air.

"By all accounts," Naphta chimed in, "there will be a fine fat feeding for the senses." In oils and in marbles, a humanistic taste would celebrate the glories of the senses—of the sinful body whose flesh it had saved from putrefaction. There was nothing surprising about that—it was of a piece with its fastidiousness in the matter of corporal punishment.

Thus they came upon the subject of torture—introduced by Wehsal, to whom, it seemed, it made a particular appeal. "The question," now—-what were the gentlemen's views about it? He, Ferdinand, when he was "on the road," liked to visit those quiet retreats in the centres of ancient culture, where such research into the conscience of man used to be carried on. He had seen the torture--chambers of Nuremberg and Regensburg, he had made a study of them, and been edified. They had certainly devised a number of ingenious ways of man--handling the body for the good of the soul. There had never been any outcry—-they rammed the famous choke--pear, itself such a very tasty morsel, into the victim's mouth, and after that silence reigned.

"*Porcheria!*" Settembrini muttered.

Ferge professed his respect for the choke--pear, and the whole silent activity. But anything worse than the pinning back of his pleura he was sure had never been devised, not even in those times.

That had been done for his good!

The obdurate soul, offended justice, these warranted a temporary lack of mercy. But in fact, the torture was an invention of the human reason.

Settembrini presumed that the speaker was not quite in his senses.

Oh, yes, he was pretty well in possession of them. It was Herr Settembrini, the professed æsthete, who was probably not altogether familiar with the history of the development of mediæval jurisprudence. There had been, in fact, a process of continuous rationalization, in the course of which reason had taken the place of God, who had been shoved out of the department of justice. In other words, trial by battle had fallen into disuse, because it had been observed that the stronger man conquered even when he was in the wrong. It had been people of Herr Settembrini's kidney, the doubters and critics, who had made the observation, and brought about the Inquisition, which superseded the old naïve procedure. Justice no longer relied on the intervention of God in favour of the truth, but aimed to get it out of the accused by confession. No sentence without confession—-you could hear that still among the people, for the instinct lodged deep with them; the chain of evidence might be as strong as it liked, but if there had been no confession, there would remain a lurking feeling that the sentence was illegitimate. But how get at the confession? How procure the truth, out of the mass of circumstance and suspicion? How look into the heart, the brain, of a man who denied and concealed? If the spirit was recalcitrant, there remained the body, which could be got at. The torture was recommended to reason, as a means to an end, the end of bringing out the indispensable confession. But it was Herr Settembrini who had demanded and introduced confession, and he, accordingly, who was responsible for torture.

The humanist implored the others not to believe a word of all this. Herr Naphta was indulging in a diabolical joke. If the position had really been what he said, if it were true that the horrible thing was actually an invention of the human reason, that only showed how grievously she always needed sustaining and enlightening, and how little ground the instinct--worshippers had for their fear that things could ever be too much directed by reason on this earth! But the speaker was of course in error. The judicial abomination they were discussing could not be laid at the door of the human reason, because it went back to an original belief in hell. The rack, the pincers, the screws and tongs you saw in these chambers of torment and martyrdom represented the effort of a childish and deluded fancy to emulate what it piously believed to be the sufferings of the eternally damned. But that was not all. They thought to assist the evil--doer, whose spirit they assumed to be wrestling after confession, while his flesh, the evil principle, set itself against the soul's desire: they had it in mind to do him a service of love, in breaking his body by torture. It was a madness of asceticism—-

"How about the ancient Romans—-did they harbour the same delusion?"

"The Romans? *Ma che!*"

"But they employed the torture as a judicial instrument."

Logical impasse. Hans Castorp tried to help out—as if it were his *metier* to guide such a conversation! Of his own accord, he flung into the arena the question of capital punishment. Torture, he said, was abolished—though examining magistrates still had ways of making an accused person pliable. But the death penalty persisted, it seemed impossible to do without it. It was practised by the most civilized nations. The French system of deportation had worked very badly. There was nothing feasible to do with certain half--human beings, except to make them a head shorter!

They were *not* "certain half--human beings" Settembrini corrected him. They were men, like the Engineer, like himself, Settembrini—-only weak--willed victims of a defective social system. He cited the case of an abandoned criminal, the kind always referred to by the prosecuting attorneys as a "beast in human form," who had covered the walls of his cell with verse, and not at all bad verse either, much better than most prosecuting attorneys ever managed to write.

That cast a somewhat singular light on the art of verse--writing, Naphta retorted, but was not otherwise worth answering.

Hans Castorp said he was not surpiseed to hear that Naphta favoured the death penalty. To his mind, Naphta was as revolutionary as Settembrini, only in a conservative direction—a reactionary revolutionist.

Herr Settembrini, with a confident smile, assured them that the world, after passing through a period of inhuman reaction, would always return to the normal order of things. But Herr Naphta preferred to discredit art sooner than admit that it might have a humanizing effect upon a sunken wretch. He need not expect, by such fanatical talk, to make much headway with light--seeking youth. He, Settembrini, had the honour to belong to a newly--formed league, the scope of which was the abolition of capital punishment in all civilized countries. It was not yet settled where the first congress should meet; but one thing was sure, that those who addressed it would have plenty of arguments at hand. He submitted some of them forthwith: the ever--present possibility that justice might err and judicial murder be committed; the hope of reformation, which it was never possible to disregard; the biblical injunction "Vengeance is mine."

Then he referred to the theory that the State, in its function not as the wielder of force, but as the instrument of human betterment, may not repay evil with evil; he attacked the conception of guilt, on the ground of scientific determinism; and lastly, he repudiated the whole theory of punishment.

On top of which "light--seeking youth" had to stand by while Naphta neatly wrung the neck of all these arguments, one after the other. He derided the humanist's reluctance to shed blood, and his reverence for human life. He said that the latter was characteristic of our intensely bourgeois age, our policy of molly--coddle. Even so, its inconsistency was apparent. For let an idea arise that went beyond considerations of personal safety and well--being—and such ideas were the only ones worthy of human beings, and thus in a higher sense were the normal field of human activity—and the individual would, even under average emotional stress, be sacrificed without scruple to the higher claim. Nay, more: the individual, of his own free will, would expose himself without a thought. The philanthropy of his honoured opponent would eliminate from life all its stern and mortal traits; it would castrate life, as would the determinism of its so--called science. But determinism would never succeed in doing away with the conception of guilt. It could only add to its authority and its awfulness. Oh, so he demanded that the unhappy victim of social maladjustment be convinced of his own sinfulness, and tread in full conviction the path to the scaffold?

"Quite. The evil--doer is filled with his guilt as with himself. For he is as he is, and can and will not be otherwise—and therein lies his guilt."

Naphta shifted the ground of the discussion from the empiric to the metaphysical. He went on to say that in behaviour, in action, determinism did indeed rule; there was no freedom of choice. But in being, the man is as he has wished to be, and as, until his last breath, he has never ceased to wish to be. He has revelled in slaying, and does not pay too dear in being slain. Let him die, then, for he has gratified his heart's deepest desire.

"Deepest desire?"

"Deepest desire."

They all gritted their teeth. Hans Castorp gave a little cough, Wehsal set his jaw awry. Herr Ferge breathed a sigh, Settembrini shrewdly remarked: "There is a kind of generalization that has a distinctly personal cast. Have you ever had a desire to commit murder?"

"That is no concern of yours. But if I had, I should laugh in the face of any ignorant humanitarianism that tried to feed me on skilly till I died a natural death. It is absurd for the murderer to outlive the murdered. They two, alone together, as two beings are together in only one other human relationship, have, like them, the one acting, the other suffering him, shared a secret that binds them for ever together. They belong to each other."

Settembrini said frigidly that he lacked the brains necessary to the understanding of this death--and--murder mysticism——and he really didn't miss them. No offence intended; Herr Naphta's religious gift did undoubtedly far surpass his own, but he protested that he was not envious. His own nature had an unconquerable craving for fresh air; it kept him somewhat aloof from a sphere where reverence——and not merely the unthinking reverence of youth——was paid to suffering, and that in a spiritual as well as a physical sense. In that sphere, it was plain, virtue, reason, and healthiness counted for nothing, vice and disease were honoured in a wondrous way.

Naphta concurred. He said that being virtuous and healthy did not, in fact, constitute being in a state of religion at all. It would clear the air to have it plainly stated that religion had nothing to do with reason and morality.

"For," he added, "it has nothing to do with life. Life is based on conditions and built up on foundations which are partly the result of experience, and partly belong to the domain of ethics. We call the first kind time, space, and causality; the second, morality and reason. But one and all of these are not only foreign to, utterly a matter of indifference to the nature of religion; they are even hostile to it. For they are precisely what make up life—-the so--called normal life, which is to say, arch Philistinism, ultra--bourgeoisiedom, the absolute antithesis of which, the very genius of antithesis to which, is the life of religion."

Naphta went on to say that he would not deny to the other sphere the possibility of genius. There was much to admire in the monumental respectability, the majestic Philistinism of the middle--class consciousness. But one must never forget that as it stood, straddle--legged, firmly planted on earth, hands behind the back, chest well out, it was the embodiment of irreligion.

Hans Castorp, like a schoolboy, put up his hand. He wished, he said, not to offend either side. But since they were talking about progress, and thus, to a certain extent also, about politics, and the republic of eloquence and the civilization of the educated Occident, he might say that it seemed to him the difference—-or, if Herr Naphta insisted, the antithesis—-between life and religion went back to that between time and eternity. Only in time was there progress; in eternity there was none, nor any politics or eloquence either. There, so to speak, one laid one's head back in God, and closed one's eyes. And that was the difference between religion and morality—-he was aware that he had put it very badly.

The way he put it, Settembrini remarked, naïve as it was, was less objectionable than his fear of giving offence, his inclination to give ground to the Devil. Oh, as far as the Devil was concerned, they two had talked about him aforetime, hadn't they? "O *Satana, O ribellione.*" But which devil was it he had been giving ground to just now? Was it Carducci's one—-rebellion, activity, critical spirit—-or was it the other? It was pretty dangerous having a devil on either hand, like this; how in the Devil's name should we get out of it?

That, Naphta said, was no proper description of the state of affairs as Herr Settembrini looked at them. For the distinctive feature of his cosmos was that he made God and the Devil two distinct persons or principles, with "life" as a bone of contention between them—-which, by the by, was just the way the Middle Ages had envisaged them. But in reality, God and the Devil were at one in being opposed to life, to bourgeoisiedom, reason and virtue, since they together represented the religious principle.

"What a disgusting hodge--podge— *che guazzabuglio proprio stomachevole!*" Good and evil, sanctification and criminal conduct, all mixed up together! Without judgment! Without direction! Without the possibility of repudiating what was vile!

Did Herr Naphta realize what it was he denied and disavowed in the presence of youth, when he flung God and the Devil together and in the name of this mad two--inoneness refused to admit the existence of an ethical principle? He denied every standard of values, he denied goodness! Horrible!—-Very well, then there existed neither good nor evil, nothing but a morally chaotic All! There was not even the individual in possession of a critical faculty—-there was only the all--consuming, the all--levelling universal communalty, and mystic immersion in her!

It was delicious, Herr Settembrini's thinking of himself as an individualist! For to be that, one had at least to recognize the difference between morality and blessedness, which our honoured illuminant and monist most certainly did not! A society in which life was stupidly conceived as an end in itself, with no questions asked about its ulterior meaning and purpose, was governed by a tribal and social ethic, indeed, a vertebrate morality, if you liked, but certainly not by individualism. For individualism belonged, singly and solely, in the realm of the religious and mystical, in the so--called "morally chaotic All." And this morality of Herr Settembrini's, what was it, what did it want? It was life--bound, and thus entirely utilitarian; it was pathetically unheroic. Its end and aim was to make men grow old and happy, rich and comfortable——and that was all there was to it. And this Philistine philosophy, this gospel of work and reason, served Herr Settembrini as an ethical system. As far as he, Naphta, was concerned, he would continue to deny that it was anything but the sheerest and shabbiest bourgeoisiedom.

Settembrini enjoined him to be calm——his own voice shaking with passion. He found Herr Naphta's talk about bourgeoisiedom simply insufferable——and God knew why he should put on that contemptuous, aristocratic air! As if the opposite of life——and we all knew what that was——was likely to be more refined than life itself!

New cries, new catchwords! Now it was the "aristocratic principle." Hans Castorp, all flushed and depleted from taxing his brains in the cold, shaky as to his capacity for clear expression, hot and cold with his own audacity, heard himself babble that always since a child he had pictured death to himself as wearing a starched ruff, or at least a sort of half--uniform, with a stand--up collar, while life, on the other hand, wore an ordinary collar. His words sounded, even to himself, like a drunken impropriety; he hastened to assure the company that that was not at all what he had meant to say. And yet——wasn't it a fact that one couldn't imagine certain people dead, simply because they were so very ordinary? That must mean they were very fit for life, but could not die, because unfit for the consecration of death.

Herr Settembrini said he was confident Hans Castorp uttered such stuff merely for the sake of being contradicted. The young man would find him ever ready to lend a hand in the intellectual warfare, against attacks like the present. The Engineer had used the expression "fit for life"; had he intended it in a derogatory sense? To him it was synonymous with "worthy of life," the two conceptions being perfectly harmonious, and suggesting by a natural process of association another equally beautiful, "worthy of love." One might with truth say that he who was worthy of the one was fully worthy of the other. And both together, loveworthy and life--worthy, made up the true nobility.

Hans Castorp found that charming—-most edifying. Herr Settembrini had quite won him over with his plastic theory. Say what you like—-and there was a lot to be said for the idea that illness had something solemn and ennobling about it—-yet after all, you couldn't deny that illness was an accentuation of the physical, it did throw man back, so to speak, upon the flesh and to that extent was detrimental to human dignity. It dragged man down to the level of his body. Thus it might be argued that disease was un--human.

On the contrary, Naphta hastened to say. Disease was very human indeed. For to be man was to be ailing. Man was essentially ailing, his state of unhealthiness was what made him man. There were those who wanted to make him "healthy," to make him "go back to nature," when, the truth was, he never had been "natural." All the propaganda carried on to--day by the prophets of nature, the experiments in regeneration, the uncooked food, fresh--air cures, sun--bathing, and so on, the whole Rousseauian paraphernalia, had as its goal nothing but the dehumanization, the animalizing of man. They talked of "humanity," of nobility—-but it was the spirit alone that distinguished man, as a creature largely divorced from nature, largely opposed to her in feeling, from all other forms of organic life. In man's spirit, then, resided his true nobility and his merit—-in his state of disease, as it were; in a word, the more ailing he was, by so much was he the more man. The genius of disease was more human than the genius of health. How, then, could one who posed as the friend of man shut his eyes to these fundamental truths concerning man's humanity? Herr Settembrini had progress ever on his lips: was he aware that all progress, in so far as there was such a thing, was due to illness, and to illness alone? In other words, to genius, which was the same thing? Had not the normal, since time was, lived on the achievements of the abnormal? Men consciously and voluntarily descended into disease and madness, in search of knowledge which, acquired by fanaticism, would lead back to health; after the possession and use of it had ceased to be conditioned by that heroic and abnormal act of sacrifice. That was the true death on the cross, the true Atonement.

"Aha!" thought Hans Castorp. "You unorthodox Jesuit, you, with your interpretations of the Crucifixion! It's plain why you never became a priest, *joli jésuite à la petite tache humide!* Now roar, lion!" he mentally addressed Herr Settembrini. And the lion roared. He characterized all Naphta had said as quibbling, sophistry, and confusion.

"Say it!" he cried to his opponent, "say it in your character as schoolmaster, say it in the hearing of plastic youth, say straight out, that the soul is——disease! Verily you will thereby encourage them to a belief in the spiritual. Disease and death as nobility, life and health as vulgarity——what a doctrine whereby to hold fast the neophyte to the service of humanity! *Davvero, è criminoso!*" And like a crusader he entered the lists in defence of the nobility of life and health, of that which nature gave, for the soul of which one did not need to fear. "The Form," he said; and Naphta rejoined bombastically: "The Logos." But he who would have none of the Logos answered: "The Reason," and the man of the Logos retorted with "The Passion."

It was confusion worse confounded.

"The Object," cried one, the other: "The Ego!" "Art" and "critique" were bandied back and forth, then once more "nature" and "soul," and as to which was the nobler, and concerning the "aristocratic problem." But there was no order nor clarity, not even of a dualistic and militant kind. Things went not only by contraries, but also all higgledy--piggledy. The disputant not only contradicted each other, they contradicted themselves. How often had Settembrini not spent his oratory in praise of criticism, as being the aristocratic principle? Yet now it was for its opposite, for "art," that he made the same claim. How often had Naphta not stood for instinct, what time Settembrini called nature a blind force, mere *"factum et fatum,"* before which reason and human pride must never abdicate! But here now was Naphta on the side of the soul and disease, wherein alone true nobility and humanity resided, while Settembrini flung himself into advocacy of nature and her noble sanity, regardless of his inconsistency on the score of emancipation from her. The "Object" and the "Ego" were no less involved in confusion—-yes, and here the confusion, moreover, remained constant, was the most literal and incorrigible; so that nobody any longer knew who was the devout and who the free--thinker. Naphta sharply forbade Settembrini to call himself an individualist, for so long as he denied the antithesis between God and nature, saw in the problem of man's inward conflict no more than the struggle between individual and collective interest, and was vowed to a materialistic and bourgeois ethic, in which life became an end in itself, limited to utilitarian aims, and the moral law subserved the interest of the State. He, Naphta, was well aware that man's inner conflict based upon the antagonism between the sensible and the supra--sensible; it was he, not Settembrini, who represented the true, the mystical individualism. He, not Settembrini, was in reality the free--thinker, the man who looked for guidance within himself. Hans Castorp reflected that if that were true, then what about the "anonymous and communal"—-not to mention any other contradiction? And what about those striking comments he had made to Father Unterpertinger on the subject of Hegel's Catholicism, and the affinity between Catholicism and politics, and the category of the objective which they together comprised? Had not statecraft and education always been the special province of the Society to which Naphta belonged? And what an education! Herr Settembrini himself was certainly a zealous pedagogue, zealous to the point of tedium; but he could simply not compete with Naphta in the matter of ascetic, self--mortifying objectivity. Absolute authority, iron discipline, coercion, submission, the Terror! All that might have its own value, but it paid scant homage to the individual and the dignity of his critical faculty. It was the army regulations of the Prussian Frederick, the Exercise--book of the Spanish Loyola all over again; it was rigid, it was devout, to the very marrow. But one question remained to be asked: how had Naphta arrived at this savage absolutism, he who, by his own account, believed not at all in pure knowledge or unfettered research, in other words not in truth, the objective, scientific truth, to strive after which was for Ludovico Settembrini the highest law of human morality. Here was the object of his rigid devotion, whereas Naphta with reprehensible looseness referred truth back to mankind itself, and declared that that was truth which advantaged man. Wasn't it the most utter bourgeoisiedom, the sheerest utilitarian Philistinism, to make truth depend on the interest of mankind? It certainly could not be considered strict objectivity, there was much more free--thinking and subjectivity about it than Leo Naphta would admit—-it was, indeed, quite as much politics as Herr Settembrini's didactic phrase: "Freedom is the law of love of one's kind." That, obviously, was to make freedom, as Naphta made truth, depend upon man, and thus was more orthodox than liberal. But here again were distinctions that tended to disappear in the process of definition. Ah, this Settembrini—-it was not for nothing he was a man of letters, son of a politician and grandson of a humanist! He had lofty ideas about emancipation and criticism—-and chirruped to the girls in the street. On the other hand, knife--edged little Naphta was bound by the strictest sort of vows; yet in thought he was almost a libertine, whereas the other was a very fool of virtue, in a manner of speaking. Herr Settembrini was afraid of "Absolute Spirit," and would like to see it everywhere wedded to democratic progress; he was simply outraged at the religious licence of his militant opponent, which would jumble up together God and the Devil, sanctification and bad behaviour, genius and disease, and which knew no standards of value, no rational judgment, no exercise of the will. But who then was the orthodox, who the freethinker? Where lay the true position, the true state of man? Should he descend into the all--consuming all--equalizing chaos, that ascetic--libertine state; or should he take his stand on the "Critical--Subjective," where empty bombast and a bourgeois strictness of morals contradicted each other? Ah, the principles and points of view constantly did that; it became so hard for Hans Castorp's civilian responsibility to distinguish between opposed positions, or even to keep the premises apart from each other and clear in his mind, that the temptation grew well--nigh irresistible to plunge head foremost into Naphta's "morally chaotic All." The confusion, the crosspurposes, became general, and Hans Castorp suspected that the antagonists would have been less exacerbated had not the dispute bitten into their very souls. They had got up meantime to the Berghof. Then the three who lived there walked back with the others as far as their door, where they stood about in the snow for some further while, and Settembrini and Naphta continued to dispute. It was apparent to Hans Castorp that their zeal was the zeal of the schoolmaster, bent on making an impression upon his plastic mind. Herr Ferge reiterated that it was all too much for him; while Wehsal, so soon as they had got off the themes of torture and corporal punishment, showed small interest. Hans Castorp stood with bent head and burrowed with his stick in the snow, pondering the vasty confusion of it all.

They broke off at last. There were no limits to the subject—-but they could not go on for ever. The three guests of the Berghof took their way home, and the two disputants had to go into the cottage together, the one to seek his silken cell, the other his humanistic cubby--hole with the pulpit--desk and the water--bottle. Hans Castorp betook himself to his balcony, his ears full of the hurly--burly and the clashing of arms, as the army of Jerusalem and that of Babylon, under the *dos banderas*, came on in battle array, and met each other midst tumult and shoutings.

Snow

Daily, five times a day, the guests expressed unanimous dissatisfaction with the kind of winter they were having. They felt it was not what they had a right to expect of these altitudes. It failed to deliver the renowned meteorological specific in anything like the quantity indicated by the prospectus, quoted by old inhabitants, or anticipated by new. There was a very great failure in the supply of sunshine, an element so important in the cures achieved up here that without it they were distinctly retarded. And whatever Herr Settembrini might think of the sincerity of the patients' desire to finish their cure, leave "home" and return to the flat--land, at any rate they insisted on their just dues. They wanted what they were entitled to, what their parents or husbands had paid for, and they grumbled unceasingly, at table, in lift, and in hall. The management showed a consciousness of what it owed them by installing a new apparatus for heliotherapy. They had two already, but these did not suffice for the demands of those who wished to get sunburnt by electricity——it was so becoming to the ladies, young and old, and made all the men, though confirmed horizontallers, look irresistibly athletic. And the ladies, even though aware of the mechanicocosmetical origin of this conquering--hero air, were foolish enough to be carried away by it. There was Frau Schönfeld, a red--haired, red--eyed patient from Berlin. In the salon she looked thirstily at a long--legged, sunken--chested gallant, who described himself on his visiting--card as "*Aviateur diplomé et Enseigne de la Marine allemande.*" He was fitted out with the pneumothorax and wore "smoking" at the midday meal but not in the evening, saying this was their custom in the navy. "My God," breathed Frau Schönfeld at him, "what a tan this demon has——he gets it from the helio—-it makes him look like a hunter of eagles!" "Just wait, nixie!" he whispered in her ear, in the lift, "I'll make you pay for looking at me like that!" It made gooseflesh and shivers run over her. And along the balconies, past the glass partitions, the demon eagle--hunter found his way to the nixie.

But the artificial sun was far from making up for the lack of the real one. Two or three days of full sunshine in the month——it was not good enough, gorgeous though these were, with deep, deep velvety blue sky behind the white mountain summits, a glitter as of diamonds and a fine hot glow on the face and the back of the neck, when they dawned resplendent from the prevailing thick mantle of grey mist.

Two or three such days in the course of weeks could not satisfy people whose lot might be said to justify extraordinary demands from the external world. They had made an inward contract, by the terms of which they resigned the common joys and sorrows proper to flat--land humanity, and in exchange were made free of a life that was, to be sure, inactive, but on the other hand very lively and diverting, and care--free to the point of making one forget altogether the flight of time. Thus it was not much good for the Hofrat to tell them how favourably the Berghof compared with a Siberian mine or a penal settlement, nor to sing the praises of the atmosphere, so thin and light, well--nigh as rare as the empty universal ether, free of earthly admixture whether good or bad, and even without actual sunshine to be preferred to the rank vapours of the plain. Despite all he could say, the gloomy disaffection gained ground, threats of unlicensed departure were the order of the day, were even put into execution, without regard for the warning afforded by the melancholy return of Frau Salomon to the fold, now a "life member," her tedious but not serious case having taken that turn by reason of her self--willed visit to her wet and windy Amsterdam.

But if they had no sun, they had snow. Such masses of snow as Hans Castorp had never till now in all his life beheld. The previous winter had done fairly well in that respect, but it had been as nothing compared to this one. The snow--fall was monstrous and immeasurable, it made one realize the extravagant, outlandish nature of the place. It snowed day in, day out, and all through the night. The few roads kept open were like tunnels, with towering walls of snow on either side, crystal and alabaster surfaces that were pleasant to look at, and on which the guests scribbled all sorts of messages, jokes and personalities. But even this path between walls was above the level of the pavement, and made of hard--packed snow, as one could tell by certain places where it gave way, and let one suddenly sink in up to the knee. One might, unless one were careful, break a leg. The benches had disappeared, except for the high back of one emerging here and there. In the town, the street level was so raised that the shops had become cellars, into which one descended by steps cut in the snow.

And on all these lying masses more snow fell, day in, day out. It fell silently, through air that was moderately cold, perhaps ten to fifteen degrees of frost. One did not feel the cold, it might have been much less, for the dryness and absence of wind deprived it of sting. The mornings were very dark, breakfast was taken by the light of the artificial moon that hung from the vaulted ceiling of the dining--room, above the gay stencilled border. Outside was the reeking void, the world enwrapped in greywhite cotton--wool, packed to the window--panes in snow and mist. No sight of the mountains; of the nearest evergreen now and again a glimpse through the fog, standing laden, and from time to time shaking free a bough of its heavy load, that flew into the air, and sent a cloud of white against the grey. At ten o'clock the sun, a wan wisp of light, came up behind its mountain, and gave the indistinguishable scene some shadowy hint of life, some sallow glimmer of reality; yet even so, it retained its delicate ghostliness, its lack of any definite line for the eye to follow. The contours of the peaks dissolved, disappeared, were dissipated in the mist, while the vision, led on from one pallidly gleaming slope of snow to another, lost itself in the void. Then a single cloud, like smoke, lighted up by the sun, might spread out before a wall of rock and hang there for long, motionless.

At midday the sun would half break through, and show signs of banishing the mist. In vain——yet a shred of blue would be visible, and suffice to make the scene, in its strangely falsified contours, sparkle marvellously far and wide. Usually, at this hour, the snowfall stopped, as though to have a look at what it had done; a like effect was produced by the rare days when the storm ceased, and the uninterrupted power of the sun sought to thaw away the pure and lovely surface from the new--fallen masses. The sight was at once fairylike and comic, an infantine fantasy. The thick light cushions plumped up on the boughs of trees, the humps and mounds of snow--covered rockcropping or undergrowth, the droll, dwarfish, crouching disguise all ordinary objects wore, made of the scene a landscape in gnome--land, an illustration for a fairytale. Such was the immediate view—-wearisome to move in, quaintly, roguishly stimulating to the fancy. But when one looked across the intervening space, at the towering marble statuary of the high Alps in full snow, one felt a quite different emotion, and that was awe of their majestic sublimity.

Afternoons between three and four, Hans Castorp lay in his balcony box, well wrapped, his head against the cushion, not too high or too low, of his excellent chair, and looked out at forest and mountain over his thick--upholstered balustrade. The snow--laden firs, dark--green to blackness, went marching up the sides of the valley, and beneath them the snow lay soft like down pillows. Above the tree line, the mountain walls reared themselves into the grey--white air: huge surfaces of snow, with softly veiled crests, and here and there a black jut of rock. The snow came silently down. The scene blurred more and more, it inclined the eye, gazing thus into woolly vacuity, to slumber. At the moment of slipping off one might give a start—-yet what sleep could be purer than this in the icy air? It was dreamless. It was as free from the burden—-even the unconscious burden—-of organic life, as little aware of an effort to breathe this contentless, weightless, imperceptible air as is the breathless sleep of the dead. When Hans Castorp stirred again, the mountains would be wholly lost in a cloud of snow; only a pinnacle, a jutting rock, might show one instant, to be rapt away the next. It was absorbing to watch these ghostly pranks; one needed to keep alert to follow the transmutations, the veiling and unveiling. One moment a great space of snow--covered rock would reveal itself, standing out bold and free, though of base or peak naught was to be seen. But if one ceased to fix one's gaze upon it, it was gone, in a breath.

Then there were storms so violent as to prevent one's sitting on the balcony for the driven snow which blew in, in such quantity as to cover floor and chair with a thick mantle. Yes, even in this sheltered valley it knew how to storm. The thin air would be in a hurly--burly, so whirling full of snow one could not see a hand's breadth before one's face. Gusts strong enough to take one's breath away flung the snow about, drew it up cyclone--fashion from the valley floor to the upper air, whisked it about in the maddest dance; no longer a snow--storm, it was a blinding chaos, a white dark, a monstrous dereliction on the part of this inordinate and violent region; no living creature save the snow--bunting—-which suddenly appeared in troops—-could flourish in it.

And yet Hans Castorp loved this snowy world. He found it not unlike life at the seashore. The monotony of the scene was in both cases profound. The snow, so deep, so light, so dry and spotless, was the sand of down below. One was as clean as the other: you could shake the snow from boots and clothing, just as you could the fine--ground, dustless stone and shell, product of the sea's depth—-neither left trace behind. And walking in the snow was as toilsome as on the dunes; unless, indeed, a crust had come upon it, by dint of thawing and freezing, when the going became easy and pleasant, like marching along the smooth, hard, wet, resilient strip of sand close to the edge of the sea.

But the storms and high--piled drifts of this year gave pedestrians small chance. They were favourable only for skiing. The snow--plough, labouring its best, barely kept free the main street of the settlement and the most indispensable paths. Thus the few short feasible stretches were always crowded with other walkers, ill and well: the native, the permanent guest, and the hotel population; and these in their turn were bumped by the sleds as they swung and swerved down the slopes, steered by men and women who leaned far back as they came on, and shouted importunately, being obsessed by the importance of their occupation. Once at the bottom they would turn and trundle their toy sledges uphill again.

Hans Castorp was thoroughly sick of all the walks. He had two desires: one of them, the stronger, was to be alone with his thoughts and his stock--taking projects; and this his balcony assured to him. But the other, allied unto it, was a lively craving to come into close and freer touch with the mountains, the mountains in their snowy desolation; toward them he was irresistibly drawn. Yet how could he, all unprovided and foot bound as he was, hope to gratify such a desire? He had only to step beyond the end of the shovelled paths---an end soon reached upon any of them---to plunge breast--high in the snowy element.

Thus it was Hans Castorp, on a day in his second winter with those up here, resolved to buy himself skis and learn to walk on them, enough, that is, for his purposes. He was no sportsman, had never been physically inclined to sport; and did not behave as though he were, as did many guests of the cure, dressing up to suit the mode and the spirit of the place. Hermine Kleefeld, for instance, among other females, though she was constantly blue in the face from lack of breath, loved to appear at luncheon in tweed knickers, and loll about after the meal in a basket--chair in the hall, with her legs sprawled out. Hans Castorp knew that he would meet with a refusal were he to ask the Hofrat to countenance his plan. Sports activities were unconditionally forbidden at the Berghof as in all other establishments of the kind. This atmosphere, which one seemed to breathe in so effortlessly, was a severe strain on the heart, and as for Hans Castorp personally, his lively comment on his own state, that "the getting used to being up here consisted in getting used to not getting used," had continued in force. His fever, which Rhadamanthus ascribed to a moist spot, remained obstinate. Why else indeed should he be here? His desire, his present purpose was then clearly inconsistent and inadmissible. Yet we must be at the pains to understand him aright. He had no wish to imitate the fresh--air faddists and smart pseudo--sportsmen, who would have been equally eager to sit all day and play cards in a stuffy room, if only that had been interdicted by authority. He felt himself a member of another and closer community than this small tourist world; a new and a broader point of view, a dignity and restraint set him apart and made him conscious that it would be unfitting for him to emulate their rough--and--tumble in the snow. He had no escapade in view, his plans were so moderate that Rhadamanthus himself, had he known, might well have approved them. But the rules stood in the way, and Hans Castorp resolved to act behind his back.

He took occasion to speak to Herr Settembrini of his plan——who for sheer joy could have embraced him. "*Si, si, si!* Do so, do so, Engineer, do so with the blessing of God!

Ask after nobody's leave, but simply do it! Ah, your good angel must have whispered you the thought! Do it straightway, before the impulse leaves you. I'll go along, I'll go to the shop with you, and together we will acquire the instruments of this happy inspiration. I would go with you even into the mountains, I would be by your side, on winged feet, like Mercury's——but that I may not. May not! If that were all, how soon would I do it! That I cannot is the truth, I am a broken man.——But you——it will do you no harm, none at all, if you are sensible and do nothing rash. Even——even if it did you harm——just a little harm——it will still have been your good angel roused you to it. I say no more. Ah, what an unsurpassable plan! Two years up here, and still capable of such projects——ah, yes, your heart is sound, no need to despair of you. Bravo, bravo!

By all means pull the wool over the eyes of your Prince of Shadows! Buy the snowshoes, have them sent to me or Lukaçek, or the chandler below--stairs. You fetch them from here to go and practise, you go off on them——"

So it befell. Under Herr Settembrini's critical eye——he played the connoisseur, though innocent of sports——Hans Castorp acquired a pair of oaken skis, finished a light--brown, with tapering, pointed ends and the best quality of straps. He bought the iron--shod staff with the little wheel, as well, and was not content to have his purchases sent, but carried them on his shoulder to Settembrini's quarters, where he arranged with the grocer to take care of them for him. He had looked on enough at the sport to know the use of his tools; and choosing for his practice--ground an almost treeless slope not far behind the sanatorium, remote from the hubbub of the spot where other beginners learned the art, he began daily to make his first blundering attempts, watched by Herr Settembrini, who would stand at a little distance, leaning on his cane, with legs gracefully crossed, and greet his nursling's progress with applause. One day Hans Castorp, steering down the cleared drive toward the Dorf, in act to take the skis back to the grocer's, ran into the Hofrat. Behrens never recognized him, though it was broad day, and our beginner had well--nigh collided with him. Shrouded in a haze of tobacco--smoke, he stalked past regardless.

Hans Castorp found that one quickly gets readiness in an art where strong desire comes in play. He was not ambitious for expert skill, and all he needed he acquired in a few days, without undue strain on wind or muscles. He learned to keep his feet tidily together and make parallel tracks; to avail himself of his stick in getting off; he learned how to take obstacles, such as small elevations of the ground, with a slight soaring motion, arms outspread, rising and falling like a ship on a billowy sea; learned, after the twentieth trial, not to trip and roll over when he braked at full speed, with the right Telemark turn, one leg forward, the other bent at the knee. Gradually he widened the sphere of his activities. One day it came to pass that Herr Settembrini saw him vanish in the far white mist; the Italian shouted a warning through cupped hands, and turned homewards, his pedagogic soul well--pleased.

It was beautiful here in these wintry heights: not mildly and ingratiatingly beautiful, more as the North Sea is beautiful in a westerly gale. There was no thunder of surf, a deathly stillness reigned, but roused similar feelings of awe. Hans Castorp's long, pliant soles carried him in all directions: along the left slope to Clavadel, on the right to Frauenkirch and Claris, whence he could see the shadowy massif of the Amselfluh, ghostlike in the mist; into the Dischma valley, or up behind the Berghof in the direction of the wooded Seehorn, only the top of which, snow--covered, rose above the tree line, or the Drusatschâ forest, with the pale outline of the Rhätikon looming behind it, smothered in snow. He took his skis and went up on the funicular to the Schatzalp; there, rapt six thousand feet above the sea, he revelled at will on the gleaming slopes of powdery snow——whence, in good weather, there was a view of majestic extent over all the surrounding territory.

He rejoiced in his new resource, before which all difficulties and hindrances to movement fell away. It gave him the utter solitude he craved, and filled his soul with impressions of the wild inhumanity, the precariousness of this region into which he had ventured. On his one hand he might have a precipitous, pine--clad declivity, falling away into the mists; on the other sheer rock might rise, with masses of snow, in monstrous, Cyclopean forms, all domed and vaulted, swelling or cavernous. He would halt for a moment, to quench the sound of his own movement, when the silence about him would be absolute, complete, a wadded soundlessness, as it were, elsewhere all unknown. There was no stir of air, not so much as might even lightly sway the treeboughs; there was not a rustle, nor the voice of a bird. It was primeval silence to which Hans Castorp hearkened, when he leaned thus on his staff, his head on one side, his mouth open. And always it snowed, snowed without pause, endlessly, gently, soundlessly falling.

No, this world of limitless silences had nothing hospitable; it received the visitor at his own risk, or rather it scarcely even received him, it tolerated his penetration into its fastnesses, in a manner that boded no good; it made him aware of the menace of the elemental, a menace not even hostile, but impersonally deadly. The child of civilization, remote from birth from wild nature and all her ways, is more susceptible to her grandeur than is her untutored son who has looked at her and lived close to her from childhood up, on terms of prosaic familiarity. The latter scarcely knows the religious awe with which the other regards her, that awe which conditions all his feeling for her, and is present, a constant, solemn thrill, in the profoundest depth of his soul. Hans Castorp, standing there in his puttees and long--sleeved camel's--hair waistcoat, on his skis *de luxe*, suddenly seemed to himself exceedingly presumptuous, to be thus listening to the primeval hush, the deathlike silence of these wintry fastnesses. He felt his breast lightened when, on his way home, the first chalets, the first abodes of human beings, loomed visible through the fog. Only then did he become aware that he had been for hours possessed by a secret awe and terror. On the island of Sylt he had stood by the edge of the thundering surf. In his white flannels, elegant, self--assured, but most respectful, he had stood there as one stands before a lion's cage and looks deep into the yawning jaws of the beast, lined with murderous fangs. He had bathed in the surf, and heeded the blast of the coast--guard's horn, warning all and sundry not to venture rashly beyond the first line of billows, not to approach too nearly the oncoming tempest——the very last impulse of whose cataract, indeed, struck upon him like a blow from a lion's paw. From that experience our young man had learned the fearful pleasure of toying with forces so great that to approach them nearly is destruction. What he had not then felt was the temptation to come closer, to carry the thrilling contact with these deadly natural forces up to a point where the full embrace was imminent. Weak human being that he was——though tolerably well equipped with the weapons of civilization——what he at this moment knew was the fascination of venturing just so far into the monstrous unknown, or at least abstaining just so long from flight before it, that the adventure grazed the perilous, that it was just barely possible to put limits to it, before it became no longer a matter of toying with the foam and playfully dodging the ruthless paw——but the ultimate adventure, the billow, the lion's jaws, and the sea.

In a word, Hans Castorp was valorous up here——if by valour we mean not mere dull matter--of--factness in the face of nature, but conscious submission to her, the fear of death cast out by irresistible oneness. Yes, in his narrow, hypercivilized breast, Hans Castorp cherished a feeling of kinship with the elements, connected with the new sense of superiority he had lately felt at sight of the silly people on their little sleds; it had made him feel that a profounder, more spacious, less luxurious solitude than that afforded by his balcony chair would be beyond all price. He had sat there and looked abroad, at those mist--wreathed summits, at the carnival of snow, and blushed to be gaping thus from the breastwork of material well--being. This motive, and no momentary fad—-no, nor yet any native love of bodily exertion—-was what impelled him to learn the use of skis. If it was uncanny up there in the magnificence of the mountains, in the deathly silence of the snows—-and uncanny it assuredly was, to our son of civilization—-this was equally true, that in these months and years he had already drunk deep of the uncanny, in spirit and in sense. Even a colloquy with Naphta and Settembrini was not precisely the canniest thing in the world, it too led one on into uncharted and perilous regions. So if we can speak of Hans Castorp's feeling of kinship with the wild powers of the winter heights, it is in this sense, that despite his pious awe he felt these scenes to be a fitting theatre for the issue of his involved thoughts, a fitting stage for one to make who, scarcely knowing how, found it had devolved upon him to take stock of himself, in reference to the rank and status of the *Homo Dei.*

No one was here to blow a warning to the rash one—-unless, indeed, Herr Settembrini, with his farewell shout at Hans Castorp's disappearing back, had been that man. But possessed by valorous desire, our youth had given the call no heed—-as little as he had the steps behind him on a certain carnival night. *"Eh, Ingegnere, un po' di ragione, sa!"* " Yes, yes, pedagogic Satana, with your *ragione* and your *ribellione"* he thought. "But I'm rather fond of you. You are a wind--bag and a handorgan man, to be sure. But you mean well, you mean much better, and more to my mind, than that knife--edged little Jesuit and Terrorist, apologist of the Inquisition and the knout, with his round eye--glasses—-though he is nearly always right when you and he come to grips over my paltry soul, like God and the Devil in the mediæval legends."

He struggled, one day, powdered in snow to the waist, up a succession of snowshrouded terraces, up and up, he knew not whither. Nowhither, perhaps; these upper regions blended with a sky no less misty--white than they, and where the two came together, it was hard to tell. No summit, no ridge was visible, it was a haze and a nothing, toward which Hans Castorp strove; while behind him the world, the inhabited valley, fell away swiftly from view, and no sound mounted to his ears. In a twinkling he was as solitary, he was as lost as heart could wish, his loneliness was profound enough to awake the fear which is the first stage of valour. "*Præterit figura huius mundi,*" he said to himself, quoting Naphta, in a Latin hardly humanistic in spirit. He stopped and looked about. On all sides there was nothing to see, beyond small single flakes of snow, which came out of a white sky and sank to rest on the white earth. The silence about him refused to say aught to his spirit. His gaze was lost in the blind white void, he felt his heart pulse from the effort of the climb—-that muscular organ whose animal--like shape and contracting motion he had watched, with a feeling of sacrilege, in the x--ray laboratory. A naïve reverence filled him for that organ of his, for the pulsating human heart, up here alone in the icy void, alone with its question and its riddle.

On he pressed; higher and higher toward the sky. Walking, he thrust the end of his stick in the snow and watched the blue light follow it out of the hole it made. That he liked; and stood for long at a time to test the little optical phenomenon. It was a strange, a subtle colour, this greenish--blue; colour of the heights and deeps, ice--clear, yet holding shadow in its depths, mysteriously exquisite. It reminded him of the colour of certain eyes, whose shape and glance had spelled his destiny; eyes to which Herr Settembrini, from his humanistic height, had referred with contempt as "Tartar slits" and "wolf's eyes"—-eyes seen long ago and then found again, the eyes of Pribislav Hippe and Clavdia Chauchat. "With pleasure," he said aloud, in the profound stillness. "But don't break it— *c'est à visser, tu sais.*" And his spirit heard behind him words of warning in a mellifluous tongue.

A wood loomed, misty, far off to the right. He turned that way, to the end of having some goal before his eyes, instead of sheer white transcendence; and made toward it with a dash, not remarking an intervening depression of the ground. He could not have seen it, in fact; everything swam before his eyes in the white mist, obliterating all contours. When he perceived it, he gave himself to the decline, unable to measure its steepness with his eye.

The grove that had attracted him lay the other side of the gully into which he had unintentionally steered. The trough, covered with fluffy snow, fell away on the side next the mountains, as he observed when he pursued it a little distance. It went downhill, the steep sides grew higher, this fold of the earth's surface seemed like a narrow passage leading into the mountain. Then the points of his skis turned up again, there began an incline, soon there were no more side walls; Hans Castorp's trackless course ran once more uphill along the mountain--side.

He saw the pine grove behind and below him, on his right, turned again toward it, and with a quick descent reached the laden trees; they stood in a wedge--shaped group, a vanguard thrust out from the mist--screened forests above. He rested beneath their boughs, and smoked a cigarette. The unnatural stillness, the monstrous solitude, still oppressed his spirit; yet he felt proud to have conquered them, brave in the pride of having measured to the height of surroundings such as these.

It was three in the afternoon. He had set out soon after luncheon, with the idea of cutting part of the long rest--cure, and tea as well, in order to be back before dark. He had brought some chocolate in his breeches pocket, and a small flask of wine; and told himself exultantly that he had still several hours to revel in all this grandeur. The position of the sun was hard to recognize, veiled as it was in haze. Behind him, at the mouth of the valley, above that part of the mountains that was shut off from view, the clouds and mist seemed to thicken and move forward. They looked like snow—-more snow—-as though there were pressing demand for it! Like a good hard storm. Indeed, the little soundless flakes were coming down more quickly as he stood. Hans Castorp put out his arm and let some of them come to rest on his sleeve; he viewed them with the knowing eye of the nature--lover. They looked mere shapeless morsels; but he had more than once had their like under his good lens, and was aware of the exquisite precision of form displayed by these little jewels, insignia, orders, agraffes—-no jeweller, however skilled, could do finer, more minute work. Yes, he thought, there was a difference, after all, between this light, soft, white powder he trod with his skis, that weighed down the trees, and covered the open spaces, a difference between it and the sand on the beaches at home, to which he had likened it. For this powder was not made of tiny grains of stone; but of myriads of tiniest drops of water, which in freezing had darted together in symmetrical variation—-parts, then, of the same anorganic substance which was the source of protoplasm, of plant life, of the human body. And among these myriads of enchanting little stars, in their hidden splendour that was too small for man's naked eye to see, there was not one like unto another; an endless inventiveness governed the development and unthinkable differentiation of one and the same basic scheme, the equilateral, equiangled hexagon. Yet each, in itself—-this was the uncanny, the anti--organic, the life--denying character of them all—-each of them was absolutely symmetrical, icily regular in form. They were too regular, as substance adapted to life never was to this degree—-the living principle shuddered at this perfect precision, found it deathly, the very marrow of death—-Hans Castorp felt he understood now the reason why the builders of antiquity purposely and secretly introduced minute variation from absolute symmetry in their columnar structures.

He pushed off again, shuffling through the deep snow on his flexible runners, along the edge of the wood, down the slope, up again at random, to his heart's content, about and into this lifeless land. Its empty, rolling spaces, its dried vegetation of single dwarf firs sticking up through the snow, bore a striking resemblance to a scene on the dunes. Hans Castorp nodded as he stood and fixed the likeness in his mind. Even his burning face, his trembling limbs, the peculiar and half--intoxicated mingled sensations of excitement and fatigue were pleasurable, reminding him as they did of that familiar feeling induced by the sea air, which could sting one like whips, and yet was so laden with sleepy essences. He rejoiced in his freedom of motion, his feet were like wings. He was bound to no path, none lay behind him to take him back whence he had come. At first there had been posts, staves set up as guides through the snow——but he had soon cut free from their tutelage, which recalled the coastguard with his horn, and seemed inconsistent with the attitude he had taken up toward the wild. He pressed on, turning right and left among rocky, snow--clad elevations, and came behind them on an incline, then a level spot, then on the mountains themselves——how alluring and accessible seemed their softly covered gorges and defiles! His blood leaped at the strong allurement of the distance and the height, the ever profounder solitude. At risk of a late return he pressed on, deeper into the wild silence, the monstrous and the menacing, despite that gathering darkness was sinking down over the region like a veil, and heightening his inner apprehension until it presently passed into actual fear. It was this fear which first made him conscious that he had deliberately set out to lose his way and the direction in which valley and settlement lay——and had been as successful as heart could wish. Yet he knew that if he were to turn in his tracks and go downhill, he would reach the valley bottom——even if some distance from the Berghof——and that sooner than he had planned. He would come home too early, not have made full use of his time. On the other hand, if he were overtaken unawares by the storm, he would probably in any case not find his way home. But however genuine his fear of the elements, he refused to take premature flight; his being scarcely the sportman's attitude, who only meddles with the elements so long as he knows himself their master, takes all precautions, and prudently yields when he must——whereas what went on in Hans Castorp's soul can only be described by the one word challenge. It was perhaps a blameworthy, presumptuous attitude, even united to such genuine awe. Yet this much is clear, to any human understanding: that when a young man has lived years long in the way this one had, something may gather——may accumulate, as our engineer might put it——in the depths of his soul, until one day it suddenly discharges itself, with a primitive exclamation of disgust, a mental "Oh, go to the devil!" a repudiation of all caution whatsoever, in short with a challenge. So on he went, in his seven--league slippers, glided down this slope too and pressed up the incline beyond, where stood a wooden hut that might be a hayrick or shepherd's shelter, its roof weighted with flat stones. On past this to the nearest mountain ridge, bristling with forest, behind whose back the giant peaks towered upward in the mist. The wall before him, studded with single groups of trees, was steep, but looked as though one might wind to the right and get round it by climbing a little way up the slope. Once on the other side, he could see what lay beyond. Accordingly Hans Castorp set out on this tour of investigation, which began by descending from the meadow with the hut into another and rather deep gully that dropped off from right to left.

He had just begun to mount again when the expected happened, and the storm burst, the storm that had threatened so long. Or may one say "threatened" of the action of blind, nonsentient forces, which have no purpose to destroy us——that would be comforting by comparison——but are merely horribly indifferent to our fate should we become involved with them. "Hullo!" Hans Castorp thought, and stood still, as the first blast whirled through the densely falling snow and caught him. "That's a gentle zephyr——tells you what's coming." And truly this wind was savage. The air was in reality frightfully cold, probably some degrees below zero; but so long as it remained dry and still one almost found it balmy. It was when a wind came up that the cold began to cut into the flesh; and in a wind like the one that blew now, of which that first gust had been a forerunner, the furs were not bought that could protect the limbs from its icy rigours. And Hans Castorp wore no fur, only a woollen waistcoat, which he had found quite enough, or even, with the faintest gleam of sunshine, a burden. But the wind was at his back, a little sidewise; there was small inducement to turn and receive it in the face; so the mad youth, letting that fact reinforce the fundamental challenge of his attitude, pressed on among the single tree--trunks, and tried to outflank the mountain he had attacked.

It was no joke. There was almost nothing to be seen for swimming snow--flakes, that seemed without falling to fill the air to suffocation by their whirling dance. The icy gusts made his ears burn painfully, his limbs felt half paralysed, his hands were so numb he hardly knew if they held the staff. The snow blew inside his collar and melted down his back. It drifted on his shoulders and right side; he thought he should freeze as he stood into a snowman, with his staff stiff in his hands. And all this under relatively favouring circumstances; for let him turn his face to the storm and his situation would be still worse. Getting home would be no easy task—-the harder, the longer he put it off.

At last he stopped, gave an angry shrug, and turned his skis the other way. Then the wind he faced took his breath on the spot, so that he was forced to go through the awkward process of turning round again to get it back, and collect his resolution to advance in the teeth of his ruthless foe. With bent head and cautious breathing he managed to get under way; but even thus forearmed, the slowness of his progress and the difficulty of seeing and breathing dismayed him. Every few minutes he had to stop, first to get his breath in the lee of the wind, and then because he saw next to nothing in the blinding whiteness, and moving as he did with head down, had to take care not to ran against trees, or be flung headlong by unevennesses in the ground. Hosts of flakes flew into his face, melted there, and he anguished with the cold of them. They flew into his mouth, and died away with a weak, watery taste; flew against his eyelids so that he winked, overflowed his eyes and made seeing as difficult as it was now almost impossible for other reasons: namely, the dazzling effect of all that whiteness, and the veiling of his field of vision, so that his sense of sight was almost put out of action. It was nothingness, white, whirling noth--ingness, into which he looked when he forced himself to do so. Only at intervals did ghostly--seeming forms from the world of reality loom up before him: a stunted fir, a group of pines, even the pale silhouette of the hay--hut he had lately passed.

He left it behind, and sought his way back over the slope on which it stood. But there was no path. To keep direction, relatively speaking, into his own valley would be a question far more of luck than management; for while he could see his hand before his face, he could not see the ends of his skis. And even with better visibility, the host of difficulties must have combined to hinder his progress: the snow in his face, his adversary the storm, which hampered his breathing, made him fight both to take a breath and to exhale it, and constantly forced him to turn his head away to gasp. How could anyone—-either Hans Castorp or another and much stronger than he—-make head? He stopped, he blinked his lashes free of water drops, knocked off the snow that like a coat of mail was sheathing his body in front—-and it struck him that progress, under the circumstances, was more than anyone could expect.

And yet Hans Castorp did progress. That is to say, he moved on. But whether in the right direction, whether it might not have been better to stand still, remained to be seen. Theoretically the chances were against it; and in practice he soon began to suspect something was wrong. This was not familiar ground beneath his feet, not the easy slope he had gained on mounting with such difficulty from the ravine, which had of course to be retraversed. The level distance was too short, he was already mounting again. It was plain that the storm, which came from the south--west, from the mouth of the valley, had with its violence driven him from his course. He had been exhausting himself, all this time, with a false start. Blindly, enveloped in white, whirling night, he laboured deeper and deeper into this grim and callous sphere.

"No, you don't," said he, suddenly, between his teeth, and halted. The words were not emotional, yet he felt for a second as though his heart had been clutched by an icy hand; it winced, and then knocked rapidly against his ribs, as it had the time Rhadamanthus found the moist cavity. Pathos in the grand manner was not in place, he knew, in one who had chosen defiance as his rôle, and was indebted to himself alone for all his present plight. "Not bad," he said, and discovered that his facial muscles were not his to command, that he could not express in his face any of his soul's emotions, for that it was stiff with cold. "What next? Down this slope; follow your nose home, I suppose, and keep your face to the wind——though that is a good deal easier said than done," he went on, panting with his efforts, yet actually speaking half aloud, as he tried to move on again: "but something has to happen, I can't sit down and wait, I should simply be buried in six--sided crystalline symmetricality, and Settembrini, when he came with his little horn to find me, would see me squatting here with a snow--cap over one ear." He realized that he was talking to himself, and not too sensibly——for which he took himself to task, and then continued on purpose, though his lips were so stiff he could not shape the labials, and so did without them, as he had on a certain other occasion that came to his mind. "Keep quiet, and get along with you out of here," he admonished himself, adding: "You seem to be woolgathering, not quite right in your head, and that looks bad for you."

But this he only said with his reason——to some extent detached from the rest of him, though after all nearly concerned. As for his natural part, it felt only too much inclined to yield to the confusion which laid hold upon him with his growing fatigue. He even remarked this tendency and took thought to comment upon it. "Here," said he, "we have the typical reaction of a man who loses himself in the mountains in a snow--storm and never finds his way home." He gasped out other fragments of the same thought as he went, though he avoided giving it more specific expression. "Whoever hears about it afterwards, imagines it as horrible; but he forgets that disease——and the state I am in is, in a way of speaking, disease——so adjusts its man that it and he can come to terms; there are sensory appeasements, short circuits, a merciful narcosis——yes, oh yes, yes. But one must fight against them, after all, for they are two--faced, they are in the highest degree equivocal, everything depends upon the point of view. If you are not meant to get home, they are a benefaction, they are merciful; but if you mean to get home, they become sinister. I believe I still do. Certainly I don't intend—in this heart of mine so stormily beating it doesn't appeal to me in the least—to let myself be snowed under by this idiotically symmetrical crystallometry."

In truth, he was already affected, and his struggle against oncoming sensory confusion was feverish and abnormal. He should have been more alarmed on discovering that he had already declined from the level course—this time apparently on the other slope. For he had pushed off with the wind coming slantwise at him, which was ill--advised, though more convenient for the moment. "Never mind," he thought, "I'll get my direction again down below." Which he did, or thought he did—- or, truth to tell, scarcely even thought so; worst of all, began to be indifferent whether he had done or no. Such was the effect of an insidious double attack, which he but weakly combated. Fatigue and excitement combined were a familiar state to our young man—whose acclimatization, as we know, still consisted in getting used to not getting used; and both fatigue and excitement were now present in such strength as to make impossible any thought of asserting his reason against them. He felt as often after a colloquy with Settembrini and Naphta, only to a far greater degree: dazed and tipsy, giddy, a--tremble with excitement. This was probably why he began to colour his lack of resistance to the stealing narcosis with half--maudlin references to the latest--aired complex of theories. Despite his scornful repudiation of the idea that he might lie down and be covered up with hexagonal symmetricality, something within him maundered on, sense or no sense: told him that the feeling of duty which bade him fight against insidious sensory appeasements was a purely ethical reaction, representing the sordid bourgeois view of life, irreligion, Philistinism; while the desire, nay, craving, to lie down and rest, whispered him in the guise of a comparison between this storm and a sand--storm on the desert, before which the Arab flings himself down and draws his burnous over his head. Only his lack of a burnous, the unfeasibility of drawing his woollen waistcoat over his head, prevented him from following suit——this although he was no longer a child, and pretty well aware of the conditions under which a man freezes to death.

There had been a rather steep declivity, then level ground, then again an ascent, a stiff one. This was not necessarily wrong; one must of course, on the way to the valley, traverse rising ground at times. The wind had turned capriciously round, for it was now at Hans Castorp's back, and that, taken by itself, was a blessing. Owing, perhaps, to the storm, or the soft whiteness of the incline before him, dim in the whirling air, drawing him toward it, he bent as he walked. Only a little further——supposing one were to give way to the temptation, and his temptation was great; it was so strong that it quite lived up to the many descriptions he had read of the "typical danger--state." It asserted itself, it refused to be classified with the general order of things, it insisted on being an exception, its very exigence challenged comparison—— yet at the same time it never disguised its origin or aura, never denied that it was, so to speak, garbed in Spanish black, with snow--white, fluted ruff, and stood for ideas and fundamental conceptions that were characteristically gloomy, strongly Jesuitical and anti--human, for the rack--and--knout discipline which was the particular horror of Herr Settembrini, though he never opposed it without making himself ridiculous, like a hand--organ man for ever grinding out "*ragione*" to the same old tune. And yet Hans Castorp did hold himself upright and resist his craving to lie down. He could see nothing, but he struggled, he came forward. Whether to the purpose or not, he could not tell; but he did his part, and moved on despite the weight the cold more and more laid upon his limbs. The present slope was too steep to ascend directly, so he slanted a little, and went on thus awhile without much heed whither. Even to lift his stiffened lids to peer before him was so great and so nearly useless an effort as to offer him small incentive. He merely caught glimpses: here clumps of pines that merged together; there a ditch or stream, a black line marked out between overhanging banks of snow. Now, for a change, he was going downhill, with the wind in his face, when, at some distance before him, and seeming to hang in the driving wind and mist, he saw the faint outline of a human habitation.

Ah, sweet and blessed sight! Verily he had done well, to march stoutly on despite all obstacles, until now human dwellings appeared, in sign that the inhabited valley was at hand. Perhaps there were even human beings, perhaps he might enter and abide the end of the storm under shelter, then get directions, or a guide if the dark should have fallen. He held toward this chimerical goal, that often quite vanished in mist, and took an exhausting climb against the wind before it was reached; finally drew near it——to discover, with what staggering astonishment and horror may be imagined, that it was only the hay--hut with the weighted roof, to which, after all his striving, by all his devious paths, he had come back.

That was the very devil. Hans Castorp gave vent to several heart--felt curses——of which his lips were too stiff to pronounce the labials. He examined the hut, to get his bearings, and came to the conclusion that he had approached it from the same direction as before——-namely, from the rear; and therefore, what he had accomplished for the past hour——as he reckoned it——had been sheer waste of time and effort. But there it was, just as the books said. You went in a circle, gave yourself endless trouble under the delusion that you were accomplishing something, and all the time you were simply describing some great silly arc that would turn back to where it had its beginning, like the riddling year itself. You wandered about, without getting home. Hans Castorp recognized the traditional phenomenon with a certain grim satisfaction——-and even slapped his thigh in astonishment at this punctual general law fulfilling itself in his particular case.

The lonely hut was barred, the door locked fast, no entrance possible. But Hans Castorp decided to stop for the present. The projecting roof gave the illusion of shelter, and the hut itself, on the side turned toward the mountains, afforded, he found, some little protection against the storm. He leaned his shoulder against the roughhewn timber, since his long skis prevented him from leaning his back. And so he stood, obliquely to the wall, having thrust his staff in the snow; hands in pockets, his collar turned up as high as it would go, bracing himself on his outside leg, and leaning his dizzy head against the wood, his eyes closed, but opening them every now and then to look down his shoulder and across the gully to where the high mountain wall palely appeared and disappeared in mist.

His situation was comparatively comfortable. "I can stick it like this all night, if I have to," he thought, "if I change legs from time to time, lie on the other side, so to speak, and move about a bit between whiles, as of course I must. I'm rather stiff, naturally, but the effort I made has accumulated some inner warmth, so after all it was not quite in vain, that I have come round all this way. Come round—not coming round—that's the regular expression they use, of people drowned or frozen to death.—I suppose I used it because I arn not quite so clear in the head as I might be. But it is a good thing I can stick it out here; for this frantic nuisance of a snow--storm can carry on until morning without a qualm, and if it only keeps up until dark it will be quite bad enough, for in the dark the danger of going round and round and *not* coming round is as great as in a storm. It must be toward evening already, about six o'clock, I should say, after all the time I wasted on my circular tour. Let's see, how late is it?" He felt for his watch; his numbed fingers could scarcely find and draw it from his pocket. Here it was, his gold hunting--watch, with his monogram on the lid, ticking faithfully away in this lonely waste, like Hans Castorp's own heart, that touching human heart that beat in the organic warmth of his interior man.

It was half past four. But deuce take it, it had been nearly as much before the storm burst. Was it possible his whole bewildered circuit had lasted scarcely a quarter of an hour? " 'Coming round' makes time seem long," he noted. "And when you *don't* 'come round'—-does it seem longer? But the fact remains that at five or half past it will be regularly dark. Will the storm hold up in time to keep me from running in circles again? Suppose I take a sip of port—it might strengthen me."

He had brought with him a bottle of that amateurish drink, simply because it was always kept ready in flat bottles at the Berghof, for excursions—though not, of course, excursions like this unlawful escapade. It was not meant for people who went out in the snow and got lost and night-bound in the mountains. Had his senses been less befogged, he must have said to himself that if he were bent on getting home, it was almost the worst thing he could have done. He did say so, after he had drunk several swallows, for they took effect at once, and it was an effect much like that of the Kulmbacher beer on the evening of his arrival at the Berghof, when he had angered Settembrini by his ungoverned prattle anent fish-sauces and the like—Herr Ludovico, the pedagogue, the same who held madmen to their senses when they would give themselves rein. Hans Castorp heard through thin air the mellifluous sound of his horn; the orator and schoolmaster was nearing by forced marches, to rescue his troublesome nursling, life's delicate child, from his present desperate pass and lead him home.—All which was of course sheer rubbish, due to the Kulmbacher he had so foolishly drunk. For of course Herr Settembrini had no horn, how could he have? He had a hand-organ, propped by a sort of wooden leg against the pavement, and as he played a sprightly air, he flung his humanistic eyes up to the people in the houses. And furthermore he knew nothing whatever of what had happened, as he no longer lived in House Berghof, but with Lukaçek the tailor, in his little attic room with the water-bottle, above Naphta's silken cell. Moreover, he would have no right nor reason to interfere—no more than upon that carnival night on which Hans Castorp had found himself in a position quite as mad and bad as this one, when he gave the ailing Clavdia Chauchat back *son crayon*—his, Pribislav Hippe's, pencil. What position was that? What position could it be but the horizontal, literally and not metaphorically the position of all long-termers up here? Was not he himself used to lie long hours out of doors, in snow and frost, by night as well as day?

And he was making ready to sink down when the idea seized him, took him as it were by the collar and fetched him up standing, that all this nonsense he was uttering was still inspired by the Kulmbacher beer and the impersonal, quite typical and traditional longing to lie down and sleep, of which he had always heard, and which would by quibbling and sophistry now betray him.

"That was the wrong way to go to work," he acknowledged to himself. "The port was not at all the right thing; just the few sips of it have made my head so heavy I cannot hold it up, and my thoughts are all just confused, stupid quibbling with words. I can't depend on them—-not only the first thought that comes into my head, but even the second one, the correction which my reason tries to make upon the first—-more's the pity. '*Son crayon!*' That means her pencil, not his pencil, in this case; you only say *son* because *crayon* is masculine. The rest is just a pretty feeble play on words. Imagine stopping to talk about that when there is a much more important fact; namely, that my left leg, which I am using as a support, reminds me of the wooden leg on Settembrini's hand--organ, that he keeps jolting over the pavement with his knee, to get up close to the window and hold out his velvet hat for the girl up there to throw something into. And at the same time, I seem to be pulled, as though with hands, to lie down in the snow. The only thing to do is to move about. I must pay for the Kulmbacher, and limber up my wooden leg."

He pushed himself away from the wall with his shoulder. But one single pace forward, and the wind sliced at him like a scythe, and drove him back to the shelter of the wall. It was unquestionably the position indicated for the time; he might change it by turning his left shoulder to the wall and propping himself on the right leg, with sundry shakings of the left, to restore the circulation as much as might be. "Who leaves the house in weather like this?" he said. "Moderate activity is all right; but not too much craving for adventure, no coying with the bride of the storm. Quiet, quiet—-if the head be heavy, let it droop. The wall is good, a certain warmth

[613]

seems; to come from the logs—-probably the feeling is entirely subjective.—-Ah, the trees, the trees!

Oh, living climate of the living—-how sweet it smells!"

It was a park. It lay beneath the terrace on which he seemed to stand—-a spreading park of luxuriant green shade--trees, elms, planes, beeches, birches, oaks, all in the dappled light and shade of their fresh, full, shimmering foliage, and gently rustling tips. They breathed a deliciously moist, balsamic breath into the air. A warm shower passed over them, but the rain was sunlit. One could see high up in the sky the whole air filled with the bright ripple of raindrops. How lovely it was! Oh, breath of the homeland, oh, fragrance and abundance of the plain, so long foregone! The air was full of bird song—-dainty, sweet, blithe fluting, piping, twittering, cooing, trilling, warbling, though not a single little creature could be seen. Hans Castorp smiled, breathing gratitude. But still more beauties were preparing. A rainbow flung its arc slanting across the scene, most bright and perfect, a sheer delight, all its rich glossy, banded colours moistly shimmering down into the thick, lustrous green. It was like music, like the sound of harps commingled with flutes and violins. The blue and the violet were transcendent. And they descended and magically blended, were transmuted and re--unfolded more lovely than before. Once, some years earlier, our young Hans Castorp had been privileged to hear a world--famous Italian tenor, from whose throat had gushed a glorious stream to witch the world with gracious art. The singer took a high note, exquisitely; then held it, while the passionate harmony swelled, unfolded, glowed from moment to moment with new radiance. Unsuspected veils dropped from before it one by one; the last one sank away, revealing what must surely be the ultimate tonal purity—-yet no, for still another fell, and then a well--nigh incredible third and last, shaking into the air such an extravagance of tear--glistening splendour, that confused murmurs of protest rose from the audience, as though it could bear no more; and our young friend found that he was sobbing.—-So now with the scene before him, constantly transformed and transfigured as it was before his eyes. The bright, rainy veil fell away; behind it stretched the sea, a southern sea of deep, deepest blue shot with silver lights, and a beautiful bay, on one side mistily open, on the other enclosed by mountains whose outline paled away into blue space. In the middle distance lay islands, where palms rose tall and small white houses gleamed among cypress groves. Ah, it was all too much, too blest for sinful mortals, that glory of light, that deep purity of the sky, that sunny freshness on the water! Such a scene Hans Castorp had never beheld, nor anything like it. On his holidays he had barely sipped at the south, the sea for him meant the colourless, tempestuous northern tides, to which he clung with inarticulate, childish love. Of the Mediterranean, Naples, Sicily, he knew nothing. And yet——he *remembered*. Yes, strangely enough, that was recognition which so moved him. "Yes, yes, its very image," he was crying out, as though in his heart he had always cherished a picture of this spacious, sunny bliss. Always——and that always went far, far, unthinkably far back, as far as the open sea there on the left where it ran out to the violet sky bent down to meet it.

The sky--line was high, the distance seemed to mount to Hans Castorp's view, looking down as he did from his elevation onto the spreading gulf beneath. The mountains held it embraced, theiï tree--clad foot--hills running down to the sea; they reached in half--circle from the middle distance to the point where he sat, and beyond. This was a mountainous littoral, at one point of which he was crouching upon a sunwarmed stone terrace, while before him the ground, descending among undergrowth, by moss--covered rocky steps, ran down to a level shore, where the reedy shingle formed little blue--dyed bays, minute archipelagoes and harbours. And all the sunny region, these open coastal heights and laughing rocky basins, even the sea itself out to the islands, where boats plied to and fro, was peopled far and wide. On every hand human beings, children of sun and sea, were stirring or sitting. Beautiful young human creatures, so blithe, so good and gay, so pleasing to see——at sight of them Hans Castorp's whole heart opened in a responsive love, keen almost to pain.

Youths were at work with horses, running hand on halter alongside their whinnying, head--tossing charges; pulling the refractory ones on a long rein, or else, seated bareback, striking the flanks of their mounts with naked heels, to drive them into the sea. The muscles of the riders' backs played beneath the sun--bronzed skin, and their voices were enchanting beyond words as they shouted to each other or to their steeds. A little bay ran deep into the coast line, mirroring the shore as does a mountain lake; about it girls were dancing. One of them sat with her back toward him, so that her neck, and the hair drawn to a knot above it smote him with loveliness. She sat with her feet in a depression of the rock, and played on a shepherd's pipe, her eyes roving above the stops to her companions, as in long, wide garments, smiling, with outstretched arms, alone, or in pairs swaying gently toward each other, they moved in the paces of the dance. Behind the flute--player——she too was white--clad, and her back was long and slender, laterally rounded by the movement of her arms—-other maidens were sitting, or standing entwined to watch the dance, and quietly talking. Beyond them still, young men were practising archery. Lovely and pleasant it was to see the older ones show the younger, curly--locked novices, how to span the bow and take aim; draw with them, and laughing support them staggering back from the push of the arrow as it leaped from the bow. Others were fishing, lying prone on a jut of rock, waggling one leg in the air, holding the line out over the water, approaching their heads in talk. Others sat straining forward to fling the bait far out. A ship, with mast and yards, lying high out of the tide, was being eased, shoved, and steadied into the sea. Children played and exulted among the breaking waves. A young female, lying outstretched, drawing with one hand her flowered robe high between her breasts, reached with the other in the air after a twig bearing fruit and leaves, which a second, a slender--hipped creature, erect at her head, was playfully withholding. Young folk were sitting in nooks or the rocks, or hesitating at the water's edge, with crossed arms clutching either shoulder, as they tested the chill with their toes. Pairs strolled along the beach, close and confiding, at the maiden's ear the lips of the youth. Shaggyhaired goats leaped from ledge to ledge of the rocks, while the young goatherd, wearing perched on his brown curls a little hat with the brim turned up behind, stood watching them from a height, one hand on his hip, the other holding the long staff on which he leaned.

"Oh, lovely, lovely," Hans Castorp breathed. "How joyous and winning they are, how fresh and healthy, happy and clever they look! It is not alone the outward form, they seem to be wise and gentle through and through. That is what makes me in love with them, the spirit that speaks out of them, the sense, I might almost say, in which they live and play together." By which he meant the friendliness, the mutual courteous regard these children of the sun showed to each other, a calm, reciprocal reverence veiled in smiles, manifested almost imperceptibly, and yet possessing them all by the power of sense association and ingrained idea. A dignity, even a gravity, was held, as it were, in solution in their lightest mood, perceptible only as an ineffable spiritual influence, a high seriousness without austerity, a reasoned goodness conditioning every act. All this, indeed, was not without its ceremonial side. A young mother, in a brown robe loose at the shoulder, sat on a rounded mossy stone and suckled her child, saluted by all who passed with a characteristic gesture which seemed to comprehend all that lay implicit in their general bearing. The young men, as they approached, lightly and formally crossed their arms on their breasts, and smilingly bowed; the maidens shaped the suggestion of a curtsy, as the worshipper does when he passes the high altar, at the same time nodding repeatedly, blithely and heartily. This mixture of formal homage with lively friendliness, and the slow, mild mien of the mother as well, where she sat pressing her breast with her forefinger to ease the flow of milk to her babe, glancing up from it to acknowledge with a smile the reverence paid her—-this sight thrilled Hans Castorp's heart with something very close akin to ecstasy. He could not get his fill of looking, yet asked himself in concern whether he had a right, whether it was not perhaps punishable, for him, an outsider, to be a party to the sunshine and gracious loveliness of all these happy folk. He felt common, clumsybooted. It seemed unscrupulous. A lovely boy, with full hair drawn sideways across his brow and falling on his temples, sat directly beneath him, apart from his companions, with arms folded on his breast—not sadly, not ill--naturedly, quite tranquilly on one side. This lad looked up, turned his gaze upward and looked at him, Hans Castorp, and his eyes went between the watcher and the scenes upon the strand, watching his watching, to and fro. But suddenly he looked past Hans Castorp into space, and that smile, common to them all, of polite and brotherly regard, disappeared in a moment from his lovely, purely cut, half--childish face. His brows did not darken, but in his gaze there came a solemnity that looked as though carven out of stone, inexpressive, unfathomable, a deathlike reserve, which gave the scarcely reassured Hans Castorp a thorough fright, not unaccompanied by a vague apprehension of its meaning.

He too looked in the same direction. Behind him rose towering columns, built of cylindrical blocks without bases, in the joinings of which moss had grown. They formed the façade of a temple gate, on whose foundations he was sitting, at the top of a double flight of steps with space between. Heavy of heart he rose, and, descending the stair on one side, passed through the high gate below, and along a flagged street, which soon brought him before other propylæa. He passed through these as well, and now stood facing the temple that lay before him, massy, weathered to a grey--green tone, on a foundation reached by a steep flight of steps. The broad brow of the temple rested on the capitals of powerful, almost stunted columns, tapering toward the top—sometimes a fluted block had been shoved out of line and projected a little in profile. Painfully, helping himself on with his hands, and sighing for the growing oppression of his heart, Hans Castorp mounted the high steps and gained the grove of columns, it was very deep, he moved in it as among the trunks in a forest of beeches by the pale northern sea. He purposely avoided the centre, yet for all that slanted back again, and presently stood before a group of statuary, two female figures carved in stone, on a high base:

mother and daughter, it seemed; one of them sitting, older than the other, more dignified, right goddesslike and mild, yet with mourning brows above the lightless empty eye--sockets; clad in a flowing tunic and a mantle of many folds, her matronly brow with its waves of hair covered with a veil. The other figure stood in the protecting embrace of the first, with round, youthful face, and arms and hands wound and hidden in the folds of the mantle.

Hans Castorp stood looking at the group, and from some dark cause his laden heart grew heavier still, and more oppressed with its weight of dread and anguish. Scarcely daring to venture, but following an inner compulsion, he passed behind the statuary, and through the double row of columns beyond. The bronze door of the sanctuary stood open, and the poor soul's knees all but gave way beneath him at the sight within. Two grey old women, witchlike, with hanging breasts and dugs of fingerlength, were busy there, between flaming braziers, most horribly. They were dismembering a child. In dreadful silence they tore it apart with their bare hands—

Hans Castorp saw the bright hair blood--smeared——and cracked the tender bones between their jaws, their dreadful lips dripped blood. An icy coldness held him. He would have covered his eyes and fled, but could not. They at their gory business had already seen him, they shook their reeking fists and uttered curses——soundlessly, most vilely, with the last obscenity, and in the dialect of Hans Castorp's native Hamburg. It made him sick, sick as never before. He tried desperately to escape; knocked into a column with his shoulder——and found himself, with the sound of that dreadful whispered brawling still in his ears, still wrapped in the cold horror of it, lying by his hut, in the snow, leaning against one arm, with his head upon it, his legs in their skis stretched out before him.

It was no true awakening. He blinked his relief at being free from those execrable hags, but was not very clear, nor even greatly concerned, whether this was a hay--hut, or the column of a temple, against which he lay; and after a fashion continued to dream, no longer in pictures, but in thoughts hardly less involved and fantastic.

"I felt it was a dream, all along," he rambled. "A lovely and horrible dream. I knew all the time that I was making it myself——the park with the trees, the delicious moisture in the air, and all the rest, both dreadful and dear. In a way, I knew it all beforehand. But how is it a man can know all that and call it up to bring him bliss and terror both at once? Where did I get the beautiful bay with the islands, where the temple precincts, whither the eyes of that charming boy pointed me, as he stood there alone? Now I know that it is not out of our single souls we dream. We dream anonymously and communally, if each after his fashion. The great soul of which we are a part may dream through us, in our manner of dreaming, its own secret dreams, of its youth, its hope, its joy and peace——and its blood--sacrifice. Here I lie at my column and still feel in my body the actual remnant of my dream——the icy horror of the human sacrifice, but also the joy that had filled my heart to its very depths, born of the happiness and brave bearing of those human creatures in white. It is meet and proper, I hereby declare that I have a prescriptive right to lie here and dream these dreams. For in my life up here I have known reason and recklessness. I have wandered lost with Settembrini and Naphta in high and mortal places. I know all of man. I have known mankind's flesh and blood. I gave back to the ailing Clavdia Chauchat Pribislav Hippe's lead--pencil. But he who knows the body, life, knows death. And that is not all; it is, pedagogically speaking, only the beginning. One must have the other half of the story, the other side. For all interest in disease and death is only another expression of interest in life, as is proven by the humanistic faculty of medicine, that addresses life and its ails always so politely in Latin, and is only a division of the great and pressing concern which, in all sympathy, I now name by its name: the human being, the delicate child of life, man, his state and standing in the universe. I understand no little about him, I have learned much from 'those up here,' I have been driven up from the valley, so that the breath almost left my poor body. Yet now from the base of my column I have no meagre view. I have dreamed of man's state, of his courteous and enlightened social state; behind which, in the temple, the horrible blood--sacrifice was consummated. Were they, those children of the sun, so sweetly courteous to each other, in silent recognition of that horror? It would be a fine and right conclusion they drew. I will hold to them, in my soul, I will hold with them and not with Naphta, neither with Settembrini. They are both talkers; the one luxurious and spiteful, the other for ever blowing on his penny pipe of reason, even vainly imagining he can bring the mad to their senses. It is all Philistinism and morality, most certainly it is irreligious. Nor am I for little Naphta either, or his religion, that is only a *guazzabuglio* of God and the Devil, good and evil, to the end that the individual soul shall plump into it head first, for the sake of mystic immersion in the universal. Pedagogues both! Their quarrels and counter--positions are just a *guazzabuglio* too, and a confused noise of battle, which need trouble nobody who keeps a little clear in his head and pious in his heart. Their aristocratic question!

Disease, health! Spirit, nature! Are those contradictions? I ask, are they problems?

No, they are no problems, neither is the problem of their aristocracy. The recklessness of death is in life, it would not be life without it—-and in the centre is the position of the *Homo Dei*, between recklessness and reason, as his state is between mystic community and windy individualism. I, from my column, perceive all this. In this state he must live gallantly, associate in friendly reverence with himself, for only he is aristocratic, and the counter--positions are not at all. Man is the lord of counterpositions, they can be only through him, and thus he is more aristocratic than they. More so than death, too aristocratic for death—-that is the freedom of his mind. More aristocratic than life, too aristocratic for life, and that is the piety in his heart. There is both rhyme and reason in what I say, I have made a dream poem of humanity. I will cling to it. I will be good. I will let death have no mastery over my thoughts. For therein lies goodness and love of humankind, and in nothing else. Death is a great power. One takes off one's hat before him, and goes weavingly on tiptoe. He wears the stately ruff of the departed and we do him honour in solemn black. Reason stands simple before him, for reason is only virtue, while death is release, immensity, abandon, desire. Desire, says my dream. Lust, not love. Death and love——no, I cannot make a poem of them, they don't go together. Love stands opposed to death. It is love, not reason, that is stronger than death. Only love, not reason, gives sweet thoughts. And from love and sweetness alone can form come: form and civilization, friendly, enlightened, beautiful human intercourse——always in silent recognition of the bloodsacrifice. Ah, yes, it is well and truly dreamed. I have taken stock. I will remember. I will keep faith with death in my heart, yet well remember that faith with death and the dead is evil, is hostile to humankind, so soon as we give it power over thought and action. *For the sake of goodness and love, man shall let death have no sovereignty over his thoughts.*—— And with this——I awake. For I have dreamed it out to the end, I have come to my goal. Long, long have I sought after this word, in the place where Hippe appeared to me, in my loggia, everywhere. Deep into the snow mountains my search has led me. Now I have it fast. My dream has given it me, in utter clearness, that I may know it for ever. Yes, I am in simple raptures, my body is warm, my heart beats high and knows why. It beats not solely on physical grounds, as finger-nails grow on a corpse; but humanly, on grounds of my joyful spirits. My dream word was a draught, better than port or ale, it streams through my veins like love and life, I tear myself from my dream and sleep, knowing as I do, perfectly well, that they are highly dangerous to my young life. Up, up! Open your eyes! These are your limbs, your legs here in the snow! Pull yourself together, and up! Look——fair weather!"

The bonds held fast that kept his limbs involved. He had a hard struggle to free himself——but the inner compulsion proved stronger. With a jerk he raised himself on his elbows, briskly drew up his knees, shoved, rolled, wrestled to his feet; stamped with his skis in the snow, flung his arms about his ribs and worked his shoulders violently, all the while casting strained, alert glances about him and above, where now a pale blue sky showed itself between grey-bluish clouds, and these presently drew away to discover a thin sickle of a moon. Early twilight reigned: no snowfall, no storm. The wall of the opposite mountain with its shaggy, tree--clad ridge stretched out before him plain and peaceful. Shadow lay on half its height, but the upper half was bathed in palest rosy light. How were things in the world? Was it morning? Had he, despite what the books said, lain all night in the snow and not frozen? Not a member was frost--bitten, nothing snapped when he stamped, shook and struck himself, as he did vigorously, all the time seeking to establish the facts of his situation. Ears, toes, finger--tips, were of course numb, but not more so than they had often been at night in his loggia. He could take his watch from his pocket—-it was still going, it had not stopped, as it did if he forgot to wind it. It said not yet five—-it was in fact considerably earlier, twelve, thirteen minutes. Preposterous! Could it be he had lain here in the snow only ten minutes or so, while all these scenes of horror and delight and those presumptuous thoughts had spun themselves in his brain, and the hexagonal hurly vanished as it came? If that were true, then he must be grateful for his good fortune; that is, from the point of view of a safe home--coming. For twice such a turn had come, in his dream and fantasy, as had made him start up—-once from horror, and again for rapture. It seemed, indeed, that life meant well by her lone--wandering delicate child.

Be all that as it might, and whether it was morning or afternoon—-there could in fact be no doubt that it was still late afternoon—-in any case, there was nothing in the circumstances or in his own condition to prevent his going home, which he accordingly did: descending in a fine sweep, as the crow flies, to the valley, where, as he reached it, lights were showing, though his way had been well enough lighted by reflection from the snow. He came down the Brehmenbühl, along the edge of the forest, and was in the Dorf by half past five. He left his skis at the grocer's, rested a little in Herr Settembrini's attic cell, and told him how the storm had overtaken him in the mountains. The horrified humanist scolded him roundly, and straightway lighted his spirit--kettle to brew coffee for the exhausted one——the strength of which did not prevent Hans Castorp from falling asleep as he sat.

An hour later the highly civilized atmosphere of the Berghof caressed him. He ate enormously at dinner. What he had dreamed was already fading from his mind. What he had thought——even that selfsame evening it was no longer so clear as it had been at first.

A Soldier, and Brave

Hans Castorp had had frequent word from his cousin, short messages, at first full of good news and high spirits, then less so, then at length communications that sought to hide something truly sad to hear. The succession of postcards began with the joyous announcement that Joachim was with the colours, and a description of the fanatical ceremony in which, as Hans Castorp ironically couched it in his reply, he had taken the vows of poverty, chastity, and obedience. One after another Joachim passed easily through the stages of his chosen vocation, whose difficulties were smoothed away by the interest of his superiors and his own passionate love for the service. All this he described to his cousin in his brief messages. He was dispensed from the duty of going to the military academy, as he had already studied some semesters, and from the cornetcy. By the New Year he would be promoted to a subalternship——and sent a photograph of himself in the uniform of an officer. His utter devotion to the spirit of the hierarchy he served, that straitly honourable hierarchy, the bonds of whose organization were like iron, and which yet in its crabbedly humorous way knew how to yield something to the weakness of the flesh, was plain in every hasty line. He related anecdotes illustrating the quaintly complex attitude of his cranky, fanatical sergeant--major toward him, the blundering young subordinate, in whom he yet envisaged the ordained superior of to--morrow, who already had the right to enter the officers' casino. It was all very fantastic and droll. Then he told of being admitted to prepare for the officers' examination. By the beginning of April he was a lieutenant. Manifestly there was no happier man, none with more single--minded devotion of his whole being to the chosen career. With a sort of shamefaced beatitude he told of going past the Rathaus for the first time, in full uniform, how the sentry had saluted, and he nodded to him from a distance. He spoke of the small vexations and rewards of the service, of the wonderfully satisfying comradeship, of the sheepish loyalty of his Bursch, of funny occurrences on the parade--ground and in instruction; of inspection, of love--feasts. Also he occasionally mentioned social affairs, visits, dinners, balls. Not a word of his health.

Until toward summer. Then he wrote that he was in bed, on sick--leave, a catarrh, a matter of a few days. By the beginning of June he was back. But at the middle of the month he had crocked up again, and complained bitterly of his luck. He could not conceal his worry lest he should miss the August general manœuvres, toward which he was already eagerly looking. Rubbish! in July he was as sound as a berry, weeks long. But then an examination, made advisable by his accursed fluctuations of temperature, suddenly appeared on the horizon. As to the result of this examination, Hans Castorp for long weeks heard nothing; and when he heard, perhaps out of mortification, perhaps because of his physical state, it was not Joachim who wrote. His mother, Louisa Ziemssen, telegraphed. She said the physicians thought it necessary for Joachim to go on sick--leave for some weeks: high mountains indicated immediate departure advised reserve two rooms reply prepaid signed Aunt Louisa. It was at the end of July when Hans Castorp, lying in his balcony, ran through this dispatch, then read it, and read it again. He nodded as he did so, not with his head but with his whole torso, and said between his teeth: "*Si, si, si*," like Herr Settembrini.

"Joachim is coming back!" ran through him like tidings of great joy. But he grew subdued at once, on the thought "H'm, this *is* bad news! One might almost call it a mess. The deuce! That went fast. Ripe for 'home' again. The mother coming with him"—-Hans Castorp said the mother, not Aunt Louisa, his family feeling having grown unconsciously very faded. "That is serious. And directly before the manœuvres he has been so on fire to go to. H'm, it's certainly a skin game, it's playing it low down on poor Joachim, it's the very opposite of the ideal. By which I mean that the body triumphs, it wants something different from the soul, and puts it through——a slap in the face of all those lofty--minded people who teach that the body is subordinate to the soul. Seems to me they don't know what they are talking about, because if they were right, a case like this would put the soul in a pretty equivocal light. *Verbum sap.*——- I know what I mean. The question I raise is how far they are right when they set the two over against each other; and whether they aren't rather in collusion, playing the same game. That's something that never occurs to the lofty--minded gentry. Not that I am for a moment saying anything against Joachim and his 'doggedness.' He is the soul of honour——but what is honour, is what I want to know, when body and soul act together? Is it possible you have not been able to forget a certain refreshing perfume, a tendency to giggle, a swelling bosom, all waiting for you at Frau Stöhr's table?——He is coming back!" he returned to the thought with the same joyous sensation. "He comes in bad shape, it is true, but we shall be together again, I shan't live up here all by myself. And that's a good thing. It won't be quite as it was before, his room is taken. That Mrs. Macdonald sits there and coughs, a voiceless sort of cough, and keeps looking at the picture of her little son, on her table or in her hand. But she is at the last stage. If nobody else has engaged it, why——but for the present it must be another one. Twenty--eight is free, so far as I know. I'll go down to the office——and to Behrens too. This is news. On the one hand it is bad news, on the other grand news——and in any case a change. I'd like to wait for the 'Comrade' though, he'll be coming along presently, and just ask him if he is still of the opinion, in a case like this, that the physical is to be regarded as secondary."

He went to the office before tea. The room he had in mind, on the same corridor as his own, was free, and there would be a place for Frau Ziemssen. He hastened to Behrens, and found him in the "lab," a cigar in one hand, and in the other a test--tube of dull--coloured fluid.

"Herr Hofrat, what do you think?" he began.

"That there's always the devil to pay," responded the pneumotomist. "Here we have Rosenheim, from Utrecht," said he, and waved his cigar at the test--tube. "Gaffky ten. And Schmitz the manufacturer comes along and tells me he's been spitting on the pavement——with Gaffky ten, if you please. I'm supposed to blow him up. Well, if I blow him up, it will be the deuce and all, because he's as touchy as a bear with a sore head, and he and his family occupy three rooms in the establishment. If I give him what for, the management gives me the same——pressed down and running over. You see what kind of trouble I get into every minute——and me so anxious to go my own simple way, unspotted from the world."

"Silly business," Hans Castorp said, with the ready understanding of the old inhabitant. "I know them both. Schmitz is immensely proper and pushful, and Rosenheim is plenty smeary. But there may be other sore spots, besides the hygienic. They are both friendly with Doña Perez from Barcelona, at the Kleefeld's table——that's the basic trouble, I should think. If I were you I'd just call attention to the rule in general, and then shut my eye to the rest."

"Don't I just? I've got functional blepharospasm already from doing nothing else. But what are you about down here?"

Hans Castorp came out with the sad yet thrilling news.

Not that the Hofrat was surprised, nor would have been in any case. But he had also been kept informed of Joachim's progress; Hans Castorp told him, whether asked or unasked, and he knew that Joachim had been in bed in May.

"Aha," said he. "And what did I tell you? What did I tell both of you, not once but a hundred times, in so many words? So now you have it. Nine months he's had his heart's desire, and been living in a fool's paradise. Well, it wasn't a snakeless paradise——it was infected, more's the pity. But he wouldn't believe what his little ole Behrens told him, and so he's had bad luck, like the rest of them, when they don't believe what their little ole Behrens says, and come too late to their senses. He's got as far as lieutenant, anyhow, there's that to say. But what's the use of it? The good Lord sees your heart, not the braid on your jacket, before Him we are all in our birthday suits, generals and common men alike ..." He rambled on, rubbed his eyes with his huge hands, still holding the cigar between his fingers; then he said Hans Castorp must excuse him for this time. A berth for Joachim would of course be found, when he came his cousin should stick him into bed, without delay. So far as he, Behrens, was concerned he bore nobody any grudge, he would be ready to welcome home the prodigal and like a fond parent kill the fatted calf.

Hans Castorp telegraphed. He spread the news of his cousin's return, and all those who had been the young man's friends were glad and sorry and both quite sincerely; for his clean and chivalrous personality had been universally approved, and there was a sort of unspoken feeling that Joachim had been the best of the lot up here. We mention no one in particular; but incline to think that in some quarters a certain satisfaction was felt in the knowledge that Joachim must give up the soldier's career and return to the horizontal, and in all his immaculateness become one of them up here again. Frau Stöhr, of course, had had her ideas all along; time had now justified the rather unfeeling hints she threw out when Joachim went down, and she was not above saying I told you so. "Pretty rotten," she called it. She had known it for that from the first, and only hoped that Ziemssen by his pigheadedness had not made it putrid. Her choice of words was conditioned by sheer innate vulgarity. How much better it was to stop at one's post, as she did; she too had her life down below, in Cannstadt, a husband and two children, but she could contain herself ... No reply came to the telegram. Hans Castorp remained in ignorance of the hour or day of his cousin's coming, and thus could not receive him at the station when, three days later, he and his mother simply arrived. Lieutenant Joachim, laughing and excited, burst upon his cousin in the evening rest--cure.

It had just begun. The same train brought them as had Hans Castorp, when years ago, years that had been neither long nor short, but timeless, very eventful yet 'the sum of nothing,' he had first come to this place. The time of year was the same too—-one of the very first days of August. Joachim, as we said, went gaily into Hans Castorp's room, or rather out of it into the loggia, with a rapid tread, and laughing, breathless, incoherent, greeted his cousin. He had put all that long way behind him, those miles of territory and that lake that was like a sea, and then wound high up the narrow passes—-and there he stood, as though he had never been away. His cousin started up from the horizontal and greeted him with a shout and "Well, well, well!"

His colour was fresh, thanks to his open--air life, or perhaps to the flush of travel. He had hurried directly to his cousin's room without going first to his own, in order to greet his old--time companion, while his mother was putting herself to rights in the chamber assigned her. They were to eat in ten minutes, of course in the restaurant. Hans Castorp could surely have a little something more with them, or at least take a glass of wine. And Joachim pulled him over to number twenty--eight, where the scene was reminiscent of that long--ago evening when Hans Castorp arrived. Now it was Joachim, who, feverishly talking, washed up at the shining wash--hand--basin, while Hans Castorp looked on, surprised and in a way disappointed to see his cousin in mufti. He had always pictured him as an officer; but here he was in grey "uni," looking like everybody else. Joachim laughed, and said he was naïve. He had left his uniform at home, of course. It was not such a simple matter with a uniform—-you couldn't wear it just any place. "Oh, thanks awfully," said Hans Castorp. But Joachim seemed unaware of any offence in his own remark and went on, asking about matters and things in the Berghof, not only without the least touch of condescension, but even rather moved by the home--coming. Then Frau Ziemssen appeared through the door connecting their two rooms, and greeted her nephew in a way some people have on these occasions; namely, as though pleasurably surprised to find him here. She spoke with subdued melancholy, in part caused by fatigue, in part with reference to Joachim's state—-and they went down to dinner.

Louisa Ziemssen had the same gentle and beautiful dark eyes as Joachim. Her hair, that was quite as black, but mingled now with many threads of grey, was confined by a nearly invisible net; an arrangement characteristic of the mild and measured composure of her personality, which was simple, and at the same time dignified and pleasing. Hans Castorp felt no surprise to see that she was puzzled, even a little put out, by Joachim's liveliness, his rapid breathing and headlong talk, which were probably foreign to his manner either at home or on the journey, besides giving the lie to his actual condition. For herself she was impressed with the sadness of this return, and would have found a subdued bearing more suitable. How could she enter into Joachim's turbulent emotions, due in part to the sensation that he was come home, which for the moment outweighed all else, and in part to the stimulus of the incomparably light, empty, yet kindling air he was once breathing? All that was totally dark to her. "My poor lad," she thought, as she watched him and his cousin abandoned to mirth, telling each other a hundred anecdotes, asking each other a hundred questions, throwing themselves back in their chairs with peals of laughter.

"Children, children!" she protested more than once; and finally levelled a mild reproof at behaviour which might rather have gladdened her heart: "Why, Joachim, I have not seen you like this for many a long day. It seems as though you needed to come back here to be as you were on the day of your promotion." No more was needed to quench Joachim's lively mood. He turned completely round, fell silent and ate none of the sweet, though it was most toothsome, a chocolate *soufflé* with whipped cream. Hans Castorp did what he could in his cousin's stead, though his own hearty dinner

was only an hour behind him. Joachim looked up no more—
-obviously because his eyes were full of tears.

Such a result was as far as possible from Frau Ziemssen's intention.
It was really more for decorum's sake that she had tried to introduce
a little sobriety into the mood of her son, not realizing that precisely
the middle course, the golden mean, was impossible up here, and
only a choice of extremes offered. When she saw him break down,
she seemed not far from tears herself, and most grateful to her
nephew for his gallant efforts to redress the balance of the situation.
Yes, he said, Joachim would find there had been changes in the
population of the Berghof, there were new people, but on the other
hand, some that had gone away were come back again. For instance,
the great--aunt and her charges sat once more at Frau Stöhr's table,
and Marusja laughed as much as ever.

Joachim said nothing. But Frau Ziemssen was thereby reminded
that they had chanced to meet someone who sent greetings, which
she must deliver while she thought of it. It was in a restaurant in
Munich, where they had spent a day between two night journeys. A
lady—a not unsympathetic person, though unaccompanied, and
with rather too level brows—had come up to their table to greet
Joachim. She had been a patient up here, Joachim would know—

"Frau Chauchat," Joachim said, in a low voice. She was spending
some time in a cure in the Allgäu, and intended to go to Spain in the
winter. She sent greetings. Hans Castorp was no raw youth, he had
control over the nerves that might have made the blood rush to or
leave his face. He said: "Oh, so she has emerged from behind the
Caucasus again, has she? And she is going to Spain?"

The lady had mentioned a place in the Pyrenees. A pretty, or at
least a charming woman. Pleasant voice, pretty gestures. But free
manners, slack, Frau Ziemssen thought. "She spoke to us as though
we were old friends, told about herself, asked questions, though it
seems Joachim had never actually known her. I thought it rather
odd."

[631]

"That is the East——and the illness," replied Hans Castorp. "One mustn't try to measure her by humanistic standards." He thought he remembered that she had intended to make a journey into Spain. H'm, Spain. That country too lay remote from the humanistic mean, though on the side of austerity rather than of softness. There it was not lack but excess of form that obtained; death itself was in the guise of form, not dissolution——black, refined, sanguinary, Inquisition, stiff ruff, Loyola, the Escurial, *et cetera*—— h'm, yes, it was interesting; he wondered what Frau Chauchat would say to Spain. She'd probably get over banging doors——and perhaps a combination of the two extremes would bring her closer to the humane mean. Yet something pretty awful, terroristic, might come to pass if the East went to Spain … No, he neither paled nor flushed; but the impression the news had made upon him betrayed itself none the less; on such talk as this nothing but perplexed silence could supervene. Joachim, of course, was less taken aback than his mother, being acquainted from aforetime with his cousin's mental volatility up here. But a great perturbation showed in Frau Ziemssen's eyes, as though her nephew had uttered some gross impropriety; and after a painful pause she broke up the gathering by rising from table, with a phrase or so intended to gloze over the situation. Before they separated, Hans Castorp told them that Behrens's order was for Joachim to remain in bed at least on the morrow, or until he had come to examine him. The rest would be decided later. Soon the three relatives lay each in his room, with the door open to the freshness of the summer night in this altitude, and each with his thoughts: Hans Castorp's were chiefly concerned with Frau Chauchat's return, to be expected within six months' time.

So this was young Joachim's home--coming——for a little after--cure. That way of putting it had obviously been the one given out down below, and it passed current here too, even Hofrat Behrens taking it up, though the first thing he did was to sentence Joachim to four weeks in the "caboose" by way of repairing the most obvious damage, acclimatizing him anew, and putting his house in order as far as temperature was concerned. He was careful to avoid setting any limit for the "aftercure." Frau Ziemssen, sensible, discerning, never very sanguine save at Joachim's bedside, mentioned the autumn, perhaps October, as the terminus, and Behrens acquiesced, at least to the extent of saying that anyhow they would be further on then than they were now. Frau Ziemssen liked him immensely. His bearing toward her was courtly; he called her "my dearest lady," looking deferentially down upon her with his bloodshot eyes; and he talked such extravagant corps--student jargon that despite her depression she always had to laugh. "I know he is in the best of hands," she said; and after a week's stay went back to Hamburg, as Joachim had no need of care, and his cousin was always with him.

"Set your heart at rest," Hans Castorp said to Joachim, sitting by his bed in number twenty--eight. "You'll get off by the autumn, the old 'un has more or less committed himself to that. You can look forward to it as a terminus——October. In that month some people go to Spain, and you can go back to your *bandera*, to distinguish yourself *ex supererogatione* ..."

It became his daily task to console his cousin for the disappointment of missing the manœuvres, which were beginning in these August days. Joachim could think of nothing else, and expressed the greatest self--contempt at this cursed slackness that had come over him in the last minute.

"*Rebellio carnis*," Hans Castorp said. "What can you do about it? The bravest officer can do nothing——even St. Anthony had his little experiences. Good Lord, don't the manœuvres come every year——and surely you know how time flies up here. You haven't been gone long enough not to get back into step quite easily, and before you can turn round your little after--cure will be over."

But the refreshment of his sense of time, caused by Joachim's stay in the valley, had been so considerable that he could not help looking forward with dread to the next four weeks. Everybody, it is true, did his best to make time light for him; the sympathy felt on all hands for the clean personality of the young officer expressed itself in many visits. Settembrini came, was very affectionate and charming, and called Joachim *Capitana*, instead of Lieutenant as before. Naphta too visited him, and all the old acquaintances in the house availed themselves of a free quarter--hour to sit by his bed, repeat the phrase about the little after--cure, and hear his news. The ladies were Stöhr, Levi, Iltis and Kleefeld, the gentlemen Ferge, Wehsal, and others. They even brought him flowers. When the four weeks were up he left his bed, the fever being so far brought under control that it would not harm him to move about. He began taking his meals in the dining--room, at his cousin's table, sitting between him and the brewer's wife, Frau Magnus, opposite Herr Magnus, the place that had once been Uncle James's, and for a few days Frau Ziemssen's as well.

Thus the young people began to live once more side by side. Yes, to make it all even more as it had been, Mrs. Macdonald breathed her last, with the picture of her little son in her hand, and her room, next his cousin's, reverted to Joachim, after it had been thoroughly freed of bacteria by means of H_2CO. More exact, indeed, it was to say that Joachim now lived next door to Hans Castorp, instead of the reverse: the latter was now the old inhabitant, and his cousin shared his existence only provisionally and temporarily. Joachim stuck stiffly by the October terminus—though his nervous system refused to some extent to lend itself to the humanistic norm, and prevented a compensatory radiation of heat.

The cousins resumed their visits to Settembrini and Naphta and their walks with those two devoted opponents. When they were joined by A. K. Ferge and Wehsal, which often happened, they formed a group of six, and before this considerable audience the two opposed spirits carried on an endless duel, which we could not reproduce in any fullness without losing ourselves, as it did daily, in an infinitude of despair. Hans Castorp chose to regard his own poor soul as the object of their dialectic rivalry. He had learned from Naphta that Settembrini was a Freemason, which fact impressed him as much as Settembrini's earlier statement that Naphta was a Jesuit.

He was quite absurdly surprised to hear that there still existed such things as Freemasons; and diligently plied the terrorist with questions about the origin and significance of this curious body, which in a few years would celebrate its two--hundredth birthday. When Settembrini spoke behind his back of Naphta and his intellectual tendencies, it was always on an appealing note of warning, with a hint that the subject had more than a little of the diabolic about it. But when Naphta did the same, he made unaffectedly merry over the sphere which the other represented, and gave Hans Castorp to understand that the things for which Settembrini fought were all of them dead issues; free--thought and bourgeois enlightenment were the pathetic delusions of yesterday, though prone to the self--deception which made them a laughing--stock: namely, that they were still full of revolutionary life. Said Naphta: "Dear me, his grandfather was a *carbonaro*— in other words a charcoal--burner. From him he gets the charcoal--burner's faith in reason, freedom, human progress, the whole box of tricks belonging to the classicistic--humanistic virtue--ideology. You see, what perplexes the world is the disparity between the swiftness of the spirit, and the immense unwieldiness, sluggishness, inertia, permanence of matter. We must admit that this disparity would be enough to excuse the spirit's lack of interest in reality, for the rule is that it has sickened long before of the ferments that bring revolution in their train. In very truth, dead spirit is more repulsive to the living than dead matter, than granite for example, which makes no claim to be alive. Such granite, the relic of an ancient reality left so far behind by the spirit that it refuses any longer to associate with it the conception of reality, continues a sluggish existence, and by its bald and dull continuance prevents futility from becoming aware that it is futile. I am speaking in general terms, but you will know how to apply my words to that humanistic freethought which imagines itself to be still in a heroic attitude of resistance to authority and domination. Ah, and the catastrophes, by virtue of which it thinks to manifest its vitality, the ever--delayed spectacular triumphs at which it is preparing to assist, and thinks one day to celebrate! The living spirit would die of ennui at the bare thought of these, were it not aware that from such catastrophes it alone can emerge as the victor, welding as it does the elements of the old and the new to create the true revolution.——

How is your cousin to--day, Hans Castorp? You know what profound sympathy I feel for him."

"Thanks, Herr Naphta. Everyone seems to feel the same, such a good lad as he is. Even Herr Settembrini admits him very much into his good graces, despite his dislike of a sort of terrorism there is in Joachim's profession. And now I hear Herr Settembrini is a Mason! Imagine! I must say that gives me to think. It sets his personality in a new light, and clarifies certain things for me. Does he go about putting his foot at the right angle and shaking hands with a particular grip? I have never seen anything——"

"Our worthy third--degree friend has probably got beyond such childishness,"

Naphta thought. "I imagine the lodges have curtailed their rites a good deal, in response to the lamentable arid Philistinism of our time. They would probably blush for the ceremonial of former periods as an extravagant mummery, and not without reason, for it would be absurd to present their atheistic republicanism in the guise of a mystery. I don't know with what species of horrors they may have tested Herr Settembrini's constancy; they may have led him blindfold through dark passages, and made him wait in gloomy vaults before the hall of the conclave, full of mirrored lights, burst upon his eyes. They may have solemnly catechized him, menaced his bare breast with swords to the accompaniment of a death's--head and three tapers. You must ask himself; but I fear you will get small satisfaction, for even if the procedure was much tamer than this, in any case he will have been sworn to silence."

"Sworn? To silence? They do that too, then?"

"Certainly. Silence and obedience."

"Obedience too. But listen, Professor, it seems to me then, he has no occasion to stick at the terrorism in my cousin's profession. Silence, and obedience! I could never have believed a free--thinker like Herr Settembrini would submit to such out--and--out Spanish conditions and vows. I perceive that Freemasonry has something quite military and Jesuitical about it."

"And your perceptions are perfectly correct," Naphta responded. "Your diviningrod twitches, and knocks. The idea of the society is rooted in and inseparably bound up with the absolute. By consequence, it is terroristic; that is to say, anti--liberal. It lifts the burden from the individual conscience, and consecrates in the name of the Absolute every means even to bloodshed, even to crime. There is some support for the view that the vows of the brotherhood were once symbolically sealed in blood. A brotherhood can never be purely contemplative. By its very nature it must be executive, must organize. You probably do not know that the founder of the Illuminati, a society which for a long time was nearly identified with Freemasonry, was a former member of the Society of Jesus?"

"No, that is certainly news to me."

"Adam Weishaupt formed his secret benevolent order entirely upon the model of the Society of Jesus. He himself was a Mason, and the most reputable lodge members of the time were Illuminati. I am speaking of the second half of the eighteenth century, which Settembrini would not hesitate to characterize as the period of the degeneration of his fraternity. Actually it was the period of its highest flower, as of all secret societies in general, a time when Masonry attained to a higher life, of which it was later 'purged' by men of the stamp of our friend of humanity here. In that time he would certainly have belonged to those who reproached it with Jesuitry and obscurantism."

"Were there grounds for the reproach?"

"Yes—-if you choose to call it that. The shallow free--thinking of the day was of that opinion. It was the period when the Fathers of

our faith sought to animate the society by breathing into it Catholic-
-hierarchical ideas——at that time there was actually a Jesuit lodge of
Freemasonry at Clermont, in France. And it was the time when
Rosicrucianism made its entrance into the lodges, that remarkable
brotherhood, which, you will note, was a peculiar union of purely
rational ideas of political and social improvement and a millennial
programme, with elements distinctly oriental, Indian and Arabic
philosophy and magical nature--lore. The reform and revision of the
lodges which then took place was in the direction of strict observance
in a definitely irrational and mystical, magical--alchemical sense, to
which the Scottish Rite owes its existence. These are degrees of
knighthood which were added to the old military ranks of apprentice,
journeyman, and master; upper ranks which issued in the hieratical,
and were full of Rosicrucian mysticism. There ensued a sort of
castingback to certain spiritual and knightly orders which existed in
the Middle Ages, for instance the Templars, you know, who took the
vows of poverty, chastity, and obedience before the Patriarch of
Jerusalem. Even to--day there is an upper degree in Freemasonry
which bears the title 'Grand Duke of Jerusalem.' "

"It's all news to me, Herr Naphta. But I'm getting to know Herr
Settembrini's tricks. 'Grand Duke of Jerusalem'——-that's not bad, not
bad at all. You ought to call him that some time, by way of a joke.
The other day he called you *'doctor angelicus.'*

Why not take your revenge?"

"Oh, there are a host more such titles in the upper reaches of the
Knights Templars. There are a Past Grand Master, a Knight of the
East, a Grand High--priest——the thirtyfirst degree is called Noble
Prince of the Royal Mysteries. You observe that all these names have
reference to oriental mysticism. The reappearance of the Templars,
indeed, means nothing else than the entrance of such conceptions, the
presence of irrational ferments in a world given over to rational-
-utilitarian ideas of social improvement. This it was which lent
Freemasonry a new brilliance and charm, and explains the great
number of recruits to it at that period of its history. It drew to itself all

the elements which were weary of the rationalistic twaddle of the century, and thirsting for a stronger draught of life. The success of the order was such that the Philistine complained of it for estranging men from domestic happiness and destroying their reverence for women."

"Then it is not surprising that Herr Settembrini does not love to be reminded of the golden age of his order."

"No, he does not love to be reminded that there was a time when it drew upon its head all the hatred felt by free--thinkers, atheists, and encyclopædists for the whole complex of Church, Catholicism, monk, Middle Ages——you heard that the Masons were accused of obscurantism——"

"Why? I should be glad to hear why, more precisely."

"I will tell you. The Strict Observance meant the broadening and deepening of the traditions of the order, it meant referring its historical origin back to the cabalistic world, the so--called darkness of the Middle Ages. The higher degrees of Freemasonry were initiates of the *'physica et mystica,'* the representatives of a magic natural science, they were in the main great alchemists."

"I shall have to put on my thinking--cap and try to recall what alchemy is——generally speaking, I mean. Alchemy: transmuting into gold, the philosopher's stone, *aurum potabile.*"

"In the popular mind, yes. More informedly put, it was purification, refinement, metamorphosis, transubstantiation, into a higher state, of course; the *lapis philosophorum*, the male--female product of suiphur and mercury, the *res bina*, the double--sexed *prima materia*, was no more, and no less, than the principle of levitation, of the upward impulse due to the working of influences from without. Instruction in magic, if you like."

Hans Castorp was silent. He glanced slantwise upward, and blinked.

"The primary symbol of alchemic transmutation," Naphta said, "was *par excellence* the sepulchre."

"The grave?"

"Yes, the place of corruption. It comprehends all hermetics, all alchemy, it is nothing else than the receptacle, the well--guarded crystal retort wherein the material is compressed to its final transformation and purification."

"Hermetics—-what a lovely word, Herr Naphta! I've always liked the word hermetic. It sounds like magicking, and has all sorts of vague and extended associations. You must excuse my speaking of such a thing, but it reminds me of the conserve jars that our housekeeper in Hamburg—-Schalleen, we call her, without any Miss or Mrs.—-keeps in her larder. She has rows of them on her shelves, air--tight glasses full of fruit and meat and all sorts of things. They stand there maybe a whole year—-you open them as you need them and the contents are as fresh as on the day they were put up, you can eat them just as they are. To be sure, that isn't alchemy or purification, it is simple conserving, hence the word conserve. The magic part of it lies in the fact that the stuff that is conserved is withdrawn from the effects of time, it is hermetically sealed from time, time passes it by, it stands there on its shelf shut away from time. Well, that's enough about the conserve jars. It hasn't much to do with the subject. Pardon me, you were going to enlighten me further."

"Only if you wish me to do so. The learner must be of dauntless courage and athirst for knowledge, to speak in the style of our theme. The grave, the sepulchre, has always been the emblem of initiation into the society. The neophyte coveting admission to the mysteries must always preserve undaunted courage in the face of their terrors; it is the purpose of the Order that he should be tested in them, led down into and made to linger among them, and later fetched up from them by the hand of an unknown Brother. Hence the winding passages, the dark vaults, through which the novice is made to wander; the black cloth with which the Hall of the Strict Observance was hung, the cult of the sarcophagus, which played so important a rôle in the ceremonial of meetings and initiations. The path of mysteries and purification was encompassed by dangers, it led through the pangs of death, through the kingdom of dissolution; and the learner, the neophyte, is youth itself, thirsting after the miracles of life, clamouring to be quickened to a demonic capacity of experience, and led by shrouded forms which are the shadowing--forth of the mystery."

"Thank you so much, Professor Naphta. That is splendid. That is what the teaching of hermetics is like, then; it can't hurt me to have heard something about it too."

"The less so that it is a guide to the ultimate; to the absolute recognition of the transcendental, and therewith to our end and aim. The alchemistic ritual of the lodges, in later centuries, led many a noble and inquiring spirit to that end——to which I need give no name, for it cannot have escaped you that the successive degrees of the Scottish Rite were only a surrogate, a substitute of the Hierarchy, that the alchemistic learning of the Master--Mason fulfilled itself in the mystery of transubstantiation, and that the hidden guidance which the lodge vouchsafed to its pupils has its prototype just as plainly in the means of grace, as the symbolic mummeries of lodge ceremonial have theirs in the liturgical and architectural symbolism of our Holy Catholic Church."

"Ah, indeed!"

"But even that is not all. I have already suggested that the derivation of the lodge from that craftsmanly and honourable masonic guild is only a historical extension. The Strict Observance invested it with a much deeper human basis. The secrets of the lodge have, in common with certain mysteries of our Church, the clearest connexion with the ceremonial mysteries and ritual excesses of primitive man. I refer, so far as the Church is concerned, to the love-

-feast, the sacramental enjoyment of body and blood; as for the lodge—-"

"One moment. One moment for a marginal note. Even in the strict communion to which my cousin belongs, they have so--called love--feasts. He has often written to me about them. I suppose they are very respectable affairs——except possibly they get a little drunk, but nothing like what it is at the corps--students'——"

"As for the lodge, however, I am thinking of the cult of the sepulchre, to whom I referred you before. In both cases it has to do with a symbolism of the ultimate, with elements of orgiastic primitive religion, with wild sacrificial rites by night, to the honour of dying and transforming, death, metamorphosis, resurrection. You will recall that the mysteries of Isis, and the Eleusinian mysteries too, were served by night, and in caverns. In Freemasonry there are present a host of Egyptian survivals, and there were, among the secret societies, some that called themselves Eleusinian. There were lodges that held feasts of Eleusinian mysteries and aphrodistic rites which finally did introduce the female element; feasts of roses, to which reference is made in the three blue roses on the Masonic apron, and which often passed over into the bacchantic."

"What's this, what's this I hear, Professor Naphta? All this Freemasonry? And I must reconcile with it all my ideas of our enlightened Herr Settembrini?"

"You would do him very great injustice if you imagined he knew anything about it. I told you that he, or his like, purified the lodge of all the elements of higher life. They humanized it, they modernized it. God save the mark! They rescued it from false gods and restored it to usefulness, reason and progress, for making war upon princes and priests, in short for social amelioration. In it they once more discuss nature, virtue, moderation, the fatherland. In a word, it is a god--forsaken bourgeoisiedom, in the form of a club."

"What a pity! Too bad about the feasts of roses! I mean to ask Settembrini if he hears anything about them nowadays."

"The noble knight of the T--square!" scoffed Naphta. "You must remember that it has been no easy matter for him to get admitted inside the gates of the temple of humanity. He is as poor as a church--mouse, and they not only demand the higher, the humanistic culture—-save the mark—-but also one must belong to the possessing classes, to be able to stand the dues and entrance fees. Culture and possessions—-there is the bourgeoisie for you! There you have the pillars of the liberal world--republic."

"In any case," laughed Hans Castorp, "we have it all right before our eyes."

"And yet," Naphta added, after a pause, "I would counsel you not to take this man and what he stands for as altogether a laughing matter; since we are on the subject, let me warn you to be on your guard. The insipid is not synonymous with the harmless. Stupidity is not necessarily free from suspicion. These people have watered their wine, that was once such a fiery draught, but the idea of the brotherhood itself remains strong enough to stand a good deal of water. It preserves the remnant of a fruitful mystery, and there is as little doubt that the lodge mixes in politics, as that there is more to see in our amiable Herr Settembrini than just his simple self, and that powers stand behind him, whose representative and emissary he is."

"An emissary?"

"That is, a proselyter, a seeker of souls."

"And what kind of emissary are you, may I ask?" Hans Castorp thought. Aloud he said: "Thank you, Professor Naphta. I am genuinely grateful for your advice and warning. What do you think? Suppose I go a storey higher—-in so far as one can speak of a storey—-and touch up our disguised lodge--brother a bit? The learner must be of dauntless courage, athirst for knowledge. But cautious too, of course. It's well to take precautions when one deals with emissaries."

He might with impunity seek further information from Herr Settembrini, for that gentleman could not reproach Naphta with any lack of discretion; indeed, he had never made any secret of his membership in the harmonious band of brothers. The *Rivista della Massoneria* lay open upon his table; Hans Castorp had simply never noticed it. Enlightened by Naphta, he led the conversation round to the subject of the "kingly art," as though Settembrini's connexion with it had never been a matter of doubt, and he met with very little reticence. True, there were points upon which the literary man was silent. When they were touched upon he closed his lips with ostentation, being obviously bound by those terroristic vows of which Naphta had spoken; this when Hans Castorp encroached on trade secrets, as it were, outward forms of the organization, and his own position within it. But otherwise he was almost too expansive; and held forth at length, giving the seeker after information a considerable picture of the extent of the society, which spread almost all over the world, with twenty thousand lodges and a hundred and fifty grand lodges, in round numbers, and had penetrated civilizations like Haiti and the Negro republic of Liberia. Also he had much to tell of the great names whose bearers had been Masons: Voltaire, Lafayette and Napoleon, Franklin and Washington, Mazzini and Garibaldi; among the living, the King of England, and besides him, a large group of people in whose hands lay the conduct of the nations of Europe, members of governments and parliaments. Hans Castorp expressed respect, but no surprise. It was the same with the student corps, he said. The members of these held together in after life, and they looked after their people well, so that it was hard to get into any important official hierarchy if you had not been a corps--student. For that reason it was perhaps not so logical of Herr Settembrini to argue that the membership of those important personages in the society was flattering to it; since on the other hand it might be assumed that the occupation of so many important posts by Freemasons gave evidence of the power of the society, which certainly mixed in politics, perhaps more than Herr Settembrini was willing to admit.

Settembrini smiled, fanning himself with the magazine, which he still held in his hand. Did Hans Castorp intend to put him a case? Had he in mind to betray him into incautious utterances upon the political character, the essentially political spirit of the lodge? "Useless *furberia*, Engineer. We admit that we are political, admit it openly, unreservedly. We care nothing for the odium that is bound up with the word in the eyes of certain fools—they are at home in your own country, Engineer, and almost nowhere else. The friend of humanity cannot recognize a distinction between what is political and what is not. There is nothing that is not political. Everything is politics."

"That's flat."

"I know there are people who think well to refer to the originally unpolitical nature of Masonic thought. But these people play with words, and set limits which have long since become imaginary and without significance. In the first place, the Spanish lodges, at least, have had a political coloration from the very first."

"I should imagine so."

"You can imagine very little, Engineer. Do not fancy that you are inclined to profound thought; the best you can do is to be receptive and to take to heart—I say this in your own interest, as well as in the interest of your country and of Europe—what I am about to impress upon you: namely, that in the second place, Masonic thought was never unpolitical, at any time—could not be. If it believed itself to be so, it was in error as to its own essential characteristics. What are we? Master-builders and builders on a building. The purpose of all is one, the good of the whole the fundamental tenet of the brotherhood. What is this good, what is this building? It is the true social structure, the perfecting of humanity, the new Jerusalem. But tell me which that is, political or non-political? The social problem, the problem of our common existence, is in itself politics, politics through and through, and nothing else than politics. Whoever devotes himself to the cause—and he does not deserve the name of man that would withhold himself from that devotion——belongs to politics, foreign and domestic; he understands that the art of the Freemason is the art of government——"

"Art of——"

"That Illuminist Freemasonry had the regent degree——"

"That is fine, Herr Settembrini: art of government, degree of regent——I like all that very much. But tell me something: are you Christians, you Masons?"

"Perché?"

"I beg your pardon, I will ask another question; I'll put it more simply and generally. Do you believe in God?"

"I will reply to you. But why do you ask?"

"I was not trying to draw you, just now. But there is a story in the Bible of the Pharisees testing our Lord with a Roman coin, and he tells them to render unto Cæsar the things that are Cæsar's, and unto God the things that are God's. It seemed to me this distinction is the distinction between the political and the non--political. If there is a God, then there is also this distinction. Do Freemasons believe in God?"

"I bound myself to answer. You are speaking of a unity which we seek to bring about, but which to--day, alas, does not exist. If it comes to exist——and I repeat that we labour with silent assiduity upon this great task——then indeed the religious creed of the Freemason will be unanimous, and it will be *'Écrasez l'infame!'* "

"Will that be obligatory? It would hardly be tolerant."

"The problem of tolerance, my dear Engineer, is rather too large for you to tackle. Do not forget that tolerance becomes crime, if extended to evil."

"God would be the evil?"

"Metaphysics is the evil. It is for no purpose but to put to sleep the energy which we should apply to the building of the temple of society. An example is afforded by the action of the Grand Orient of France a generation ago. He struck the name of God out of his writings. We Italians followed him."

"How Catholic!"

"In what sense do you——"

"I mean I find it enormously Catholic, to strike out God."

"What you wish to express is——"

"Nothing worth listening to, Herr Settembrini. Don't pay too much attention to my prattle. It just struck me that atheism may be enormously Catholic, and as though one might strike out God merely the better to be Catholic."

Herr Settembrini allowed a pause to ensue; but it was clear that he only did so out of pedagogic deliberation. He answered, after a measured silence: "Engineer, I am far from wishing to wound or mortify you in your adhesion to Protestantism. We were speaking of tolerance; it is surely superfluous for me to emphasize that far from mere toleration, I feel for Protestantism, as the historical opponent of the enslavement of knowledge, the most profound admiration. The invention of printing and the Reformation are and remain the two outstanding services of central Europe to the cause of humanity. Without question. But after what you have just said I do not doubt you will understand me when I reply that after all it is only one side of the question, and there is another. Protestantism conceals elements——the very personality of your reformer concealed elements.——I am thinking of elements of quiescent beatitude, hypnotic abstraction, which are not European, but foreign to the laws of life that govern our busy continent. Look at him, this Luther! Observe the portraits we have, in early and later life. What sort of cranial formation is that, what cheek-bones, what a singular emplacement of the eye! My friend, that is Asia! I should be surprised, I should be greatly surprised, if there were not Wendish, Slavic, Sarmatic elements in play there. And if the mighty apparition of this man—for who would deny that it was mighty?—had not flung a fatal preponderance into one of the two scales which in your country hang so dangerously even, into the scale of the East, so that the other even to--day is still outweighed and flies up in the air—-"

Herr Settembrini walked from the humanistic folding--desk in the little window, where he had been standing, up to the table, nearer his pupil, who was sitting on the cot against the wall, his elbows on his knees and his chin in his hands.

"Caro!" Herr Settembrini said. *"Caro amico!* There will be decisions to make, decisions of unspeakable importance for the happiness and the future of Europe; it will fall to your country to decide, in her soul the decision will be consummated. Placed as she is between East and West, she will have to choose, she will have to decide finally and consciously between the two spheres. You are young, you will have a share in this decision, it is your duty to influence it. And therefore let us thank the fates that brought you up here to this horrible region, thus giving me opportunity to work upon your plastic youth with my not unpractised, not wholly flagging eloquence, and make you feel the responsibility which—-which your country has in the face of civilization—-"

Hans Castorp sat, his chin in his hand. He looked out of the mansard window, and in his simple blue eyes there was a certain obstinacy. He was silent.

"You are silent," Herr Settembrini said, moved. "You and your native land, you preserve a silence which seems to cover a reservation—and which gives one no hint of what goes on in your depths. You do not love the Word, or you have it not, or you are chary with it to unfriendliness. The articulate world does not know where it is with you. My friend, that is perilous. Speech is civilization itself. The word, even the most contradictious word, preserves contact—-it is silence which isolates. The suspicion lies to hand that you will seek to break your silence with deeds. You will ask Cousin Giacomo" (Settembrini had taken to calling Joachim Giacomo, for convenience sake) "to step out in front of your silence,

'And thrice he smites, and thrice his blows

Deal death, before him fly his foes ...' "

Hans Castorp began to laugh, and Herr Settembrini smiled too, satisfied for the moment with the effect of his plastic words.

"Good," he said. "Very good, let us laugh, you will always find me ready to do that. Laughter, says the classic, is a sunbeam of the soul. We have wandered from the point, we have taken up questions which, I admit, have much to do with the difficulties encountered by us in our preparatory efforts to establish a Masonic worldfederation." Herr Settembrini went on to speak of the idea of this world--federation, which had originated in Hungary, the hoped--for realization of which was destined to consummate the world--power of Freemasonry. Casually he displayed letters from foreign potentates of the society: one from the very hand of the Swiss Grand Master, Brother Quartier la Tente, of the thirty--third degree; and discussed the proposal to make Esperanto the official language of the body. His zeal elevated him to the sphere of policy; he directed his gaze hither and yon, estimated the prospects of revolutionary thought in his own country, in Spain, in Portugal. He was in contact by letter, it appeared, with persons who were at the head of the Portuguese lodge, and there, without much doubt, things were ripening to a decisive event. Hans Castorp would think of him when, before very long, it came to an upset in that country. Hans Castorp promised to do so.

It should be remarked that these Masonic conferences between the pupil and the two mentors took place separated in time, before Joachim's return. The following conversation, however, occurred during his second stay up here, and in his presence, nine weeks after he arrived, at the beginning of October. Hans Castorp retained a clear memory of this gathering in the autumn sunshine, before the Kurhaus in the Platz, where they sat sipping cooling drinks; for it was just at that time he began to feel a secret concern about Joachim——though its ground was not one usually thought very important, being merely a sore throat and hoarseness, quite harmless afflictions, which yet appeared to Hans Castorp in a somewhat peculiar light——the same light, one might say, that he saw in the depths of Joachim's eyes. Those eyes had always, we know, been large and mild, but to-day, precisely on this very day, had seemed to grow larger and deeper, with a musing, yes, we must even say an ominous expression, together with the above--mentioned light. It would have been false to say that Hans Castorp did not like the look of them; he did, only that it disquieted him. And, in short, one cannot, by their very nature, speak of these impressions otherwise than vaguely and confusedly. As for the talk——a controversy, of course, between Settembrini and Naphta——it was an affair of itself, only slightly connected with those earlier and private utterances on the subject of Freemasonry. Ferge and Wehsal were there, and the interest was general, although not all the parties were equal to the situation. Herr Ferge, for instance, was quite definitely not. But a dispute carried on as though it were a matter of life and death, yet with all the polished elegance of a fulldress debate——as were, indeed, all engagements between Settembrini and Naphta——such a dispute is in itself highly diverting to hear, even for those who understand but little of it or its bearing. Strangers sitting near them listened in amaze to the exchange of words and were chained to the spot by the passion and brilliance displayed. All this took place, as we said, in front of the Kurhaus, after tea. The four guests from the Berghof had met Settembrini there, and by chance Naphta also. They sat together about a little metal table, with various drinks and soda, or anise and vermouth. Naphta, who regularly took his tea here, had ordered wine and cake, obviously a reminiscence from his student days. Joachim moistened his aching throat with a lemonade made of fresh lemons, very strong and sour; it had an astringent effect which soothed the ache. Settembrini was drinking sugar--and--water through a straw, with a gusto that made it the rarest of beverages.

[650]

He jested: "What do I hear, Engineer? What are these rumours that fly about? Your Beatrice is returning? Your guide through all the nine circles of Paradise? I must hope that you will not entirely scorn the friendly hand of your Virgil. Our ecclesiastic here will tell you that the world of the *medio evo* is not complete when Franciscan mysticism is not counterbalanced by the opposite pole of Thomistic cognition." They laughed over these erudite jests, and looked at Hans Castorp, who laughed back, raising his glass to his "Virgil." But it is unbelievable what endless academic strife arose in the next hour out of Herr Settembrini's high--sounding but harmless remark. Naphta, having been in a manner challenged, straightway girded up his loins, and fell foul of the Latin poet, whom Settembrini was known to admire to the point of idolatry, even placing him higher than Homer, while Naphta had more than once expressed contempt for him and for the whole of Latin poetry, and did not fail to seize this opportunity to do so again. It was a complaisant limitation of the great Dante, due to his period, that he took so seriously this mediocre versifier and in his poem assigned him so high a rôle—-even though Herr Ludovico did ascribe rather too freemasonly a meaning to it. But what was there to this courtly laureate and lickspittle of the Julian house, this urban *litterateur* and eulogist, who was without a spark of creative genius, whose soul, if he had one, was second--hand, and who was certainly no poet, but a Frenchman in an Augustan full--bottomed wig!

Herr Settembrini had no doubt that the speaker would find ways and means of reconciling his scorn of the golden age of Rome with his office as teacher of Latin. Yet he, Settembrini, could not avoid calling attention to the serious conflict in which such judgments involved Herr Naphta with his own favourite centuries, when Virgil was not only not despised, but his greatness was recognized in the most naïve way; namely, by making a seer and magician of him.

It was vain, Naphta responded, for Herr Settembrini to invoke the simplicity of those primitive times, the victorious element which preserved its creative vitality even while endowing that which it conquered with a demonic quality. But in truth, the Fathers of the early Church were never weary of warning the faithful against the lies of the old philosophers and poets, in particular of cautioning them not to be corrupted by the voluptuous eloquence of Virgil; and to--day, at a time when again an age is declining to its fall, and we see the approaching dawn of another proletarian morn, the time is ripe to feel with them. Finally, in order to leave nothing unanswered, Herr Ludovico might be assured that he, the speaker, did his duty by the small civilian task which Herr Settembrini had been so kind as to mention, with all due *reservatio mentalis;* though there was indeed a certain irony in his conforming to the standards of a classic and rhetorical educational system, whose survival the most optimistic observer could not predicate for more than a few decades.

"You studied them," Settembrini cried out, "you studied them till you sweated, those old poets and philosophers; you have sought to make their priceless heritage your own, as you used the building--stones of their monuments to erect your churches. For well you knew that your proletarian soul could of its own strength bring no art form to birth; and you hoped to defeat antiquity with its own weapons. So it will ever be, history will repeat itself. Your crude immaturity must go to school to the power which you would like to persuade yourself and others to despise; for without discipline you could not endure in the sight of man, and there is but one kind, that which you call the bourgeois, but which is in reality the human." Herr Settembrini went on. A matter of decades? The end of the humanistic principles of education?

Only politeness prevented him from a burst of laughter both unaffected and mocking. A Europe that knew how to preserve its immortal treasures would serenely pass over any proletarian apocalypse of which it here and there pleased people to dream and resume its ordered programme of the reign of classic reason.

It was, Naphta rejoined bitingly, just this ordered programme about which Herr Settembrini seemed not to be very well informed. That which he took for granted was precisely that which was being called in question: namely, whether the Mediterranean, classic, humanistic tradition was bound up with humanity and so coexistent with it, or whether it was but the intellectual garb and appurtenance of a bourgeois liberal age, with which it would perish. History would decide this; he would recommend Hen Settembrini not to lull himself in the secure triumph of his Latin conservatism. All his hearers, but with especial bitterness Herr Settembrini himself, listened to this brazen characterization on the part of little Naphta. He, Herr Settembrini, the avowed servant of progress, a conservative! He twisted violently his flowing moustaches, and seeking for a return blow left the enemy time for a further onslaught upon the classical ideal in education, the rhetorical and literary spirit which characterized the whole of the European educational system, and its splenetic partisanship of the formal and grammatical, which was nothing else than an accessory to the interests of bourgeois class supremacy, and had long been an object of ridicule to the people. They had no idea what an utter joke our doctors' degrees and the whole system fostered by our educational mandarins had become in the minds of the proletariat; as also the public school system, which was the instrument of the domination of the middle classes, maintained in the delusion that popular education is merely watered scholarship. The sort of training and education required by the people in their struggle against the crumbling bourgeois kingdom they had long known how to find elsewhere than in these governmental establishments for compulsory training; one day all the world would realize that our system, which had developed out of the cloister school of the Middle Ages, was a ridiculous bureaucracy and anachronism, that nobody in the world any longer owes his education to his schooling, and that a free and public instruction through lectures, exhibitions, cinematographs, and so forth was vastly to be preferred to any school course.

Herr Settembrini said that Naphta had served up to their audience a mixture of revolution and obscurantism, in which, however, the obscurantist element outweighed the other, to an unsavoury extent.

[653]

Herr Settembrini was pleased to see his concern for the enlightenment of the people, but his pleasure was marred by the fear that what really actuated Herr Naphta was an instinctive tendency to involve both people and world in analphabetic darkness.

Naphta smiled. "That bogy!" he said. Herr Settembrini believed himself to have uttered a word of terror, to have displayed the head of the gorgon, quite convinced that everybody would promptly pale at the sight. He, Naphta, regretted to disappoint his partner in the dialogue, but the fact was, the sight of the humanistic horror of illiteracy simply made him laugh. Verily, one must be a classical literary man, a *précieux*, a *seicentist*, a Marinist, a Jack--of--all--trades of the *estilo culto*, to attach such exaggerated educational value to knowing how to write, as to imagine that where that knowledge was lacking a night of the spirit must reign. Did Herr Settembrini remember that the greatest poet of the Middle Ages, Wolfram von Eschenbach, could neither read nor write? It had been thought blameworthy, in the Germany of that time, to send a boy to school unless he was to be a priest; and this popular--aristocratic scorn of the literary arts was always the sign of fundamental nobility of soul; the literary person, true son of humanism and bourgeoisiedom, could always, certainly, read and write—-whereas the noble, the soldier, and the people never could, or barely—-but he could do and understand nothing else in all the wide world, being nothing but a Latinistic windbag, who had power over language, but left life to people who were fit for it. Which was the reason why the literary person always conceived of politics as an empty bag of wind; that is, of rhetoric and "literature," which in political jargon were called radicalism and democracy—-and so on, and so on.

But now Herr Settembrini sprang into the breach. His opponent, he cried, was rash to expose his preference for the intense barbarism of certain epochs, and to pour scorn upon a love of literary form—-without which no human nature was possible or thinkable, never had been and never would be! Fundamental nobility? Only misanthropy could so characterize the absence of letters, a rude and tongue--tied materialism. Rather you could only rightly so characterize a certain lordly luxuriance, the *generosità* which displayed itself in ascribing to form a human value independent of its content——the cult of speech as an art for art's sake, the inheritance bequeathed by the Græco--Roman culture, which the humanists, the *uomini letterati*, had restored, restored at least to the Romance nations, and which was the source of every later significant idealism, even political. "Yes, my dear sir! That which you would disparage as a divorce between literature and life is nothing but a higher unity in the diadem of the beautiful; I am under no apprehension as to the side on which highhearted youth will choose to fight, in a struggle where the opposing camps are literature and barbarism."

Hans Castorp had been only half listening to the dialogue, being preoccupied by the fundamental nobility of the soldierly representative then present——or rather by the strange new expression in his eyes. He started slightly as he felt himself challenged by Herr Settembrini's last words, and made such a face as he had the time the humanist would have solemnly constrained him to a choice between East and West: a face full of reserve and obstinacy. He said nothing. They forced everything to an issue, these two——as perhaps one must when one differed——and wrangled bitterly over extremes, whereas it seemed to him, Hans Castorp, as though somewhere between two intolerable positions, between bombastic humanism and analphabetic barbarism, must be something which one might personally call the human. He did not express his thought, for fear of irritating one or other of them; but, wrapped in his reserve, listened to one goading the other on, each leading the other from hundredthly to thousandthly, and all because of Herr Settembrini's original little joke about Virgil. The Italian would not give over; he brandished the word, he made it prevail. He threw himself into the fray as the defender of literary genius, celebrated the history of the written word, from the moment when man, yearning to give permanency to his knowledge or emotions, engraved word--symbols upon stone. He spoke of the Egyptian god Thoth, identical with the thrice--renowned

Hermes of Hellenism; who was honoured as the inventor of writing, protector of libraries, and inciter to all literary efforts. He bent the knee metaphorically before that Trismegistus, the humanistic Hermes, master of the palæstra, to whom humanity owed the great gift of the literary word and agonistic rhetoric—-which incited Hans Castorp to the remark that this Egyptian person had apparently been a politician, playing in the grand style the same rôle as that Herr Brunetto Latini who had sharpened the wits of the Florentines, taught them the art of language and how to guide their State according to the rules of politics. Naphta put in that Herr Settembrini was slightly disingenuous: his picture of Thoth--Trismegistus had a good deal of the reality smoothed away. He had been, in fact, an ape, moon and soul deity, a peacock with a crescent moon on his head, and in his Hermes aspect, a god of death and of the dead, a soul--compeller and tutelary soul--guide, of whom late antiquity made an arch--enchanter, and the cabalistic Middle Ages the Father of hermetic alchemy.

Hans Castorp's brain reeled. Here was blue--mantled death masquerading as a humanistic orator; and when one sought to gaze at closer range upon this pedagogic and literary god, benevolent to man, one discovered a squatting ape--faced figure, with the sign of night and magic on its brow. He waved it away with one hand, which he laid over his eyes. But upon that darkness wherein he sought refuge from complete bewilderment, there broke the voice of Herr Settembrini, continuing to chant the praises of literature. All greatness, both contemplative and active, he said, had been bound up with it from all time; and mentioned Alexander, Cæsar, Napoleon, named the Prussian Frederick and other heroes, even Lasalle and Moltke. It disturbed him not a whit that Naphta referred him to China, where such a witless idolatry of the alphabet obtained as had never been the case in any other land, and where one might become a field--marshal if one could draw the forty thousand word--symbols of the language—-a standard, one would think, directly after a humanistic heart!—-Ah, Naphta well knew—-pitiable scoffer though he was!—-that it was a matter not of drawing symbols but of literature as a human impulse, of its spirit, which was Spirit itself, the miraculous conjunction of analysis and form. This it was that awakened the understanding of all things human, that operated to weaken and dissolve silly prejudices and convictions, that brought about the civilizing, elevating, and betterment of the human race. While it developed extreme ethical sensitiveness and refinement, far from being fanatical, it preached honest doubt, fairness, tolerance. The purifying, healing influence of literature, the dissipating of passions by knowledge and the written word, literature as the path to understanding, forgiveness and love, the redeeming might of the word, the literary spirit as the noblest manifestation of the spirit of man, the writer as perfected type, as saint—-in this high key was Herr Settembnni's apologetic pitched. But alas, his antagonist was not struck dumb—-on the contrary, he straightway set about with malicious, brilliant criticism to undermine the humanist's panegyric. He declared himself to the party of conservation and of life, and struck out against the decadent spirit which hid itself behind all that seraphic cant. The marvellous conjunction to which Herr Settembrini referred, in a voice all quavering with emotion, was nothing but a deception and juggling, for the form which the literary spirit prided itself on uniting with the principle of examination and division was only an apparent, a lying form, no true, adequate, natural, living form. These so--called reformers of humanity did indeed take the words purification and sanctification in their mouths, but what they really meant and intended was the emasculation, the phlebotomy of life. Yes, their theory and moving spirit were in violation of life; and he who would destroy passion, that man desired nothing less than pure nothingness—-pure, at least, in the sense that pure was the only adjective which could be applied to nothingness. It was just here that Herr Settembrini showed himself for that which he was: namely, the man of progress, liberalism, and middleclass revolution. For the progress was pure nihilism, the liberal citizen was quite precisely the advocate of nothingness and the Devil; yes, he denied God, the conservatively and positively Absolute, by swearing to the devilish anti--Absolute. And yet with his deadly pacificism thought himself monstrously pious. But he was anything else than pious, he was a traitor to life, before whose stern inquisition and *Vehmgericht* he deserved to be put to the question——and so forth.

Thus did Naphta astutely go about to turn Herr Settembrini's pæan the wrong way and represent himself as the incarnation of the cherishing severity of love——so that it was again impossible to distinguish which side was in the right, where God stood and where the Devil, where death and where life. Our readers will believe us that his antagonist insisted on giving him tit for tat, paying in the newest--minted coin, receiving in his turn another just as good; thus the conversation proceeded, on the lines laid down. But Hans Castorp attended no longer. Joachim had remarked that he believed he had a feverish cold, and did not quite know what to do about it, as colds were not "*reçus*" up here. The duellists had paid him no heed, but Hans Castorp kept, as we have said, an eye on his cousin, and so got up, in the midst of a speech, relying on Ferge and Wehsal to display adequate thirst for further pedagogic disputation. On the way home he and Joachim agreed that it was best to invoke the official channels in matters like colds and sore throats. In other words, they would ask the bathing--master to see the Oberin, in order that something might be done to relieve the sufferer. It was well done. That very evening, directly after dinner, Adriatica knocked at Joachim's door, Hans Castorp being present, and asked what were the wishes of the young officer.

"Sore throat? Hoarseness?" she repeated; "what sort of antics are these, young'un?" and undertook to pierce him with her eye. It was not Joachim's fault that their glances failed to meet, hers swerved aside. Yet she would continue to try, though experience must have taught her it was not given her to succeed in the undertaking. With the help of a sort of metal shoehorn from her pocket, she looked at the patient's tonsils, Hans Castorp standing by with the lamp. Rising on tiptoes to peer into Joachim's throat, she asked: "Tell me, young 'un, do you ever swallow the wrong way?"

What could he answer? For the moment, while she peered into his throat, nothing; but even after she was done, he was at a loss. Naturally, in the course of his life, when eating or drinking he had swallowed the wrong way; but everybody did the same, and surely that could not be what she meant. He asked why: he could not remember the last time.

It was no matter, she said. It had merely occurred to her. He had taken a cold, she added, to the astonishment of the cousins, for colds were in the ordinary way taboo. In any case, it would be necessary to have the Hofrat's laryngeal mirror for further examination of the throat. She left some formamint, and a bandage with a guttapercha sheath, to be used for a moist compress during the night. Joachim availed himself of both, finding they gave relief. He continued to use them; but his hoarseness persisted, it even grew worse in the next few days, though the sore throat largely disappeared.

His fever proved imaginary—at least the thermometer gave no more than the usual result, that, namely, which together with the results of the Hofrat's examinations kept our ambitious Joachim here for his little after--cure, instead of letting him return to the colours. The October terminus had slipped by and no man named it, neither the Hofrat nor the cousins between themselves. They let it pass, in silence, with downcast eyes. From the diagnosis which Behrens dictated at the monthly examinations *to* the psychically expert assistant sitting at his table, and from the results shown by the photographic plate, it was all too clear that though there had once been a departure, of which the best that could be said was that it had been decidedly risky, this time there was nothing for it but iron self--discipline, until such a day as entire immunity might be won, for the fulfilment of the oath and the service of the flat--land.

Such was the decree with which, one and all, they silently pretended to be in agreement. But the truth was, neither of the cousins was sure the other believed it; if they did not meet each other's eyes, it was because of the doubt both pairs of eyes sought to hide, and because the eyes had met before. That, of course, often happened, after the colloquy on the subject of literature, during which Hans Castorp had first remarked the strange new light and ominous expression in the depths of his cousin's eyes. And happened once at table. Joachim suddenly choked violently, and could scarcely get his breath. While he gasped behind his serviette, and his neighbour, Frau Magnus, performed the time--honoured service of slapping him on the back, the cousins' eyes met, in a way more alarming to Hans Castorp than the incident itself, that being something that might happen to anyone. Then Joachim closed his eyes and left the table, his face covered with his serviette, to cough himself out in the garden. Ten minutes later he came back, smiling, if rather pale, and with excuses on his lips for the disturbance. He went on again with his hearty meal, and no one thought afterwards even of wasting a word on so trifling an episode. But some days later, at second breakfast, the thing occurred again; this time there was no meeting of eyes, at least on the part of the cousins, for Hans Castorp bent over his plate and went on eating without seeming to notice. But after the meal they spoke of it, and Joachim freed his mind on the subject of that damned female who had put the thing in his head with her silly question and somehow or other set a spell on him. Yes, it was obviously a case of suggestion, Hans Castorp agreed, and as such rather amusing, despite its annoying side. And Joachim, having named it, seemed able to counteract the spell; he was careful at table, and did not choke any more frequently than persons not bewitched. Not until nine or ten days later did it occur again—-where there was simply nothing to be said.

But he was summoned out of his order to Rhadamanthus. The Oberin had so arranged it, probably with good sense; since there was a laryngeal mirror at hand, it was well to make use of that clever little device for the relief of the obstinate hoarseness or even total lack of voice from which he suffered for hours at a time, and the sore throat, which recurred whenever he omitted to keep his throat passages soft by various salivating medicaments. Not to mention, indeed, that though he choked as other people do, and no more frequently, this was only by dint of the very greatest care, which hindered him at his meals, and made him late in finishing.

The Hofrat, then, mirrored, reflected, peered deep into Joachim's throat, and when he had done, Joachim went straight to his cousin's balcony to give him the result. He said, half whispering, as it was the hour for the afternoon cure, that it had been bothersome, and tickled a good deal. Behrens had rambled on about an inflamed condition, and said the throat must be painted every day; they were to begin tomorrow, as the medicament had to be put up. An inflamed condition, then, and it was to be painted. Hans Castorp, his head full of far--reaching associations, having to do for instance with the lame concierge, and that lady who had gone about for a week holding her ear, and need not have troubled herself, would have liked to put more questions. But he refrained, inwardly resolving to see the Hofrat privately, and said to Joachim he was glad the trouble was being treated, and that the Hofrat had taken it personally in hand. He was top--hole in his line, he would soon put it right. Joachim nodded without looking at him, turned and went into his balcony.

What troubled our honour--loving Joachim? In these last days his eyes had grown so shy, so uncertain in their glance. Fräulein von Mylendonk's efforts had suffered shipwreck only the other day against his mild dark gaze; but now had she tried, she might even have succeeded. For Joachim avoided meeting people's eyes; and even when he met them, as he sometimes must notwithstanding, for his cousin looked at him a good deal, Hans Castorp was not greatly the wiser. He sat now in his balcony much cast down, and tempted to see the chief upon the spot, but refrained, for Joachim must have heard him get up; it was better to wait, and see Behrens later in the afternoon.

That proved impossible. It seemed he simply could not lay eyes on the Hofrat; either that evening, or in the course of the two following days. It was difficult to prevent Joachim from noticing; but that could not fully account for the fact that Rhadamanthus was not to be brought to bay. Hans Castorp sought and asked for him through the house; was sent here or there where he would be certain to find him, and found only that he had gone. Behrens was present at a meal, indeed, but sat far off Hans Castorp, at the "bad" Russian table, and disappeared before the sweet. Once or twice, seeing him stand in talk with Krokowski, with the Oberin, with a patient, on the stairs or in the passage, Hans Castorp thought he had him, and only needed to wait. But chancing to turn away his eyes a minute, he looked back to find him vanished. On the fourth day he succeeded. From his balcony he saw his prey below, giving directions to the gardener; slipped forth of his covers and ran down. He saw the Hofrat's back, as he was paddling in the direction of his own house, set off at a smart pace after him, even took the liberty of calling, but the Hofrat paid no heed. At last, breathless, he caught up his quarry and brought him to a stand.

"What are you doing here?" demanded the Hofrat, and goggled his eyes. "Shall I get an extra--special copy of the house rules printed for you? Seems to me this is the rest period. Your curve and your x--ray don't justify you in playing the independent gentleman, so far as I know. I ought to set up a scarecrow to gobble up people who have the cheek to come down and walk about in the garden at this hour."

"Herr Hofrat, I absolutely must speak to you for a moment."

"I've been observing for some days that you thought you had. You've been laying traps for me, as though I were a female and the object of your passion. What do you want?"

"It is on account of my cousin, Herr Hofrat. Pardon me——he is coming to you to have his throat painted.——I feel sure the thing is all right——it is quite harmless, isn't it, if you will pardon my asking?"

"You are always for having everything harmless, Castorp——that is the nature of you. You rather like mixing in matters that are not harmless, but you treat them as though they were and think to find favour in the eyes of God and man. You're a bit of a hypocrite, Castorp, and a bit of a coward; your cousin puts it very euphemistically when he calls you a civilian."

"That may all be, Herr Hofrat. The weaknesses of my character are beyond question. But that is just the point——at the moment they are not in question: what I've been trying for three days to ask you is——"

"That I'll wrap up the dose in jelly for you——isn't that it? You want to badger me into abetting your damned hypocrisy, so that you can sleep in comfort, while other people have to wake and watch and grin and bear it."

"But, Herr Hofrat, why are you so hard on me? I actually want to——"

"Yes, yes, hardness isn't your line, I know. Your cousin's a different sort, quite another pair of shoes. He knows. *He knows*—— and keeps quiet. Understand? He doesn't go about hanging on to people's coat--tails and asking them to help him pull the wool over his eyes! He knows what he did, and what he risked, and he is the kind to bite his teeth together on it. That's the kind of thing a man, that is a man, can do: unfortunately it isn't in the line of a fascinating biped like yourself. But I warn you, Castorp, if you are going to give way to your civilian feelings and set up a howl, I'll simply show you the door. What we need now is a *man*. You understand?"

Hans Castorp was silent. Nowadays he too turned mottled when he changed colour, being too copper--tinted to grow really pale. At last, with twitching lips, he said: "Thank you, Herr Hofrat. I understand now——at least, I feel sure you would not speak to me so——so solemnly if it weren't serious with Joachim. But I dislike scenes very much——you do me injustice there. If the thing requires judgment and discretion, I think I can promise you I shall not be wanting."

"You set great store by your cousin, Hans Castorp?" asked the Hofrat, as suddenly he gripped the young man's hand, and looked at him with his blue, blood--veined, protruding eyes, under their white eyelashes.

"What is there to say, Herr Hofrat? A near relation, and——and my good friend and only companion up here"——Hans Castorp gulped and turned one foot about on its toes as he stood.

The Hofrat hastened to let go his hand.

"Well, then be as good to him as you can, these next six or eight weeks," he said.

"Just turn yourself loose and give free rein to your native harmlessness. That will help him the most. I'll be here too, to help make things comfortable, and befitting the officer and gentleman he is."

"It's the larynx, isn't it?" Hans Castorp asked, inclining his head in answer.

"*Laryngea*," Behrens assented. "Breaking down fast. The mucous membrane of the trachea looks bad too. Maybe yelling commands in the service set up a *locus minoris resistentiæ* there. But we must always be ready for such little diversions. Not much hope, my lad; really none at all, I suppose. Of course, we'll try everything that's good and costs money."

"The mother," began Hans Castorp.

"Later on, later on. No hurry. Use your discretion, and see that she comes into the picture at the right time. And now get back where you belong. He will miss you——it can't be pleasant for him to feel himself discussed behind his back."

Daily Joachim went to be painted, in the fine autumn weather. In white flannel trousers and blue blazer, he would come back late from his treatment, neat and military; would enter the dining--room, make his little bow, courteous and composed, in excuse of his tardiness, and sit down to his meal, which was specially prepared, for he no longer ate the regular food, on account of the danger of choking; he received minces and broths. His table--mates grasped quickly the state of affairs. They returned his greetings with unusual warmth, and addressed him as Lieutenant. When he was not there they asked after him of Hans Castorp; and even people from the other tables came up to inquire. Frau Stöhr wrung her hands, and exhausted herself in vulgar lamentations. But Hans Castorp replied only in monosyllables, admitted the seriousness of the affair, yet to a certain extent made light of it, in the honourable design not to betray his cousin untimely.

Daily they took their walks together, thrice covering the prescribed distance, to which the Hofrat had now strictly limited Joachim, in order to husband his strength. Hans Castorp walked at his cousin's left. They had been used to walk as chance had it, but now he held consistently to the left. They did not talk much; uttered the phrases proper to the daily routine, and little else. On the subject that lay between them there is nothing to say, especially between people of traditional reserve, who could scarcely bring themselves to utter each other's first names. Sometimes it did well up insistently in Hans Castorp's civilian breast, as though it must out. But it could not: the painful, rebellious feeling sank away again, and he was still.

With bowed head Joachim walked beside him. He gazed earthwards—-as though looking at the earth. How strange! He walked so *comme il faut*, so much as he had always been; he greeted people with his wonted courtliness, he set store, as always, by his outward appearance and *bienséance*— and he belonged to the earth. Well, thither we all belong, soon or late. But so young; with such joyous goodwill to his chosen service—-to belong to the earth so young, is bitter. Bitterer, harder to understand, for him who knew and walked beside him than for the devoted one himself, whose knowledge, even though he knew and kept silent, was academic in its nature, was in a way less his own concern than his companion's. It is a fact that a man's dying is more the survivors' affair than his own. Whether he realizes it or not, he illustrates the pertinence of the adage: So long as we are, death is not; and when death is present, we are not. In other words, between death and us there is no rapport; it is something with which we have nothing to do—-and only incidentally the world and nature. And that is why all living creatures can contemplate it with composure, with indifference, unconcern, with egoistic irresponsibility. Of this state of mind Hans Castorp observed much in his cousin, in these weeks; and comprehended that Joachim, knowing, yet did not know; that it was not hard for him to preserve a decorous silence on the subject, for the reason that his inward relation to it was, so to speak, merely theoretic. So far as it came into practical consideration with him, it was regulated by a healthy sense of the fitness of things, which made him as little likely to discuss it as he was to talk about other functional indecencies of which we are all aware, by which our life is conditioned, but on the subject of which we yet preserve *bienséance.*

So they walked and kept silence between them upon all such unseemly natural concerns. Even the complaints which at first Joachim had so frequently and loudly voiced at missing the manœuvres, and neglecting the service in general, he voiced no more. Yet why, despite all his unconscious bearing, did that sad, shrinking look creep back into his gentle eyes? And that flickering glance—-over which the Frau Directress, had she tried, might now have triumphed? Was it because he saw how big--eyed and hollow--cheeked he was grown?—-for so he was, in these few weeks, much more than during his whole stay down below, and his bronze skin turned from day to day more brown and leathery. As though circumstances which to Herr Albin were but an opportunity to enjoy the boundless advantages of shame, were to the young officer a source of chagrin and self--contempt. Before what, before whom, did his once frank and open glance seek to swerve aside? How strange is this shame of the living creature that slips away into a corner to die, convinced that he may not expect from outward nature any reverence or regard for his suffering and death! Convinced, and rightly: a troop of swallows on exultant wing will give no heed to a maimed comrade, nay, they will even peck him with their beaks. But the example is from the lower reaches of nature. Hans Castorp's heart indeed, his humanly pitying and loving heart, swelled in his breast to see this dark, instinctive shame rise in Joachim's eyes. He walked on his left side expressly; and when there came a little rise to surmount, would help his cousin, who had grown by now unsteady on his feet; would put his arm across his shoulder; overcoming his shyness, would even leave it there a while, until Joachim shook it off pettishly and said: "Don't, it looks silly—-as if we were drunk, coming along like that."

But there came a moment when Hans Castorp saw in a different light the sadness in Joachim's eyes. It was when the latter received the order to keep his bed, at the beginning of November. The snow lay deep. By then he found it too difficult to eat even the minces and porridge they prepared for him, as every second mouthful went the wrong way. The change to liquid nourishment was indicated, and Behrens sent him to bed, in order to conserve his strength. The evening before, the last evening he was about, Hans Castorp saw him talking to Marusja, Marusja of the ready laugh, the orange--scented handkerchief, the bosom fair to outward eye. After dinner, during the social half--hour, Hans Castorp came out of the music--room to look for his cousin, and saw him by the tiled stove, near Marusja's rocking--chair, which Joachim held tipped back with his left arm, so that she looked up in his face from a half--lying posture, with her round brown eyes, and he bent over her, talking softly and disjointedly. She smiled every now and then, and shrugged her shoulders, nervously, deprecatingly. The onlooker hastened to withdraw; though he saw that he was not the only one to watch the little scene, unobserved or at least unheeded by Joachim. The sight shook Hans Castorp more than any sign of failing strength he had seen all these weeks in his cousin: Joachim in conversation, sunk in conversation, with Marusja, at whose table he had sat so long without exchanging a syllable with her, but in reason and honour kept his eyes cast down, and sternly refused to be aware of her person or existence, though he went all mottled whenever she was mentioned in his presence—-"Ah, yes, he is a lost man," thought Hans Castorp, and sat down on a chair in the music--room, to give Joachim time for this one farewell indulgence.

From now on, Joachim took up the horizontal. Hans Castorp sitting in his excellent chair wrote to Louisa Ziemssen. To his earlier reports he added that Joachim had now taken to his bed; that he had said nothing, but the wish to have his mother by him could be read in his eyes, and Hofrat Behrens agreed that it would be well. He put it all with great delicacy. And Louisa Ziemssen, as was not surprising, took the earliest possible train and came to her son. Three days after the humanely worded letter went off she arrived, and Hans Castorp engaged a sleigh and fetched her from the station in a snow--storm. As the train drew in, he took care to compose his features, that the mother might not receive a shock, nor on the other hand be lulled by false hopes. How often had such meetings taken place on this platform, how often this arrival in haste, this anguished searching of features as the traveller descended from the train!

Frau Ziemssen gave the impression that she had run all the way from Hamburg on foot. Flushed of face, she drew Hans Castorp's hand between hers to her breast, and looking at him as though she feared to hear, put her hurried, almost shamefaced queries. He parried them by thanking her for having come so quickly, saying it was splendid to have her, and how delighted Joachim would be. Yes, he was in bed now; it was too bad, but had to be, on account of the liquid diet, which must naturally weaken him to some extent. If necessary, of course, there were other expedients---for instance, artificial nourishment. But she would see for herself.

She saw; and beside her, Hans Castorp saw too. Up to that moment he had not been fully aware of the changes the last weeks had made in Joachim---the young have not much eye for such things. But now he looked with the eyes of the newly arrived mother, as though he had not seen Joachim for weeks; and realized clearly and distinctly, as doubtless she did too, and beyond a doubt Joachim himself clearest of all, that he was a *moribundus*. He took Frau Ziemssen's hand and held it---his own was as yellow and wasted as his face. And his ears, because of the emaciation, stood out almost disfiguringly. Yet despite this blemish, the one affliction of his young days, and despite the austere expression illness set upon his features, their manly beauty seemed intensified——the lips, perhaps, beneath the small black moustache, looked a shade too full by contrast with the hollow cheek. Two lengthwise folds had graven themselves in the yellow surface of his brow; his eyes, deep in their bony sockets, were larger and more beautiful than ever, Hans Castorp never tired of looking at them. For all the distressed and wavering look was gone, now Joachim lay in bed; there was only that earlier light in their dark, quiet depths——yes, there was the "ominous" look as well. He did not smile, he took his mother's hand and whispered her a welcome. He had not even smiled on her entrance; and this immobility of his mien said all.

Louisa Ziemssen was a brave soul. She did not dissolve in grief at sight of her dear son. The almost invisible net that confined and kept in order her hair was symbolic of her composed and self--controlled bearing. Phlegmatic, energetic, as they all were on her native heath, she took in hand the care of Joachim, spurred on by his appearance to engage all her maternal powers in the struggle, and persuaded that if anything could save him, it must be her watchful and devoted care. Not to spare herself, but only from a sense of style, did she consent to call in a nurse. It was Sister Berta, Alfreda Schildknecht, who came with her little black bag. Frau Ziemssen's zeal left her little to do, by day or night, and she had plenty of time to stand in the corridor, with her eye--glass ribbon behind her ear, and keep an eye to all that went on. She was a prosaic soul, this Protestant sister. Once, when she was alone in the room with Hans Castorp and the patient, who was not asleep but lay on his back with open eyes, she actually made the remark: "Who would have dreamed I should ever come to tend the last illness of either of you?"

Hans Castorp, horrified, shook his fist at her, but she scarcely grasped his meaning; she was far from any thought of sparing Joachim's feelings, and too matter--of--fact to dream that anyone, least of all the next of kin, could be in any doubt as to the character and issue of this illness. "There," she said, and held a handkerchief wet with cologne to Joachim's nose, "take a little comfort, Herr Leutnant, do!" And after all, she was right: there could be little sense, at this hour, in keeping up the pretence. It was more for the sake of the tonic effect that Frau Ziemssen still spoke to her son, in a brisk, encouraging voice, of his recovery. For two things were unmistakable: first, that Joachim was approaching death in full consciousness, and second, that he consented to his state, and was in harmony with himself. Only in the last week—the end of November—did cardiac weakness show itself. There were hours when he grew confused, no longer realized his condition, and spoke of an early return to the colours, spoke even of the autumn manœuvres, which he imagined were still going on. Then it was Hofrat Behrens ceased to hold out any hope, and told the relatives the end was a matter of hours. The condition is as regular as it is pathetic, this forgetful, credulous self-deception, that attacks even masculine spirits at the hour when the lethal process nears its culmination. As impersonal, as true to type, as independent of the individual consciousness as the temptation to slumber that overpowers the man benumbed by cold, or the walking in circles of one who has lost his way. Hans Castorp's grief and concern did not prevent him from objective observation of these phenonema, nor from making shrewd if baldly expressed remarks upon them in conversation with Naphta and Settembrini, when he reported to them on his cousin's condition. He even drew upon himself a rebuke from Settembrini, for saying he thought the current conception in error which would have it that a philosophical credulity and belief that all is for the best is the mark of a sound nature, as pessimism and cynicism are of morbidity. For if this were true, it would not be precisely the hopeless final stage that displayed an optimism so abnormally rosy as to make the preceding depression seem by comparison a crassly healthy manifestation of life. He was glad at the same time to be able to tell his friends that though Rhadamanthus gave them no hope, yet the hopelessness was not of the most painful character, for he prophesied a gentle, painless end, despite Joachim's blooming youth.

"Idyllic—affair of the heart, my dear lady," Behrens said, and held Louisa Ziemssen's hand in his own two, the size of shovels, looking down at her with his goggling, watery, blood-shot eyes. "I'm tremendously glad it is taking such a gratifying course, and he doesn't need to go through with œdema of the glottis or any indignity of that sort, he will be spared a lot of messing about. The heart is giving out rapidly, lucky for him and for us; we can do our duty with camphor injections and the like, without much chance of drawing things out. He will sleep a good deal at the end, and his dreams will be pleasant, I think I can promise you that; even if he shouldn't go off in his sleep, still it will be a short crossing, he'll scarcely notice, you may rely upon it. It's so in the majority of cases, at bottom—I know what death is, I am an old retainer of his; and believe me, he's overrated. Almost nothing to him. Of course, all kinds of beastliness can happen beforehand—but it isn't fair to count those in, they are as living as life itself, and can just as well lead up to a cure. But about death—no one who came back from it could tell you anything, because we don't realize it. We come out of the dark and go into the dark again, and in between lie the experiences of our life. But the beginning and the end, birth and death, we do not experience; they have no subjective character, they fall entirely in the category of objective events, and that's that."

Which was the Hofrat's way of administering consolation. We may hope that the reasonable Frau Ziemssen drew comfort therefrom; his assurances, at least, were in a very large degree justified by the event. Joachim, in these days, slept many hours, out of weakness, and probably dreamed of the flat-land and the service and whatever else was pleasant to him to dream. When he roused, and they asked how he felt, he would answer a little incoherently, yet always that he felt well and happy. This though he had scarcely any pulse, and at the end could no longer feel the hypodermic needle. His body was insensitive, you might have burned or pinched the flesh, he was past feeling. Great physical changes had taken place since the mother's coming. Shaving had grown burdensome to him, for some eight or ten days it had not been done, and he had now a strong growth of beard, setting off with a black frame his waxen face and gentle eyes. It was the warrior's beard, the beard of the soldier in the field; they all found it manly and becoming. But because of this beard Joachim had suddenly grown from a stripling to a ripe man—though perhaps not because of it alone. He was living fast, his life whirred away like the mechanism of a watch; he passed at a gallop through stages not granted him in time to reach; and in the last four--and--twenty hours became a grey old man. The cardiac weakness caused a facial swelling that gave the effect of strain, and made upon Hans Castorp the impression that dying must at the very least be a great effort, though of course Joachim, thanks to various sensory adjustments and a merciful narcosis of the system, was not aware of it. The puffing of the features was mostly about the lips; the inside of the mouth also seemed dry or semi--paralysed, making Joachim mumble like an old man—which annoyed him excessively. If he could only, he said thickly, get rid of it he would be quite all right, but it was a cursed nuisance.

In what sense he meant the "quite all right" was not clear—in fact, he showed the typical tendency to ambiguousness, made more than one remark of doubtful or double sense, seemed to know and yet not to; once, when it was very evident that a wave of the oncoming dissolution broke over him, he shook his head and said self--pityingly that he felt very bad, he had never felt so bad before.

After that he became austere, forbidding, even gruff; would not listen to any soothing fictions or pretence, but stared before him and made no reply. Louisa Ziemssen had sent for a young clergyman, who, to Hans Castorp's regret, did not appear in a starched ruff, but wore bands instead. After he had prayed with Joachim, the patient assumed an official tone and air, and uttered his wishes in the form of short commands.

At six o'clock in the afternoon he began making a strange continuous movement with his right hand, with the chain bangle on the wrist: passing it across the bed--cover, at about the hips, lifting it as he drew it back and toward him, with a raking motion, as though he were gathering something in.

At seven o'clock he died; Alfreda Schildknecht was in the corridor, the mother and cousin were alone with him. He had sunk down in the bed, and curtly ordered them to prop him up. While Frau Ziemssen, with her arm about his shoulders, tried to do so, he said hurriedly that he must write out an application for an extension of his leave and hand it in at once; and even while he said this, the "short crossing" came to pass, as Hans Castorp, reverently watching in the light of the red--shaded table--lamp, quickly perceived. His gaze grew dim, the unconscious tension of the features relaxed, the strained and swollen look about the lips notably diminished; the beauty of early manhood visited once more our Joachim's quiet brow, and all was over.

Louisa Ziemssen turned sobbing away; it was Hans Castorp who bent over the moveless, breathless form, closed the eyes with the tip of his ring--finger, and laid the hands together on the coverlet. Then he too stood and wept, tears ran down his cheeks, like those that had smarted the skin of the English officer of marines: those clear drops flowing in such bitter abundance every hour of our day all over our world, till in sheer poetic justice we have named the earth we live in after them; that alkaline, salty gland--secretion, which is pressed from our system by the nervous stress of acute pain, whether physical or mental. It contained, as Hans Castorp knew, a certain amount of mucin and albumen as well.

The Hofrat came, summoned by Sister Berta. He had been there a half--hour earlier, and given a camphor injection; had scarcely been absent for more than the moment of the "short crossing." "Ay," said he simply, "he has it behind him now," and lifted the stethoscope from Joachim's breast. And he pressed both their hands, nodding his head; standing with them awhile by the bed, and looking into Joachim's moveless visage, with the warrior beard. "Crazy young one," he said: jerking his head towards the recumbent form. "Crazy chap. Would force it, you know——of course, that's the way of the service down there, all force, all compulsion—-he joined the service while he was febrile, he took a life--and--death chance. Field of honour, you know—-slipped away from us, and now he's dead on the field. Honour was the death of him, and death—-well, you might put it the other way round too. At any rate, he's gone—-'had the honour to take his leave.' A madman, a crazy chap." And he left, tall and stooped, his neck--bone very prominent.

It had been decided to take Joachim home; and House Berghof assumed the arrangements, doing all that was necessary or that could add to the dignity or stateliness of the occasion. Mother and cousin needed not to lift a finger. By next day Joachim lay in his silk dress--shirt, with flowers about him on the coverlet, looking, in the midst of all this white, more beautiful than immediately after death. Every trace of strain was gone from the features, they had composed themselves, growing cold, into a silent purity of form. Curling dark locks fell upon the yellowish brow, that seemed to be of some fine brittle stuff between wax and marble; through the crisp hair of the beard, the lips showed full and curling. An antique helmet would have become this head—-as many of the guests remarked, who came to take last leave of Joachim. Frau Stöhr, as she looked, wept with abandon. "A hero, he was a hero," cried she, and demanded that the *Erotica* be played at his grave.

"Be quiet," hissed Settembrini, at her side. He and Naphta were with her in the room. Greatly moved, with both hands he waved the onlookers toward the bed and summoned them to mourn with him. "*Un giovanotto tanto simpatico, tanto stimabile,*" said he repeatedly.

And Naphta, without looking at him, or relaxing his contained manner, apparently could not refrain from saying, low and bitingly: "I am glad to see that despite your enthusiasm for freedom and progress, you have some feeling for serious things."

Settembrini pocketed the affront. Perhaps he felt conscious, under the circumstances of the moment, of the superiority of Naphta's position over his own; may even have sought to balance this by the lively expression of his grief, especially when Leo Naphta further presumed on his advantage, while he had it, and sententiously added: "The mistake you literary men make is in thinking that only the spirit makes for virtue. It is nearer the truth to say that only where there is no spirit is there true virtue."

"Goodness," thought Hans Castorp, "but that was a Pythian remark! Made like that with the lips snapped together afterwards, it quite staggers one—for the moment, that is." In the afternoon the metallic coffin arrived. The removal of Joachim to this stately receptacle, decorated with lions' heads and rings, was the sole affair of the man who came along with it, a black--clad functionary of the undertaking establishment which had the arrangements in hand. He wore a sort of short dress--coat, and the weddingring on his plebian hand had almost grown into the flesh. One inclined to feel that he exhaled an odour of death from his garments—-pure prejudice, of course, and groundless. This specialist let it be known that all his spiriting had to be done behind the scenes, and a proper and dress--parade appearance presented to the surviving relatives. Hans Castorp felt fairly suspicious of the fellow and all his works. He assented to Frau Ziemssen's withdrawal, but was not minded to be bowed from the scene himself. He stood by and lent a hand, grasping the figure under the shoulders and helping carry it over to the coffin, upon whose coverlet and tasselled cushions Joachim presently lay ensconced high and solemnly, among candelabra provided by the house.

On the next day but one appeared a phenomenon which determined Hans Castorp to take inward leave of that quiet form, to void the field and leave it to the professional guardian of the amenities: Joachim, whose expression had been so noble and serious, began now to smile in his warrior beard. Hans Castorp did not conceal from himself that this smile had in it the seeds of corruption; he knew in his heart that time was pressing. It was good that the coffin was now to be closed, the lid screwed on; that the hour for removal was at hand. Hans Castorp, laying aside traditional reserve, lightly touched with his lips the icy forehead of that which once was Joachim; and though conscious still of mistrustful sentiments toward the man behind the scenes, yet submissively followed Louisa Ziemssen from the room.

We let the curtain fall, for the last time but one. While it rustles down, let us take our stand in spirit with Hans Castorp on his lonely height, and gaze down with him upon a damp burial--ground in the flat--land; see the flash of a sword as it rises and falls, hear the word of command rapped out, and three salvoes, three fanatical salutes reverberating over Joachim Ziemssen's root--pierced grave.

CHAPTER VII
By the Ocean of Time

Can one tell—-that is to say, narrate—-time, time itself, as

such, for its own sake?

That would surely be an absurd undertaking. A story which read: "Time passed, it ran on, the time flowed onward" and so forth—-no one in his senses could consider that a narrative. It would be as though one held a single note or chord for a whole hour, and called it music. For narration resembles music in this, that it *fills up* the time. It "fills it in" and "breaks it up," so that "there's something to it," "something going on"—-to quote, with due and mournful piety, those casual phrases of our departed Joachim, all echo of which so long ago died away. So long ago, indeed, that we wonder if the reader is clear how long ago it was. For time is the medium of narration, as it is the medium of life. Both are inextricably bound up with it, as inextricably as are bodies in space. Similarly, time is the medium of music; music divides, measures, articulates time, and can shorten it, yet enhance its value, both at once. Thus music and narration are alike, in that they can only present themselves as a flowing, as a succession in time, as one thing after another; and both differ from the plastic arts, which are complete in the present, and unrelated to time save as all bodies are, whereas narration—-like music—-even if it should try to be completely present at any given moment, would need time to do it in.

So much is clear. But it is just as clear that we have also a difference to deal with. For the time element in music is single. Into a section of mortal time music pours itself, thereby inexpressibly enhancing and ennobling what it fills. But a narrative must have two kinds of time: first, its own, like music, actual time, conditioning its presentation and course; and second, the time of its content, which is relative, so extremely relative that the imaginary time of the narrative can either coincide nearly or completely with the actual, or musical, time, or can be a world away. A piece of music called a "Five--minute Waltz" lasts five minutes, and this is its sole relation to the time element. But a narrative which concerned itself with the events of five minutes, might, by extraordinary conscientiousness in the telling, take up a thousand times five minutes, and even then seem very short, though long in relation to its imaginary time. On the other hand, the contentual time of a story can shrink its actual time out of all measure. We put it in this way on purpose, in order to suggest another element, an illusory, even, to speak plainly, a morbid element, which is quite definitely a factor in the situation. I am speaking of cases where the story practises a hermetical magic, a temporal distortion of perspective reminding one of certain abnormal and transcendental experiences in actual life. We have records of opium dreams in which the dreamer, during a brief narcotic sleep, had experiences stretching over a period of ten, thirty, sixty years, or even passing the extreme limit of man's temporal capacity for experience: dreams whose contentual time was enormously greater than their actual or musical time, and in which there obtained an incredible foreshortening of events; the images pressing one upon another with such rapidity that it was as though "something had been taken away, like the spring from a broken watch "from the brain of the sleeper. Such is the description of a hashish eater. Thus, or in some such way as in these sinister dreams, can the narrative go to work with time; in some such way can time be dealt with in a tale. And if this be so, then it is clear that time, while the medium of the narrative, can also become its subject. Therefore, if it is too much to say that one can tell a tale *of* time, it is none the less true that a desire to tell a tale *about* time is not such an absurd idea as it just now seemed. We freely admit that, in bringing up the question as to whether the time can be narrated or not, we have done so only to confess that we had something like that in view in the present work. And if we touched upon the further question, whether our readers were clear how much time had passed since the upright Joachim, deceased in the interval, had introduced into the conversation the above--quoted phrases about music and time——remarks indicating a certain alchemistical heightening of his nature, which, in its goodness and simplicity, was, of its own unaided power, incapable of any such ideas——we should not have been dismayed to hear that they were not clear. We might even have been gratified, on the plain ground that a thorough--going sympathy with the experiences of our hero is precisely what we wish to arouse, and he, Hans Castorp, was himself not clear upon the point in question, no, nor had been for a very long time——a fact that has conditioned his romantic adventures up here, to an extent which has made of them, in more than one sense, a "time--romance."

How long Joachim had lived here with his cousin, up to the time of his fateful departure, or taken all in all; what had been the date of his going, how long he had been gone, when he had come back; how long Hans Castorp himself had been up here when his cousin returned and then bade time farewell; how long——dismissing Joachim from our calculations——Frau Chauchat had been absent; how long, since what date, she had been back again (for she did come back); how much mortal time Hans Castorp himself had spent in House Berghof by the time she returned; no one asked him all these questions, and he probably shrank from asking himself. If they had been put him, he would have tapped his forehead with the tips of his fingers, and most certainly not have known——a phenomenon as disquieting as his incapacity to answer Herr Settembrini, that long--ago first evening, when the latter had asked him his age. All which may sound preposterous; yet there are conditions under which nothing could keep us from losing account of the passage of time, losing account even of our own age; lacking, as we do, any trace of an inner time--organ, and being absolutely incapable of fixing it even with an approach to accuracy by ourselves, without any outward fixed points as guides. There is a case of a party of miners, buried and shut off from every possibility of knowing the passage of day or night, who told their rescuers that they estimated the time they had spent in darkness, flickering between hope and fear, to be some three days. It had actually been ten. Their high state of suspense might, one would think, have made the time seem longer to them than it actually was, whereas it shrank to less than a third of its objective length. It would appear, then, that under conditions of bewilderment man is likely to under--rather than over--estimate time.

No doubt Hans Castorp, were he wishful to do so, could without any great trouble have reckoned himself into certainty; just as the reader can, in case all this vagueness and involvedness are repugnant to his healthy sense. Perhaps our hero himself was not quite comfortable either; though he refused to give himself any trouble to wrestle clear of vagueness and involution and arrive at certainty of how much time had gone over his head since he came up here. His scruple was of the conscience—yet surely it is a want of conscientiousness most flagrant of all not to pay heed to the time!

We do not know whether we may count it in his favour that circumstances advantaged his lack of inclination, or perhaps we ought to say his disinclination. When Frau Chauchat came back—-under circumstances very different from those Hans Castorp had imagined, but of that in its place—when she came back, it was the Advent season again, and the shortest day of the year; the beginning of winter, astronomically speaking, was at hand. Apart from arbitrary time--divisions, and with reference to the quantity of snow and cold, it had been winter for God knows how long, interrupted, as always all too briefly, by burning hot summer days, with a sky of an exaggerated depth of blueness, well--nigh shading into black; real summer days, such as one often had even in the winter, aside from the snow—and the snow one might also have in the summer! This confusion in the seasons, how often had Hans Castorp discussed it with the departed Joachim! It robbed the year of its articulation, made it tediously brief, or briefly tedious, as one chose to put it; and confirmed another of Joachim's disgusted utterances, to the effect that there was no time up here to speak of, either long or short. The great confusion played havoc, moreover, with emotional conceptions, or states of consciousness like "still" and "again"; and this was one of the very most gruesome, bewildering, uncanny features of the case. Hans Castorp, on his first day up here, had discovered in himself a hankering to dabble in that uncanny, during the five mighty meals in the gaily stenciled dining--room; when a first faint giddiness, as yet quite blameless, had made itself felt.

Since then, however, the deception upon his senses and his mind had assumed much larger proportions. Time, however weakened the subjective perception of it has become, has objective reality in that it brings things to pass. It is a question for professional thinkers—-Hans Castorp, in his youthful arrogance, had one time been led to consider it—-whether the hermetically sealed conserve upon its shelf is outside of time. We know that time does its work, even upon Seven--Sleepers. A physician cites a case of a twelve--year--old--girl, who fell asleep and slept thirteen years; assuredly she did not remain thereby a twelve--year--old girl, but bloomed into ripe womanhood while she slept. How could it be otherwise? The dead man—-is dead; he has closed his eyes on time. He has plenty of time, or personally speaking, he is timeless. Which does not prevent his hair and nails from growing, or, all in all—-but no, we shall not repeat those free--and--easy expressions used once by Joachim, to which Hans Castorp, newly arrived from the flat--land, had taken exception. Hans Castorp's hair and nails grew too, grew rather fast. He sat very often in the barber's chair in the main street of the Dorf, wrapped in a white sheet, and the barber, chatting obsequiously the while, deftly performed upon the fringes of his hair, growing too long behind his ears. First time, then the barber, performed their office upon our hero. When he sat there, or when he stood at the door of his loggia and pared his nails and groomed them, with the accessories from his dainty velvet case, he would suddenly be overpowered by a mixture of terror and eager joy that made him fairly giddy. And this giddiness was in both senses of the word: rendering our hero not only dazed and dizzy, but flighty and light--headed, incapable of distinguishing between "now" and "then," and prone to mingle these together in a timeless eternity.

As we have repeatedly said, we wish to make him out neither better nor worse than he was; accordingly we must report that he often tried to atone for his reprehensible indulgence in attacks of mysticism, by virtuously and painstakingly striving to counteract them. He would sit with his watch open in his hand, his thin gold watch with the engraved monogram on the lid, looking at the porcelain face with the double row of black and red Arabic figures running round it, the two fine and delicately curved gold hands moving in and out over it, and the little second--hand taking its busy ticking course round its own small circle. Hans Castorp, watching the second--hand, essayed to hold time by the tail, to cling to and prolong the passing moments. The little hand tripped on its way, unheeding the figures it reached, passed over, left behind, left far behind, approached, and came on to again. It had no feeling for time limits, divisions, or measurements of time. Should it not pause on the sixty, or give some small sign that this was the end of one thing and the beginning of the next? But the way it passed over the tiny intervening unmarked strokes showed that all the figures and divisions on its path were simply beneath it, that it moved on, and on. —- Hans Castorp shoved his product of the Glashütte works back in his waistcoat pocket, and left time to take care of itself.

How make plain to the sober intelligence of the flat--land the changes that took place in the inner economy of our young adventurer? The dizzying problem of identities grew grander in its scale. If to--day's now—-even with decent goodwill—-was not easy to distinguish from yesterday's, the day before's or the day before that's, which were all as like each other as the same number of peas, was it not also capable of being confused with the now which had been in force a month or a year ago, was it not also likely to be mingled and rolled round in the course of that other, to blend with it into the always? However one might still differentiate between the ordinary states of consciousness which we attached to the words "still," "again," "next," there was always the temptation to extend the significance of such descriptive words as "tomorrow," "yesterday," by which "to--day" holds at bay "the past" and "the future." It would not be hard to imagine the existence of creatures, perhaps upon smaller planets than ours, practising a miniature time--economy, in whose brief span the brisk tripping gait of our second--hand would possess the tenacious spatial economy of our hand that marks the hours. And, contrariwise, one can conceive of a world so spacious that its time system too has a majestic stride, and the distinctions between "still," "in a little while," "yesterday," "to--morrow," are, in its economy, possessed of hugely extended significance. That, we say, would be not only conceivable, but, viewed in the spirit of a tolerant relativity, and in the light of an already--quoted proverb, might be considered legitimate, sound, even estimable. Yet what shall one say of a son of earth, and of our time to boot, for whom a day, a week, a month, a semester, ought to play such an important rôle, and bring so many changes, so much progress in its train, who one day falls into the vicious habit——or perhaps we should say, yields sometimes to the desire——to say "yesterday" when he means a year ago, and "next year" when he means to--morrow? Certainly we must deem him lost and undone, and the object of our just concern.

There is a state, in our human life, there are certain scenic surroundings——if one may use that adjective to describe the surroundings we have in mind——within which such a confusion and obliteration of distances in time and space is in a measure justified, and temporary submersion in them, say for the term of a holiday, not reprehensible. Hans Castorp, for his part, could never without the greatest longing think of a stroll along the ocean's edge. We know how he loved to have the snowy wastes remind him of his native landscape of broad ocean dunes; we hope the reader's recollections will bear us out when we speak of the joys of that straying. You walk, and walk——never will you come home at the right time, for you are of time, and time is vanished. O ocean, far from thee we sit and spin our tale; we turn toward thee our thoughts, our love, loud and expressly we call on thee, that thou mayst be present in the tale we spin, as in secret thou ever wast and shalt be!——A singing solitude, spanned by a sky of palest grey; full of stinging damp that leaves a salty tang upon the lips.——We walk along the springy floor, strewn with seaweed and tiny mussel--shells. Our ears are wrapped about by the great mild, ample wind, that comes sweeping untrammelled blandly through space, and gently blunts our senses. We wander— -wander—-watching the tongues of foam lick upward toward our feet and sink back again. The surf is seething; wave after wave, with high, hollow sound, rears up, rebounds, and runs with a silken rustle out over the flat strand: here one, there one, and more beyond, out on the bar. The dull, pervasive, sonorous roar closes our ears against all the sounds of the world. O deep content, O wilful bliss of sheer forgetfulness! Let us shut our eyes, safe in eternity! No——for there in the foaming grey--green waste that stretches with uncanny foreshortening to lose itself in the horizon, look, there is a sail. There? Where is there? How far, how near? You cannot tell. Dizzyingly it escapes your measurement. In order to know how far that ship is from the shore, you would need to know how much room it occupies, as a body in space. Is it large and far off, or is it small and near? Your eye grows dim with uncertainty, for in yourself you have no sense--organ to help you judge of time or space.——We walk, walk. How long, how far? Who knows? Nothing is changed by our pacing, there is the same as here, once on a time the same as now, or then; time is drowning in the measureless monotony of space, motion from point to point is no motion more, where uniformity rules; and where motion is no more motion, time is no longer time.

The schoolmen of the Middle Ages would have it that time is an illusion; that its flow in sequence and causality is only the result of a sensory device, and the real existence of things in an abiding present. Was he walking by the sea, the philosopher to whom this thought first came, walking by the sea, with the faint bitterness of eternity upon his lips? We must repeat that, as for us, we have been speaking only of the lawful licence of a holiday, of fantasies born of leisure, of which the wellconducted mind wearies as quickly as a vigorous man does of lying in the warm sand. To call into question our human means and powers of perception, to question their validity, would be absurd, dishonourable, arbitrary, if it were done in any other spirit than to set bounds to reason, which she may not overstep without incurring the reproach of neglecting her own task. We can only be grateful to a man like Herr Settembrini, who with pedagogic dogmatism characterized metaphysics as the "evil principle," to the young man in whose fate we are interested, and whom he had once subtly called "life's delicate child." We shall best honour the memory of one departed, who was dear to us, if we say plainly that the meaning, the end and aim of the critical principle can and may be but one thing: the thought of duty, the law of life. Yes, lawgiving wisdom, in marking off the limits of reason, planted precisely at those limits the banner of life, and proclaimed it man's soldierly duty to serve under that banner. May we set it down on the credit side of Hans Castorp's account, that he had been strengthened in his vicious time--economy, his baleful traffic with eternity, by seeing that all his cousin's zeal, called doggedness by a certain melancholy blusterer, had but the more surely brought him to a fatal end?

Mynheer Peeperkorn

Mynheer Peeperkorn, an elderly Dutchman, spent some time at House Berghof, that establishment which, in its prospectus, so correctly described itself as "international." Pieter Peeperkorn—-such was his name, so he called himself, as for instance, 'Pieter Peeperkorn will now take unto himself a Hollands gin"—-was a colonial Dutchman, a man from Java, a coffee--planter. His slightly faded nationality is scarcely sufficient ground for introducing him at this late day into our story. God knows we have had racial mixtures a--plenty in the famous cure conducted with such many--tongued efficiency by Herr Hofrat Behrens! There was the Egyptian princess who had given the Hofrat the extraordinary coffee--machine and sphinx cigarettes, a sensational person with cropped hair and beringed fingers yellow with nicotine, who went about——except at the main meal of the day, for which she made full Parisian toilet——in a sack coat and well--pressed trousers; and who scorned the world of men, to lay hot and heavy, though fitful siege to an insignificant little Roumanian Jewess called plain Frau Landauer, while Lawyer Paravant for her royal highness's *beaux yeux* neglected his mathematics and altogether played the fool for love. This princess, in addition to her own colourful personality, had among her little suite a Moorish eunuch, a weak and sickly man, who yet, despite his basic and constitutional lack——upon which Caroline Stönr loved to dwell——clung to life more desperately than most, and was quite inconsolable over the conclusions Hofrat Behrens drew from the transparency they made of his dusky inside.

Mynheer Peeperkorn, then, compared with such phenomena, might seem well--nigh colourless. And it is true that this part of our story might, like an earlier chapter, bear the caption "A Newcomer." But the reader need not fear that in him another occasion for pedagogic strife has arrived upon the scene. No, Mynheer Peeperkorn was not the man to be the bearer of logical confusion. He was quite a different man, as we shall see. Yet he brought sore dismay and perplexity upon the hero of our tale, as will shortly be very evident.

Mynheer Peeperkorn arrived at the Dorf station by the same evening train as Frau Chauchat. They drove up in the same sleigh to House Berghof, and supped together in the restaurant. The arrival, in short, was not only coincident but concurrent, and continued in that sense, Mynheer taking his place beside the returned wanderer at the "good" Russian table, opposite the doctor's seat——the place Popoff had occupied, what time he performed his wild and equivocal antics. The companionship troubled our good Hans Castorp——that it should turn out like this had never entered his mind. The Hofrat, after his own fashion, had announced the day and hour of Clavdia's return. "Well, Castorp, old top," he said, "there's always a reward for faithful waiting. To--morrow the little puss will be slinking back——

-I've had a dispatch." But not a word that she might not come alone. Perhaps he did not know that she and Peeperkorn were travelling together; at least, he showed surprise when Hans Castorp, the day after, as much as took him to task.

"Don't know myself where she picked him up," he declared. "I take it they met on the return from the Pyrenees. Alas, poor Strephon! Tut, my lad, you'll have to put up with it, no use pulling a long face. They're thick as thieves, it seems, have even their luggage in common. The man's larded with money, from what I hear. Retired coffeeking, Malayan valet, plutocratic is no word for it. But he hasn't come up here for fun. A catarrhal condition due to alcoholism——and from what I can see he is threatened with tropical fever, malignant, intermittent, you know; protracted, obstinate. You'll have to be patient with him."

"Don't mention it," replied Hans Castorp, loftily. "And what about you?" he said to himself. "I wonder what your feelings are; you didn't come off scot--free either, or I miss my guess, you blue--in--the--face widower, with your oil--painting technique. Old dog in the manger! You needn't tell me: so far as Peeperkorn is concerned, I'm certain we're companions in misery."——"Quaint creature," he continued aloud, and shrugged. "An original, certainly. He's so lean——yet he's robust; that is the impression he makes, at least that's the impression I got at breakfast. Lean, and robust, those are the adjectives, I think, though they aren't commonly used together. He is certainly tall and broad, and likes to stand with his legs apart and his hands in his trouser pockets——which, I observe, are put in running up and down, not like yours and mine and most people's of our class. And when he stands there and talks, in his guttural Dutch voice, there's something unmistakably robust about him. But he has a sparse whisker, you could almost count the hairs; and his eyes are very small and pale, hardly any colour to them at all. He keeps trying to open them wide, and has made a lot of wrinkles, regular corrugations, that turn up on the temples and run straight across his forehead, and his forehead is high and red, with long wisps of white hair. He wears a clerical waist--coat, but his tail--coat is check. These are the impressions I got this morning."

Behrens answered: "I see you've taken his number——you're right, too, for you will have to come to terms with his being here."

"Yes, I expect we shall," said Hans Castorp. We have left it to him to describe the unlooked--for guest, and he has not come badly off—-we could scarcely add anything essential to the picture. He had a good view; as we know, he had in Clavdia's absence moved closer to the "good" Russian table; the one where he now sat stood parallel with hers, only rather farther away from the verandah door. Both he and Peeperkorn were on the inner and narrow side of their respective tables, and thus, in a way, neighbours, Hans Castorp being slightly in the Dutchman's rear, very advantageously placed to observe him, as also to look at the three--quarter view which Frau Chauchat's profile presented. We might round out Hans Castorp's description by a few notes: as, that the Dutchman's nose was large and fleshy, his mouth large too, and bare of moustaches, the lips of irregular shape, as though chapped. His hands were fairly broad, with long, pointed nails; he used them freely as he talked, and he talked almost continuously, though Hans Castorp failed to get his drift. Those adequate, compelling, cleanly attitudes of the hands——so varied, so full of subtle nuances——possessed a technique like that of an orchestral conductor. He would curve forefinger and thumb to a circle; extend the palm, that was so broad, with nails so pointed, to hush, to caution, to enjoin attention——and then, having by such means led up to some stupendous utterance, produce an anticlimax by saying something his audience could not quite grasp. Yet this, perhaps, was less a disappointment than it was a conversion of expectancy into ecstatic amaze; for the speaking gesture made good what he did not say, and was of itself alone vastly satisfying and diverting. Sometimes, indeed, after leading up to his climax, he left it out altogether. He would lay his hand tenderly on the arm of the young Bulgarian scholar next him, or on Frau Chauchat's on the other side; then lift it obliquely for silence, create suspense for what he was about to say, wrinkling high his brows, so that the lines running upwards from the outer corners of his eyes were deepened like those on a mask; he would look down on the cloth before his neighbour's place, and from his thick, distorted lips words of the highest import seemed about to issue then, after more pause, he would breathe an outward breath, give up the struggle, nod, as though to say "As you were," and return undelivered to his coffee, which was served to him of extra strength, in his own machine.

After the draught he would proceed thus, choking off with one hand the conversation, making a silence round him, as a conductor hushes the confused sounds of tuning instruments and collects his orchestra to begin a number; mastering at will any situation, for could anything resist that regal head, with its aureole of white hair and its pallid eyes, the great folds of the brows, the long whisker and shaven raw upper lip? They were silent, they looked at him and smiled, they waited, anticipatorily nodding. He spoke.

In rather a low voice he said: "Ladies and gentlemen. Very well. Very well indeed. Very. Settled. But will you keep in mind, and——not for one moment——not one moment——lose sight of the fact——but no more. On this point not another word. What is incumbent upon me to say is not so much——it is in the first place simply this: it is our duty——we lie under a solemn——an inviolable No! No, ladies and gentlemen! It was not thus——it was not thus that I——how mistaken to imagine that I——quite right, ladies and gentlemen! Set——tled. Let us drop the subject. I feel we understand each other, and now——to the point!"

He had said absolutely nothing. But look, manner, and gestures were so peremptory, perfervid, pregnant, that all, even Hans Castorp, were convinced they had heard something of high moment; or, if aware of the total lack of matter and sequence in the speech, certainly never missed it. We wonder how it might appear to a deaf person. Perhaps the impressiveness of what he saw would make him draw an altogether wrong conclusion as to what he might have heard but for his infirmity——and cause him to suffer accordingly. Such people incline to mistrust and bitterness. On the other hand, a young Chinaman at the other end of the table, who possessed too little of the language to understand what had been said, but had yet assiduously listened and looked, clapped his hands and called out: "*Très bien, très bien.*"

And Mynheer Peeperkorn came "to the point." He drew himself up, swelled his broad chest, buttoned the check frock--coat over the clerical waistcoat; the pose of his white head was regal. He beckoned to a "dining--room girl"—-it was the dwarf—and though busily engaged, she at once obeyed his weighty summons, and stood, milk jug and coffee--pot in hand, by his chair. She too felt drawn to look at him with an ingratiating smile on her large, old face; she too was rapt by the pallid gaze beneath the deep--wrinkled brow; by the lifted hand, whose thumb and forefinger were joined in an O, while the other three with their lanceolate nails stood stiffly up.

"My child," said he, "very well. Very well indeed—-very. You are small—-what is that to me? On the contrary. I find it a positive good, I thank God, that you are as you are; I thank God you are so small and full of character. What I want of you is also small and full of character. But in the first place, what is your name?"

She said, smiling and stammering, that her name was Emerentia.

"Splendid," cried Peeperkorn, throwing himself back in his chair and stretching out his arm toward her. He cried it in the tone of one who would say "Wonderful! Is not everything wonderful?"—-"My child," he went on, with a perfectly serious face, almost sternly, "you surpass all my expectations. Emerentia! You utter it so modestly—-yet, taken with your person, it holds out such boundless possibilities. Beautiful. Worth dwelling upon, communing with in the depths of one's—-in order to—-understand me, my child: as a term of endearment—the pet name. It might be Rentia. Though Emchen would equally warm and fortify the heart—-in short, for the moment, I will abide by Emchen. Emchen, then, 'Emchen my child, attend. A little bread, my love. But hold! Let no misunderstanding come between us——for in your somewhat over life--size face I seem to read——bread, Renzchen, bread; yet not baker's bread, of which in this place we have enough and to spare, in all conceivable forms. Not corn that is baked, my angel, but corn that is burnt——in other words, distilled. Bread of God, bread of sunshine, little pet name; bread for the laving of man's weary spirit. But I still have misgivings——whether the sense of this word I would even consider substituting for it another, the beautiful word cordial——if here we did not encounter a new danger, that it might be understood in the ordinary thoughtless sense——No more, Rentia. Settled. Set——tled, and out of the question. Rather would I, in consideration of the debt of honour I acknowledge, right cordially to rejoice your characteristic smallness——a gin, love, and haste thee. A Schiedamer, Emerentia. Bring me one hither."

"A geneva, sir," repeated the dwarf, and spun three times round on herself, seeking a place for her jugs, which she finally deposited on Hans Castorp's table, quite near him, obviously not wishing to burden Herr Peeperkorn with the same. She put wings to her feet, and he soon received his desire. The little glass was so full that the "bread" overflowed and bedewed the plate. He took the grain distillation between thumb and middle finger, and held it toward the light. "Pieter Peeperkorn," he declared, "will now take unto himself a glass of Hollands." He appeared to chew the liquid somewhat, then swallowed it down; "And now," he said, "I look on you all with new eyes."

He lifted Frau Chauchat's hand from the cloth, carried it to his lips and laid it back, letting his own rest for some while upon it.

An odd man, and of great personal weight, though incoherent. The population of the Berghof were enthusiastic over him. It was reported that he had only lately retired from his colonial interests and transferred them to the continent. He was said to have a magnificent house at The Hague, and another at Scheveningen. Frau Stöhr called him a money magnet (the unhappy woman meant magnate) and indicated the string of pearls Frau Chauchat had worn in the evening since her return to the Berghof. These pearls, Frau Stöhr considered, were scarcely a token of affection from the transCaucasian husband; more likely they came out of the common travelling-trunk. She winked and jerked her head in the direction of Hans Castorp, whose discomfiture she parodied with her mouth drawn down—-no, illness and affliction had had no power to refine Caroline Stöhr; her jeers over the young man's disappointment positively went beyond bounds. He preserved his composure, and corrected her blunder, not unadroitly. It was magnate, not magnet she had meant to say, he told her. Moneymagnate. But magnet was not so bad after all—-certainly Herr Peeperkorn had a good deal that was attractive about him. The schoolmistress, Fräulein Engelhart, with a wry smile, flushing dully, but not looking at him as she spoke, asked how he liked the new guest. He replied, quite calmly, that he found Mynheer Peeperkorn a "blurred personality"; a personality, that is, undoubtedly, though blurred. The precision of the characterization showed objectivity and poise; it dislodged the schoolmistress from her position. Ferdinand Wehsal, too, made oblique reference to the unexpected circumstances of Frau Chauchat's return; and got from Hans Castorp proof that a look may be every whit as telling and unequivocal as the articulate word. "You paltry wretch," said the stare with which Hans Castorp measured the Mannheimer—-said it without the shadow of a doubt of its meaning. Wehsal understood that look, and pocketed it up; even nodded and showed his bad teeth; but from that time forward he ceased to carry Hans Castorp's overcoat, when they went their walks with Naphta, Settembrini, and Ferge. But dear me, Hans Castorp could carry his own coat, couldn't he—-and much preferred to; he had only let the poor creature take it now and then out of sheer good feeling. However, there was no doubt everybody in the circle knew that Hans Castorp was hard hit by the wholly unforeseen circumstance, which frustrated all the hopes he had cherished against the return of his carnival partner. It would be putting it even better to say that she had rendered nugatory all his hopes; that, precisely, was the mortifying fact.

His designs had been of the most discreet and delicate, he had meant nothing clumsy or abrupt. He would not even fetch her from the station—-what a mercy, indeed, he had not thought of doing so! Uncertain whether a woman—-upon whom illness had conferred such a degree of freedom—-uncertain whether she would even admit the fantastic adventures of a dream dreamed on carnival night, in a foreign tongue to boot! Whether she would even wish in the first instance to be reminded of them. No, there would be no exigence, no clumsy pressing of claims. Admitted that his relations with the slant--eyed sufferer went beyond the limits prescribed by the traditions of the Occident; the uttermost formality of civilization, even for the moment apparent forgetfulness—-was indicated as the suitable procedure. A respectful greeting from table to table—-only that, for the time, no more. A courtly approach as occasion indicated, an easy inquiry after the health of the traveller. The actual meeting would follow in good time, as a reward for his chivalrous reserve.

All this fine feeling, now, had become null and void—-Hans Castorp's conduct being deprived of choice, and therewith of merit. The presence of Mynheer Peeperkorn effectively disposed of any tactics save utter aloofness. On the evening of the arrival, Hans Castorp had seen from his loge the sleigh come up the winding drive. On the box next the coachman sat the Malayan valet, a yellow little man with a fur collar to his overcoat, and a bowler hat. At the back, his hat over his brows, sat the stranger, beside Clavdia. That night Hans Castorp got little sleep. Next morning he heard for the asking the name of the mysterious new arrival; heard likewise that the two travellers occupied neighbouring suites on the first floor. He was early at breakfast, and sat in his place erect but pale, awaiting the slamming of the glass door. It did not come. Clavdia's entrance was noiseless; for Mynheer Peeperkorn closed the door behind her—tall and broad, his white hair flaring above his lofty brow, he followed the familiar gliding tread of his companion, as with head stuck out before her she slipped to her chair. Yes, she was unchanged. Regardless of his programme, Hans Castorp devoured her, with his sleep--weary eyes.

[693]

There was the red--blond hair, no more elaborately dressed than of yore, wound in the same simple braid about her head; there were the "prairie--wolf's eyes," the rounding neck, the lips that seemed fuller than they actually were, thanks to the prominent cheek--bones, which gave the cheeks that exquisite flat or slightly concave look.—-Clavdia! he thought, and thrilled. He fixed his eyes on the unexpected guest; not without a toss of the head for the splendid masklike impression the person made; not without summoning a sneer at pretensions which, however justified by present possession, were invalidated by the past—-by certain very definite events in the past—-for instance in the field of amateur portraiture. Hans Castorp knew, for had not those events visited himself with justifiable pangs?—-Even her way of turning, before she sat down, to present herself, as it were, to the room, she had as of yore. Mynheer Peeperkorn assisted at the little ceremony, standing behind her while it took place, and then seating himself at Clavdia's side.

As for that courtly salute from table to table—-nothing came of it. Clavdia's eyes, when she presented herself, had passed over Hans Castorp's person and his whole vicinity, and rested upon the far corner of the room. At the next meal it was the same. And the more meals passed without any response to his gaze than this blank and indifferent passing--over, the more impracticable became the project of the courtly salute. After supper the two travelling--companions sat in the small salon, on the sofa together, surrounded by their table--mates; and Peeperkorn, his magnificent visage flaming against the flashing white of hair and beard, drank out the bottle of red wine he had ordered at table. At each of the main meals he drank one, or two, or two and a half bottles, in addition to the "bread" which he took even at early breakfast. Obviously the system of this kingly man stood in more than common need of moistening. He took in fluid likewise in the form of extra--strong coffee, many times a day, drinking it out of a large cup, even after dinner—-or rather, he drank it during dinner, along with the wine. Wine and coffee, Hans Castorp heard him say, were both good for fever—-quite aside from their cordial and refreshing properties—-very good against the intermittent tropical fever which had kept him in bed for several hours the second day after he arrived. The Hofrat called it quartan fever: it took the Dutchman about every fourth day, first with a chill, then with a fever, then with a mighty sweat. He was said to have also an inflamed spleen, from the same cause.

Vingt Et Un

A little time passed, some three or four weeks—-this on our own reckoning, since on Hans Castorp's we cannot depend. They brought no great change. On our hero's part they witnessed an abiding scorn of the unforeseen circumstances which kept him in undeserved exile, of, in particular, that circumstance which called itself Pieter Peeperkorn, when it took unto itself a glass of gin—-the disturbing presence of that kingly, incoherent man, which upset Hans Castorp far more than had the presence of the "organ--grinder" in the old days. His brows took on two querulous vertical wrinkles, and five times daily he contracted them as he sat and looked at the returned traveller—-glad despite himself to be able to look at her—-and at the high--and--mighty presence sitting there all unaware what a poor light past events shed on his present pretensions.

One evening the social hour happened to be livelier than usual—-which it might be at any time without especial cause. A Hungarian student played spirited gipsy waltzes on his fiddle; and Hofrat Behrens, who chanced to be present for a quarter--hour with Dr. Krokowski, got somebody to play the melody of the "Pilgrims' Chorus" on the bass notes of the piano, while he himself operated in a skipping movement with a brush over the treble, and parodied the violin counterpoint. Everybody laughed; and the Hofrat, nodding benevolent approval of his own sprightly performance, withdrew amid applause. The gaiety prolonged itself, there was more music, people sat down with drinks beside them to dominoes and bridge, trifled with the optical instruments, or stood in groups talking. Even the Russian circle mingled with the others in hall and music--room.

Mynheer Peeperkorn was to be seen among them—-or rather, he could not but be seen, wherever he was, his kingly head towering high above any scene, and dwarfing it by the sheer weight and majesty of his person. Those who stood about him, drawn first by the reports of the man's wealth, soon hung absorbed upon his personality. Forgetful of all else, they stood laughing and nodding, spellbound by the pallid eye, by the brow's mighty folds, by the compulsion of the gestures his longnailed hands performed. And never, for one moment, were they conscious of any lack in his incoherent, rhapsodic, literally futile remarks.

If we look about for our friend Hans Castorp, we shall find him in the reading--and writing--room, where once (but that "once" is vague, not the teller nor the reader of this story, nor yet its hero, being any longer clear upon the degree of its "onceness")—-where once he had received certain very important communications touching the history of human progress. It was quiet here—-only two or three other persons shared his retreat. At one of the double tables, under the electric light, a man was writing; and a lady with two pairs of glasses on her nose sat by the bookshelves and turned over the leaves of an illustrated magazine. Hans Castorp sat near the open door to the music--room, with his back to the portières, on a chair that happened to be standing there, a plush--covered chair in Renaissance style, with a high straight back, and no arms. He held a newspaper as though to read it, but instead was listening with his head on one side to the snatches of music and talk from the next room. His brows were dark, his thoughts seemed not on harmonies bent, but rather on the thorny path of his present disillusionment. Bitter, bitter was the weird of our young man, who had borne out the long waiting only to be gulled at the end. Indeed he seemed not far from a sudden determination to fling his paper upon the chair he sat in, to escape by the hall door and exchange the empty gaieties of the salon for the frosty solitude of his balcony, and the society of his Maria.

"And your cousin, Monsieur?" a voice suddenly asked above and behind his shoulder. It was a voice enchanting to his ear; it seemed his senses had been expressly contrived to perceive its sweet--and--bitter huskiness as the very height and summit of earthly harmonies; it was the voice that once had said to him: "Certainly. But be careful not to break it"——a compelling, fateful voice. And if he heard aright, it had asked him about Joachim.

Slowly he let his newspaper fall, and turned his face up a little, so that the crown of his head came against the straight back of his chair. He even closed his eyes, but quickly opened them, and gazed somewhere into space——the expression on the poor wight's face was well--nigh that of a sleep--walker, or clairvoyant. He wished she might ask again, but she did not, he was not even sure she still stood behind him, when, after all that pause, so tardily and with scarce audible voice he answered: "He is dead. He went down below to the service, and he died."

He realized that this "dead" was the first word to fall between them; likewise, simultaneously, that she was not sure of expressing herself in his tongue, and chose short and easy phrases to condole in. Still standing behind and above him, she said: "Oh, woe, alas! That is too bad! Quite dead and buried? Since when?"

"Some time ago. His mother came and took him back with her. He had grown a beard, a soldier's beard. They fired three salvoes over his grave."

"He deserved them. He was a very good young man. Far better than most other people——than some others one knows."

"Yes, he was good and brave. Rhadamanthus always talked about his doggedness. But his body would have it otherwise. *Rebellio carnis*, the Jesuits call it. He always set store by his body——in the highest sense. However, his body thought otherwise, and snapped its fingers at doggedness. But it is more moral to lose your life than to save it."

"Monsieur is still the philosophizing *fainéant*, I see. But Rhadamanthus? Who is that?"

"Behrens. That is Settembrini's name for him."

"Ah, Settembrini. Him I know. That Italian who—-whom I did not like. He was not *hu*—- man. He had—-arrogance." The voice dwelt on the word human—-dreamily, fanatically; and accented arrogance on the final syllable. "He is no longer here? And I am so stupid, I do not know what is Rhadamanthus."

"A humanistic allusion. Settembrini has moved away. We've philosophized a lot of late, he and I and Naphta."

"Who is Naphta?"

"His adversary."

"If he is that, then I would gladly make his acquaintance.—-Did I not tell you your cousin would die if he went down to be a soldier?"

And Hans Castorp answered as he had vowed and dreamed: "*Tu l'as su*," he said.

"What are you thinking of?" she asked him.

There was a long pause. He did not retract, he waited, with the crown of his head pressed against the chair--back, and his gaze half tranced, to hear her voice again; and again he was not sure she was still there, again he was afraid the broken music might have drowned her departing footsteps. At last it came again: "And Monsieur did not go down to his cousin's funeral?"

He replied: "No, I bade him adieu up here, before they shut him away, when he had begun to smile in his beard. His brow was cold—- *tu sais comme les fronts des morts sont froids?*"

"Again! What a way is that to address a lady whom one hardly knows!"

"Must I speak not humanly, but humanistically?"

"*Quelle blague!* You were here all the time?"

"Yes. I waited."

"Waited—-for what?"

"For thee!"

A laugh came from above him, a word that sounded like "Madman!"—-"For me?

How absurd it is— *ils ne t'auraient pas laissé partir."*

"Oh, yes, Behrens would have, once—-he was furious. But it would have been folly. I have not only the old scars that come from my school--days, but the fresh places that give me my fever."

"Still fever?"

"Yes, still, a little—- or nearly always. It is intermittent. But not an intermittent fever."

"Des allusions?"

He was silent. He still gazed somnambulantly, but his brows were gathered. After a while he asked: *"Et toi—-où as--tu été?"*

A hand struck the back of the chair. *"Toujours ce tutoyer! Mais c'est un sauvage!—-*

Where have I been? All over. In Moscow"—-the voice pronounced it Muoscow—-" in Baku—-in some German baths, in Spain."

"Oh, in Spain. Did you like it?"

"So--so. The travelling is bad. The people are half Moorish. Castile is bare and stark. The Kremlin is finer than that castle or monastery, or whatever it is, at the foot of the mountains—-"

"Yes, the Escurial."

"Yes, Philip's castle. An inhuman place. I preferred the folk--dancing in Catalonia, the *sardana* to the bagpipes. *Moi, j'ai dansé aussi moi!* they take each other's hands and dance in a ring—-the whole square is full of dancing people. *C'est charmant.* That is *hu*—- man. I bought a little blue cap, such as all the men and boys of the people wear down there, almost like a fez—-the *boina.* I shall wear it in the rest--cure, and other places, perhaps. Monsieur shall judge if it becomes me."

"What monsieur?"

"Sitting here in this chair."

"Not Mynheer Peeperkorn?"

"He has already pronounced judgment——he says I look charming in it."

"He said that——all of it? Did he really finish the sentence, so it could be understood?"

"Ah! It seems Monsieur is out of temper? Monsieur would be spiteful, cutting? He would laugh at people who are much greater and better, and——more *hu*—-man than himself and his——his *ami bavard de la Méditerranée, son maître et grand parleur*—-put together. But I cannot listen——"

"Have you my x--ray portrait?" he interrupted, crest--fallen.

She laughed. "I must look it out."

"I carry yours here. And on my bedside table I have a little easel——-"

He did not finish. Before him stood Peeperkorn. He had searched for his travellingcompanion, entered through the portières and stood in front of Hans Castorp's chair, behind which he saw her talking; stood like a tower, so close to Hans Castorp as to rouse the latter from his trance, and make him realize that it was in place to get up and be mannerly. But they were so close he had to slide sidewise from his seat, and then the three stood in a triangle, the centre of which was the chair.

Frau Chauchat complied with the requirements of the civilized West, by presenting the gentlemen to each other, Hans Castorp to Peeperkorn as "an acquaintance of a former stay." Superfluous to account for Herr Peeperkorn. She gave his name, and the Dutchman bent a look upon the young man, out of his colourless eyes, beneath the astonishing arabesque of wrinkles that made his face so like an old idol's; gave him a look, and put out his hand, which was freckled on the back, and would have looked like a sea--captain's, Hans Castorp thought, but for the lanceolate finger--nails. For the first time, he stood under the immediate influence of Peeperkorn's impressive personality (personality was the word that always occurred to one in reference to this man, one knew straightway that this was a personality; and the more one saw of him the more one was convinced that a personality must look not otherwise than as he did) and his unstable youth felt the weight of this broad--shouldered, red--faced man in the sixties, with his aureole of white hair, his cracked lips and the chin--whisker that strayed long and scanty over the clerical waistcoat. Peeperkorn's manner was courtesy itself.

"My dear sir," he said, "with the greatest of pleasure. Don't mention it. I am entirely your man. In making your acquaintance, I distinctly feel—-as a young man, you inspire me with confidence. I like you. I—-don't mention it. Settled, sir, settled. You suit me."

What could Hans Castorp do? Peeperkorn's gestures were conclusive, peremptory. He liked Hans Castorp. It was "settled." And his satisfaction gave Peeperkorn an idea, which he indicated by means of speaking gesture. His fair companion, coming to the rescue, elaborated and made it vocal.

"My child," he said. "Very well. Very well indeed. Very. But how would it be—-?

Pray understand me. Our life here is but brief. Our power to do it justice is but—-

These are facts, my child. Laws. In—-ex—-orable. In short, my child, in short and in brief—-" He paused, in an impressive attitude, which suggested that he would defer to another's judgment but disclaim responsibility if, despite his warning, an error were committed.

Frau Chauchat was obviously skilled in interpreting his half--uttered wishes. She said: "Why not? We might remain down a little longer, make a party, perhaps, and drink a bottle of wine together." She turned to Hans Castorp. "Make haste! Why are you waiting? We must have company, we three are not enough. Who is still in the salon? Ask anyone who is there, fetch some of your friends down from their balconies. We will ask Dr. Ting--fu from our table."

Peeperkorn rubbed his hands.

"Very good," he said. "Absolutely. Capital. Do as you are bid, young man, make haste! Let us make a little company, play, and eat and drink. Let us feel that—-settled, young man. Absolutely."

Hans Castorp took the lift to the second storey. He knocked at Ferge's door, who in his turn fetched Wehsal and Herr Albin from their chairs in the main rest--hall below. Lawyer Paravant and the Magnus couple were still in the hall, Frau Stöhr and the Kleefeld in the salon. A large table was set up under the centre chandelier, chairs and serving--tables put about. Mynheer courteously greeted each guest as he appeared, with a glance of the pallid eyes and a lifting of the masklike brows. They sat down, twelve together, Hans Castorp between his kingly host and Clavdia Chauchat. Cards and counters were produced, they decided on some rounds of *vingt et un*. Peeperkorn summoned the dwarf and in his most impressive manner ordered wine—-white Chablis of '06, three bottles for a start—-and dessert, whatever *pâtisseries* and dried fruits were to be had. He rubbed his hands in high glee as the good things came in, and communicated his sentiments in broken phrases which were none the less entirely successful, at least in the direction of establishing his "personality." He laid both hands on his neighbour's arm, then raised his long forefinger with the pointed nail, and claimed and received the admiration of the table for the splendid golden colour of the wine in the rummers, for the sugar that sweated from the Malaga grapes, for a certain sort of little salt and poppy--seed pretzel. These, he declared, were divine, and with an imperious gesture nipped in the bud any possible protest against the strength of his adjective. He had taken charge of the bank at first, but soon turned it over to Herr Albin and was understood to say that the charge of it hindered his unfettered enjoyment.

The gambling was to him quite evidently a minor consideration. The stakes were very low, a mere trifle in his view, though the bidding, at his suggestion, began at fifty *rappen*, a considerable sum to most of those present. Lawyer Paravant and Frau Stöhr went white and red by turns; the latter suffered pangs of indecision when called on to decide whether it was too high for her to buy at eighteen. She squealed aloud when Herr Albin with chill routine dealt her a card so high as to confound her hopes over and over. Peeperkorn laughed heartily.

"Squeal away, madame, squeal away," said he. "It sounds shrill and full of life, it wells up from depths—drink, madame, drink and refresh yourself for new efforts." He filled her glass, also his neighbour's and his own, ordered three more bottles, and clicked glasses with Wehsal and Frau Magnus the inly wasted one; they two seeming to stand in most need of enlivenment. Faces flushed more and more, from the effects of the truly marvellous wine—only Dr. Ting--fu's remained unchangingly yellow, with jet--black slits of eyes. He staked very high, with his little suppressed giggle, and was shamelessly lucky. Lawyer Paravant, his gaze a--swim, challenged fate by putting ten francs on an only moderately hopeful opening card, bought until he was pale in the face, and then won twice his money back; for Herr Albin had rashly doubled on the strength of an ace he received. Not only the persons involved felt the shock of these events; the whole circle shared the shattering effect. Even Herr Albin, whose sangfroid outdid the croupiers of Monte Carlo, where, according to him, he was an old habitué, now scarcely mastered his excitement. Hans Castorp played high, so did Frau Stöhr and the Kleefeld, Frau Chauchat as well. They went the rounds: played *Chemin de fer*, " My aunt, your aunt," and the perilous *Différence*. There were outbursts of jubilation and despair, explosions of rage, attacks of hysterical laughter——all due to the reaction of this unlawful pleasure upon their nerves; and all perfectly serious and genuine. The chances and changes of life itself would have called up in them no other reaction.

But it was not solely——or even chiefly——the play and the wine that made the little circle so tense, that flushed their cheeks and opened their eyes so wide, or evoked such breathless excitement, such almost painful concentration on the moment's business. It was rather the effect of a commanding nature in their midst, a "personality"; it was Mynheer Peeperkorn who held the gathering in the hollow of his mobile gesturing hand, and enforced it, by the spectacle of his countenance, by his pallid gaze beneath the monumental creases of his brow, by his words, and his compelling pantomime, to take the mood of the hour. No matter what he said; it was highly incomprehensible, and the more so the more wine he drank. Yet they hung on his lips, they could not take their eyes from the little round made by his finger and thumb, with the pointed nails stiffly erect beside it; or from the majestic, speaking face; they utterly succumbed to feelings which for self--forgetfulness and intensity far exceeded the accustomed gamut of these people. The tribute they paid was too much for some of them——Frau Magnus, at least, felt very poorly; threatened to faint, but stoutly refused to retire, and contented herself with the chaise--longue, where she lay awhile with a wet--napkin over her forehead, and then rejoined the group at the table. Peeperkorn put down her plight to lack of nourishment. He expressed himself in this sense, with impressive disjointedness, forefinger aloft. People must nourish themselves properly, he gave them to understand, in order to do justice to life's manifold claims. And he ordered sustenance for the company: platters of cold meat, joint and roast; tongue, goose, ham, sausage, whole dishes of délectables, all garnished with little radishes, butter--balls, and parsley, gay as flower--beds. They found a welcome, despite the lately consumed supper, which, it were superfluous to tell the reader, had lacked nothing in heartiness. But Mynheer Peeperkorn, after a few bites, dismissed the whole as "kickshaws"——

-dismissed them with a scorn which gave dismaying evidence of the uncertain temper of this lordly man. Yes, he waxed choleric, turned upon one of the company who tried to defend the collation. He swelled with rage, struck the table with his fist, and cursed the food for garbage, fit for the dust--bin. This reduced the offender to silence, for certainly Peeperkorn, as host and dispenser of the good cheer, might find fault with its quality if he chose. But his rage, however disproportionate, became him magnificently, Hans Castorp saw that. It did not misrepresent or render him petty: it wrought his incoherence, which no one in the group could have had the heart to connect with the mixture of wine he had drunk, to so royal a pitch that they all with one accord agreed, and took not another bite of the offending viands. Frau Chauchat set to work to mollify her companion's mood. She stroked his great sea--captain's hand, as it rested on the cloth after the blow he had struck, and said cajolingly that they might order something else, a hot dish, perhaps, if the *chef* could be won over. "Very good, my child," Peeperkorn said, assuaged. And passed, without abating his dignity, from a full torrent of wrath to a state of appeasement, as he took Clavdia's hand and kissed it. He ordered omelets for himself and the company, for each person a fine large *omelette aux fines herbes*, to help them do justice to the demands life made on them. And accompanied the order with a hundred--franc note as a sweetener for the staff.

His placidity was fully restored by the appearance of the steaming dishes, with their burden of canary--yellow besprent with green, which dispersed a mild warm fragrance of eggs and butter upon the air. They fell to with Peeperkorn, who ate and presided over the enjoyment, with broken words and compelling gesture enjoining upon everybody a perfervid appreciation of these gifts of God. He ordered a Hollands all round to go with the omelets; the transparent liquor gave out a healthy grain odour, mingled with just the faintest whiff of juniper—and Peeperkorn laid upon them all to drink it reverently.

Hans Castorp smoked, Frau Chauchat as well; the latter Russian cigarettes with a mouthpiece, from a lacquered box with a *troika* going full speed on the lid, which lay to hand on the table before her. Peeperkorn made no objection to his neighbours' enjoyment, but did not smoke himself—-he never had done so. If they understood him aright, he considered the use of tobacco one of those over--refined enjoyments the cultivation of which robbed of their majesty the simpler pleasures of life—those gifts and claims to which our power of feeling was even at best scarcely equal. "Young man," said he to Hans Castorp, holding him by the power of his pale eye and his developed gesture: "Young man—-the simple—-the holy. Good—-you understand me.

A bottle of wine, a steaming dish of eggs, pure grain spirit—-let us absorb such things as these, exhaust them, satisfy their claims, before we—-Positively, sir. Not a word. I have known men and women, cocaine eaters, hashish smokers, morphine takers—-My dear friend, very good. Very good indeed. Very. Let them. We cannot judge, or condemn. But the simple, the great, the primeval gifts of God—-to them they were unequal in the first place. Settled, my friend. Condemned, rejected. They could not respond.—-Your name, young man? Good. I knew it, but I had forgotten. Not in cocaine, not in opium, not in vice as such does the viciousness lie. The unpardonable—-the—-unpardonable—-sin—-"

He paused. Tall and broad, he bent toward his neighbour; paused and maintained a marvellously expressive silence. His forefinger was raised, his mouth a broken line beneath the bare, red upper lip, which was somewhat raw from the razor, the horizontal folds of his bald forehead rose to meet the white aureole of his hair; the small pale eyes stared wide, and Hans Castorp seemed to read in them some flicker of horror at the crime, the great transgression, the unforgivable sin, which seeking to expound he stood there now, charming the silence with all the force of a commanding though incoherent personality. Hans Castorp thought it a disinterested horror, yet with something too of a personal kind, something that touched the kingly creature near: fear, perhaps, but not of any mean or narrow sort; that was very like panic flickering up momentarily in the eyes. Hans Castorp——despite the grounds he had for hostile misinterpretation of Frau Chauchat's majestic friend——was by nature too respectful not to feel shocked at the revelation.

He cast down his eyes, and nodded, to give his neighbour the satisfaction of being understood.

"You are quite right," he said. "It may easily be a sin——and a sign of impotence——to indulge in the refinements of life, at the same time being inadequate to its great, simple, sacred gifts. If I understood you aright, Herr Peeperkorn, that was your meaning. And though I hadn't thought of it in that light, I may say that I agree with you, now that you mention it. It probably happens seldom enough that these sound and simple gifts of life have real justice done them. The majority of human beings are too heedless, too flabby, too corrupt, too worn out inwardly to give them their due, I feel sure of that."

The mighty one was immensely pleased. "Young man," he said, "positively. Will you permit me——not a word. I beg you to drink with me——no heel--taps——arm--in--arm. I do not, at this moment, propose to you the brotherly thou; I was about to do so, but it would no doubt be precipitate. Somewhat. In the near future, however. Depend upon it. Or, if you insist upon the present——"

Hans Castorp demurred.

"Excellent, young man. 'Impotence'——very good. Very. Gives one the shivers.

'Corrupt'——very good too. 'Gifts'——not so good——'claims' better. The holy, the feminine claims life makes upon manly honour and strength——"

Hans Castorp was suddenly driven to realize that Peeperkorn was very drunk. Still, his drunkenness was not debasing, there was no loss of dignity; rather it combined with the nobility of his nature to produce an immense and awe--inspiring effect. Bacchus himself,

thought Hans Castorp, without detriment to his godhead, leaned for
support on the shoulders of his troop. Everything depended upon *who*
was drunk——a drunken personality was far from being the same as a
drunken tinker. He took care not to abate, even inwardly, his respect
for this overwhelming person, whose gestures had grown lax, and his
tongue stammering.

"Brother," said Peeperkorn. His great torso lolled back in free and
regal intoxication against his chair. His arm lay stretched along the
cloth and he tapped the table with fist lightly clenched. "Brother--in-
-blood——prospective. In the near future——after a proper interval for
reflection.——Very good. Set——tled.——Life, young man, is a female.
A sprawling female, with swelling breasts close to each other, great
soft belly between her haunches, slender arms, bulging thighs, half-
-closed eyes. She mocks us. She challenges us to expend our
manhood to its uttermost span, to stand or fall before her. To stand or
fall. To *fall*, young man——do you know what that means? The defeat
of the feelings, their overthrow when confronted by life——that is
impotence. For it there is no mercy, it is pitilessly, mockingly
condemned.——Not a word, young man! Spewed out of the mouth.
Shame and ignominy are soft words for the ruin and bankruptcy, the
horrible disgrace. It is the end of everything, the hellish despair, the
Judgment Day..."

The Dutchman had flung back his mighty torso more and more,
his kingly head sank lower on his breast, he seemed to be dozing as
he talked. But with the last word he lifted the fist that had been lying
relaxed on the table, and brought it down with a crash, making our
slim young Hans Castorp, overwrought as he was with wine and
play, and the singularity of the whole scene, jump, and in startled
awe look at the mighty one. "The Judgment Day!" How the phrase
suited the man! Hans Castorp did not remember ever hearing it
uttered, except perhaps at catechism. And no wonder, he said to
himself. Who else would have thought of using it like that——or, more
correctly, who would have been big enough to take the thunderbolt in
his mouth? Naphta, perhaps, when he talked his vindictive rubbish——

-but it would have been cheek. Whereas Peeperkorn's utterance seemed to hold the sound of the last trump, majestic, biblical. "Good Lord, what a personality!" he felt for the hundredth time. "At last I've come in contact with a real character——and it turns out to be Clavdia's——." Not too clear--headed himself, he turned his wineglass about on the table, one hand in his trouser pocket, one eye clipped shut against the smoke of the cigarette he held in the corner of his mouth. Certainly he would have done better to keep quiet. What was his feeble pipe, after the rolling thunder of Jove? But his two democratic mentors had trained him to discussion——for they were both democratic, though one of them struggled against it——and habit betrayed him into one of his naïve commentaries.

"Your remarks, Mynheer Peeperkorn," (what an expression! Does one make "remarks" about the Day of Judgment?) "lead back my mind to what you said previously about vice: that it consists in an affront to the simple, what you call the holy, or, as I might say, the classic, gifts which life offers us; the larger gifts, by contrast with the later and 'cultivated' ones, the refinements, which you 'indulge in,' as one of us put it, whereas one 'consecrates oneself' to the great gifts and pays them homage. But just here, it seems to me, lies the excuse for vice (you must pardon me, but I incline by nature to excuses, though there is nothing 'large' about them——I am quite clear on that point) in so far as it is a result of impotence. About the horrors of impotence you have said things of such magnitude that I am quite confounded, as you see me sit here. But in my view, a vicious man appears not at all insensible of your horrors; on the contrary he does them full justice, since it is the abdication of his feelings before the classical gifts of life that drives him to vice. Thus we need not see in vice any affront to life, it may just as well be regarded as homage to it; on the other hand, so far as the refinements represent s *timulantia*, as they say——means of excitation or intoxication——so far as they sustain or increase the power to feel, then life is their purpose and meaning, the desire for feeling, the impotent striving after feeling——I mean——"

What was he talking about? Was it not democratic and unblushing enough that he had said "as one of us put it"——thus coupling himself and a personality like Peeperkorn? Had certain events in the past——which shed a dubious light on present pretensions——given him courage to utter the impertinence? Were the gods wishful to destroy him, when they moved him to embark on this foolhardy analysis of "vice"?

Now let him look to it to extricate himself; for surely he has invoked the whirlwind. Mynheer Peeperkorn, during Hans Castorp's harangue, had sat flung back in his chair, his head still sunk on his breast. It was uncertain even whether he had been listening. But now, slowly, as the young man's utterance grew more involved, he began to erect himself to his full sitting height, the majestic head inflamed; the pattern of furrows on his brow expanded upwards, his little eyes opened in pallid menace. Obviously a storm was brewing beside which the other had been a passing cloud. Mynheer's under lip pressed wrathfully against the upper, the corners of his mouth drew down, the chin protruded. Slowly he raised his right arm above his head; the fist clenched and remained poised aloft, ready for summary execution upon the democratic prattler, who for his part was panic-stricken——yet not without a thrill of precarious joy at this spectacle of regal rage.

He repressed an inclination to flight, and hastened to say, disarmingly: "Of course, I have failed to express my meaning. The whole thing is simply a question of scale. If a thing has size, one cannot call it vice. Vice is petty. Of their nature, so are the *raffine-- ments*. They are never on the grand scale. But since the most primitive times man has had to his hand a resource, a means of mounting to the heights of feeling, which belongs among the classic gifts of life: a resource, simple, sacred, in the grand style, if I may so express myself. I mean the grape, wine, the gift of the gods to man, as we are told of old time. A God invented it, and with its invention civilization began. For we are told that, thanks to the art of planting and treading the vine, man emerged from his barbaric state, and achieved culture; even to--day where the grape grows, those people are accounted, or account themselves, possessed of a higher culture than the Cimmerians, a fact which is worthy our attention. For it indicates that civilization is not a thing of the reason, of being sober and articulate; it has far more to do with inspiration and frenzy, the joys of the winecup——if I may make so bold as to ask, have I not expressed your attitude in the matter?"

A sly dog, this Hans Castorp. Or, as Herr Settembrini with literary feeling had put it, a "wag." To rush into controversy with personalities, to be even forward of speech——but then to know how to extricate himself when need was, and his coat--tails, as it were, all but on fire! In the first place, he had given them an impromptu but quite respectable *apologia* for drinking; into which, *en passant*, he had slipped a reference to "civilization"——of which there was just then small trace in Mynheer Peeperkorn's primitive and menacing attitude; and lastly, he had got round him, put him in the wrong, by asking him, quite simply, a question which one can scarcely answer and maintain the threatening pose or the raised fist. And accordingly the Dutchman relaxed from his neolithic rage, slowly his arm sank again till it rested on the table, his face lost its swollen look, the storm passed over with no trace but the last mutter of thunder, he even seemed to entertain the thought of clicking glasses again; and now Frau Chauchat came to the rescue, by calling her companion's attention to the gradual disintegration of the party.

"My friend," she said to him, in French, "you are neglecting your other guests. You devote yourself too exclusively to this gentleman---important though your conversation with him doubtless is——and the others have stopped playing, I fear they grow tired--shall we say good--night?"

Peeperkorn turned his attention to the circle. It was true: they were demoralized. Lethargy and boredom sat on every brow; the guests were out of hand, like a neglected class. Several were on the point of falling asleep. Peeperkorn took a firm grip on the reins he had let fall. "Ladies and gentlemen!" he summoned them, with raised forefinger——and that pointed finger was like a waving standard or the flash of an unsheathed sword, as his words were like the rallying--cry of the leader, which brings to a stand the threatened rout. It had its effect in a trice. They picked themselves up, they pulled themselves together, they looked again with smiles into their host's pale eyes beneath his masklike brows. He held them all, he pressed them afresh into service of his personality, sinking the tip of his forefinger till it met the tip of his thumb, and erecting the three others straight and stiff with their long nails. He stretched out his sea--captain's hand, checking them, warning them, and words issued from his cracked lips——words utterly irrelevant and indistinct, yet exerting on their spirits a resistless power, thanks to the reserves of personality behind them.

"Ladies and gentlemen. Very good, very good indeed. Very. The flesh, ladies and gentlemen, is——not another word. No, permit me to say——weak, so the Scripture has it. Weak. Inclined to be unequal to claims——but I appeal to your——in short, ladies and gentlemen, in short *and* in brief, I ap——peal! You will say to me: 'Sleep.' Very good, ladies and gentlemen, very good, very. I love and honour sleep. I venerate the deep, sweet, refreshing bliss of it. Sleep is one of the— -what did you call them, young man?——one of the classic gifts of life——the first, the very first, the highest, ladies and gentlemen. But you will recall, you will remember——Gethsemane. 'And took with him Peter and the two sons of Zebedee ... Then saith he unto them: ... Tarry ye here and watch with me.' You remember? 'And he cometh unto the disciples and findeth them asleep, and saith unto Peter: What, could ye not watch with me one hour?' Immense, my friends. Heart--piercing moving to the last——very. 'And came and found them asleep again, for their eyes were heavy. And saith unto them: Sleep on now, and take your rest, behold the hour is at hand.' Ladies and gentlemen, that pierces the heart, it sears——"

In truth, they were all cut to the quick, they were crushed. He had folded his hands across his chest, upon His scanty beard, and laid his head on one side. His eyes had grown dim with feeling as the words expressive of the lonely anguish of death fell from his chapped lips. Frau Stöhr sobbed. Frau Magnus heaved a heavy sigh. Lawyer Paravant saw it was incumbent upon him to represent the sense of the meeting. In a voice solemnly sunk, he assured their honoured host that the circle was his to command. Herr Peeperkorn mistook them. Here they were, blithe as the dawn, jolly as sand--boys, ready for anything. This, he said, was a priceless evening, so festive, so out of the ordinary. Such was their feeling, and no one of them had any present idea of availing himself of life's good gift of sleep. Mynheer Peeperkorn could count on them, one and all.

"Splendid, excellent," Peeperkorn cried, and stood erect again. He unclasped his hands and spread them wide and high before him, palms outward——it looked like a heathen prayer. His majestic physiognomy, but now imprinted with Gothic anguish, blossomed once more in pagan jollity. Even a sybaritic dimple appeared in his cheek.

"The hour is at hand," said he, and sent for the wine--card. He put on a horn--rimmed pince--nez, the nose--piece of which rode high up on his forehead, and ordered champagne, three bottles of Mumm & Co., *Cordon rouge*, extra dry, with *petits fours*, toothsome cone--shaped little dainties in lace frills, covered with coloured frosting and filled with chocolate and *pistache* cream. Frau Stöhr licked her fingers after them. Herr Albin nonchalantly removed the wire from the first bottle, and let the mushroomshaped cork pop to the ceiling; elegantly he conformed to the ritual, holding the neck of the bottle wrapped in a serviette as he poured. The noble foam bedewed the cloth. Every glass rang as the guests saluted, then drank the first one empty at a draught, electrifying their digestive organs with the ice--cold, prickling, perfumed liquid. Every eye sparkled. The game had come to an end, no one troubled to take cards or gains from the table. They gave themselves over to a blissful *far niente*, enlivened by scraps of conversation in which, out of sheer high spirits, no one hung back. They uttered thoughts that in the thinking had seemed primevally fresh and beautiful, but in the saying somehow turned lame, stammering, indiscreet, a perfect gallimaufry, calculated to arouse the scorn of any sober onlooker. The audience, however, took no offence, all being in much the same irresponsible condition. Even Frau Magnus's ears were red, and she admitted that she felt "as though life were running through her"—-which Herr Magnus seemed not over--pleased to hear. Hermine Kleefeld leaned against Herr Albin's shoulder as she held her glass to be filled. Peeperkorn conducted the Bacchanalian rout with his long--fingered gestures, and summoned additional supplies: coffee followed the champagne, "Mocha double," with fresh rounds of "bread," and pungent liqueurs: apricot brandy, chartreuse, *crème de vanille*, and maraschino for the ladies. Later there appeared marinated *filets* of fish, and beer; lastly tea, both Chinese and camomile, for those who had done with champagne and liqueurs and did not care to return to a sound wine, as Mynheer himself did; he, Frau Chauchat, and Hans Castorp working back after midnight to a Swiss red wine. Mynheer Peeperkorn, genuinely thirsty, drank down glass after glass of the simple, effervescent drink.

The party held together for another hour, partly because they were all too leadenfooted and befuddled to rise, partly because this method of spending the hours of the night appealed to them by its novelty; partly by the weight of Peeperkorn's personality, and the blasting example of Peter and his brethren, to which they all shamed to yield. Generally speaking, the female section seemed less compromised than the male. For the men, flushed or sallow, sat with their legs sprawled before them, puffing out their cheeks. Now and then they would make a half--mechanical effort to lift the glass, but their hearts were no longer in it. The women were more enterprising. Hermine Kleefeld, bare elbows on the table, propped up her head, her cheeks in her hands, and showed the giggling Ting--fu all the enamel of her front teeth. Frau Stöhr, with her chin and shoulder coquettishly meeting, sought to reawaken Lawyer Paravant to desire. Frau Magnus's state was such that she had seated herself on Herr Albin's lap and was pulling both his ears by their lobes—-a sight in which

Herr Magnus appeared to find relief. The company had urged Anton
Karlowitsch Ferge to regale them with the story of the pleura--shock;
but his tongue was too thick, he could not manage it, and honourably
avowed his incapacity, which was greeted by the company as
occasion for another drink. Wehsal all at once began to weep bitterly,
from some unplumbed depth of wretchedness. They brought him
round with coffee and cognac; but the episode roused Peeperkorn's
lively interest, who looked at his quivering chin, from which tears
dripped, and with raised forefinger and lifted masklike brows called
the attention of the company to the phenomenon.

"That is—-" he said. "Ah—-with your permission, that is—-holy.
Dry his chin, my child, take my serviette—-or, still better, let it drip.
He himself has done so. Holy, holy, my friends. In every sense.
Christian and pagan. A primitive phenomenon, of the first—-the very
first—-No. No, that is to say—-"

This oft--repeated phrase set the key for all the running comment
with which he accompanied his production of gesture—-gesture that
by now, in all conscience, had grown more than a little burlesque. He
had a way of lifting that little circlet formed by thumb and forefinger
to a poise above his ear, and coyly twisting his head away from it—
-one watched him as one might an elderly priest of some oriental cult,
with the skirts of his robe snatched up, doing a dance before the
sacrificial altar. Again, flung back in Olympian repose, with one arm
stretched out on the back of his neighbour's chair, he beguiled them
all to their confusion, by painting a vivid and irresistible scene of a
dark, frosty winter morning, when the yellow gleam of the night-
-lamp reveals the network of bare boughs outside the pane, rigid in
the harsh and penetrating mist of early dawn. So telling was the
picture, so universal its appeal—-actually, they all shivered;
particularly when he went on to speak of rising in such a dawn, and
squeezing a great sponge filled with ice--cold water over neck and
shoulders. The effective sensation he characterized as "holy." But all
this was a digression, an aside thrown out to illustrate receptivity for
life; a fantastic impromptu, let fall merely to renew and reassert the

[715]

whole irresistible compulsion of his presence and his sensations upon the scene of abandoned night--revelry. He made love to every female creature within reach, without discrimination or respect of person; tendering such offers to the dwarf that the crippled creature's large old face was wreathed in smiles. He paid Frau Stöhr compliments that made the vulgar creature bridle more extravagantly than ever, and become almost senseless with affectation. He supplicated—-and received—-a kiss from Fräulein Kleefeld, upon his thick, chapped lips. He even coquetted with the forlorn Frau Magnus—-and all this without detriment to the delicate homage he paid his companion, whose hand he would every now and then carry gallantly to his lips. "Wine—-" he said, "women; they are—-that is—-pardon me—-Gethsemane—-Day of Judgment ..."

Toward two o'clock word flew about that "the old man"—-in other words, Hofrat Behrens—-was approaching by forced marches. Panic reigned among the nerveless company. Chairs and ice--pails were upset. They fled through the library. Peeperkorn raged at the precipitate breaking--up of the festivities, in kingly choler struck the table with his fist and called after the retreating "cowardly slaves"—-but allowed Frau Chauchat and Hans Castorp to calm him with the consideration that the banquet had already lasted some six hours, and must in any case some time come to an end. He lent an ear when they murmured something about the "holy" boon of sleep, and yielded to their efforts to lead him away to bed.

"Let me lean upon you, my child! And you, young man, on my other side," he said. They helped him lift his unwieldy body from table, gave him the support of their arms, and he walked with wide steps between them bedwards, his mighty head sunk on his lifted shoulder. First one and then the other of his aides was carried to one side by his staggering pace. It is probable that he was merely indulging himself in the regal luxury of being thus supported and piloted; presumably he could have gone by himself. But he scorned the effort. If made it would have been solely for the unworthy purpose of disguising his state, and of this he was royally unashamed, revelling in the fun of making his companions stagger with him from side to side. He even said, on the way: "Children—-nonsense. Of course I'm not—at this moment. You ought to see—-ridiculous—-"

"Ridiculous, of course," Hans Castorp agreed. "It certainly is. We are giving the classical gifts of life their due, staggering in their honour. Seriously, on the other hand: I've had my share too; but any so--called drunkenness to the contrary, I fully recognize the honour of helping such a tremendous personality to bed; I am not so drunk I don't know that in the matter of size I don't hold a candle—-"

"Come, come, chatterbox," Peeperkorn said, and they moved rhythmically on toward the stairs, drawing Frau Chauchat with them.

The report of the Hofrat's approach had been a bogy. Perhaps the weary little waitress was responsible, thinking thereby to break up the party. Peeperkorn scented the false alarm, and would have turned back for another drink. But they both set to work to talk him out of the idea, and he let himself be moved on.

The Malayan valet, in white cravat and black silk slippers, awaited his master in the corridor before their apartments. He bowed low, laying his hand upon his breast.

"Kiss each other," commanded Peeperkorn. "Young man, kiss this lovely woman good--night, upon her brow," said he to Hans Castorp. "She will have no objection to receiving and responding to—-do it to my health, with my blessing." But Hans Castorp declined.

"No, Your Majesty," he said. 'fl beg your pardon. It would not do."

Peeperkorn, in the arms of his valet, drew up his arabesques and demanded to know why.

"Because your companion and I can exchange no kisses on the brow," Hans Castorp responded. "I hope you sleep well. No, no, that is the sheerest nonsense, however you look at it."

Frau Chauchat, for her part, was moving toward her door; Peeperkorn gave way, and let the unwilling suitor go, though looking at him awhile over his and the Malay's shoulders, his wrinkled brows drawn high in astonishment at an insubordination his kingly temper was seldom called upon to brook.

Mynheer Peeperkorn (Continued)

Mynheer Peeperkorn remained in House Berghof the whole winter—-what there was left of it—-and on into the spring; and there took place, among others, a memorable excursion (in which Settembrini and Naphta joined) into the Fluela valley, to see the waterfall. This occurred at the end of his stay. At the end? Did he remain no longer, then? No. He went away? Yes—-and no. How yes and no? Pray let us have no prying into secrets—-in the fullness of time we shall know. We are aware that Lieutenant Ziemssen died, not to speak of other less admirable performers of the dance of death. Then Peeperkorn's malignant tropical fever carried him off? No, not so—-but why so impatient? Let us not forget the condition of life as of narration: that we can never see the whole picture at once—-unless we propose to throw overboard all the God--conditioned forms of human knowledge. Let us at least pay time so much honour as the nature of our story permits—-little enough, in all conscience; for it has begun to rush pell--mell and helter--skelter; or, if the words suggest too much noise and confusion, shall we say it is going like the wind? The little hand on time's clock trips away as though measuring seconds; but God knows how much time it is covering when it whisks round heedless of the divisions it passes over! So much is certain, that we have been up here years. Our brains reel, surely this is an evil dream, though dreamed with nor hashish nor opium; a censor of morals would rebuke us for it. Yet how much logical clarity, how much pure light of reason have we opposed to the stealing vague? Not by chance, may we say, have we kept company with intellectual lights like Naphta and Settembrini, instead of surrounding ourselves with incoherent Peeperkorns! And this leads us to a comparison, which in many respects, notably that of scale, must result in favour of this latest arrival on the scene. It did so in Hans Castorp's own mind. He lay, considering matters, in his loge, and admitted to himself that his two over--vocal mentors, the self--elected guardians of his soul, were dwarfed beside Pieter Peeperkorn. Almost he inclined to call them what Peeperkorn in his royal cups had called him, Hans Castorp—-chatterboxes. He was well pleased that hermetic pedagogy should have given him this too: contact with an out--and--out personality.

True, this personality was the companion of Clavdia Chauchat's travels, and as such a greatly disturbing element. But that was another matter, and one which Hans Castorp did not allow to prejudice his judgment. He persisted in his sincere and respectful if also rather forward sympathy for this man on the grand scale, regardless of his partnership in the travelling--trunks of the woman of whom once, on a carnival night, Hans Castorp had borrowed a lead--pencil. That was his way; though we know some people, male and female, will not understand such a lack of sensibility, preferring that our hero should hate Peeperkorn, avoid him, call him an old dotard, a drivelling old sot. Instead of which we see him by Peeperkorn's bedside in his attacks of fever—-prattling to him (the word applies to his own share in the conversation, not the majestic Peeperkorn's) and with the receptivity of inquiring youth on his travels, letting himself be played on by the power of the personality. All this Hans Castorp did, and all this we report of him, indifferent to the danger that someone may thereby be reminded of Ferdinand Wehsal, who once was wont to carry Hans Castorp's overcoat. The comparison is not pertinent—-for our hero was no Wehsal. Depths of self--abasement were not his line. But he was no "hero" either: which is to say, he would never let his relation to the masculine be conditioned by the feminine. True to our principle of making him out neither better nor worse than he was, we assert that he simply declined—-not expressly and consciously, but quite naïvely, declined to let his judgment of his own sex be perverted by romantic considerations. Nor his sense of what was formative in experience. The female sex may find this offensive; we believe Frau Chauchat did feel some involuntary chagrin over the fact——a biting remark or so escaped her, to which we shall refer later on. But surely it was this very characteristic of his which rendered him so irresistible an object for pedagogic rivalry.

Pieter Peeperkorn lay grievously ill, the day after that evening of cards and champagne we have described——and no wonder. Nearly all the participants in those long--drawn--out, exhausting revels were the same. Hans Castorp was no exception, his head ached to splitting; which did not prevent him from paying a visit to the bedside of his last night's host. He craved permission through the Malay, whom he met in the corridor; and it was readily granted.

He entered the Dutchman's double bedroom through the salon which separated it from Frau Chauchat's. It was larger and more luxuriously furnished than most of the Berghof rooms, with satin--upholstered arm--chairs and curly--legged tables. A thick, soft carpet covered the floor, and the beds——they were not the usual hygienic dyingbed of the establishment, but very stately indeed, of polished cherry--wood with brass mounting, and above them hung a little canopy without curtains, like one umbrella sheltering both.

Pieter Peeperkorn lay in one of the two; its red satin coverlet was strewn with papers, books, and letters, and he was reading the *Telegraaf* through his horn--rimmed pince--nez with the high nose--piece. The coffee--machine stood on a chair at the bedside, and a half--empty bottle of the same simple effervescent red wine was on the night--table, among vials of medicine. Hans Castorp was rather put off to see the Dutchman wearing not a white night--shirt, but a long--sleeved woollen vest, buttoned at the wrists and collar--less, cut round in the neck, and clinging to the old man's powerful torso, his broad shoulders and breast. This undress threw into even greater relief the splendid humanity of his head on the pillow; in it he looked more remote than ever from the conventional and middle--class, suggesting on the one hand the *homme du peuple*, on the other a portrait--bust.

"By all means, young man," he said, taking off the horn spectacles by the nose--piece. "Come in. Don't mention it—-on the contrary." Hans Castorp sat down by the bed, and concealed his surprise—-for it was that rather than admiration which he felt, however sympathetically—-under a burst of cordial and lively chatter, which Peeperkorn seconded with magnificent *disjecta membra* and much play of gesture. He looked very "poorly," yellow and in evident distress; a good deal affected by the attack of fever he had had toward morning, and the subsequent exhaustion—-in part undoubtedly the result of his last night's bout. "We were pretty—-last night, you know—-carried it pretty far," he said. "But you are—-Good. With you there were no further—-but my age, and the condition I am in—-my child," he turned with mild yet quite perceptible severity to Frau Chauchat, who just then entered the room from the salon, "very well, very well indeed. Very. But I repeat—-ought to have been prevented." Something like an approach to his regal fit of rage rose in face and voice. The injustice, the unreason of the reproof were obvious to anybody who tried to imagine the storm that would have burst on the head of one seriously thinking to disturb him in his drink. But such are the moods of the great. Frau Chauchat moved to and fro in the room, after greeting Hans Castorp, who rose as she entered, without a handshake, but with a smile and nod, and a "Pray don't disturb yourself"—-in his *tête-- à--tête*, that was, with Mynheer. She busied herself about the room, summoned the Malay to take the coffee--machine, then withdrew awhile, and on her return, softfooted, took part standing in the others' talk. Hans Castorp got an impression that she was there on guard. It was all very well for her to come back to the Berghof in company with a personality. But when the long--suffering lover took leave to evince regard for the personality, as man for man, then she betrayed uneasiness in pointed phrases like "Pray don't disturb yourself" and the like. They cost Hans Castorp a smile, which he bent his head to hide, though inwardly aglow. Peeperkorn poured him out a glass of wine from the bottle on the night--table. Under the circumstances the best thing, in the Dutchman's opinion, was to begin where one had left off; and that innocent effervescent wine had the same effect as soda--water. They touched glasses. Hans Castorp, as he drank, looked at the freckled, sea--captain's hand, with its pointed nails, the woollen band buttoned round the wrist. It took up the glass, carried it to the thick, cracked lips; the throat, so like a statue's and yet rather like a day labourer's, worked up and down as it swallowed the wine. Peeperkorn indicated the medicine bottle on the table, a brown liquid, of which he took a spoonful from Frau Chauchat's hand. It was an antipyretic, chiefly quinine, he baid. He made his guest try its characteristic bitter and pungent taste; and had much to say in praise of the wonderworking, germ--destroying properties of the drug, its tonic quality, its wholesome effect in regulating the temperature. It slowed down protein catabolism, promoted assimilation, in short it was a boon to mankind, a wonderful cordial, tonic and stimulant——an intoxicant as well, for one could get quite tipsy on it, he said, making the last night's suggestive gesture of fingers and head like a pagan priest at his ritual dance.

Yes, a wonderful substance, cinchona. It had not been three hundred years since European pharmacology made its acquaintance; not a century since the alkaloid had been isolated which was its active principle; isolated and, to a certain extent, analysed, for it would be too much to say that chemistry knew all there was to know about it, or was in a position to reproduce it synthetically. Our pharmacology need not be too arrogant over its science; for the state of its knowledge on the subject of quinine was a fair example of the rest. It had various facts about the operation of this or that drug; but was very often embarrassed to know the causes of the effect produced. If the young man were to survey the field of our toxicological knowledge, he would find that no one could tell him anything of the elementary properties conditioning the effects of the so--called poisons. For example, take the venom of snakes: all that was known of these animal substances was that they belonged to the albuminoid group, and consisted of various proteids, none of which produced a violent effect, except in this certain——and most uncertain——

-combination. Introduced into the blood--circulation, the effect was astonishing indeed, considering how far we were from being accustomed to think of albumen as a poison. The truth was, Peeperkorn said, and lifted his head from the pillow, elevated the arabesques on his brow, and gave point to his remarks by the little circle and the upright finger--tips——the truth was, in the world of matter, that all substances were the vehicle of both life and death, all of them were medicinal and all poisonous, in fact therapeutics and toxicology were one and the same, man could be cured by poison, and substances known to be the bearer of life could kill at a thrust, in a single second of time.

He spoke very impressively, and with unwonted coherence, of drugs and poisons, and Hans Castorp listened and nodded; less concerned with the content of his speech——he seemed to have the subject much at heart——than with silently exploring this extraordinary personality, which in the end remained as inexplicable as the operation of the snake--poison he was discussing. In the world of matter, Peeperkorn said, everything depended on dynamics, all else being entirely hypothetical. Quinine was one of the medicinal poisons; one of the strongest of these. Four grammes could make one deaf and giddy and short--winded; it acted like atropine on the visual organs, it was as intoxicating as alcohol; workers in quinine factories had inflamed eyes and swollen lips and suffered from affections of the skin. Peeperkorn described the cinchona, the quinine--tree, in the primeval forests of the Cordilleras, three thousand metres above sea--level. Its bark, called Peruvian or Jesuits' bark, came late to Spain, long after the natives of South America knew its use. He spoke of the enormous quinine plantations owned by the Dutch government in Java, whence yearly many million pounds of the coils of reddish bark, like cinnamon, were shipped to Amsterdam and London. In fact, said Peeperkorn, bark, the wood--fibre itself, from the epidermis to the cambium, contained, almost always, extraordinary dynamic virtue, for good or evil. The knowledge of drugs possessed by the coloured races was far superior to our own. In certain islands east of

[723]

Dutch New Guinea, youths and maidens prepared a love charm from the bark of a tree—it was probably poisonous, like the manzanilla tree, or the *antiaris toxicaria*, the deadly upas--tree of Java, which could poison the air round with its steam and fatally stupefy man and beast. This bark they powdered and mixed with coconut shavings, rolled the mixture into a sheet and toasted it, then sprinkled a brew in the face of the reluctant one, who was straightway inflamed with love for the sprinkler. Sometimes it was the bark of the root that contained the principle, as was the case with a certain creeper growing in the Malay Archipelago, called *strychnos tieuté*, from which the natives prepared the *upas-- radsha*, by adding snake--venom. This drug caused immediate death when introduced into the circulation—-as for instance by means of an arrow—-but nobody could explain how it operated. All that seemed clear was that the upas had a dynamic relation with strychnine ... Peeperkorn, by this time, was sitting erect in his bed; now and then, with a hand that slightly trembled, conveying the wineglass to his cracked lips, to take great, thirsty draughts. He went on to speak of the "crows'--eye" tree of the Coromandel Coast, from the orange--yellow berries of which—-the crows' eyes—-was extracted the most powerful alkaloid of all, strychnine. His voice sank to a whisper, and the great folds of his brow rose high, as he described to Hans Castorp the ash--grey boughs, the strikingly glossy foliage and yellow--green blossoms; the picture of this tree conjured up in the mind's eye of the young man was luridly, almost hysterically garish—-it made him shudder. But here Frau Chauchat intervened, saying it was not good for Mynheer Peeperkorn to talk any longer, it tired him too much. She disliked to interfere, but Hans Castorp would forgive her if she suggested that they had had enough for the time. The young man accordingly took his leave. But often, in the months that followed, did Hans Castorp sit by the bed of that kingly man, when he kept it after an attack of fever; Frau Chauchat being within hearing, as she moved about the rooms, and sometimes taking part with a few words. They spent much time together when Peeperkorn was free of fever; for the Dutchman, on his good days, seldom failed to gather round him a select company, to play and drink and otherwise divert themselves and rejoice the inner man. These reunions took place either in the salon, as on the first occasion, or in the restaurant; and Hans Castorp had a habitual place between the great man and his languid companion. They even went abroad together, took walks with Herr Ferge and Wehsal, Naphta and Settembrini, those opposed spirits, whom they could hardly fail to meet. Hans Castorp counted himself fortunate in presenting them to Peeperkorn, and even, in the end, to Clavdia Chauchat. He troubled not at all whether the acquaintance was to these pedagogues' liking or not. Secure in the knowledge that they needed a tree whereon to sharpen their pedagogical tusks, he reckoned on their putting up even with unwelcome society, in order to continue in enjoyment of his own.

And he was not wrong in thinking that the members of this motley group would at least get used to not getting used to each other. Strangeness, tension, even suppressed hostility there was of course enough between them; it is surely rather remarkable that a comparatively insignificant personality could have held them together. That he did so must be laid to a certain shrewd geniality native to him, which found everything fish that came to his net, and not only bound to him people of the most diverse tastes and characters, but exerted enough power to bind them to each other.

Again, how involved were the relations between the various members of our group!

Let us con them a little, as Hans Castorp himself did, with shrewd, yet friendly eye, as they went their ways together. There was the unhappy Wehsal, consumed by his louring passion for Frau Chauchat; who grovelled before Peeperkorn and Hans Castorp, the one on grounds of the past, the other for the sake of the compelling present. And there was Clavdia Chauchat herself, charming, soft--stepping invalid, the property of Peeperkorn—-surely by choice and conviction, yet uneasy and sharptongued to see her carnival cavalier on such good terms with her sovereign lord. The irritation was probably the same in kind as that which coloured her feeling toward

Herr Settembrini, the humanist and haranguer, whom she could not
abide, calling him arrogant, not *"hu—- man."* Dearly would she have
liked to ask this mentor of Hans Castorp's the meaning of certain
words in his own Mediterranean tongue, of which, though less
contemptuously, she was as ignorant as he of hers: the words he had
flung after the altogether nice young German, quite correct and of
good family, on that carnival night when at length he had summoned
courage to approach her.——Hans Castorp was in love up to his ears,
so much was true; not in the accepted blissful sense, but as one loves
when the case is out of all reason, and cannot be celebrated in any
pretty little flat--land ditties we know of. He was badly smitten, quite
subjugated, endured all the orthodox pangs; yet was the man to
retain, even in his slavery, a certain sense of proportion, which told
him that his devotion was worth something to the fair one with the
Tartar eyes; not too blind in his abasement to measure its worth by
Settembrini's own attitude toward her. The Italian was as distant as
the dictates of humanistic courtesy would permit; while she was only
too obviously piqued by his bearing. The position with regard to Leo
Naphta was scarcely more——or, from Hans Castorp's point of view,
scarcely less——favourable. True, there was here no fundamental
antagonism such as set Herr Ludovico's being against hers and all its
works. Also, the language difficulty was less, and they sometimes
strolled and talked apart, Clavdia and the knife--edged little man;
discussed books, and questions of political philosophy, upon which
both held radical views. Hans Castorp, in his simplicity, would
sometimes take part. Yet Frau Chauchat could not but be aware of a
certain haughty aloofness in Naphta's bearing. Its source was the
caution of the parvenu, a feeling of insecurity in this unfamiliar
society. But in truth his Spanish terrorism had little in common with
her roving, door--slamming, all--too--human humanity. And there
was moreover the subtle, scarcely perceptible animosity felt by both
pedagogues on the score of this disturbing female element that came
between them and their fledgling, and united them in an unspoken,
primitive hostility, at least as potent as their long--standing conflict
with each other. If Hans Castorp was aware of these sentiments they

could hardly escape his charmer's feminine intuition. Was there something of the same aversion in the attitude of the two dialecticians toward Pieter Peeperkorn? At least, Hans Castorp thought he discerned it, though perhaps he went out to meet it, and took malicious pleasure in watching tongue--tied majesty in contact with his two "auditors," as, with reference to his stocktaking activities, he jestingly called them——though distinctly feeling that the word was but a definition by contraries! Mynheer, in the open, was not so impressive as in the house. He wore a soft felt hat drawn down on his brows, covering the blaze of white hair and the forehead's extraordinary folds, reducing, as it were, the scale of his features, even the commanding large red nose. He looked better standing than walking; for he took small steps, and with each one of them shifted the full weight of his body on to the leg he had advanced——it was the comfortable gait of an old man, but it was not kingly. He stooped slightly too, or rather, shrank together; though even so he overlooked Herr Ludovico, and was a whole head taller than little Naphta. But it was not his height alone that made his presence oppressive——oh, quite as oppressive as Hans Castorp had anticipated!——to the two politicians.

Yes, they suffered by comparison——so much was perceptible not only to the connoisseur's watchful eye, but very probably to the feelings of those concerned, the tongue--tied giant as well as the two insignificant and over--articulate others. Peeperkorn treated both with distinguished attention, a respect which Hans Castorp would have called ironic had he not known that irony is not on the grand scale. Kings are never ironical——not even in the sense of a direct and classic device of oratory, to say nothing of any other kind. The Dutchman's manner toward Hans Castorp's friends was rather mocking than ironic. He made beautiful fun of them, either openly or veiled in exaggerated respect. "Oh, yes, yes," he would say, with his finger threatening their direction, the head and smiling lips turned away, "this is——these are——ladies and gentlemen, I call your attention——cerebrum, cerebral, you understand!

No, no—-positively. Extraordinary—-displays great—-" In revenge, they looked at each other, pantomimed despair, angled for Hans Castorp's glance; but he refused to be drawn.

Settembrini however attacked Hans Castorp directly, and confessed to pedagogic concern.

"Lord, what a stupid old man you have there, Engineer," said he. "What is it you see in him? What good can he do you? I am at a loss. I should understand—-though scarcely approve—-your putting up with his society in order to enjoy that of his mistress. But it is obvious that you are even more interested in him than in her. Come to the aid of my understanding, I implore you."

Hans Castorp laughed. "By all means," said he. "Absolutely. That is to say—-very good. Very good indeed." He tried to imitate Peeperkorn's gestures. "Yes, yes," he went on, laughing, "you find it stupid, Herr Settembrini, and I admit it is unclear, which in your eyes is even worse. Stupid—-well, there are so many kinds of stupidity, and cleverness is one of the worst. There, I have made an epigram—-a *bon mot!* What do you think of it?"

"Very good. I look forward eagerly to your collection of aphorisms. Perhaps there is still time to beg you not to forget some comment we once made on the anti--social nature of paradox."

"I won't indeed, Herr Settembrini. I certainly will not. No, my *mot* was not in the nature of paradox, I assure you. I only meant to indicate the difficulty I really find in distinguishing between stupidity and cleverness. It is so hard to draw a line—-one goes over into the other.—-I know you hate all that mystical *guazzabuglio;* you are all for values, judgment, and judgment of values; and I'm sure you are right. But this about stupidity and—-on my honour, it's a complete mystery; and after all, it is allowable to think about mysteries, isn't it, so long as one is honestly bent on getting to the bottom of them? But I ask you. Can you deny that he puts us all in his pocket? That's expressing it crudely, perhaps—-but, so far as I can see, you can't deny it. He puts us all in his pocket; somehow or other, he has the right to laugh at us all—but where does he get it? Where does it come from? How does he do it? Certainly it's not that he's so clever. I admit that you can't talk about his cleverness. He's inarticulate—-it's more feeling with him, feeling is just his mark, if you'll excuse my language. No, as I say, it's not out of cleverness, not on intellectual grounds at all, that he can do as he likes with us. You would be right to deny it. It isn't the point. But not on physical either. It's not the massive shoulders, or the strength of his biceps; not because he could knock us down if he liked. He isn't conscious of his power; if he does take a notion, he can easily be put off it with a couple of civilized words.—-So it is not physical. And yet the physical has something to do with it; not in a muscular sense—-it's something quite different, mystical; because so soon as the physical has anything to do with it, it becomes mystical, the physical goes over into the spiritual, and the other way on, and you can't tell them apart, nor can you cleverness and stupidity. But the result is what we see, the dynamic effect—-he puts us in his pocket. We've only one word for that—-personality. We use it in another, more regular sense too, in which we are all personalities—-morally, legally, and otherwise. But that is not the sense in which I am using it now. I am speaking of the mystery of personality, something above either cleverness or stupidity, and something we all have to take into account: partly to try to understand it; but partly, where that is not possible, to be edified by it. You are all for values; but isn't personality a value too? It seems so to me, more so than either cleverness or stupidity, it seems positive and absolute, like life—-in short, something quite worth while, and calculated to make us trouble about it. That's what I wanted to say in answer to what you said about stupidity."

Nowadays, when Hans Castorp relieved his mind, he did not hem and haw, become involved and stick in the middle. He said his say to the end like a man, rounded off his period, let his voice drop and went his way; though he still got red, and at heart was still afraid of the silence he knew would follow when he had done, to give him time to feel mortified at what he had expressed.

Herr Settembrini let it have full sway before he said: "You deny that you are hunting paradoxes; but at the same time you well know that I love them as much as I do mysteries. In making a mystery of the personality, you run a risk of idol--worship. You do reverence to a hollow mask. You see mystery in mystification, in one of those counterfeits with which a malicious demon of physical form loves sometimes to mock us. Have you ever frequented theatrical circles? You know those physiognomies in which the features of Julius Cæsar, Beethoven, and Goethe unite---the happy possessor of which has only to open his mouth to prove himself the most pitiable fool on God's earth?"

"Very good, a freak of nature," said Hans Castorp. "But not alone a freak of nature, not simply a hoax. For since these people are actors, they must have a gift, and the gift itself is beyond cleverness and stupidity, it is after all a value. Mynheer Peeperkom has a gift, say what you like; and thus it is he can stick us all in his pocket. Put Herr Naphta in one corner of the room, and let him deliver a discourse on Gregory the Great and the City of God---it would be highly worth listening to---and put Mynheer Peeperkorn in the other, with his extraordinary mouth and the wrinkles on his forehead, and let him not say a word except 'By all means---capital---settled, ladies and gentlemen!' You will see everybody gather round Peeperkorn, and Herr Naphta will be sitting there alone with his cleverness and his City of God, though he may be uttering such penetrating wisdom that it pierces through marrow and cucumber, as Behrens says---"

"Take shame to yourself for bowing down to success," Herr Settembrini adjured him. *"Mundus vult decipi.* I do not claim that people ought to flock about Herr Naphta. He is too full of guile for my taste. But I am inclined to range myself on his side, in the imaginary scene you have conjured up with such relish. Will you despise logic, precision, discrimination? Will you contemn them, in favour of some suggestion---hocus--pocus and emotional charlatanry? If you will, then the devil has you in his---"

"But he can often talk as coherently as you please," said Hans Castorp, "when he gets interested. The other day he was telling me about dynamic drugs and Asiatic poison--trees; it was so interesting it was almost uncanny—-interesting things are always a bit uncanny—-but the interest was not so much in what he was saying as it was taken in connexion with his personality, which made it interesting and uncanny at once."

"Ah, yes, your weakness for Asia is well known to me. True, I cannot oblige with marvels such as those," the Italian said, so bitterly that Hans Castorp hastened to assure him how much he valued his conversation and instruction from quite another angle, and that it had not occurred to him to make comparisons which would be unjust to both sides. Herr Settembrini paid no heed, he spurned the politeness, and went on: "In any case, Engineer, you must permit me to admire your serene objectivity. It approaches the fantastic, you will admit. The way things stand: this zany has taken away your Beatrice from you, yet you—-it is unheard of."

"These are temperamental differences, Herr Settembrini. We have different views as to what is knightly and warm--blooded. You, a southerner, would prescribe poison and dagger, at least you would conceive the affair in its social and passionate aspect, and want me to act like a game--cock. That would of course be masculine and gallant, in a social sense. But with me it is different. I am not at all masculine in the sense that I see in another man only a rival male and nothing more. Perhaps I am not masculine at all—-certainly I am not in the sense which I tend to call 'social,' I don't exactly know why. What I do is to question my sad heart whether I have any ground of complaint against the man. Has he really insulted me? But an insult must be of intent, otherwise it can be none. And as for his having 'done anything' to me, there I should have to apply to *her*—- and I have no right to, certainly not with regard to Peeperkorn. For he is a quite extraordinary personality, which by itself is something for women, and then he is hardly a civilian, like me, he is a sort of military, a bit like my poor cousin, in that he has a *point d'honneur*, a sore spot, as it were, which is feeling, life.——I know I am talking nonsense, but I'd rather go rambling on, and partly expressing something I find it difficult to express, than to keep on transmitting faultless platitudes. That must be a military trait in my character, after all, if I may say so——"

"You may say so," Settembrini acquiesced. "A trait at least worthy of praise. The courage to recognize and express——that is the quality that makes literature——that is humanism."

Thus they parted on good terms, Herr Settembrini having given the conversation this placable turn. It was the wiser course; his position had not been so strong he could afford to push the argument to extremes. A conversation dealing with jealousy was rather slippery ground for him; at one point he would have been obliged to admit that his own position——as a pedagogue——was scarcely masculine in the social and cockfighting sense, else why should the prepotent Peeperkorn disturb his tranquillity, in the same way Naphta and Frau Chauchat did? Lastly, the Italian could not hope to argue his pupil out of interest in a personality to whose native superiority he himself and his partner in cerebral gymnastic were willy--nilly constrained to bow.

They were on safer ground when they could sustain the conversation in the realms of the intellectual, and hold the attention of their audience by one of their elegant and impassioned debates, academic, yet conducted as though the matter discussed were the most burning question of the time, or of all time. They were of course almost the sole support of such discussions; while these lasted; they did, to some extent, neutralize the effect of "bigness" purveyed by a certain member of their group, who could only accompany them by a running play of wrinkles, gestures, and snatches of mockery. But even that was enough to cast a shadow, rob their brilliant performance of some of its gloss, emasculate it, as it were, set up a cross--current perceptible to them all, though Peeperkorn himself remained unconscious, or conscious to a degree impossible for them to guess. Neither side could get any advantage, both were embarrassed, and the stamp of futility set upon their debate. We might put it like this: that their life--and--death duel of wits came to be carried on always with vague subterranean reference to "bigness" walking beside them, and to be deflected from its orbit by the magnetism "bigness" exerted. One cannot characterize otherwise this puzzling, for the two disputants maddening, posture of affairs. One can only add that had there been no Pieter Peeperkorn, party feeling would have run higher on both sides; as when Leo Naphta defended the arch--revolutionary nature of the Church, against Settembrini's dogmatic assertion that that great historic power was to be looked upon merely as the protectress of the sinister forces of reaction; whereas all the forces that made for life and future, and looked undismayed on change and resolution, he claimed for the principles of enlightenment; science and progress, which had their rise in an epoch of quite opposed tendencies, the famous century that witnessed the rebirth of classical culture. He drove home his convictions with a graceful play of word and gesture. Whereupon Naphta, with chilling acuity, undertook to show——and showed too, with devastating clarity——that the Church, as the embodiment of the religious and ascetic ideal, was remote indeed from posing as the champion and support of the existing order, in other words of secular culture and civil law——rather had she from the beginning inscribed upon her radical banner the programme of their extirpation root and branch; that absolutely everything beloved and cherished of the bourgeoisie, the conservative, the cowardly, and the impotent——the State, family life, secular art and science——was consciously or unconsciously hostile to the religious idea, to the Church, whose innate tendency and permanent aim was the dissolution of all existing worldly orders, and the reconstitution of society after the model of the ideal, the communistic City of God.

After that, Settembrini took the floor——and well he knew how to avail himself of it. It was lamentable, he said——this confusion of luridly revolutionary doctrine with a general insurrection of all the powers of evil. The Church's love of innovation had for centuries manifested itself in putting to the question the living idea, wherever she found it; throttling it, quenching it in smoke at the stake; to--day she announces through her emissaries that she rejoices in revolution, that her goal is the uprooting of freedom, culture, and democracy, which she intends to replace by barbarism and the dictatorship of the mob. Yea, verily, a fearsome mixture of contradictory consistency and consistent contradiction ...

His opponent, Naphta retorted, displayed no lack of the same qualities. By his own account, he was a democrat; yet his words sounded neither democratic nor egalitarian; but rather displayed a reprehensible and arrogant aristocratism, as when he alluded to the delegated dictatorship of the proletariat as mob rule! However, where the Church was in question, assuredly he showed himself a democrat; for the Church was admittedly the most aristocratic force in the history of mankind; an aristocracy in the last and highest sense, that of the spirit. For the ascetic spirit---if the pleonasm might be pardoned him---the spirit that would deny and destroy the world, was aristocracy itself, a pure culture of the aristocratic principle. It could never be popular; and the Church, accordingly, had at all times been unpopular. A little research into the cultural history of the Middle Ages would convince Herr Settembrini of the stout resistance which the people---in the widest sense---opposed to the things of the Church. There were for instance monkish figures, the invention of popular fantasy, who, quite in the spirit of Luther, had set up wine, women, and song in opposition to the ascetic idea. All the instincts of secular heroism, all warlike spirit, all court poetry, set themselves in more or less open conflict with the religious idea and the hierarchy. For all that was "the world," all that was "the common people," compared with the aristocracy of the spirit represented by Church.

Herr Settembrini thanked him for jogging his memory. The figure of the monk Ilsan in the *Rosengarten* he did indeed find refreshing by comparison with this muchlauded aristocracy of the grave. He, the speaker, was no friend to the German Reformation; but they would find him ever ready to defend whatever of democratic individualism there was in its teaching, against any and every clerical and feudal craving for dominion over the individual.

"Aha!" cried Naphta. So Herr Settembrini would condemn the Church for lack of democracy, for being wanting in a sense of the value of human personality? But what of the humane freedom from prejudice evinced by canonical law? For whereas Roman law made the possession of legal rights dependent upon citizenship, and Germanic law upon individual freedom and membership in the tribe, ecclesiastical law, orthodoxy, was alone in divorcing legal rights from either national or social considerations, and asserting that slaves, serfs, and prisoners of war were all capable of making wills and inheriting property.

Settembrini bitingly remarked that he might mention, as not entirely irrelevant in this connexion, the so--called "canonical portion," which subtracted a substantial sum from every testamentary bequest. And he spoke of priestly demagoguery, which began to vent its thirst for power in exaggerated solicitude for the under dog, when the top dog would none of it. The Church, he asserted, cared more about the quantity of souls she got hold of than their quality—which certainly reflected upon her pretensions to spiritual refinement.

So the Church lacked refinement? Herr Settembrini's attention was invited to the inexorable aristocratism which underlay the idea that shame could be inherited: the passing on of guilt to the---democratically considered---innocent descendants; for example, the illegitimacy and lifelong pollution of natural children. But the Italian bade him be silent: in the first place, because his human feelings rose up in arms against Naphta's words, and in the second, because he had had enough of such quibbles, and saw in the shifts of his opponent's apologetics only the same old infamous and devilish cult of nihilism, which wanted to be called Spirit, and found so legitimate, so sacrosanct the admittedly existent hatred of the ascetic principle. But here Naphta begged to be forgiven for laughing outright. The nihilism or the Church! The nihilism of the most realistic system of government in the history of the world! Herr Settembrini, then, had never been touched by a breath of that ironic humanity which made constant concession to the world and the flesh, cleverly veiling the letter and letting the spirit rule, not to put too sore a constraint on nature? He had never heard of the ecclesiastical conception of indulgence, under which was to be classified one of the sacraments of the Church—-namely, marriage, not in itself an absolute good, like the other sacraments, but only a protection against sin, countenanced in order to set bounds to sensual desire; that the ascetic principle, the ideal of complete chastity, might be upheld, without at the same time opposing an unpolitic harshness to the flesh?

Herr Settembrini, of course, could not refrain from protesting against this hideous conception of "policy"; against the gesture of a shrewd and sinister complaisance, made by the "Spirit"—-or what called itself so—-against the imaginary guilt of its opposite, which it pretended to deal with in a "politic" sense, but which in reality stood in no need of the pernicious indulgence it proffered; against the accursed dualism of a conception which bedevilled the universe—-that is to say, life—as well as life's dark opposite, the Spirit—for if life was evil, the Spirit, as pure negation, must be so too. And he broke a lance in defence of the blamelessness of sensual gratification—-hearing which, Hans Castorp could not but think of the humanistic cuddy under the roof, with its standing desk, rush--bottomed chairs, and water--bottle. Naphta asserted that sensual gratification was never blameless—-nature, he said, always had a bad conscience in respect of the spiritual. The ecclesiastical policy of indulgence practised by the Spirit he designated as "Love"—-this to refute the nihilism of the ascetic principle. Hans Castorp felt how very odd indeed the word sounded in the mouth of sharp, skinny little Naphta.

So it went on—-we know already how it went, and so did Hans Castorp. We have listened, as he did, for a little while, in order to learn how such a peripatetic passageat--arms fares, in what way it is blown upon, by the presence of a personality. It seemed as though a secret impulse to animadvert upon the presence of Peeperkorn quenched the leaping spark of wit, and called up that sense of weary devitalization that comes over us when an electric connexion fails to connect. Yes, that was it. No spark leaped nimbly from pole to pole, no flash of lightning, no current. The intellect which should in its own opinion have neutralized the presence was neutralized by it—as Hans Castorp, amazed and curious, perceived.

Revolution, conservation—he looked at Peeperkorn, saw him stalking along, not particularly majestic on foot, with his slumping gait, his hat drawn over his brows; saw his thick lips with their broken line, heard him say, jerking his head mockingly in the direction of the debaters: "Yes, yes—cerebrum, highly cerebral, you understand. Very; that is—it shows"—and behold, in a trice, the current cut off! Dead. As a doornail. They tried another tack, invoked more powerful spells, came on the "aristocratic problem," on popularity and exclusiveness. Not a spark. Despite itself, what they said sounded personal. Hans Castorp saw Clavdia's traveling-companion as he lay under the red satin coverlet, in his collarless woollen shirt, half ancient *ouvrier*, half royal bust. And the nerve of the debate quivered and died. They tried to galvanize it into life. Negation, cult of nihilism on the one hand, on the other the positive assertion of life, and the inclining of the heart unto love. But where was the spark, where the current, directly one looked at Mynheer, as one did, irresistibly, as though magnetized? They simply were not there—which remained, to use Hans Castorp's expression, neither more nor less than a mystery. He took note, for his collection of aphorisms, that either one expresses a mystery in the simplest words, or leaves it unexpressed. But to get this one expressed, one could only say straight out that Pieter Peeperkorn, with his kingly mask, and bitter, irregular mouth, was both, now this, now that; both seemed to fit him and to neutralize each other when one looked at him—both this and that, the one and the other. Yes, this stupid old man, this commanding cipher! He did not paralyse the opposition by cross-purposes and confusion, like Naphta, he was not like him equivocal, or was so in an entirely different way, in a positive way, this staggering mystery, which so naïvely set at naught not only cleverness and stupidity, but so much else in the way of opposed views invoked by Settembrini and Naphta, in order to stimulate interest, to their own pedagogical ends. The personality, it appeared, was not pedagogically inclined——yet what a find, what a prize, for inquiring youth on its travels! Fascinating it was to watch riddling royalty when the conversation turned on marriage and sin, indulgences, the guilt or innocence of pleasures of the sense! His head would sink upon his shoulder or chest, the calamitous lips part as the mouth relaxed into pathetic curves, the nostrils dilate as with pain, the folds on the forehead rose until the eyes were fixed in a wide, suffering gaze.——It was a picture of bitterness and woe. And behold, as one looked, this martyr's visage blossomed into wantonness. The head was roguishly on a side, the still open lips wreathed in wickedly suggestive smiles, the sybaritic little dimple appeared in one cheek—-he was again the dancing priest, and jerked his head as before, mockingly, in the direction of so much cerebration, as they heard him say: "Ah, yes, yes, absolutely! But isn't there a——are there not—-sacraments of pleasure——you understand——"

Still, as we said, Hans Castorp's diminished friends and teachers were always well served when they could wrangle. They were in their element, whereas the personality was not. Though one might have two views of the rôle he played when wrangling was the order of the day. But on the other hand, when the scene changed from the sphere of the intellectual to the strictly earthly and practical, and dealt with questions, and in fields, where commanding natures prove their worth——then there were no two views possible. For then the others were undone, then they were cast in the shade, then they drew in their horns, and Peeperkorn came out, grasped the sceptre, arranged, decided, "settled." Was there any wonder, then, that he behaved so as to bring that state of things about, that he sought to override logomachy? He suffered, while it held sway, or if it held sway for long. But not in his vanity. Of that Hans Castorp felt assured. For vanity is not on the grand scale, nor is greatness vain. No,

Peeperkorn's need of reality had other grounds. It sprang, to put it baldly, from fear: from a characteristic infirmity of minds on the grand scale, from the sensitively and passionately cherished *point d'honneur* which Hans Castorp had struggled to explain to Herr Settembrini, describing it as in a sense a military trait.

"Ladies and gentlemen," the Dutchman said, and lifted his sea--captain's hand, with its nails like lance--heads, in entreaty and monition. "Ladies and gentlemen. Very good. Very. Asceticism. Indulgences. Lust of the flesh. By all means. Most important. Most debatable. But may I——I should like to——I fear we may commit a serious error. Are we not irresponsibly neglecting——one of our highest——" He drew in a deep breath.

"Ladies and gentlemen. This air——this characteristic thawing air, with its somewhat enervating breath, full of memories and promises of spring——we should not breathe it in to breathe it out in——-Really.——I must implore you. We must not. It is an insult. We should give it out only in the form of praise——of complete and utter——enough, ladies and gentlemen. I interrupt myself——in honour of——" He did, indeed, stand still, bent backward, shading his brows with his hat. They followed his gaze. "May I," said he, "may I draw your attention upwards——high in the sky, to that black, circling point against the blue, intensely blue, shading into black——that is a bird of prey. It is, if I am not mistaken——look, ladies and gentlemen, look, my child. It is an eagle. Most emphatically I call your attention——-look, it is no buzzard, no vulture, it is an eagle. If you were as far--sighted as my advancing age——yes, my child, advancing——my hair is white. You would see, as plainly as I do, the blunt pinions——it is a golden eagle. He circles directly overhead, he hovers, not a single beat of his wing——at a tremendous height in the blue, and with his keen, far--sighted eyes under the prominent bony structure of his brows he is peering earthwards. The eagle, ladies and gentlemen, the bird of Jove, king of his kind, the lion of the upper air. He has feathered gaiters, and a beak of iron, with a sudden hook at the end; claws of enormous strength, their talons curving inwards, the front ones overlapped by the long hinder one in an iron clutch. Look!" And he tried to put his long fingers in the posture of an eagle's claw. "Gaffer, why are you circling and spying up there?" He turned his head upwards again.

"Strike! Strike downward, with your iron beak into head and eyes, tear out the belly of the creature God gives you——-splendid! Splendid! Absolutely! Bury your talons in its entrails, make your beak drip with its blood——"

He had wrought himself to a pitch. All interest in Settembrini's and Naphta's antinomies was fled away. But the vision of the eagle remained——-even though they ceased talking about it, and devoted themselves to the programme they were carrying out under Mynheer's lead. They stopped at an inn to eat and drink——-quite out of hours, but with an appetite whetted by silent memories of the eagle. There was a feasting and a tippling, such as always went on where Mynheer was, in Dorf or Platz, or the inns at Claris and Klosters, whither they had gone in the little train. Under his tutelage, they tasted the "classic" gifts of life: coffee and cream with fresh bread, moist cheese and fragrant Alpine butter, heavenly--tasting with hot roasted chestnuts. They drank red Veltliner, to their hearts' content. Peeperkorn accompanied the impromptu meal with a fire of ejaculations; or incited Anton Karlowitsch Ferge to talk, that good--natured sufferer, who abhorred all high thoughts, but could hold forth so acceptably on the subject of the manufacture of rubber shoes in Russia. He described how the rubber mass was treated with sulphur and other substances, and the finished, glossy product subjected to a heat of over two hundred degrees to "vulcanize" it. He talked about the polar circle, for his business trips had more than once taken him thither; about the midnight sun, and eternal winter at the North Cape——-all this out of his scraggy throat, from beneath his bushy moustaches. Up there, he said, the steamers looked tiny, next the gigantic cliffs, on the steel--grey surface of the sea. And a yellow radiation was diffused over great tracts of the heavens——-the northern lights. The whole thing had seemed spooky to him, Anton Karlowitsch: the scene and himself to boot.

Thus Herr Ferge, the complete outsider, the only member of the group who stood detached from its complicated relationships. But now that we speak of these, it will be well to relate two conversations, two priceless conversations *à deux*, which our unheroic hero had, the first with Clavdia Chauchat, the second with the present companion of her travels; one in the hall, on an evening when the disturbing element lay above with a fever; the other on an afternoon by Mynheer's bedside.

It was half dark in the hall. The social activities had been brief and languid, the guests withdrew early to the evening cure or else took their wilful way into town, to dance and game. A single light burned in the hall ceiling——and in the adjoining salons dimness reigned. But Hans Castorp knew that Frau Chauchat, who had taken dinner without her protector, was not gone upstairs after it, but still lingered in the writingroom, so he did the same. He sat by the tiled hearth, in the back part of the hall, which was raised by one step from the rest, and separated by arches supported on two columns; in a rocking--chair such as that one Marusja had leaned back in, on the evening Joachim had spoken with her for the first and last time. He was, permissibly at this hour, smoking a cigarette.

She came, he heard her approaching step and the sound of her frock; fanning the air with a letter she held by one corner, and saying, in her Pribislav voice: "The porter has gone. Do give me a *timbre poste*."

She was wearing a thin dark silk this evening, cut round in the neck, with filmy sleeves finished by a buttoned cuff at the wrists. It was the cut he loved. She wore the pearls, they gleamed palely in the half light. He looked up into her Khirgiz face.

"*Timbre?*" he repeated, "I have none."

"No? *Tant pis pour vous*. Not prepared to do a lady a favour?" She pouted and shrugged her shoulders. "I am disappointed. You ought to be more precise and dependable. I imagined you having a compartment in your pocket--book, nice neat little sheets of all denominations."

"Why should I? I never write a letter. To whom should I write? I seldom do, even a card, and that is already stamped. I have no one to write to. I have no contact with the flat--land, it has fallen away. We have a folk--song that says: 'I am lost to the world'—-so it is with me."

"Well, then, lost soul, at least give me a *papiros*," said she, and sat down opposite him on a bench with a linen cushion, one leg over the other. She stretched out her hand. "With those, at least, you are provided." She took a cigarette, negligently, from the silver case he held out to her, and availed herself of his little pocket--device, the flame of which lighted up her face. The indolent "Give me a cigarette," the taking it without thanks, bespoke the spoiled, luxurious female; yet even more it betokened a human companionship and mutual "belonging," an unspoken give and take which came both thrilling and tender to his love--lorn sense.

He said: "Yes, I always have them. I am always provided, one must be. How should I get on without them? I have, as they say, a passion for them. To tell the truth, however, I am hardly a very passionate man, though I have my passions, phlegmatic ones."

"I am extraordinarily relieved," she said, breathing out, as she spoke, the smoke she had inhaled, "to hear that you are not a passionate man. But how should you be? You would have degenerated. Passionate—-that means to live for the sake of living. But one knows that you all live for sake of experience. Passion, that is self--forgetfulness. But what you all want is self--enrichment. *C'est ça.* You don't realize what revolting egoism it is, and that one day it will make you an enemy of the human race?"

"Well, well, well! Enemy of the human race! How can you make such a general statement, Clavdia? Have you something definite and personal in your mind, when you say we don't live for the sake of life, but for the sake of enriching ourselves?

Women don't usually moralize like that, so abstractly. Oh, morality, and that! A subject for Naphta and Settembrini to quarrel over. It belongs to the realm of the Great Confusion. Whether one lives for oneself, or for the sake of life—-one doesn't know oneself, no one can know that precisely and certainly. I mean, the limits are fluid. There is egoistic devotion, and there is devoted egoism. I think, on the whole, that it is as it is in love. Of course, it is probably immoral of me that I cannot very well attend to what you say to me about morality for being so happy that we are sitting here as we once did, and then never again, even since you came back. And that I may tell you there was never anything so lovely as the way those cuffs suit your hand, and the soft flowing silk your arm—your arm, that I know so well—-"

"I am going."

"Oh, please, please not! I promise to have proper regard for the circumstances, and the—-personalities."

"As one would expect, from a man without passion!"

"Yes, you see—-you mock at me when I—-and then, when I—-you say you will leave me—-"

"Pray speak a little more connectedly, if you expect me to understand you."

"So I am not to have any benefit from all your practice in guessing the meaning of disconnected sentences? Is that fair, I ask—-or I would if I did not know that it is not a matter of justice at all—-"

"No, justice is a phlegmatic passion. In contrast to jealousy—-when phlegmatic people are jealous, they always make themselves ridiculous."

"There—-ridiculous. Then grant me my phlegm. I repeat, how could I do without it?

For instance, how else could I have endured to wait so long?"

"I beg pardon?"

"*Aussi longtemps pour toi.*"

"*Voyons, mon ami.* I say no more about the form of address you persist in, in your folly. You will tire of it—-and then, I am not prudish, not an outraged middle--class housewife—-"

"No, for you are ill. Your illness gives you freedom. It makes you—-wait, I must hunt for the word—-it makes you—- *spirituelle!*"

"We shall speak of that another time. It was something else I meant. Something I demand to hear. You shall not pretend I had anything to do with your waiting—-if you did wait—-that I encouraged you to it, or even permitted it. You must admit explicitly that the opposite was the case—-"

"Certainly, Clavdia, with pleasure. You never asked me to wait, I did it on my own. I can quite understand your laying stress on the point—-"

"Even when you make admissions, there is always some impertinence about them. You are impertinent by nature—-not only with me, but in general—-God knows why. Your admiration, your very humility, is an impertinence. Don't think I can't see it. I ought not to speak with you at all, and certainly not when you dare to talk about waiting for me. It is inexcusable that you are still here. You should have been long ago at your work, *sur le chantier*, or wherever it was."

"Now that, Clavdia, is not *spirituel*—- it even sounds conventional. You are just talking. You can't mean it in Settembrini's sense—-and however else, then? I cannot take it seriously. I will not go off without permission, like my poor cousin, who, as you said he would, died because he tried to do service down below, and who knew himself, I suppose, that he would die, but preferred death to doing service up here any longer. Well, it was for that he was a soldier. But I am not. I am a civilian, for me it would be deserting the colours to do what he did, and go and serve the cause of progress down in the flat--land, despite what Behrens says. It would be the greatest disloyalty and ingratitude, to the illness, and its *spirituel* quality, and to my love for you, of which I bear scars both old and new——and to your arms I know so well, even admitting that it was in a dream, a highly *spirituel* dream, that I learned to know them, and that you had no responsibility for my dream, and were not bound by it, nor your freedom infringed on——"

She laughed, cigarette in mouth, so that the Tartar eyes became narrow slits; leaning back against the wainscoting, her hands resting on the bench on either side of her, one leg crossed over the other, and swinging,her foot in its patent--leather shoe.

"*Quelle générosité! Pauvre petit! Oh la la, vraiment*—— Precisely thus I have always imagined *un homme de génie!*"

"Don't, Clavdia. I am no *homme de génie*—— as little as I am a personality. Lord, no. But chance——call it chance——brought me up here to these heights of the spirit——you, of course, do not know that there is such a thing as alchemistic--hermetic pedagogy, transubstantiation, from lower to higher, ascending degrees, if you understand what I mean. But of course matter that is capable of taking those ascending stages by dint of outward pressure must have a little something in itself to start with. And what I had in me, as I quite clearly know, was that from long ago, even as a lad, I was familiar with illness and death, and had in the face of all common sense borrowed a lead pencil from you, as I did again on carnival night. But unreasoning love is *spirituel;* for death is the *spirituel* principle, the *res bina*, the *lapis philosophorum*, and the pedagogic principle too, for love of it leads to love of life and love of humanity. Thus, as I have lain in my loge, it has been revealed to me, and I am enchanted to be able to tell you all about it. There are two paths to

[745]

life: one is the regular one, direct, honest. The other is bad, it leads through death——that is the *spirituel* way."

"You are a quaint philosopher," she said. "I will not assert that I have understood all your involved German ideas; but it sounds human and good, and you are good, a good young man. You have truly behaved *en philosophe*, one must say that for you——"

"Too much *en philosophe* for your taste, eh, Clavdia?"

"No more impertinences. They become tiresome. That you waited for me was silly——uncalled for. But you are not angry, because you waited in vain?"

"It was hard, Clavdia, even for a man phlegmatic in his passions. Hard for me and hard of you to come back with him like that——for of course you knew through Behrens that I was here and waiting for you. But I have told you I regard it as a dream, what we had together, and I admit that you are free. And I waited after all not quite in vain, for here you are, we sit together as once we did, I can hear the piercing sweetness of your voice, known to my ear from so long ago; and beneath this flowing silk are your arms, your arms that I know——-even though upstairs there lies your protector, in a fever, the mighty Peeperkorn, whose pearls you wear——"

"And with whom, for your own profit and enrichment, you have struck up such a friendship."

"Do not grudge me it, Clavdia, Settembrini reproached me with it too. But that is conventional prejudice. The man is a boon——for God's sake, is he not a personality?

He is already old——yes; but even so, I could well understand how you as a woman could love him madly. You do love him madly?"

"All honour to thy philosophy, my little German Hänschen," she said, and lightly stroked his hair. "But I could not find it in my heart to speak to you of my love for him. It would not be *hu*—- man."

"Ah, why not, Clavdia? It is my belief that love of humanity begins where poorspirited people believe it leaves off. We can speak quite quietly of him. You love him passionately?"

She bent to toss her cigarette--end in the grate, and then sat with folded arms.

"He loves me," she said, "and his love makes me proud and grateful, and devoted to him. *Tu peux comprendre çela.* Or else you are not worthy the friendship he feels for you. His feeling forced me to follow and serve him. What else could I do? You may judge. Is it possible for any human being to disregard his love?"

"*Not* possible," Hans Castorp confirmed. "No, of course, it was out of the question. How could a woman bring herself to disregard his feeling, and his anguish over that feeling——to forsake him, as it were, in his Gethsemane——"

"*Tu n'es pas du tout stupide,*" said she, her slanting eyes fixed in a reverie. "You understand things. 'Anguish over the feeling——' "

"Not much understanding is needed to know that you had to follow him——though, or rather because, there must be much that is troubling in his love."

"*C'est exact.* Troubling. There is much care with him, you know, many difficulties." She had taken his hand, and played absently with the fingers——but suddenly she knitted her brows, she looked up and said: "*Mais——dis--moi: ce if est pas un peu——ordinaire, que nous parlons de lui, comme ça?*"

"No, Clavdia. Surely not. Far from it. Surely it is no more than human. You love the word, and I love to hear you say it, in your quaint pronunciation. My cousin Joachim did not like it——on military grounds. He thought it meant general licence and flabbiness; and in that sense, as an unlimited *guazzabuglio* of self--indulgence, I have my own suspicions of it, I confess. But in the sense of freedom, goodness, *esprit*, then it is great, we can freely apply it to our talk about Peeperkorn and the care and pain he causes you. Of course, they are the result of his sore spot——his dread of denying the feelings, that makes him love so much what he calls the classic gifts of life, the gift of Bacchus, liquid refreshment——we may speak of that in all reverence, for even in that weakness his scale is kingly and we shall lower neither him nor ourselves by speaking of it."

"It is not a question of us," she said. She had folded her arms again. "One would not be a woman if one were not willing to bear humiliation for the sake of a man like that, on the grand scale, as you say, when one is the object of his feeling and of his suffering from it."

"Absolutely, Clavdia. Well said. For then even the humiliation is on the grand scale, and from the height of it the woman can look down on poor creatures built on smaller lines, and speak to them with such contempt as was in your voice when you said, about the postage stamps: 'You ought to be more precise and dependable!' "

"You are hurt? You must not be. Let us put those feelings away, send them to Jericho. Do you agree? I have been wounded too sometimes——I will confess it, since we are sitting together like this. I have been angry with your phlegm, and your being such friends with him, on account of your egoistic craving for experience. Yet I was glad too, and grateful for the respect you paid him. You were loyal; if you were a bit impertinent too, after all I could make allowance for that."

"Very kind of you."

She looked at him. "You are incorrigible, it seems. And certainly I can't quite tell how much *esprit* you have——but deep you are, a deep young man. Well, very good, one can do with it, and be friends. Shall we be friends, shall we make a league——not against but for him? Will you give me your hand on it? I am often frightened.——

Sometimes I am afraid of the solitude with him——the inward solitude, *tu sais*—— he is——frightening; sometimes I am afraid something may happen to him——it makes me shudder.——I should be glad to feel I had someone beside me. *En fin*— if you care to know—that was why I came back here with him— *chez toi.*"

They sat knee to knee, he with his rocking-chair tipped toward her, she on her bench. Her last words were breathed close to his face, and she pressed his hand as she spoke. He said: "To me? Oh, Clavdia! That is beautiful beyond words! You came back to me with him? And yet will you say my waiting was silly and wrong and fruitless? It would be very inept of me to refuse, not to know how to value your friendship, friendship with me for his sake—"

She kissed him on the mouth. It was a Russian kiss, the kind that is exchanged in that spreading, soulful land, at high religious feasts, as a seal of love. But when a notoriously "deep" young man and a lady still young, and of such insinuating charm, exchange it, we are involuntarily reminded of Dr. Krokowski's ingenious if not wholly unobjectionable method of treating the subject of love, in that slightly fluctuating sense, so that no one was ever quite sure whether it was earthly or heavenly, spiritual or fleshly love he had in mind. Are we so treating it, or were Clavdia Chauchat and Hans Castorp, when they exchanged their Russian kiss? But what will the reader say if we simply refuse to go into the question? To try to make a clean-cut distinction between the passionate and the soulful—that would, no doubt, be analytical. But we feel that it would also be inept—to borrow Hans Castorp's useful word—and certainly not in the least "genial." For what would "clean-cut" be? The subject is so equivocal, the limits so fluctuating. We make bold to laugh at the idea. Is it not well done that our language has but one word for all kinds of love, from the holiest to the most lustfully fleshly? All ambiguity is therein resolved: love cannot but be physical, at its furthest stretch of holiness; it cannot be impious, in its utterest fleshliness. It is always itself, as the height of shrewd "geniality" as in the depth of passion; it is organic sympathy, the touching sense-embrace of that which is doomed to decay. In the most raging as in the most reverent passion, there must be *caritas*. The meaning of the word varies? In God's name, then, let it vary; That it does so makes it living, makes it human; it would be a regrettable lack of "depth" to trouble over the fact.

So while these youthful lips meet in their Russian kiss, let us darken our little stage and change the scene. For now, instead of the dimness of the hall we have the rather pensive light of a declining spring day in the season of melting snows; and our hero is seated in his wonted place at the bedside of Mynheer Peeperkorn, in friendly and respectful converse with that great man. Frau Chauchat, after the tea hour, at which she had appeared alone, as at the previous three meals, had gone shopping in the Platz, and Hans Castorp announced himself for his usual visit to the Dutchman. First of all to show him attention and help him pass the time; but also to be edified by the motions of the great man's personality. In short, out of "varying" motives, varying as life varies. Peeperkorn laid aside the *Telegraaf* and tossed the horn-rimmed eyeglasses upon it. He reached his visitor a broad, sea-captain's hand, and his thick chapped lips, on which sat a distressed expression, moved vaguely. Red wine and coffee were as usual to hand; the coffee things stood on a chair, stained brown from recent use—Mynheer had taken his regular afternoon drink, hot and strong, with sugar and cream, and was in a perspiration. His face with its fringe of white hair was flushed, and little beads stood on brow and upper lip.

"I am sweating somewhat," he said. "Come in, young man, come in. On the contrary. Sit down. It is a sign of weakness when one takes a hot drink and sweats thereafter. Will you—-quite right—-a handkerchief—thank you." The flush soon faded and gave place to the yellowish pallor which was Mynheer's facial *teint* after a bad attack. The fever had been severe this morning, and in all three stages, the cold, the hot, the moist; Peeperkorn's little eyes looked tired beneath the lined, masklike brow. He said: "It is—-by all means, young man. I would like to express my—the word is—-

Positively. Appreciative—-very kind of you to visit an ailing old man—-"

"Not at all, Mynheer Peeperkorn. I am the one to be grateful, for permission to sit here a little; I get a great deal more out of it than you—I assure you my motives are not altruistic. But what sort of description is that of yourself—-an ailing old man? It would never occur to anyone to call you that. It gives an entirely false picture."

"Very good," responded Mynheer. He closed his eyes for a second or so, leaning his majestic head against the pillows, the chin raised, the fingers with their long nails folded on his kingly chest, the muscles of which showed beneath the *tricot* shirt. "You are right, young man, or, rather, you mean it well. I am sure. It was pleasant yesterday—-yes, yesterday afternoon, at that hospitable spot—-the name of which I have now forgotten where we ate the excellent salami and scrambled eggs—-and that sound native wine—-"

"It was gorgeous," Hans Castorp confirmed. "We certainly are filled up—-the Berghof chef would not have been pleased to see us putting it in—-one and all; he'd have felt insulted. That was genuine salami, the real thing; Herr Settembrini ate it with tears in his eyes. He is a patriot, you must know, a democratic patriot. He has consecrated his burgher's pike on the altar of humanity, so that salami may be taxed at the Brenner frontier."

"That is no matter," Peeperkorn declared. "He is most chivalrous and courteous and very affable in conversation—-a gallant gentleman, though obviously unable to change his clothing with any frequency."

"None at all," said Hans Castorp, "none at all! I know him well, have been friendly with him for a long time; he was kind enough to take me up, because he found I was a 'delicate child of life.' That is an expression we use between us, the sense of which is not obvious without the context. He has taken much pains to influence me for my good. But never, summer or winter, have I seen him wear anything but those check trousers and that threadbare double--breasted coat. He wears the old things with great dignity, there *is* something gallant about him, I agree with you there. The way he does it is a triumph

[751]

over poverty—-I like better to see it than little Naphta's elegance, that always seems suspicious—-a work of darkness, as it were, and he gets the money for it in some hole--and--corner way, I understand."

"A chivalrous and affable gentleman," repeated Peeperkorn, passing over Hans Castorp's remarks about little Naphta. "But also—-forgive me the reservation—-not free from prejudice. Madame, my companion, has no great opinion of him—-you may have seen. She feels little sympathy—-no doubt because she perceives the same prejudice to exist toward herself. Not a word, young man. I am far from—-comment on Herr Settembrini and your friendly feelings for him—-No more! I should not think of saying that in any point—-he has failed in any respect in knightly courtesy. My dear friend—-irreproachable, very. But there is—-a line drawn, a certain—-a withdrawal—-which makes comprehensible Madame Chauchat's—-"

"Feeling against him. Perfectly natural. Perfectly justified. Pardon me, Mynheer Peeperkorn, for taking the words out of your mouth. I venture to do so in the consciousness that you will not misunderstand me. When one thinks how women are made (you smile, to hear a person of my youth and inexperience making general observations on this subject)—-how dependent a woman's feeling for a man is upon his feeling for her—-it is not surprising. Women, if you will permit me so to express myself, are creatures not of action but of reaction; they do not initiate, they are inactive in the sense that they are passive. May I, even at the risk of being tiresome, try to follow that a little further? Woman, so far as I have been able to observe, regards herself, in a love--affair, as the object. She lets it come; she does not make a free choice, she only chooses on the basis of the man's having chosen, and even then, even then, I must repeat, her choice is suspect, it is prejudiced by the very fact that she has been chosen—-provided, of course, the man is not *too* poor a specimen, and even so—-Good Lord, what unalloyed drivel I'm talking! But when one is young, everything seems new and astonishing. You ask a woman: 'Do you love him?' And she tells you: 'He loves me so much!' and rolls her eyes up, or else rolls them down. Imagine an answer like that from one of us—-if you will pardon me putting us in the same category. Perhaps there are men who would answer like that, but they are poorspirited creatures—-their women wear the breeches, if you will forgive the expression. I should like to know what kind of self--appraisement is at the bottom of the feminine answer. Is it that the woman thinks she owes a man boundless devotion merely because he has conferred the favour of his choice upon so lowly a creature? Or does she see in the man's love an infallible sign of her personal excellence? I've often asked myself these questions, when I have been thinking quietly alone."

"Primitive—-traditional mysteries you touch on there, young man, applying your glib little phrases to the sacred conditions of our existence," responded Peeperkorn.

"Man is intoxicated by his desire, woman demands and expects to be intoxicated by it. Hence our holy duty of feeling, hence the shame in unfeelingness, in powerlessness to awaken the woman to desire. Will you take a glass of red wine with me? I will drink, for I am thirsty. I have given out a considerable amount of water to--day."

"Thanks, Mynheer Peeperkorn. I do not usually take anything at this hour; but I am always ready to drink a swallow or so to your health."

"Then take the wineglass. There is only one, I will use the water--glass. It won't insult this simple wine to drink it out of an ordinary tumbler—-" He poured out the wine, with Hans Castorp's help, as his hand trembled slightly, and drank thirstily, as though it had been water.

"That is refreshing," he said. "Won't you have some more? No? Permit me to fill my glass"—-the second time, he spilled some wine; the turned--over sheet was stained with dark--red spots. "I repeat," he said, with one lancelike finger reared up, "I repeat, that therein lies our duty, our sacred duty to feel. Feeling, you understand, is the masculine force that rouses life. Life slumbers. It needs to be roused, to be awakened to a drunken marriage with divine feeling. For feeling, young man, is godlike. Man is godlike, in that he feels. He is the feeling of God. God created him in order to feel through him. Man is nothing but the organ through which God consummates his marriage with roused and intoxicated life. If man fails in feeling, it is blasphemy; it is the surrender of His masculinity, a cosmic catastrophe, an irreconcilable horror——" He drank.

"Permit me to relieve you of your glass," Hans Castorp said. "I find your train of thought highly edifying, Mynheer Peeperkorn. You are developing a theology there, in which you ascribe to man a highly honourable, if perhaps rather a one--sided religious function. There is, if I may say so, a certain austerity in your conception, it has its alarming side. Pardon me. All religious austerity is naturally somewhat alarming to people who are built on modest lines. I have no thought of criticizing the conception, I should like simply to return to your remark about certain prejudices, which, according to your observations, Herr Settembrini has on the subject of Madame. I have known Herr Settembrini for some time, more than a year, for years, in fact. And I can assure you that his prejudices, in so far as they exist, are in no case of a petty or bourgeois character. It would be absurd to think so. It can only be a question of prejudice in a general sense, impersonal, relating to certain pedagogic principles, which, in my character as a delicate child of life, Herr Settembrini has been at pains to——but that would lead us too far. It is a very complex subject, into which I could not——"

"And you love Madame?" Mynheer suddenly asked. He turned toward his visitor that kingly countenance, with the sore, writhen mouth and the pale little eyes under the arabesque of lines on the brow.

Hans Castorp started. He stammered: "I——that is——I feel great respect for Frau Chauchat, certainly, in her character as——"

"Pray!" said Peeperkorn, stretching out his hand with that gesture which held back the flow of words. Having thus made a free space for what he was about to say, "Let me," he went on, "let me repeat, that

I am far from reproaching this Italian gentleman with any actual offence against the rules of chivalry. I levelled this reproach against no one——no one. But it occurs to me——Understand me, young man, I am gratified, very. Your presence rejoices my heart. At the same time, I say to myself: your acquaintance with Madame is older than ours. You were a companion of her earlier sojourn up here. And she is a woman of the rarest charms, and I am only an ailing old man. How does it happen——to--day, as I was unable to accompany her, she goes down unattended to the village to make purchases——there is no harm in that, none at all. But doubtless——am I then to ascribe it to the——what was it you said?——the pedagogic principles of Signor Settembrini that you——I beg you not to misunderstand me——"

"Not at all, Mynheer Peeperkorn. Absolutely not. Not in the least. I act independently. On the contrary, Herr Settembrini has even taken occasion to——I regret to see that you have spilled wine on your sheets, Mynheer Peeperkorn. May I not——we usually put salt on while the spots are fresh——"

"It does not matter," said Peeperkorn, fixing his guest with his glance.

Hans Castorp changed colour. He said, with a hollow smile: "Everything up here is out of the ordinary. The spirit of the place, if I may put it so, is not conventional. The sufferer, whether man or woman, is privileged. The laws of chivalry are thus forced rather into the background. You are for the moment indisposed, Mynheer Peeperkorn, an acute indisposition. Your companion *is* relatively well. I think I do as Madame would wish in representing her here beside you, in her absence——in so far as there can be any talk of representing her, ha ha!——instead of representing you with her and offering to attend her into the village. How indeed should I come to be playing the cavalier to Madame? I have no title to the position, no mandate, and I have, I must admit, a strong sense of mine and thine. In short, I find my position is correct, in face of the general situation, and also the very genuine feelings I entertain for you, Mynheer

Peeperkorn. You asked me, I believe, a question, and I think what I have said should be a satisfactory answer to it."

"A very amiable answer," Peeperkorn responded. "I listen with involuntary pleasure, young man, to your fluent little phrases. Your tongue runs on, it springs over stock and stone, and rounds off all the sharp corners. But satisfactory——no. Your answer does not quite satisfy me——you must forgive me for disappointing you. Austere, my dear friend——you used the word with reference to some of my remarks just now. But in yours too I seem to note a certain austerity, they seem a little stiff and forced, and not in harmony with your nature, though I am acquainted with the phenomenon through your bearing in one respect and therefore recognize it now. I mean the formal manner you assume toward Madame——and toward no one else in our little circle, on our walks and excursions. And of which you owe me an explanation. It is a duty, an obligation. I am not mistaken. I have confirmed my observation too many times, and it is unlikely it has not been remarked by others as well——with the difference that these others may perhaps——or even probably——-possess a key which I do not."

Mynheer spoke with uncommon precision and clarity this afternoon, despite the exhaustion consequent upon his fever. There was scarcely a trace of his usual rhapsodic style. He half sat in his bed, his powerful shoulders and splendid head turned toward his guest; one arm was stretched out over the coverlet, with the freckled, sea--captain's hand erect at the end of the woollen sleeve, forming the ring of precision. The lance--tipped fingers were aloft. And his lips formed the words, as precisely, as "plastically," as Herr Settembrini himself could have wished, and rolled the *r* in his throat in words like probably and austerity.

"You smile," he went on. "You seem to be busy searching the tablets of your memory and finding them blank. But there can be no doubt that you know what I mean. I do not say that you do not sometimes address Madame, or that you do not answer her, as occasion arises. But I repeat, you do so with a definite constraint, an evasiveness, and, in fact, an avoidance of one certain form. One gets the impression that there has been a one--sided wager; it is as though you had eaten a philippina with Madame, and made up that you will not address her with the usual form of address. In short, you never use the third person plural. You never say *She* to Madame."

"But Mynheer Peeperkorn—-how absurd—-what sort of philippina would that be?"

"May I mention the circumstance—-you are surely aware of it yourself—-that you have just grown pale to the lips?"

Hans Castorp did not look up. He bent over and busied himself with the red stains on the sheet. "It had to come to that, I suppose," he thought. "It had to come out.—-

And I suppose I even helped it on myself. I can see that now. Did I really go pale? It may be. For now we've certainly come to grips. What will happen? Shall I keep on lying? It might still go—-but I won't. I'll just sit tight a few minutes and look at these blood--stains—-I mean wine--stains—-on the sheet." They were both silent. The stillness lasted some two or three minutes—-and gave evidence how much under such circumstances these very small units of time can expand.

It was Pieter Peeperkorn who first spoke. "On the evening when I first had the pleasure of making your acquaintance," he said, beginning in a singsong tone, and letting his voice fall at the end, as though embarked on a long recitative, "we had a little celebration, sat very late eating and drinking and making merry, and then, in an elevated mood, of spirit free and unrestrained, arm in arm we sought our beds. As we parted, here at my door, the idea came to me to ask you to salute Madame on the brow, as a good friend from her former visit up here. You bluntly refused, rejected the idea on the ground that it would be preposterous. You will not deny that the expression itself demanded an explanation—-an explanation for which you have remained until now in my debt. Are you willing to absolve yourself of it?"

"Ah, so he noticed that too," Hans Castorp thought, and bent closer over the winestains, one of which he scratched with his middle finger. "The fact is I suppose I wanted him to notice it, or I should not have said it. But what to say now? My heart is pounding. Will there be an exhibition of royal rage? Perhaps I'd best keep an eye on his fist, he may be holding it over me already. Certainly I am in a fine position—between the devil and the deep blue sea, as it were."

And suddenly he felt his right wrist grasped by the hand of Peeperkorn.

"Hullo!" he thought. "Why should I be sitting here with my tail between my legs?

Have I done him any injury? Not in the least. Let him talk to the man in Daghestan before he does to me. And after that somebody else, and so on. And then me. And what has he to complain of about me? Nothing, so far. Then why should my heart be pounding like this? It is high time I sit up and look him in the eye—with all due respect to his personality, of course."

He did so. The great man's face was yellow, the eyes pale beneath the forehead's heavy folds, a bitter expression sat on the wounded lips. They looked each other in the eye, the splendid old man and the insignificant young one, and Peeperkorn continued to hold Hans Castorp by the wrist. At last he said, gently: "You were Clavdia's lover when she was here before."

Hans Castorp bowed his head once more but lifted it again straightway, took a deep breath, and began: "Mynheer Peeperkorn! It is in the highest degree repugnant to me to tell you a lie. I am searching for a means of avoiding it, but this is not easy. I should be boasting if I say yes, lying if I say no. Let me explain in what sense this is to be taken. I lived a long time, oh, a very long time in this house with Clavdia—I beg pardon, with the present companion of your travels—before making her acquaintance. Our relations—or, rather, my relation to her was never the social one; I can only say of it that its beginnings are shrouded in darkness. In my thoughts I have never named Clavdia but with the thou—and never in reality either. For on the evening when, casting off certain pedagogic restraints of which we were speaking, I made bold to approach her, upon a pretext furnished me by the long--ago past, it was carnival. It was an evening of masks and freedom, an irresponsible hour, when the thou was in force, and by the power of magic and dreams, somehow had—full sway. And—it was also the eve of Clavdia's departure."

"Full sway," repeated Peeperkorn. "You have put that very—-very—-well." He released Hans Castorp's hand, and began with his own huge ones to massage both sides of his own face, eyes, cheeks, and chin. Then he folded his hands upon the winebespotted sheet, and laid his head on the left shoulder, the one toward his guest, with the effect that his face was lightly turned away.

"I have given you the best answer I could, Mynheer Peeperkorn," Hans Castorp said. "I have tried to say neither too much nor too little. I was concerned to let you see that it is in a way open to us to count that evening—-when the thou had full sway, and it was the eve of Clavdia's departure—-or not to count it. It was an extraordinary occasion, almost outside the calendar, intercalated, so to speak, a twenty--ninth of February. It would have been only half a lie if I had simply denied the truth of what you said."

Peeperkorn made no answer.

"I preferred," Hans Castorp began again, after a pause, "to tell you the truth, rather than run the risk of losing your favour, which, I openly admit, would be a sensible loss to me, I may say a blow, a real blow, comparable to the one I received when Frau Chauchat returned hither as the companion of your travels. I have risked letting this happen, because I have long wished and hoped that there might be understanding between myself and the man for whom I entertained feelings of the most extraordinary respect and reverence. It seemed finer, more 'human' to me—you know that is Clavdia's favourite word, and how she pronounces it, in that enchanting, husky drawl of hers——than silence and dissimulation; and in that sense a weight was lifted from my heart when you put your question."

No answer.

"One thing more, Mynheer Peeperkorn," Hans Castorp went on. "There was another thing that made me wish to make a clean breast of it to you: and that was the personal experience I had with the irritating effect of uncertainty, being let in for suspicions that could be neither confirmed nor dismissed. You know now who it was——before this present relationship was established which it would be absurd of me not to respect——with whom Clavdia spent——or experienced, or committed——that twenty-ninth of February. It is clear to you now. But for my part I have never been able to know——though of course I realized that anyone in my situation has to reckon with the past——by which I really mean predecessors——and though I also realized that Hofrat Behrens is an amateur portrait-painter, and had, in the course of many sittings, made a capital portrait of her, with a treatment of the skin so very lively and realistic that——between ourselves——it gave me very seriously to think. I have tormented myself no end with that riddle, and still do."

"You still love her?" Peeperkorn asked, without changing his position, his face still turned away. The large room fell more and more into twilight.

"You will pardon me, Mynheer Peeperkorn," answered Hans Castorp, "but my feeling for you, which is one of the highest respect and admiration, will not permit me to speak of my feeling for the present companion of your travels,"

"And does she——" Peeperkorn asked, with lowered voice, "does she still return your feeling?"

"I do not say," answered Hans Castorp, "I do not say that she ever returned it. That is scarcely credible. We were touching upon this subject earlier in the afternoon, when we spoke of the responsive nature of women. There is nothing much about me to fall in love with. I am not built on a grand scale, as you can see. The possibility of—-of a twenty--ninth of February could only be ascribed to feminine receptivity on the basis of the man's choice already made. I must say that when Í refer to myself as a man, it seems to me a sort of self--advertising and bad taste—-but at all events, Clavdia is a woman."

"She was responsive to your feeling," murmured Peeperkorn, with wry lips.

"How much more so to yours," said Hans Castorp. "And in all probability to many another. One has to face that, when—-"

"Stop!" Peeperkorn said, still turned away, but with a gesture of the palm toward his interlocutor. "Is it not rather—-common—-of us to talk about her?"

"I don't feel it so, Mynheer Peeperkorn. I think I can set your mind at rest on that point. These are human topics we are treating of; human in the sense that they have to do with freedom and the *spirituel*—- you must pardon me if I use a rather ambiguous terminology, but I needed the expression lately, and made it my own."

"Very good, go on," Peeperkorn said in a low voice.

Hans Castorp spoke in a low voice, too, and sat on the edge of his chair by the bed, bent toward the kingly old man, his hands between his knees.

"For she is certainly a most *spirituel* being," he said, "and the husband beyond the Caucasus—-you know, of course, that she has a husband beyond the Caucasus—-gives her her freedom, whether out of stupidity or intelligence I don't know, I don't know the chap. But it is a good thing he does, for it is her illness grants it to her—-and whoever falls into our situation will do well to follow his example, and not complain, either of the past or of the future."

"You don't complain?" asked Peeperkorn, and turned his face. It seemed ashen in the twilight, the pale, weary eyes stared out beneath the great folds of brow, the large chapped lips stood half open, like the mouth of a tragic mask.

"I hardly thought it was a question of myself," Hans Castorp answered modestly.

"What I meant was that you should not complain, nor deprive me of your friendship because of events in the past. That is what concerns me at this hour."

"But aside from that," Peeperkorn said, "I must involuntarily have been the cause of much suffering on your part."

"If you put the question," responded Hans Castorp, "and if I answer yes, my answer must not be taken to mean that I did not know how to value the enormous privilege of knowing you; for that privilege was indissolubly bound up with the suffering."

"I thank you, young man, I thank you. I value the courtesy of your little phrases. But, aside from our acquaintance——"

"It is difficult," Hans Castorp said, "to divorce the two; and the idea does not commend itself to me that I should divorce them in order to be free to reply in the affirmative to your question. The very fact that it was a personality like you in whose company Clavdia returned could only make more distressing and involved her coming back in the company of anybody whatever. It gave me a quarter of an hour, I assure you, and still does, that I do not deny; I have purposely kept as much as I could to the positive element, that is my sincere feeling of honour and reverence for you, Mynheer Peeperkorn——in which there mingled a spice of malice against your mistress; for women are never at ease when their lovers come to terms."

"True enough," Peeperkorn said, and ran his hand over mouth and chin to conceal a smile, as though he were afraid Madame Chauchat might see it. Hans Castorp too smiled discreetly——and then they both nodded, in mutual understanding.

"This little revenge," went on Hans Castorp, "was granted me at the end, because, so far as I personally am concerned, I have a quarrel after all, not with Clavdia, not with you, Mynheer Peeperkorn, but with my lot in general, my destiny. I will try to tell you about it, in so far as I can, now that I am secure in the honour of your confidence, and in this altogether exceptional and extraordinary twilight hour."

"Pray do so," said Peeperkorn, courteously, and Hans Castorp went on.

"I have been up here a long time, Mynheer Peeperkorn, years. How long I hardly know myself, but it has been years of my life. My cousin, to visit whom I came up, in the first instance, was a soldier, an upright and honourable soul, but that was no help to him—he died, and left me, and I remained here alone. I was no soldier, but a civilian, I had a profession, as you may have heard, a good, two-fisted job, which is even supposed to do its share in drawing together the nations of the earth—but somehow it did not draw me. I admit this freely; but the reasons for it I cannot describe otherwise than to say that they are veiled in obscurity, the same obscurity that envelops the origin of my feeling for Madame your mistress—I call her that expressly to show that I am not thinking of undermining the situation as it exists—my feeling for Clavdia Chauchat, and my intimate sense of her being, which I have had since the first moment her eyes met mine and bewitched me, enchanted me, you understand, beyond all reason. For love of her, in defiance of Herr Settembrini, I declared myself for the principle of unreason, the *spirituel* principle of disease, under whose ægis I had already, in reality, stood for a long time back; and I remained up here, I no longer know precisely how long. I have forgotten, broken with, everything, my relatives, my calling, all my ideas of life. When Clavdia went away, I waited here for her return, so that now I am wholly lost to life down below, and dead in the eyes of my friends. That is what I meant when I spoke of my destiny, and said there might be some justice in a complaint over my present state. I have read a story—no, I saw it in the theatre: a good-natured youth, a soldier like my cousin, who comes to know a charming gipsy—charming she was, with a flower behind her ear, a wild and fatal creature, who so bewitches him that he goes off altogether, sacrifices everything to her, deserts the colours, joins the smugglers, dishonours himself in every way. Well, when he has got so far, she for her part has had enough of him, and takes up with a matador, a forceful personality with a magnificent baritone voice. The end of it all is that the little soldier, white as a sheet, shirt open at the throat, stabs his mistress with his knife in front of the circus—-which, after all, she brought upon herself. It is rather a pointless story after all: how did I come to think of it?"

Mynheer Peeperkorn, at mention of the knife, had shifted his position in the bed, with a quick motion to one side, turning his face toward his guest, and looking him piercingly in the eye. Now he pulled himself to a more comfortable posture, supporting himself on one elbow, and said: "Well, young man, I have listened to you, and I have the whole picture. On my side, let me make you an honourable declaration. Were my hair not white, my limbs not racked with fever, you would see me ready to give you satisfaction, man to man, weapon to weapon, for the injury I unwittingly did you, and that which my companion added to it, for which likewise it is mine to atone. Positively, my friend—-you would see me at your service. But as matters lie, you must let me make a different proposal. It is this: I recall an exalted moment, when our acquaintance was very young, when I felt myself pleasantly impressed by your native parts, and stood ready to offer you the brotherly thou; but then perceived that the moment was premature. Very good. I stand again to--day at that moment, I return to it, I declare that the period of probation has come to an end. Young man, we are brothers. Your phrase was that the thou had full sway—-very good, let ours likewise have full sway, let us give free rein to brotherly feeling. The satisfaction which age and incapacity prevent me from giving you, I offer in another form, in the form of a brotherly alliance, such as one forms against a third party, against the world, against all and sundry; let us swear it to each other in the name of our feeling for somebody. Take your wineglass, young man, I will use the water--glass again, it does the crude new wine no shame——" With his trembling hand he filled the glasses, Hans Castorp hastening to assist him.

"Take it," repeated Peeperkorn, "take my arm, let us drink so, let us drink it out——positively, young man. Very. Here is my hand. *Art thou satisfied?"*

"That is no word for it, of course, Mynheer Peeperkorn," said Hans Castorp. He had not found it easy to drink out the full glass at a draught; he spilled a little and dried his knee with his handkerchief. "I might better say that I am immensely happy, and can hardly grasp how this has all come about, it is like a dream. What an immense honour for me! How I have deserved it I scarcely know, certainly in no active sense. It is not surprising that at first it seems entirely too bold, and I doubt if I shall be able to fetch it out——especially in Clavdia's presence, who is not quite so likely to be pleased with the new arrangement, all at once."

"Leave that to me," responded Peeperkorn; "the rest is a matter of practice and habit. Go, now, young man. Leave me, my son. The night has fallen, our loved one may return any moment, and a meeting between you just now would perhaps not be quite well--advised."

"Farewell, Mynheer Peeperkorn," Hans Castorp said, and rose. "Yes, it has grown dark. I can imagine Herr Settembrini coming in suddenly and turning on the light, to let reason and convention reign——it is a weakness of his. Good--bye until to--morrow. I leave you, so proud, so joyful, as I could never have dreamed it was possible for me to be. And now you will have at least three good days, and free of fever, and that rejoices me as much as though it were myself. Brother, good--night!"

Mynheer Peeperkorn (Conclusion)

A waterfall is always an attractive goal for an excursion. We scarcely know how to explain why Hans Castorp, with all his native love of falling water, had never visited the picturesque cascade in the valley of the Fluela. His cousin's strong sense of duty to the service had probably prevented him, during Joachim's time; the latter's purposeful attitude had tended to confine their activities to the close vicinity of the Berghof. But even since that time—-if we except the winter excursions on skis—-Hans Castorp's relations with the mountain scenery had been extremely conservative, not to say monotonous. The young man found a curious pleasure in the contrast between the limitations of his physical sphere and the broad scope of his mental operations. However, when it was proposed that his little group of seven people should make a driving excursion to the waterfall, he readily assented.

It was the blissful month of May, oft celebrated in the pleasant little ditties of the flat--land. Up here the air was fresh, the temperature scarcely ingratiating; but at least the snow was gone. It might, indeed, snow again; during the last few days there had been flurries of gigantic flakes, but it did not lie, it only made wet. The winter drifts had wasted away, they were gone, save for vestiges here and there; and the green slopes, the open paths, tempted the spirit to rove.

The group had been less socially occupied of late weeks owing to the illness of its ruling spirit, the prepotent Pieter Peeperkorn. His fever refused to yield to the beneficent working of the climate or the skilled ministrations of so excellent a doctor as Hofrat Behrens. He was obliged to spend much time in bed, not only on the days when the quartan fever held sway, but on others too. There was trouble with his liver and spleen, Behrens told those who tended him; the digestion was not what it should be—-in short, the Hofrat did not neglect to point out that the condition seemed to indicate a danger of chronic debility, not to be ignored.

Mynheer Peeperkorn had presided at only one evening festivity in all these weeks; and the group had taken but one short walk. Hans Castorp was rather relieved than otherwise at this state of affairs; for the pledge he had drunk with Clavdia Chauchat's protector made him difficulties, in general conversation, of the same kind he had to deal with in the case of Frau Chauchat herself, namely the avoidance of the formal mode of address—-as though, as Peeperkorn said, they had eaten a philippina together. He was fertile in expedients to get round it or simply leave it out; nevertheless, the favour accorded him by Peeperkorn had doubled his present dilemma.

But now the excursion to the waterfall was the order of the day; Peeperkorn himself had arranged it, and felt equal to the effort. It was the third day after the usual attack, and he announced that he wished to take advantage of it. He did not, indeed, appear at the early meals of the day, but took them, in company with Madame Chauchat, in their salon, as they often did of late. But Hans Castorp received word, through the lame concierge, to be ready for a drive an hour after the midday meal, and further, to communicate with Ferge and Wehsal, Settembrini and Naphta, and to engage two landaus for three o'clock.

Accordingly, at this hour they assembled before the portal of the Berghof—-Hans Castorp, Ferge and Wehsal. and awaited the pair from the *appartements de luxe;* whiling the time by holding out lumps of sugar on the palms of their hands, for the horses to nip them up with thick, moist black lips. Their companions appeared with no great delay on the threshold; Peeperkorn's kingly head seemed narrower; he lifted his hat as he stood in a long, rather shabby ulster, by Madame Chauchat's side, and his lips shaped a vague form of greeting to the company in general. Then he descended and shook hands with the three gentlemen, who met him at the foot of the steps. He laid his left hand on Hans Castorp's shoulder, saying: "Well, young man, and how goes it, my son?"

"Topping, thanks, I hope it's mutual," responded the young man.

The sun shone, the day was beautiful and bright. But they had done well to don overcoats, driving would be cool. Madame Chauchat too wore a warm belted mantle of some woolly stuff with a pattern of large checks, and a small fur about her shoulders. The rim of her felt hat was turned down at one side by the olive--green veil she wore bound under her chin; an effect so charming that it was actual pain to most of the beholders——Ferge being the only man there not in love with her. To his disinterested state was probably due the temporary advantage he presently enjoyed, of being selected to sit opposite Mynheer and Madame in the first landau, while Hans Castorp mounted with Wehsal into the second, catching as he did so a mocking smile that for a moment visited Frau Chauchat's face. The others would be called for at their lodgings. The Malayan servant joined the party with a capacious basket, from the top of which protruded the necks of two winebottles. He bestowed it under the back seat of the first landau, took his place by the coachman on the box and folded his arms; the horses started up, and the carriages, with the brakes against their wheels, drove down the drive.

Wehsal had seen Frau Chauchat's smile, and expressed himself on the subject to his companion, showing his bad teeth as he talked.

"Did you see," he asked, "how she was laughing at you for having to drive alone with me? Yes, yes, a man like me is always fair game. Do you find it so disgusting to have to sit next to me?"

"Pull yourself together, Wehsal, and stop talking in that poor--spirited way," Hans Castorp admonished him. "Women are for ever smiling, at anything, just for the sake of smiling; there is no sense in attending to it. Why do you always cry yourself down?

You have your advantages and your disadvantages, like the rest of us. For instance, you can play out of the *Midsummer Night's Dream*, and it's not everybody who can. Will you play for us again soon' "

"Yes, you think you can talk to me condescendingly, like that," retorted the wretched soul, "and you don't know what cheek there is in your consolation and how it just lowers me the more. You have the right to, though. You are laughing out of the wrong corner of your mouth now; but once you were in the seventh heaven, and felt her arms about your neck——oh, God, it burns me in the pit of my stomach when I think of it—-and you are conscious of all you have had, when you look down on me and my torments and think what a beggarly wretch I am."

"You haven't a pretty way of expressing yourself, Wehsal. I don't need to conceal my opinion of it, since you reproach me with being cheeky: it is really very repulsive and probably intentional on your part; you lay yourself out to be disgusting and humiliate yourself, the whole time. Are you really so desperately in love with her?"

"Fearfully," answered Wehsal, with a head--shake. "Words cannot express what I have had to endure from my craving for her. I wish I could say it will be the death of me——but the trouble is, one can neither die nor live. It was a bit better while she was away, I was gradually beginning to forget her. But since she came back, and I have her daily before my eyes, I get attacks——I bite my hand and strike about me, and am beside myself. Such things ought not to be; yet one cannot wish not to have them. Whoever is in that state cannot wish not to be, it would be like wishing not to live, because it has bound itself up with life. What good would it do to die? Afterwards——afterwards, yes, gladly. In her arms it would be bliss. But before——no; it would be preposterous, because life is longing, and longing is life——it cannot go against itself, that is the cursed catch in the game. Even when I say cursed, it is only a way of talking, as though I were somebody else, for in myself I cannot feel it so. There are many kinds of torture, Castorp, and whichever one you are under, your one desire and longing is to be free of it. But the torture of fleshly lust is the only one you can never wish to be free of, except through satisfaction. Never, never in any other way, never at any price. So it is; the man who is not suffering from it doesn't dwell on it; but the man who is learns to know our Lord Jesus Christ, and his tears run down. Good Lord in heaven, what a thing it is, that the flesh can crave the flesh like that, simply because it is not its own flesh, but belongs to another soul——how strange, and yet, when you come to look at it, how unassuming, how friendly, how almost apologetic! One might say, almost, if that is all he wants, in God's name let him have it! What is it I want, Castorp? Do I want to kill her? Do I want to shed her blood? I only want to fondle her. Dear, good Castorp, don't despise me for whining like this——but after all, couldn't she let me have my way? There would be something higher about it, Castorp; I am not a beast of the field, in my way I am a man too. Pure fleshly desire casts about, here, there, and everywhere; it is not bound, not fixed, and so we call it animal. But when it is fixed upon a human being, with a human face, then we begin talking about love. It is not that I just crave her carnal part, to enjoy as if she were a fleshand--blood doll; if there were one least little thing different about her face, it might be that I should not crave her at all——which shows that I love her soul, and love her with my soul. For love of the face is love of the soul——"

"Why, Wehsal, what's the matter with you? You are off your head, you don't know how you are going on——"

"But that is just it," pursued the unhappy wretch, "that she has a soul, that she is a creature made up of soul and body. And her soul will have absolutely nothing to do with mine, nor her body either, and thence come, oh, God, the torments I suffer, and therefore is my desire condemned to shame, and my body must mortify itself for ever. Why will she know nothing of me, Castorp, either body or soul, and why is my desire a horror to her? Am I not a man? Even if I am repulsive? I swear to you that I am, that I would give her more than all the others who have lain there, once she opened to me the bliss of her embrace, of her arms, which are beautiful because her soul is so. There is not a glory of the flesh I would not offer her, Castorp, if it were only a matter of the body, not of the countenance, if it were not her accursed soul that will have none of me, without which I should have no longing for her body——that is the devil's treadmill in which I eternally go round and round."

"Hush, Wehsal, hush, the coachman can understand you. He does not turn his head, on purpose, but I can see by the expression of his back that he is listening."

"Yes, you're right, he is listening, and he understands. There you have again the thing I am talking about, and can see what it is like. If I were speaking of—-of palingenesis, or hydrostatics, he would not understand, and would not listen, he would not have the faintest idea about it, nor care to have. There is no popular understanding for those things. But this business of body and soul, the last and highest and most ghastly private matter in the world, is also the most universal—-everybody can understand it and laugh at anyone suffering from it, whose days are a torture of desire and his nights a torment of hell. Castorp, dear Castorp, let me make my little moan to you—-you don't know the sort of nights I have. Every night I dream of her, ah, what do I not dream of her, it makes me burn inside even to think of it! And all the dreams end the same way: she gives me a box on the ear, slaps me in the face, sometimes spits at me, with her face all distorted with disgust, and then I awake, covered with sweat and drowned in shame and desire—-"

"That will do, Wehsal. We will sit quiet now, and make up our minds to hold our tongues until we reach the grocer's and someone gets in with us. That is my wish. I don't want to wound you, and I admit that your mental state is a quite choice and par--ticular mess. But you know the story about the maiden who by way of being punished for something had snakes and toads hop out of her mouth, a snake or a toad for every word she spoke. The book does not say what she did about it, but I should think she finally had to keep her mouth shut."

"But every human being needs to express what he feels," said Wehsal complainingly, "to relieve himself, my dear Castorp, when he is in the state I am in!"

"And every human being has the right to do it, too, if you like. But my dear Wehsal, it seems to me there are certain rights a man simply does not assert."

After which, according to Hans Castorp's desire, they were silent. Moreover, they were now arrived at the grocer's vine--clad cottage, where they needed not to linger at all, for Naphta and Settembrini stood waiting in the street; the one in his shabby fur, the other in a yellowish--white spring overcoat, copiously stitched, and looking almost foppish. They all bowed and exchanged greetings, and Naphta took his place beside Ferge in the first landau, which now contained four persons, while Herr Settembrini added himself to the other two in the second carriage. Wehsal gave up his place on the back seat, and the Italian lolled there elegantly, as though on his native Corso; in his very best mood, and bubbling over with *esprit*.

He talked about the pleasure of driving, the charm of sitting still and being moved along at the same time amid a changing scene; showed a fatherly interest in Hans Castorp, even patted the forlorn Wehsal's cheek and bade him forget his own unsympathetic ego in admiration of the blithe exterior world, to which the Italian pointed with a spacious gesture of his hand in its worn leather glove.

It was a delightful drive. The horses, all four of them sturdy, glossy, well--fed beasts, with a blaze on each forehead, covered the excellent road at a steady pace. There was no dust. The route was bordered here and there by crumbling rock tufted with grass and flowers. Telegraph--poles flew past. Their way wound along the mountain forests in pleasant curves that invited the interest and led it on; in the sunny distance glimmered mountain heights still partly covered with snow. They left behind their own accustomed valley, and the change of scene refreshed their spirits. At the edge of the forest they drew up, having decided to cover on foot the remainder of the distance to the goal they had in mind—-a goal of which they had been for some time aware, by reason of the sound that came to their ears, at first scarcely perceptible, but steadily increasing in volume. They all heard, directly they dismounted, that far--away, sibilant, vibrating roar, that distant murmuring of water, as yet so faint that they would suddenly lose the sound and pause to listen again.

"It is mild enough now," Settembrini said. He had often been here before. "But when you come close, it is brutal, at this time of the year. You won't be able to hear yourselves think—-mark my words."

Thus they entered the woods, along a path strewn with damp pine--needles: Pieter Peeperkorn first, leaning on Madame Chauchat's arm, his soft black hat drawn down on his brows, walking with his slumping gait; behind them Hans Castorp, hatless, like the other gentlemen, hands in pockets, head on one side, whistling softly as he looked about; then Naphta and Settembrini, then Ferge and Wehsal, last the Malay with the tea--basket on his arm. They all talked about the wood.

For the wood was not quite usual, it had a peculiarity which made it picturesque, exotic, even uncanny. It abounded in a hanging moss that draped and wreathed and wrapped the trees: the matted web of this parasitic plant hung and dangled in long, pallid beards from the branches, so that scarcely any pine--needles were visible for the shrouding veil. A complete, a bizarre transformation, a bewitched and morbid scene. For the trees were sick of this rank growth, it threatened to choke them to death—-so all the visitors felt, as the little train wound along the path toward the sound, and the hissing and splashing swelled slowly to a mighty tumult that justified Settembrini's prediction. A turn in the path revealed the bridge and the rocky ravine down which the torrent poured. At the moment their eyes perceived it, their ears seemed saluted with the maximum of sound—-for which infernal was the only right word. The volume of water fell perpendicularly in a single cascade, perhaps nine or ten feet high, and of considerable breath, and foaming white shot away over the rocks. The frantic noise of its falling seemed to mingle all possible intensities and variations of sound—-hissing, thundering, roaring, bawling, whispering, crashing, crackling, droning, chiming—-truly it was enough to drive one senseless. The visitors went very close, on the slippery rocks at the bottom of the chasm, and stood looking, bespattered with its spray, enveloped in its mist, their ears stopped by its insensate clamour. They exchanged glances and head--shakes and rather intimidated smiles as they stood regarding this spectacle, this long catastrophe of foam and fury, whose preposterous roaring deafened them, frightened them, bewildered their senses of sight and hearing, so that they even imagined they heard above, below, and on all sides, cries of warning, trumpet--calls, hoarse human voices.

Gathered in a little group behind Mynheer Peeperkorn, Frau Chauchat surrounded by the five gentlemen, they stood and looked into the surging waters. The others could not see the Dutchman's face, but they saw him take off his hat, and breathe in the freshness with expanding chest. They communicated by looks and signs, for words would have been useless, even shrieked immediately into the ear, against that raging thunder. Their lips formed soundless phrases of wonder and admiration. Hans Castorp, Settembrini, and Ferge proposed, by nods and signs, to climb up the side of the ravine in which they stood, and look down upon the water from above. It was not difficult: a series of narrow steps cut in the rock led up to an upper storey, so to speak, of the forest. They climbed it, one behind the other, reached the bridge which spanned the water just where it arched to pour downward, and leaning on the rail, waved to the party below. Then they crossed over and climbed laboriously down on the other side of the stream, whence they rejoined their friends by a second bridge over the whirling torrent.

Tea--drinking was now indicated; and more than one of them said it might be well to withdraw a little from the din in order to enjoy that refreshment in comfort, not totally dumb, not utterly deafened and dazed. But they learned that Peeperkorn thought otherwise. He shook his head, and pointed several times with violence toward the ground. His distorted lips curled back with the emphasis of the "Here!" they shaped. What could the others do? In such matters he was accustomed to command, and the weight of his personality would always have been decisive, even if he had not been, as he was, master and mover of the expedition. Size itself is tyrannical, autocratic; thus it has always been, thus it will remain. Mynheer desired to eat in sight, in thunderous hearing of the waterfall, it was his mighty will. Who did not wish to go hungry must acquiesce. Most of them felt dissatisfied. Herr Settembrini saw that all chance of conversation, of a human interchange of ideas, would be out of the question, and flung up his hand with a gesture of resigned despair. The Malay hastened to carry out his master's will. Two camp--stools were set up against the rocks for Monsieur and Madame, and at their feet upon a cloth he spread out the contents of the basket: coffee--apparatus and glasses, thermos bottles, cake and wine. The others found places on boulders, or against the railing of the foot--bridge, holding their cups of hot coffee in their hands, their plates on their knees; they ate silently, amid the clamour. Peeperkorn sat with his coat--collar turned up and his hat on the ground beside him, drinking port out of a monogrammed silver cup, which he emptied many times. And suddenly he began to speak. Extraordinary man! It was impossible for him to hear his own voice, still more for the others to catch a syllable of what he let transpire without its in the least transpiring. But with the winecup in his right hand, he raised his forefinger, stretching his left arm palm outwards toward the water. They saw his kingly features move in speech, the mouth form words, which were as soundless as though spoken into empty, etherless space. No one dreamed he would continue; with embarrassed smiles they watched this futile activity, thinking every moment it would cease. But he went on, with tense, compelling gesture, to harangue the clamour that swallowed his words; directing upon this or that one of the company by turns the gaze of his pale little weary eyes, spanned wide beneath the lifted folds of his brow; and whoever felt himself addressed was constrained to nod back again, wide--eyed, openmouthed, hand to ear, as though any sort of effort to hear could better the utterly hopeless situation. He even stood up! There, in his crumpled ulster, that reached nearly to his heels, the collar turned up; bare--headed, cup in hand, the high brow creased with folds like some heathen idol's in a shrine, and crowned by the aureole of white hair like flickering flames; there he stood by the rocks and spoke, holding the circle of thumb and forefinger, with the lancelike others above it, before his face, and sealing his mute and incomprehensible toast with that compelling sign of precision. Such words as they were accustomed to hearing from him, they could read on his lips or divine from his gestures: "Settled" and "Absolutely!"—-but that was all. They saw his head sink sideways, the broken bitterness of the lips, they saw the man of sorrows in his guise. But then quite suddenly flashed the dimple, the sybaritic roguishness, the garment snatched up dancewise, the ritual impropriety of the heathen priest. He lifted his beaker, waved it half--circle before the assembled guests, and drank it out in three gulps, so that it stood bottom upwards. Then he handed it with outstretched arm to the Malay, who received it with an obeisance, and gave the sign to break up the feast.

They all bowed and thanked him as they hastened to do his bidding. Those crouching on the ground sprang up, the others jumped down from the railing. The little Javanese in his stiff hat and turned--up collar gathered the remnants of the meal. They went back along the path in the same order as they had come, through the draped, uncanny grove, to the high road and the waiting carriages.

This time Hans Castorp mounted with Alynheer and Madame, and sat opposite the pair with the humble Ferge, to whom all high thoughts were vain. Scarcely a word was spoken on the homeward drive. Mynheer sat with his jaw dropped and his hands palm upward on the carriage rug spread across his and Madame's knees. Settembrini and Naphta dismounted and took their leave before the carriages crossed the track and the watercourse, and Wehsal drove alone as far as the portal of the Berghof, where the party separated.

Was Hans Castorp's sleep this night rendered light and fitful by portents of which his soul knew naught—-so that the slightest variation in the usual nightly peace of the Berghof, the faintest commotion, the barely perceptible sound of running, was enough to fetch him broad awake, to make him sit up in bed? He had been, in fact, awake for some time before a knock came on his door, as it did shortly after two o'clock. He answered at once, composed, alert and energetic, and heard the voice of one of the nurses in the house, saying in high, uncertain tones that Frau Chauchat would be glad if he would come at once to the first storey. Briskly he responded, sprang up and flung on some clothing, ran his fingers through his hair, and went down; not slow, not fast, and more in uncertainty as to the how than the what, in the meaning of these summons. The door to Peeperkorn's salon stood open, also that to his bedroom, where all the lights were burning. The two physicians, the Directress, Madame Chauchat, and the Malay were within, the last--named dressed not as usual, but in a sort of national costume, with a striped garment like a shirt, very long wide sleeves, a gaily coloured skirt, and a curious, cone--shaped hat made of yellow cloth on his head. He wore an ornament of amulets on his breast, and stood with folded arms at the head of the bed, wherein Pieter Peeperkorn lay on his back, his arms stretched out before him. Hans Castorp, paling, took in the scene. Frau Chauchat sat with her back toward him in a low chair at the foot of the bed. Her elbows rested on the coverlet, her chin was in her hands, whose fingers were buried in her upper lip, and she gazed into the face of her protector.

"Evening, m' boy," said Behrens, who stood talking in low tones with Krokowski and the Oberin, and nodded ruefully to Hans Castorp, with his upper lip drawn back. He was in his surgeon's coat, from the pocket of which a stethoscope stuck out, wore embroidered slippers and no collar. "It's all up with him," he added in a whisper.

"Gone for good, o'er the border and awa'. Come have a look--run your experienced eye over him—-you'll agree there's nothing for us to do."

Hans Castorp approached the bed on tiptoe. The Malay without turning his head followed the movement, until his eyeballs showed white. The young man assured himself by a side glance that Frau Chauchat was paying no heed; then stood by the bed in his accustomed posture, his weight on one leg, his head on one side, his hands folded across his stomach, reverently, reflectively gazing. Pieter Peeperkorn lay under the red satin coverlet, in his *tricot* shirt, as Hans Castorp had so often seen him. His hands were veined a bluish black, likewise parts of his face; a considerable disfigurement, though the kingly features remained unaltered. Beneath the white aureole of hair the masklike folds carved by the habitual gesture of a lifetime ran in a row of four or five, straight across the brow and then in a right angle down the temples; they were more striking than ever, by contrast with the drooping lids and the repose of the features. The cracked lips were slightly parted. The . cyanosis indicated abrupt stoppage, a violent apoplectic arrest of the vital functions.

Hans Castorp stood awhile, reverently, observing all this; hesitating to move, expectant of being addressed by the "widow." As he was not, and could not bring himself to disturb her, he turned toward the little group of other persons present. Behrens jerked his head in the direction of the salon, and Hans Castorp followed him thither.

"Suicide?" he asked, subdued but terse.

"Rather," said the Hofrat, with a shrug, and added: "up to the hilt. To the *nth* power. Have you ever seen a toy like this before?" he went on, and drew out of the pocket of his smock an irregularly shaped case, from which he took a small object and presented it to the young man's notice. "Nor I either. But it is well worth seeing. We live and learn. It's a fantastic little gadget, and ingenious. I took it out of his hand. Take care, if it drips on your skin it will blister."

Hans Castorp turned the puzzling little object in his hands. It was made of steel, gold, ivory, and rubber, wonderful to see. There were two curving prongs of bright steel, extremely sharp--pointed; a slightly spiral centre portion of gold--inlaid ivory, in which the prongs were somewhat movable and could sink up to a point; and a bulb of semi--hard black rubber. The whole thing was only about two inches long.

"What is it?" Hans Castorp asked.

"That," answered Behrens, "is an organized hypodermic syringe. Or, if you like, it is a copy of the mechanism of the cobra's bite.

Understand? You don't seem to," he went on, as Hans Castorp continued to stare at the bizarre little instrument. "These are the teeth. They are not solid all the way, there is a canal inside, the thickness of a hair; you can see the issue of it quite plainly, here just above the point. They are also open at the base, of course, and communicate with the excretory duct of the bulb, which runs into the ivory middle part. When the teeth bite, they sink in a little, and the pressure on the reservoir shoots the contents into the canals, so that the poison gets into circulation the moment the fangs sink in the flesh. Perfectly simple, when you see it like that; you just have to get the idea. He probably had it made after his own design."

"Surely," Hans Castorp said.

"The amount must have been very small," continued the Hofrat. "What it lacked in quantity it made up for in——"

"Dynamic," Hans Castorp finished for him.

"Well, yes. What it was we shall soon find out. It will be worth knowing too, it has something curious to teach us. Shall we wager that the native on duty over there, who dressed himself up like that for the night's work, could tell us all we want to know? I suspect it is a combination of animal and vegetable poisons, the most powerful known, for it must have worked like lightning. Everything points to its having taken away his breath, paralysed his respiration, you know, quick suffocation, probably easy and painless."

"God grant it," said Hans Castorp piously, handed the uncanny toy back to the Hofrat and returned to the bedchamber.

Madame Chauchat and the Malay were there alone. And this time Clavdia lifted her face toward the young man as he neared the bed.

"You had a right to be called," she said.

"It was kind of you," he answered, "and you are right." He availed himself of the third person plural as used by the peoples of the cultured West. "We were brothers. I feel shamed in the depth of my soul that I tried to hide it, and used circumlocutions before other people. Were you with him at the last?"

"The servant called me when all was over," she answered.

"He was built on such a grand scale," Hans Castorp began again, "that he considered it a blasphemy, a cosmic catastrophe, to be found wanting in feeling. For you must know, he regarded himself as the instrument of God's marriage. That was a piece of majestic tomfoolery—when one is moved one can say things that sound crass and irreverent, but are after all more solemn than the conventional religious formulas."

"*C'est une abdication*," she said. "He knew of our folly?"

"I was not able to prevent it, Clavdia. He guessed, when I refused to kiss you on the forehead, in his presence. At this moment, his presence is rather symbolic than actual—but will you let me do it now?"

She moved her head toward him, in a little nod, the eyes closed. He pressed his lips on her brow. The brown, doglike eyes of the Malay servant watched the scene, rolling sidewise, until the whites showed.

The Great God Dumps

Once more we hear Herr Hofrat Behren's voice—let us give it our ear. For we hear it perhaps for the last time. Some day even the story itself will come to an end. Long has it lasted; or, rather, the pace of its contentual time has so increased that there is no more holding it, even its musical time is running out. Perhaps we shall have no further opportunity to hear the lively cadences of the Rhadamanthine tongue. The Hofrat said to Hans Castorp: "Castorp, old cock, you're bored. Chap--fallen, I see it every day, disgust and ennui are written on your brow. You're collapsed like a punctured tire—if some first--class excitement doesn't come along every day, you pull a face as though you were saying: 'H'm, small potatoes *and* few in the hill!' Am I right, or am I not?"

[780]

Hans Castorp said never a word——a sure sign that his inward man was indeed pervaded with gloom.

"Right, then, of course, as I always am," Behrens answered himself. "Well, I can't have you spreading the toxin of your disaffection all over my community, you disgruntled citizen, you. I must convince you that you are not forgotten of God and man, that the powers above have an eye, an unchanging eye upon you, and ceaselessly ponder your welfare. Old Behrens hasn't forsaken you yet, my lad. Well, joking aside, I've been thinking about your case, and in the watches of the night something has come to me. I might almost speak of a revelation——in short, I promise great things from my new idea, nothing more nor less than your complete cure and triumphal progress down to the flat--land, before you can say Jack Robinson."

"Yes," he went on, after a pause for effect, "you may well open your eyes"——Hans Castorp had done nothing of the sort, merely blinked at him rather sleepy and distraught——"of course you haven't an idea how old Behrens can say such a thing. Well, it's like this: it cannot have escaped your acute apperceptions that there is something about your case that doesn't hold water. The symptoms of infection have not for a long time corresponded to the local condition, which is undoubtedly very much improved. It's not only since yesterday that I've been thinking about it. Here is your latest photo, take it and hold it up to the light. See there! The sheerest pessimist and cavillar——as the Kaiser says——could not see very much in it to find fault with. Some of the foci are absorbed, the area is smaller and more clearly defined, which you are experienced enough to know is a sign of healing. Nothing here to explain the unreliability of your domestic heater, my man. The doctor finds himself under the necessity of casting about for another cause." Hans Castorp's bow conveyes at most a civil interest.

"You would think old Behrens must admit to having made a mistake in the treatment? Well, if you did, you've come a cropper again; sized the thing up wrong, and old Behrens too. The treatment was not wrong, but it was just possibly one--sided. The possibility has occurred to me that your symptoms were not necessarily to be referred to tuberculosis alone——because it is out of the question to refer them to it any longer. There must be some other source of trouble. In my view, you've got cocci."

"Yes," he repeated with increase of emphasis, and in acknowledgment of the bow with which Hans Castorp accepted his statement, "it is my profound conviction that you have streps——which, of course, is not necessarily alarming."

Of alarm there could be no talk: Hans Castorp's face expressed at most a sort of ironic recognition, either of his companion's acuteness, or of the new dignity with which the Hofrat had hypothetically invested him.

"No call for panic," he varied his theme. "Everybody has cocci. Any ass can have streps. You needn't be puffed up. It is not very long since we have known that one can have streptococci in the blood without showing any symptoms of infection. And many of my colleagues are as yet unacquainted with the situation which confronts us, namely, that a man can even have tubercular bacilli in his blood without being any the worse for it. We aren't more than three steps from the conception that tuberculosis is a disease of the blood."

Hans Castorp politely found that truly remarkable.

"When I say streps," Behrens began again, "you must not picture a well--known or severe type of illness. If this little one has really settled down and made itself at home in you, the bacteriological blood--test will show it. But whether it is really the cause of the fever——supposing it is present——that we can only tell from the effect of the streptovaccine treatment. This, my dear friend, is the technique, and I promise myself unheard--of results. Tuberculosis is the most long--winded thing in the world; but affections of this sort can be cured very quickly to--day; if you react to the inoculations, you will be as sound as a bell inside six weeks. Well, what do you say to that? That little ole Behrens has his head on his shoulders, what?"

"It is only a hypothesis for the moment, isn't it?" Hans Castorp said languidly.

"But a demonstrable hypothesis! A highly fruitful hypothesis!" the Hofrat responded. "You'll see how fruitful it is, when the cocci begin to grow in our culture. To--morrow afternoon we'll rap you; we'll let your blood according to the sacred rites of the village barber. It's diverting in itself, and may have miraculous results."

Hans Castorp declared himself ready for the diversion, and thanked the Hofrat in due form for his efforts in his behalf. He put his head on one side and watched Behrens paddle off. It was true: the intervention had come at the critical moment, Rhadamanthus had not been far out in the description he gave of Hans Castorp's face and air. The new undertaking was put forth—-quite explicitly, there had been no attempt to wrap it up—-in order to tide him over the crisis he was in, which betrayed itself by a bearing very like the departed Joachim's, when he was mentally working himself up to a certain desperate resolve.

And further. It seemed to Hans Castorp that not only he himself had arrived at this point, but that all the world, "the whole show," as he said, had arrived there with him; he found it hard to differentiate his particular case from the general. He had experienced the extravagant ending of his connexion with a certain personality. A commotion had ensued in the house. There had been a farewell between Clavdia Chauchat and himself, the surviving member of a severed brotherhood; a farewell, uttered in the shadow of a tragic renunciation, and followed by her second departure from the Berghof. Now all these events had put the young man in a frame of mind to find life itself not precisely canny. Everything appeared to have gone permanently and increasingly awry, as though a demonic power—-which had indeed for a long time given hints of its malign influence—-had suddenly taken control, in a way to induce secret consternation and almost thoughts of flight. The name of the demon was Dumps.

The reader will accuse the writer of laying it on pretty thick when he associates two such ideas as these, and ascribes to mere staleness a mystical and supernatural character. But we are not indulging in flights of fancy. We are adhering strictly to the personal experience of our simple--minded hero, which in some way defying exact definition it has been given us to know, and which indicates that when all the uses of this world unitedly become flat, stale, and unprofitable, they are actually possessed by a demonic quality capable of giving rise to the feelings we have described. Hans Castorp looked about him. He saw on every side the uncanny and the malign, and he knew what it was he saw: life without time, life without care or hope, life as depravity, assiduous stagnation; life as dead.

Yet it was occupied too, it had activities of various kinds, pursued simultaneously; now and again one of these would assume the proportions of a craze, and subordinate everything to itself. Old residents experienced the periodic revival of more than one of these fads. So for instance amateur photography, always playing an important rôle at the Berghof, had twice become a perfect mania, lasting weeks and months on end. Everywhere one saw people absorbedly bent over cameras supported in the pit or their stomachs, focusing and snapping the shutter; and floods of snapshots were handed round at table. It became a point of honour to do the developing oneself. The supply of dark--rooms in the establishment was not sufficient, the bedroom windows and doors were draped with black cloth, and people busied themselves by dim red lights over chemical baths, until something caught fire, the Bulgarian student at the "good" Russian table was nearly reduced to ashes, and a prohibitory decree went forth from the management. Next they tired of ordinary photography, the fashion veered to flashlights and colour photography after Lumière. They were enthusiastic over groups of people with startled, staring eyes in livid faces dazed by the magnesium flare, resembling the corpses of the murdered set upright. Hans Castorp had a framed diapositive, showing him with a copper--coloured visage, a brassy buttercup in his buttonhole, standing among buttercups in a poisonously green meadow, with Frau Stöhr on one side of him in a sky--blue blouse, and Fräulein Levi on the other in a blood--red sweater.

Then there was the collecting of postage stamps, a considerable interest at all times, but rising periodically to an obsession. Everybody pasted, haggled, exchanged, took in philatelic magazines, carried on correspondence with special vendors, foreign and domestic, with societies and private owners; astonishing sums were spent for rare specimens, even by people whose means were scarcely adequate to their expenses at the Berghof.

Postage stamps would have their day, and give way to the next folly on the list, which might be the accumulation and endless munching of all possible brands of chocolate. Everybody's mouth was stained brown, and the Berghof kitchen offered its most elaborate delicacies to captious and indifferent diners who had lost their appetites to *Milka--nut, Chocolat à la crème d'amandes, Marquis--napolitains,* and gold--besprinkled cats' tongues.

Pig--drawing, a diversion introduced by high authority on a long--ago carnival evening, had had its little day, and led up to geometrical teasers which for a time consumed all the mental powers of the Berghof world, and even the last thoughts and energies of the dying. Weeks on end the house was under the spell of a complicated figure consisting of not less than eight circles, large and small, and several engaged triangles, the whole to be drawn free--hand without lifting the pen—-or, as a further refinement, to be drawn blindfold. Lawyer Paravant, the virtuoso of this kind of mental concentration, finally succeeded in performing the feat, perhaps with some loss of symmetry; but he was the only one.

We know on the authority of the Hofrat that Lawyer Paravant studied mathematics; we know too the disciplinary grounds of his devotion to that branch of learning, and its virtue in cooling and dulling the edge of fleshly lusts. If the guests of the Berghof had more generally applied themselves to the same study, the necessity for certain recent rulings would most likely have been obviated. The chief of these dealt with the passage across the balconies, at the end of the white glass partitions that did not quite reach to the balustrade. These were now extended by means of little doors, which the bathing--master had it in charge to lock every night——and did so, to a general accompaniment of smirks and sniggers. Since that time, the chambers in the first storey had become popular, because they afforded a passage across the verandah roof beyond the balustrade. But this disciplinary departure had not been introduced on Lawyer Paravant's account. He had long since overcome the severe attack caused by the presence of the Egyptian Fatme, and she had been the last to challenge his natural man. Since her time he had flung himself with redoubled conviction into the arms of the clear--eyed goddess, of whose soothing powers Hofrat Behrens had so morally discoursed. There was one problem to which day and night he devoted all his brains, all the sporting pertinacity which once——before the beginning of this prolonged and enforced holiday, that even threatened at times to end in total quiescence——had gone to the convicting of criminals. It was——the squaring of the circle.

In the course of his studies, this retired official had convinced himself that the arguments on which science based the impossibility of the proposition were untenable; and that an overruling providence had removed him, Paravant, from the world of the living, and brought him here, having selected him to transfer the problem from the realms of the transcendental into the realms of the earthly and exact. By day and night he measured and calculated; covered enormous quantities of paper with figures, letters, computations, algebraic symbols; his face, which was the face of an apparently sound and vigorous man, wore the morose and visionary stare of a monomaniac; while his conversation, with consistent and fearful monotony, dealt with the proportional number pi, that abandoned fraction which the debased genius of a mathematician named Zachariah Dase one day figured out to the two--hundredth decimal place——purely for the joy of it and as a work of supererogation, for if he had figured it out to the two--thousandth, the result, as compared with unattainable mathematical exactitude, would have been practically unchanged. Everybody shunned the devoted Paravant like the plague; for whomever he succeeded in buttonholing, that unhappy wretch had to listen to a torrent of red--hot oratory, as the lawyer strove to rouse his humaner feelings to the shame that lay in the defilement of the mind of man by the hopeless irrationality of this mystic relation. The fruitlessness of for ever multiplying the diameter of the circle by pi to find its circumference, of multiplying the square of the radius by pi to find its area, caused Lawyer Paravant to be visited by periodic doubt whether the problem had not been unnecessarily complicated, since Archimedes' day; whether the solution were not, in actual fact, a child's affair for simpleness. Why could not one rectify the circumference, why could one not also convert every straight line into a circle? Lawyer Paravant felt himself, at times, near a revelation. He was often seen, late in the evening, sitting at his table in the forsaken and dimly lighted dining--room, with a piece of string laid out before him, which he carefully arranged in circulai shape, and then suddenly, with an abrupt gesture, stretched out straight; only to fall thereafter, leaning on his elbows, into bitter brooding. The Hofrat sometimes lent him a helping hand at the sorry sport, and generally encouraged him in his freak. And the sufferer turned to Hans Castorp too, again and yet again, with his cherished grievance, finding in the young man much friendly understanding and a sympathetic interest in the mystery of the circle. He illustrated his pet despair to the young man by means of an exact drawing, executed with vast pains, showing a circle between two polygons, one inscribed, the other circumscribed, each polygon being of an infinite number of tiny sides, up to the last human possibility of approximation to the circle. The remainder, the surrounding curvature, which in some ethereous, immaterial way refused to be rationalized by means of the calculable bounding lines, that, Lawyer Paravant said, with quivering jaw, was pi. Hans Castorp, for all his receptivity, showed himself less sensitive to pi than his interlocutor. He said it was all hocus--pocus; and advised Paravant not to overheat

[787]

himself with his cat's--cradle; spoke of the series of dimensionless points of which the circle consisted, from its beginning—which did not exist—to its end—which did not exist either; and of the overpowering melancholy that lay in eternity, for ever turning on itself without permanence of direction at any given moment—spoke with such tranquil resignation as to exert on Lawyer Paravant a momentary beneficent effect.

It was a consequence of our good Hans Castorp's nature that more than one of his fellow--patients made a confidant of him; several of them possessing some *idée fixe* or other and suffering because they could get no hearing from the callous majority. There was an elderly man from somewhere in the back blocks of Austria, a one--time sculptor, with white moustaches, a hooked nose and blue eyes; who had conceived a project, financial and political in its scope, and drawn it up most meticulously in a calligraphic hand, colouring the important points in sepia. The main feature of the scheme was that every newspaper subscriber should bind himself to contribute a daily quantum of forty grammes of old newspaper, collected on the first of every month; which in one year would amount to a lump quantity of 1400 grammes, and in twenty years to not less than 288 kilogrammes. Reckoning at twenty pfennig the kilo, this would come to fifty--seven marks and sixty pfennig. Five million subscribers, it was calculated, would in the course of twenty years deliver a quantity of old newspaper valued at the enormous sum of 288 million marks; of which two--thirds might be reckoned off to the new subscriptions, which would thus pay for themselves, the other third, amounting to about a million marks, remaining to be devoted to humanitarian projects, such as financing free establishments for tuberculous patients, encouraging struggling talent, and so on. The plan was elaborated even to the design for a centimetre price--column, from which the organization for collecting the old paper could read off each month the value of the paper collected, and the stamped form to be used as a receipt in exchange for payment. It was an excellent plan from every point of view. The wanton waste and destruction of news-

-print, thrown away or burnt up by the unenlightened, was a betrayal of our forests and of our political economy. To save and conserve paper meant to save cellulose, meant the conservation of our forests, the protection of human material that was used up in the manufacture of cellulose and paper—-human material and capital. Furthermore, since newspaper might easily come to have four times the value of wrapping--paper and pasteboard, it would become an economic factor of considerable importance, and the basis of fruitful governmental and communal assessments, and thus lighten for newspaper readers the burden of taxation. In short, the plan was good, it was every way incontrovertible. The uncanny air of futility, or even a sort of sinister crackbrainedness, which hung about it was due to the addled fanaticism with which the former artist pursued and supported an economic idea, about which he was obviously so little serious that he made not the smallest effort to put it into execution. Hans Castorp, nodding, with his head on one side, listened to the man, as with fevered eloquence he made propaganda for his idea; observing at the same time in himself the contempt and repulsion which diminished his partisanship for the inventor against the indifference of the thoughtless world.

Some of the patients studied Esperanto, and knew enough to converse a little in that artificial jargon at their meals. Hans Castorp listened gloomily, but admitted to himself that there were other things even worse. A group of English who had been here for a short time, introduced a parlour game which consisted in the question, asked by the first player of his neighbour: "Have you ever seen the Devil with a nightcap on?" To which the person asked must reply: "No, I've never seen the Devil with a nightcap on," and then repeat the question in his turn, and so on. It was insufferable. Yet Hans Castorp found the patience--players even worse. They were to be seen all over the house, at every hour of the day, laying out their cards; a passion for that diversion having assumed such proportions at the Berghof as to turn the place into a den of vice. Hans Castorp had the more ground for horror, in that he himself fell a temporary victim to the plague—-was, indeed, one of the severest cases. It was the patience called "elevens" that proved his undoing, the game in which the cards are laid out in three rows of three deep, and any two cards that together make eleven covered anew as they come uppermost, as well as the three face--cards, until by good luck the pack is dealt out. It seems inconceivable that such a simple procedure could prove fascinating to the point of bewitchment—-yet so it was. Hans Castorp, like so many others, experienced it—-always with drawn and frowning brows, for this particular form of debauch is never a merry one. He was given over to the whims of the card--goblins, ensnared by the fitful and fickle favour of fortune, which sometimes let the face--cards and elevens pile up so that the game was over before the third tier was laid, when the fleeting triumph would stimulate the nerves to new efforts. But next time perhaps, the ninth and last card would fall without any possibility of covering anything, or else the game, having aroused flattering hopes, would obstinately stick at the last moment. Everywhere, at all hours of the day, he played patience—-and at night under the stars, and in the morning in his pyjamas; played at table, played almost in his sleep. He shuddered, but he played. Thus one day Herr Settembrini found him—-and disturbed him, as even from the beginning it had been his mission to do.

"*Accidente!*" said he. "What, Engineer, you are playing cards?"

"Not precisely playing cards," Hans Castorp told him. "I am just laying them out, to have a tussle with abstract chance. The tricks it plays intrigue me, it is as inconsistent as the wind. It fawns on you, and then suddenly puts up its back and won't budge. This morning, directly I got up, it came three times running, once in two rows, which is a record. But will you believe it, this is the thirty--third time I have played it without once going even halfway through?"

Herr Settembrini looked at him, as so often he had looked in the course of the years, with melancholy black eyes.

"At all events, you are preoccupied," he said. "It does not look as though I could find here the consolation I seek, nor balsam for my inward wound."

"Wound?" echoed Hans Castorp, laying afresh.

"The world situation puzzles me," the Freemason sighed. "The Balkan Federation will go through, Engineer, all the information I receive points that way. Russia is working feverishly for it. And the combination is aimed against the Austro--Hungarian monarchy, which must fall before any of the Russian programme can be realized. You understand my scruples. Austria, as of course you are aware, I hate with all my strength. But shall I, on that account, lend support and countenance in my soul to the Sarmatian despotism, which is about to set the torch to the whole of our highly civilized continent? Yet on the other hand, diplomatic collaboration, to however small an extent, between my own country and Austria, I should regard as dishonourable. These are conscientious scruples which---"

"Seven and four," said Hans Castorp. "Eight and three. Knave, queen, king. It is coming out. You have brought me luck, Herr Settembrini."

The Italian was silent. Hans Castorp felt the black eyes, the eyes of reason and morality, bent in sorrow upon him. He played on for a while; then, resting his cheek in his hand, looked up at his mentor with the innocent, impenitent air of a naughty child.

"Your eyes," the master said, "vainly seek to hide the fact that you are conscious of your state."

"*Placet experiri,*" Hans Castorp was so pert as to reply to him. Herr Settembrini left; and the abandoned one sat long, at his table in the middle of his white room, his chin supported on his hand, and brooded; shuddering in the very core of him at the cross--purposes everything in the world had got into, at the grinning and grimacing of the demons and ape--headed gods into whose hands it had fallen, at their unbridled domination, the name of which was "The Great God Dumps." An apocalyptic, evil name, calculated to give rise to mysterious fears. Hans Castorp sat and rubbed his brow and his heart with the flat of his hand. He was frightened. It seemed to him "all this" could come to no good, that a catastrophe was impending, that long-suffering nature would rebel, rise up in storm and whirlwind and break the great bond which held the world in thrall; snatch life beyond the "dead point" and put an end to the "small potatoes" in one terrible Last Day. He longed to flee—as we have seen already. It was fortunate, then, that the heads had their unchanging eyes upon him, that they knew how to read his face, and were ready to tide him over the hard place with new and fruitful diversions.

They had declared, the heads, in the accents of a corps-student, that they were on track of the actual causes of the instability of Hans Castorp's heating economy. And those causes, according to their scientific pronouncement, were so easy to come at that a veritable cure and legitimate dismissal to the flat-land had leaped into the foreground. The young man's heart throbbed stormily with manifold emotions, when he stretched out his arm for the blood-letting. Going slightly pale, and blinking, he expressed his admiration for the splendid ruby colour of his life-blood, as it mounted in the glass container. The Hofrat himself, assisted by Dr. Krokowski and a Sister of Mercy, performed the slight but portentous operation. Then passed several days, occupied in Hans Castorp's mind with the question how this blood of his, this part of himself, would behave out of his control and under the eye of science.

At first, the Hofrat said one could not expect it to grow straight off. Later, he said it was unfortunate nothing had grown, as yet. But there came a day when he approached Hans Castorp at breakfast, where he sat at the upper end of the "good" Russian table, in the place once occupied by his great brother-in-blood, and whimsically congratulated him on the fact that the coccus was definitely established in one of the cultures they had prepared. It was now a question of probabilities: whether the symptoms of infection were to be referred to the insignificant amount of tubercle bacillus, or to the streptococci, which, also, were only present in small quantity. He, Behrens, must think it over. They were not finished with the cultures yet. He showed them to Hans Castorp in the "lab": a red, coagulate blood, in which tiny grey points were discernible. Those were the cocci. But any ass might have cocci, and tubercular bacilli too. If not for the symptoms of infection, they were not worth noticing. Outside his body, under the eyes of science, Hans Castorp's blood went on bearing witness. The morning came when the Hofrat in his sprightly phraseology announced that not only on the first culture, but on all the others as well, cocci had subsequently grown, in large quantities. It was not yet certain that they were all streptococci, but it was more than probable that they were the cause of the existing infection——or such part of it as had not been due to the previously existing and perhaps not quite conquered tubercular infection. And the conclusion the Hofrat drew was——a streptovaccine! The prognosis was extraordinarily favourable, there was not the slightest risk about the procedure, so in any case it could do no harm to try it. As the serum was prepared from Hans Castorp's own blood, the inoculation with it could introduce into his system no deterrent not already present there. At worst, the experiment would have a negative result——which could hardly be called unfavourable, since even without it the patient must stop on in any case!

Hans Castorp could not go quite that far. He submitted to the treatment, though he found it absurd, contemptible. This inoculation of himself with part of himself seemed a singularly cheerless procedure, an incestuous abomination, a self--to--self which could have nothing but a fruitless, hopeless result. Such was his ignorant and hypochondriac judgment, right only as to the unfruitfulness of the result, but there wholly. The diversion lasted for weeks. Sometimes it seemed to do harm——which was of course not the case——sometimes good, which, it followed, must equally not be the case. The result was negative——without being explicitly so called and announced. The whole undertaking died a natural death, and Hans

Castorp went on playing patience—-and gazing into the eye of the demon, whose unbridled sway he foresaw would come to an end of horror.

Fullness of Harmony

What new acquisition of House Berghof was it which at length released our longstanding friend from his patience--playing mania, and flung him into the arms of another passion, nobler, though at bottom no less strange? We are about to relate, being ourselves much taken by the mysterious object, and eager to communicate our enthusiasm.

The excellent management, in its sleepless concern for the happiness of its guests, had considered matters, there in the bowels of the earth, had resolved, and acted. It acquired, at a cost which we need not go into, but which must surely have been considerable, a new device for the entertainment of the patients, and added it to those already installed in the largest of the reception--rooms of House Berghof. Was it some clever artifice, of the same nature as the stereopticon, the kaleidoscope, or the cinematographic cylinder? Yes—-and yet, again, no, far from it. It was not an optical toy which the guests discovered one evening in the salon, and greeted with applause, some of them flinging their hands above their heads, others stooping over and clapping in their laps. It was an acoustical instrument. Moreover, the simple devices above--mentioned were not to be compared with it—-they were outclassed, outvalued, outshone. This was no childish peep--show, like those of which all the guests were sick and tired, at which no one ever looked after the first few weeks. It was an overflowing cornucopia of artistic enjoyment, ranging from grave to gay. It was a musical apparatus. It was a gramophone.

We are seriously concerned lest the term be understood in an unworthy, outworn sense, and ideas attach to it which are applicable only to the primitive form of the instrument we have in mind, never to the elegant product evolved by a tireless application of technical means to the Muses' own ends. My dear friends, we implore you to realize that the instrument we describe was not that paltry box with a handle to it, a disk and shaft atop and a shapeless brass funnel attached, which used to be set up on the table outside country inns, to gratify the ears of the rude with its nasal braying. This was a case finished in dull ebony, a little deeper than broad, attached by a cord to an electric switch in the wall, and standing chastely on its special table. With the antediluvian mechanism described above, it had nothing in common. You lifted the prettily bevelled lid, which was automatically supported by a brass rod attached on the inside, and there above a slightly depressed surface was the disk, covered with green cloth, with a nickelled rim, and nickelled peg upon which one fitted the hole in the centre of the hard--rubber record. At the right, in front, was a time--regulating device, with a dial and figures like a watch; at the left, the lever, which set the mechanism going or stopped it; and behind, also on the left, the hollow, curving, club--shaped, nickel--plated arm, with its flexible joints, carrying the flat round sound--box at the end, with a fitment into which the needle was screwed. If you opened the double doors at the front of the box, you saw a set of slanting shelves, rather like a blind, stained black like the case——and that was all.

"Newest model," the Hofrat said. "Latest triumph of art, my children; A--I, copperbottomed, *superfinísimo*, nothing better on the market in this line of goods"——he managed to give the words the twang of an eager and ignorant salesman. "This is not just a machine," he went on, taking a needle out of one of the gay little metal boxes ranged on the table, and fitting it into the holder, "it's a Stradivarius, a Guarneri; with a resonance, a vibration—— *dernier raffinemang*, Polyhymnia patent, look here in the inside of the lid. German make, you know, we do them far and away better than anybody else. The truly musical, in modern, mechanical form, the German soul up to date. And here's the libretto," he said, and gestured with his head toward a little case on the wall, filled with broad--backed albums. "I turn it all over to you, it is yours. But take care of it; I commend it to the solicitude of the public. Shall we shoot it off once, just for fun?"

The patients implored him to do so. Behrens drew out a fat magic tome, turned over the heavy leaves, and chose a paper envelope, which showed a coloured title through a round hole on the front. He placed the record on the disk, set it in motion, waited until it was at full speed, and then carefully set the fine steel point upon the edge of the plate. There was a low, whetting sound. He let the lid sink, and at the same moment, from the open doors in front, from between the slats of the blind, or, rather, from the box as a whole, came a burst of music, with a hubbub of instruments, a lively, bustling, insistent melody: the first contagious bars of an Offenbach overture. They listened, their lips parted in smiles. They could scarcely believe their ears at the purity and faithful reproduction of the colour of the wood--wind. A solo violin preluded whimsically; the bowing, the *pizzicato*, the sweet gliding from one position to another, were all clearly audible. It struck into the melody of the waltz, "*Ach, ich habe sie verloren*" ; the orchestral harmony lightly bore the flattering strain—enchanting it was to hear it taken up by the ensemble and repeated as a sounding *tutti*. Of course, it was scarcely like a real orchestra playing in the room. The volume of sound, though not to any extent distorted, had suffered a diminution of perspective. If we may draw a simile from the visual field, it was as though one were to look at a painting through the wrong end of an opera--glass, seeing it remote and diminutive, though with all its luminous precision of drawing and colour. The vivid, consummate piece of music was reproduced in all the richness of its light--hearted invention. The finish was abandon itself, a galop with a drolly hesitating beginning, a shameless *cancan* that called up a vision of top--hats waved in the air, flying skirts and tossing knees, and seemed never to come to the end of its triumphal jollification. But at length the mechanism stopped automatically. It was over. There was cordial applause. They called for more, and it was forthcoming. A human voice welled out from the casket, a masculine voice at once soft and powerful, with orchestral accompaniment. It was a famous Italian baritone; the marvellous organ swelled out to the full extent of its natural register, there could be no talk here of any diminution or veiling of the sound. If one sat in an adjoining room and did not see the instrument, it seemed not otherwise than as though the artist stood in the salon in his own person, notes in hand, and sang. He sang an *aria di bravura* in his own tongue— *Eh, U barbiere! "Di qualità, di qualità! Figaro qua, Figaro là, Figaro, Figaro, Figaro!"* The listeners almost died of laughter at his *falsetto parlando*, at the contrast between the deep voice and the tongue--splitting facility with which it rendered the words. The musical followed and admired the art of his phrasing, his breathing--technique. He was a master in the irresistible, a virtuoso of the Italian *da capo* school; he must have come forward to the footlights and flung up his arm, as he held the last tone before the closing tonic, so that the audience involuntarily burst out in shouts of applause before he ceased. It was beyond words.

Followed a French horn, playing, with delicate scrupulosity, variations on a folksong. A soprano voice, with the loveliest freshness and precision, the most exquisite *staccato*, trilled and warbled an air from *La Traviata*. The spirit of a world--famed violinist played as though behind veils a romance by Rubinstein, to a piano accompaniment that sounded thin and cold, like a spinet. The wonder--box seemed to seethe: it poured out the chimes of bells, harp glissandos, the crashing of trumpets, the long rolling of drums. Lastly, dance records were put in. There were specimens of the new imported dance, the tango, in the taste of a water--side dive, calculated to make a Viennese waltz sound sedate and grand--fatherly by contrast. Two couples displayed the fashionable steps, Behrens having by now withdrawn with the admonition that a needle should be used no more than once, and the whole instrument handled "as though it were made of eggs." Hans Castorp took his place as operator.

But why precisely Hans Castorp? In this wise. With suppressed eagerness he had opposed those who had thought to take over, on the Hofrat's departure, the changing of plate and needle, the switching on and off of the current. "Let me do it," he said to them, gently putting them aside; and they gave way, first because he wore an air of having known all about it for years, and second because they cared little to take their pleasures actively, instead of sitting to be served to as much and such enjoyment as they could comfortably and unbored receive.

Not so Hans Castorp. While the Hofrat was introducing his new toy to the guests, the young man had remained in the background, not laughing or applauding, but following the performance with tense interest, rubbing an eyebrow round with two fingers, as he had on occasion a way of doing. Several times he restlessly shifted his position, even went into the reading--room to listen from there; then took up his stand close to Behrens, with his hands behind his back, and an enigmatic expression on his face, fixing the casket with his eye, and observing the simple operation of it. But within him something was saying: "Hold on! This is an epoch. This thing was sent to me!" He was filled with the surest foreknowledge of a new passion, a new enchantment, a new burden of love. The youth in the flat--land, who at first sight of a maiden marvels to find himself pierced to the heart with love's barbed arrow, feels not greatly different. Jealousy followed hard upon. Public property, was it? Had that feeble curiosity the right, or the strength, to possess anything? "Let me do it," he had said between his teeth, and they were content it should be so. They danced a little more, to the rollicking pieces he ran off; asked for another vocal number, an operatic duet, the barcarole from the *Contes d'Hoffmann*, which sounded lovely enough. When he closed the lid they all flocked off, chattering in their ephemeral pleasure over the new toy, these to the evening rest--cure, those to bed. He had been waiting for them to go. They left behind all as it was, the boxes of needles open, the plates and albums strewn about. It was like them. He made as though to follow, but then left them on the stairs, turned back to the salon, closed all the doors, and stopped there half the night, busy as a bee.

He made himself acquainted with the new possession, and worked in undisturbed enjoyment through the contents of the heavy albums. There were twelve, in two sizes, with twelve records each; many of the flat, round, black disks were inscribed on both sides, not only with the continuation of a piece of music, but also because many of the plates held two distinct records. Here was a world to conquer, large enough that even to survey it was a difficult task at first, and bewildering; yet a world full of beautiful possibilities. He played some twenty or thirty records; using a kind of needle that moved softly over the plate and lessened the sound, in order that his activity might not offend the silence of the night. But twenty or thirty were scarcely the eighth part of the riches that lay asking to be enjoyed. He must be content tonight with looking over the titles, only choosing one now and again to set upon the disk and give it voice. To the eye one was like another, except for the coloured label in the centre of each hardrubber plate; each and all were covered to the centre or nearly so with concentric circles; but it was these fine lines that held all imaginable music, the happiest inspirations from every region of the art, in choicest reproduction.

There were many overtures, and single symphonic movements, played by famous orchestras, the names of whose conductors were given on the record. There was a long list of *lieder*, sung to piano accompaniment by famous prima donnas; some of these were the lofty and conscious creation of individual artists, others simple folksongs, still others fell between the two categories, in that they were products of an intellectual art, and at the same time sprang from all that was profoundest and most reverent in the feeling and genius of a people—artificial folk--songs, one might call them, if the word artificial need not be taken to cast a slur on the genuineness of their inspiration. One of these Hans Castorp had known from childhood; but from now on began to attach to it a quite special love and clothe it with many associations, as shall be seen hereafter. What else was there—or, simply—what was there not? Operas aplenty. An "international troupe of famous artists, male and female, displayed their highly trained, God--given talent in *arias*, *duos*, ensembles illustrating various periods and localities in the history of the opera—-to discreet orchestral accompaniment. The opera of the south, a high--hearted, light--hearted ravishment; the German, racy of the people, whimsical, hobgoblinish; and both grand and comic opera in the French style. But was that all? Oh, no. A succession of chamber music followed, quartets and trios, instrumental solo numbers for violin, 'cello, flute; concert numbers with violin or flute obbligato, piano solos—-and then there were the light diversions, the "couplets," the topical and popular numbers, played in the first instance by some small orchestra or other, and needing a coarse needle to render them suitably.

Hans Castorp, bustling and solitary, sifted and classified it all, and tried a fraction of it upon the instrument. At a late hour, as late as on the occasion of the first carouse with Pieter Peeperkorn of majestic memory, he went flushed of cheek to bed, where from two to seven he dreamed of the wonder--box. He saw in his sleep the disk circling about the peg, with a swiftness that made it almost invisible and quite soundless. Its motion was not only circular, but also a peculiar, sidling undulation, which communicated itself to the arm that bore the needle, and gave this too an elastic oscillation, almost like breathing, which must have contributed greatly to the *vibrato* and *portamento* of the stringed instruments and the voices. Yet it remained unclear, sleeping as waking, how the mere following out of a hair--line above an acoustic cavity, with the sole assistance of the vibrating membrane of the sound--box, could possibly reproduce such a wealth and volume of sound as filled Hans Castorp's dreaming ear.

Next morning he was early in the salon, even before breakfast; and comfortably sitting with folded hands, listened to a glorious baritone voice, singing to a harp accompaniment: *"Blick' ich umher in diesem edlen Kreise."* The harp sounded perfectly natural, there was no distortion or diminution of the sound that poured out of the casket accompanying the swelling, breathing, articulating human voice—it was simply amazing! And there could be on earth nothing more tender than the next number he chose: a duet from a modern Italian opera, a simple, heartfelt mingling of emotion between two beings, one part taken by the world--famous tenor who was so well represented in the albums, the other by a crystal--clear and sweet little soprano voice; nothing more lovely than his *"Da mi il braccio, mia piccina"* and the simple, sweet, succinct little melodic phrase in which she replies.

Hans Castorp started as the door opened in his rear. It was the Hofrat, looking in on him; in his clinical coat, the stethoscope showing in his breast pocket, he stood there a moment, with his hand on the door--knob, and nodded at the distiller of sweet sounds. Hans Castorp, over his shoulder, replied to the nod, and the chief's blue--cheeked visage, with its one--sided moustache, disappeared as he drew the door to behind him. Hans Castorp returned to his invisible, melodious pair of lovers.

Later in the day, after the noon and evening meals, he had a changing audience for his performance—unless one must reckon him in with the audience, instead of as the dispenser of the entertainment. Personally he inclined to the latter view. And the Berghof population agreed with him, to the extent that from the very first night they silently acquiesced in his self--appointed guardianship of the instrument. They did not care, these people. Aside from their ephemeral idolatry of the tenor, luxuriating in the melting brilliance of his own voice, letting this boon to the human race stream from him in cantilenas and high feats of virtuosity, notwithstanding their loudly proclaimed enthusiasm, they were without real love for the instrument, and content that anyone should operate it who was willing to take the trouble. It was Hans Castorp who kept the records in order, wrote the contents of each album on the inside of the cover, so that each piece might be found at once when it was wanted, and "ran" the instrument. Soon he did it with ease and dexterity. The others would have spoiled the plates by using worn--out needles, would have left them lying about on chairs, would have tried all sorts of imbecile tricks, playing some noble and stately piece of music at breakneck speed and pitch, or setting the indicator at zero, so that nothing but a hysterical trilling or a long expiring groan came from the instrument. They had tried all that already. Of course, they were ill; but they were also pretty crude. After a while, Hans Castorp simply took the key of the little cabinet that held the needles and albums, and kept it in his pocket, so that his permission must needs be asked if anyone desired to play.

Evening, after the social quarter--hour, when the guests were gone, was his best time. He remained in the salon, or returned stealthily thither, and played until deep in the night. He found there was less danger than he had feared of disturbing the nightly rest of the house; for the carrying power of this ghostly music proved relatively small. The vibrations, so surprisingly powerful in the near neighbourhood of the box, soon exhausted themselves, grew weak and eerie with distance, like all magic. Hans Castorp was alone among four walls with his wonder--box; with the florid performance of this truncated little coffin of violin--wood, this small dull--black temple, before the open double doors of which he sat with his hands folded in his lap, his head on one side, his mouth open, and let the harmonies flow over him.

These singers male and female whom he heard, he could not see; their corporeal part abode in America, in Milan, Vienna, St. Petersburg. But let them dwell where they might, he had their better part, their voices, and might rejoice in the refining and abstracting process which did away with the disadvantages of closer personal contact, yet left them enough appeal to the sense, to permit of some command over their individualities, especially in the case of German artists. He could distinguish the dialect, the pronunciation, the local origin of these; the character of the voice betrayed something of the soul--stature of individuals, and the level of their intelligence could be guessed by the extent to which they had neglected or taken advantage of their opportunities. Hans Castorp writhed when they failed. He bit his lips in chagrin when the reproduction was technically faulty; he was on pins and needles when the first note of an often--used record gave a shrill or scratching sound—-which happened more particularly with the difficult female voice. Still, when these things happened, he bore with them, for love makes us forbearing. Sometimes he bent over the whirring, pulsating mechanism as over a spray of lilac, rapt in a cloud of sweet sound; or stood before the open case, tasting the triumphant joy of the conductor who with raised hand brings the trumpets into place precisely at the right moment. And he had favourites in his treasure--house, certain vocal and instrumental numbers which he never tired of hearing.

One group of records contained the closing scenes of a certain brilliant opera, overflowing with melodic genius, by a great countryman of Herr Settembrini, the doyen of dramatic music in the south, who had written it to the order of an oriental prince, in the second half of the last century, to celebrate the completion of a great technical achievement which should bind the peoples of the earth together. Hans Castorp had learned something of the plot, knew the main lines of the tragic fate of Radames, Amneris, and Aida; and when he heard it from his casket could understand well enough what they said. The incomparable tenor, the royal alto with the wonderful sob in her register, and the silver soprano he understood perhaps not every word they said, but enough, with his knowledge of the situation, and his sympathy in general for such situations, to feel a familiar fellow--feeling that increased every time he listened to this set of records, until it amounted to infatuation.

First came the scene of the explanation between Radames and Amneris: the king's daughter has the captive brought before her, whom she loves, whom she would gladly save for her own, but that he has just thrown all away for the sake of a barbarian slave—-fatherland and honour and all. Though he insists that in the depth of his soul honour remains untarnished. But this inner unimpairment avails him little, under the weight of all that indisputable guilt and crime, for he has become forfeit to the spiritual arm, which is inexorable toward human weakness, and will certainly make short work of him if he does not, at the last moment, abjure the slave, and throw himself into the royal arms of the alto with the sob in her register—-who, so far as her voice went, richly deserved him. Amneris wrestles fervidly with the mellifluous but tragically blind and infatuated tenor, who sings nothing at all but "In vain" and "I cannot," when she addresses him with despairing pleas to renounce the slave, for that his own life is in the balance. "I cannot" ... "Once more, renounce her" ... "In vain thou pleadest"—-and deathly obstinacy and anguished love blend together in a duet of extraordinary power and beauty, but absolutely no hope whatever. Then comes the terrifying repetition of the priestly formulas of condemnation, to the accompaniment of Amneris's despair; they sound hollowly from below, and them the unhappy Radames does not reply to at all.

"Radames, Radames," sings the high--priest peremptorily, and points out the treason he has committed.

"Justify thyself," all the priests, in chorus, demand.

The high--priest calls attention to his silence, and they all hollowly declare him guilty.

"Radames, Radames," sings the high--priest again. "The camp thou hast left before the battle."

And again: "Justify thyself." "Lo, he is silent," the highly prejudiced presiding officer announces once more; and all the priests acain unanimously declare him guilty.

"Radames, Radames," for the third time comes the inexorable voice. "To Fatherland, to honour and thy King, thy oath thou hast broken"—-"Justify thyself," resounded again. And finally, for the third time, *Fellonia,* the priestly chorus proclaims, after noting that Radames has again remained absolutely silent. So then there is nothing for it: the chorus announces the evil--doer for judgment, proclaims that his doom is sealed, that he must die the death of a deserter and be buried alive beneath the temple of the offended deity.

The outraged feelings of Amneris at this priestly severity had to be imagined, for here the record broke off. Hans Castorp changed the plate, with as few movements as possible, his eyes cast down. When he seated himself again, it was to listen to the last scene of the melodrama, the closing duet of Radames and Aida, sung in the underground vaults, while above their heads in the temple the cruel and bigoted priests perform the service of their cult, spreading forth their arms, giving out a dull, murmurous sound. "*Tu—in qitesta tomba?*" comes the inexpressibly moving, sweet and at the same time heroic voice of Radames, in mingled horror and rapture. Yes, she has found her way to him, the beloved one for whose sake he has forfeited life and honour, she has awaited him here, to die with him; and the exchange of song between the two, broken at times by the muffled sound of the ceremonies above them, or blending and harmonizing with it, pierced the soul of our solitary night--watcher to its very depth, as much by reason of the circumstances as by the melodic expression of them. They sang of heaven, these two; but truly the songs were heavenly themselves, and heavenly sweet the singing of them. That melodic line resistlessly travelled by the voices, solo and *unisono*, of Radames and Aida; that simple, rapturous ascent, playing from tonic to dominant, as it mounts from the fundamental to the sustained note a half--tone before the octave, then turning back again to the fifth——it seemed to the listener the most rarefied, the most ecstatic he had ever heard. But he would have been less ravished by the sounds, had not the situation which gave them birth prepared his spirit to yield to the sweetness of the music. It was *so* beautiful, that Aida should have found her way to the condemned Radames, to share his fate for ever! The condemned one protested, quite properly, against the sacrifice of the precious life; but in his tender, despairing "*No, no, troppo sei bella*" was the intoxication of final union with her whom he had thought never to see again. It needed no effort of imagination to enable Hans Castorp to feel with

Radames all this intoxication, all this gratitude. And what, finally, he felt, understood, and enjoyed, sitting there with folded hands, looking into the black slats of the jalousies whence it all issued, was the triumphant idealism of the music, of art, of the human spirit; the high and irrefragable power they had of shrouding with a veil of beauty the vulgar horror of actual fact. What was it, considered with the eye of reason, that was happening here? Two human beings, buried alive, their lungs full of pit gas, would here together——or, more horrible still, one after the other——succumb to the pangs of hunger, and thereafter the process of putrefaction would do its unspeakable work, until two skeletons remained, each totally indifferent and insensible to the other's presence or absence. This was the real, objective fact—-but a side, and a state of affairs quite distinct, of which idealism and emotion would have none, which was triumphantly put in the shade by the music and the beauty of the theme. The situation as it stood did not exist for either operatic Radames or operatic Aida. Their voices rose *unisono* to the blissful sustained note leading into the octave, as they assured each other that now heaven was opening, and the light of its eternity streaming forth before their yearning eyes. The consoling power of this aesthetic palliation did the listener good, and went far to account for the special love he bore this number of his programme.

He was wont to rest from these terrors and ecstasies in another number, brief, yet with a concentrated power of enchantment; peaceful, compared with the other, an idyll, yet *raffiné*, shaped and turned with all the subtlety and economy of the most modern art. It was an orchestral piece, of French origin, purely instrumental, a symphonic prelude, achieved with an instrumentation relatively small for our time, yet with all the apparatus of modern technique and shrewdly calculated to set the spirit adreaming. Here is the dream Hans Castorp dreamed: he lay on his back in a sunny, flowerstarred meadow, with his head on a little knoll, one leg drawn up, the other flung over——and those were goat's legs crossed there before him. His fingers touched the stops of a little wooden pipe, which he played for the pure joy of it, his solitude on the meadow being complete. He held it to his lips, a reed pipe or little clarinet, and coaxed from it soothing head--tones, one after the other, just as they came, and yet in a pleasing sequence. The care--free piping rose toward the deep--blue sky, and beneath the sky stretched the branching, wind--tossed boughs of single ash--trees and birches whose leaves twinkled in the sun. But his feckless, day--dreaming, half--melodious pipe was far from being the only voice in the solitude. The hum of insects in the sunwarmed air above the long grass, the sunshine itself, the soft wind, the swaying treetops, the twinkling leaves—all these gentle vibrations of the midsummery peace set themselves to his simple piping, to give it a changeful, ever surprisingly choice harmonic meaning. Sometimes the symphonic accompaniment would fade far off and be forgot. Then goat--legged Hans would blow stoutly away, and by the naïve monotony of his piping lure back Nature's subtly colourful, harmonious enchantment; until at length, after repeated intermission, she sweetly acceded. More and higher instruments came in rapidly, one after another, until all the previously lacking richness and volume were reached and sustained in a single fugitive moment that yet held all eternity in its consummate bliss. The young faun was joyous on his summer meadow. No "Justify thyself," was here; no challenge, no priestly court--martial upon one who strayed away and was forgotten of honour. Forgetfulness held sway, a blessed hush, the innocence of those places where time is not; "slackness" with the best conscience in the world, the very apotheosis of rebuff to the Western world and that world's insensate ardour for the "deed." The soothing effect of all which upon our nightwalking music--maker gave this record a special value in his eyes. There was a third. Or rather there were many, a consecutive group of three or four, a single tenor *aria* taking up almost half the space of a whole black rubber plate. Again it was French music—an opera Hans Castorp knew well, having seen and heard it repeatedly. Once, at a certain critical juncture now far in the past, he had made its action serve him for an allegory. The record took up the play at the second act, in the Spanish tavern, in crude Moorish architecture, a shawl-

[807]

-draped, roomy cellar like the floor of a barn. One heard Carmen's voice, a little brusque, yet warm, and very infectious in its folk--quality, saying she would dance before the sergeant; one heard the rattle of castanets. But in the same moment, from a distance, the blare of trumpets swelled out, bugles giving a military signal, at which sound the little sergeant starts up. "One moment, stop!" he cries, and pricks up his ears like a horse. Why? What was it then, Carmen asked; and he: "Dost thou not hear?" astonished that the signal did not enter into her soul as into his. "Carmen, 'tis the retreat!" It is the trumpets from the garrison, giving the summons. "The hour draws nigh for our return," says he, in operatic language. But the gipsy girl cannot understand, nor does she wish to. So much the better, she says, half stupidly, half pertly; she needs no castanets, for here is music dropped from the sky. Music to dance by, tra--la, tra--la! He is beside himself. His own disappointment retreats before his need to make clear to her how matters stand, and how no love--affair in the world can prevent obedience to this summons. How is it she cannot understand anything so fixed, so fundamental? "I must away, the signal summons me, to quarters!" he cries, in despair over a lack of understanding that doubly burdens his heavy heart. And now, hear Carmen! She is furious. Outraged to the depths of her soul, her voice is sheer betrayed and injured love—-or she makes it sound so. "To quarters? The signal?" And her heart? Her faithful, loving heart, just then, in its weakness, yes, she admitted, in its weakness, about to while away an hour with him in dance and song? "Tan--ta--ra!" And in a fury of scorn she sets her curled hand to her lips and imitates the horns: "Taran--tara!" And that was enough to make the fool leap up, on fire to be off! Good, then, let him be off, away with him! Here are helmet, sabre, and hanger—-away, away, away with him, let him be off, let him be off, off to the barracks! He pleads for mercy. But she goes on, scorching him with her scorn, mocking him, taking his place and showing in pantomime how at the sound of the horn he lost what little sense he had. Tan--tara! The signal! O heaven! he will come too late! Let him go, let him be off, for the summons sounds, and he, like a fool, makes to go, at the very moment when she would dance for him. From this time, so she will account his love!

He is in torments. She cannot understand. The woman, the gipsy girl, cannot, will not understand. Will not—for in her rage and scorn speaks something more and larger than the moment and the personal: a hatred, a primeval hostility against that principle, which in the accents of these Spanish bugles—or French horns—called to the lovelorn little soldier. Over that it was her deepest, her inborn, her more than personal ambition to triumph. And she possesses a very simple means: she says that if he goes he does not love her—precisely that which José cannot bear to hear. He beseeches her to let him speak. She will not. Then he compels her—it is a deucedly serious moment, dull notes of *fatality* rise from the orchestra, a gloomy, ominous motif, which, as Hans Castorp knew, recurred throughout the opera, up to its fatal climax, and formed also the first phrase of the soldier's *aria*, on the next plate, which had now to be inserted.

"See here thy flow'ret treasured well"—how exquisitely José sang that! Hans Castorp played this single record over and over, and listened with the deepest participation. As far as its contents went, it did not fetch the action much further; but its imploring emotion was moving in the highest degree. The young soldier sang of the flower Carmen had tossed him at the beginning of their acquaintance, which had been everything to him, in the arrest he had suffered for love of her. He confesses: "Sometimes I cursed the hour I met thee, and tried all vainly to forget thee"—only next moment to rue his blasphemy, and pray on his knees to see her once more. And as he prayed—striking the same high note as just before on the "To see thee, Carmen," but now the orchestration lends all the resources of its enchantment to paint the anguish, the longing, the desperate tenderness, sweet despair, in the little soldier's heart—ah, there she stood before his eyes, in all her fatal charm; and clearly, unmistakably, he felt that he was undone, for ever lost—on the word undone came a sobbing whole--tone grace--note to the first syllable—

[809]

-lost and for ever undone. "Then would an ecstasy steal o'er me," he despairingly asseverated in a recurrent melody repeated wailingly by the orchestra, rising two tones from the tonic and thence returning ardently to the fifth: "Carmen, my own," he repeats, with infinite tenderness but rather tasteless redundancy, going all the way up the scale to the sixth, in order to add: "My life, my soul belongs to thee"—-after which he let his voice fall ten whole tones and in deepest emotion gave out the "Carmen, I love thee!" shuddering forth the words in anguish from a note sustained above changing harmonies, until the "thee" with the syllable before it was resolved in the full accord. "Yes, ah, yes," said Hans Castorp, with mournful satisfaction, and put on the finale: where they are all congratulating young José because the meeting with the officer has cut off his retreat, and now it only remains open to him to desert, as Carmen, to his horror, had before now demanded he should.

"Away to the mountains, away, away,

Share in our life, careless and gay,"

they sang in chorus—-one could understand the words quite well:

"Freely to roam, the world our home,

Gaily to pass o'er land and sea

And enjoy, all else excelling,

Sweet liberty!"

"Yes, yes," he said, as before; and passed on to a fourth record, something very dear and good.

It is not our fault that it was French again, nor are we responsible for its once more striking the military note. It was an intermezzo, a solo number, the Prayer from Gounod's *Faust*. The singer, a character warmly sympathetic to our young man's heart, was called in the opera Valentine; but Hans Castorp named him by another and dearly familiar, sadness--evoking name; whose onetime bearer he had come largely to identify with the operatic character whom the wonder--box was making vocal—-though the latter to be sure had a much more beautiful voice, a warm and powerful baritone. His song was in three parts: the first consisting of two closely related "corner"—-strophes, religious in character, almost in the style of the Protestant chorale, and a middle--strophe, bold and *chevaleresque*, war--like, light--hearted, yet God--fearing too, and essentially French and military. The invisible character sang:

"Now the parting hour has come

I must leave my lovéd home"

and turned under these circumstances to God, imploring Him to take under His special care and protection his beloved sister. He was going to the wars: the rhythm changed, grew brisk and lively, dull care and sorrow might go hang! He, the invisible singer, longed to be in the field, to stand in the thickest of the fray, where danger was hottest, and fling himself upon the foe—-gallant, God--fearing, altogether French. But if, he sang, God should call him to Himself, then would He look down protectingly on "thee"—-meaning the singer's sister, as Hans Castorp was perfectly aware, yet the word thrilled him to the depths, and his emotion prolonged itself as the hero sang, to a mighty choral accompaniment:

"O Lord of heaven, hear my prayer!

Guard Marguerite within Thy shelt'ring care!"

There the record ceased. We have dwelt upon it because of Hans Castorp's especial penchant; but also because it played a certain rôle on a later and most strange occasion. And now we come back to the fifth and last piece in his group of high favourites: this time not French, but something especially and exemplarily German; not opera either, but a *lied*, one of those which are folk--song and masterpiece together, and from the combination receive their peculiar stamp as spiritual epitomes. Why should we beat about the bush? It was Schubert's "Linden--tree," it was none other than the old, old favourite, *"Am Brunnen vor dem Tore."*

It was sung to piano accompaniment by a tenor voice; and the singer was a lad of parts and discernment, who knew how to render with great skill, fine musical feeling and finesse in recitative his simple yet consummate theme. We all know that the noble *lied* sounds rather differently when given as a concert--number from its rendition in the childish or the popular mouth. In its simplified form the melody is sung straight through; whereas in the original art--song, the key changes to minor in the second of the eight--line stanzas, changes back again with beautiful effect to major in the fifth line; is dramatically resolved in the following "bitter blasts" and "facing the tempest"; and returns again only with the last four lines of the third stanza, which are repeated to finish out the melody. The truly compelling turn in the melody occurs three times, in its modulated second half, the third time in the repetition of the last half--strophe "Ay, onward, ever onward." The enchanting turn, which we would not touch too nearly in bold words, comes on the phrases "Upon its branches fair," "A message in my ear," "Yet ever in my breast"; and each time the tenor rendered them, in his clear, warm voice, with his excellent breathing--technique, with the suggestion of a sob, arid so much sensitive, beauty--loving intelligence, the listener felt his heart gripped in undreamed--of fashion; with an effect the singer knew how to heighten by head--tones of extraordinary ardour on the lines "I found my solace there," and "For rest and peace are here." In the repetition of the last line, "Here shouldst thou find thy rest," he sang the "shouldst thou" the first time yearningly, at full strength, but the second in the tenderest flute--tones.

So much for the song, and the rendering of it. For the earlier selections, we may flatter ourselves, perhaps, that we have been able to communicate to the reader some understanding, more or less precise, of Hans Castorp's intimate emotional participation in the chosen numbers of his nightly programme. But to make clear what this last one, the old "Linden--tree," meant to him, is truly a ticklish endeavour; requiring great delicacy of emphasis if more harm than good is not to come of the undertaking.

Let us put it thus: a conception which is of the spirit, and therefore significant, is so because it reaches beyond itself to become the expression and exponent of a larger conception, a whole world of feeling and sentiment, which, whether more or less completely, is mirrored in the first, and in this wise, accordingly, the degree of its significance measured. Further, the love felt for such a creation is in itself "significant": betraying something of the person who cherishes it, characterizing his relation to that broader world the conception bodies forth—-which, consciously or unconsciously, he loves along with and in the thing itself.

May we take it that our simple hero, after so many years of hermetic--pedagogic discipline, of ascent from one stage of being to another, has now reached a point where he is conscious of the "meaningfulness" of his love and the object of it? We assert, we record, that he has. To him the song meant a whole world, a world which he must have loved, else he could not have so desperately loved that which it represented and symbolized to him. We know what we are saying when we add—-perhaps rather darkly—-that he might have had a different fate if his temperament had been less accessible to the charms of the sphere of feeling, the general attitude of mind, which the *lied* so profoundly, so mystically epitomized. The truth was that his very destiny had been marked by stages, adventures, insights, and these flung up in his mind suitable themes for his "stock--taking" activities, and these, in their turn, ripened him into an intuitional critic of this sphere, of this its absolutely exquisite image, and his love of it. To the point even that he was quite capable of bringing up all three as objects of his conscientious scruples!

Only one totally ignorant of the tender passion will suppose that such scruples can detract from the object of love. On the contrary, they but give it spice. It is they which lend love the spur of passion, so that one might almost define passion as misgiving love. But wherein lay Hans Castorp's conscientious and stocktaking misgiving, as to the ultimate propriety of his love for the enchanting *lied* and the world whose image it was? What was the world behind the song, which the motions of his conscience made to seem a world of forbidden love?

It was death.

What utter and explicit madness! That glorious song! An indisputable masterpiece, sprung from the profoundest and holiest depths of racial feeling; a precious possession, the archetype of the genuine; embodied loveliness. What vile detraction!

Yes. Ah, yes! All very fine. Thus must every upright man speak. But for all that, behind this so lovely and pleasant artistic production stood——death. It had with death certain relations, which one might love, yet not without consciously, and in a "stocktaking" sense, acknowledging a certain illicit element in one's love. Perhaps in its original form it was not sympathy with death; perhaps it was something very much of the people and racy of life; but spiritual sympathy with it was none the less sympathy with death. At first blush proper and pious enough, indisputably. But the issues of it were sinister.

What was all this he was thinking? He would not have listened to it from one of you. Sinister issues. Fantastical, dark--corner, misanthropic, torture--chamber thoughts, Spanish black and the ruff, lust not love——and these the issues of pure--eyed loveliness!

Unquestioning confidence, Hans Castorp knew, he had never placed in Herr Settembrini. But he remembered now an admonition the enlightened mentor had given him in past time, at the beginning of his hermetic career, on the subject of "spiritual backsliding" to darker ages. Perhaps it would be well to make cautious application of that wisdom to the present case. It was the backsliding which Herr Settembrini had characterized as "disease"; the epitome itself, the spiritual phase to which one backslid——that too would appeal to his pedagogic mind as "diseased"? And even so? Hans Castorp's loved nostalgic lay, and the sphere of feeling to which it belonged——morbid? Nothing of the sort. They were the sanest, the homeliest in the world. And yet——This was a fruit, sound and splendid enough for the instant or so, yet extraordinarily prone to decay; the purest refreshment of the spirit, if enjoyed at the right moment, but the next, capable of spreading decay and corruption among men. It was the fruit of life, conceived of death, pregnant of dissolution; it was a miracle of the soul, perhaps the highest, in the eye and sealed with the blessing of conscienceless beauty; but on cogent grounds regarded with mistrust by the eye of shrewd geniality dutifully "taking stock" in its love of the organic; it was a subject for self--conquest at the definite behest of conscience.

Yes, self--conquest—that might well be the essence of triumph over this love, this soul--enchantment that bore such sinister fruit! Hans Castorp's thoughts, or rather his prophetic half--thoughts soared high, as he sat there in night and silence before his truncated sarcophagus of music. They soared higher than his understanding, they were alchemistically enhanced. Ah, what power had this soul--enchantment! We were all its sons, and could achieve mighty things on earth, in so far as we served it. One need have no more genius, only much more talent, than the author of the *"Lindenbaum,"* to be such an artist of soul--enchantment as should give to the song a giant volume by which it should subjugate the world. Kingdoms might be founded upon it, earthly, alltoo--earthly kingdoms, solid, "progressive," not at all nostalgic—in which the song degenerated to a piece of gramophone music played by electricity. But its faithful son might still be he who consumed his life in self--conquest, and died, on his lips the new word of love which as yet he knew not how to speak. Ah, it was worth dying for, the enchanted *lied!* But he who died for it, died indeed no longer for it; was a hero only because he died for the new, the new word of love and the future that whispered in his heart.

These, then, were Hans Castorp's favourite records.

Highly Questionable

Edhin Krokowski's lectures had in the swift passage of the years taken an unexpected turn. His researches, which dealt with psycho--analysis and the dream--life of humanity, had always had a subterranean, not to say catacombish character; but now, by a transition so gradual that one scarcely marked it, they had passed over to the frankly supernatural, and his fortnightly lectures in the dining--room——the prime attraction of the house, the pride of the prospectus, delivered in a drawling, foreign voice, in frock--coat and sandals from behind a little covered table, to the rapt and motionless Berghof audience——these lectures no longer treated of the disguised activities of love and the retransformation of the illness into the conscious emotion. They had gone on to the extraordinary phenomena of hypnotism and somnambulism, telepathy, "dreaming true," and second sight; the marvels of hysteria, the expounding of which widened the philosophic horizon to such an extent that suddenly before the listener's eyes would glitter darkly puzzles like that of the relation of matter to the psychical, yes, even the puzzle of life itself, which, it appeared, was easier to approach by uncanny, even morbid paths than by the way of health.

We say this because we consider it our duty to confound those flippant spirits who declared that Dr. Krokowski had resorted to mystification for the sake of redeeming his lectures from hopeless monotony; in other words, with purely emotional ends in view. Thus spoke the slanderous tongues which are everywhere to be found. True, the gentlemen at the Monday lectures flicked their ears harder than ever to make them hear; Fräulein Levi looked, if possible, even more like a wax figure wound up by machinery. But these effects were as legitimate as the train of thought pursued by the mind of the learned gentleman, and for that he might claim that it was not only consistent but even inevitable. The field of his study had always been those wide, dark tracts of the human soul, which one had been used to call the subconsciousness, though they might perhaps better be called the superconsciousness, since from them sometimes emanates a knowingness beyond anything of which the conscious intelligence is capable, and giving rise to the hypothesis that there may subsist connexions and associations between the lowest and least illumined regions of the individual soul and a wholly knowing All--soul. The province of the subsconscious, "occult" in the proper sense of the word, very soon shows itself to be occult in the narrower sense as well, and forms one of the sources whence flow the phenomena we have agreed thus to characterize. But that is not all. Whoever recognizes a symptom of organic disease as an effect of the conscious soul--life of forbidden and hystericized emotions, recognizes the creative force of the psychical within the material——a force which one is inclined to claim as a second source of magic phenomena. Idealist of the pathological, not to say pathological idealist, he sees himself at the point of departure of certain trains of thought which will shortly issue in the problem of existence, that is to say in the problem of the relation between spirit and matter. The materialist, son of a philosophy of sheer animal vigour, can never be dissuaded from explaining spirit as a mere phosphorescent product of matter; whereas the idealist, proceeding from the principle of creative hysteria, is inclined, and very readily resolved, to answer the question of primacy in the exactly opposite sense. Take it all in all, there is here nothing less than the old strife over which was first, the chicken or the egg——a strife which assumes its extraordinary complexity from the fact that no egg is thinkable except one laid by a hen, and no hen that has not crept out of a previously postulated egg.

Well then, it was such matters as these that Dr. Krokowski discussed in his lectures. He came upon them organically, logically, legitimately——that fact cannot be overemphasized. We will even add that he had already begun to treat of them before the arrival of Ellen Brand upon the scene of action, and the progress of matters into the empirical and experimental stage.

Who was Ellen Brand? We had almost forgotten that our readers do not know her, so familiar to us is the name. Who was she? Hardly anybody, at first glance. A sweet young thing of nineteen years, a flaxen--haired Dane, not from Copenhagen but from Odense--on--Fünen, where her father had a butter business. She herself had been in commercial life for a couple of years or so; with a sleeve--protector on her writing--arm she had sat over heavy books, perched on a revolving stool in a provincial branch of a city bank——and developed temperature. It was a trifling case, probably more suspected than real, though Elly was indeed fragile, fragile and obviously chlorotic—-distinctly sympathetic too, giving one a yearning to lay one's hand upon the flaxen head——as the Hofrat regularly did, when he spoke to her in the dining--room. A northern freshness emanated from her, a chaste and glassy, maidenly chaste atmosphere surrounded her, she was entirely lovable, with a pure, open look from childlike blue eyes, and a pointed, fine, High--German speech, slightly broken, with small typical mispronunciations. About her features there was nothing unusual. Her chin was too short. She sat at table with the Kleefeld, who mothered her.

Now this little Fräulein Brand, this little Elly, this friendly--natured little Danish bicycle--rider and stoop--shouldered young counter--jumper, had things about her, of which no one could have dreamed, at first sight of her transparent small personality, but which began to discover themselves after a few weeks; and these it became Dr. Krokowski's affair to lay bare in all their extraordinariness.

The learned man received his first hint in the course of a general evening conversation. Various guessing games were being played; hidden objects found by the aid of strains from the piano, which swelled higher when one approached the right spot, and died away when the seeker strayed on a false scent. Then one person went outside and waited while it was decided what task he should perform; as, exchanging the rings of two selected persons; inviting someone to dance by making three bows before her; taking a designated book from the shelves and presenting it to this or that person——and more of the same kind. It is worthy of remark that such games had not been the practice among the Berghof guests. Who had introduced them was not afterwards easy to decide; certainly it had not been Elly Brand, yet they had begun since her arrival.

The participants were nearly all old friends of ours, among them Hans Castorp. They showed themselves apt in greater or less degree—-some of them were entirely incapable. But Elly Brand's talent was soon seen to be surpassing, striking, unseemly. Her power of finding hidden articles was passed over with applause and admiring laughter. But when it came to a concerted series of actions, they were struck dumb. She did whatever they had covenanted she should do, did it directly she entered the room; with a gentle smile, without hesitation, without the help of music. She fetched a pinch of salt from the dining--room, sprinkled it over Lawyer Paravant's head, took him by the hand, led him to the piano and played the beginning of a nursery ditty with his forefinger; then brought him back to his seat, curtseyed, fetched a footstool and finally seated herself at his feet, all of that being precisely what they had cudgelled their brains to set her for a task.

She had been listening.

She reddened. With a sense of relief at her embarrassment they began in chorus to chide her; but she assured them she had not blushed in that sense. She had not listened, not outside, not at the door, truly, truly she had not!

Not outside, not at the door?

"Oh, no"—-she begged their pardon. She had listened after she came back, in the room, she could not help it.

How not help it?

Something whispered to her, she said. It whispered and told her what to do, softly, but quite clearly and distinctly.

Obviously that was an admission. In a certain sense she was aware, she had confessed, that she had cheated. She should have said beforehand that she was no good to play such a game, if she had the advantage of being whispered to. A competition loses all sense if one of the competitors has unnatural advantages over the others. In a sporting sense, she was straightway disqualified—-but disqualified in a way that made chills run up and down their backs. With one voice they called on Dr. Krokowski, they ran to fetch him, and he came. He was immediately at home in the situation, and stood there, sturdy, heartily smiling, in his very essence inviting confidence. Breathless they told him they had something quite abnormal for him, an omniscient, a girl with voices. Yes, yes? Only let them be calm, they should see. This was his native heath, quagmirish and uncertain footing enough for the rest of them, yet he moved upon it with assured tread. He asked questions, and they told him. Ah, there she was—-come, my child, is it true, what they are telling me? And he laid his hand on her head, as scarcely anyone could resist doing. Here was much ground for interest, none at all for consternation. He plunged the gaze of his brown, exotic eyes deep into Ellen Brand's blue ones, and ran his hand down over her shoulder and arm, stroking her gently. She returned his gaze with increasing submission, her head inclined slowly toward her shoulder and breast. Her eyes were actually beginning to glaze, when the master made a careless outward motion with his hand before her face. Immediately thereafter he expressed his opinion that everything was in perfect order, and sent the overwrought company off to the evening cure, with the exception of Elly Brand, with whom he said he wished to have a little chat.

A little chat. Quite so. But nobody felt easy at the word, it was just the sort of word Krokowski the merry comrade used by preference, and it gave them cold shivers. Hans Castorp, as he sought his tardy reclining--chair, remembered the feeling with which he had seen Elly's illicit achievements and heard her shamefaced explanation; as though the ground were shifting under his feet, and giving him a slightly qualmish feeling, a mild seasickness. He had never been in an earthquake; but he said to himself that one must "experience a like sensation of unequivocal alarm. But he had also felt great curiosity at these fateful gifts of Ellen Brand; combined, it is true, with the knowledge that their field was with difficulty accessible to the spirit, and the doubt as to whether it was not barren, or even sinful, so far as he was concerned—-all which did not prevent his feeling from being what in fact it actually was, curiosity. Like everybody else, Hans Castorp had, at his time of life, heard this and that about the mysteries of nature, or the supernatural. We have mentioned the clairvoyante greataunt, of whom a melancholy tradition had come down. But the world of the supernatural, though theoretically and objectively he had recognized its existence, had never come close to him, he had never had any practical experience of it. And his aversion from it, a matter of taste, an aesthetic revulsion, a reaction of human pride—- if we may use such large words in connexion with our modest hero—-was almost as great as his curiosity. He felt beforehand, quite clearly, that such experiencess whatever the course of them, could never be anything but in bad taste, unintelligible and humanly valueless. And yet he was on fire to go through them. He was aware that his alternative of "barren" or else "sinful," bad enough in itself, was in reality not an alternative at all, since the two ideas fell together, and calling a thing spiritually unavailable was only an a--moral way of expressing its forbidden character. But the *"placet experiri"* planted in Hans Castorp's mind by one who would surely and resoundingly have reprobated any experimentation at all in this field, was planted firmly enough. By little and little his morality and his curiosity approached and overlapped, or had probably always done so; the pure curiosity of inquiring youth on its travels, which had already brought him pretty close to the forbidden field, what time he tasted the mystery of personality, and for which he had even claimed the justification that it too was almost military in character, in that it did not weakly avoid the forbidden, when it presented itself. Hans Castorp came to the final resolve not to avoid, but to stand his ground if it came to more developments in the case of Ellen Brand. Dr. Krokowski had issued a strict prohibition against any further experimentation on the part of the laity upon Fräulein Brand's mysterious gifts. He had pre--empted the child for his scientific use, held sittings with her in his analytical oubliette, hypnotized her, it was reported, in an effort to arouse and discipline her slumbering potentialities, to make researches into her previous psychic life. Hermine Kleefeld, who mothered and patronized the child, tried to do the same; and under the seal of secrecy a certain number of facts were ascertained, which under the same seal she spread throughout the house, even unto the porter's lodge. She learned, for example, that he who—or that which—whispered the answers into the little one's ear at games was called Holger. This Holger was the departed and etherealized spirit of a young man, the familiar, something like the guardian angel, of little Elly. So it was he who had told all that about the pinch of salt and the tune played with Lawyer Paravant's forefinger?

Yes, those spirit lips, so close to her ear that they were like a caress, and tickled a little, making her smile, had whispered her what to do. It must have been very nice when she was in school and had not prepared her lesson to have him tell her the answers. Upon this point Elly was silent. Later she said she thought he would not have been allowed. It would be forbidden to him to mix in such serious matters—and moreover, he would probably not have known the answers himself. It was learned, further, that from her childhood up Ellen had had visions, though at widely separated intervals of time; visions, visible and invisible. What sort of thing were they, now—-invisible visions? Well, for example: when she was a girl of sixteen, she had been sitting one day alone in the living--room of her parents' house, sewing at a round table, with her father's dog Freia lying near her on the carpet. The table was covered with a Turkish shawl, of the kind old women wear three--cornered across their shoulders. It covered the table diagonally, with the corners somewhat hanging over. Suddenly Ellen had seen the corner nearest her roll slowly up. Soundlessly, carefully, and evenly it turned itself up, a good distance toward the centre of the table, so that the resultant roll was rather long; and while this was happening, the dog Freia started up wildly, bracing her forefeet, the hair rising on her body. She had stood on her hind legs, then run howling into the next room and taken refuge under a sofa. For a whole year thereafter she could not be persuaded to set foot in the living--room.

Was it Holger, Fräulein Kleefeld asked, who had rolled up the cloth? Little Brand did not know. And what had she thought about the affair? But since it was absolutely impossible to think anything about it, little Elly had thought nothing at all. Had she told her parents? No. That was odd. Though so sure she had thought nothing about it, Elly had had a distinct impression, in this and similar cases, that she must keep it to herself, make a profound and shamefaced secret of it. Had she taken it much to heart?

No, not particularly. What was there about the rolling up of a cloth to take to heart?

But other things she had—-for example, the following:

A year before, in her parent's house at Odense, she had risen, as was her custom, in the cool of the early morning and left her room on the ground--floor, to go up to the breakfast--room, in order to brew the morning coffee before her parents rose. She had almost reached the landing, where the stairs turned, when she saw standing there close by the steps her elder sister Sophie, who had married and gone to America to live. There she was, her physical presence, in a white gown, with, curiously enough, a garland of moist water--lilies on her head, her hands folded against one shoulder, and nodded to her sister. Ellen, rooted to the spot, half joyful, half terrified, cried out: "Oh, Sophie, is that you?" Sophie had nodded once again, and dissolved. She became gradually transparent, soon she was only visible as an ascending current of warm air, then not visible at all, so that Ellen's path was clear. Later, it transpired that Sister Sophie had died of heart trouble in New Jersey, at that very hour.

Hans Castorp, when Fräulein Kleefeld related this to him, expressed the view that there was some sort of sense in it: the apparition here, the death there—-after all, they did hang together. And he consented to be present at a spiritualistic sitting, a tabletipping, glass--moving game which they had determined to undertake with Ellen Brand, behind Dr. Krokowski's back, and in defiance of his jealous prohibition. A small and select group assembled for the purpose, their theatre being Fräulein Kleefeld's room. Besides the hostess, Fräulein Brand, and Hans Castorp, there were only Frau Stöhr, Fräulein Levi, Herr Albin, the Czech Wenzel, and Dr. Ting--Fu. In the evening, on the stroke of ten, they gathered privily, and in whispers mustered the apparatus Hermine had provided, consisting of a medium--sized round table without a cloth, placed in the centre of the room, with a wineglass upside--down upon it, the foot in the air. Round the edge of the table, at regular intervals, were placed twenty--six little bone counters, each with a letter of the alphabet written on it in pen and ink. Fräulein Kleefeld served tea, which was gratefully received, as Frau Stöhr and Fräulein Levi, despite the harmlessness of the undertaking, complained of cold feet and palpitations. Cheered by the tea, they took their places about the table, in the rosy twilight dispensed by the pink--shaded table--lamp, as Fräulein Kleefeld, in concession to the mood of the gathering, had put out the ceiling light; and each of them laid a finger of his right hand lightly on the foot of the wineglass. This was the prescribed technique. They waited for the glass to move.

That should happen with ease. The top of the table was smooth, the rim of the glass well ground, the pressure of the tremulous fingers, however lightly laid on, certainly unequal, some of it being exerted vertically, some rather sidewise, and probably in sufficient strength to cause the glass finally to move from its position in the centre of the table. On the periphery of its field it would come in contact with the marked counters; and if the letters on these, when put together, made words that conveyed any sort of sense, the resultant phenomenon would be complex and contaminate, a mixed product of conscious, half--conscious, and unconscious elements; the actual desire and pressure of some, to whom the wish was father to the act, whether or not they were aware of what they did; and the secret acquiescence of some dark stratum in the soul of the generality, a common if subterranean effort toward seemingly strange experiences, in which the suppressed self of the individual was more or less involved, most strongly, of course, that of little Elly. This they all knew beforehand—-Hans Castorp even blurted out something of the sort, after his fashion, as they sat and waited. The ladies' palpitation and cold extremities, the forced hilarity of the men, arose from their knowledge that they were come together in the night to embark on an unclean traffic with their own natures, a fearsome prying into unfamiliar regions of themselves, and that they were awaiting the appearance of those illusory or halfrealities which we call magic. It was almost entirely for form's sake, and came about quite conventionally, that they asked the spirits of the departed to speak to them through the movement of the glass. Herr Albin offered to be spokesman and deal with such spirits as manifested themselves—-he had already had a little experience at seances.

Twenty minutes or more went by. The whisperings had run dry, the first tension relaxed. They supported their right arms at the elbow with their left hands. The Czech Wenzel was almost dropping off. Ellen Brand rested her finger lightly on the glass and directed her pure, childlike gaze away into the rosy light from the table--lamp. Suddenly the glass tipped, knocked, and ran away from under their hands. They had difficulty in keeping their fingers on it. It pushed over to the very edge of the table, ran along it for a space, then slanted back nearly to the middle; tapped again, and remained quiet.

They were all startled; favourably, yet with some alarm. Frau Stöhr whimpered that she would like to stop, but they told her she should have thought of that before, she must just keep quiet now. Things seemed in train. They stipulated that, in order to answer yes or no, the glass need not run to the letters, but might give one or two knocks instead.

"Is there an Intelligence present?" Herr Albin asked, severely directing his gaze over their heads into vacancy. After some hesitation, the glass tipped and said yes.

"What is your name?" Herr Albin asked, almost gruffly, and emphasized his energetic speech by shaking his head.

The glass pushed off. It ran with resolution from one point to another, executing a *zigzag* by returning each time a little distance toward the centre of the table. It visited H, O, and L, then seemed exhausted; but pulled itself together again and sought out the G, and E, and the R. Just as they thought. It was Holger in person, the spirit Holger, who understood such matters as the pinch of salt and that, but knew better than to mix into lessons at school. He was there, floating in the air, above the heads of the little circle. What should they do with him? A certain diffidence possessed them, they took counsel behind their hands, what they were to ask him. Herr Albin decided to question him about his position and occupation in life, and did so, as before, severely, with frowning brows; as though he were a cross--examining counsel. The glass was silent awhile. Then it staggered over to the P, zigzagged and returned to O. Great suspense. Dr. Ting--Fu giggled and said Holger must be a poet. Frau Stöhr began to laugh hysterically; which the glass appeared to resent, for after indicating the E it stuck and went no further. However, it seemed fairly clear that Dr. Ting--Fu was right.

What the deuce, so Holger was a poet? The glass revived, and superfluously, in apparent pridefulness, rapped yes. A lyric poet, Fräulein Kleefeld asked? She said ly—-ric, as Hans Castorp involuntarily noted. Holger was disinclined to specify. He gave no new answer, merely spelled out again, this time quickly and unhesitatingly, the word poet, adding the T he had left off before.

Good, then, a poet. The constraint increased. It was a constraint that in reality had to do with manifestations on the part of uncharted regions of their own inner, their subjective selves, but which, because of the illusory, half--actual conditions of these manifestations, referred itself to the objective and external. Did Holger feel at home, and content, in his present state? Dreamily, the glass spelled out the word tranquil. Ah, tranquil. It was not a word one would have hit upon oneself, but after the glass spelled it out, they found it well chosen and probable. And how long had Holger been in this tranquil state? The answer to this was again something one would never have thought of, and dreamily answered; it was "A hastening while." Very good. As a piece of ventriloquistic poesy from the Beyond, Hans Castorp, in particular, found it capital. A "hastening while" was the time--element Holger lived in: and of course he had to answer as it were in parables, having very likely forgotten how to use earthly terminology and standards of exact measurement. Fräulein Levi confessed her curiosity to know how he looked, or had looked, more or less. Had he been a handsome youth? Herr Albin said she might ask him herself, he found the request beneath his dignity. So she asked if the spirit had fair hair.

"Beautiful, brown, brown curls," the glass responded, deliberately spelling out the word brown twice. There was much merriment over this. The ladies said they were in love with him. They kissed their hands at the ceiling. Dr. Ting--Fu, giggling, said Mister Holger must be rather vain.

Ah, what a fury the glass fell into! It ran like mad about the table, quite at random, rocked with rage, fell over and rolled into Frau Stöhr's lap, who stretched out her arms and looked down at it pallid with fear. They apologetically conveyed it back to its station, and rebuked the Chinaman. How had he dared to say such a thing——did he see what his indiscretion had led to? Suppose Holger was up and off in his wrath, and refused to say another word! They addressed themselves to the glass with the extreme of courtesy. Would Holger not make up some poetry for them? He had said he was a poet, before he went to hover in the hastening while. Ah, how they all yearned to hear him versify! They would love it so!

And lo, the good glass yielded and said yes! Truly there was something placable and good--humoured about the way it tapped. And then Holger the spirit began to poetize, and kept it up, copiously, circumstantially, without pausing for thought, for dear knows how long. It seemed impossible to stop him. And what a surprising poem it was, this ventriloquistic effort, delivered to the admiration of the circle—-stuff of magic, and shoreless as the sea of which it largely dealt. Sea--wrack in heaps and bands along the narrow strand of the broad--flung bay; an islanded coast, girt by steep, cliffy dunes. Ah, see the dim green distance faint and die into eternity, while beneath broad veils of mist in dull carmine and milky radiance the summer sun delays to sink!

No word can utter how and when the watery mirror turned from silver into untold changeful colour--play, to bright or pale, to spreading, opaline and moonstone gleams—or how, mysteriously as it came, the voiceless magic died away. The sea slumbered. Yet the last traces of the sunset linger above and beyond. Until deep in the night it has not grown dark: a ghostly twilight reigns in the pine forests on the downs, bleaching the sand until it looks like snow. A simulated winter forest all in silence, save where an owl wings rustling flight. Let us stray here at this hour—-so soft the sand beneath our tread, so sublime, so mild the night! Far beneath us the sea respires slowly, and murmurs a long whispering in its dream. Does it crave thee to see it again? Step forth to the sallow, glacierlike cliffs of the dunes, and climb quite up into the softness, that runs coolly into thy shoes. The land falls harsh and bushy steeply down to the pebbly shore, and still the last parting remnants of the day haunt the edge of the vanishing sky. Lie down here in the sand! How cool as death it is, how soft as silk, as flour! It flows in a colourless, thin stream from thy hand and makes a dainty little mound beside thee. Dost thou recognize it, this tiny flowing? It is the soundless, tiny stream through the hour--glass, that solemn, fragile toy that adorns the hermit's hut. An open book, a skull, and in its slender frame the double glass, holding a little sand, taken from eternity, to prolong here, as time, its troubling, solemn, mysterious essence ...

Thus Holger the spirit and his lyric improvisation, ranging with weird flights of thought from the familiar sea--shore to the cell of a hermit and the tools of his mystic contemplation. And there war more; more, human and divine, involved in daring and dreamlike terminology—-over which the members of the little circle puzzled endlessly as they spelled it out; scarcely finding time for hurried though rapturous applause, so swiftly did the glass zigzag back and forth, so swiftly the words roll on and on. There was no distant prospect of a period, even at the end of an hour. The glass improvised inexhaustibly of the pangs of birth and the first kiss of lovers; the crown of sorrows, the fatherly goodness of God; plunged into the mysteries of creation, lost itself in other times and lands, in interstellar space; even mentioned the Chaldeans and the zodiac; and would most certainly have gone on all night, if the conspirators had not finally taken their fingers from the glass, and expressing their gratitude to Holger, told him that must suffice them for the time, it had been wonderful beyond their wildest dreams, it was an everlasting pity there had been no one at hand to take it down, for now it must inevitably be forgotten, yes, alas, they had already forgotten most of it, thanks to its quality, which made it hard to retain, as dreams are. Next time they must appoint an amanuensis to take it down, and see how it would look in black and white, and read connectedly. For the moment, however, and before Holger withdrew to the tranquillity of his hastening while, it would be better, and certainly most amiable of him, if he would consent to answer a few practical questions. They scarcely as yet knew what, but would he at least be in principle inclined to do so, in his great amiability?

The answer was yes. But now they discovered a great perplexity--what should they ask? It was as in the fairy--story, when the fairy or elf grants one question, and there is danger of letting the precious advantage slip through the fingers. There was much in the world, much of the future, that seemed worth knowing, yet it was so difficult to choose. At length, as no one else seemed able to settle, Hans Castorp, with his finger on the glass, supporting his cheek on his fist, said he would like to know what was to be the actual length of his stay up here, instead of the three weeks originally fixed. Very well, since they thought of nothing better, let the spirit out of the fullness of his knowledge answer this chance query. The glass hesitated, then pushed off. It spelled out something very queer, which none of them succeeded in fathoming, it made the word, or the syllable Go, and then the word Slanting and then something about Hans Castorp's room. The whole seemed to be a direction to go slanting through Hans Castorp's room, that was to say, through number thirty--four. What was the sense of that? As they sat puzzling and shaking their heads, suddenly there came the heavy thump of a fist on the door.

They all jumped. Was it a surprise? Was Dr. Krokowski standing without, come to break up the forbidden session? They looked up guiltily, expecting the betrayed one to enter. But then came a crashing knock on the middle of the table, as if to testify that the first knock too had come from the inside and not the outside of the room. They accused Herr Albin of perpetrating this rather contemptible jest, but he denied it on his honour; and even without his word they all felt fairly certain no one of their circle was guilty. Was it Holger, then? They looked at Elly, suddenly struck by her silence. She was leaning back in her chair, with drooping wrists and finger--tips poised on the table--edge, her head bent on one shoulder, her eyebrows raised, her little mouth drawn down so that it looked even smaller, with a tiny smile that had something both silly and sly about it, and gazing into space with vacant, childlike blue eyes. They called to her, but she gave no sign of consciousness. And suddenly the night--table light went out.

Went out? Frau Stöhr, beside herself, made great outcry, for she had heard the switch turned. The light, then, had not gone out, but been put out, by a hand——a hand which one characterized afar off in calling it a "strange" hand. Was it Holger's? Up to then he had been so mild, so tractable, so poetic——but now he seemed to degenerate into clownish practical jokes. Who knew that a hand which could so roundly thump doors and tables, and knavishly turn off lights, might not next catch hold of someone's throat? They called for matches, for pocket torches. Fräulein Levi shrieked out that someone had pulled her front hair. Frau Stöhr made no bones of calling aloud on God in her distress: "O Lord, forgive me this once!" she moaned, and whimpered for mercy instead of justice, well knowing she had tempted hell. It was Dr. Ting--Fu who hit on the sound idea of turning on the ceiling light; the room was brilliantly illuminated straightway. They now established that the lamp on the night--table had not gone out by chance, but been turned off, and only needed to have the switch turned back in order to burn again. But while this was happening, Hans Castorp made on his own account a most singular discovery, which might be regarded as a personal attention on the part of the dark powers here manifesting themselves with such childish perversity. A light object lay in his lap; he discovered it to be the "souvenir" which had once so surprised his uncle when he lifted it from his nephew's table: the glass diapositive of Clavdia Chauchat's x--ray portrait. Quite uncontestably he, Hans Castorp, had not carried it into the room.

He put it into his pocket, unobservably. The others were busied about Ellen Brand, who remained sitting in her place in the same state, staring vacantly, with that curious simpering expression. Herr Albin blew in her face and imitated the upward sweeping motion of Dr. Krokowski, upon which she roused, and incontinently wept a little. They caressed and comforted her, kissed her on the forehead and sent her to bed. Fräulein Levi said she was willing to sleep with Frau Stöhr, for that abject creature confessed she was too frightened to go to bed alone. Hans Castorp, with his retrieved property in his breast pocket, had no objection to finishing off the evening with a cognac in Herr Albin's room. He had discovered, in fact, that this sort of thing affected neither the heart nor the spirits so much as the nerves of the stomach——a retroactive effect, like seasickness, which sometimes troubles the traveller with qualms hours after he has set foot on shore.

His curiosity was for the time quenched. Holger's poem had not been so bad; but the anticipated futility and vulgarity of the scene as a whole had been so unmistakable that he felt quite willing to let it go at these few vagrant sparks of hell--fire. Herr Settembrini, to whom he related his experiences, strengthened this conviction with all his force.

"That," he cried out, "was all that was lacking. Oh, misery, misery!" And cursorily dismissed little Elly as a thorough--paced impostor.

His pupil said neither yea nor nay to that. He shrugged his shoulders, and expressed the view that we did not seem to be altogether sure what constituted actuality, nor yet, in consequence, what imposture. Perhaps the boundary line was not constant. Perhaps there were transitional stages between the two, grades of actuality within nature; nature being as she was, mute, not susceptible of valuation, and thus defying distinctions which in any case, it seemed to him, had a strongly moralizing flavour. What did Herr Settembrini think about "delusions"; which were a mixture of actuality and dream, perhaps less strange in nature than to our crude, everyday processes of thought? The mystery of life was literally bottomless. What wonder, then, if sometimes illusions arose—-and so on and so forth, in our hero's genial, confiding, loose and flowing style.

Herr Settembrini duly gave him a dressing--down, and did produce a temporary reaction of the conscience, even something like a promise to steer clear in the future of such abominations. "Have respect," he adjured him, "for your humanity, Engineer!

Confide jn your God--given power of clear thought, and hold in abhorrence these luxations of the brain, these miasmas of the spirit! Delusions? The mystery of life?

Caro mio! When the moral courage to make decisions and distinctions between reality and deception degenerates to that point, then there is an end of life, of judgment, of the creative deed: the process of decay sets in, moral scepsis, and does its deadly work." Man, he went on to say, was the measure of things. His right to recognize and to distinguish between good and evil, reality and counterfeit, was indefeasible; woe to them who dared to lead him astray in his belief in this creative right. Better for them that a millstone be hanged about their necks and that they be drowned in the depth of the sea.

Hans Castorp nodded assent—-and in fact did for a while keep aloof from all such undertakings. He heard that Dr. Krokowski had begun holding seances with Ellen Brand in his subterranean cabinet, to which certain chosen ones of the guests were invited. But he nonchalantly put aside the invitation to join them—-naturally not without hearing from them and from Krokowski himself something about the success they were having. It appeared that there had been wild and arbitrary exhibitions of power, like those in Fräulein Kleefeld's room: knockings on walls and table, the turning off of the lamp, and these as well as further manifestations were being systematically produced and investigated, with every possible safeguarding of their genuineness, after Comrade Krokowski had practised the approved technique and put little Elly into her hypnotic sleep. They had discovered that the process was facilitated by music; and on these evenings the gramophone was pre--empted by the circle and carried down into the basement. But the Czech Wenzel who operated it there was a not unmusical man, and would surely not injure or misuse the instrument; Hans Castorp might hand it over without misgiving. He even chose a suitable album of records, containing light music, dances, small overtures and suchlike tunable trifles. Little Elly made no demands on a higher art, and they served the purpose admirably. To their accompaniment, Hans Castorp learned, a handkerchief had been lifted from the floor, of its own motion, or, rather, that of the "hidden hand" in its folds. The doctor's waste--paper--basket had risen to the ceiling; the pendulum of a clock been alternately stopped and set going again "without anyone touching it," a table--bell "taken" and rung—-these and a good many other turbid and meaningless phenomena. The learned master of ceremonies was in the happy position of being able to characterize them by a Greek word, very scientific and impressive. They were, so he explained in his lectures and in private conversations, "telekinetic" phenomena, cases of movement from a distance; he associated them with a class of manifestations which were scientifically known as materializations, and toward which his plans and attempts with Elly Brand were directed. He talked to them about biopsychical projections of subconscious complexes into the objective; about transactions of which the medial constitution, the somnambulic state, was to be regarded as the source; and which one might speak of as objectivated dream--concepts, in so far as they confirmed an ideoplastic property of nature, a power, which under certain conditions appertained to thought, of drawing substance to itself, and clothing itself in temporary reality. This substance streamed out from the body of the medium, and developed extraneously into biological, living end--organs, these being the agencies which had performed the extraordinary though meaningless feats they witnessed in Dr. Krokowski's laboratory. Under some conditions these agencies might be seen or touched, the limbs left their impression in wax or plaster. But sometimes the matter did not rest with such corporealization. Under certain conditions, human heads, faces, full--length phantoms manifested themselves before the eyes of the experimenters, even within certain limits entered into contact with them. And here Dr. Krokowski's doctrine began, as it were, to squint; to look two ways at once. It took on a shifting and fluctuating character, like the method of treatment he had adopted in his exposition of the nature of love. It was no longer plain--sailing, scientific treatment of the objectively mirrored subjective content of the medium and her passive auxiliaries. It was a mixing in the game, at least sometimes, at least half and half, of entities from without and beyond. It dealt—-at least possibly, if not quite admittedly—-with the non--vital, with existences that took advantage of a ticklish, mysteriously and momentarily favouring chance to return to substantiality and show themselves to thair summoners—-in brief, with the spiritualistic invocation of the departed.

Such manifestations it was that Comrade Krokowski, with the assistance of his followers, was latterly striving to produce; sturdily, with his ingratiating smile, challenging their cordial confidence, thoroughly at home, for his own person, in this questionable morass of the subhuman, and a born leader for the timid and compunctious in the regions where they now moved. He had laid himself out to develop and discipline the extraordinary powers of Ellen Brand and, from what Hans Castorp could hear, fortune smiled upon his efforts. Some of the party had felt the touch of materialized hands. Lawyer Paravant had received out of transcendency a sounding slap on the cheek, and had countered with scientific alacrity, yes, had even eagerly turned the other cheek, heedless of his quality as gentleman, jurist, and onetime member of a duelling corps, all of which would have constrained him to quite a different line of conduct had the blow been of terrestrial origin. A. K. Ferge, that good--natured martyr, to whom all "highbrow" thought was foreign, had one evening held such a spirit hand in his own, and established by sense of touch that it was whole and well shaped. His clasp had been heart--felt to the limits of respect; but it had in some indescribable fashion escaped him. A considerable period elapsed, some two months and a half of biweekly sittings, before a hand of other--worldly origin, a young man's hand, it seemed, came fingering over the table, in the red glow of the papershaded lamp, and, plain to the eyes of all the circle, left its imprint in an earthenware basin full of flour. And eight days later a troop of Krokowski's workers, Herr Albin, Frau Stöhr, the Magnuses, burst in upon Hans Castorp where he sat dozing toward midnight in the biting cold of his balcony, and witn every mark of distracted and feverish delight, their words tumbling over one another, announced that they had seen Elly's Holger——he had showed his head over the shoulder of the little medium, and had in truth "beautiful brown, brown curls." He had smiled with such unforgettable, gentle melancholy as he vanished!

Hans Castorp found this lofty melancholy scarcely consonant with Holger's other pranks, his impish and simple--minded tricks, the anything but gently melancholy slap he had given Lawyer Paravant and the latter had pocketed up. It was apparent that one must not demand consistency of conduct. Perhaps they were dealing with a temperament like that of the little hunch--backed man in the nursery song, with his pathetic wickedness and his craving for intercession. Holger's admirers had no thought for all this. What they were determined to do was to persuade Hans Castorp to rescind his decree; positively, now that everything was so brilliantly in train, he must be present at the next seance. Elly, it seemed, in her trance had promised to materialize the spirit of any departed person the circle chose.

Any departed person they chose? Hans Castorp still showed reluctance. But that it might be any person they chose occupied his mind to such an extent that in the next three days he came to a different conclusion. Strictly speaking it was not three days, but as many minutes, which brought about the change. One evening, in a solitary hour in the music--room, he played again the record that bore the imprint of Valentine's personality, to him so profoundly moving. He sat there listening to the soldierly prayer of the hero departing for the field of honour:

"If God should summon me away,

Thee I would watch and guard alway,

O Marguerite!"

and, as ever, Hans Castorp was filled by emotion at the sound, an emotion which this time circumstances magnified and as it were condensed into a longing; he thought: "Barren and sinful or no, it would be a marvellous thing, a darling adventure! And he, as I know him, if he had anything to do with it, would not mind." He recalled that composed and liberal "Certainly, of course," he had heard in the darkness of the x--ray laboratory, when he asked Joachim if he might commit certain optical indiscretions. The next morning he announced his willingness to take part m the evening seance; and half an hour after dinner joined the group of familiars of the uncanny, who, unconcernedly chatting, took their way down to the basement. They were all old inhabitants, the oldest of the old, or at least of long standing in the group, like the Czech Wenzel and Dr. Ting--Fu; Ferge and Wehsal, Lawyer Paravant, the ladies Kleefeld and Levi, and, in addition, those persons who had come to his balcony to announce to him the apparition of Holger's head, and of course the medium, Elly Brand.

[836]

That child of the north was already in the doctor's charge when Hans Castorp passed through the door with the visiting--card: the doctor, in his black tunic, his arm laid fatherly across her shoulder, stood at the foot of the stair leading from the basement floor and welcomed the guests, and she with him. Everybody greeted everybody else, with surprising hilarity and expansiveness—it seemed to be the common aim to keep the meeting pitched in a key free from all solemnity or constraint. They talked in loud, cheery voices, poked each other in the ribs, showed everyway how perfectly at ease they felt. Dr. Krokowski's yellow teeth kept gleaming in his beard with every hearty, confidence--inviting smile; he repeated his "Wel—-come" to each arrival, with special fervour in Hans Castorp's case—-who, for his part, said nothing at all, and whose manner was hesitating. "Courage, comrade,"

Krokowski's energetic and hospitable nod seemed to be saying, as he gave the young man's hand an almost violent squeeze. No need here to hang the head, here is no cant nor sanctimoniousness, nothing but the blithe and manly spirit of disinterested research. But Hans Castorp felt none the better for all this pantomime. He summed up the resolve formed by the memories of the x--ray cabinet; but the train of thought hardly fitted with his present frame; rather he was reminded of the peculiar and unforgettable mixture of feelings—-nervousness, pridefulness, curiosity, disgust, and awe—-with which, years ago, he had gone with some fellow students, a little tipsy, to a brothel in Sankt--Pauli.

As everyone was now present, Dr. Krokowski selected two controls—-they were, for the evening, Frau Magnus and the ivory Levi—-to preside over the physical examination of the medium, and they withdrew to the next room. Hans Castorp and the remaining nine persons awaited in the consulting--room the issue of the austerely scientific procedure—-which was invariably without any result whatever. The room was familiar to him from the hours he had spent here, behind Joachim's back, in conversation with the psycho--analyst. It had a writing--desk, an arm--chair and an easychair for patients on the left, the window side; a library of reference--books on shelves to right and left of the side door, and in the further right--hand corner a chaise--longue, covered with oilcloth, separated by a folding screen from the desk and chairs. The doctor's glass instrument--case also stood in that corner, in another was a bust of Hippocrates, while an engraving of Rembrandt's "Anatomy Lesson" hung above the gas fire--place on the right side wall. It was an ordinary consulting--room, like thousands more; but with certain temporary special arrangements. The round mahogany table whose place was in the centre of the room, beneath the electric chandelier, upon the red carpet that covered most of the floor, had been pushed forward against the left--hand wall, beneath the plaster bust; while a smaller table, covered with a cloth and bearing a red--shaped lamp, had been set obliquely near the gas fire, which was lighted and giving out a dry heat. Another electric bulb, covered with red and further with a black gauze veil, hung above the table. On this table stood certain notorious objects: two table--bells, of different patterns, one to shake and one to press, the plate with flour, and the paper--basket. Some dozen chairs of different shapes and sizes surrounded the table in a half--circle, one end of which was formed by the foot of the chaise--longue, the other ending near the centre of the room, beneath the ceiling light. Here, in the neighbourhood of the last chair, and about half--way to the door, stood the gramophone; the album of light trifles lay on a chair next it. Such were the arrangements. The red lamps were not yet lighted, the ceiling light was shedding an effulgence as of common day, for the window, above the narrow end of the writing--desk, was shrouded in a dark covering, with its open--work cream--coloured blind hanging down in front of it.

After ten minutes the doctor returned with the three ladies. Elly's outer appearance had changed: she was not wearing her ordinary clothes, but a night--gownlike garment of white *crêpe*, girdled about the waist by a cord, leaving her slender arms bare. Her maidenly breasts showed themselves soft and unconfined beneath this garment, it appeared she wore little else.

They all hailed her gaily. "Hullo, Elly! How lovely she looks again! A perfect fairy!

Very pretty, my angel!" She smiled at their compliments to her attire, probably well knowing it became her. "Preliminary control negative," Krokowski announced. "Let's get to work, then, comrades," he said. Hans Castorp, conscious of being disagreeably affected by the doctor's manner of address, was about to follow the example of the others, who, shouting, chattering, slapping each other on the shoulders, were settling themselves in the circle of chairs, when the doctor addressed him personally.

"My friend," said he, "you are a guest, perhaps a novice, in our midst, and therefore I should like, this evening, to pay you special honour. I confide to you the control of the medium. Our practice is as follows." He ushered the young man toward the end of the circle next the chaise--longue and the screen, where Elly was seated on an ordinary cane chair, with her face turned rather toward the entrance door than to the centre of the room. He himself sat down close in front of her in another such chair, and clasped her hands, at the same time holding both her knees firmly between his own. "Like that," he said, and gave his place to Hans Castorp, who assumed the same position.

"You'll grant that the arrest is complete. But we shall give you assistance too. Fräulein Kleefeld, may I implore you to lend us your aid?" And the lady thus courteously and exotically entreated came and sat down, clasping Elly's fragile wrists, one in each hand.

Unavoidable that Hans Castorp should look into the face of the young prodigy, fixed as it was so immediately before his own. Their eyes met—but Elly's slipped aside and gazed with natural self--consciousness in her lap. She was smiling a little affectedly, with her lips slightly pursed, and her head on one side, as she had at the wineglass seance. And Hans Castorp was reminded, as he saw her, of something else: the look on Karen Karstedt's face, a smile just like that, when she stood with Joachim and himself and regarded the unmade grave in the Dorf graveyard.

The circle had sat down. They were thirteen persons; not counting the Czech Wenzel, whose function it was to serve Polyhymnia, and who accordingly, after putting his instrument in readiness, squatted with his guitar at the back of the circle. Dr. Krokowski sat beneath the chandelier, at the other end of the row, after he had turned on both red lamps with a single switch, and turned off the centre light. A darkness, gently aglow, lay over the room, the corners and distances were obscured. Only the surface of the little table and its immediate vicinity were illumined by a pale rosy light. During the next few minutes one scarcely saw one's neighbours; then their eyes slowly accustomed themselves to the darkness and made the best use of the light they had—-which was slightly reinforced by the small dancing flames from the chimney--piece.

The doctor devoted a few words to this matter of the lighting, and excused its lacks from the scientific point of view. They must take care not to interpret it in the sense of deliberate mystification and scene--setting. With the best will in the world they could not, unfortunately, have more light for the present. The nature of the powers they were to study would not permit of their being developed with white light, it was not possible thus to produce the desired conditions. This was a fixed postulate, with which they must for the present reckon. Hans Castorp, for his part, was quite satisfied. He liked the darkness, it mitigated the queerness of the situation. And in its justification he recalled the darkness of the x--ray room, and how they had collected themselves, and "washed their eyes" in it, before they "saw."

The medium, Dr. Krokowski went on, obviously addressing his words to Hans Castorp in particular, no longer needed to be put in the trance by the physician. She fell into it herself, as the control would see, and once she had done so, it would be her guardian spirit Holger, who spoke with her voice, to whom, and not to her, they should address themselves. Further, it was an error, which might result in failure, to suppose that one must bend mind or will upon the expected phenomena. On the contrary, a slightly diffused attention, with conversation, was recommended. And Hans Castorp was cautioned, whatever else he did, not to lose control of the medium's extremities.

"We will now form the chain," finished Dr. Krokowski; and they did so, laughing when they could not find each other's hands in the dark. Dr. Ting--Fu, sitting next Hermine Kleefeld, laid his right hand on her shoulder and reached his left to Herr Wehsal, who came next. Beyond him were Herr and Frau Magnus, then A. K. Ferge; who, if Hans Castorp mistook not, held the hand of the ivory Levi on his right——and so on. "Music!" the doctor commanded, and behind him his neighbour the Czech set the instrument in motion and placed the needle on the disk. "Talk!" Krokowski bade them, and as the first bars of an overture by Millöcker were heard, they obediently bestirred themselves to make conversation, about nothing at all: the winter snow--fall, the last course at dinner, a newly arrived patient, a departure, "wild" or otherwise——artificially sustained, half drowned by the music, and lapsing now and again. So some minutes passed.

The record had not run out before Elly shuddered violently. A trembling ran through her, she sighed, the upper part of her body sank forward so that her forehead rested against Hans Castorp's, and her arms, together with those of her guardians, began to make extraordinary pumping motions to and fro.

"Trance," announced the Kleefeld. The music stopped, so also the conversation. In the abrupt silence they heard the baritone drawl of the doctor. "Is Holger present?"

Elly shivered again. She swayed in her chair. Then Hans Castorp felt her press his two hands with a quick, firm pressure.

"She pressed my hands," he informed them.

"He," the doctor corrected him. "He pressed your hands. He is present. Wel——come, Holger," he went on with unction. "Wel—

-come, friend and fellow comrade, heartily, heartily wel—-come. And remember, when you were last with us," he went on, and Hans Castorp remarked that he did not use the form of address common to the civilized West—-"you promised to make visible to our mortal eyes some dear departed, whether brother soul or sister soul, whose name should be given to you by our circle. Are you willing? Do you feel yourself able to perform what you promised?"

Again Elly shivered. She sighed and shivered as the answer came. Slowly she carried her hands and those of her guardians to her forehead, where she let them rest. Then close to Hans Castorp's ear she whispered: "Yes."

The warm breath immediately at his ear caused in our friend that phenomenon of the epidermis popularly called goose--flesh, the nature of which the Hofrat had once explained to him. We mention this in order to make a distinction between the psychical and the purely physical. There could scarcely be talk of fear, for our hero was in fact thinking: "Well, she is certainly biting off more than she can chew!" But then he was straightway seized with a mingling of sympathy and consternation springing from the confusing and illusory circumstance that a blood--young creature, whose hands he held in his, had just breathed a yes into his ear.

"He said yes," he reported, and felt embarrassed.

"Very well, then, Holger," spoke Dr. Krokowski. "We shall take you at your word. We are confident you will do your part. The name of the dear departed shall shortly be communicated to you. Comrades," he turned to the gathering, "out with it, now! Who has a wish? Whom shall our friend Holger show us?"

A silence followed. Each waited for the other to speak. Individually they had probably all questioned themselves, in these last few days; they knew whither their thoughts tended. But the calling back of the dead, or the desirability of calling them back, was a ticklish matter, after all. At bottom, and boldly confessed, the desire does not exist; it is a misapprehension precisely as impossible as the thing itself, as we should soon see if nature once let it happen. What we call mourning for our dead is perhaps not so much grief at not being able to call them back as it is grief at not being able to want to do so.

This was what they were all obscurely feeling; and since it was here simply a question not of an actual return, but merely a theatrical staging of one, in which they should only see the departed, no more, the thing seemed humanly unthinkable; they were afraid to look into the face of him or her of whom they thought, and each one would willingly have resigned his right of choice to the next. Hans Castorp too, though there was echoing in his ears that large--hearted "Of course, of course" out of the past, held back, and at the last moment was rather inclined to pass the choice on. But the pause was too long; he turned his head toward their leader, and said, in a husky voice: "I should like to see my departed cousin, Joachim Ziemssen."

That was a relief to them all. Of those present, all excepting Dr. Ting--Fu, Wenzel, and the medium had known the person asked for. The others, Ferge, Wehsal, Herr Albin, Paravant, Herr and Frau Magnus, Frau Stöhr, Fräulein Levi, and the Kleefeld, loudly announced their satisfaction with the choice. Krokowski himself nodded well pleased, though his relations with Joachim had always been rather cool, owing to the latter's reluctance in the matter of psycho--analysis.

"Very good indeed," said the doctor. "Holger, did you hear? The person named was a stranger to you in life. Do you know him in the Beyond, and are you prepared to lead him hither?"

Immense suspense. The sleeper swayed, sighed, and shuddered. She seemed to be seeking, to be struggling; falling this way and that, whispering now to Hans Castorp, now to the Kleefeld, something they could not catch. At last he received from her hands the pressure that meant yes. He announced himself to have done so, and—-

"Very well, then," cried Dr. Krokowski. "To work, Holger! Music," he cried.

"Conversation!" and he repeated the injunction that no fixing of the attention, no strained anticipation was in place, but only an unforced and hovering expectancy. And now followed the most extraordinary hours of our hero's young life. Yes, though his later fate is unclear, though at a certain moment in his destiny he will vanish from our eyes, we may assume them to have been the most extraordinary he ever spent.

They were hours——more than two of them, to be explicit, counting in a brief intermission in the efforts on Holger's part which now began, or rather, on the girl Elly's——of work so hard and so prolonged that they were all toward the end inclined to be fainthearted and despair of any result; out of pure pity, too, tempted to resign an attempt which seemed pitilessly hard, and beyond the delicate strength of her upon whom it was laid. We men, if we do not shirk our humanity, are familiar with an hour of life when we know this almost intolerable pity, which, absurdly enough no one else can feel, this rebellious "Enough, no more!" which is wrung from us, though it *is* not enough, and cannot or will not be enough, until it comes somehow or other to its appointed end. The reader knows we speak of our husband--and fatherhood, of the act of birth, which Elly's wrestling did so unmistakably resemble that even he must recognize it who had never passed through this experience, even our young Hans Castorp; who, not having shirked life, now came to know, in such a guise, this act, so full of organic mysticism. In what a guise! To what an end! Under what circumstances! One could not regard as anything less than scandalous the sights and sounds in this red--lighted lying--in chamber, the maidenly form of the pregnant one, barearmed, in flowing night--robe; and then by contrast the ceaseless and senseless gramophone music, the forced conversation which the circle kept up at command, the cries of encouragement they ever and anon directed at the struggling one: "Hullo, Holger! Courage, man! It's coming, just keep it up, let it come, that's the way!" Nor do we except the person and situation of the "husband"---if we may regard in that light our young friend, who had indeed formed such a wish——sitting there, with the knees of the little "mother" between his own, holding in his her hands, which were as wet as once little Leila's, so that he had constantly to be renewing his hold, not to let them slip.

For the gas fire in the rear of the circle radiated great heat.

Mystical, consecrate? Ah, no, it was all rather noisy and vulgar, there in the red glow, to which they had now so accustomed their eyes that they could see the whole room fairly well. The music and shouting were so like the revivalistic methods of the Salvation Army, they even made Hans Castorp think of the comparison, albeit he had never attended at a celebration by these cheerful zealots. It was in no eerie or ghostly sense that the scene affected the sympathetic one as mystic or mysterious, as conducing to solemnity; it was rather natural, organic——by virtue of the intimate association we have already referred to. Elly's exertions came in waves, after periods of rest, during which she hung sidewise from her chair in a totally relaxed and inaccessible condition, described by Dr. Krokowski as "deep trance." From this she would start up with a moan, throw herself about, strain and wrestle with her captors, whisper feverish, disconnected words, seem to be trying, with sidewise, jerking movements, to expel something; she would gnash her teeth, once even fastened them in Hans Castorp's sleeve.

This had gone on for more than an hour when the leader found it to the interest of all concerned to grant a brief intermission. The Czech Wenzel, who had introduced an enlivening variation by closing the gramophone and striking up very expertly on his guitar, laid that instrument aside. They all drew a long breath and broke the circle. Dr. Krokowski strode over to the wall and switched on the ceiling lamp; the light flashed up glaringly, making them all blink. Elly, bent forward, her face almost in her lap, slumbered. She was busy too, absorbed in the oddest activity, with which the others appeared familiar, but which Hans Castorp watched with attentive wonder. For some minutes together she moved the hollow of her hand to and fro in the region of her hips: carried the hand away from her body and then with scooping, raking motion drew it towards her, as though gathering something and pulling it in. Then, with a series of starts, she came to herself, blinked in her turn at the light with sleep--stiffened eyes and smiled.

She smiled affectedly, rather remotely. In truth, their solicitude seemed wasted; she did not appear exhausted by her efforts. Perhaps she retained no memory of them. She sat down in the chair reserved for patients, by the writing--desk near the window, between the desk and the screen about the chaise--longue; gave the chair a turn so that she could support her elbow on the desk and look into the room; and remained thus, receiving their sympathetic glances and encouraging nods, silent during the whole intermission, which lasted fifteen minutes.

It was a beneficent pause, relaxed, and filled with peaceful satisfaction in respect of work already accomplished. The lids of cigarette--cases snapped, the men smoked comfortably, and standing in groups discussed the prospects of the seance. They were far from despairing or anticipating a negative result to their efforts. Signs enough were present to prove such doubting uncalled for. Those sitting near the doctor, at the far end of the row, agreed that they had several times felt, quite unmistakably, that current of cool air which regularly whenever manifestations were under way streamed in a definite direction from the person of the medium. Others had seen lightphenomena, white spots, moving conglobations of forces showing themselves at intervals against the screen. In short, no faint--heartedness! No looking backward now they had put their hands to the plough. Holger had given his word, they had no call to doubt that he would keep it.

Dr. Krokowski signed for the resumption of the sitting. He led Elly back to her martyrdom and seated her, stroking her hair. The others closed the circle. All went as before. Hans Castorp suggested that he be released from his post of first control, but Dr. Krokowski refused. He said he laid great stress on excluding, by immediate contact, every possibility of misleading manipulation on the part of the medium. So

[846]

Hans Castorp took up again his strange position vis--à--vis to Elly; the white light gave place to rosy twilight, the music began again, the pumping motions; this time it was Hans Castorp who announced "trance." The scandalous lying--in proceeded.

With what distressful difficulty! It seemed unwilling to take its course—how could it? Madness! What maternity was this, what delivery, of what should she be delivered? "Help, help," the child moaned, and her spasms seemed about to pass over into that dangerous and unavailing stage obstetricians call eclampsia. She called at intervals on the doctor, that he should put his hands on her. He did so, speaking to her encouragingly. The magnetic effect, if such it was, strengthened her to further efforts. Thus passed the second hour, while the guitar was strummed or the gramophone gave out the contents of the album of light music into the twilight to which they had again accustomed their vision. Then came an episode, introduced by Hans Castorp. He supplied a stimulus by expressing an idea, a wish; a wish he had cherished from the beginning, and might perhaps have profitably expressed before now. Elly was lying with her face on their joined hands, in "deep trance." Herr Wenzel was just changing or reversing the record when our friend summoned his resolution and said he had a suggestion to make, of no great importance, yet perhaps—possibly—of some avail. He had—that is, the house possessed among its volumes of records—a certain song, from Gounod's *Faust*, Valentine's Prayer, baritone with orchestral accompaniment, very appealing. He, the speaker, thought they might try the record.

"Why that particular one?" the doctor asked out of the darkness.

"A question of mood. Matter of feeling," the young man responded. The mood of the piece in question was peculiar to itself, quite special—he suggested they should try it. Just possible, not out of the question, that its mood and atmosphere might shorten their labours.

"Is the record here?" the doctor inquired.

[847]

No, but Hans Castorp could fetch it at once.

"What are you thinking of?" Krokowski promptly repelled the idea. What? Hans Castorp thought he might go and come again and take up his business where he had left it off? There spoke the voice of utter inexperience. Oh, no, it was impossible. It would upset everything, they would have to begin all over. Scientific exactitude forbade them to think of any such arbitrary going in and out. The door was locked. He, the doctor, had the key in his pocket. In short, if the record was not now in the room—-

He was still talking when the Czech threw in, from the gramophone: "The record is here."

"Here?" Hans Castorp asked.

"Yes, here it is, *Faust*, Valentine's Prayer." It had been stuck by mistake in the album of light music, not in the green album of *arias*, where it belonged; quite by chance—-or mismanagement or carelessness, in any case luckily—-it had partaken of the general topsyturvyness, and here it was, needing only to be put on.

What had Hans Castorp to say to that? Nothing. It was the doctor who remarked: "So much the better," and some of the others chimed in. The needle scraped, the lid was put down. The male voice began to choral accompaniment: "Now the parting hour has come."

No one spoke. They listened. Elly, as the music resumed, renewed her efforts. She started up convulsively, pumped, carried the slippery hands to her brow. The record went on, came to the middle part, with skipping rhythm, the part about war and danger, gallant, god--fearing, French. After that the finale, in full volume, the orchestrally supported refrain of the beginning.

"O Lord of heaven, hear me pray ..."

Hans Castorp had work with Elly. She raised herself, drew in a straggling breath, sighed a long, long, outward sigh, sank down and was still. He bent over her in concern, and as he did so, he heard Frau Stöhr say, in a high, whining pipe: "Ziems—-sen!"

He did not look up. A bitter taste came in his mouth. He heard another voice, a deep, cold voice, saying: "I've seen him a long time."

The record had run off, with a last accord of horns. But no one stopped the machine. The needle went on scratching in the silence, as the disk whirred round. Then Hans Castorp raised his head, and his eyes went, without searching, the right way.

There was one more person in the room than before. There in the background, where the red rays lost themselves in gloom, so that the eye scarcely reached thither, between writing--desk and screen, in the doctor's consulting--chair, where in the intermission Elly had been sitting, Joachim sat. It was the Joachim of the last days, with hollow, shadowy cheeks, warrior's beard and full, curling lips. He sat leaning back, one leg crossed over the other. On his wasted face, shaded though it was by his head--covering, was plainly seen the stamp of suffering, the expression of gravity and austerity which had beautified it. Two folds stood on his brow, between the eyes, that lay deep in their bony cavities; but there was no change in the mildness of the great dark orbs, whose quiet, friendly gaze sought out Hans Castorp, and him alone. That ancient grievance of the outstanding ears was still to be seen under the head--covering, his extraordinary head--covering, which they could not make out. Cousin Joachim was not in mufti. His sabre seemed to be leaning against his leg, he held the handle, one thought to distinguish something like a pistol--case in his belt. But that was no proper uniform he wore. No colour, no decorations; it had a collar like a *litewka* jacket, and side pockets. Somewhere low down on the breast was a cross. His feet looked large, his legs very thin, they seemed to be bound or wound as for the business of sport more than war. And what was it, this headgear? It seemed as though Joachim had turned an army cook--pot upside--down on his head, and fastened it under his chin with a band. Yet it looked quite properly warlike, like an old--fashioned foot--soldier, perhaps. Hans Castorp felt Ellen Brand's breath on his hands. And near him the Kleefeld's rapid breathing. Other sound there was none, save the continued scraping of the needle on the run--down, rotating record, which nobody stopped. He looked at none of his company, would hear or see nothing of them; but across the hands and head on his knee leaned far forward and stared through the red darkness at the guest in the chair. It seemed one moment as though his stomach would turn over within him. His throat contracted and a four--or fivefold sob went through and through him. "Forgive me!" he whispered; then his eyes overflowed, he saw no more.

He heard breathless voices: "Speak to him!" he heard Dr. Krokowski's baritone voice summon him, formally, cheerily, and repeat the request. Instead of complying, he drew his hands away from beneath Elly's face, and stood up.

Again Dr. Krokowski called upon his name, this time in monitory tones. But in two strides Hans Castorp was at the step by the entrance door and with one quick movement turned on the white light.

Fräulein Brand had collapsed. She was twitching convulsively in the Kleefeld's arms. The chair over there was empty.

Hans Castorp went up to the protesting Krokowski, close up to him. He tried to speak, but no words came. He put out his hand, with a brusque, imperative gesture. Receiving the key, he nodded several times, threateningly, close into the other's face; turned, and went out of the room.

Hysterica Passio

With the swift--changing years, a spirit began to walk in House Berghof: a spirit of immediate descent, or so Hans Castorp surmised, from that other demon whose baleful name we have spoken. With the facile curiosity of inquiring youth on its travels, he had studied this new demon, yes, had even discovered in himself an alarming aptitude, in common with the rest of the world up here, to pay him extensive homage. This new evil genius had, like the other, always been present, as it were, in the germ, but now it began to spread itself; Hans Castorp had by nature no great predilection for becoming its slave; yet with something like horror he observed that even he, when he let himself go ever so little, fell victim to a contagion so general that scarce anyone in the circle escaped it.

What was this, then, that was in the air? A rising temper. Acute irritability. A nameless rancour. A universal tendency to envenomed exchange of words, to outbursts of rage––yes, even to fisticuffs. Embittered disputes, bouts of uncontrolled shrieking, by pairs and by groups, were of daily occurrence; and the significant thing was that the bystanders, instead of being disgusted with the participants, or seeking to come between them, actually sympathized with one side or the other to the extent of being themselves involved in the quarrel. They would pale and tremble, their eyes would glitter provocatively, their mouths set with passion. They envied those actively engaged the chance, the justification for screaming; a gnawing desire to do likewise possessed mind and body, and he who could not summon strength to flee apart, was soon willy--nilly in the midst of the mêlée. The fruitless dissensions, the mutual recriminations, in the face of authorities bent on accommodation but themselves falling with alarming ease a prey to the general temptation to brawl––these become frequent occurrences in House Berghof. A patient might issue forth of the house in tolerable tranquillity and not know at all in what frame he would return. A member of the "good" Russian table, an elegant dame from the provinces, from Minsk, still young, and a light case, with only three months prescribed, betook herself one day to the village to make purchases at the French *lingerie* shop; fell there into a quarrel with the modiste, of such dimensions that she came back in a state of violent excitement, suffered a hemorrhage, and was thenceforth incurable. The husband was summoned, and informed that her stay up here would terminate only with her life.

Her case aptly illustrates the general mood. Albeit with some distaste, we cite others. Our readers may remember the greedy schoolboy in the round spectacles, who sat at Frau Salomon's table and had a habit of cutting up all the food on his plate into a sort of mess, and gulping it down, now and again wiping his eyes with his serviette behind his heavy spectacle--lenses. He had sat here, still a schoolboy, or rather still a former schoolboy, all this time, gobbled and wiped, without drawing upon his person more than the most cursory attention. But now, one morning at early breakfast, out of a blue sky, he was overtaken by such a transport of disorder that half the dining--room started up at the noise coming from his quarter. He sat there all pale and shrieking, and it was at the dwarf waitress standing near him that he shrieked. "You lie," he yelled, his voice breaking. "It's ice--cold, this tea you have brought me is ice--cold, I tell you. Try it yourself before you lie to me again about it——it is just lukewarm wash--water, try if it isn't, not fit for a decent person to drink! How do you dare think of bringing me ice--cold tea and setting it in front of me and actually persuading yourself that I would drink such hog--wash? I won't drink it! I won't!" he screamed, and began pounding with his fists on the table, till the dishes rang. "I will have hot tea——boiling hot——that is my right before God and man——boiling hot; I'd rather die on the spot than take a drop of this——you damned dwarf, you!" he fairly bellowed, and with the words appeared to fling off the last vestige of restraint and go stark mad, shaking his fist at Emerentia, literally showing her his foaming teeth. He went on, stamping, pounding, yelling "I will" and "I won't"; while the dining--room displayed the now usual scene. There was tense and alarming participation in the schoolboy raving. Some of the guests even sprang up and glared, fists doubled, teeth clenched; others sat white and trembling, their eyes cast down. And they still glared or trembled, long after the schoolboy had spent himself, and sat in a collapse before his fresh tea, not drinking. What was all this?

Among the Berghof community was a former business man, some thirty years old. His case was long--standing, he had wandered for years from one establishment to another. This man was a confirmed anti--Semite, out of conviction and the sporting instinct. He devoted a joyous consistency to the game, and the preaching of this negative gospel was the pride and content of his life. Business man he had been, he was so no more, he was nothing more in the world, but he was still an anti--Semite. His illness was serious, he had a burdensome cough, and made a sound as though he sneezed with his lung, a short, high--pitched, uncanny sound. But he was no Jew, and that was his one positive characteristic. His name was Wiedemann, a Christian name, not a filthy Jewish. He took in a paper called the *Arian Sun;* and would talk in this wise: "I arrive at the A— -sanatorium, in B—. When I go to sit down in my chair in the rest- -hall, whom do I find on my right hand? Herr Hirsch! And whom do I find on my left? Herr Wolf! Of course, I leave," And so on.

Wiedemann had a quick, threatening glance. It was literally as though he had a punching--ball hanging close in front of his nose, and squinted at it, seeing nothing whatever beyond. The prejudice that haunted him was grown to an itch, a ceaseless persecution--mania, which led him to smell out the vileness hidden or disguised in his neighbourhood and hold it up to scorn. Wherever he went, he suspected, he gibed, he vented his spleen; in short, his days were filled with hunting out and hounding down all his fellow--creatures who did not possess that inestimable advantage which was the only one he had.

The prevailing temper in House Berghof, which we have been indicating, aggravated Wiedemann's complaint to an abnormal pitch. Naturally, he could not fail here to come into contact with persons suffering from the disability of which he was free; and so it came to a scene, at which Hans Castorp was present, and which will serve us as further illustration of our theme.

For there was another man. No possibility of concealing what he was, the case was clear. The man's name was Sonnenschein, than which he could bear no filthier; and thus he became for Wiedemann the punching--ball in front of his nose, at which he squinted with his threatening glare, at which he struck, not so much to drive it away as to set it in motion that it might rasp his nerves the more.

Sonnenschein, like the other, was a business man born and bred. He too was critically ill, and illness made him sensitive. A friendly man, not at all a dull one, by nature rather playful, he hated Wiedemann for his gibes and stabs as Wiedemann hated him; and one afternoon things came to a head down in the hall, they fell on each other like beasts.

It was a horrid sight. They scuffled like small boys, but with the grimness of grown men when things have got to such a pitch. They clawed at each other's faces, clutched throats or noses, grappled, hewed loose from each other and rolled together on the floor, spat, kicked, worried, and foamed at the mouth. The "management" came running and by main strength dragged them asunder, scratched and bitten. Herr Wiedemann, bleeding and frothing, his face brutish with rage, displayed a phenomenon Hans Castorp had never before seen and had always supposed a figure of speech: his hair stood on end. He staggered away. Herr Sonnenschein, with one black eye, a bleeding lacuna in the curling black locks about his brow, was led into the bureau, where he sat down, buried his face in his hands and wept bitterly.

Thus Wiedemann and Sonnenschein. All those who saw the encounter trembled hours after. Let us turn from it to a real affair of honour, which by contrast with such ignominy will seem almost refreshing. This affair of honour occurred at about the same period, and, on account of the solemn formality with which it was conducted, deserved the name, even to the point of absurdity. Hans Castorp did not assist in person at the successive episodes; but was informed of its involved and dramatic course by means of certain documents, protocols and formal declarations, touching the affair, circulated not only in the house and without, not only in the village, the canton, and the country, but even abroad and in America; and presented for the consideration of persons who most certainly were not in the faintest degree interested in the circumstances.

It was a Polish affair, a "pain in the honour," having its seat in the heart of the Polish group which had lately collected in the Berghof, a little colony, which preempted the "good" Russian table—Hans Castorp, be it said in passing, sat there no longer, having moved thence to the Kleefeld's, then to Frau Salomon's, finally to Fräulein Levi's. Social relations in the Polish group were so elegant, so courtly, so polished, that one could only elevate one's eyebrows and be prepared for anything. There was a married couple, and an unmarried young female who stood in friendly relations with one of the gentlemen; the rest were male, with such names as von Zutawski, Cieszynski, von Rosinski, Michael Lodygowski, Leo von Asarapetian, and others. Now it fell out that one of them, named Japoll, drinking champagne in the restaurant with two others of the party, made, in their presence, remarks of a certain nature about the wife of Herr von Zutawski, and about the young lady, named Kryloff, who was the intimate friend of Herr Lodygowski. And from this circumstance arose all the proceedings, acts, and formalities, which were the theme of a widely circulated composition. Hans Castorp read:

"Declaration, translated from the Polish original: On the 27th of March, 19—, M. Stanislaw von Zutawski addressed himself to MM. Dr. Anton Cieszynski and Stefan von Rosinski, with the request that they should betake themselves to M. Kasimir Japoil and in his name demand satisfaction in the usual way for the 'calumny and detraction' which the said M. Kasimir Japoll had been guilty of against M. Stanislaw von Zutawski's wife, Mme. Jadwiga von Zutawska, in the presence of and in conversation with MM. Janusz Teofil Lenart and Leo von Asarapetian.

"When the above conversation, which took place at the end of November, came, indirectly, to M. von Zutawski's knowledge, he took immediate steps to assure himself of the fact and the circumstances of the calumny and detraction. On the previous day, the 27th of March, 19—, he was able to confirm the fact of the said calumny and detraction by the mouth of an immediate witness to the conversation in which the offensive words and insinuations had been uttered. And thus M. Stanislaw von Zutawski was constrained to apply without delay to the undersigned and to authorize them to institute honourable proceedings against the said M. Kasimir Japoll.

"The undersigned make the following statement:

"1. On the basis of a protocol of the 9th of April, 19——, drawn up at the instance of one party, written at Lemberg by M. Zdzistaw Zygulski and Tadeusz Kadyi in the affair of M. Ladislaw Goduleczny versus M. Kasimir Japoll; and further, on the basis of the declaration of the court of honour of the 18th of June, 19——, drawn up in Lemberg with reference to the same affair, both which documents agree in establishing that M. Kasimir Japoll, 'in consequence of repeated conduct not to be reconciled with the principles of honour, cannot be regarded as a gentleman,'

"2. the undersigned, having reference to the significant conclusions to be deduced from the foregoing, assert and confirm the absolute impossibility of any longer considering M. Kasimir Japoll as capable of affording satisfaction,

"3. and the undersigned, for their own persons, consider it inadmissible, with reference to a man who stands outside the pale of honour, to act either as principals or as seconds in any affair of honour.

"With reference to this state of affairs, the undersigned inform M. Stanislaw von Zutawski that it would be fruitless to proceed against M. Kasimir Japoll according to the procedure laid down in affairs of honour; and recommend him instead to have recourse to a criminal court, in order to prevent further injury on the part of a person otherwise incapacitated from giving satisfaction.——Dated and signed: Dr. Anton Cieszynski. Stefan von Rosinski."

And further, Hans Castorp read: "Protocol" of witnesses to the affair between M. Stanislaw von Zutawski, M. Michael Lodygowski, "and MM. Kasimir Japoll and Janusz Teofil Lenart, in the bar of the Kurhaus in K——and on the 2d of April, 19——, between 7.30 and 7.45.

"As M. Stanislaw von Zutawski, with reference to the representations of his friends, MM. Dr. Anton Cieszynski and Stefan von Rosinski, in connexion with the occurrences of the 27th of March, 19—, had after mature consideration come to the conclusion that the taking of the judicial steps which they recommended against M. Kasimir Japoll for the calumny and detraction uttered against his wife Jadwiga would afford him no satisfaction whatever, since "1. There was a justifiable suspicion that M. Kasimir Japoll would not appear before the court, and since, he being an Austrian subject, further proceedings would be difficult if not impossible,

"2. and since furthermore, a legal chastisement of M. Kasimir Japoll would in no wise atone for the insult by which he had sought to injure and defame the name and family of M. Stanislaw von Zutawski,

"now therefore, M. Stanislaw von Zutawski took what appeared to him the shortest, most thorough, and in view of the circumstances most appropriate course, after having indirectly ascertained that M. Kasimir Japoll purposed leaving the place on the following day, "and, on the 2d of April, 19—, between 7.30 and 7.45 in the evening, in the presence of his wife Jadwiga and MM. Michael Lodykowski and Ignaz von Mellin, administered several boxes on the ear to M. Kasimir Japoll, who was seated in the company of M. Janusz Teofil Lenart and two unknown young women, in the American bar of the Kurhaus, imbibing alcoholic drinks.

"Immediately thereafter, M. Michael Lodygowski boxed the ears of M. Kasimir Japoll, stating that he did so in return for the insult offered to Fräulein Kryloff and himself; "and immediately thereafter M. Michael Lodygowski boxed the ears of M. Janusz Teofil Lenart, in return for the unqualifiable injury offered to M. and Mme. von Zutawski, and further, "without losing a moment, M. Stanislaw von Zutawski likewise, and repeatedly, boxed the ears of M. Janusz Teofil Lenart for the calumnious defamation of his wife as well as of Mlle. Kryloff.

"MM. Kasimir Japoll and Janusz Teofil Lenart remained entirely passive during the whole of the above proceedings. Dated and signed: Michael Lodygowski, Ign. v. Meilin."

The prevailing temper did not permit Hans Castorp to laugh, as he would otherwise surely have done, at this rapid fire of boxes on the ear. Instead, he quaked as he read. The irreproachable bearing of the one side, the contemptibleness and total lack of selfrespect of the other were both apparent in the document, which was, despite its frigid objectivity, so impressive as to move him deeply. So it was with them all. The Polish *affaire d'honneur* was conned far and wide, and discussed through clenched teeth. A counterblast by Herr Kasimir Japoll fell rather flat. The substance of it was that Zutawski had been perfectly well aware that he, Japoll, had been declared incapable of giving satisfaction by some conceited puppy in Lemberg, once on a time, and that his whole proceeding had been a pretence, since he knew full well it would not issue in a duel. Furthermore, the sole and only reason Zutawski had declined to institute proceedings was that all the world, himself included, was aware that his wife Jadwiga had provided him with a complete assortment of horns; as to the truth of which fact Japoll would have found nothing easier than to give evidence; and that lastly the appearance of the Kryloff before a court would have been little edifying for anybody concerned. Anyhow, it was only his own honour that had been impeached, not that of his partner in the famous conversation; von Zutawski had entrenched himself behind the fact in order not to involve himself in any danger. As for the rôle played by Herr von Asarapetian in the whole affair, he preferred not to speak of it, but for the encounter in the Kurhaus bar, he, Japoll, though ready of tongue and wit, was admittedly of very feeble strength; he was at a great physical disadvantage with Zutawski and his friends and the uncommonly powerful Zutawska; while the two young ladies who were in his and Lenart's society were lively creatures enough, but timid as rabbits. Under the circumstances, and in order to avoid a free fight and public scandal, he had compelled Lenart, who would have put himself on the defensive, to be quiet, and to suffer in God's name the transient social contact with MM. von Zutawski and Lodygowski, which had not hurt them at all, and which had been regarded in the light of a pleasantry by the bystanders.

Thus Japoll, for whom, of course, not much could be said. His defence did not greatly invalidate the elegant contrast of honour with pusillanimity presented by the document on the other side; the less because he had not the manifolding facilities disposed of by his opponents, and could only distribute a few typed duplicates of his reply. The protocol, on the contrary, everyone received, even the most uninterested. Naphta and Settembrini, for instance, had copies sent them, which Hans Castorp saw in their hands, and remarked, to his surprise, that they too perused them with bitter concentration. For him the ruling temper of the Berghof was too much——he was powerless to dissipate its mood by a burst of blithe and cleansing laughter, but this he had confidently expected to hear from Herr Settembrini. Alas, no, even the unclouded eye of the Freemason was dimmed by the prevailing spleen; it weighed on his spirit, stilling his mirth; it made him susceptible to the rasping provocation of the tale of the ear--boxing. Moreover he, the protagonist of Life, was suffering in spirit from the state of his health. Slowly, remorselessly, with deceptive interludes of brighter hope, it grew worse. He despised, he scorned it, and himself; but had reached the point where it obliged him, every few days, to take to his bed.

His housemate and antagonist was no better off. The organic disease which had been the cause——or must we say pretext——for the untimely end to his activities within his order, made rapid progress; even the high and thin conditions of life up here could not give it pause. Naphta too was often confined to his bed; the crack in his voice was more cracked than ever when he talked; and as his fever increased he talked more, and more malignantly, than ever. That ideal opposition to the forces of disease and death, the forced surrender of which before the superior power of abject nature gave Herr Settembrini such pain, was foreign to little Naphta. His way of taking the deterioration of his physical part was not with sorrow or aversion, but with a sort of jeering levity, an unnatural lust of combat, a mania of intellectual doubt, denial, and distraction, that was a sore irritant to the other's melancholy, and daily embittered more the intellectual quarrel between them. Hans Castorp, of course, could only speak of those at which he was present; but he felt tolerably sure he did not miss any; that his presence, the presence of the bone of pedagogic contention, was necessary, to give rise to a disputation of any magnitude. And though he did not spare Herr Settembrini the pain of finding Naphta's gibes worth hearing, he had to admit that these were latterly going beyond all bounds and often enough overstepping the border--line of mental sanity.

For this sufferer possessed neither the power nor the good will to rise above his illness; but rather saw all the world in its sign and image. In the presence of Herr Settembrini's quivering resentment, who would sooner have drawn his nursling away from the room or even stopped his ears, Naphta declared that matter was so bad a material that the spirit could not be realized within it. Any effort in that direction was sheer folly; nothing could come of it but distortion and fatuity. What had been the net result of the vainglorious French Revolution—-what but the capitalistic bourgeois State? A magnificent outcome, truly! And one it was hoped to improve upon, forsooth, by making the horror universal! A world--republic! That would bring happiness, beyond a doubt. Progress? It was the cry of the patient who constantly changes his position thinking each new one will bring relief. The unconfessed but secretly quite general desire for war was another manifestation of the same condition. It would come, this war, and it would be a good thing, though the consequences of it would not be those anticipated by its authors. Naphta sneered at the security of the bourgeois State. He took occasion to animadvert upon it one day in autumn as they were walking on the main street. It came on to rain, and suddenly, as though at the word of command, all the world put up its umbrellas. Which served Naphta as a symbol of the cowardice and vulgar softness engendered by civilized life. An incident like the going--down of the *Titanic* was like the writing on the wall: it flung people back upon primitive conditions and fears, and thus was salutary. Afterwards, of course, came the great outcry that transportation must be safeguarded. Always the greatest outcry whenever security was threatened. It was pathetic; and the flabby humanitarianism of it went hand in hand with the wolfish cruelty and baseness of the economic conflict within the bourgeois State. War, war! For his part, he was for it; the general hankering seemed to him comparatively creditable.

Herr Settembrini introduced the word justice into the discussion, and sought to apply this lofty principle as a preventive measure against political catastrophes both foreign and domestic. But as soon as he did so, Naphta, who just previously had found the spiritual too high ever to succeed in manifesting itself in material form, now set to work to cast doubts on, to derogate from, that very spiritual. Justice! Was it, as a conception, worth worshipping? Was it first--class? Was it of divine origin? God and Nature were not even--handed, they played favourites, they exercised the right of choice, they graced one individual with dangerous distinction, to another granted the easy common lot. And as for the man of action——for him justice was on the one hand a paralysing weakness, doubt itself, on the other a trumpet--call to unscrupulous deeds. And since, in order to remain within the moral code, such a man had always to correct "justice" in the second sense by "justice" in the first, where then was the Absolute, the radical, in the conception? Moreover, one was "just" according to one standard *or* according to the other. All the rest was liberalism——in which nobody nowadays took any stock. Justice, in short, was an empty husk, a stock--in--trade of bourgeois rhetoric; to get down to business, one had always to know which justice one was dealing with: the one which would give a man his own, or the one which would give everybody alike.

Out of his shoreless stream of words, we have hit upon these in illustration of the way he sought to confound the reason. But even worse was the way he talked about science——in which he did not believe. He did not believe, he said, in it, because it was permissible to exercise choice, whether to believe in it or not. It was a belief, like any other, only worse, stupider than any; the word science was the expression of the silliest realism, which did not blush to take at their face value the more than dubious reflections of objects in the human intellect; to pass them current, and to shape out of them the sorriest, most spiritless dogma ever imposed upon humanity. Was not the idea of a material world existing by and for itself the most laughable of all selfcontradictions? But the modern natural sciences, as dogma, rested upon the metaphysical postulate that time, space, and causality, the forms of cognition, in which all phenomena are enacted, are actual conditions, existing independently of our knowledge of them. This monistic position was an insult to the spirit. Space, time, and causality—in monistic language, evolution: here was the central dogma of a freethinking, atheistical, bastard religion, by virtue of which one thought to supersede the first book of Moses, and oppose the pure light of knowledge to a stultifying fable—as though Haeckel had been present at the creation! Empiricism! The universal ether—based on exact knowledge, of course? The atom, that pretty mathematical joke of the smallest, the indivisible particle of matter—its existence had been demonstrated, undoubtedly? The doctrine of the illimitability of time and space was, surely, based on experience? In fact, anybody with a very little logic could make very merry over the theory of the endlessness and the reality of space and time; and could arrive at the result of—nothing: that is, at the view that realism is your true nihilism. How? Quite simply; since the relation to infinity of any size you chose to postulate was as zero. There was no size to the infinite; in eternity was neither duration nor change. In the spatially infinite, since every distance was, mathematically, as zero, there could not even be two points close together, to say nothing of two bodies, or of motion as such. He, Naphta, stated this, in order to counter the arrogance of materialistic science, which gave out for absolute knowledge its astronomical quackery, its windbaggery about the universe. Pitiable human kind, that by a vain mustering of meaningless figures have let themselves be driven to a conclusion of their own insignificance, to the destruction of any emphasis upon their own importance! It might be tolerable that human reason and knowledge should confine themselves to the terrestrial, and within this sphere treat as actual their experience with the subjective object. But let them go beyond that, let them once attempt to grapple with the riddle of eternity, and invent so--called cosmologies and cosmogonies, and it was beyond a jest; the presumptuousness of it reached a climax. What blasphemous rubbish, to reckon the "distance" of any star from the earth in terms of trillions of kilometres, or in light years, and to imagine that with such a parade of figures the human spirit was gaining an insight into the essence of infinity and eternity—-whereas infinity had absolutely nothing whatever to do with size, nor yet eternity with duration or distance in time; they had nothing in common with natural science, being, as they were, the abrogation of that which we called nature! Verily, the simplicity of a child, who thinks the stars are holes in the tent of heaven, through which the eternal brightness shines, was a thousand times more to his mind than the whole hollow, preposterous, overweening drivel of monistic science on the subject of the "universe."

Settembrini asked him if that about the stars represented his own personal belief. He answered that on this point he reserved to himself the freedom, and the humblemindedness, of doubt. From which again it might be seen what he understood by freedom, and whither such a conception of it might lead. If only Herr Settembrini had not ground for the fear that Hans Castorp found all this highly worth listening to! Naphta's malicious wit lay in ambush, to spy out the weaknesses of the naturecompelling forces of progress, and convict its standard--bearers and pioneers of human relapses into the irrational. Aviators, flying men, he said, were mostly a bad lot, untrustworthy, above all exceedingly superstitious. They carried mascots on board with them, pigs and ravens and such--like; they spat three times in different directions, they wore the gloves of lucky flyers. How could such primitive unreason be reconciled with the conception of the

[863]

universe which underlay their calling? The contradiction diverted him, he held forth upon it *in extenso*. But such illustrations of Naphta's malevolence are without number——let us abandon them for the all--toopertinent tale we have to tell. One afternoon in February, the gentlemen arranged an excursion to Monstein, some hour and a half from the village by sleigh. The party consisted of Naphta and Settembrini, Hans Castorp, Ferge and Wehsal. In two one--horse sleighs, Hans Castorp with the humanist, Naphta with Ferge and Wehsal, the last--named sitting with the coachman, they left the greengrocer's at about three o'clock in the afternoon, and well bundled up drove off to the friendly music of bells, that sounds so pleasant through still, snowy air. They took the right--hand road, past Frauenkirch and Claris, southwards. Storm--clouds pushed up rapidly from that direction, and soon the only streak of blue in the sky lay behind them, over the Rhätikon. The cold was severe, the mountains misty. The road, a narrow, railingless shelf between mountain wall and abyss, rose steeply into the fir forests. They went at a foot--pace. Coasting--parties rode downhill toward them, and had to dismount as they met. Sometimes from round a bend in the road would come the clear and warning sound of other bells; sleighs driven tandem would be approaching and some skill was required to pass in the narrow road. Near their destination was a beautiful view of a rocky stretch of the Zügenstrasse. They disentangled themselves from their wraps and climbed out in front of the little Monstein inn, that called itself a Kurhaus, and went on foot a few steps further to get the view south--west toward the Stulsergrat. The gigantic wall, three thousand metres high, was shrouded in vapours. Only one jagged tooth reared itself heavenward out of the mist——superterrestrial, Valhallari, far and faint and awesomely inaccessible. Hans Castorp admired it immensely, and summoned the others to follow suit. It was he who with due respect dubbed it inaccessible——and afforded Herr Settembrini the chance of saying that this particular rock was considerably frequented. And, in general, that there were few spots where man had not set his foot. That was rather tall talk, retorted Naphta; and mentioned Mount Everest, which to date had icily refused to surrender to man's importunity, and seemed likely to continue to do so. The humanist was put out. They returned to the Kurhaus, before which stood other unharnessed sleighs beside their own.

One might have lodgment here; in the upper story were numbered rooms, and on the same floor the dining--room, furnished in peasant style, and well heated. They ordered a bite from the obliging landlady: coffee, honey, white bread and "pear bread," a sort of sweetmeat, the speciality of the place; red wine was sent out to the coachman. At the other tables were sitting Swiss and Dutch visitors.

We should have been glad to relate that our friends, being warmed and cheered by the hot and excellent coffee, proceeded to elevating discourse. But the statement would be inexact. For the discourse, after the first few words, took the form of a monologue by Naphta, and even as a monologue was conducted in a manner singularly offensive, from the social point of view; the ex--Jesuit flatly turning his back on Herr Settembrini, completely ignoring the other two gentlemen, and devoting himself to Hans Castorp, to whom he held forth with marked affability.

It would have been hard to give a name to the subject of this discourse, to which Hans Castorp listened, nodding from time to time as though in partial agreement. We may presume that it was scarcely a connected argument, but rather moved loosely in the realms of the intellectual; in general pointing out, with an accompanying comment which we may characterize as cheerless, the equivocal nature of the spiritual phenomena of life, the changeful aspects and contentious unserviceability of the great abstract conceptions man has based on them, and indicating in what a rainbow--hued garment the Absolute appears upon this earth.

At any rate, we might take as the nucleus of his lecture the problem of freedom, which he treated in the sense of confusion. He spoke, among other matters, of the Romantic movement, at the beginning of the nineteenth century, and its fascinating double meaning; pointing out how before it the conceptions of reaction and revolution went down, in so far as they were not incorporated in a new and higher one. For it was of course utterly absurd to try to associate the conception of revolution solely with progress and victoriously advancing enlightenment. The Romantic movement in Europe had been above all a movement of liberation: anti--classic, anti--academic, directed against French classicism, the old school of reason, whose defenders it derided as "powdered wigs."

And Naphta began upon wars of liberation, talked of Fichtean enthusiasms, of a singing, frenzied popular uprising against that unbearable tyranny, as which, unfortunately—-he tittered—-freedom, that is to say the revolutionary idea, had taken shape. Very droll it was: singing loudly, the people had set out to shatter the revolutionary tyranny for the benefit of reactionary princely authority—-and this they did in the name of freedom.

The youthful listener would perceive the distinction, even the opposition, between foreign and domestic freedom; also note the ticklish question, which unfreedom was soonest—-he he!—-which least compatible with a nation's honour.

Freedom, indeed, was a conception rather romantic than illuminating. Like romanticism, it inevitably limited the human impulse to expansion; and the passionate individualism in them both had similar repressive results. Individualistic thirst for freedom had produced the historic and romantic cult of nationalism, which was warlike in character, and was called sinister by humanitarian liberalism, though the latter also preached individualism, only the other way about. Individualism was romantic--mediæval, in its conviction of the infinite, the cosmic, importance of the single human being, whence was deduced the doctrine of the immortality of the soul, the geocentric doctrine, and astrology. But on the other hand, individualism was an aspect of liberalizing humanism, which inclined to anarchy and would in any case protect the precious individual from being offered up on the altar of the general. Such was individualism, in its two aspects—-all things unto all men.

[866]

One had to admit that the freedom-- *pathos* had produced the most brilliant enemies of freedom, the most brilliant knights--errant of tradition at war with irreverent, destructive progress. Naphta cited Arndt, who cursed industrialism and glorified the nobility; and Görres, the author of Christian mysticism. Perhaps his hearer would ask what mysticism had to do with progress? Had it not been anti--scholastic, antidogmatic, anti--priestly? One was, indeed, compelled to recognize in the Hierarchy a force making for freedom: had it not set limits to the boundless pretensions of monarchy? But the mysticism of the end of the Middle Ages had shown its liberal character as forerunner of the Reformation——he he!——which in its turn had been an inextricable and tangled weave, a weft of freedom with a warp of mediævalism.

ᴧᴧOh, yes, what Luther did possessed the merit of demonstrating crudely and vividly the dubious character of the deed itself, the deed in general. Did Naphta's listener know what a deed was? A deed, for example, was the murder of Councillor Kotzebue by Sand, the theological student and member of the *Burschenschaft*. What was it, to speak the language of criminology, had put the weapon into the hand of young Sand? Enthusiasm for freedom, of course. But looked at more nearly, it had rather been moral fanaticism, and the hatred of light foreign ways. Kotzebue had been in the employ of Russia, in the service of the Holy Alliance, and thus Sand's shot had presumably been fired for freedom; which again declined into improbability by virtue of the circumstance that there were several Jesuits among his nearest friends. In short, whatever the "deed" might be, it was in any case a poor way of making one's meaning clear; as also it contributed little toward the clarification of intellectual problems.

"Might I take the liberty of inquiring if you will be bringing these scurrilities of yours to an end before long?"

Herr Settembrini put the question in withering tones. He had been drumming on the table, and twisting his moustaches. But now his patience was exhausted. It was too much. He sat upright, and more than upright, he sat, so to speak, on tiptoe, for only his shanks touched the chair; and with flashing black eyes faced the enemy, who turned toward him in assumed surprise.

"What, may I ask, was the expression you were pleased to use?" Naphta countered.

"I was pleased to say," said the Italian, swallowing, "I am pleased to say, that I am resolved to prevent you from continuing to molest a defenceless youth with your equivocations."

"I invite you, sir, to take heed to your words."

"The reminder, sir, is unnecessary. I am accustomed to take heed to my words. They will precisely fit the fact if I say that your way of misleading unsettled youth, of dissipating and undermining his moral and intellectual powers, is *infamous*, and cannot receive a stronger chastisement than it merits."

With the word infamous, Settembrini struck the table with the flat of his hand, and pushing back his chair, stood up. It was a signal for the rest to do likewise. People looked across from the other tables—-or, rather, from one, as the Swiss guests had left and only the Dutchmen remained, listening in amazement.

At our table they all stood there stiffly: Hans Castorp and the two antagonists, with Ferge and Wehsal opposite. All five were pale and wide--eyed, with twitching lips. Might not the three onlookers have made an effort to calm the troubled waters, to lighten the atmosphere with a jest, or bring affairs to a peaceful conclusion with some kind of human appeal? They did not try. The prevailing temper prevented them. They stood, all trembling, with hands that clenched involuntarily into fists. Even A. K. Ferge, to whom all elevated thoughts were foreign, who disclaimed from its inception any power to measure the seriousness of the dispute—-even he was convinced that this was a quarrel *à outrance*, and that there was nothing to do but let it take its course. His good--natured moustaches worked violently up and down.

There was a stillness, in which could be heard the gnashing of Naphta's teeth. To Hans Castorp, this was an experience like the one with Wiedemann's hair. He had supposed it to be a figure of speech, something which did not actually occur. Yet here was Naphta, and in the silence his teeth could be heard to grate; a horribly unpleasant, a wild, incredible sound, which yet evinced a self--control equally fearsome, for he did not storm, but said in quite a low voice, though with a sort of cackling half--laugh;

"Infamous? Chastisement? Ah, so the bleating sheep have taken to butting? Have we driven the policemen of civilization so far that they draw their weapons? That *is* a triumph; won in passing; I must say, considering what mild provocation sufficed to summon to arms the guardians of our morality! As for the rest, sir, it will follow in due course. The chastisement too. I hope your civilian principles will not prevent you from knowing what you owe me——else I shall be forced to put these principles to a test that——"

Herr Settembrini drew himself up; the movement was so expressive that Naphta went on: "Ah, I see, that will not be necessary. I am in your way, you are in mine——good. We will transfer the settlement of our differences to a suitable place. For the moment, only this: your sentimental solicitude for the scholastic interpretation of the Jacobin Revolution envisages a pedagogic crime in my manner of leading youth to doubt, of throwing categories to the winds, of robbing ideas of their academic dignity. And your anxiety is justified; for it happens on account of your humanity, be assured of that——happens and is done. For your humanity is to--day nothing but a tail end, a stale classicistic survival, a spiritual ennui; it is yawning its head off, while the new Revolution, *our* Revolution, my dear sir, is coming on apace to give it its quietus. We, when we sow the seeds of doubt deeper than the most up--to--date and modish freethought has ever dreamed of doing, we well know what we are about. Only out of radical scepsis, out of moral chaos, can the Absolute spring, the anointed Terror of which the time has need. This for your instruction, and my justification. For the rest we must turn over the page. You will hear from me."

"And you will find a hearing, sir," Settembrini called after him, as the Jesuit left his place and hurried to the hat--stand to seek his cloak. Then the Freemason let himself fall back with a thud on his hard chair, and pressed both hands to his heart.

"Distruttore! Cane arabbiato! Bisogna ammazzarlo!" burst from him, pantingly. The others still stood at the table. Ferge's moustaches went on wagging up and down. Wehsal's jaw was set hard awry. Hans Castorp was imitating his grandfather's famous attitude, for his neck was all a--tremble. They were thinking how little they had expected such an outcome as this to their excursion. And all of them, even Herr Settembrini, felt how fortunate it was that they had come in two sleighs. It simplified the return. But afterwards?

"He challenged you," Hans Castorp said, heavily.

"Undoubtedly," answered Herr Settembrini, and cast a glance upward at his neighbour, only to turn away again at once and lean his head on his hand.

"Shall you take it up?" Wehsal wanted to know.

"Can you ask?" answered Settembrini, and looked a moment at him too.

"Gentlemen," he said then, and sat up, having brought himself again to perfect control, "I regret the outcome of our pleasure excursion; but in life one must be prepared to reckon with such events. Theoretically I disapprove of the duel, I am of a law--abiding temper. In practice, however, it is another matter. There are situations where—quarrels that—in short, I am at this man's service. It is well that in my youth I fenced a little. A few hours' practice will make my wrist supple again. Shall we go?

The rendezvous will have to be made. I assume our gentleman will already have ordered them to put to the horses."

Hans Castorp had moments, during the drive home, and afterwards, when he became giddy in contemplation of what lay before them. Still more, when it subsequently appeared that Naphta would not hear of cut and thrust, but insisted on a duel with pistols. And he, as the injured party, had the choice of weapons. There were moments, we say, when Hans Castorp was able, to a certain extent, to free himself from embroilment with the prevailing temper and tell himself that all this was madness, and must be prevented.

"If even there were a real injury," he cried, in discussion with Herr Settembrini, Ferge and Wehsal—Naphta, on the way home, had invited the last-named to be his second, and he acted as intermediary between the factions. "An affront like that, purely civilian and social! If one of them had dragged the other's good name in the dirt, if it was a question of a woman, or anything else really momentous, that you could take hold of, so that you felt there was no possibility of reconciliation! For such cases the duel is the last resort; and when honour is satisfied and the affair has gone off with credit to all parties, and the antagonists part friends, as they say, why, then it seems a very good arrangement, quite useful and practical, too, in complicated cases. But what was it he did? I don't mean to stand up for him, I only ask what the insult consisted in. He threw the categories to the winds, as you say, and robbed conceptions of their academic dignity. And you felt yourself insulted thereby—justifiably, let us assume—"

"Assume?" repeated Herr Settembrini, and looked at him.

"Oh, justifiably, quite justifiably! He affronted you. But he did not insult you. There is a difference. Permit me to say so. It was a matter of abstractions, an intellectual disagreement. On intellectual topics he could affront you, perhaps, but not insult you. That is axiomatic, any court of honour would tell you the same, I swear to God they would. And so neither was your answer to him, about infamy and chastisement an insult; because it was in an intellectual sense, the whole affair was in the intellectual sphere, and has nothing to do with the personal, and an insult can only be personal. The intellectual can never be personal, that is the conclusion and the explanation of the axiom, and therefore——"

"You err, my friend," answered Settembrini, with closed eyes. "You err first of all in the assumption that the intellectual cannot assume a personal character. You should not think that," he said, and smiled a peculiarly fine and painful smile. "The point at which you go wrong is in your estimation of the things of the mind, in general. You obviously think they are too feeble to engender conflicts and passions comparable for sternness with those real life brings forth, the only issue of which can be the appeal to force. *All incontro!* The abstract, the refined--upon, the ideal, is at the same time the Absolute——it is sternness itself; it contains within it more possibilities of deep and radical hatred, of unconditional and irreconcilable hostility, than any relation of social life can. It astonishes you to hear that it leads, far more directly and inexorably than these, to radical intimacy, to grips, to the duel and actual physical struggle? The duel, my friend, is not an "arrangement," like another. It is the ultimate, the return to a state of nature, slightly mitigated by regulations which are chivalrous in character, but extremely superficial. The essential nature of the thing remains the primitive, the physical struggle; and however civilized a man is, it is his duty to be ready for such a contingency, which may any day arise. Whoever is unable to offer his person, his arm, his blood, in the service of the ideal, is unworthy of it; however intellectualized, it is the duty of a man to remain a man."

Thus was Hans Castorp put in his place. What should he answer? He preserved a depressed and brooding silence. Herr Settembrini had spoken with composure, logically. But his words sounded strange in his mouth. His thoughts were not his own thoughts, the idea of the duel was one he would never have come upon of himself. He had only taken it over from the terroristic little Naphta. And what he said was but an expression of the strength of that prevailing temper, whose tool and underling Herr Settembrini's fine understanding had become. What? The intellectual, simply because it was so stern, must lead relentlessly to the animal, to the issue of physical combat?

Hans Castorp set himself against it—-or at least he tried, only to discover, in affright, that even he was powerless to do so. In him too the prevailing temper was strong, he was not the man to win free. There was an area of his brain where memory showed him Wiedemann and Sonnenschein grappled like animals; and with horror he understood that at the end of everything only the physical remained, only the teeth and the nails. Yes, they must fight; only thus could be assured even that small mitigation of the primitive by the rules of chivalry. Hans Castorp offered to act as Herr Settembrini's second.

The offer was refused. No, it was not fitting, it would not do, he was told: first by Herr Settembrini himself, with that fine, rueful smile; then, after brief consideration, by Ferge and Wehsal, who also, without specified reason, found it would not do for Hans Castorp to assist at the encounter in this capacity. As a neutral party, perhaps—-the presence of such an one was a part of the prescribed chivalrous mitigations—-he might be present. Even Naphta, through his second, let it be known that this was his view, and Hans Castorp was satisfied. As witness, or as neutral party, in either case he was able to exert his influence upon the details of the procedure now to be discussed and settled—-an influence which proved necessary indeed.

For Naphta's proposals went beyond all bounds. He demanded a distance of five paces, and, if necessary, three exchanges of fire. These insane conditions he sent by Wehsal the very evening of the quarrel; Wehsal had succeeded in fully identifying himself with Naphta's mad ideas, and partly as representative, but certainly also in accordance with his personal taste, obstinately insisted upon them. Settembrini, of course, found nothing in them to object to. But Ferge, as second, and the neutral Hans Castorp, were beside themselves, and the latter fell heavily upon the wretched Wehsal. Was he not ashamed to bring forward such frantic and inhuman ideas to meet a case where the injury was purely abstract, not sensible at all? As though pistols were not bad enough, that they must add these murderous conditions! Where did the chivalrous mitigation come in? He might as well suggest firing across a handkerchief!

He, Wehsal, was not going to be fired at five paces off—it was easy for him to be blood--thirsty! And so forth. Wehsal shrugged his shoulders, as much as to say that precisely that extreme case was a contingency; thus reducing to silence Hans Castorp, who was inclined to forget the fact. But he succeeded, during the negotiations of the following day, in fixing the number of shots at one instead of three, and in dealing with the question of distance so as to arrange that the combatants should be placed fifteen paces apart, and have the right to advance five paces before firing. But in exchange for these concessions, he had to promise that no attempt should be made at reconciling the parties.——It was discovered that none of them had any pistols. Herr Albin had. Besides the shiny little revolver with which he loved to frighten the ladies, he had a pair of officer's pistols from Belgium in a velvet case: Browning automatics, with brown wooden butts holding the magazine, blued steel mechanism and shining barrels, with crisp little sights atop. Hans Castorp had seen them in Herr Albin's room, and against his own convictions, out of sheer compulsion from the prevailing temper, offered to borrow them. He made no concealment of the purpose they were to serve, but appealing to the young swaggerer's honour, readily swore him to secrecy. Herr Albin instructed him how to load the pistols, and they tested both weapons with blank shots in the open.

All this took time: two days and three nights intervened between the quarrel and the meeting. The place was of Hans Castorp's choosing: that picturesque blue--blossoming scene of his retreat and stock--taking activities. On this spot the affair should take place, on the third morning, as soon as there should be light enough to see. The evening before, rather late, it occurred to Hans Castorp, by this time thoroughly wrought up, that there ought to be a physician present.

He immediately advised with Ferge, who foresaw great difficulty. Rhadamanthus himself was an old corps--student; but it would be impossible to ask the head of the establishment to act in an illegal affair, and between patients to boot. It was scarcely likely a doctor could be found who would be willing to lend a hand in a pistol duel between two severe cases. As for Krokowski, for all his brain, it was a question whether the technique of wound treatment would be his strong point.

Wehsal, who was present, announced that Naphta had already expressed himself to the effect that he wanted no doctor. He was not going to the meeting--place to be salved and bandaged, but to lay about him, and that in grim earnest. It sounded a sinister declaration enough; but Hans Castorp tried to interpret it as meaning that Naphta felt there would be no need of a physician. Ferge too bore back a message from Herr Settembrini, that they might dispose of the question, it did not interest him. It was thus not unreasonable to hope that both antagonists had resolved not to let it come to the shedding of blood. Two nights had passed since the quarrel, and there would be yet a third. Time cools, time clarifies; no mood can be maintained quite unaltered through the course of hours. In the early dawn, standing weapon in hand, neither of the combatants would be the same man as on the evening of the quarrel. They would be going through it, if at all, mechanically, in obedience to the demands of honour, not, as they would have at first, of their own free will, desire, and conviction; and such a denial of their actual selves in favour of their past ones, it must somehow be possible to prevent.

Hans Castorp's reflections proved in the event not far from justified; but justified in a manner unlike anything he could have dreamed. So far as Herr Settembrini was concerned, he was entirely right. But had he suspected in what direction Leo Naphta would have altered his intentions beforehand, or at the decisive moment, not even the prevailing temper, of which all this was the outcome, could have driven him to let the affair go on.

At seven o'clock next morning, the sun showed no sign of making an appearance above the mountain; yet day was dawning, difficultly, in a reek of mist, as Hans Castorp, after a restless night, left the Berghof to go to the rendezvous. The maidservants cleaning the hall looked after him in wonder. The house door, however, was unbolted; Ferge and Wehsal, alone or in company, had undoubtedly passed that threshold, the one to accompany Settembrini, the other Naphta, to the field of battle. He, Hans, went alone, his capacity of neutral not permitting him to attach himself to either party.

He moved mechanically, under the compulsion of honour, under pressure from the prevailing temper. It was necessary for him to be present at the encounter——that went without saying. Impossible to stop away and await the event in bed, in the first place because——but he did not finish his firstly, but hastened on to secondly, which was that one could not leave the thing to itself. Thus far, thank Heaven, nothing dreadful had happened; and nothing dreadful need happen, it was really highly improbable that anything would. They had had to get up and dress by artificial light. and breakfastless, in the bitter frost, betake themselves to the appointed spot. But once there, under the influence of his, Hans Castorp's presence, the whole thing would surely be turned aside, work out for good——in some manner not yet foreseen, and best left unguessed at, since experience showed that even the simplest events always worked out differently from what one would have thought beforehand.

All which notwithstanding, this was the unpleasantest morning within his memory. He felt stale and seedy, his teeth tended to chatter; in the depth of his being he was prone to mistrust his own powers of self--control. These were such singular times. The lady from Minsk, who shattered her health on the point of a quarrel with her *corsetière*, the raging schoolboy, Wiedemann and Sonnenschein, the Polish earboxes——drearily he thought of them. Simply he could not picture two people, before his eyes, in his presence, standing up to shoot at each other, spill each other's blood. But when he remembered what it had come to, what he had actually seen, in the case of Wiedemann and Sonnenschein, then he misdoubted himself, misdoubted all the world, and shivered in his fur jacket; though at the same time a feeling of the extraordinariness, the abnormality of all this, heightened by the quality of the early morning air, began now surprisingly to elevate and stimulate him.

In the dusk of that slow--brightening dawn, moved by such mingled and fluctuating hopes and feelings, he mounted the narrow path along the slope, from the village end of the bob--run; arrived at the deeply drifted woods, crossed the little wooden bridge over the course, and followed a way among the tree--trunks trodden by feet in the snow rather than cleared by any shovel. He walked fast, and very soon overtook Settembrini and Ferge, the latter holding the case of pistols with one hand under his cloak. Hans Castorp did not hesitate to join them, and, coming abreast, was aware of Naphta and Wehsal, only a few paces in advance.

"Cold morning; at least eighteen degrees of frost," said he, in the purity of his intentions, but started at the frivolity of his own remark, and added: "Gentlemen, I am convinced——"

The others were silent. Ferge's good--natured moustache wagged up and down.

After a while Settembrini came to a pause, took Hans Castorp's hand, laid his own other one upon it, and spoke.

"My friend, I will not kill. I will not. I will offer myself to his bullet, that is all that honour can demand. But I will not kill, you may trust me."

He released the young man and walked on. Hans Castorp was deeply moved. After a few steps he said: "That is splendid of you, Herr Settembrini. Now——on the other side——if he, for his part—— "

But Herr Settembrini shook his head. Hans Castorp reflected that if one party did not fire, the other would surely not be able to bring himself to do it either; and his heart perceptibly lightened. Everything was going well, his predictions seemed about to be verified.

They crossed the foot--bridge over the gorge, where the waterfall hung stiff and silent. Naphta and Wehsal were walking up and down before the bench now upholstered with thick white cushions of snow:

the bench on which Hans Castorp, lying to await the end of his nose--bleeding, had experienced such lively memories out of the distant past. Naphta was smoking a cigarette, and Hans Castorp questioned himself if he should do the same, but found he had no faintest desire. It seemed to him an affectation in the other. With the pleasure he always felt in these surroundings, he looked about at them in their icy state and found them not less beautiful than in the season of their blue blossom--time. The fir that jutted so boldly into the picture had its trunk and branches laden with snow.

"Good--morning," he said cheerily, with the idea of lending the scene a note of the natural, which should help to dissipate its evil bearing—-but was out of luck, for nobody answered. The greetings consisted in silent bows, so stiff as to be almost imperceptible. However, he was resolved to convert the energy from his walk, the splendid warmth engendered by brisk motion in the cold air, at once and without delay to good purpose; and so began: "Gentlemen, I am convinced—-"

"You will develop your convictions another time," Naphta cut him off icily. "The weapons, if you please," he added, in the same arrogant tone. Hans Castorp, thus slapped on the mouth, had to look on while Ferge brought out the fatal *étui* from beneath his cloak, and handed one pistol to Wehsal to pass on to Naphta. Settembrini took the other from Ferge's hand. The latter in a murmur asked them to make a space, and began measuring off the ground. He marked off the outer limits by lines dug with his heel in the snow, the inner by means of two canes, his own and Settembrini's. Our good--natured sufferer, what sort of work was this for him? Hans Castorp could not trust his eyes. Ferge was long--legged, he took proper strides, the fifteen paces, at least, were a goodly distance—-but the cursed canes, alas, were not far apart at all. Certainly, he was acting in all honour; but what a grip the prevailing temper had upon him, to enforce him to a procedure so monstrous in its significance!

Naphta had flung his fur cloak on the ground, so that its mink lining showed. Pistol in hand, he moved to one of the outer barriers directly it was established, and while Ferge was still marking off the other. When that was fixed, Settembrini took up his position, his shabby fur coat open in front. Hans Castorp wrenched himself out of a stealing paralysis, and flung himself once more into the breach.

"Gentlemen," he said, choking, "don't be hasty. It is my duty, after all——"

"Silence!" cried out Naphta sharply. "Give the signal."

But no one gave the signal. It had not been arranged for. Somebody, of course, ought to say: "Fire!" but it had not been realized that it was the office of the neutral party to give the dread sign——at least, it had not been mentioned. Hans Castorp remained silent, and nobody spoke in his place.

"We will begin," Naphta declared. "Come forward, sir, and fire," he called across to his antagonist, and began himself to advance, holding the pistol at arm's length, directed at Settembrini——an unbelievable sight. Settembrini did the same. At the third step the other, without firing, was already at the barrier——the Italian raised the pistol very high, and fired. The shot awaked repeated echoes, the mountains flung back the sound and the rebound, the valley reverberated with the shock, until it seemed to Hans Castorp people must come running.

"You fired in the air," Naphta said collectedly to Settembrini, letting his own weapon sink.

Settembrini answered: "I fired where it pleased me to fire."

"You will fire again!"

"I have no such intention. It is your turn." Herr Settembrini, lifting his face toward the sky, had turned himself somewhat side--wise to his opponent. It was touching to realize that he had heard one should not offer one's breast full face to an opponent's fire; and that he was acting according to the regulations.

"Coward!" Naphta shrieked; and with this human shriek confessing that it takes more courage to fire than be fired upon, raised his pistol in a way that had nothing to do with duelling, and shot himself in the head.

Piteous, unforgettable sight! He staggered, or tottered, while the mountains played ball with the sound of his shot, a few steps backward, flinging out his legs jerkily; executed a right turn with his whole body, and fell with his face in the snow. They all stood a moment rigid. Settembrini, hurling his weapon from him, was first at Naphta's side.

"Infelice!" he cried. *"Che cosa fai, per l'amor di Dio?"*

Hans Castorp helped him turn the body over. They saw the blackened red hole in the temple. They looked into a face that one would do well to cover with the silk handkerchief, one corner of which hung out of Naphta's breast pocket.

The Thunderbolt

Seven years Hans Castorp remained amongst those up here. Partisans of the decimal system might prefer a round number, though seven is a good handy figure in its way, picturesque, with a savour of the mythical; one might even say that it is more filling to the spirit than a dull academic half--dozen. Our hero had sat at all seven of the tables in the dining--room, at each about a year, the last being the "bad" Russian table, and his company there two Armenians, two Finns, a Bokharian, and a Kurd. He sat at the "bad" Russian table, wearing a recent little blond beard, vaguish in cut, which we are disposed to regard as a sign of philosophic indifference to his own outer man. Yes, we will even go further, and relate his carelessness of his person to the carelessness of the rest of the world regarding him. The Authorities had ceased to devise him distractions. There was the morning inquiry, as to whether he had slept well, itself purely rhetorical and summary; and that aside, the Hofrat did not address him with any particularity; while Adriatica von Mylendonk—-she had, at the time of which we write, a stye in a perfect state of maturity—-did so seldom, in fact scarcely ever. They let him be. He was like the scholar in the peculiarly happy state of never being "asked" any more; of never having a task, of being left to sit, since the fact of his being left behind is established, and no one troubles about him further—-an orgiastic kind of freedom, but we ask ourselves whether, indeed, freedom ever is or can be of any other kind. At all events, here was one on whom the authorities no longer needed to keep an eye, being assured that no wild or defiant resolves were ripening in his breast. He was "settled," established. Long ago he had ceased to know where else he should go, long ago he had ceased to be capable of a resolve to return to the flat--land. Did not the very fact that he was sitting at the "bad" Russian table witness a certain abandon? No slightest adverse comment upon the said table being intended by the remark! Among all the seven, no single one could be said to possess definite tangible advantages or disadvantages. We make bold to say that here was a democracy of tables, all honourable alike. The same tremendous meals were served here as at the others; Rhadamanthus himself occasionally folded his huge hands before the doctor's place at the head; and the nations who ate there were respectable members of the human race, even though they boasted no Latin, and were not exaggeratedly dainty at their feeding. Time—-yet not the time told by the station clock, moving with a jerk five minutes at once, but rather the time of a tiny timepiece, the hand of which one cannot see move, or the time the grass keeps when it grows, so unobservably one would say it does not grow at all, until some morning the fact is undeniable—-time, a line composed of a succession of dimensionless points (and now we are sure the unhappy deceased Naphta would interrupt us to ask how dimensionless points, no matter how many of them, can constitute a line), time, we say, had gone on, in its furtive, unobservable, competent way, bringing about changes. For example, the boy Teddy was discovered, one day—-not one single day, of course, but only rather indefinitely from which day—-to be a boy no longer. No more might ladies take him on their laps, when, on occasion, he left his bed, changed his pyjamas for his knickerbockers, and came downstairs. Imperceptibly that leaf had turned. Now, on such occasions, he took them on his instead, and both sides were as well, or even better pleased. He was become a youth; scarcely could we say he had bloomed into a youth; but he had shot up. Hans Castorp had not noticed it happening, and then, suddenly, he did. The shooting--up, however, did not suit the lad Teddy; the temporal became him not. In his twenty--first year he departed this life; dying of the disease for which he had proved receptive; and they cleansed and fumigated after him. The fact makes little claim upon our emotions, the change being so slight between his one state and his next.

But there were other deaths, and more important; deaths down in the flat--land, which touched, or would once have touched, our hero more nearly. We are thinking of the recent decease of old Consul Tienappel, Hans's great--uncle and foster--father, of faded memory. He had carefully avoided unfavourable conditions of atmospheric pressure, and left it to Uncle James to stultify himself; yet an apoplexy carried him off after all; and a telegram, couched in brief but feeling terms——feeling more for the departed than for the recipient of the wire——was one day brought to Hans Castorp where he lay in his excellent chair. He acquired some black--bordered note--paper, and wrote to his uncle--cousins: he, the doubly, now, so to say, triply orphaned, expressed himself as being the more distressed over the sad news, for that circumstances forbade him interrupting his present sojourn even to pay his great--uncle the last respects. To speak of sorrow would be disingenuous. Yet in these days Hans Castorp's eyes did wear an expression more musing than common. This death, which could at no time have moved him greatly, and after the lapse of years could scarcely move him at all, meant the sundering of yet another bond with the life below; gave to what he rightly called his freedom the final seal. In the time of which we speak, all contact between him and the flat--land had ceased. He sent no letters thither, and received none thence. He no longer ordered Maria Mancini, having found a brand up here to his liking, to which he was now as faithful as once to his old--time charmer: a brand that must have carried even a polar explorer through the sorest and severest trials; armed with which, and no other solace, Hans Castorp could lie and bear it out indefinitely, as one does at the sea--shore. It was an especially well cured brand, with the best leaf wrapper, named "Light of Asia"; rather more compact than Maria, mouse--grey in colour with a blue band, very tractable and mild, and evenly consuming to a snow--white ash, that held its shape and still showed traces of the veining on the wrapper; so evenly and regularly that it might have served the smoker for an hour--glass, and did so, at need, for he no longer carried a timepiece. His watch had fallen from his night--table; it did not go, and he had neglected to have it regulated, perhaps on the same grounds as had made him long since give up using a calendar, whether to keep track of the day, or to look out an approaching feast: the grounds, namely, of his "freedom." Thus he did honour to his abiding--everlasting, his walk by the ocean of time, the hermetic enchantment to which he had proved so extraordinarily susceptible that it had become the fundamental adventure of his life, in which all the alchemistical processes of his simple substance had found full play. Thus he lay; and thus, in high summer, the year was once more rounding out, the seventh year, though he knew it not, of his sojourn up here.

Then, like a thunder--peal—-

But God forbid and modesty withhold us from speaking overmuch of what the thunder--peal bore us on its wave of sound! Here rodomontade is out of place. Rather let us lower our voice to say that then came the peal of thunder we all know so well; that deafening explosion of long--gathering magazines of passion and spleen. That historic thunder--peal, of which we speak with bated breath, made the foundations of the earth to shake; but for us it was the shock that fired the mine beneath the magic mountain, and set our sleeper ungently outside the gates. Dazed he sits in the long grass and rubs his eyes—-a man who, despite many warnings, had neglected to read the papers.

His Mediterranean friend and mentor had ever tried to prompt him; had felt it incumbent upon him to instruct his nursling, the object of his solicitude, in what was going on down below; but his pupil had lent no ear. The young man had indeed, in a stocktaking way, preoccupied himself with this or that among the subjective shadows of things; but the things themselves he had heeded not at all, having a wilful tendency to take the shadow for the substance, and in the substance to see only shadow. For this, however, we must not judge him harshly, since the relation between substance and shadow has never been defined once and for all.

Long ago it had been Herr Settembrini who brought sudden illumination into the room, sat down beside the horizontal Hans and sought to influence and instruct him upon matters of life and death. But now it was the pupil, who, seated with his hands between his knees, at the bedside of the humanist, or near his couch in the cosy and retired little mansard study, with the *carbonaro* chairs and the water--bottle, kept him company and listened courteously to his utterances upon the state of Europe—for in these days Herr Ludovico was seldom on his legs. Naphta's violent end, the terroristic deed of that desperate antagonist, had dealt his sensitive nature a blow from which it could scarcely rally; weakness and infirmity had since been his portion. He could no longer work on the *Sociological Pathology*; the League waited in vain for that lexicon of all the masterpieces of letters having human suffering for their central theme. Herr Ludovico had perforce to limit to oral efforts his contribution to the organization of progress; and even so much he must have foregone had not Hans Castorp's visits given him opportunity to spread his gospel.

His voice was weak, but he spoke with conviction, at length and beautifully, upon the self--perfecting of the human spirit through social betterment. Softly, as though on the wings of doves, came the words of Herr Ludovico. Yet again, when he came to speak of the unification and universal well--being of the liberated peoples, there mingled a sound—he neither knew nor willed it, of course—as of the rushing pinions of eagles. That was the political key, the grandfatherly inheritance that united in him with the humanistic gift of the father, to make up the *littérateur*— precisely as humanism and politics united in the lofty ideal of civilization, an ideal wherein were blended the mildness of doves and the boldness of eagles. That ideal was only biding its time, until the day dawned, the Day of the People, when the principle of reaction should be laid low, and the Holy Alliance of civic democracies take its place. Yes, here seemed to sound two voices, with differing counsels. For Herr Settembrini was a humanitarian, yet at the same time, half explicitly, he was warlike too. In the duel with the outrageous little Naphta he had borne himself like a man. But in general it still remained rather vague what his position was to be, when humanity in an outburst of enthusiasm united itself with politics in support of a triumphant and dominating world--civilization, and the burgher's pike was dedicated upon the altar of humanity. There was some doubt whether he would then hold back his hand from the shedding of blood. Yes, it seemed the prevailing temper more and more held sway in the Italian's mind and view; the boldness of the eagle was gradually outbidding the mildness of the dove.

Not infrequently his attitude toward the existing great political systems was divided, embarrassed, disturbed by scruples. The diplomatic *rapprochement* between his country and Austria, their co--operation in Albania, had reflected itself in his conversation: a co--operation that raised his spirits in that it was directed against Latinless half--Asia—knout, Schlüsselburg, and all—yet tormented them in that it was a misbegotten alliance with the hereditary foe, with the principle of reaction and subjugated nationalities. The autumn previous, the great French loan to Russia, for the purpose of building a network of railways in Poland, had awakened in him similar misgivings. For Herr Settembrini belonged to the Francophile party in his own country, which was not surprising when one recalled that his grandfather had compared the six days of the July Revolution to the six days of the creation, and seen that they were as good. But the understanding between the enlightened republic and Byzantine Scythia was too much for him, it oppressed his breast, and at the same time made him breathe quicker for hope and joy at the thought of the strategic meaning of that network of railways. Then came the Serajevo murder, for everyone excepting German Seven--Sleepers a storm--signal; decisive for the informed ones, among whom we may reckon Herr Settembrini. Hans Castorp saw him shudder as a private citizen at the frightful deed, while in the same moment his breast heaved with the knowledge that this was a deed of popular liberation, directed against the citadel of his loathing. On the other hand, was it not also the fruit of Muscovite activity, and as such giving rise to great heart--searchings? Which did not hinder him, three weeks later, from characterizing the extreme demands of the monarchy upon Servia as a hideous crime and an insult to human dignity, the consequences of which he could foresee well enough, and awaited in breathless excitement.

In short, Herr Settembrini's feelings were as complex as the fatality he saw fast rolling up, for which he sought by hints and half--words to prepare his pupil, a sort of national courtesy and compunction preventing him from speaking out. In the first days of mobilization, the first declaration of war, he had a way of putting out both hands to his visitor, taking Hans Castorp's own and pressing them, that fairly went to our young noodle's heart, if not precisely to his head. "My friend," the Italian would say, "gunpowder, the printing--press, yes, you have certainly given us all that. But if you think we could march against the Revolution— *Caro!* ..."

During those days of stifling expectation, when the nerves of Europe were on the rack, Hans Castorp did not see Herr Settembrini. The newspapers with their wild, chaotic contents pressed up out of the depths to his very balcony, they disorganized the house, filled the dining--room with their sulphurous, stifling breath, even penetrated the chambers of the dying. These were the moments when the "SevenSleeper," not knowing what had happened, was slowly stirring himself in the grass, before he sat up, rubbed his eyes—-yes, let us carry the figure to the end, in order to do justice to the movement of our hero's mind: he drew up his legs, stood up, looked about him. He saw himself released, freed from enchantment—-not of his own motion, he was fain to confess, but by the operation of exterior powers, of whose activities his own liberation was a minor incident indeed! Yet though his tiny destiny fainted to nothing in the face of the general, was there not some hint of a personal mercy and grace for him, a manifestation of divine goodness and justice? Would Life receive again her erring and "delicate" child—-not by a cheap and easy slipping back to her arms, but sternly, solemnly, penitentially—-perhaps not even among the living, but only with three salvoes fired over the grave of him a sinner? Thus might he return. He sank on his knees, raising face and hands to a heaven that howsoever dark and sulphurous was no longer the gloomy grotto of his state of sin. And in this attitude Herr Settembrini found him—-figuratively and most figuratively spoken, for full well we know our hero's traditional reserve would render such theatricality impossible. Herr Settembrini, in fact, found him packing his trunk. For since the moment of his sudden awakening, Hans Castorp had been caught up in the hurry and scurry of a "wild" departure, brought about by the thunder--peal. "Home"—-the Berghof—-was the picture of an ant--hill in a panic: its little population was flinging itself, heels over head, five thousand feet downwards to the catastrophe--smitten flat--land. They stormed the little trains, they crowded them to the footboard—-luggageless, if needs must, and the stacks of luggage piled high the station platform, the seething platform, to the height of which the scorching breath from the flat--land seemed to mount—-and Hans Castorp stormed with them. In the heart of the tumult Ludovico embraced him, quite literally enfolded him in his arms and kissed him, like a southerner—-but like a Russian too—-on both his cheeks; and this, despite his own emotion, took our wild traveller no little aback. But he nearly lost his composure when, at the very last, Herr Settembrini called him "Giovanni" and, laying aside the form of address common to the cultured West, spoke to him with the thou!

"*E così in giù,* " he said. "*Così vai in giù finalmente—addio, Giovanni mio!* Quite otherwise had I thought to see thee go. But be it so, the gods have willed it thus and not otherwise. I hoped to discharge you to go down to your work, and now you go to fight among your kindred. My God, it was given to you and not to your cousin, our *Tenente!* What tricks life plays! Go, then, it is your blood that calls, go and fight bravely. More than that can no man. But forgive me if I devote the remnant of my powers to incite my country to fight where the Spirit and *sacro egoismo* point the way. *Addio!*"

Hans Castorp thrust out his head among ten others, filling the little open windowframe. He waved. And Herr Settembrini waved back, with his right hand, while with the ring--finger of his left he delicately touched the corner of his eye.

What is it? Where are we? Whither has the dream snatched us? Twilight, rain, filth. Fiery glow of the overcast sky, ceaseless booming of heavy thunder; the moist air rent by a sharp singing whine, a raging, swelling howl as of some hound of hell, that ends its course in a splitting, a splintering and sprinkling, a crackling, a coruscation; by groans and shrieks, by trumpets blowing fit to burst, by the beat of a drum coming faster, faster—There is a wood, discharging drab hordes, that come on, fall, spring up again, come on.—Beyond, a line of hill stands out against the fiery sky, whose glow turns now and again to blowing flames. About us is rolling plough--land, all upheaved and trodden into mud; athwart it a bemired high road, disguised with broken branches and from it again a deeply furrowed, boggy field--path leading off in curves toward the distant hills. Nude, branchless trunks of trees meet the eye, a cold rain falls. Ah, a signpost! Useless, though, to question it, even despite the half--dark, for it is shattered, illegible. East, west? It is the flat--land, it is the war. And we are shrinking shadows by the way--side, shamed by the security of our shadowdom, and noways minded to indulge in any rodomontade; merely led hither by the spirit of our narrative, merely to see again, among those running, stumbling, drum--mustered grey comrades that swarm out of yonder wood, one we know; merely to look once more in the simple face of our one--time fellow of so many years, the genial sinner whose voice we know so well, before we lose him from our sight.

They have been brought forward, these comrades, for a final thrust in a fight that has already lasted all day long, whose objective is the retaking of the hill position and the burning villages beyond, lost two days since to the enemy. It is a volunteer regiment, fresh young blood and mostly students, not long in the field. They were roused in the night, brought up in trains to morning, then marched in the rain on wretched roads——on no roads at all, for the roads were blocked, and they went over moor and ploughed land with full kit for seven hours, their coats sodden. It was no pleasure excursion. If one did not care to lose one's boots, one stooped at every second step, clutched with one's fingers into the straps and pulled them out of the quaking mire. It took an hour of such work to cover one meadow. But at last they have reached the appointed spot, exhausted, on edge, yet the reserve strength of their youthful bodies has kept them tense, they crave neither the sleep nor the food they have been denied. Their wet, mud--bespattered faces, framed between strap and grey--covered helmet, are flushed with exertion——perhaps too with the sight of the losses they suffered on their march through that boggy wood. For the enemy, aware of their advance, have concentrated a barrage of shrapnel and large--calibre grenades upon the way they must come; it crashed among them in the wood, and howling, flaming, splashing, lashed the wide ploughed land.

They must get through, these three thousand ardent youths; they must reinforce with their bayonets the attack on the burning villages, and the trenches in front of and behind the line of hills; they must help to advance their line to a point indicated in the dispatch their leader has in his pocket. They are three thousand, that they may be two thousand when the hills, the villages are reached; that is the meaning of their number. They are a body of troops calculated as sufficient, even after great losses, to attack and carry a position and greet their triumph with a thousand--voiced huzza——not counting the stragglers that fall out by the way. Many a one has thus fallen out on the forced march, for which he proved too young and weak; paler he grew, staggered, set his teeth, drove himself on——and after all he could do fell out notwithstanding. Awhile he dragged himself in the rear of the marching column, overtaken and passed by company after company; at length he remained on the ground, lying where it was not good to lie. Then came the shattering wood. But there are so many of them, swarming on——they can survive a bloodletting and still come on in hosts. They have already overflowed the level, rain--lashed land; the high road, the field road, the boggy ploughed land; we shadows stand amid and among them. At the edge of the wood they fix their bayonets, with the practised grips; the horns enforce them, the drums roll deepest bass, and forward they stumble, as best they can, with shrill cries; nightmarishly, for clods of earth cling to their heavy boots and fetter them. They fling themselves down before the projectiles that come howling on, then they leap up again and hurry forward; they exult, in their young, breaking voices as they run, to discover themselves still unhit. Or they are hit, they fall, fighting the air with their arms, shot through the forehead, the heart, the belly. They lie, their faces in the mire, and are motionless. They lie, their backs elevated by the knapsack, the crowns of their heads pressed into the mud, and clutch and claw in the air. But the wood emits new swarms, who fling themselves down, who spring up, who, shrieking or silent, blunder forward over the fallen.

Ah, this young blood, with its knapsacks and bayonets, its mud--befouled boots and clothing! We look at it, our humanistic--æsthetic eye pictures it among scenes far other than these: we see these youths watering horses on a sunny arm of the sea; roving with the beloved one along the strand, the lover's lips to the ear of the yielding bride; in happiest rivalry bending the bow. Alas, no, here they lie, their noses in fiery filth. They are glad to be here——albeit with boundless anguish, with unspeakable sickness for home; and this, of itself, is a noble and a shaming thing——but no good reason for bringing them to such a pass.

There is our friend, there is Hans Castorp! We recognize him at a distance, by the little beard he assumed while sitting at the "bad" Russian table. Like all the others, he is wet through and glowing. He is running, his feet heavy with mould, the bayonet swinging in his hand. Look! He treads on the hand of a fallen comrade; with his hobnailed boot he treads the hand deep into the slimy, branch--strewn ground. But it is he. What, singing? As one sings, unaware, staring stark ahead, yes, thus he spends his hurrying breath, to sing half soundlessly:

"And loving words I've carven

Upon its branches fair—-"

He stumbles, No, he has flung himself down, a hell--hound is coming howling, a huge explosive shell, a disgusting sugar--loaf from the infernal regions. He lies with his face in the cool mire, legs sprawled out, feet twisted, heels turned down. The product of a perverted science, laden with death, slopes earthward thirty paces in front of him and buries its nose in the ground; explodes inside there, with hideous expense of power, and raises up a fountain high as a house, of mud, fire, iron, molten metal, scattered fragments of humanity. Where it fell, two youths had lain, friends who in their need flung themselves down together—-now they are scattered, commingled and gone.

Shame of our shadow--safety! Away! No more!—-But our friend? Was he hit? He thought so, for the moment. A great clod of earth struck him on the shin, it hurt, but he smiles at it. Up he gets, and staggers on, limping on his earth--bound feet, all unconsciously singing:

"Its waving branches whi—-ispered

A mess—-age in my ear—-"

and thus, in the tumult, in the rain, in the dusk, vanishes out ot our sight. Farewell, honest Hans Castorp, farewell, Life's delicate child! Your tale is told. We have told it to the end, and it was neither short nor long, but hermetic. We have told it for its own sake, not for yours, for you were simple. But after all, it was your story, it befell you, you must have more in you than we thought; we will not disclaim the pedagogic weakness we conceived for you in the telling; which could even lead us to press a finger delicately to our eyes at the thought that we shall see you no more, hear you no more for ever.

Farewell—and if thou livest or diest! Thy prospects are poor. The desperate dance, in which thy fortunes are caught up, will last yet many a sinful year; we should not care to set a high stake on thy life by the time it ends. We even confess that it is without great concern we leave the question open. Adventures of the flesh and in the spirit, while enhancing thy simplicity, granted thee to know in the spirit what in the flesh thou scarcely couldst have done. Moments there were, when out of death, and the rebellion of the flesh, there came to thee, as thou tookest stock of thyself, a dream of love. Out of this universal feast of death, out of this extremity of fever, kindling the rain--washed evening sky to a fiery glow, may it be that Love one day shall mount?

END OF THE BOOK

CPSIA information can be obtained
at www.ICGtesting.com
Printed in the USA
LVHW111715201020
669305LV00005B/1093

9 786257 120258